A MERSEY KILLING

MERSEY MURDER MYSTERIES
BOOK I

ACKNOWLEDGMENTS

So many people were instrumental in various ways in helping to ensure *A Mersey Killing* came to final fruition, it would take too long to mention them all, but hopefully those whose names are not mentioned here will know who you are, and how grateful I am to each and every one of you. Some, however, I felt I must include by name, so here goes.

Thanks must go to my publisher, Miika Hannila at Next Chapter Publishing, who had such faith in the book that he issued a contract for it before the first chapter was completed, and likewise to Mario Domina, CEO of ThunderBall Films, who optioned the book for movie adaptation at around the same time. Such confidence in one's work is truly rewarding for an author.

On a more personal level, sincere and loving thanks go to all the members of my extended family in the great city of Liverpool. Mostly my father's cousins and their descendants, my thoughts and recollections of you all helped mould most of the characters in the following story. The wonderful, typical Liverpudlian personalities of 'Aunty Ada' and 'Aunty Alice' combined to become Connie Doyle, and cousin George appears as George Thompson. Ron and Iris, with whom we stayed often in my early teens, helped me to form some of the personalities that make up many of the background characters.

A word of gratitude goes to my cousin, Rachael Tiffen, who graciously allowed me to use the names of her children, Ethan and Clemency as characters, and to Ethan and Clemmy personally for giving me their personal approval for me to do so. I hope you enjoy reading the book. As an author, I find it so much easier to develop a character who is based on the reality of a personal acquaintance. It enables me to add substance to the character that might otherwise be difficult to incorporate effectively.

I owe a debt of thanks also to my fellow author and dog lover, Carole Gill, the successful author of a number of bestselling horror novels. Read her vampire books if you dare! During a period of technical difficulty towards the end of the book, when it looked as if the final completion of *A Mersey Killing* might be delayed by many weeks, her help and support proved invaluable. A million thanks, Carole.

Similar thanks go to the aforementioned Mario Domina, who also helped immensely during this period.

To all the people of the wonderful city of Liverpool, thank you for being there, and for providing me with the inspiration for *A Mersey Killing*.

As always, I save my final thanks for my dear wife, Juliet, my fiercest critic during the writing of all my books. If she doesn't like it, it doesn't go into the final manuscript. Her patience, (often worn thin), and unerring support have been as always, a tower of strength time during the entire writing process.

INTRODUCTION

The year is 1961, and the city of Liverpool is just beginning to rock to the sounds of the new wave of popular music finding its way to the UK from the United States. At the birth of what would become known as 'The Swinging Sixties' four young men come together with dreams of pop stardom in their eyes, and begin following that dream in Liverpool's various clubs, some with illustrious names such as The Cavern and The Iron Door, but mostly in those venues little known outside the great port city. Playing for minimum fees, here, in the environment that would spawn such names as The Beatles, Gerry and the Pacemakers and more, Brendan Kane and the Planets begin their journey towards eventual recognition.

In what will become a sweeping tale of almost epic proportions, we skip to the eve of the millennium. It is 1999, and as the city of Liverpool undergoes a transforming programme of modernization and redevelopment, workers on a project to reclaim an old disused wharf and dockside warehouse uncover the skeletal remains of a long dead murder victim. Both kneecaps of the victim appear to bear the marks of a classic IRA 'kneecapping' and before long, Detective Inspector Andy Ross and his assistant, Detective Sergeant Clarissa (Izzie) Drake, find themselves involved in an investigation that sends them back in time, back to those heady days of the sixties when the city rocked to the sound of the new brand of British popular music, but when passions greater than anything they at first envisage had led to the ultimate crime, cold-blooded murder! A chance clue leads to the eventual identification of the remains, and to a new mystery, involving a young woman, missing for over thirty years. When a new murder occurs, connected to the investigation, Ross realises the case is not quite as 'cold' as it first appeared, and begins a race against time to prevent further killings as the past and present collide and the case takes a new sinister turn.

AUTHOR'S NOTE

A Mersey Killing is a work of fiction, and as such, the main characters and many of the places mentioned with the work that follows are the creations of the author's mind and are not intended to be confused with any real persons, living or dead. It has been necessary, however, in order to create a work that is credible and believable to make certain references to actual people, places, and events in order to invoke the time and era of the book's setting, i.e. the city of Liverpool in the early nineteen-sixties. Where this has happened, it has been done with the greatest reverence and respect for those mentioned in passing, none of whom are actual participants in the fictional work, and that the reader will soon realise are there merely to help create the ambience of a very special time in the world of music, and in the wonderful vibrant city that gave birth to the phenomenon that came to be known as 'The Swinging Sixties.'

SPELLING AND GRAMMAR

Please note that this book is written in British, (UK) English, and here in the UK, many spellings differ from those in the USA. Also, many of the characters in the book speak the local Liverpudlian dialect, which means I have amended the spellings and grammatical use of certain words to indicate the phonetic pronunciation of the words affected.

CHAPTER 1

OPENING BARS

The Cavern Club in the spring of 1961 was, to use the idiom of the day, 'really rocking'. A raucous crowd of teenagers was dancing, screaming and in some cases, eating a typical Cavern lunch of sandwiches, soft drinks, (the club had no liquor licence), or maybe tea or coffee. Rory Storm and the Hurricanes, a popular local group of the day, completed their set and the crowded club, built in a converted, disused warehouse, filled with the sound of the clapping and cheering of happy and almost delirious youth. The drummer of the band, one Ringo Starr, would later rise to worldwide fame as a member of The Beatles, but their days of taking the music world by storm still lay a little way in the future. For now, he grinned at the applause, as did the other members of the group, who reveled in the ovation they received from the appreciative young audience. Like the Beatles, Rory Storm and the Hurricanes would later be signed by the iconic musical entrepreneur, Brian Epstein, without, sadly, achieving the fame of Liverpool's most marketable asset of the sixties, but for now, they were content to be one of the most popular groups on the ever growing local music scene. At the time, 'beat' music and rock 'n roll was only allowed in The Cavern Club during their lunchtime sessions, the club being a 'Skiffle Club' where only a smattering of jazz would be allowed to deviate from the norm. That would all change very soon thanks to the burgeoning sound of the sixties that would emanate from the streets of the great seaport.

Holding both arms out to his sides and lowering his palms in a request for quiet from the gathered throng of teenagers, Rory Storm smiled and spoke in a voice loud enough to be heard over the general hubbub of the club.

"Thanks, everyone. It's great to be appreciated. It's time for us to take a break, but I know you're gonna love the next group who're about to step up here for you. It's their first time here at the Cavern, so let's all give a real big Cavern welcome to *Brendan Kane and the Planets!*"

The audience cheered and clapped and as the sound rose until it seemed to bounce back from the brick walls of the club, Rory turned to his left and beckoned to the waiting group, positioned off stage, waiting for the moment to make their debut.

"Come on, Brendan, fellas," Rory shouted and the debutantes virtually ran onto the stage to yet more cheers from the throng of eager youth, always happy to hear and appreciate the latest groups to hit the local music scene. Comprising Brendan himself, the group's lead vocalist and rhythm guitarist, he was followed onto the compact Cavern stage by lead guitarist Mickey Doyle, drummer Phil Oxley and Mickey's younger brother Ronnie on bass. Without preamble the group launched into the first of the two numbers they would perform that day, their own arrangement of Chuck Berry's classic hit, *Roll Over Beethoven*. Within seconds of them beginning the club was rocking to the sound of the new group on the scene and Brendan Kane's voice, powerful and resonant, had the audience enraptured.

"Wow, that boy can sing!" "Fab" and other superlatives were soon being exchanged by the young listeners whose discerning ears were fast becoming attuned to recognition of those groups or singers who had the right musical sound and most importantly, voices that could make them stand out from the crowd in a rapidly expanding local music scene. As the last strains of the music died away at the end of their performance, the watching audience spontaneously burst into a rousing chorus of applause, whistles, and cheers, and Brendan looked hopefully towards the side of the stage, where the club's resident D.J, knowing a good thing when he saw, (and heard) it, held one finger up, signaling that the group could perform one more song, that being double what they'd expected to play that day.

Brendan quickly mouthed "Coming home" to the group members and Mickey Doyle's fingers began to pick out the opening melody of a song he and Brendan had written together. With a resonating beat and a 'catchy' guitar melody running through the song, any risk the group had taken in performing their own composition rather than one of the standards of the day soon evaporated as the audience foot-tapped and jigged their way through the new song, which the group was performing in public for the first time.

"That was great," said the club's D.J as the group left the stage to yet more rapturous applause. "You lads have a really good sound. I want you to come back again, and soon."

"That'll be terrific," Brendan replied, a beaming smile on his face. "How soon?"

"How're you fixed for next week?"

"Well, we're at The Iron Door on Tuesday."

"What about Thursday lunchtime?"

Brendan quickly looked questioningly at the other members of the group. He knew they'd have to arrange time off work or simply absent themselves from their jobs if they were to fulfill the engagement, but each one unhesitatingly nodded their agreement.

"Okay, we'll be here," he replied.

After staying at the club long enough to smoke a couple of cigarettes each and drink a coffee or a Coca-Cola, Brendan and the Planets made their way through the smoke-laden atmosphere and the happy crowd, towards the exit, accompanied by much back slapping and complimentary comments from a number of the youngsters who'd obviously enjoyed their performance. *Perhaps*, thought Brendan as the group loaded their gear into the old Bedford van they regularly borrowed from Phil Oxley's father, *we might just have a decent shot of making something of the music business.* Phil drove carefully, not wanting to damage his precious drum kit or the others' guitars and equipment and one by one, dropped the group members off at their homes, or, in Brendan's case, outside the bookshop where he worked. Mr. Mason, the shop owner, didn't mind giving Brendan time off to attend his gigs, as, being forward-thinking, he realized that many of the younger crowd who knew Brendan were already visiting his shop regularly and he'd cleverly begun to stock a wide range of products, magazines and American comics that ensured a steady turnover from the new branch of his clientele. *Maybe*, he thought, *I ought to start stocking a few records, just in case.*

Mr. Mason cheerfully welcomed Brendan back to work, where the young man soon managed to lose himself in daydreams of future stardom as he went about the rest of his day's work.

CHAPTER 2

LIVERPOOL, 1999

Clarissa Drake stood looking down, maybe thirty feet or so, towards the bottom of the old, dried up dock. Turning to the young man beside her, she spoke quietly, as she shivered in the early morning mist that drifted across the landscape from the nearby River Mersey.

"You know, Derek, if I didn't know better, I'd say he looks pleased to see us."

Before the young man could reply, a deep voice from behind them made them both jump slightly.

"Now then, Izzie, how many times have I told you about that sense of humour of yours?

Turning to face the man behind the voice, Detective Sergeant Clarissa, (Izzie) Drake, found herself staring into the eyes of her boss, Detective Inspector Andy Ross. Detective Constable Derek McLennan stood beside her, trying to make himself look small and insignificant in an effort to avoid the wrath of his boss. D.I. Ross in fact, despite his words, had an almost imperceptible grin on his face as he looked sternly at his sergeant.

"I'm sorry sir, but you know how it always affects me, seeing something like this. I'm just trying to lighten the moment a bit if you know what I mean."

The tall, swarthy-skinned Inspector took a step forward and looked down at the sight that had brought them here in the first place, the grinning rictus of the skull certainly looking to all intents and purposes appearing, as Izzie intimated, pleased to be revealed from its long incarceration in the clinging mud that had only now decided to reveal its macabre secret.

Ross knew it had to have been there a long time, as the small wharf and dockside had been abandoned for many years and only now, in the course of urban renovation and improvement, had the collective mass of mud and detritus of years of neglect been slowly cleared away until the discovery of the remains brought all work to a halt. He turned to face the sergeant and the young detective constable who remained rooted to the spot beside her.

"Right then, let's get on with it. Izzie, try not to assign or assume gender until the doc has examined the remains, as well, OK?"

Izzie nodded her understanding.

"And Constable?" Ross looked into the eyes of the young detective.

"Sir?"

"I'm not going to chew your head off for standing next to the sergeant while she makes frivolous comments, so no need to look like you're about to be sent back to uniform, or fed to the Chief Superintendent for supper, okay?"

"Yes, sir, okay sir, I mean thank you, sir."

"How long you been in the detective division, lad?"

"Six months, sir."

"Lots to learn my boy, lots to learn. Now, let's get on with the job."

"Right sir, McLennan replied, following Izzie as she began the descent of the iron-runged ladder that led down to the muddy and rank smelling river bed below.

Ross quickly followed the two until all three officers stood quietly looking at the recently revealed skeletal remains that lay half in and half out of the mostly hard-packed surface of the ground that would once have been the bed of a busy and thriving riverside wharf.

The detectives took care not to approach too close to the remains, not wanting to disturb the scene before the medical examiner had had the opportunity to inspect the scene.

"Anyone know who the duty M.E. is?" Ross asked of no-one in particular.

Izzie Blake provided him with the answer.

"One of the paramedics up there said it's Fat Willy, sir."

Ross groaned. The nickname Blake used referred to Doctor William Nugent, a brilliant but terribly overweight police surgeon, an expert in forensic pathology, whose unfortunate weight problems had provided the members of Merseyside Constabulary with the excuse to make jokes at his expense, always behind his back of course. A rather dour Scot, the doctor's accent contrasted with the predominantly local Liverpool accent possessed by most of the local constabulary, some of whom found it difficult to keep up with the doctor's words at times, though he seemed to have no difficulty with the Liverpudlian accent, having lived in the city for as many years as anyone could remember. Nugent was also something of a stickler for the

rules and Ross knew he'd better be on his toes and not cause any disturbance to the scene before him, lest he incur the wrath of the good doctor.
Ross held both arms out to his sides, as though indicating an invisible
barrier.

"Right, people, no-one gets any closer than this until the doctor arrives.
Now, tell me what you see. You first, Sergeant."

Izzie Drake peered down at the skeletal remains and paused, as she
gathered her thoughts. The skull and upper body were for the most part,
fully exposed with the abdominal area still covered by a thick layer of
mud and silt, and the lower legs and feet also exposed to the chill morning
air.

"Well, sir looks to me as though the body has laid there for some time.
If you look at the wall of the dock above us, we can see that the mud and
silt must have reached up at least ten feet before the workmen started on
the reclamation job."

Ross looked up, nodding his agreement with his sergeant, also taking
time to notice the faded lettering on the side of the disused brick built
warehouse, which read 'Cole and Sons, Importers,' many of the letters now
indistinct and barely readable. He made a mental note to check how long
the warehouse had lain empty and whether Cole and Sons had been the
last company to have used the facility. Izzie continued.

"Whoever the victim is, or was, must have lain buried beneath the mud
and silt for years, to have ended up so deep."

"Agreed," said Ross. "Go on, what else?"

"I'd lay odds on the fact this is a suspicious death. I just don't see
anyone dying of natural causes and not being reported missing or nobody
having the faintest clue where he or she was last seen, that kind of thing."

McLennan butted in.

"Unless the victim had a heart attack, or slipped and fell in the water
all those years ago, no witnesses, and was just never found."

"Well done, Constable McLennan," said Ross. "That's good thinking.
We may have to do a massive trawl of the missing person records once the
doc gives us an idea of how long the remains have been down here.
Anything else, Izzie?"

"Not yet, sir. I think we need to get the doctor's opinion before we
begin formulating our own theories."

As if on cue, first of all a wide shadow, and then a large figure
appeared on the dockside above, followed by the booming voice of Doctor
Nugent.

"Well now, Inspector Ross. I see you've got something interesting for
me this morning?" The Scottish accent was easily discernible to those
around the pathologist.

"Morning, Doctor. Yes. Been here a while, I'd say, but I'd appreciate
your professional opinion before we jump to conclusions."

"Aye, well, it's good to hear you're learning a thing or two. I take it no-one's disturbed the remains?"

"No, we've stayed well back to give you an undisturbed area around the victim."

"Aye well, I'd better be comin' doon then, eh? Francis, come on man, and bring your camera."

As if by magic the diminutive figure of Francis Lees, the pathologist's assistant appeared at his side, looking down at the death scene.

"What the hell are you waiting for man? Get doon the ladder there and wait for me at the bottom. And make sure to catch me if I slip on those old rusty rungs."

The detectives looked at each other and smiled. The thought of Nugent's bulk falling from the ladder on to the hapless Lees gave them a moment of humour in the midst of their other wise grim task. The thought that Nugent's weight would probably force poor Lees's body into the mud and silt, suffocating the poor man, made him think they may end up with two bodies to remove from the dock before the day was out.

Lees quickly made his way down the ladder and dutifully stood almost to attention, his camera slung over his shoulder, as Nugent ponderously made his way down the rusting ladder, thankfully arriving safely at the bottom less than a minute after his assistant. Ross couldn't help but admire the way the pathologist, despite his bulk, managed to make his way down the ladder almost gracefully, and without any apparent difficulty.

"Now, let's see what we've got, eh?" said Nugent as he and Lees began their own examination of the scene. Lees's camera flashed incessantly as he photographed the partially revealed skeletal remains from every possible angle. Nugent knelt in the mud beside the skeleton and began a close examination. Ross, knowing the doctor's routine all too well, couldn't resist a quick question.

"See anything yet that might help us, Doctor?"

"Sshhh," Nugent urged.

"Does he think the corpse is going to talk to him?" McLennan whispered quietly to Izzie.

"Ah heard that, young man," Nugent snapped at the young detective. "Ah like tae work in peace if you don't have any objections."

"Of course, Doctor, sorry," said McLennan, blushing visibly.

"Aye, well, anyway, in response to your question, Inspector Ross, I do believe I have something for you."

"Already, Doctor?"

"Aye, already, but it doesn't take a genius in this case to ascertain that, in my humble opinion, you'll be looking for a murderer I think."

Ross and Izzie Drake looked at each other, exchanging knowing glances. Both knew instinctively this was going to be a potentially long and difficult case to crack.

"How can you be sure so quickly?" he asked the pathologist.

"Aye, well, I dinna think this hole in the skull got here by accident."

Nugent beckoned the inspector closer and pointed to the rear of the skull, which he'd raised carefully just clear of the mud. There, the two men looked closely at the gaping hole in the back of the skull, larger than would have been left by a bullet but still conversant with some form of blunt force trauma.

"Couldn't that have been caused by an accident, Doc?"

"Under certain circumstances, it may have been, Inspector Ross, but not in this case, I think."

"Why so certain?" asked the policeman.

Nugent pointed to a point about twelve inches to the right of the skull. Ross could see that the doctor, in the course of his close examination had uncovered the unmistakable form of a hammer.

"I'll wager a month's salary that yon hammer is your murder weapon, Inspector," said Nugent. "There's some staining on the hammer head that may be blood, and the shape and size of the hammer head would appear to match the shape of the wound in this poor unfortunate soul's head. I'll be able to confirm it when we get the remains back to the lab, but for now, I'm satisfied you have a murder on your hands. No chance of fingerprints after so long I'm afraid which leads me to the bad news that I believe the remains have possibly lain here for a long time, years in fact."

"Any idea of gender?" asked Izzie Drake.

"Not yet, Sergeant, but looking at the size of the feet, I'd hazard a guess at male," Nugent replied. "Inspector, I dinna want to disturb the remains too much where they lie at present. Can you arrange for a team to dig out the entire area surrounding the skeleton and transport the lot back to my lab? I can carry out a thorough examination there and give you as much information as the deceased is willing to reveal to me."

Ross groaned inwardly. It would be a massive task to remove the remains from their resting place, mud and all, without disturbing or destroying the skeleton, but at least once it was out of the way he and his team could carry out an intensive search of the surrounding area for clues to the identity of the victim or to the full nature of the crime. At least the possibility that this was indeed the murder site might make his task a little simpler, no need to go searching the length of the river bank for miles in both directions.

"I'll make the arrangements, Doc. Please, once you get the remains to your lab…"

"I know, Inspector. You'd like my findings as soon as possible."

"Thanks, yes, Doc. I know it's not as if I can see a quick solution to this one, but anything we can do to find out who this was, and when the murder occurred, might just help us bring a killer to justice."

"I wish you luck, Inspector, I really do," Nugent said as he rose from his position and beckoned Lees to follow him, and the pair began the ascent up the ladder back up to the dockside.

"Anything to add, Constable?" Ross directed the question at McLennan.

"Just a question really, sir."

"OK, ask away."

"Well sir, this dock or wharf or whatever the correct term is, was once connected to the Mersey by that channel, right?" McLennan pointed along the narrow channel along which the ships would have approached the dock from the river, unloaded at the dockside and then turned round in the basin they now stood in before heading back out to the Mersey.

"Right," said Ross, "so what's the question?"

"It's just that I don't see how they could block off the whole River Mersey so they could drain the dock and the channel, sir. How the heck did they manage it?"

"Good question, McLennan and I'm glad to see you're thinking about this. I'm no engineer but I think you'll find they drive large metal pilings into the river bed, erect some sort of temporary dam, then use massive pumps of some sort to drain the water from this side. When it's dry, they can then build the new reinforced river bank you now see at the end of the channel, thus re-directing the flow of the Mersey. They must have done this many times during all the redevelopment of the dock area, because I know there are a hell of a lot of these old inlets and channels that had to be closed off to the river before the developers could start work on their so-called urban redevelopment and improvement of the old dock area."

"Right, sir, I see. I was just trying to work out if the clearing of the channel might have any bearing on the timing of the death of the victim."

"Good thought, Constable, but of course, it could have happened any time when the dock was still operational or after closure as far as my thinking goes. But listen, you keep thinking lad, okay? That's what a good detective does, all the time, lots of thinking, mainly small points but then one day you just might hit on something important. The other thing we need to consider is whether the body was carried here by the tide and simply washed up here. The actual murder site and original dump site could be almost anywhere."

McLennan smiled, pleased the inspector had listened to his points and didn't think he was wasting his time, but wished he'd thought of the inspector's last point.

Ross next took out his mobile phone, and spent the next few minutes making arrangements for a specialist recovery team to attend the scene and remove the remains and the surrounding mud and silt in one large excavation, for transportation to the forensic lab, in order for Doctor Nugent to carry out what Ross knew would be a painstaking examination. There wasn't much they could do for the present, not until the remains had been removed and they had the opportunity to carry out a detailed examination of the surrounding area. Ross knew he'd have to call in a few uniformed officers as well as the members of his own team of detectives, and his own boss, Detective Chief Inspector Harry Porteous wouldn't be best pleased at the overtime bill that would probably ensue from a case that on the surface, at least, appeared to offer little hope of a quick and easy solution.

"Well," said Izzie as she and Ross stood staring at the remains, McLennan having been dispatched by Ross to begin the arrangements to have the remains carefully removed and taken to the lab.

"Well indeed, Sergeant," Ross replied, thoughtfully. "Well, indeed."

CHAPTER 3

LIVERPOOL, SEPTEMBER, 1962

Brendan Kane and his fellow musicians sat around the kitchen table in Brendan's parents home, a small two up, two down red-brick terraced house, much like thousands of others in the city. The young men sat around Brendan's Mum's kitchen table, with drummer Phil, unable to keep his hands still, constantly fiddling with a bottle of Camp Coffee in one hand and another of Heinz Tomato Ketchup in the other. To one side of the room, a small coal fire burned in the hearth, adding warmth and a feeling of cozy security to the room. Near the fire, a load of washing stood draped over a wooden clothes horse, the smell of damp washing adding to the homely feel of the room. Despite the domestic warmth and atmosphere of his parents' home, like many others of his own age, Brendan nurtured dreams of being able to move up in the world, to leave behind the rather grim and humdrum workaday existence endured by his Mum and Dad and others of their generation. His father, Dennis, had spent his entire working life as a docker, a hard life, with much physical toil required on a daily basis. The years had taken their toll on Dennis Kane, and Brendan, despite having the greatest of respect for his father, wanted more from life, a house with a garden instead of a front door that opened straight onto the street, a few of the modern conveniences perhaps, like a dishwashing machine similar to those he'd seen in the shops in the city centre, and one of the new fangled automatic washing machines. Brendan knew his Mum was luckier than most, in owning her twin tub machine with the spin-dryer that took the worst of the water out of the clothes. Still, the washing draped on the clothes-horse was a reminder that his mother still did a great deal of washing by hand and dried it the best she could in front of the fire.

Like the rest of the group, he felt his best chance of achieving his dreams just might be through their music. He'd received his guitar, a second-hand but good condition twin pick-up Hofner, as a Christmas present one year from his parents, who were well aware of their son's love of music, and who'd scrimped and saved for months in order to buy their son the instrument and a second-hand amplifier to go with it. Second-hand or not, to young Brendan, the guitar had been, and still was, the greatest gift his parents could ever have given him, and he was determined to pay them back for their financial sacrifice, just as soon as he could.

"Listen up lads," said Brendan, as he pointed to a stack of papers laid out on the table in front of him. "Here's the receipts for every gig we've done so far. We're doing okay locally, but I think we need to try and branch out, you know, like, maybe get a recording contract."

"Christ, Brendan," Mickey replied, flicking back a permanently annoying lock of hair that always fell across right eye, "We'd all love to do that, man, but getting a recording contract isn't as easy as that, and you know it."

The others all nodded their agreement with Mickey's statement.

"Yeah, look, I know that, but that guy Brian Epstein, you know, his Dad owns a furniture shop in town? Brian's the manager of the music department and he's started out managing some of the local beat groups. He's signed The Beatles, and we've played the same stage as them, right? Someone told me they've got a recording contract already with a record coming out next month. They wrote it themselves, it's called *Love me Do*. I heard last week he's also got Gerry and the Pacemakers on his books and a couple of others, and they're all local and doing okay under his guidance."

Phil Oxley joined in the conversation.

"Yeah, I've seen him around in some of the clubs, like The Cavern, The Iron Door, places like that."

"But has he ever seen us and heard us play?" asked young Ronnie.

"Exactly," said Brendan. "We need to make sure he's there in one of those clubs when we're on stage, make sure he hears and likes us. Then maybe we'll get picked up by him, too."

"Yeah, but he's not the only manager in the business, is he?" said, Ronnie. "I know for a fact that a couple of groups have had demo recordings made at Pete Kemp's studio in the city centre. Maybe we could do that and send copies of the demo off to Mr. Epstein and some of the big recording companies, you know, like Decca, E.M.I. and Polydor?"

"Sure, Ronnie," said Brendan. "We could do that, spend a load of dosh we haven't got on getting a demo made, and then buy enough copies to send around the industry, only for some producer's assistant to listen to a few bars if we're lucky and then throw the disc in the bin. We only get three pounds a gig man, and we have to pay Phil's dad a bit towards the petrol we use when he lends us his van, so we ain't got a whole lot of spare cash to throw away on a demo that hardly anyone will hear."

"But how do other groups manage then?" asked Ronnie. "Surely lots of record companies do have people who listen to new talent when they get the demos in the post?"

Mickey chimed in.

"Ronnie, I think what Brendan's getting at is that most of the groups whose demos get heard are probably sent in by their managers, who already know the producers and such like at Decca and places like that."

"Yeah, exactly," said Brendan. "That's why we need someone like Brian Epstein to notice us. It doesn't have to be him of course, but he's local, and we've probably got more chance of being heard and spotted by him than by anyone else, and we don't exactly know many managers of pop groups personally, do we?"

"Okay," said Ronnie. "What do you think we should do then, Brendan? How do we get him to see and hear us? We can't exactly go begging to him, can we? You know, *'Please Mr. Epstein, we're real good. Come and listen to us and sign us up.'*

"We use our brains, Ronnie. That's what we do. Look here," Brendan said. "These receipts show we make a small profit on every gig, not a lot, sure, but enough to maybe get a few leaflets printed. My idea is to get them printed with a few of our 'coming soon' dates, you know, when we've maybe got three or four bookings lined up and we make sure copies of the leaflet are delivered to his dad's shop, to the music department and to his office. I've found out he's got one in town, where he runs his management stuff from. Then we get that gorgeous sister of yours, Mickey, to help us out."

"And what do we want Marie to do, exactly?" asked Mickey.

"Well, she's a real looker, right, and she and her mates go out to the clubs regular to listen to the music, right?" They all nodded in agreement, apart from Mickey, who appeared unsure of just what Brendan was about to suggest.

"What we do is, we ask her to go to a few of the clubs where we know he hangs out and see if she can get to talk to him, just drop him a few hints about this really great group she's heard, that's us of course, and that he ought to go to The Iron Door, or wherever we're booked that week, and listen to us. She can tell him lots of kids are following us and that we've got a great sound. What bloke can resist a really good looking bird like your sis, Mickey?"

"Sounds good," Mickey replied, "but how do we know which clubs he's going to be at so Marie can try and talk to him?"

"Yes, I know, that's the one big problem with my plan. Maybe she could spend a week or two doing her best to corner him and then we get the leaflets posted, sharpish like, and distribute them so he gets copies just after talking to Marie, and we might get lucky."

"Bloody hell, Brendan, there's a load of ifs, buts, and maybes in there, don't you think?" asked Ronnie.

"I know Ronnie, but come on fellas, don't you think it's worth a try?"

After another five minutes of discussion, with no-one having come up with a better idea to try to gain the recognition of the man they saw as a way into the recording industry, they reached an agreement, and Mickey promised he'd speak to his sister Marie, who he agreed would probably be pleased to enlist her friends in helping them to put Brendan's grand plan into operation.

After another half hour of discussion and agreeing to meet at Brendan's house at seven p.m on Friday night before going on to a gig at the newly-opened Pelican Club, the group went their separate ways, leaving Brendan to clear away the receipts and the mugs that had held their frequent cups of tea, leaving his Mum's kitchen as clean as possible when she came home after her shift at the launderette.

The front door opened soon afterwards, and Brendan's Dad walked into the house, having spent an hour at the pub, enjoying a pint or two with his friends. He made his way straight to the kitchen, where Brendan was sitting at the table, deep in thought.

"Hey, son, how you doing?" Dennis asked.

"Alright, Dad, Just thinking stuff, you know."

"Aye lad, you do a lot of that there thinking, don't you? I hope you're going to stick at that new job of yours and not turn into too much of a dreamer over all that music stuff you and your mates are so keen on. There's no future in that life, you should know that."

Brendan sighed. He and his father had had this conversation many times in recent months.

"You're wrong, Dad, really. There's a real future out there if you're good enough, and I know me and the lads have a real chance if we can just get spotted. That's what we've been talking about before you came home."

"Oh aye? And just what does Mr. Mason think of all this 'beat music' lark, eh? He's got some patience, I'll say that for him, letting you have time off to go and play that so-called music of yours during the day."

"It's only the odd hour here and there, Dad, when we get a lunchtime gig, and then I'm only actually away from the shop for a couple of hours, and one of them's me lunch hour anyway, and Mr. Mason says he thinks I should follow me dreams, we all should."

Dennis Kane waved a dismissive hand in his son's direction. No way would the hardened old dock worker ever understand the modern generation.

"Aye well, if you say so, son, if you say so. Now be a good lad and put the kettle on and make your old Dad a nice cup of tea, eh?"

Brendan nodded at his father, rose from the table and picked up the kettle from the cooker hob next to the sink unit, quickly filling it and putting it on to boil on the gas ring, all dreams of being a future pop star, for the moment, like the slowly boiling kettle, placed on the back burner.

One day, Dad, I'll prove you wrong, and make you proud of me, he thought, without actually saying the words. He knew he'd never convince his Dad until maybe he and the group actually made it big, and perhaps even then his Dad wouldn't think being a musician and singer was what he'd deem a 'proper job.

The kettle whistled as it came to the boil and Brendan dutifully made the tea, and Dennis took his with a quick "Thanks, son," and made his way into the small parlour at the front of the house, and turned on the small black and white television in the corner, the one Brendan hoped to one day turn into one with a glorious colour screen, like the ones in that big shop in the city.

Brendan took his own cup of steaming hot tea upstairs with him to his bedroom, where he turned on his small portable transistor radio which he kept permanently tuned to Radio Luxemburg, lay down on his bed and allowed himself to drift into his daydream of music stardom as the latest sounds of the pop charts assailed his brain, the tea soon growing cold as he became lost in the early sounds of the sixties.

CHAPTER 4

MERSEYSIDE POLICE HEADQUARTERS, 1999

On the sixth day after the discovery of the remains, Ross sat alone at his desk in his small but functional office at police headquarters. The painstaking task of removing the remains from the abandoned dock had taken almost two days to achieve, and the inspector now awaited the results of the post-mortem on the unfortunate soul whose last resting place had gone unmarked and unrecognized for God knows how many years. After six years as a Detective Inspector, Ross had to admit to himself that this could turn out to be his most baffling case to date. As a rule, most murders tended to follow a similar pattern. Either through love, jealousy, hatred or for financial reasons, one individual would one day snap and instigate the death of another. In the majority of cases, the body would be found sooner rather than later, and certainly not years later, as in the current case. Of course, identifying the victim helped, and again was usually achieved fairly quickly even when no identification was present on the body. Only in rare cases did it take a length of time for the police with all their modern resources to identify a murder victim. This time, however, things were very different. In the case of the skeletal remains which even now, Dr. Nugent and his assistant, Lees were carrying out an autopsy of sorts on, there was no hope of fingerprint identification and the few items of trace evidence found in the vicinity after the removal of the body had provided little if any hints that would put a name to the victim, and without a name for the deceased, any hope of finding the killer would prove minimal.

Ross picked up the report that lay on his desk, a single sheet of paper that contained the list of items recovered from the mud and silt that had accumulated around the decomposing body over the years. The remains of one boot, obviously a man's had survived in enough detail to be estimated at a size ten. Nugent, of course, had been correct in his assumption the remains were those of a man. Perhaps the other boot had degraded and been washed away with the tidal flow from the dock while it was still operational, Ross hypothesized. Next, a few coins, totalling six shillings and tenpence in pre-decimalisation currency, that had probably been in the deceased's pockets had been found, cleaned and from the date of the most recently minted coin discovered it was possible to assume with some degree of certainty that the murder had taken place no later than nineteen sixty six.

"Bloody hell," Ross spoke aloud, "that's over thirty years ago. How the hell am I supposed to find this poor sod's killer if I can't even find out who he was?"

"Talking to yourself, now, are we, sir?" came the voice of Izzie Drake from the doorway. Ross had been so engrossed in his personal thoughts he hadn't heard her knock gently before entering his office.

"Well, there wasn't anyone else here to listen, was there, Sergeant?" he replied, quickly regaining his composure after initially appearing surprised at Drake's sudden appearance.

"I'm here now, though, sir. You managed to come up with anything new from looking at that list?"

Ross quickly scanned the short list of items once again, for probably the tenth time since the forensic team had compiled it, and sighed before replying. The actual items found were currently in the evidence locker down in the basement of the headquarters building, and the two detectives had spent a few hours trying to glean something, anything, from staring at the assortment on the day they'd been brought in, under Izzie's supervision after she'd led the team in a painstaking search of the dock.

"I'm no miracle worker, that's for sure, Izzie. I mean, what have we got? A bit of an old boot, a few coins, a few pieces of cloth that may or may not have been part of the victim's clothing, a metal comb, a few drinks cans, various makes of beer and soft drinks apparently identifiable, a few glass bottles, whole and in pieces and that strange piece of plastic one of your searchers picked up. Any or all of this stuff could just as easily have been thrown into the water by someone not connected to the murder. We just don't know, and I can't see how we're ever going to know, if you want the truth."

"I know sir. It seems like an impossible and pretty thankless task if you ask me. Doesn't the chief superintendent realize we're on a hiding to nothing with this one?"

"He probably does, Izzie, but he puts a bit of pressure on D.C.I Porteous to get a result and he puts the pressure on me and we just have to do our best."

Izzie Drake walked across to the window of Ross's office, and appeared to stare into space for a few seconds. Ross recognized this as one of Izzie's regular ways of gathering her thoughts and waited patiently for her to speak. She turned back from the window, and as Ross looked at her expectantly, she voiced her thoughts.

"Look, sir, I know this a wild thought, but what about the guys in the cold case squad? Our skeleton might just refer back to one of their cases."

Merseyside Police did in fact have one of the best cold case units in the North of England, as the inspector knew only too well, and Ross deliberated for a few seconds before replying to his sergeant.

"Under normal circumstances I'd probably agree with you, but, and it's a big but, I know for a fact that the Cold Case Squad have to work under very specific terms of reference. The most important prerequisite for them to become involved in a case is that, quite simply, there has to be a case for them to become *involved* in. In other words, it has to be a case that already exists on the unsolved books, and sadly for us, in this case, as we have no identity for our victim, we have nothing to cross reference it against, to see if they have our victim listed in any past crime statistics."

"Damn it," said Drake. "I really thought I might be on to something there."

Ross smiled.

"You still might be, Izzie. If we can find out who our victim is, and he's listed in an unsolved case file somewhere then Cold Case might be interested in taking the case over, if the boss agrees."

"And why wouldn't he, sir?"

"Simple, Izzie. Because if he thinks there's any mileage for positive publicity to be gained from his own murder squad solving an old case, he's unlikely to want to hand it to the wrinkly squad."

Drake sighed.

"Internal politics at work again, eh, sir?"

"'Fraid so, Izzie."

Before they could continue their discussion, the phone on Ross's desk rang. Drake moved to leave the office, but he held up a hand to tell her to stay where she was. The call might be important to their case, and indeed, after a minute of what Drake took to be serious listening by her boss, he spoke into the mouthpiece.

"Okay, thanks, Doc. Sergeant Drake and I will be with you shortly."

Izzie looked intently at Ross as he hung up on Doctor Nugent.

"Results of the autopsy, or should I say examination of the bones, I assume, sir?"

Ross nodded his head and spoke as he quickly tidied the papers on his desk into a neat pile and then placed them in the top left drawer of his desk, locking it with a key which hung on the key ring that also contained his car keys.

"Such as it was, yes. Our dour but brilliant pathologist says he's come up with one or two things, but he'd rather explain to us in person rather then over the phone. Of course, that's his usual stance, always wanting to over-dramatise any little bit of trivia he might have discovered, and present it like he's bloody Sherlock Holmes or something, so let's not get too excited until we see and hear what he has to say."

"Understood, sir, but, from what you just said, I'm assuming he's found something of interest?"

"According to the good doctor, yes he has. So, let's get on over to the mortuary, and see what he has for us."

"Right, sir. Should we tell D.C.I. Porteous we're going over there?"

"No point, Izzie, not unless or until we have something to report to him. If he needs me he can always reach me through my mobile, and I'd rather talk to him with something positive to report rather than just give him my travel itinerary for the morning. Just tell D.C. McLennan where we're going just in case the boss does ask where we are while we're gone. Go on, and give D.C. Ferris a heads-up too. He might need to get in touch if he comes up with anything."

Drake returned to the squad room where she quickly brought the two Detective Constables up to date. McLennan was busy going through missing persons files going back for a number of years, though how he hoped to cross reference a name with an as yet unidentified skeleton was anybody's guess, and the older and more experienced D.C. was studying the photographs taken by the crime scene techs, of all the various items of detritus and rubbish, or potential evidence, however you looked at it, discovered around the victim's remains.

Ten minutes later, she was behind the wheel of the Mondeo pool car assigned to Ross, as they made the short drive to the city mortuary. Hopefully, they would find something of interest in the results of Doctor Nugent's examination of the mystery skeleton.

CHAPTER 5

THE MORTUARY, 1999

Drake and Ross stepped into the sunlight as they alighted from the Mondeo in the car park outside the mortuary building. As Ross stretched to his full height, relieving the stiffness in his neck and back, Izzie Drake couldn't help but admire the man who she worked closely with.

Detective Inspector Andy Ross might be the wrong side of forty, but his full head of dark brown hair and his healthy skin tone gave him the look of a man almost ten years younger. Drake had noticed a framed photo of his parents in his office soon after she'd started working under Ross, and had commented on the handsome couple in the picture. Ross explained that his father, a military policeman at the time, had met his mother during a posting to the Far East in the fifties, and fell in love with the beautiful dark-skinned daughter of a wealthy shipping merchant. Apparently Ross's mother came from an old Anglo-Indian family, with a strong hint of Spanish blood in the mix, hence her mother's maiden name of Martinez. It was therefore easy for Izzie to see where her boss got his good looks from.

Izzie often envied Ross's wife, Maria, a doctor in general practice not far from where they now stood, looking at the entrance to the mortuary building. She wished she could meet a man with the looks, integrity and self-assurance of Andy Ross, but her luck with men never seemed to follow a straight or true course. Maybe one day, but for now, work took priority over everything else.

"Ready, Sergeant?" Ross asked as Izzie pressed the button on the remote and the car answered with a beep as the door locks engaged.

"Ready as I'll ever be, sir. God, I do hate these places."

"Don't we all? I doubt this place is anyone's favourite place to be on a warm, sunny day, except of course, someone like our friendly neighborhood pathologist, the good Doctor Nugent."

"Not forgetting his faithful hound, Lees, of course," Izzie chuckled as she spoke.

Ross joined in Izzie's lighthearted banter for a few seconds.

"God, yes. I must say, Lees is almost more cadaverous than some of the poor sods in this place, looks like a good meal might kill him."

"He's good at his job though, eh, sir? Doctor Nugent won't have anyone else assisting him, so I've heard."

"True. Well, here goes."

The two detectives stood at the entrance to the building where an intercom system was in place, beside a small keyboard which only staff had the code to, in order to effect immediate entry. A notice adjacent to a small silver button read 'Press here for entry' and Ross duly pressed where indicated. Almost immediately, a tinny disembodied voice squeaked from the small speaker above the button.

"Hello. Please state your name and business."

"Detective Inspector Ross and Sergeant Drake, Merseyside Police, for Doctor Nugent. We're expected."

"Ah yes, I have your names here. Please push the door when the buzzer sounds, Inspector."

Ross and Drake entered the building as instructed and walked a short distance along the corridor immediately inside the door, quickly arriving at another door beside which a small window looked into an equally small cubicle. Within, a young man sat at a small desk with a computer screen and keyboard in front of him, obviously the disembodied voice from moments earlier, Ross surmised. The man wore a lapel badge that gave his name as Peter Foster, the title Mortuary Reception below the name. Foster spoke to the detectives through a grill in the glass partition that separated him from mortuary visitors.

"Good morning, may I see your identification please, Inspector Ross, Sergeant Drake?"

Both officers produced their warrant cards and passed them through the small gap at the bottom of the glass. Foster checked them carefully. Ross couldn't remember seeing him here on previous visits to the building.

"You new here?" he inquired of Foster.

"Been here a month, Inspector," he replied as he passed the warrant cards back to the detectives. "Sorry if I seem over careful, but we've been instructed to be very fastidious and only allow authorized personnel into the actual examination suites."

"No need to apologise for doing your job the right way, Mr. Foster," Ross replied. "It's a rare thing to find nowadays."

Foster smiled, grateful to the inspector for putting him at ease. Ross assumed not everyone was as understanding as he was about being held up in their attempts to enter the 'business end' of the mortuary, as he thought of it.

"Thank you, Inspector," Foster smiled again. "I presume you know your way to the autopsy rooms?"

Ross noted the change in terminology; Foster acknowledging his professional status rather than using the terms presumably used with grieving relatives and so on.

"We do indeed."

"Doctor Nugent is in Autopsy Room Two," said Foster, as he handed over two 'visitor' badges which Ross and Drake proceeded to pin on their jackets.

"Thanks for your help, Mr. Foster," Ross smiled at the young man, who beamed an equally expansive smile back at the detectives.

"You're welcome, Inspector. Please remember to hand the badges back to me before you leave the building."

Ross nodded and the two walked through the door that opened magically as Foster pressed a switch, out of sight to those outside his small but functional cubicle, which, Ross thought, he probably thought of as his office.

As soon as they entered the next corridor the two officers became instantly aware that they were now in what could best be described as the 'mortuary, proper' as their olfactory senses were assailed by the smell familiar to such establishments the world over, that heady mix of formaldehyde and disinfectant. Their nostrils twitched involuntarily as they followed the wide corridor, its walls a pallid 'hospital green' in colour, until it suddenly opened up into a large circular room with large double doors spaced evenly around it, each bearing a small plaque carrying the room, or 'autopsy suite' number.

"At least we don't have to watch any bodies being sliced and diced this time," Izzie Drake said with a tinge of relief in her voice.

"Something to be grateful for, I suppose, Izzie," Ross replied, himself relieved that he wouldn't need to avail himself of the 'Vick's Vaporub he and most other police officers usually smeared under their nose to help combat the smell of decomposition and putrefaction. No need either, to dress themselves in the surgical scrubs usually worn when attending autopsies either, as Nugent had advised earlier on the phone. No matter how many autopsies he'd attended over the years, Andy Ross had never been able to get used to the odours associated with the process of post-mortem examinations. With nothing but a set of skeletal remains on the table today, both detectives would be spared the gruesome sights and smells of a regular autopsy.

They paused for a second or two outside the doors to autopsy room two, then Ross slowly eased one of the double doors open enough for himself and Drake to pass through. The detectives walked in to the room, which contained all the usual paraphernalia associated with the process in hand, steel autopsy table with channels at the sides for the blood to drain along into waiting receptacles at the end of the table, a set of large cold-boxes set into the far wall, where the bodies would be stored and further tables and counter tops, all in gleaming steel, holding saws, drills, cutting tools and everything a proficient pathologist could ask for in order to determine his or her findings.

As the door slowly closed silently and automatically behind them, both Ross and Drake found themselves staring in surprise at the sight before their eyes. In the centre of the room the skeletal remains lay, displayed in the middle of the autopsy table, with Doctor Nugent standing on the opposite side of the table to the detectives, facing them as they entered the room. With his back to them, Francis Lees was busily dictating something into a small hand-held recorder, probably on Nugent's instructions, his voice low and inaudible from where they stood.

What took Ross and Drake by surprise however was that, for the first time in either officer's memory, there was a third person in the room with the pathologist and his assistant. Ross in particular was quite amazed as he took in the sight of an extremely beautiful blonde-haired woman, dressed not in surgical scrubs as Nugent and Lees always were, despite Nugent's instructions to the opposite to Ross, but in an extremely expensive looking light blue skirt suit, the hem of the skirt ending just above the knee, revealing just enough for Ross to appreciate a terrific pair of legs. Topped off with a short white lab coat, the newcomer looked more like a consulting psychiatrist then a pathologist and Ross knew immediately that something was definitely different about this examination of Nugent's, that much was for sure. Ross led the way as he and Drake approached the trio at the table.

* * *

"Ah, Inspector Ross, and the good Sergeant Drake, come in, come in," Nugent urged, "I have someone here I'd like you to meet."

Avoiding the urge to reply that such news was rather obvious, Ross instead replied, "I see, Doctor, and just who is this lady that we are to have the pleasure of meeting?"

"Well," Nugent went on, "As you know, I'm pretty much acknowledged as one of the leading pathologists in the country, and there's not much that leaves me floundering, but this time, I did feel the need to consult another expert in order to give you a true picture of what these remains might mean to your investigation."

Ross ignored Nugent's blatant statement of his own self-importance and waited as the pathologist continued. "Allow me to introduce you to Doctor Hannah Lewin. Hannah's an old friend of mine, and she's a professor of forensic anthropology, at Cambridge."

"Forensic anthropology?" Ross queried.

"Aye, Inspector Ross. My speciality is in working with something a little, er, fresher than our friend on the table, and knowing Hannah was in town for a lecture at the University, I took the opportunity to ask her opinion of our remains."

"I see," said Ross, reaching out to shake hands with Hannah Lewin. The woman however, held her hands up, and stepped back, Ross able to see she was wearing rubber autopsy gloves. "Oops, sorry, Doctor, or should I say professor?"

"Hannah is fine, Inspector," she smiled at him. "I never like all these grandiose titles, do you?"

"Well, no, I suppose not, then you must call me Andy, and this is Izzie," Ross replied, as he nodded in the Drake's direction.

A flicker of recognition passed across Ross's face as he went on, "I think I've heard of you, Hannah. Didn't you assist the police down south with the identification of the bones found in the old factory building in Herefordshire a couple of years ago?"

"You're quite right, Andy," Hannah replied. "It was in Leominster to be precise, an old shoe factory that Samuel Metcalfe used as a burial site for his victims, nine of them to be precise. I was able to determine cause of death and also individual identifications for the majority of the remains."

"Ha, got you," Izzie suddenly exclaimed. "I've seen you on the telly too. You were on that show that told the history of the Viking bones at the settlement in Hillingdale last year, weren't you?"

Hannah Lewin smiled at Izzie's remark.

"I was indeed, Sergeant, er, sorry, Izzie. Are you interested in such things?"

"A real history buff, that's me," Izzie replied. "I love to learn from the past, and the history of our country is really what shapes its future, don't you think?"

"Certainly," said the anthropologist, impressed with Izzie's enthusiasm.

Ross gave an exaggerated cough, eager to bring the conversation back to their reason for being in the autopsy suite. Hannah returned to her professional persona as she spoke again.

"I'm really pleased to meet you both. Doctor Nugent has told me you're very good at your jobs. He speaks highly of you, don't you, William?"

Nugent grunted, obviously feeling a little uncomfortable at Hannah Lewin's bluntness.

"Aye, well, no need to go making them big-headed now, is there lass?"

"Oh, don't be so gruff, William. Now, shall we get on with what we're here for?"

"Aye. Let's do that," Nugent went on, relieved to be back on familiar territory. He looked at Ross and Drake as he now spoke in his usual, professional tones. "As you know, there was really nothing but bones when we finally extracted the remains from the dockside river bed. The lack of hair or any tissue after so many years of immersion, first in the water and then in the mud and silt that had built up in the disused dock area had ruined any chances we may have had of obtaining a good DNA sample and of course, even then, we wouldn't have known what the hell to compare any such sample with. Facial recognition was definitely out of the question, and that's when I thought Hannah's expertise might be of assistance to us."

"You're sure it's been there since before the dock was drained, then?" Drake asked the pathologist.

"Aye lass, I'm pretty sure of it. You see, we know the dock was drained about ten years ago, as part of the urban regeneration plan for the whole docks area. If the body had been tossed in there after draining, it would, I'm sure have been discovered sooner and would not have sunk into the river bed and been buried in the mud as it was when we found him. Hannah has conducted a pretty extensive initial examination in the time she's had available and has some findings to report to you, I'm pleased to say."

"Anything you can add to the investigation will help, I'm sure," Ross replied. "We have very little to go on so far."

"Well, I can't actually tell you too much, but I do have one or two points of interest to give you," Hannah Lewin replied.

As Ross and Drake waited, she picked up a clipboard from the side of the autopsy table and began her report to the detectives.

CHAPTER 6

LIVERPOOL, MARCH 1963

The crowd had gone home, and Brendan and the group sat quietly around a table at The Iron Door Club, sipping Coca-Cola through straws as they waited for Marie to bring Mr. Oxley's van round to the front, Mickey's sister having taken on the role of driver for the group whenever she had a free evening. The group's drum kit and instruments were waiting at the rear entrance ready to be loaded into the van as the boys relaxed after another night in the smoky atmosphere of the club.

"Still no sign of our big break then, Brendan," said Mickey. "Even your great master plan didn't work did it? Marie and her mates did all they could to get that Epstein fella in the right place at the right time and we know he's been in a couple of clubs when we've been playing so he must have heard us."

"If he has, that means he doesn't rate us," said Phil Oxley, a hint of sadness in his voice. "Why don't we just admit we're not as good as we think we are? The Beatles are number two in the charts with *Please Please Me*, it's great, and they write all their own stuff, while we turn up everywhere and play cover versions of other people's music. We're just not original enough Brendan. You've got a great voice, lad, but we don't have what it takes to write enough of our own songs, and maybe that's what's holding us back."

Brendan Kane nodded sadly at his friend, knowing in his heart of hearts that Phil was probably correct in his summing up. Yet, something in his heart refused to allow him to give up on his dreams, at least not yet.

Before he could reply to Phil's depressing statement, Marie bounced into the club and called out to the group.

"OK, you lot, who's for home then? Come on, get loaded up, we haven't got all night, you know. I've got work in the morning and need some sleep, even if you lot don't."

The little group began to rise from their seats but, as they did so, Phil Oxley raised a hand to signal them to stay put.

"Listen everyone, before we go, I've got some more bad news."

"Oh God, Phil, what is it now?" asked Brendan, as tiredness suddenly washed over him like a tidal wave. He wanted nothing more than to get home and sleep. He too didn't want to be late for work the next day. Mr. Mason was a great boss, but wouldn't tolerate a lame excuse like sleeping in because he'd been out late at a gig.

Phil's face took on a serious look as the others slumped back into their seats, Marie standing just behind Mickey, anxious to leave and get them all home. She'd keep the van parked outside her home overnight as usual and return it to Mr. Oxley's home the next day as always, on her way to work.

"It's about the van, actually," said Phil. "Dad says he's still okay with us using it at night, but, well, things are a bit tight at present. He's had to let his mate Mick go, and he used his own van to make deliveries during the day, and there just isn't enough work to keep them both 'gainfully employed' as Dad puts it.

Phil's father had been a ship's carpenter, a highly qualified tradesman, until the shipyard where he worked suffered a downturn in new ship-building contracts. Along with others, he'd suffered the ignominy of redundancy, but had used his redundancy payout wisely and started a small, but initially profitable business, creating hand-made furniture. His friend, Mick Donnelly had joined him as a part-time employee, working with Dave Oxley on the manufacturing side of the business and then using his own small van to make deliveries to the homes of customers. With Mick gone, Dave would need his own van to be available every day, and the group would have to manage without his generous loan of the vehicle.

"Maybe you could use the drum kits most of the clubs have in place, Phil," said Mickey, knowing that Phil's drum kit was the largest piece of equipment they had to move from place to place. Most clubs possessed amplifiers they could use for their electric guitars, though he knew it would still be a problem for everyone carrying their instruments, including the acoustic guitars they often used through the streets of Liverpool, on foot or on buses.

"Are you kidding me?" Phil said, a hint of anger in his voice. "I saved every penny I earned from me paper round for three years, and me Mam and Dad paid the rest of the cash for them drums. I know they're second-hand, but they give me the right sound I want, and I'm not about to start using some heap of old crap that everyone and his uncle has probably used for years, and don't forget, I paid three quid to get our name stenciled on the front."

Bassist, Ronnie, always the quiet member of the group now spoke up.

"So, what do we do now, then? Do we give up, pack in the group, like?"

"Not if I can help it," Brendan replied, firmly. "There has to be a way we can carry on. We just need to think it through."

"We can tell the clubs we can only do evening gigs from now on." Ronnie suggested.

"Yeah, then they'll think we're being uncooperative," said Mickey.

Brendan thought for a few seconds, and then said, "Look, for now, nights it is, no daytime gigs, okay? Phil, tell your Dad thanks from all of us. We really appreciate him letting us use the van all this time, and tell him we understand how things stand for him, and we hope business'll get better for him, real soon."

Phil breathed a small sigh of relief. He'd expected a row of some sort after making such an announcement. All in all, he thought, Brendan and the others had taken things pretty well, so far, though he still had another bit of bad news to share with his mates.

"Thanks, Brendan, I'll tell him what you said, but, well, there is one more thing."

Seeing hesitation in Phil's expression, Brendan pressed him further.

"Oh Christ, Phil, for fuck's sake, spit it out, man. How much worse can things get?" Suddenly remembering that Marie was standing behind Mickey, he added, quickly, "Sorry about the language, Marie, love." Marie just nodded at him, knowing he was more than a little worked up.

"It's the petrol," Phil went on. "Dad hasn't minded us using his fuel, up to now, I mean, he knows they're only short trip to most of the clubs and round our houses like, and we pay a bit towards the fuel, but with money short and everything…"

"Is that all?" Brendan sighed. "Tell your Dad we'll put an extra gallon a week in the tank, Phil. That should cover the few miles we clock up when we use it. If we don't have any gigs some weeks, we'll give it a miss, but if we all chip in a bit from our take from each gig, we'll hardly notice a couple of shillings a month."

The club manager was gesticulating to Brendan from the club exit. He needed to lock up and wanted Brendan and the group to leave him in peace to get on with it and allow him to go home. Brendan acknowledged him with a wave, and within a couple of minutes the group was in the van, Marie at the wheel, heading for their various drop-offs.

That night, sitting at the kitchen table, his parents fast asleep upstairs, a sleepless Brendan Kane held his head in his hands, as a wave of depression swept over him. Despite his outward display of positivity in front of the other members of the group, he had a sinking feeling in his gut that was telling him the days of Brendan Kane and the Planets might be numbered.

If they were, he needed to formulate a new plan if he was ever going to achieve his dream of pop stardom. Later, in bed, with just the sound of his old Westclox Big Ben alarm clock ticking away on his bedside cabinet, and the occasional creaking sound as the house seemed to settle itself down for the night, the germ of an idea began to grow in the recesses of his mind. The others might not be too keen, he thought, but there was a way forward, and Brendan became determined to explore the avenue that had just revealed itself to him in his most private of thoughts. He suddenly heard the sound of his Dad experiencing a coughing fit in the next bedroom. The thin walls of their house meant that little was private between rooms, particularly in the dead of night, and Brendan was quite used to the occasional sounds of his parents indulging in passionate love-making, though how they still managed it at their age he really couldn't comprehend. *For Christ's sake*, he always thought as the sound of his father's heavy breathing and his mother's gasping, combined with the banging of the headboard against the adjoining wall had kept Brendan awake many a night, *they're in their bloody forties!* Brendan just couldn't imagine being that old, and now he listened as the coughing gradually died away and all fell silent once again.

Brendan's Dad smoked around twenty cigarettes a day, and despite the advent of filter tipped cigarettes which were supposed to reduce the recently announced health risks associated with smoking, Dennis Kane happily continued to smoke the same Capstan Full Strength unfiltered cigarettes he'd always enjoyed. In his mind, filter tips were meant for women and 'pansies', not for 'real' men. He didn't know of one single man down at the docks who smoked filter tipped cigarettes. Brendan's Mum smoked the new brand, Cadets, and even if he'd occasionally smoke one of his wife's cigarettes if he'd run out of Capstan, Dennis would invariably break off the tip and smoke it 'neat' as he put it.

Brendan would occasionally smoke one of his Dad's cigarettes, surreptitiously 'nicked' from his father's packet, as Dennis would never dream of keeping count of his smokes, though he'd happily give one to Brendan if he asked. Trouble was, they made Brendan cough a lot and the last thing he wanted was to break into a coughing fit in the middle of a performance, so he was determined not to become a regular smoker and limited his indulgence to the odd one when he felt in need of a quick 'lift' such as was provided by the nicotine in the little white sticks, and never of course, on the day of a gig. Brendan had noticed his father had been coughing a lot more recently, just a 'smoker's cough' his Dad called it, but Brendan worried his Dad might be suffering from some kind of chest disease as a result of a lifetime's inhaling of the smoke. For now though, such thoughts died away in tune to the gathering silence from the next room and, still thinking of his new master plan for his own future, Brendan Kane drifted into a dreamless, peaceful sleep.

CHAPTER 7

HANNAH LEWIN'S REPORT, 1999

"Before I tell you what I've ascertained so far, I need to ask you something,"

"Go ahead, ask me anything," Ross replied, wondering just what was in the mind of Hannah Lewin.

"When you searched the area around the site where the remains were found, I presume you found various items?"

"We did, but we have to consider the fact this was a wharf, a dock for loading and unloading of ships, and all sorts of rubbish will have been thrown into the water over the years, and a fair amount since it closed down."

"I know that, Inspector,"

"Andy, please," he interrupted.

"Yes, sorry, Andy. Anyway you found this hammer, right?"

Hannah held up the hammer that had found in close proximity to the skeleton.

"Well, actually, it was Doctor Nugent who found it, as he carried out his initial examination of the remains at the scene. It was quite close by and had obviously also been disturbed by the digger when they were clearing the dock."

"No other tools? Any specific metallic fragments, drinks cans excluded?"

"No, just the hammer. Doctor Nugent thought it may have been the murder weapon."

William Nugent gave a sort of nervous cough, untypical of the man, as he waited for Hannah to continue. Before she did, she beckoned with her hand to draw the two detectives closer to the remains on the table.

"Well, for once, my friend William is in error."

Nugent coughed again, and began to speak.

"Yes, but…"

"Oh, do shut up, please, William. Nobody says you were negligent. You weren't in a position to make a full examination in situ so you couldn't have been expected to see the rest."

Nugent appeared mollified by Hannah's words and stood back a little to allow her to go on.

"Look here," she said, as the detectives moved closer to the table. She held the hammer closer to the skull until it was lined up with the hole that was previously thought to be the cause of death.

"What are we looking at?" asked Izzie Drake.

"Here," said Lewin. "The small perforation in the skull was almost certainly made by the hammer but from the small indentation present, I can almost certainly say this blow, though it would have certainly incapacitated the victim and possibly caused a loss of consciousness, really did not pierce the skull sufficiently far to cause any damage within the brain cavity. And, once the skeleton had been fully cleared of the thick sludge and mud that covered the midsection, we saw these."

Hannah pointed towards the skeletal legs, and Ross and Drake's eyes followed her finger until it came to a stop, and both detectives immediately knew exactly what she was indicating to them.

"Bloody hell," said Ross.

"Oh shit," added Drake.

"Exactly," said Hannah Lewin.

"Not quite what you expected us to find, eh, Inspector?" came the voice of William Nugent, over Ross's shoulder.

"That's why you wanted to know if we found any metallic fragments?"

"Yes, it would have helped of course, but it doesn't change the fact that your victim was shot in both kneecaps before he ended up in the river. I hoped you might have found the remains of the bullets or shell casings from the shooting. They would have helped me to identify the type of ammunition used and therefore give you a possible identification of the type of murder weapon. As it is, I can still hazard a guess, but you need facts, not guesses really."

Both Ross and Drake continued to appear a little shell-shocked at this new revelation. Ross's thought immediately went back in time to his teens, when the TV news and the newspapers were full of stories about 'The Troubles' in Northern Ireland, and the IRA's use of kneecapping as a means of spreading fear among the community, and often used as a deterrent when applied to those they believed had betrayed their cause, perhaps by talking to the police or the troops deployed in that benighted province during that sad time. He decided not to mention those thoughts right now; that being something he would save for discussion between himself and Drake back at the station. The inspector let up a silent prayer that if and when they identified the victim, he wouldn't find himself embroiled in a case involving the terrible and bloody events that had taken place back in sixties Belfast. With the Northern Irish capital lying just across the Irish Sea from Liverpool he knew the chances were high that any number of IRA members and members of their opposition in the loyalist community factions had at any given time used the port of Liverpool as an entry and exit point for their forays to mainland Britain, and the ramifications of having to investigate an IRA killing on his home turf were enough to make Ross shiver involuntarily. For now, though, he eventually asked,

"So, you don't think the blow to the head was fatal, and we now know the victim was kneecapped as well, before being killed, as there'd be little point doing such a thing post-mortem, so I have to ask you, what do you think killed the poor bugger?"

Hannah Lewin stood looking down at the pitiful-looking assembly of bones that lay before them on the cold steel of the autopsy table for a full twenty seconds before finally replying to Ross's question.

"Well, I'd agree with your assumption regarding the bullet wounds to the knees, absolutely no point in taking such measures against a corpse. They certainly would have been excruciatingly painful, but, like the blow to the head, not fatal in themselves, and therefore the only assumption I can make, and it is only an assumption, based on the lack of confirming evidence, is that your victim was probably shot first, and then, while on the ground he was struck on the head and then thrown alive into the water."

Izzie Drake, her face a mask of a mixture of anger and horror now asked,

"Are you saying they, whoever they were, just tossed him in the river like a piece of rubbish and left him to drown?"

"That's my best guess, Sergeant," Hannah Lewin replied. "There doesn't appear to be any other answer to the question of how your victim found his way into the water, does there?"

"That's just horrible," said Drake, who then went on, "What makes you sure the body was thrown into the water, and not into the dried up dock after it had been closed off from the river?"

"That's where we come to the rest of the results of my examination," said Hannah Lewin.

"Please go on, Hannah," Ross encouraged her.

"Well, from the state of the bones I can tell you there is enough evidence to suggest they were immersed in water for a long period of time. Also, there was sufficient detritus found in the immediate vicinity of the remains after cleaning to be able to date some of it, the drink cans for example, and under the remains we found these coins, none of which bears a date later than 1963, not conclusive I know, but they were probably in the victim's pockets and fell through the bones as the clothes gradually deteriorated in the water, hence them being found in the mud immediately below the remains. There were four old cans in the mud we cleared away, two Coca- Cola cans, one Sprite and one Tizer, and each still bore the date stamps on the base that helped me identify when those cans went on sale."

"You can determine such things after all this time?" asked the sergeant, becoming engrossed with Lewin's findings.

"Oh yes, that's not difficult at all. I've done work around the world on burial sites and communal graves and you'd be amazed at the huge data-bases that are being built up to assist in the identification of all sorts of artifacts found on and around corpses and skeletal remains."

"Amazing," said Drake, as Ross then also intervened with a question of his own.

"Okay," he said, "but, can you give me anything else at this point that will help us to identify just who the victim was?"

"I think I can," Lewin smiled at the inspector. "I can tell you that the victim was male, which Doctor Nugent of course had already ascertained, I know, and, from the shape of the skull I can tell you the victim was almost ninety nine percent of Caucasoid extraction."

"A white male then?" Ross asked, then added, "but, you said only ninety-nine percent, Hannah. Explain the one percent, please."

"This is Liverpool, after all, Inspector," she replied. "You must remember that over the years there has been a great deal of inter-marriage between people of various races, typical in most large ports around the world. Your victim may have been of mixed race origin, one British parent, the other of any other race exhibiting similar Caucasoid character-istics, but if I had to testify on the spot, I'd say yes, this poor soul was a white male of between fifteen and thirty years of age."

"Okay, I accept that," Ross said, thinking for a moment of his own, mixed-race background, and then, "The bullet-holes, Hannah? Small calibre I presume?"

"Definitely," she replied. "A shotgun would have done far more damage, particularly from close-range."

"Close-range?" asked Izzie.

"Of course. You're not going to shoot someone in the knees from long distance, Sergeant. Whoever did this had to be standing in close proximity to the victim and obviously had to be within close firing range so as to be on target with both shots, so to speak."

"You're right of course. I should have known that," Izzie said, feeling slightly foolish in front of the forensic specialist.

"Don't worry about it," Ross interjected, refusing to criticize his assistant. He knew all this new information was a lot to take in and he'd seen Izzie's face when she'd realised just how the victim had probably been eliminated. It wasn't a particularly good way to go, if there ever was such a thing. "I do have a question, though."

"Of course, please ask anything you want," Lewin replied.

"Leaving the shooting aside for a moment, why didn't the body rise to the surface? I thought dead bodies always floated after a period of time."

You're correct, of course, and under normal circumstances, a body sinks as the lungs fill with water, and stays there until bacteria in the gut and chest cavity produce enough lighter than air gasses, methane, hydrogen sulphide and good old carbon dioxide, at which point the cadaver will float to the surface like a balloon. In the case of this poor young man, something obviously prevented that, which probably means he was weighted down before being allowed to sink into the water. There would probably have been enough heavy items on a dockside for your killer, or killers to utilize as a weight. Or they may have used a number of smaller items and placed them in his pockets, or he may simply have got trapped in some underwater detritus, which held the body down and kept it from floating to the surface. I can take a look at the scene if you like. There may be something that gives me a clue as to what kept the body under water, instead of returning to the surface."

"Thank you, yes that might be a good idea. I'll arrange it and get back to you, give you an escort to accompany you. Perhaps Doctor Nugent would like to go along too?"

Nugent replied enthusiastically to Ross's suggestion.

"Aye, well, that might be a good idea, Hannah. Two sets of eyes and two minds would be better than one, don't you think? Lees can assist us on site, take photographs and record anything we find."

"A very good idea, William," Hannah Lewin responded. "If you make the arrangements, we can make our detailed study of the site whenever it's convenient for you, Andy," she said to Ross.

"Sure, Izzie, can you arrange for D.C. McLennan to pick the doctors up tomorrow morning and take them to the wharf and give them whatever assistance they need?"

"Yes, sir, I'll make sure I see to it when we return to the station," Drake replied.

That one point dealt with, Ross now moved the conversation back to the subject of just who their victim could have been. He directed another question at Hannah Lewin.

"You said you had more information that might help with identification, Hannah?"

"Yes, as a matter of fact, I do. If you look here," and she pointed to what appeared to be a small, but noticeable line across one of the lower bones of the leg. Both detectives leaned in closer to get a better look at what she was indicating. "This is the tibia, and this," she pointed again at the paler looking groove-like line in the bone, "well, this is a sign of a break

40

at some time, long healed by the time of death, possibly occurring some time in the victim's youth, maybe a sporting injury, or an accident of some kind. Oh yes, as I've previously speculated, your victim was definitely young, certainly under thirty five, and most likely around twenty years old at the time of death, give or take a year."

"I see, and you can be reasonably sure of that?" Ross asked, already knowing the answer likely to be forthcoming. Hannah Lewin struck him as not being the sort of person to make such statements without being sure of her facts.

"Of course, Andy. First of all, we have enough teeth to give us a pretty good estimate of age and then there are other contributing factors, most of which are highly scientific and probably wouldn't interest you, though they will be in my final written analysis of the remains."

"Oh, please, go ahead and humour me. Tell me just a little bit about how you determined the age of our victim."

Hannah sighed, thinking the detective was perhaps testing her skills prior to fully accepting her findings. Then again, he had a job to do.

"You really want the text book version? She asked, and as Ross smiled and nodded she simply smiled back and with the words, "Very well," she began. "There are multiple ways that we can estimate how old the person was at the time of death, it's kind of like a puzzle and as forensic scientists, we have to join the dots in order to achieve a result. So, first of all, we can estimate the age of skeletal remains by dentition. You probably know from your experience of similar cases that there are certain teeth that erupt at certain times, etc."

Both Ross and Drake nodded, both understanding Lewin so far, and the scientist carried on, sounding to Ross almost as if she was quoting directly from a text book, so sound was her knowledge, it seemed to him.

"Now, apart from the teeth, we can also determine age from the cranial suture fusion sites, long bone length, though not an exact science, and changes to the pubic symphysis surface. A young adult displays a rugged surface transversed by horizontal ridges and intervening grooves, and the surface eventually loses relief with age and is bounded around the age of 35. Additionally, we can estimate the age of a murder victim by obtaining a radiograph of specific bones in the victim's body, mainly the hand and wrist. By comparing these to an atlas of bone growth, the victim's age can usually be detected."

Hannah Lewin fell silent and looked directly into the eyes of Andy Ross. When he said nothing for a few seconds, she spoke once again.

"I did try to make it as clear and helpful as possible. I hope it made some sense to you both."

Ross smiled and looked first at Drake and then at the pathologist, before finally responding.

"Hannah, you are an undoubted expert in your field and you know damn well we were hardly able to follow any of that accurately but thank you. I believe we got the gist of what you're saying and wholeheartedly accept your findings of our victim's age, don't you agree, Sergeant?" He looked to Izzie for her response.

"If you say we agree, sir, then yes, without a doubt, we agree, most assuredly, we agree."

Izzie couldn't help but grin as she replied to the inspector, and before they knew it, the two detectives, Hannah Lewin and even the usually stiff and gruff William Nugent were laughing together. The laughter served to act as a release of the tension that had built up as Hannah Lewin had delivered her in-depth technical 'lecture' on determining the age of a human being's bones, and as they each returned to their normal, professional demeanors, the pathologist added:

"Oh yes, there was one other thing too. I think you'll find it very interesting,"

"Do go on, please," said Ross.

Lewin walked to the back of the room where a long, counter-top style table ran the length of the wall across the width of the room. Ross immediately recognized the three boxes of possible evidence his team had recovered in the vicinity of the skeleton, in a radius of ten yards from the last resting place of the remains.

"We received these earlier this morning, sent across from your own crime scene people."

William Nugent joined in the conversation again. In fact, Andy Ross was quite surprised to have witnessed the long silence from the big Scotsman, quite out of character from his own experiences with the man. Ross wondered if perhaps Nugent was a little overawed by the skill and expertise of the younger, and certainly much better looking expert who now held the attention of everyone in the room.

"Aye," he said, "And I must say your people turned up a considerably varied collection of items, most of which are probably nothing more than the detritus of many years, having been thrown into the water as nothing more than rubbish."

"Hey," Ross replied, leaping immediately to the defence of his crime scene analysts. "You need to remember, Doctor, that my people had no idea what they were looking for or what might or might not be significant to the case. That body may have lain in place for years or may have floated into its final resting place some time after death so yes; they collected anything and everything that may have a bearing on the case. They had a job to do, and they did it, whilst thanklessly crawling around in the filth and the mud beside that old wharf."

"Och, dinna get yer knickers in a twist, Inspector. I'm no criticizing your people at all. Just mentioning that there was quite a bit of stuff in there for us to wade through in order to locate anything of significance.

Perhaps in future, ye'll kindly allow me to finish ma sentence afore ye begin berating me. A'hm just doing ma job you know, same as you and the good sergeant here."

When irate or disturbed, Ross had noticed that Nugent had a habit of slipping into the broadest of Scottish dialects, clearly betraying his Glaswegian roots.

Okay, okay, truce," Ross said, smiling broadly at Nugent. "We're all tired and have been working long hours, so I apologise if I was a little quick off the mark there."

Nugent 'harumphed' and added, "Aye, well, I accept your apology, Inspector, and I apologise too if ye thought I was having a go at your people. Hannah, please go on and tell our friends here what we found."

With his rant over, Nugent's accent had moderated to his usual slight Scottish lilt, a fact Ross noticed and found instantly amusing, though he fought hard to keep himself from grinning at the humour he felt at the realisation. Izzie Drake, however, found herself thinking the same as her boss and covered her mouth with one hand, effecting a louder than necessary cough as she did her best to cover the smile that had appeared on her face.

"Are you alright?" Lewin asked, as Izzie finally brought her smile muscles under control and retuned her hand to its place at her side.

"Yes. Thank you. I'm fine, just a tickle in my throat. I'm sorry to have interrupted you, Doctor…er…sorry, I mean Hannah. Please show us what you've found. Sorry boss," she said as she turned to Ross, who knew quite well what she'd been doing.

"No problem, Sergeant Drake. Happens to us all. Please, Hannah, carry on."

Lewin lifted the lid off one of the stiff cardboard evidence boxes and lifted out a small, see-through cellophane packet and walked back to the small group gathered around the autopsy table. As she placed the packet on the table she also took another, similar packet from the right hand pocket of her white doctor's coat, which she preceded to place next to the first packet.

"When the skeletal remains had been completely cleaned this little item was found under the pelvic area, obviously having at one time been in the victim's trouser or jacket pocket. As you can see, not only is it the same material as the piece your people discovered, but when placed together, they make a rather nice fit, making them, in my opinion, two parts of the same whole."

"The piece of plastic!" Izzie exclaimed.

"Well no, not plastic actually," Lewin corrected the sergeant.

"Really?" Drake asked.

"Go on, please Hannah," Ross urged. "If it's not plastic, then just what exactly is it?"

Before replying, Hannah Lewin opened the two packets, and removed the two small pieces of material, then brought them together to show the detectives how they fitted together to form an almost perfect heart-shaped item.

"Does it remind you of anything, now?" she asked.

"Well, now you mention it, no, not really," Ross replied.

"It does resemble something I've seen before," Drake answered, "though I'm not sure what, or where."

"First of all, it's not just a piece of plastic," Lewin went on. "It's what's known as tortoiseshell and this," she held up the two pieces of material so they could all see clearly, "if I'm not very much mistaken, is a guitar pick, or plectrum, an item commonly made from the material. If I'm right, and I think you'll find I am, then it's quite probable your victim was a musician, Inspector."

"Well, blow me down," said Ross, "and it's Andy, remember. A guitar plectrum, of all things."

"Yes," Drake now added. "I knew I'd seen something like it before, way back at school, when some of the kids took guitar lessons, though I'm sure they were more of the shape of a small shield."

"They come in quite a few shapes and thicknesses," Lewin said. "I believe it depends on whether the musician was a lead or rhythm guitarist, playing a steel stringed instrument or an acoustic model or something like that, though, not being a musical person, I'm not certain on that."

Ross hesitated for a second, almost tempted to inject the lighthearted comment that he was surprised to find there was something Hannah Lewin didn't know, but diplomacy won out and instead he replied, "Hannah, thank you. If you hadn't identified it, we'd have probably ended up discounting it as just a piece of useless plastic, with no relevance to the case. Now we know we're probably looking for a possible young guitarist, dating back to the sixties, young, having suffered a broken leg at some time in his youth."

Hannah smiled. "I know it's not a lot to go on and certainly far from a positive identification, but…"

"Hey, it's a damn sight more than we had to go on before we walked in here this morning, right, Izzie?"

"Right, sir," Drake replied, as she wondered to herself just how the hell they were going to find anyone from thirty something years ago matching such a brief and sketchy description, but, as Ross had just said, it was a step forward, albeit a small one.

CHAPTER 8

LIVERPOOL, THE SUMMER OF '63

"You've got to be kiddin' us, man," Mickey Doyle shouted at Brendan's latest pronouncement.

The four group members, Brendan, Mickey, Ronnie, and Phil, together with Marie were sitting on the grass in what they all knew simply as 'The Park.' The Park was in fact a small grassed area just a couple of streets away from Brendan's home, identified, as its grand name suggested by the council's generous provision, in one corner of the fenced-in area, by a number of items of play equipment designed to amuse the younger children of the area. As well as four traditional swings the play area possessed a slide, a small roundabout, powered of course by the eager little hands that would propel it in a whirl, and a 'Bobby's Helmet', the odd, conical structure that served as a kind of rocking roundabout-cum climbing frame, and the source of many resulting accidents involving cut and bleeding knees, elbows and fingers and the occasional broken arm from the numerous accidents that seemed to proliferate during the warm sunny, summer days such as today. Brendan's favourite, in his younger days, had always been the little hand-push roundabout, which he and his pals from the local junior school would spin round and round until they couldn't go any faster, then grab a hold of one of the metal hand rails, jump on, and then bend over the small domed centre of the apparatus, peering through the small gap between the dome and the wooden slats of the seating area, and then suddenly jumping up and feeling the eerie sensation of accompanying dizziness that inevitably followed. It took quite some doing to remain in control of one's faculties in such a dizzy state and more than once,

Brendan and his mates had lost their hand-hold and fallen from the round-about, propelled by centrifugal force onto the hard concrete surface into which the structure was mounted, and of course, more cuts and bruises would be sustained, but, what the heck, it was fun, and that was what being a kid was all about, after all.

The summer holidays being in full-swing, the play area was currently busily occupied by a number of young children all enjoying the same activities Brendan and the other members of the group had indulged in some years earlier. It was from one particularly nasty fall from the Bobby's Helmet that the twelve-year old Brendan Kane had broken his left leg and subsequently spent many weeks in a plaster cast, steadily gathering the signatures of friends and relatives on the plaster-of-Paris cast, until the day it was removed, and Brendan almost reluctantly said goodbye to the crutches that had made him feel just a little important and had drawn much sympathy on his behalf from his school mates. It was a strange coincidence that lead guitarist, Mickey Doyle, had suffered a similar fracture at the age of thirteen, not from the same source, but during a school football match, an accident which in Mickey's case had left him with a barely noticeable limp, and ended his own boyhood dream of becoming a professional footballer. Mickey found himself watching as a group of young boys enjoyed an impromptu game of football, using jumpers for goal posts, just as he and his mates had done.

Now, however, the raucous laughter of the boys and the happy squeals and screams of the girls in the play area seemed to disappear into the ether as all eyes and ears among the group sitting on the grass, some hundred feet or so from the swings, turned their attention to Brendan and Mickey as a potentially explosive argument gathered strength. Marie's transistor radio was blasting out Elvis Presley's *Devil in Disguise,* the current number one in the UK Top Twenty, but Marie turned the volume down as the argument gathered momentum.

"I mean it, Brendan. How the fuck can you even think of doing this to us?" Mickey asked, his voice growing louder with almost each word that spilled angrily from his lips.

"Look, Mickey, everyone," Brendan said, defensively, "I just said the word *might*, not *definitely*, at least not yet."

"Fuck you, Brendan," Mickey went on. "You're talking about splitting the group up so you can go off and try to make it on your own. Just where the fuck would that leave the rest of us, eh? Three piggin' years we've stuck together through thick and thin, trying to make it, man. Now, just because things are a bit tough, you want to fuck us off and go and do your own thing. It stinks, man, that's what I think."

"Yeah," Phil Oxley now joined in, "You just wanna dump us, ain't that right, Brendan? Christ, man, I know we've not done so many gigs since we lost the use of the van in the daytime and the night jobs have dropped off a bit, but that's no reason to split up. We're still popular and getting book-ings, even if they're a bit fewer."

"Look," said Brendan, realising his new plans weren't exactly being received well, "I said we ought to try one last time to make a breakthrough, and if things don't work out then it might be time to think about splitting up. We wouldn't be the first group to give up you know. Not every group in the city or in the country, come to that, makes the big break, I just think that if that happens, I might stand a chance of a solo career as a singer, that's all."

"Oh yeah, and just how do you propose we go about tryin' to make this last attempt at making the breakthrough? I'm thinkin' maybe you've got some plan up your sleeve, right? Ronnie asked in a less threatening voice than the others, trying to be the voice of reason as the argument became more heated.

"Well, yeah, I have as a matter of fact, if any of you are prepared to hear me out without wanting to knock me block off."

"Go on then, mister bloody big-shot Brendan Kane," said Mickey, his voice laced with a heavy dose of sarcasm. "Let's hear your latest master plan."

Silence fell for a few seconds as Brendan gathered himself for a moment, and almost prophetically the sound of *Do You Want to Know a Secret?* from the local group, Billy J Kramer and the Dakotas, came from Marie's radio.

"Okay, then. Here's what I'm proposing," Brendan began, "I've been doing some adding up and such like and the group's bank account is pretty healthy, considering the fewer gigs we've been doing."

"It shouldn't take a fucking Einstein to work that out," Mickey inter-rupted. "We haven't exactly spent much of it apart from money for travel to gigs and replacement strings and things."

"Are you going to listen to me, or not?" Brendan bit back at his friend.

Mickey held both arms out to the side in a gesture of supplication.

"Sorry, do go on, mastermind." Mickey's voice was heavy on cynicism as they waited for Brendan to continue.

"Right, what we do is use the majority of what we have in the bank to produce a demo disc. We record a couple of covers that demonstrate our talents to their best effects, that's vocals, guitars, and drums. We show how well we harmonise together, and use two tracks that will show how diverse we can be in style and performance. Then, we send them to every major record company, and every independent producer we can think of. It won't cost the earth for the stamps, and then, we wait a reasonable time to see if we get any replies. If we do, great, but, if we go past an agreed cut-off date and we haven't heard anything positive, then we seriously consider the fact that we're just not going to make it, guys, and the time will have come to try something new."

"With the 'something new' being you going off on your own to seek your fame and fortune," Phil Oxley said, scornfully. Brendan knew he was on the verge of losing not only the support but the friendship of these three young men with whom he'd put in so many hours over the years in their attempt to break into the music business. He tried to remain calm as he went on,

"Look, fellas, it might be the best thing for all of us. You guys can keep the name of The Planets if you want to, or change it if you want. Maybe with a new lead singer, you might still have a chance of getting somewhere."

"And just maybe we'll sink like a stone being thrown into the Mersey," said Ronnie. "We'd have no chance without you fronting us, Brendan, and you know it."

Suddenly, as the sound of The Searchers' *Sweets for my Sweet* faded away on the radio, Marie Doyle unexpectedly entered the boys' argument.

"Here, you lot, listen to me a minute would you? You might not like it, but I think Brendan's right. You've all tried really hard to make it, but just how many years are youse goin' to keep floggin' away at this? I think if you were going to make it big, someone would have spotted you by now and offered you a contract. I'm not saying youse guys are crap, 'cos you're not, you're good, dead good, but so are a lot of groups out there, okay? Brendan isn't saying he wants the group to split up just like that, is he? He wants to give it one more go and if it works, you'll all be happy. If it doesn't, you can't say you never tried, and if Brendan wants to try and make a go of things on his own, then youse lot should just accept it and wish him luck. That's what I think, anyway."

A shocked silence fell over the group. Marie's defence of Brendan's idea had truly taken the others by surprise.

"Are you serious, sis?" Mickey Doyle spoke, incredulous at his sister's apparent betrayal of the group.

"Course I'm serious," she replied. "Look, listen to me. I've driven you lot all over Liverpool, Birkenhead, even as far as St.Helens, Wigan, and even bloody Southport to gigs over the years. I might not get up on stage with you and play the guitar or drums, but I feel just as much a part of this group as the rest of you, so I think I've got some say in this, don't you?"

A general murmur of agreement gave Marie the impetus to continue.

"You know as well as I do that loads of groups have started out and then folded in a lot less time than we've been together. Want me to name a few? There was The Trojans, you know, Dave Morris and his mates, The First Sound, The Lee Gibson Band, and lots more. They all gave it their best shot but had the sense to know when to quit. You lot have got to be realistic too. No one wants you to succeed more than me after all the time I've given to the group, but sometimes we can't always have what we want. All of you have been dead lucky to be able to get time off work from your bosses when we had daytime gigs, and God knows how many sickies you've all pulled from time to time, when we've got back from a late night gig and you've been too knackered to get up and go to work the next day, but that's not really professional is it?"

A kind of pall appeared to gather over the little group as Marie fell silent. The children carried on playing on the swings and roundabout, the sound of Peter, Paul and Mary's *Blowing in the Wind* issued forth from Marie's transistor radio, but all these peripheral sounds simply dimmed in the minds of the members of the Planets as Marie's words sank home and for a few seconds, no one seemed prepared to break the silence.

Eventually after what felt like an age to everyone but in fact was only the space of about ten seconds, her brother Mickey sighed heavily, and in a softer voice than the one he'd previously displayed during the voicing of his anger at Brendan, said,

"Wow, sis, you've really given this some thought haven't you?"

"Yes, Mickey, I have."

"I know you're usually the sensible one in the family, but I'm still not sure about this."

"Me neither," said Phil, while young Ronnie Doyle stayed silent, not sure how to react to his elder sister's words.

"And you think I am?" Marie said to her brother. "Come to that, do you think Brendan's sure? None of us is sure, Mickey, but nothing is certain in life is it? Brendan is being realistic, that's all, and I think we should listen to him and give things one more try, a big push to try and get you noticed and if it fails, then, well, let's do what he suggests, and at least give one of us a chance to make something of their talent. Brendan might just have a chance as a solo performer, and you never know, if he makes it, he might just need a backing group one day in the future, right Brendan?"

"Well, there's always a possibility," Brendan replied, caught on the hop by Marie's comment. The truth of the matter was that he hadn't thought things through that far ahead.

Within minutes, thanks to Marie's intervention, tacit agreement was reached to go along with Brendan's idea. It had become clear to the others that Brendan had basically made his mind up and if they were going to split up, better to do so after having a last attempt at achieving recognition in the business. At least, they all agreed, if nothing else, they'd each have a copy or two of their demo disc to play to their children or grandchildren in the future, some proof that they had at one time nearly made it as recording artists.

As they left the park on that warm, sunny, summer's afternoon, they would also have been surprised to learn that Marie had not only stood up for Brendan's idea from any altruistic sense, but that for nearly three months, she and the lead singer had been indulging in a much closer rela-tionship than any of them could have possibly dreamed about, one that would have also caused consternation in other ways if their relationship became public knowledge. There were other factors involved in the couple keeping their liaison secret, though for now, love's young dream made them both oblivious to the possible consequences of their current course of action.

A slight breeze rustled the bushes that lined the park boundary and a small gust caught the hem of Marie's new, floral summer dress, revealing a little more of her legs than she'd like, and she quickly smoothed her dress down, but not before attracting a wolf-whistle from a young man walking past on the other side of the street from the park. Mickey quickly shouted, "Fuck off, pervert," and the group couldn't help but laugh, as Marie blushed with embarrassment. As a bank of thick cloud rolled in to blank out the sun, Marie walked behind the others, lost in thought, and then turned off the radio. Somehow, the gesture seemed appropriate.

CHAPTER 9

MERSEYSIDE POLICE HEADQUARTERS, 1999

Izzie Drake stood before the mirror on the rear wall of the ladies washroom a few minutes after she and Ross returned from the mortuary. Unlike the smaller mirrors over the wash basins on the other side of the room, this one was a full-length version, thoughtfully provided by someone who'd had the foresight to realise that ladies, in particular, might want to check their overall appearance before venturing onto the streets to continue the fight against crime. In practice, it allowed uniformed officers to ensure nothing looked out of place and that their appearance was of the standard required of their position as representatives of Merseyside Police. Whatever the reason, Izzie was grateful for the chance to quickly take stock of herself after the day's earlier activity.

For some reason, despite the mortuary being one of the most antiseptically clean places she'd even known, Drake always felt as if she needed a bath or at the very least a shower, after visiting the place. It just had that effect on her, as if being surrounded by the presence of death and decomposition somehow tainted her hair, her clothes, her entire being, and as much as she tried to talk herself into ignoring such irrational feelings, the damn place still affected her like this, every time.

Peering at herself in the mirror, she saw a moderately (she thought), pretty woman, still with a youthful look about her at the age of twenty nine, her shoulder-length hair a dark brunette with a lustrous sheen that needed no special shampoos or treatments to maintain its good looks. A quick wash in the morning and she was good to go, ready to face the day and whatever it may bring, even a visit to the morgue. Izzie considered herself lucky in that respect, and her trim figure was accentuated by the well-cut navy skirt suit she'd chosen for the day's work. With the warmer weather she felt more comfortable in a skirt, though she'd be the first to admit there were times when trousers definitely proved a rather more practical option.

Satisfied with her appearance, and relieved to be back on the familiar grounds of the headquarters building, she made her way back to the C.I.D. section and in particular, the office of Andy Ross.

As she knocked and entered the D.I's office, Izzie found Ross sitting behind his desk, a cup of coffee in one hand and a copy of Hannah Lewin's preliminary report in the other. Lewin had worked fast in getting it typed up and faxed through to Ross in double-quick time.

The look on Ross's face was one she'd seen before and knew only too well.

"You've got your worried look on your face, sir."

"Very observant of you, Izzie. You're right of course. Tell me, what did you make of Doctor Lewin and her conclusions?"

"Oh, she of the very beautiful face and shapely body, and…"

"Okay, Izzie, that's enough," Ross grinned. "Any chance you can be serious here, bearing in mind my worried look, you know, the one you seem so concerned about?"

Izzie grinned back at her boss; pleased she'd been able to levitate the moment into something a little less morose.

"Well yes, right you are, sir. I know she appears to be on the ball and a complete expert in her field, so I've no reason to doubt a word she said. But, that's not what's really on your mind is it, sir? It's the bullet wounds to the kneecaps; the possible IRA connection isn't it?"

Ross smiled an ironic smile. He knew his sergeant was familiar enough with his moods and expressions to be able to read him very well indeed, one of the traits that helped them work so well together.

"I can't hide anything from you, can I, Izzie? And yes, you're quite correct in your assumption. I remember the sixties only too well, growing up with the non-stop news of gradually escalating troubles over the water in Northern Ireland. I just hope we're not walking into a potential mine-field here, with political implications if we find evidence of an IRA or Provo killing having taken place here in the city. With the peace process well underway nowadays, the last thing the politicians will want is something like this. Then again we may find the murder has nothing at all to do with the Irish, and that would at least be a weight off my mind."

"So, a nice domestic would do the trick, eh, sir?"

"No murder at all would be preferable, Sergeant, but, if we have to solve one, then yes, I'd rather it didn't have connections with either political or terrorist activity."

"So, what's our next move?"

"We need to speak to the contractors who were working on the reclamation for a start. I know Hannah and Fat Willy Nugent are going to check the site out tomorrow, but there's a chance the workmen who made the original discovery have knowledge or information they don't even realise they're in possession of."

"Such as, sir?"

"If I knew that, we wouldn't be wanting to speak to them, now would we, Izzie?"

"Very true. Anything else?"

"You know as well as I do that identifying the victim has to be our first priority. We don't have a lot to be going on with but at least Hannah Lewin has given us a couple of scraps that might help."

"You mean like the broken leg, for example?"

"Exactly. Assuming our victim is local, it might help if we can start by getting local hospitals to check their records for all youngsters between, let's say ten and fifteen to begin with, let's say twenty five to thirty five years ago. Heck of a list probably I know, but we have to begin somewhere. Local kids would obviously be treated locally so let's check all Liverpool and Birkenhead medical facilities first. It's possible our lad came to school from Birkenhead through the tunnel. I know quite a few secondary pupils made that journey, even in my day."

"You want me to take charge of that sir, or hand it to one of the team?"

"You do it, Izzie. I don't want one of the junior officers taking it on and then not being as thorough as I know you will be. It is a pretty thankless task I know, but…"

"Say no more, sir. I know what you mean. I'll get on it soon as we've finished here."

"Good, thanks Izzie. While you're doing that, I'm going to disappear for a while. I'm going to have a word with the boss, see if he has any contacts with anyone involved in the anti-terrorist people from back then. I want to know if there was any significant IRA or Loyalist activity going on in the early sixties that might have had any connection with the city. If anyone knows, the anti-terrorist squad will, I'm sure.

"We still don't know if the body was dumped in the water before or after the warehouse facility and the wharf ceased operating, do we, sir? Who do you think should check that out?"

"Let's give that to D.C. Ferris. He's got great local knowledge. God knows why that man has never managed to pass his sergeant's exams, he's a first class officer but seems a bit devoid of ambition."

"Maybe it's got something to do with his son, sir? You know, not wanting to commit to the extra hours he'd have to put in if he got his stripes."

Ross silently berated himself for forgetting an important part of one of his junior officer's backgrounds.

"I'd forgotten he has a disabled child. You're probably right, Izzie. Thanks for reminding me."

"That's okay, sir, and don't go beating yourself up just because you can't recall every aspect of every officer on the team's home lives. How he manages sometimes, I don't know. It must be awful trying to juggle his shifts with the need to make sure he or his wife can take the lad for his regular dialysis sessions and check-ups and everything."

"Very true, Izzie. So, yes, Okay, put Ferris on checking up on the old warehouse. I want to know everything possible about the place. Exactly who owned it, when it closed, who worked there, the whole kit and caboodle."

"I'll put him on it before I start checking the hospitals, sir. Anything else for now?"

"No, I think that's enough to get things moving in the right direction. So you go and do what you have to do while I go and have a word with D.C.I. Porteous."

As Izzie Drake left the office and closed the door behind her, Ross rose from behind his desk, picked up the as yet quite thin case file, and quickly followed his sergeant out of the door, and made his way to the office of the Detective Chief Inspector. Things were starting to move, albeit slowly, but any progress was better than none at all, he mused as he walked, deep in thought, to instigate his next line of inquiry.

CHAPTER 10

COLE & SONS

Detective Constable Paul Ferris was in a hurry. Dashing from the kitchen of his neat, two-bedroom semi-detached home, still chewing on a piece of toast, he grabbed his jacket from the coat hook at the bottom of the stairs, throwing it on whilst running upstairs as fast as he could. His wife, Kareen, turned and smiled at her husband as he scurried into the bedroom of their son, Aaron.

"Running late again, darling?" she grinned, as she helped five-year old Aaron on with his shirt.

"Hi, Dad," the youngster said, cheerfully.

"I have to go, Kareen," Ferris gasped, out of breath. "It's a murder inquiry and the boss has given me an important slice of the investigation to work on. I need to get to the station and go through some files before I head off to the docks."

"The docks? Who got killed? You hardly said two words last night when you came in."

"We had other things on our minds last night, remember?" said Ferris, happily remembering a very intimate evening with his wife the night before. They had always made a point of trying to avoid work talk in the evenings, and Paul hadn't mentioned his current assignment yet. He'd normally have told her about the new case over breakfast, but today was different as Kareen had to take Aaron for dialysis for his failing kidneys very early, and had been forced to forego their usual breakfast chat. Paul Ferris replied to his wife, looking at his watch as he did so.

"Well, that's it, babe, we don't know who got killed."

"What? Someone's dead and you don't know who it is? When did this happen?"

"Er, about thirty years ago."

"Thirty *years*. Are you kidding me?"

"It's a skeleton, not a body."

"Paul, make sense will you?"

"Kareen, babe, I've really got to go. Tell you later, okay?"

Quickly kissing his wife on the lips, Ferris dashed from the room, almost tripping over one of Aaron's toy cars which had been left strategically right behind where he stood.

"Be careful, Paul," Kareen shouted, but Ferris was already halfway down the stairs, and in seconds he was out the door and pressing the unlock button on his car's remote. Another twenty seconds and the Ford Escort disappeared round the corner at the end of the street and Paul Ferris began his first full day on the investigation.

* * *

Once at his desk, Ferris lost no time in booting up his computer. One of the reasons Ross loved having Ferris on his team was the D.C's aptitude and skill in all computer-related tasks. Put simply, Paul Ferris and computer technology appeared made for each other. While Ross struggled to master the art of creating and sending an email, Ferris had the talent to use a computer to produce results Ross could only dream about. The current task assigned to Ferris was, by his own standards pretty mundane and not too challenging, but that did nothing to reduce the level of importance attached to the information he'd been asked to find. Having been fully briefed the previous day by Izzie Drake, Ferris had already sent inquiries to various organizations that would hopefully provide him with what he sought.

Most important of all had been a request for information on the company of Cole and Sons, sent the previous afternoon to Companies House in London, where details of the company registration should be available. Having checked his email and seeing nothing from his contact in the capital, Ferris picked up the phone on his desk and in a couple of minutes was engaged in conversation with Jane Hill at Companies House, a useful contact he'd cultivated during a previous investigation.

"Paul Ferris, here Jane, Merseyside Police. You helped me out last year with the Briggs investigation. Hope you remember me."

"Of course, Paul. Good to hear from you. How are you? And that little boy of yours?"

"I'm fine, Jane, thanks. And Aaron's doing okay, still needs regular dialysis though. He's on the waiting list for a transplant, but, well, you know…"

"Sorry, Paul, yes, I know it's hard and very much a waiting game, but I'm sure things will work out for him. But, you didn't call me to talk about Aaron, did you? It's about the request you sent yesterday, Cole and Sons, right?"

"That's right," Ferris replied. "I know it's early, but wondered if you might have anything for me yet. This time, it's not just a fraud case we're investigating. We're looking into a murder that took place some years ago, on the wharf where Cole's warehouse is, or was, seeing as it's been closed for a long time, as far as we know."

"Hold on a minute, please Paul." He heard the sound of Jane's fingers tapping on her keyboard, followed by the sound of rustling paper, and then her voice came back on the line.

"Sorry about that. I'd done some of the checking before I went home yesterday and just wanted to confirm something before ringing you myself."

"You have something for me then, Jane?"

"Yes, I'll send you this in an email in a few minutes but for now, I'm sure you'd like to hear the gist of things, yes?"

"Yes, please Jane. Give me what you've got so far."

"Right, seems Cole and Sons of Liverpool was an old family firm, and the 'Cole' of Cole and Sons was Josiah Cole, who incorporated the business back in 1898."

"That long ago?" Ferris asked, a little surprised the warehouse had been around over a century.

"That's what it says here," Jane Hill went on, "and Josiah eventually handed over the company title to his sons, Walter and Frederick Cole, who held joint ownership of the business until the company ceased to exist, as far as our records show, in 1955."

"Right," Ferris said, thoughtfully. If what Jane said was true, and it would be of course, the warehouse either changed hands or stood empty for a long time prior to the redevelopment of the docks area. He knew he still had work to do.

"Jane, what exactly was Cole and Sons business? You know, what kind of a warehouse was it?"

"It was a bonded warehouse, Paul."

"Hmm, interesting," Ferris replied. A bonded warehouse would have held dutiable goods, wines, spirits, tobacco and so on prior to it being exported, or until duty had been paid to allow it into the UK. Definitely enough to provide a motive for nefarious goings on, he surmised, but then realised the place had probably been closed for years before the murder. *Think again, Ferris*, he thought to himself. "Don't suppose your records show what happened after the Cole's closed the place down?"

"Sorry, Paul. There's only so much we can do for you. Our records can only tell you if a business was registered at that address and as far as those records are concerned, no company has ever registered as operating from that address. Maybe the Cole brothers are still alive, and may be able to help you, or perhaps your local Chamber of Commerce will have more local knowledge of what use the place was put to, if any, after it closed down."

"Understood, Jane, and thank you. The Chamber of Commerce is the next stop on my list. Would be odd if a place like that just stood empty for so many years without being utilized in some way. Anyway, it's been good talking to you again, and thanks for all your help."

"My pleasure, Paul. Sorry, it wasn't much. Hope you find your killer before too long though. You take care of yourself, and that family of yours."

"I will, and you look after yourself too. Thanks again."

After hanging up on Jane Hill, Ferris turned his attention to the local Chamber of Commerce. The secretary of the Chamber informed the detective that the old Cole & Sons warehouse had in fact been used on a number of occasions over the years, having been rented out to various small companies or individuals on short-term leases. A mail order business, a small local company specializing in the manufacture of bespoke toilet seats, and a parcel delivery company were among those who'd rented the warehouse for varying lengths of time, anything from three months to a year, but as far as the secretary was concerned, the place had then fallen into disrepair, with a leaking roof among its drawbacks, some time around nineteen sixty five, ten years after the Coles had closed their business down. When asked by Ferris if he knew whether either of the Cole brothers was still alive, the question drew a blank reply. He was advised to have a word with the chairman of the chamber, who, he was reliably informed, had been around for as long as anyone could remember and if anyone knew anything about the Cole brothers he'd be the man. So, armed with the telephone number of George Irons, Ferris took a quick coffee break and ten minutes later picked up his phone once again.

* * *

"Well, well, Walter and Frederick Cole, now there's a blast from the past," said George Irons, after Ferris had explained the reason for his call.

"You knew them, then, Mr. Irons?"

"Oh, yes, Detective Constable, I knew them both well. They were very active in the affairs of the Chamber at one time. I was a much younger man back then and ran my own private coach business of course. Did great business with workers outings to the seaside and so on. Thirty some-thing years ago, seems like a lifetime ago, but anyway, that's not what you want to know is it? As for the brothers, they took over the bonded ware-house when their father died, and carried on a successful business until poor Walter succumbed to a heart attack quite early in life. He'd never married so the business passed completely to his brother. Freddie carried on for a year or two but quite frankly, I don't think his heart was in the business any longer and he eventually decided to pull out. I remember he put the business up for sale as a going concern, but there were no takers. Anyway, one day he announced he'd closed the place down, just like that. The workers were all laid off, all the fixtures and fittings were sold, fork lift trucks, the lot."

"How many people worked for, er, Freddie, Mr. Irons?"

"Ten, maybe twelve, if I'm not mistaken."

Ferris refrained from asking if the chairman knew any of the workers. That would be too much to ask for after so many years, and of course, he wouldn't have had anything to do with the day to day business of the warehouse.

"Well, thanks for the information, Mr. Irons. Just one more question, and I'll leave you in peace."

"It's a pleasure, Constable. Please, ask away."

"Well, the place had lain idle for years before the docklands redevelopment began. Do you know if it's been used for any other purpose over the years, and who actually owns the place?"

"Can't help with the first part of that question, I'm afraid, but as for who owns it, well, as far as I'm aware, Freddie Cole still owns the property. I'm sure he'll be able to tell you if he's rented it out at any time over the years. If he has, it would probably have been through a letting agent, and they'd be the ones to tell you what it's been used for and who rented it."

Ferris thanked George Irons, there being nothing else he felt he could learn of any relevance from the man. Next on his list had now become Frederick, 'Freddie' Cole. A quick check of the electoral register gave Ferris the address he needed and he decided that it was time to get some fresh air. A personal visit would give him the chance to get out from behind his desk and he was becoming deeply interested in the case. What, if anything did the Cole's warehouse have to do with the skeleton found deep underneath the waters, or in this case, the mud of their former dockside wharf?

Ferris left a message on the desk of Sergeant Drake, who he knew was out doing the rounds of local hospitals, before heading out of the building and was soon on the road, to the district of Wavertree, where Frederick Cole was registered as residing.

* * *

Izzie Drake, meanwhile, was enduring something of a frustrating morning. She'd been amazed at how many hospitals in the area simply didn't retain records as far back as she needed to go. Of those that did, she'd faced the usual 'patient confidentiality' argument, until she'd explained this was a murder inquiry and she wasn't looking to obtain personal medical histories of any particular patient, just that in order to identify a victim, the police needed to ascertain certain information which thankfully the various hospitals finally provided.

In the period she was looking at there had been a total of two hundred and sixty six cases of youngsters in the target age range with broken right legs in the period. She felt relieved she wasn't looking for a left leg victim, of whom there'd been over a hundred more in that time. Thankfully, she'd been able to cut that list down by deleting any who hadn't suffered the break to the femur. Next, looking at the area of the break from the photos provided by Hannah Lewin she was able to eliminate a further thirty five as the fractures had occurred too low down on the bone. She'd finally whittled the list down to forty two possibilities. As Izzie sat at her desk, feeling a headache coming on, she wondered how she could reduce the list further before presenting it to Andy Ross. She rose from her desk, walked across to the coffee machine at the far side of the C.I.D office, and poured herself a mug of very strong, black coffee, returning to her desk with her mind ticking over, still working on her next step. As Izzie opened the top drawer of her desk and took two Advil tablets from a bottle she kept there, ready to swallow when the coffee cooled a little, Paul Ferris walked into the room, fresh from his sojourn to Wavertree.

He raised a hand in greeting as he caught sight of his sergeant, and after a long and fairly hit and miss morning for both officers, it was time to compare notes.

CHAPTER 11

NEW BRIGHTON, MERSEYSIDE, 1964

The seaside resort of New Brighton, part of the town of Wallasey, sits at the northeastern tip of the Wirral peninsula, across the Mersey from its much larger neighbour, Liverpool. The resort received its name from its founder, Liverpool merchant James Atherton who, in 1830, purchased most of the land at Rock Point, and began to develop it as a genteel and fashionable resort for the gentry of the day much like other fashionable resorts of the day, and in a similar way to the better known South Coast resort of Brighton, hence 'New Brighton.' The New Brighton Tower, modelled on the famous Eiffel Tower, and the tallest in the country was opened in 1900 but closed in 1919 and was dismantled by 1921. Below the tower stood the Tower Ballroom, which remained after the tower closed and retained its use as a venue for entertainment, and hosted numerous concerts in the 1950s and 60s, including performances by The Beatles, and other international stars. Brendan Kane and the Planets made two appearances at the ballroom which would eventually be destroyed by fire in 1969.

For now, however, the resort played host to a young couple seeking something of a getaway from their usual habitat and surroundings. Brendan Kane and Marie Doyle had found themselves growing ever closer together over the preceding months, and it was now evident to both of them that their feelings were deep and of a highly romantic nature. In short, Brendan and Marie were in love.

Marie was dressed in a new cream and silver striped blouse and her new knee-length half-lined navy skirt that fitted her perfectly and accentuated the femininity of her figure. Her stockings were new, too, and she'd borrowed a pair of black shoes with two inch heels from her best friend, Clemmy. She'd bought the skirt especially for this day with Brendan, who wore a crisp blue shirt and a pair of new jeans he'd ordered from his Mother's mail-order catalogue, together with his black 'winkle-picker' shoes, highly polished as always. Marie thought he looked incredibly handsome.

Having crossed the Mersey on the early morning New Brighton Ferry and then spending an idyllic two hours listening to music on Marie's transistor radio, whilst kissing and canoodling on New Brighton Beach, Brendan and Marie now sat holding hands in a small caravan, rented by Brendan for one week on one of the popular caravan sites that had sprung up to cater for holidaymakers in the area. Though he knew he and Marie would probably only have one or two opportunities to slip away to the caravan during the week, he felt it was worth the financial outlay in order to give them these precious hours together. Living in such a close environment as they did with the group, privacy was something that didn't come easily, and the couple had no wish to make their feelings for each other public knowledge, at least not yet. Marie had stood by him when he'd made the suggestion about trying the demo disc and possibly breaking up the group if things didn't go their way, and the others might feel aggrieved if they thought she'd only supported Brendan because of her feelings for him.

Having spent months making their plans for the disc, Brendan Kane and The Planets had finally recorded their demo disc the previous week and now awaited the delivery of the consignment of their 'last chance' recording to arrive, after which they'd circulate copies of the disc as previously arranged. After that, their fate would be in the lap of the Gods, and the various record producers and recording companies.

"You're sure nobody knows we're here, Brendan?" Marie asked, nervously.

"I told you, we're totally safe here," he replied. I booked this place weeks ago, paid cash and used the name Davis, so please stop worrying."

"You do know I have to be back home by tea-time or me Mam and Dad'll wonder where I am?"

"They think you're out with the girls, right?" Brendan asked.

"Yeah, they do. They don't mind me doing stuff with the group, Brendan, but this, well, it's different isn't it?"

Brendan slowly slipped an arm round Marie's shoulder, pulling her closer to him.

"Everything's okay, Marie, honestly. You trust me, don't you?"

"Course I do, you silly bugger. I wouldn't be here with you now if I didn't trust you, would I, you dozy mare?"

Brendan laughed, a laugh Marie had always found infectious, and in seconds the couple were both giggling and then, suddenly, Brendan leaned in close and kissed her, passionately, on the lips. The kiss seemed to last for ages, and Marie finally pulled away gasping.

"Wow," she exclaimed.

"You're so beautiful, you know that don't you?" said Brendan, not really expecting a reply.

"If you say so, Brendan," Marie managed, before he kissed her again, a long, slow kiss that made her knees go weak and made her feel a dampness between her legs. Brendan didn't say anything else, but his hand slowly began to make its way under the hem of Marie's skirt, gradually feeling its way upwards along the length of her leg, stopping for a moment as his fingers reached the top of her stocking. Marie felt her breath coming in small gasps as the thrill of the moment began to overtake her.

"Don't stop, Brendan, please," she gasped, her voice husky as Brendan's hand moved higher and Marie opened her legs a little to allow him access to her private places, where no man, before today had been granted access. His fingers gently slipped into her panties and found their way in between her legs, where Brendan found her wet and ready for him to take things even further.

"Wait," she whispered in Brendan's ear, and she gently removed his hand from its place under her skirt. Marie stood up and slowly raised the hem of her skirt, allowing Brendan a view of her shapely legs and then slowly she reached behind her, unzipped the skirt and allowed it to fall to the floor. Her panties followed, and as she stepped out of the tiny white lace-trimmed knickers, Brendan gazed almost in awe at the sight before him. Marie knelt in front of him and reached up to unfasten the buttons of his shirt, which soon fell open to reveal his chest, covered in dark brown hairs, and she ran her hand through the hairs for a few seconds, bringing a tingle to his skin and Brendan felt himself growing harder in anticipation of the next few minutes. Marie moved to try to remove his jeans, but, making her wait to prolong the moment, Brendan kissed her once again before leading her by the hand into the dormer area of the caravan, where he quickly closed the curtains and pushed Marie, very gently, on to her back on the bed, which he'd made up the previous day, hoping for just such an eventuality. Marie lay on the bed, looking up at him as he slowly reached down, took her face in his hands and kissed her again. His hands reached behind her and after a little fumbling, he managed to unfasten Marie's bra, and as he pulled it from her, he was able to marvel at the sight of her perfectly formed breasts, the nipples dark and engorged and standing erect, perhaps as erect as he was at that moment. He reached out and gently took each one in turn between his fingers, manipulating them gently as Marie closed her eyes and reveled in the new and exciting feelings his attentions were setting off in her body. When he stopped using his fingers and moved closer, taking her left nipple in his mouth, Marie shuddered with the pure thrill of what was happening to her, and a small groan escaped from her lips.

"Oh, God, Brendan. What are you doing to me? I've never felt like this before. I think you should know, though, that I've never, well, you know, I've never actually done this or anything like it before."

Brendan shushed her gently, placing a finger on her lips and whispering back to her, "Neither have I."

"But, you must have," Marie exclaimed in surprise. All those gigs, the girls flocking round you, surely you..."

"Never, Marie. I've fancied you since the day we met, and I've waited all this time in case I saw some sign from you that you felt the same."

"I never knew."

"Well, you know now,"

"Mmm, "she gasped as Brendan fell silent once more and moved his mouth to take her other nipple between his lips. This time, he allowed his teeth to gently nip at her breast, and Marie could barely contain the wave of arousal that swept through her body. Brendan took hold of Marie's hand and guided it to the growing bulge in his jeans. She didn't need telling what to do as she lowered the zip and moved to unfasten his belt. As she pushed his underpants down, his erect penis sprang from within, and Marie gasped again at the sheer size and weight of the throbbing thing that she held in her hand.

Neither of them could wait any longer, and as Brendan's fingers probed inside her wet opening, she spoke in that husky, expectant voice once more, "Please Brendan, make love to me, now."

Brendan Kane didn't need any further encouragement and he pushed Marie onto her back on the bed and pushed her legs apart. Marie helped by spreading her legs wide, and as Brendan moved on top of her, she took hold of him and guided him into herself, giving out a small cry as he penetrated her for the first time.

"Are you alright?" Brendan asked as she cried out.

"Don't stop, please, don't stop," she replied.

Brendan soon settled into a slow, rhythmic movement in and out of her virgin vagina, and Marie urged him to move faster until he could no longer hold back and he felt a massive release as he ejaculated into the girl of his dreams. Marie suddenly felt a welling up of emotions coming from deep within and she cried out again as her body was overtaken by a series of spasms that seemed to go on and on, until they finally subsided, leaving her breathless and amazed at their intensity.

"Oh, my God, Brendan," she exclaimed. "That was amazing. I wonder if it's like that for everyone the first time."

His breathing returning to normal, Brendan looked down at Marie and smiled. "I don't know and don't care. All I know is it was great for us, and that's all I care about. I love you, Marie."

"I love you too, Brendan," she replied, as he slowly pulled out of her, and rolled off to lie beside her. Marie just lay there with her legs wide apart for a minute, and then, pulling herself together, she rose from the bed and reached for a box of tissues that she saw on the small shelf in the room. She self-consciously wiped herself and leaned over to pick her underwear up from the floor, and was soon dressed once again, standing beside the bed, smoothing her skirt down as Brendan finally rose, pulled up his jeans and fastened his belt and zip. They sat gazing into each other's eyes for what seemed an age, as Marie's radio played quietly in the background. Marie had discovered the pleasure of listening to the new pirate radio station, Radio Caroline, broadcasting from somewhere in the North Sea, and like many teenagers, derived an almost guilty pleasure from tuning in to the illegal broadcaster. When Kathy Kirby's *Secret Love* came bursting forth from the tiny radio's speaker, the couple stared harder at each other and almost simultaneously spoke the same words, "That's our song!"

It was impossible to say whether either one of them had thought about using any form of contraception, as neither of them mentioned it to the other. The time of general knowledge on the use of contraception and family planning was years away in the early sixties, so it was quite possible that neither one of the couple possessed much awareness or understanding on the subject. For now, both Brendan Kane and Marie Doyle were filled with the first flush of love and sated from the resulting consummation of their newly-declared feelings for one another.

A short time later, after locking up the caravan and making their way back to the beach, where they enjoyed a half hour lying on the sand together, holding hands, saying little, but occasionally staring longingly into one another's eyes, the time came for them to make their way back to the ferry terminal, where, all too soon, they were crossing the Mersey, back to Liverpool and the reality of their everyday lives. They would get the chance to return to New Brighton later in the week, but for now, home beckoned for them both. Marie would soon be sitting down to tea with her family, while Brendan would have a bite to eat and then wander down the road to the pub to enjoy a pint or two with his Dad, who, Brendan thought, hadn't been himself recently, appearing to have lost weight and coughing a lot.

As they kissed each other goodbye after the ferry docked, Brendan felt a deep longing for Marie as he watched her walk away towards her bus stop, her hips seeming to sway with additional sensuality as her flared skirt added to the sway of her hips, and later that night, both of them would dream of their time together earlier that day, and look forward with intense anticipation to their next planned visit to the caravan, their own secret place.

CHAPTER 12

LIVERPOOL 1999

"Well, Paul, any progress?" Izzie Drake asked D.C. Ferris as he took a seat in the chair at the end of her desk.

"Of a sort, Sarge," he replied, "though I'm not sure it'll get us very far with the case."

"Okay, just tell me what you discovered in deepest, darkest Wavertree."

""Strange place, Sarge. Lots of nice houses and yet there's loads of students from the university living out there, too. Did you know lots of well-known people lived there at one time, and some still do?"

"Go on then, I know you're dying to tell me who."

"For a start, John Lennon and George Harrison lived there at one time, and Kim Cattrall, you know, the actress?"

"Yes, I do happen to know who Kim Cattrall is, Paul, thank you."

"Leonard Rossiter, and lots more."

"Thanks for the celebrity guidebook tour," Drake grinned. "I take it you looked all that up on your trusty computer before you even left the building this morning?"

Ferris smiled back at her and replied, sheepishly, "Well, yesterday afternoon actually. Just wanted to check out the territory before hitting the streets, like, you know?"

"Bloody hell, Paul. You sound like something out of 'Hill Street Blues'. Come on now, what did you discover from the surviving brother?"

Ferris pulled his notebook from his pocket, opened it up to check his notes as he spoke, and began:

"Frederick, he made me call him Freddie by the way, Cole, is the last surviving member of his family. Seems he and his brother Walter, who he referred to as Wally, were always close and worked well together after the death of their father, Josiah. Freddie became sole proprietor of the business after Wally's death from a heart attack, and he carried on running the business successfully, according to him, until his wife, Mary died in a road traffic accident five years after Wally's death."

"Any suspicious circumstances surrounding the wife's death, d'you think?"

"I seriously doubt it, Sarge. He was in the car with her at the time. Poor bloke was left blind in one eye and with one leg shorter than the other as a result of the crash. Still has a limp and walks with a stick. Didn't stop him running the warehouse though, until Mary died and he told me his heart just went out of it, and he tried selling up but there were no takers."

"So, what did he do with the place?"

"He handed redundancy notices to his ten staff, paid them off more than generously, sold off the fixtures and fittings and placed the warehouse in the hands of a commercial letting agent. Over the years a few small companies and individuals rented it on short term leases but the cost of continually maintaining the fabric of the building itself made the whole thing a financial liability. When the redevelopment of the docklands area began and the council approached him with a view to him selling the warehouse and land for future redevelopment, he jumped at the chance to offload the place. He sold up, over a year ago, and as far as he's concerned, the council will probably be selling it on to some property developer who'll build luxury apartments on the site."

"And that's all you found out?"

"Well, yes, and a couple of names of the companies who leased the place, but they all seem to have come along well outside the time frame we're looking at for the murder."

Izzie Drake leaned back in her chair for a few seconds, lost in thought. Finally, she spoke again.

"It may not seem much, but you've managed to eliminate certain people and organisations from the investigation."

"I have?"

"Yes, it's now that obvious none of those who used the warehouse after Frederick Cole closed the place could have been involved if they came into the picture years after the death of the victim. If what Cole told you is true and we don't seem to have any reason to doubt his word at this point, the warehouse was closed, standing empty and mothballed at the time of the murder so the chances of the murder having anything to do with the goods that would have been stored in a bonded warehouse are also zero. Whatever happened on the wharf outside Cole and Sons' warehouse took place long after the closure and had no connection to the business previously carried out there. That may not seem much, but it is progress of a kind, Paul."

"Glad you see it that way, Sarge. How did your hospital visiting go?"

"Pretty much inconclusive, I'm afraid. I've managed to narrow the list of potential victims down to about forty five, but don't see how we can possibly trace every former kid who broke his leg back in the sixties. Some will have left town, others may have died, and some will just have dropped off the radar. I don't want to sound negative, but I'm just not sure if this case is going anywhere. If we can't identify the victim, what chance do we have? It happened over thirty years ago according to forensics, and I don't see the Chief Superintendent letting us spend too many hours on it, what with all the current crimes on the books that need resolving."

Drake knew their chances of success in the case were virtually non-existent without that vital piece of evidence that might give their victim a name. Until they had that, the remains in the old dock were just that, a set of bones, remains of a nameless victim of violence who would probably never be identified, a crime forever unsolved.

* * *

Detective Chief Inspector Harry Porteous looked across his desk at Andy Ross. He'd been unable to give his D.I. much to go on with regards to the subject of terrorist activity in the city in the nineteen-sixties. He knew Ross was fighting what appeared to be a losing battle with the skeleton case, as he thought of it, and wasn't sure just how long he should let his murder squad spend time on the problem of the bones in the dock.

"Like I said, Andy, when you first called me I spoke with my contacts at the Anti-Terrorist Squad, and as far as they're concerned, there was nothing going on in the city around that time. Of course, it's possible the IRA and the Loyalist groups used us a point of entry or exit to the mainland, but no evidence exists to suggest any terror cells were actually active here at the time."

"Right, sir, so my question is, just how far do you want us to take this inquiry?"

"I can't afford to let you spend much longer on the case, Andy. We need our people working on active cases, rather than a murder that took place thirty-odd years ago. I know every victim is entitled to justice, but if we can't I.D. the victim, we can't possible catch the killer. You say Dr. Lewin is going over the site of the discovery once again, so let's see if her search uncovers anything else. If not, and if your people haven't found anything during the inquiries you've got them conducting at present, I think we need to gradually wind this inquiry down."

Ross fully understood his boss's point, and for the most part, agreed with him, though it rankled with him that a murderer would appear to have got away with a violent killing and had managed to escape the retribution of the law for over thirty years.

"Just give me a couple of weeks, sir, please. I don't want to give up without giving this a really good try. Someone killed that young man, and I want to find the bastard who kneecapped and bludgeoned a young man and probably threw him alive into the Mersey to drown in agony."

Porteous swivelled his high-backed executive chair round until he was facing the large plate glass window that gave his office a great view over the city he and his men and women did their best to protect. He stared off into space for a few seconds, as Ross patiently sat waiting for a decision. His mind made up, the D.C.I turned his chair back to face Ross.

"One week, Andy, that's the best I can do. If you can't make any progress in that time, we close the case, and mark it unsolved, Okay?"

Ross nodded, pleased to have been given some time, at least, to pursue the case. The nameless victim still had a chance to find justice. Leaving Porteous's office, he made his way back to his office, suddenly feeling an urgent need for a strong cup of coffee, and a crisis meeting with his team of detectives.

CHAPTER 13

PROGRESS, 1999

The phone call Andy Ross received the following morning came as a pleasant surprise. The feelings of negativity and impending failure began hanging like the Sword of Damocles over the Inspector and his team since the previous afternoon. As much as none of them felt good about the possibility of allowing a murderer to go free, even after such a length of time, the prospect of being pulled off the case loomed large and such a result was abhorrent to every member of Ross's small team. Even young Detective Constable McLennan appeared to have lost some of his normally infectious enthusiasm.

"We're not going to just give up though, sir, are we?" the young D.C had asked. "I mean, it's still a body, isn't it, that is, I mean, I know it's a skeleton, but it's a victim, murdered, right? Our duty must be…"

"Please do not try to tell me what our duty is McLennan. As much as I sympathise with your youthful exuberance and sense of justice, we have a duty to follow the orders of our superior officers, and if D.C.I Porteous says we close the case in a week, we close it. If we want to keep the investigation alive, we have to identify the victim, got it?"

"Got it sir. Sorry, sir," McLennan had replied, looking rather sheepish and shamefaced at having voiced his opinions so strongly. In truth, Ross had every sympathy with young Derek McLennan. He too hated the thought that they'd quite literally unearthed a murder victim from many years earlier and due to lack of clues and identity, they could be forced to close the case almost before it had got off the ground, thus allowing the murderer to continue living in the belief that he or she had got away with their crime, scot-free.

"Ross here," he spoke as he lifted the receiver and held it to his ear.

"Andy, it's Hannah Lewin."

"Oh, hello, Doctor Lewin."

"It's Hannah, remember? And listen, you know you said William and I could go and have another ferret around the skeleton recovery site?"

"Uh huh," said Ross, suddenly feeling a sense of anticipation at the way the forensic scientist was speaking.

"Well we did, go for another dig that is, and we've just returned to the lab. I really think you should come down here and see what we found."

Now Ross was as alert as he could possibly be.

"You've got something?" he asked

"We've got something," she replied. "How long will it take you to get here?"

"I'll go find Sergeant Drake and we'll be there within the hour, and Hannah?"

"Yes?"

"Well done, and thanks."

"You don't know what we've found yet. Isn't it a bit premature to be thanking me?"

"Just let me be the judge of that, okay?"

"Okay," she replied as she replaced the phone on its cradle.

"Izzie," Ross shouted at the top of his voice. "Get in here, now, and bring McLennan with you."

Soon afterwards, Ross, Drake and young Derek McLennan were in the car heading for the mortuary. Ross had made the decision to include the young detective constable in the visit in order to give the man added experience, and in view of McLennan's earlier statement about the case, he wanted to show him that they were, in fact, doing all they possibly could. Perhaps a visit to the morgue would give McLennan something of a reality check. It might just make him aware of the difficulties the case presented, and anyway, it was time he saw how the youngest detective on his team handled such a visit.

Peter Foster was once again on duty in reception and this time smiled warmly in recognition as Ross and Drake walked up to this cubicle cum office, closely followed by D.C. McLennan,

"Back again so soon, Detective Inspector?" asked Foster. "You must like it here."

"Needs must I'm afraid, Mr. Foster. You seem a lot happier today than when we called last time."

"Ah, a good win at the weekend, Inspector, always cheers me up for the week."

"I see," said Ross, "an Everton supporter eh?"

"Correct," Foster replied,

"Me too," said Ross, and Foster beamed at him as he identified himself as a fellow fan of Everton Football Club. A wry smile on the face of McLennan gave him away as a fan of the red half of the city, in the form of Liverpool F.C. The young constable maintained a diplomatic silence in the presence of his boss.

Foster buzzed the three officers through and they were soon back in the presence of Doctors William Nugent and Hannah Lewin, Lees the assistant lurking in the background, and on this occasion, another man stood beside Hannah Lewin.

"Ah, come in, please, Inspector," William Nugent urged. "Sergeant Drake, good to see you again, and who might we having the pleasure of entertaining here?" he said indicating young Derek McLennan.

"Good morning Doctor," Ross replied. "This is Detective Constable McLennan, the newest member of my team. Thought he'd maybe learn a thing or two from joining us this morning."

"Aye, a good idea, I'm sure. Pleased tae meet ye, laddie," Nugent reached out a hand to McLennan, who shook hands firmly with the pathologist. "A fine handshake ye have, laddie. You'll go far, I'm sure."

McLennan blushed and Ross came to the rescue of his embarrassed young officer.

"And who have we here, may I ask, Doctor?" his eyes turning to indicate the newcomer. The answer came from the man himself, dressed in a plain navy blue suit, white shirt and red bow-tie which, to Andy Ross immediately screamed 'academic' who quickly walked round from the other side of the autopsy table, his hand outstretched in greeting. The man's black shoes were polished to an almost mirror finish. As Ross politely shook hands with the newcomer, the man swiftly identified himself.

"Alan Slade, Inspector. Please to meet you."

"That's *Professor* Alan Slade," Hannah Lewin interjected. "Alan's a forensic orthodontist."

"Ah, I see, I think," said Ross.

"Hannah asked me to give her a second opinion on the teeth in your mystery skull, Inspector. Hope you don't mind," Slade said.

"Not at all," Ross replied.

Hannah Lewin quickly added,

"Alan is a freelance expert in his field, Andy. I know how frustrating this case is proving to be for you and thought Alan might see something I haven't that might help identify our victim."

Ross nodded, "And have you found anything new, Professor?"

Slade glanced at Hannah before continuing.

"I can't exactly say what I've found is new compared to Hannah's previous analysis, but I can confirm that the amalgam used in the fillings in the victims mouth are a silver amalgam typically in use during the late fifties, early sixties. What we call composite amalgams came into regular use during the sixties but this amalgam pre-dates them so we can certainly say that victim received the fillings in his younger days. I've taken a full set of dental x-rays which we can normally use to generate positive identity, but we would need the patient's dental records against which we can compare the x-rays."

As a look of disappointment appeared on Ross's face, Izzie Drake spoke the very thoughts in his mind.

"So we're really nowhere nearer to a positive I.D. are we?"

"That really depends how you look at it," Slade replied. "It's probably true that a lot of dental surgeons who were actively practicing in the fifties and sixties are now either retired or deceased, but we still have a chance of making a positive identification, if your victim was treated at a practice that is still in existence. What you need to do is send copies of the x-rays to each practice in the city and ask if they match any young male patients, probably of junior school age, from your timeframe. The other thing I can confirm is that your victim was certainly no older than twenty one or maybe twenty two at the time of his death. I presume you'd like the exact details of how we determined the age, Inspector?"

"I'll take your word on that for now, Professor, but would like a written copy of your findings as soon as possible, please," Ross replied, a hint of optimism creeping into his voice. It wasn't much, but it was a tiny glimmer of hope provided by the joint efforts of the pathologists. "McLennan, as soon as we get back to the station, I'd like you to compile a list of dentists in the city, and as soon as the dental x-rays arrive you can circulate a request to all dental practices in the area in the hope that one of them might have the records of the deceased. It's a long shot after all this time, but well worth the effort."

"Will do, sir," said D.C. McLennan, as he wrote his orders up in his notebook.

"There's something else," Slade said.

"Go ahead, Professor," Ross spoke with expectation in his voice. He was beginning to warm to this dapper little man.

"Well, back in the nineteen fifties and early sixties, I do believe there was a system in operation where what were known as 'school dentists' would visit schools in the area, mostly infant and junior level I think, and carry out routine dental checks. It's possible the education department might be of some help in that area of investigation?"

"Hmm, a little more complicated to check out with all the changes in the education system over the years, but yes, thank you, Professor, it's an avenue worth pursuing if we come up empty-handed with the dentists. Anything else?"

"Just that your victim was well-fed, the teeth showing no signs of poor diet or undue decay for their age."

"Right, well, thank you for that, and thank you to you too, Hannah for having the Professor here take a look at the teeth."

"I'm glad it may have helped," said Hannah Lewin. I know I told you that teeth can play a big part in identifying the dead, but even we forensic pathologists need a point of reference in order to come up with a definite identification. But all this leads me on to the real reason William and I asked you here today."

"There's more?" Ross asked.

"Oh yes, isn't there, William?"

"Aye, that there is, lass," Nugent replied. "Go ahead, Hannah, you tell them. After all, you were the one who had the brainwave in the first place."

Lewin now asked the small group to follow her to the counter top that stood against the far wall of the room. Standing there was a battered and faded boot, still easily recognisable as being of the western, or cowboy style of footwear. In addition, propped up against the wall itself where the counter top ended was the rusted, misshaped carcass of an old bedstead, little more than a few springs and a partial frame, with one remnant of a leg barely attached at one corner.

Hannah first of all indicated the rusted old bedstead.

"One thing we discovered when I was working abroad, with mass graves or any old burial sites where water was involved, was that heavier items can often find their way down through muddy river bottoms and so on into the next layer of strata, mud, or whatever. William and I, together with Mr. Lees, spent a morning getting down 'n dirty in the old dock until we came up with this old thing, and the boot, possibly the pair to the remnants your people found. I think you might just find that this is the reason the body never floated back to the surface when it should have done."

"Of course," said Drake. "The body could have sunk and got caught in the old springs of the bedstead. The boots would have got trapped by the springs and prevented it from floating."

"That's precisely what I believe happened, Sergeant," said Lewin. "I think you might even be able to date the boot as well. It's degraded a bit but should still be identifiable. It certainly appears to have been an expensive item, not some cheap imitation leather or synthetic. Whoever owned it and its partner would have treasured such a pair of boots, I'm sure."

Feeling they'd learned all they could from the current visit, Ross thanked the three scientists and he, Drake and McLennan headed back to Merseyside Police H.Q. where McLennan eagerly separated from the two senior officers, eager to 'get his teeth' into his new role in the investigation. He knew it wouldn't be easy but was determined to do all he could to effect an identification through the dental records check. Until the x-rays arrived from Professor Slade later that day, he'd prepare the ground by compiling a list of all those dental practitioners he'd need to contact. Andy Ross and

Izzie Drake had just returned to Drake's office and were reviewing the information they had to date when the phone on Ross's desk began to ring. "Does someone have eyes in my walls, Izzie? Two minutes back in the office and the damn thing rings."

Izzie Drake smiled as she watched Ross reach out and pick up the phone.

"D.I. Ross," he snapped into the offending instrument.

After a few seconds, he spoke again.

"You have got to be joking." A pause as he listened again and then, "Well for Heaven's sake, get someone to show them to my office, right away, Miller."

Replacing the phone on its cradle, he looked at Izzie Drake and said, sounding much calmer than he felt, "That was Sergeant Miller on the reception desk downstairs. He says there are two men standing in front of him who claim to have information relating to the identity of the skeletal remains found, at the wharf near Cole and Sons warehouse. Apparently, they'll only speak to the detective in charge of the investigation. They'll be here in a minute, soon as Miller can get someone to escort them up here."

"That's amazing, sir. Let's hope they have genuine intel. Do you want me to leave you to speak to them in private?"

"No, Izzie. Stay here. Whatever these guys have to say, I want you to hear it too. Make sure you take notes of everything they have to say."

Ross quickly re-arranged the papers on his desk in an effort to make it look a little more business-like in front of his visitors, but within a minute a knock on the door signalled their arrival. *Maybe it's time our luck changed,* thought Ross as he motioned to Drake who moved to the door, to usher their potential informants into the office.

CHAPTER 14

MEMORIES

Izzie Drake thanked the female uniformed constable who'd escorted the two men up to Ross's office and led them in and repeated the names given to her by Constable Greening at the door.

"Michael and Ronald Doyle are here to see you, sir."

Ross looked at the two men, both probably in their fifties, who'd walked into the room, and, even without being told their names, he'd have had no problem in discerning them to be brothers. Although the elder of the two was rotund and showed evidence of a beer drinking habit, evidenced by his overhanging belly, and the leaner of the two appeared fit and more meticulous in his dress and demeanour, their facial characteristics were such that the familial resemblance was inescapable.

"Come in, gentlemen, please. Have a seat." Ross gestured to the two chairs Izzie had recently placed in front of his desk in preparation for the interview. The two men sat, and the elder brother spoke.

"We'd prefer Mickey and Ronnie if you don't mind."

"Sure," Ross replied. "I'm Detective Inspector Ross, and this is Detective Sergeant Drake," he went on, as he indicated Izzie, who'd taken up a standing position near the door. "The desk sergeant tells me you may have some important information for us relating to recent events?"

"Yes, we do," said Mickey. "First of all, we saw this," and he took a folded up newspaper from the inside pocket of his brown leather jacket and passed it across the desk to Ross. It was a copy of the Liverpool Echo, opened at the page where the Force's Press Liaison Officer's release to the press had been printed. It had been a short piece, merely stating that skeletal remains had been discovered in the vicinity of a former warehouse in the city's docklands area and that the police were pursuing inquiries in an attempt to identify the victim, the remains appearing to be between thirty and forty years old.

"I see, please go on."

"Well, I saw it first, and then when he came round to my house, I showed it to Ronnie and we both thought the same thing."

"And just what was this, 'same thing' you both thought of?" Ross asked.

Mickey looked as if he was on the verge of tears, and looked at his brother, who now spoke for the first time.

"We didn't just jump to conclusions, Inspector. You have to understand that this has hung over us for a long time, and we might be wrong in our assumption, but, well, we think you might have found our sister, Marie."

Ross's heart sank. Of course, the press release hadn't given any indicator of the gender of the victim, and he wondered how to let the brothers down gently. First, however, he thought it prudent to probe a little deeper.

"I'm sorry to tell you that the remains that were unearthed were those of a male, not a female, and therefore can't be the remains of your sister."

Ronnie and Mickey looked at each other, and it was plain to Ross that a certain amount of confusion existed in their minds. Perhaps a little relief that it wasn't their sister, but at the same time a continuation of some long-held stress that held both men in its thrall.

"Oh," said Mickey, and "We seem to have wasted your time, Inspector," Ronnie added.

Ross looked up at his sergeant, standing by the door, and she nodded back at him, instinctively knowing where he was about to direct the interview.

"Mickey, Ronnie, please, it might be important and helpful if you can tell us why you thought the remains could have been those of your sister. When did she go missing, and what exactly led up to her disappearance, because I'm presuming you're telling us she'd been gone for a long time?"

Mickey still appeared quite upset, and he gestured with his hands for Ronnie to tell their story. After taking a few seconds to gather his thoughts, the younger of the Doyle brothers began his tale by first passing a photograph across the desk, which Ross picked up and smiled as he saw the subject of the old black and white image.

"This was you?" he asked.

"Yes," said Ronnie. "We were both in a pop group back in the early sixties, Brendan Kane and The Planets. I know you won't have heard of us, but we did okay for a while, even played at The Cavern and The Iron Door, and all the major clubs in the area. We really thought we had a chance to follow in the footsteps of The Beatles, Gerry and The Pacemakers and their ilk. Sadly we never quite made it. Mickey was our lead guitarist, and I was the bass player. A chap called Phil Oxley was our drummer and Brendan Kane himself was lead singer and rhythm guitar."

"And Marie?" This question came from Izzie Drake, who'd moved from her place by the door to take a seat in the corner, off to the side of Ross's desk.

"Marie was our sister, of course, but not a part of the group, as such. But, back in the early days she often drove the van for us, ferrying us to and from gigs. At first, we used our Dad's van, but when his business began to fail he laid off his mate who had a van too, and we were restricted to only using it at night. Anyway, Marie was kind of like an honorary member of the group, always with us, and we'd not have got as far as we did without her."

Ross felt there was something more here, and wanted to hear the rest of the Doyle's story.

"So, what happened, Ronnie? You said you didn't make it, so what happened to the group?"

"Well, we gradually got fewer gigs when we had to stop playing at lunchtimes, and one day Brendan dropped a bombshell, saying he thought we should cut a demo disc and if it didn't get us a recording contract, he wanted us to split up, end the group, you know?"

"And you weren't too happy with that?"

"No, none of us were. We'd been together for about five years as a group by then. We probably knew he was right, deep down but we felt as if he'd betrayed us all, wanting to just give up and then he said if we did, he'd be going on to try and launch a solo career. You can imagine, that went down like a flippin' lead balloon. We were in the little park near where Brendan lived and I can remember it was a really warm summer's day. We'd been arguing about the future for a while and the thing was, when he'd first announced his plan, Marie had actually agreed with him, which kind of took the rest of us by surprise. Anyway, to cut it short, we made the demo disc at a studio in town, long closed now, by the way and Marie went and helped Brendan to mail copies to just about every recording studio and management agency in the country. As you've probably guessed it never got us anywhere and a few months later the group spilt up as we'd reluctantly agreed and Brendan went off to start what he believed would be a new, solo career."

"But that didn't work out for him either, did it, little brother?" Mickey joined the conversation, his words tinged with a bitterness he found hard to disguise.

"No, it didn't." Ronnie continued. "He tried and failed to make the breakthrough on his own. After a couple of years, his solo career had died and the last we heard, Brendan was planning on going to America. He thought he'd have a better opportunity over there, more potential exposure, as he thought the States might prove a better market for a solo singer."

At this point, Mickey Doyle felt the need to interject.

"Yeah, but there was worse to come, Inspector Ross. None of us knew that Brendan and Marie had been secretly 'carrying on' together for years, sneaking off to make love whenever they could. Marie knew our parents wouldn't approve of her having sex outside marriage. They were dead straight, you know, real old-fashioned about those things. It wasn't all as free and easy as everyone thinks back in the sixties you know."

Ronnie took over once again.

"Anyway, one day, everything came to a head. There was a massive row between us all, and well, we never saw Brendan after that day, and soon after that, Marie disappeared too, but because she was an adult, and because we had no proof whatsoever that foul play was suspected, the police at the time either couldn't or wouldn't do much when we reported her disappearance to them. To be honest, we, and Mickey here, especially, have been doing all we can to trace her over the years. When we saw that report about the skeleton in the Echo we thought…well…you know what I'm saying, right?"

Ross thought carefully as he hesitated before answering Ronnie Doyle. A theory was forming in his mind, and he needed to ask just one question to confirm whether the wild idea that had formed as he'd listened to Ronnie's story might be possible. Eventually, he decided to test his theory.

"This is all very interesting, Ronnie, but of course, my priority is identifying the remains we found at the old wharf. I sympathise with your loss in regards to your sister's disappearance, and from what you've told me I have the very strange feeling that Marie may be connected to our current case. You coming here today may just have been the 'wild card' we've been waiting for, the chance to begin putting this case together at last."

"In what way, Inspector? You said the skeleton was male, so it can't be Marie," said Ronnie, looking a little confused.

"Let me just ask you one question, please, well, maybe two."

"Okay, go ahead."

"You'd both known Brendan since you'd been boys growing up together, yes?"

Both men nodded yes.

"Can either of you tell me whether, at some time during his school life, Brendan Kane suffered a broken right leg, and whether, round about the time of him supposedly leaving you all behind to go off to America, he owned a very expensive pair of brown cowboy style boots?"

The Doyle brothers gaped open-mouthed at Ross's words. The detective might have been a mind reader as far as they were concerned.

"How the fu…er, sorry. How the heck do you know that, Inspector?" said Mickey.

"The answer's yes to both questions," added Ronnie. "He broke his leg in a playground accident and those boots were Brendan's pride and joy. He'd ordered them especially from America. How do you…?"

Ronnie fell silent in mid-sentence as he caught on to Ross's train of thought. He spoke again.

"You think those bones belong to Brendan, don't you, Inspector? You think he never went to the States; that he died all those years ago and no-one knew about it."

Andy Ross chose his next words very carefully. If the bones were indeed the mortal remains of Brendan Kane, the Doyle brothers just might be considered potential suspects, although them coming forward like this made him seriously doubt the possibility. They'd hardly come in here after all these years if they'd been responsible for putting the body in the water in the first place.

"I think there's a strong possibility, yes. I need to know a lot more before we can confirm it. For now," he turned to Izzie, "Sergeant Drake here will go and get us some coffee, and, if you're not in any great hurry, I'd like you to tell me more, and especially about the last time you saw Brendan Kane and your sister, in as much detail as possible."

Izzie Drake nodded and left the office to return soon afterwards with coffee for all four of them. Ross had allowed the men a five minute break to gather their thoughts while she'd been absent and now he turned to Ronnie once more.

"Ronnie, please, think hard, and take me back to the nineteen sixties. Tell me exactly what happened."

Ronnie Doyle closed his eyes, and as he allowed his thoughts to wander back in time, the memories came flooding back…

CHAPTER 15

1966 AND ALL THAT

Nineteen sixty-six had been a good year so far for the people of Liverpool. The blue half of Merseyside had celebrated an F.A. Cup triumph for Everton, while the reds of Liverpool had claimed the league title. All this was followed by England's memorable World Cup victory in a thrilling final at Wembley against West Germany. Musically, The Beatles continued to dominate the pop charts, with *Paperback Writer* hitting the number one position in June. Liverpool's own darling of the pop charts, Cilla Black released the beautiful *Don't Answer Me* in the summer after earlier recording the title track to the Michael Caine film, *Alfie*, with Burt Bacharach.

For the music industry in general, there had been a few trials and tribulations, with Radio Caroline South's pirate radio ship *MV Mi Amigo* running aground in January on the beach at Frinton, and in other news the country had been horrified by the terrible case of the Moors Murders which finally saw Ian Brady and Myra Hindley go on trial for the brutal torture and slayings of three children.

A wind of change swept the fashion industry. Almost overnight, Mary Quant's mini-skirt was suddenly 'in' and for the first time, the amount of leg shown by the young women of Britain showed teenage boys and men alike that women really did have legs that extended up and beyond their knees.

For the younger generation then, all seemed well, but for the former members of Brendan Kane and the Planets, life had taken an unfortunate downturn.

Following the inevitable break up of the group after the failure of their demo disc two years earlier, Brendan, still full of belief and ambition had launched himself on a grueling tour of the clubs in Liverpool and its surrounding area. He'd saved hard after the initial split with The Planets and had first taken driving lessons, and after passing his driving test had bought himself a second-hand Hillman Minx, picked up for thirty pounds at a local motor auction. He'd carried on working at the bookshop by day and would drive himself to gigs at night, usually ending up tired beyond belief by the end of each week, and having to start all over again as Monday dawned once more. At least he had his own place, having rented a small flat above a shop in the city centre. Sadly, he'd as yet failed to attract that elusive recording contract, though his dreams of stardom kept him going through the tiredness.

He and Marie continued to see each other, usually at the flat, and the couple had somehow managed to keep their relationship a secret until a few months earlier, when a friend of Mickey's had seen them kissing and romantically entangled, quite by chance in a pub in Wigan. Mickey, who, with the others had long suspected a romance between the couple, and who was now working as a bricklayer had tried to be sensible and had sat down with his sister and tried to talk her out of the relationship with Brendan, telling her it could lead to nothing. Marie however, informed her elder brother about the long-standing nature of their love affair and even though Mickey attempted to change her mind by bringing accounts clerk Ronnie in on the secret, Marie would hear none of it. Mickey and Ronnie then confronted Brendan, who refused to listen to their entreaties to end the affair.

A kind of lull ensued, as the former group members saw less and less of each other, though Brendan maintained a closer relationship with Phil Oxley than he did with the brothers, who, for the sake of their sister, maintained a civilized silence about the affair with Brendan. Phil had at least managed to remain in the music business, now playing drums regularly for a local dance band, not quite pop stardom, but it was regular work and paid well.

* * *

Brendan held Marie close as they lay together in bed in the small city centre flat. Marie's head rested on his shoulder as they relaxed in the aftermath of a particularly passionate love-making session.

"It's just not happening for me here, Marie. In England, I mean. Look how long I've been trying, first with The Planets, and now on my own. I know I can do better, I just know it."

"But Brendan, darling, just what else can you do that you haven't already tried?"

Lying naked beside him, the warmth and intense satisfaction of their recent lovemaking still coursing through her body, the truth was, Marie wasn't really too concerned about Brendan's career at that particular moment. All that changed with his next words, however.

"I can go to America. That's what else I can do, Marie."

The look of shock on Marie's face was palpable as his words struck home like an arrow to her heart.

"America? You've got to be joking, Brendan, surely."

"No joke, Babe. The States could be just the place to start and build up a whole new career."

"But nobody in America has ever heard of you. What makes you think you'll have a better chance of success over there than you've had here?"

"I've got to try something, anything or I'll go through my life wondering what might have been if I hadn't tried. I thought you'd understand that."

"Understanding is one thing, but, what about us, Brendan? Sounds as if your mind's made up and you're prepared to just bugger off to America and leave me here. I thought you loved me. I thought we had a future together, that we'd be together forever. Not much chance of that Brendan, is there, with you on the other side of the world and me stuck here in an office in Liverpool for the rest of my life?"

Brendan leaned over and tried to kiss her, but Marie turned her face away at the last minute, leaving him with a mouthful of blonde hair. Taking her head in his hands, he gently turned her face until they were facing each other once again, and with a smile on his face he said,

"Do you really think I'd just leave you here all alone?"

Marie looked questioningly at him.

"Well, I…"

"Look, you silly girl, you know I love you, always have and always will. I was going to explain things a bit better. Didn't mean for it to come out like it has, but anyway, I want to go over there and maybe try a change of name, get an agent or a manager or whatever it takes to get started in America, and I want you to come with me, you daft bugger."

"Me? Go to America with you? Are you crazy?"

"No, Marie, I'm not. Why shouldn't you come with me? We want to be together, don't we?

"I know, but me Mam and Dad'll never allow it, especially me Dad. You know how strict he is on religious things."

"Oh, come on, Marie. This is the nineteen sixties for God's sake. All that Papist and Proddie stuff is way out of date now, except for that lot over in Ireland."

"God, don't let me Dad ever hear you saying, that word, you know, Papists. He'd go ballistic."

"Give over, Marie. I bet he calls Protestants proddies, though and that's okay is it?"

"Look, I know he's a bit of an old dinosaur, but he's still me Dad. He'd never agree to me living with you over here, never mind in bloody America."

"Who said anything about living together? I meant I want you to go with me as my wife. I want you to marry me, Marie. Say you will, please."

A look of pure shock showed on Marie's face as she took in Brendan's words. She felt her hands beginning to tremble as she pulled herself up into a sitting position in the bed.

"Brendan, of course I want to marry you. You know I do, but, Mam and Dad won't allow it, you know they won't."

"Then we don't ask them. We go over to America and get married there. I've read about places where you can go, wedding chapels they call them. All you need's your birth certificate and a couple of witnesses, and you have to have some kind of blood test I think."

"What for?"

"Oh, I dunno. Probably to make sure you're not carrying any diseases or something. Anyway, if we plan it carefully and quietly we can probably be there in a couple of months."

"Two months? Oh God, Brendan, I so want to say yes, but it's all so sudden and well, a bit scary, more like a lot scary really. I mean, I couldn't just up sticks and leave without a word to anyone."

"We can wait until nearer the time and then maybe just tell Mickey, or maybe Ronnie. They love you too, even though they might be pissed off with me, and if we can show them it's what you want and it's going to make you happy, I'll bet you they won't say anything to your Mam and Dad, at least until after we've left."

Marie's head was awhirl with all Brendan had said in the last few minutes. She needed time to think. Sliding her legs out of the bed and on to the floor, she reached across and quickly slipped Brendan's blue denim shirt over her shoulders.

"Where're you going? Brendan asked, admiring her legs as she paced out of the bedroom.

"Kitchen," Marie replied. "I need a drink. Want one?"

"Sure, just a Coke, please."

Marie quickly lifted two bottles of Coca-Cola from the small fridge in the kitchen, pausing for a moment to listen to the song playing on Radio Luxembourg, Cilla Black's *Don't Answer Me*. She stood admiring Brendan's new Grundig radio as she found the bottle opener and removed the tops from two bottles of Coke, then returned to the bedroom, holding one bottle out towards Brendan, who took it from her gratefully, and took a long slug from the bottle.

"Well?" he asked.

"Let me think, Brendan. I want to say yes, you know I do, but it's a massive step."

"Okay, I understand. Let's not say anything else tonight. Just promise me you'll think about it."

"Of course I will, silly. I just need for it all to sink in, work out how to sort everything out, you know?"

In truth, Brendan had blurted out his American idea pretty much on the hoof and hadn't really thought it through. He'd no real idea about how to go about emigrating to the USA and knew he'd have to do some fast, serious fact-finding now that he'd revealed his plans to Marie. Could he really plan and execute his ideas in the space of two months. Would Marie say yes?

After he and Marie made love once more, the couple dressed, and an awkward silence descended upon them as neither appeared to know quite what to say to each other in light of the evening's turn of events. Brendan drove her home and dropped her on the corner of her street, watching her as she walked to her door, then he drove home, fell into bed, and spent a sleepless night as his mind raced, alive with thoughts of a future with Marie in a brave new world, as man and wife, with a new career and a whole new life ahead of them. He knew he had two major hurdles to overcome if he were to turn his latest dream into reality. First, he needed Marie's commitment to join him if he did manage to arrange to leave Liverpool and head for the USA, and secondly, and perhaps most important, there remained the problems that might ensue from her family when they found about their plans.

* * *

The Red River Café was hardly the most salubrious establishment in the area. Standing at the end of a row of pre-war terraced houses, close to an area bombed extensively during the war and still bearing its scars as a bombsite, the café was, nevertheless a popular meeting place for the younger generation and it was here that Brendan had arranged to meet former group member, Phil Oxley. One of the reasons for the Red River's popularity was the beautiful Wurlitzer Juke Box that stood in one corner of the establishment and Sam Beckett, owner of the café, always made sure it was filled with the latest chart hits, making his place a major attraction for the local youths and young adults, eager to sit and feed the machine with money in order to hear their latest favourites.

Arriving two minutes before the pre-arranged time, Phil walked though the café door to find Brendan waiting for him, seated at a table near the window. Phil took a seat at the Formica-topped table, and reached across to shake hands with his old friend.

"Hiya, Phil. How's things?" Brendan asked.

"I'm doing good, Brendan, thanks. How about yourself?"

"That's what I wanted to talk to you about, Phil, but hey, let's get a drink first. What'll you have?"

"Espresso for me, please," Phil replied and Brendan pushed his chair back, rose and walked to the counter. In a minute or so the satisfying hiss of the espresso machine signalled the coffee was ready and he returned to the table with two cups of espresso on a plastic tray, which he placed on the table before regaining his seat and smiling at Phil.

"So, how's it going with the dance band, Phil? Bit different from The Planets, eh?"

"It is, but they're a good crowd, the fellas in the band. Mostly a lot older than me, of course, but hey, some of that dance band music is really cool, you know? The swing sound and the big band sounds like those bands in the war played really get people up and dancing, and Bob, the bandleader says I'm one of the best drummers they've had for years, and you know, a lot of the band music was like the roots of a lot of our rock 'n roll. The Jive, the Lindy Hop and lots more all came out of the big band music during the war."

"That's good mate, it really is. But listen, I've something important to tell you, and to be honest, I could do with your advice."

"Well, there's a first. Not often you've ever been unsure enough to want my advice, mate."

Brendan smiled as he replied, "Well, there's always a first time, Phil and this is really important, and I'm just not sure what to do."

Phil realised his friend was deadly serious and he could see worry etched on Brendan's face, and so he dropped the air of flippancy he'd at first adopted and prepared to listen carefully to his friend.

* * *

Half an hour later, Brendan finally came to the end of his story, Phil having listened to his friend with only sporadic interruptions for the occasional question, and to replenish their espressos at the counter.

"So, Phil, what d'you think?" Brendan looked at Oxley hopefully after finishing presenting his ideas for the future to his friend.

"What do I think? I think you're bloody mad, Brendan Kane, that's what I think. Bloody hell, man, you've always been a bit of a dreamer, you know you have, but this is taking it to the limit, man. You've told me in your own words you don't really know much about moving to the States, so, if you're serious about this hare-brained scheme of yours, you'd better contact the US Embassy or whoever you need to get in touch with to find out if your idea even has a chance of working. You might not fit the, what do they call it…? Oh yeah, the criteria, that's the word. You might not fit the criteria they set for people wanting to go and live over there. No, be quiet and friggin' listen to me," he said quickly as he could see Brendan was about to interject and interrupt his reply. "You've asked for my help and my advice, so let me tell you what I think, then you can have another go, okay?"

Brendan nodded and Phil continued.

"As I see it, that's the first part of your problem, and probably the easiest bit to get sorted. The hard part is Marie, and I don't mean the bit about marrying her, or persuading her to go to America with you. She'd go with you like a shot, man. You'd have had to be blind, deaf and dumb not to see how much she's been love with you these last few years. Oh yes, Brendan bloody big man Kane. We all knew, even though you'd both worked hard at keeping it a secret for a long time. Eventually you couldn't disguise the looks that passed between you and we all thought you'd tell us when you wanted to and we just kept quiet and let you play your little game of secrets."

"How long had you known?" Brendan had to ask, unable to keep silent any longer.

"Oh, from soon after we cut the demo disc, not long before we packed in the group. But anyway, like I said, that's not the big problem. It's her family, Brendan. They're staunch Catholics, you know that. They're not going to take too kindly to their only daughter running off with some proddie kid to get married and then moving halfway around the bloody world to live in another bloody country. You might just win Mickey and Ronnie round in the end but it's their parents that's your problem. They'll kick up such a stink, Brendan lad, they really will."

"But they can't stop us, can they, Phil, if we really want to go?"

"You're not thinking straight, man. Look, Marie is twenty, right?"

Brendan nodded in the affirmative.

"Well then, until she's twenty-one, she can't get married without her parent's permission. That's the law, Brendan, and that's all there is to it."

"Shit," said Brendan, his face a mask of frustration. You mean we've got to wait another six months until her birthday?"

Phil thought for a few second before replying, a sudden thought giving him an idea that might just help his friend.

"There's one way you might be able to get round it, I've just remembered something"

"What? Come on, Phil, don't muck about, what is it?" Brendan asked; eager to hear of anything that might help him out of what he saw as a serious setback to his plans.

"Elope to Scotland," Phil spoke with a broad grin on his face.

"Scotland? Why the bloody hell should we go to friggin' Scotland?"

"Because, you numpty, the law's different up there, that's why. Have you never heard of people running away and eloping to Gretna Green?"

"I've heard of the place, sure, but I've never really thought about getting married before so can't say I've really thought much about those stories."

"Brendan, man, they're not stories, it's a fact. In Scotland, it's legal to get married at sixteen. All I think you have to do is qualify by living there, just for a week or two, I'm not sure, you'd have to find out. It's just over the border in Scotland. The two of you could bugger off up there, stay in a B & B or something and then get married, all nice and legal, and her parents couldn't do a thing about it when you come back as Mr. and Mrs. Brendan Kane."

The smile that appeared on Brendan's face stretched from ear to ear as he listened to Phil's potential solution to one of the major hurdles standing between him and Marie becoming a legally married couple.

"You're a bloody genius, Phil," he exclaimed. "If I can get Marie to agree to come away with me, it might just work."

"Yeah, but remember you need to find out about going to the States first, and if I were you I'd try and get Mickey and Ronnie on your side too. You're gonna need some back-up eventually when their parents do find out. They're going to want to cut your bloody legs off, and maybe other more sensitive body parts too when they find out what you've been doing with their precious Marie."

"I've hardly had much to do with them since the group split up, Phil. I know they were pissed off at me when we folded, and I've only seen them now and then since, so I doubt they'll be too happy about helping me out here."

"You're a real prat sometimes, Brendan, you know that? Sure they were mad at you. We all were, but like I said they've known about you and Marie for a while and if they weren't your friends, don't you think they'd have tried to split you up before now? Just because they were angry back then doesn't mean they're going to do anything that might hurt Marie or interfere with her happiness. Give 'em a chance, man."

"But, how? What do I say to them?"

"Tell them the truth, man, you might be surprised."

"Will you help me Phil? To set up a meeting with them, I mean? I'd feel better with you there to back me up, you know?"

"What, just in case they want to give you a good battering?" Phil laughed.

Brendan tried to return the smile but it wouldn't form on his face.

"You really don't think they'd want to…?"

"Give over, you great pillock. With Marie there with you? They're not morons you know. Anyway, yes, for old time's sake and because I happen to think you and Marie are good for each other, I'll help you."

Brendan jumped up from his seat at the table and almost ran round to the other side where he wrapped his arms round Phil's shoulders and hugged his friend.

"Thanks, Phil, I don't know how to thank you."

"Hey, be careful, you'll give people the wrong idea," Phil laughed.

Brendan drew back, smiling like a Cheshire cat and grabbed Phil's hand and shook it briskly.

"That's more like it, mate," Phil chuckled. "Well, let's have another coffee and try and work out how we're going to sort your bloody mess of a life out, eh?"

CHAPTER 16

A TIME TO TELL

"And you know all about this meeting because?" Ross asked, as Ronnie Doyle sighed, and took a couple of deep breaths as he paused in his narrative. Both the inspector and Sergeant Izzie Drake had found themselves being drawn inescapably into the past as they'd sat listening to Ronnie's story. The man could certainly weave a good tale and had the knack of being able to communicate his thoughts in a way that gave the detectives a fascinating insight not only into the subject they were discussing but into another era, a period in recent history that only those who'd lived through it could perhaps fully appreciate. They were fascinated.

"Eh? Oh, sorry, Inspector. The memories, you know? They sort of bring those days all back to life for me, if you see what I mean. It all happened so long ago and yet, now I'm talking to you about it, it could all have taken place last week, it seems so real in my mind. Anyway, you asked about the meeting in the Red River, well, it was Phil and Brendan themselves who told us about it, mostly Phil, I'll admit, when he got in touch with me and Mickey soon after him and Brendan had met in the café."

"I see, and who did he call first, you or Mickey? Do you remember?"

"It was me, Inspector," Mickey spoke quietly. It was obvious from his demeanour and facial expression that Ronnie's recollections of the past had affected him too. "He called me a couple of days after he'd met with Brendan. It was actually me who told Ronnie about it, but Ronnie spoke to Phil after that, if I remember it right."

"Yes, that's right," said Ronnie, "you did tell me first, and I agreed to speak to Phil to arrange a meeting with him, Brendan and Marie. We agreed that it should be me who talked to Marie, us being closer back in those days."

"Yeah, she was always a bit awed by me, I think. Don't know why, Maybe it was just because I was the eldest, you know, big brother and all that?"

Ross had allowed the brothers to digress slightly, wanting them to feel at ease as he gradually teased the story from them, and now he moved to get them back on track.

"Alright, Ronnie, please, can we get back to the meeting with Brendan Kane and Phil Oxley? What happened next?"

"Yeah, right, Inspector, sorry. Well now, where was I? Right, yeah, well, Mickey and me agreed that I'd talk to Marie first, make sure she was up for it, and then make arrangements to meet up with Brendan and Phil."

"And how did Marie react when you approached her and told her you'd known about her affair with Brendan for quite some time, which I'm presuming you must have done?"

"She was bloody scared shitless…oops, sorry about that Sergeant," Ronnie said, apologising for his language to Izzie Drake who merely said,

"Don't let it worry you, Mr. Doyle. I hear far worse than that from our own people within these walls every day of the week, I can assure you. Please, go on with your story."

She smiled and Ronnie Doyle relaxed again and went on with his tale.

"Okay, like I said, she was scared shi…a bit scared at first, thinking me and Mickey were mad at her, and that we'd go round and knock seven shades of shit out of Brendan Kane."

"And did you feel like doing that?" Ross asked.

"For a second or two, yes, to tell the truth, Inspector. Mind you, Brendan was bigger and tougher than me so I really wouldn't have had much chance of doing him any damage, even if I'd wanted to. I was a bit like the typical seven stone weakling, physically in those days. I've filled out a bit now of course, middle age and all that."

"How about you, Mickey? Did you feel like thumping Brendan's lights out?"

"It might come as a surprise to you, Inspector, but no, I didn't. Ever hear of Woodstock?"

"You mean the place in Oxfordshire?" Izzie interjected.

"No lass, not the one in bloody Oxfordshire. I mean the Woodstock music festival in the USA."

"I've heard of it," said Ross. "What's that got to do with your relationship with your sister?"

"Well, Woodstock didn't happen for another few years, but what I'm saying, is that even back in sixty-six, I was already a believer in free love, peace and all that stuff, you know? I might not have liked what Brendan bloody Kane did to us over the group, but hell, if he wanted to shag me sister, and she wanted it too, then bloody good luck to the pair of 'em. That was my attitude Inspector. Just 'cos I'm a big bloke, doesn't make me a violent one. You shoulda seen me in me flower power hippy shirts, complete with beads after Woodstock took place and the hippy culture took me over."

Ronnie couldn't help laughing at his brother.

"He was a right sight, Inspector, I can tell you. All 'peace, man' and bloody weird hand gestures and long lank hair. Thank God he grew out of it."

"And when did that happen, Mickey, you growing out of the hippy lifestyle?"

"When my first wife Chrissie left me for another man, Inspector. We'd met at a concert and got married within six weeks, so you can see why I wouldn't be the type to be hard on my sister, but she left me for a bloody stockbroker she met at an art gallery of all things, and well, I just drifted out of the lifestyle. Mind you, I was thirty by then."

The two brothers laughed again and Ross groaned inwardly. These two were natural jokers and he needed to keep them deadly serious if he was going to get what he wanted from them. How soon, he wondered, would either Ronnie or Mickey realise the remains at the wharf were probably those of their friend, Brendan?

"Okay, point taken, Mickey. Now, Ronnie, the meeting with Brendan and your sister, *please*. Just where and when did it take place and exactly what happened? I know it was a long time ago but please try to remember as many of the details as you possibly can, it really is important."

"Alright, sorry. It's just funny thinking of Mickey the hippy. Anyway, yes, we arranged to meet with Brendan and Marie round at Brendan's flat a few days later. We all thought it best to go there as there'd be no way our parents would find out about it if we kept it private, like. Anyway, I remember most of it as if it were yesterday."

"So, go ahead, Ronnie, take us back to nineteen sixty-six again, please. You were all at Brendan's flat, and…?"

CHAPTER 17

BRENDAN KANE & THE PLANETS REUNITED

"So, here we are, all back together again. It's been a while, eh, lads?"

Brendan Kane looked at the gathering of his old friends as they sat around the living room in his flat. He and Marie were seated side by side on the sofa, with Phil Oxley on the other side of Marie. Mickey and Ronnie had claimed an armchair each and after an uncomfortable couple of minutes following their arrival, Marie being already with him to greet them, it seemed as though a peaceful camaraderie had fallen over the room. They'd all spent a long time together as Brendan Kane and The Planets, and though their eventual split may have borne a deal of acrimony, all that seemed to be in the past and for the most part, everyone seemed pleased to be back in each other's company, much to Brendan's relief.

"Too long if you ask me," Ronnie replied.

"I thought you'd all hate my guts," said Brendan.

"We probably did, for a while," Mickey added, "but friends are friends, and we couldn't stay mad at you forever. Hell's bells, Brendan you were probably right. We'd never have made it anyway and at least we quit before the bookings dried up and we got booed off stage in some poky little working men's club somewhere."

"Hey, we weren't that bad," Brendan protested.

"Maybe not, but that's not why we're here tonight is it?"

"No, and I'm surprised you two don't want to knock my block off."

"Why?" Ronnie asked. "Just because you and Marie fell for each other? Hell, we all knew about you two ages ago, maybe not as much as we could have known, but enough to know there was something going on between you."

"So, you don't mind if we get married and if Marie comes to America with me?"

"We couldn't stop her if we tried, could we Marie?"

"No chance, Ronnie," Marie replied.

"Okay, but it's not that simple, is it, girl?" said big brother Mickey.

"I know. It's Mam and Dad isn't it? What can I do, Mickey?"

"Phil told me and Ronnie his idea, and I think that's the only way to do it."

"What, you mean me and Brendan elope to Gretna Green and then go to America as man and wife?"

"Yes, but, you've got to be really careful about how you do things. If Dad finds out what you're up to, he'll be mad as hell." Mickey fell silent and Ronnie, normally so quiet, took over again, his intellectual side clearly coming to the fore as he worked the problem out in his mind.

"Right, you arrange a short holiday in Scotland with a couple of your girlfriends, first. You can do that, yeah?" Marie nodded. "Good, you can use them as witnesses anyway. Once you've stayed there as long as you have to, you get married, and then you'll need to come back here and carry on with normal life until you can leave for the States."

"We couldn't do that, Ronnie," Marie exclaimed. "Once we're married, we want to be together, forever."

"It won't be for long, Marie. That's up to Brendan to make all the arrangements in advance."

"It all sounds a bit complicated to me," said Brendan. "I'd rather we just go one day and not come back,"

"Look, Brendan. It's up to you. We're just agreeing with Phil's plan, which sounds a good one if we want to keep it all nice and quiet so you two lovebirds can slip away without Dad finding out." Ronnie insisted.

"It's a good plan, Brendan, honest it is," said Phil.

"But it's just as easy for me and Marie to meet one day, and just board a plane or a ship or whatever and disappear from Liverpool, without going through all your cloak and dagger stuff, Phil. We can get married in America when we get there."

"And what do you think, Marie?" Phil asked the young woman.

"I just wanna be with Brendan," she answered.

The argument raged on for over an hour without any real decision being made. It was clear to the brothers that Marie would end up doing whatever Brendan wanted her to do. She was totally besotted with him and would truly follow him to the ends of the earth. They had to hope that good sense would eventually prevail. They knew that if Marie and Brendan were legally married in Scotland, their father could scream and bellow all he liked, but the marriage would be valid and they would both do their best to support their sister against their father's wrath.

The remainder of their time at Brendan's flat felt rather surreal to the Doyle brothers and to Phil Oxley. Brendan insisted on showing off his brand new Dansette record player, with its facility to hold up to ten singles on its spindle, automatically dropping the next record in turn onto the turntable after the playing arm lifted from the record.

As the Searchers' *When You Walk In The Room* played in the background, Marie left the boys for a minute, returning soon afterwards with chilled bottles of Double Diamond from Brendan's fridge. The cold pale ale was refreshing and helped them all to relax, and the record ended, the needle rose magically and another disc dropped on to the turntable, this time The Rolling Stones, one of Mickey's favourite groups, with their smash hit, *It's All Over Now*, with the brilliant Brian Jones on lead guitar. Little did any of them imagine at the time that the superb guitarist would tragically be lost to the pop scene in July 1969, drowned in his swimming pool just a month after leaving the Rolling Stones. For now, though, Mickey Doyle idolized the young man who had formed the Stones in the first place and whose musical talents helped them become one of the biggest names in the British pop industry.

Soon, however, with the future as yet unresolved, the time came for the group to go their separate ways and the Doyle brothers patiently waited outside with Phil Oxley as Marie said goodnight to Brendan, obviously, according to the time taken, Ronnie commented, accompanied by much 'snogging and groping'. Mickey playfully slapped his younger brother across the back of his head, "That's our bloody sister you're talking about, you pillock."

"So! She's got the same equipment as other girls, hasn't she? Brendan's a red blooded guy and…"

Before he could say more the street door opened and Marie stepped out to join them, waving to the figure of Brendan Kane, hidden from the brother's view. After blowing him a kiss, she skipped across to where the others waited in a huddle on the footpath and quickly linked arms with her two brothers, smiling up at each in turn, then said, cheerfully,

"We going home then, or what?"

CHAPTER 18

BACK TO THE FUTURE

"And that, Inspector Ross, was honestly the last time I saw Brendan Kane," Ronnie said as he sighed and sagged a little in his chair, a rather wistful look on his face. Ross quite correctly guessed it had taken something out of Ronnie Doyle, going back in his mind to those long ago days of his youth, and the trauma of losing his sister, though he hadn't yet told Ross anything about what eventually happened when Brendan and Marie appeared to vanish from the face of the earth. It was time to be blunt, to hit Ronnie and Mickey with his theory.

Still directing his words in Ronnie's direction, Ross began.

"Ronnie, and you too, Mickey, I know you came here today to try and help us, and you thought the remains at Cole's Wharf might have been your sister, which we've been able to discount, but the reasons we asked to go into such detail about your sister's disappearance, and believe me, I want to know much more in a minute, are twofold. One, I do believe the remains at the wharf could be very closely connected to your sister's eventual disappearance, and two, I have strong reasons, based on what you've told me, and from other evidence we've discovered, to believe the remains at Cole's Wharf are those of your old friend, Brendan Kane."

Ronnie and Mickey Doyle both looked as if someone had hit them over the head with a cricket bat. Both Ross and Izzie Drake had no doubts that the news the inspector had just delivered had struck the brothers a real sledgehammer blow, and that neither man had up to now connected the dots, and worked out where Ross had been leading throughout the current interview. They were either totally innocent of any involvement in the disappearance and subsequent murder of Brendan Kane, or, one or both of the brothers was a very good actor. Ross had to consider the possibility that one of the men sitting before him could be a cold hearted and very clever sociopathic killer, emotionless and devoid of the emotion necessary to register true emotions, and therefore he had to take things slowly and carefully.

"You can't mean that, surely, Inspector Ross," Ronnie exclaimed.

"It's not possible," said Mickey, his voice rising almost to the point of shouting. Sudden realisation had dawned on the elder Doyle brother, even if, for the moment it had escaped his younger brother. "Brendan went to America, and Marie went with him. If the skeleton you found is Brendan then that means that Marie would well be…"

Mickey suddenly choked up with the emotion of the moment, unable to complete his sentence, but by now, Ronnie had caught on to the possibilities Ross's revelation had opened up.

"So she is dead. That's what you're saying, isn't it, Inspector? If Brendan died here in Liverpool all those years ago, there's no chance Marie made it to America on her own is there? After all, why would she go without Brendan? They were fucking inseparable."

It was only at that point that Ross realised the brothers still harboured hopes that Marie might be alive, that their search through endless newspaper articles over the years had been in truth, a sort of cathartic process of elimination. With each body that wasn't Marie, the more they hoped she may yet turn up alive sometime, somewhere. It was a 'syndrome' he'd witnessed once or twice in the past with relatives of missing persons, a form of positive denial, that led hopeful parents or, in this case, siblings to refuse to accept the inevitable as long as no body could be found. For now, though, he had to push the brothers in order to ascertain every fact he could squeeze from their memories.

Ross spoke firmly but gently once again, trying to convey a calmness that might enable the two men to begin to think clearly once more.

"Look, Mickey, Ronnie, as of right now we have no idea what happened to your sister. Until the pair of you walked in here today we had no idea she had anything to do with this case, and we had no firm proof that the remains were those of Brendan Kane. But you had suspicions that your sister might not have gone with him or why come here saying you thought the remains at the wharf might be Marie? What really made you think your sister might be dead?"

Ronnie Doyle thought for a few seconds before replying.

"Look, Inspector Ross, at first we'd no idea what had happened. Yes, me and Mickey thought she'd run off with Brendan but when we heard nothing from her, and then our Mam and Dad started worrying, we had to come clean and tell them what had been going on. Even so, me and Mickey took a long time to come round to the idea that something bad, and I mean really bad, might have happened to Marie. We started searching newspapers for stories about unidentified bodies or unsolved murders against unknown victims, and when we saw the article about the skeleton at the docks, we thought, well…you know what we thought."

Ross knew the time had come to be open and honest with the two brothers. Perhaps if he could first obtain conclusive proof that the remains at the wharf were those of Brendan Kane, he might then be able to ascertain if the death of the young musician and the disappearance of Marie Doyle were connected. He now felt it extremely unlikely they wouldn't be. First of all, of course, he needed to know more.

"Okay," he said. "You remember me asking you if Brendan had ever suffered a broken leg?"

The brothers nodded in unison, words failing them both for the moment.

"Well, our victim suffered just such an injury, and we're currently conducting a survey of dentists who may have been practicing in the city around the time of death, to confirm the identity of the remains through dental records, but so far, thanks to what you've revealed today, I have to say my thoughts are leaning towards the fact that this was in fact, Brendan Kane. I want to show you something and I want you to tell me if it has any significance for either of you."

With that, Ross opened the top right hand drawer of his desk and reached inside, his hand emerging holding a small Perspex packet. He passed the packet across the desk towards Ronnie, who looked at it as if it was about to bite him. He could see something within the packet and as it came closer to him, he realised what he was looking at.

"Oh, shit," he said, his face assuming a crestfallen look.

"What is it Ronnie? What's in there?" his brother asked, a quiver of fear creeping into his voice.

Ronnie picked up the packet with the tips of two fingers, as though it contained a human body part, and passed it to his brother.

"I take it you both know what that is?" Ross asked, as Izzie Drake moved to take the packet from Mickey's trembling hand. She passed it back to Ross who returned it to his desk drawer before he spoke once more.

"A plectrum. A broken guitar plectrum," Ronnie said, quietly.

"A tortoiseshell plectrum," Mickey added. "Brendan always used one just like it."

"I'm sorry if this has shocked you both," Ross said, "but now, I want you to really think back and tell me what took place, to the best of your knowledge, between the time you last saw Brendan, and your sister's disappearance."

Both men nodded again. Mickey Doyle appeared to be on the verge of tears. Ronnie was exerting great effort in an attempt not to join his brother on the point of breakdown.

Seeing the state of the men, Ross thought a break would be in order and he asked Izzie to organize tea and coffee for all four of them. She also sent in a uniformed officer who escorted Ronnie and Mickey to the men's toilets, allowing them to relieve themselves and splash some water on their faces in an attempt to refresh themselves a little before going on with what had now become, for both men, a frightening and potentially tragic interview with Detective Inspector Ross.

A few minutes later, the Doyle brothers were returned to the office where they were soon seated once again in the identical positions in front of Ross's desk. During the short break, Ross had ascertained that his sergeant had been totally in line with this thoughts and the line of his questioning from the moment he'd first suggested the remains may be those of their old friend. He was reassured by the fact that Drake was still able to almost read his mind and think along the same lines as he did. This ability to almost think in parallel was, he believed, one of the particular strengths of the working relationship between himself and Izzie Drake. Drake soon furnished the two men with cups of very strong tea, and Ross soon took up the thread of his questioning again. This time, he felt he had to really strike hard and make the brothers realise just where his line of inquiry had been leading.

"Right lads, I know you came here today thinking you might have found some answers about the disappearance of your sister, and to be honest, I'm going to do all I can to find out what happened to her, because, although you may not have caught on so far, I do believe your sister may have been closely connected with the remains unearthed at Cole's Wharf."

"But how, Inspector? What on earth could Marie have had to do with whatever happened down at the docks all those years ago?" It was Mickey who now seemed to have assumed the mantle of spokesman for the brothers. Ross paused for a moment, turning his head to look out of his office window. A darkness had fallen on the room, and Ross could see the cause, as a bank of dark, grey clouds were sweeping across the sky, obliterating the sunshine and turning the sky a strange mixture of purple and black. Somehow, it seemed fitting, bearing in mind the information he was about to divulge. Turning quickly back to face the brothers, he spoke again, in almost hushed tones.

"I don't know, Mickey but we need to find out," Ross continued.

"We believe someone either met or lured Brendan to that wharf, probably late at night, and cold-bloodedly murdered your friend, approximately thirty five years ago. Somehow, it now appears your sister may have been involved in what took place that night"

"Murdered?" This came from Ronnie. "But why? How? Inspector Ross, if that was Brendan you found at that wharf, how did he die? Can you tell, just from the bones? Don't you need the full body or something to get all that sort of information? And how could Marie have been involved?"

"Oh, we can tell alright, Ronnie. Forensic science is highly advanced nowadays. I can tell you our pathologists have determined that Brendan was probably shot in both kneecaps to incapacitate him, then someone struck him over the head with a hammer, not enough to have caused his death, and finally threw him into the water, as the river still flowed up to the dock in those days. In other words, he was shot, bludgeoned and thrown into the Mersey to drown."

Ross waited as his words hit home. Both brothers seemed incapable of speech for a few seconds, Mickey visibly blanched, and then Ronnie finally broke the awful silence that had descended on the room.

"But, that's bloody monstrous. Brendan never did anything to deserve anything like that. Do you know who did it yet, Inspector?"

"Of course he doesn't, Ronnie, you moron," said Mickey. "After thirty five bloody years? They haven't got a friggin' clue, have you, Inspector Ross?"

"Not yet, Mickey, no. But, I'm sorry to say that if it is indeed Brendan who was murdered at the wharf, bearing in mind the information you've brought to us today, it now leads us on to another, potentially unsavoury matter."

All of a sudden, the penny dropped, and both brothers exchanged a glance as Ross's words registered.

"Oh, my God," Mickey blurted out. "So you *do* believe Marie's dead too, don't you, Inspector? She must have been with Brendan and whoever killed him probably did the same to our sister. That's what you're thinking, isn't it? We came here thinking the bones might have been Marie's, we've thought she was dead for a long time, but now you've described what happened to poor Brendan, well, it looks like she might have been murdered too. That's not what we expected you know. We always thought she'd gone off with Brendan and maybe there'd been an accident or some-thing or…"

Mickey halted in mid-sentence as his emotions overcame him and the big man suddenly slumped, silent, against the back of his chair. Ronnie took one last stab at denial.

"You still can't be sure it's Brendan, though, can you? I mean, a skeleton who broke a leg in the same place as Brendan and a broken guitar plectrum aren't exactly positive proof are they, Inspector?"

There it is again, thought Ross, *positive denial.*

"Until you two walked in here today, no, but after hearing what you've told us so far, Sergeant Drake and I are certain that the remains are those of your friend, and I'm certain the dental analysis of the skull will confirm it."

Ross didn't let on that they so far had no idea if they would actually find the dentist who'd worked on the victim.

"Maybe now you can see why it's so important that you tell us everything you can, every small detail you can recall about those last weeks when Marie still lived at home, right up until the time she and Brendan disappeared."

The brothers nodded in unison, and Ross continued.

"Okay, please carry on with your story and then, when you've done with that, I want to know precisely what happened when you reported Marie missing to the police. That would have been the Liverpool City police back in those days, wouldn't it?"

"Yeah, for what it was worth. Bloody useless lot if you ask me," Mickey grunted.

"Like I said, that's for later. For now, please, tell me about those last weeks. You said you never heard from Brendan again after the meeting at his flat, right?"

"No, Inspector," Ronnie corrected him. "We said we never *saw* him again. That's not the same as saying we never *heard* from him, which we did, about a week after the meeting. We spoke on the phone, didn't we, Mickey?"

"About a week, yeah, right," Mickey confirmed his brother's words.

"Okay, good. Right, let's hear it," said Ross.

Ronnie now took up the story once again.

"Well, the best I remember is it happened something like this, Inspector Ross. Please remember it was thirty-five years ago and it's not all as clear as it could be, but anyway, here goes…"

CHAPTER 19

END TIMES, LIVERPOOL, 1966

The typing pool at the offices of BICC, (British Insulated Callendar's Cables), known locally simply as B.I. was its usual hubbub of sound, the constant clacking of typewriter keys interspersed with the chatter of the girls who manned the machines. Towards the back of the room, Marie Doyle sat busily typing invoices as to her right, her best friend, Clemmy (Clemency) De Souza sat at the neighbouring desk, typing letters for various departmental supervisors. Clemmy and Marie shared a love of music, and when she wasn't seeing Brendan, Marie could usually be found in the company of the olive-skinned, pretty girl whose father had been a Portuguese merchant seaman. He'd met and fallen in love with a local girl when his ship had been docked in the Port of Liverpool many years ago, and Clemmy had been the first-born offspring of the marriage.

Together, the two girls would shop, visit the various clubs where live music could be heard, and would also spend many a happy Saturday morning in town, listening to the latest record releases, squeezed together in one of the listening booths in one or more of the many record shops that had blossomed across the city in keeping with the rise of the pop music industry.

In recent weeks, Clemmy had noticed a distinct change in her friend. Marie had become moody and rather withdrawn and Clemmy, though only the same age as Marie, had a feeling that something serious now weighed heavily on her friend's mind. As the two continued touch-typing, their fingers almost flying over their typewriter keys, Clemmy first made sure that Mrs. Marley, the supervisor who sat at a desk at the front of the typing pool where she could survey her territory with a quick glance around the room, wasn't looking in their direction, she leaned to her left and spoke to Marie, just loud enough to be heard by her friend, though not by any of the other girls around them.

"Why won't you tell me what's wrong, Marie?"

"I keep telling you, there's nothing wrong, Clemmy, honest there isn't."

"Good God, girl. How long have we known each other? D'you not think your best friend knows when you've got a serious problem in that head of yours? I've been waiting for you to tell me, but now I'm going to ask you straight out, are you up the duff, Marie Doyle?"

Marie almost laughed out loud at Clemmy's words, but controlled herself, not wanting to attract Mrs. Marley's attention.

"Look, Clemmy, let's talk at lunchtime, okay? I'm not supposed to say anything, but, well, you are my best friend, and to be honest, I'm bursting with excitement, but I'm not allowed to show it, and by the way, no, I'm not bloody pregnant. What kind of girl do you take me for?"

Both girls found the next hour almost intolerable as they continued beating a tattoo on the keys of their rather out of date Imperial typewriters. B.I certainly needed to modernise their equipment if the girls were to achieve the level of productivity the company demanded of its workers. Clemmy desperately yearned to learn Marie's big secret and Marie, at last, felt she could tell Clemmy her big, big news.

Finally, the lunch break arrived and the two girls quickly made their way to the canteen, where they both obtained a lunch of sausage and mashed potato, garden peas and gravy, then found a table in a corner of the vast room, at a table with no other workers in close proximity to them. Satisfied that they'd achieved a modicum of privacy, Clemmy immediately pushed Marie to open up to her.

"A'right, girl, tell. If you're not bloody pregnant, just why have you been acting so funny lately?"

Taking a deep breath, and swallowing the last of a piece of sausage with a visible gulp, Marie replied.

"Me and Brendan's goin' to America, but you're not to breathe a word to anyone, d'you understand, Clemmy De Souza, not to *anyone*, especially not to your Mam and Dad."

"Bloody hell, Marie. What's this all about, girl? You've never said nothin' about America before. Is Brendan mad or what, wanting to take you all that way, when you've never been further than bloody Birkenhead in your life?"

"That's not true, Clemmy, and you know it. What about when Mam and Dad took us on that holiday to Blackpool, and to Spain a few years ago? Saved up for years to pay for that, they did."

"Oh, right, yeah, sorry. But, it's still only Blackpool and one trip to Spain isn't it? It's not exactly Las bleedin' Vegas, Marie. I'll change what I said to you've never been out of Lancashire except for once in your life, and you can't argue with that. So, why does your boyfriend suddenly want to whisk you off to America, and just where in America is he thinkin' of, by the way? You do have some idea how big that country is, don't you, girl?"

Marie leaned across the table towards her friend and lowered her voice to what she felt was a nicely conspiratorial level.

"Keep your voice down, Clemmy, please. Look, he thinks his singing career might have a better chance of taking off in America. The music scene in Liverpool has grown a bit stale, so he says, and solo singers like him seem to have more success over there. You've only got to look at the U.S charts and all the big names over the last few years, like Bobby Darin, Bobby Vee, Elvis Presley, Ricky Nelson. There's hardly been one really big solo singer over here, not counting Cilla of course, and she's a girl."

"Get away," said Clemmy, sarcastically. "I'd never have known that, if you hadn't told me."

Marie waved a derisory hand at her friend and then continued.

"Anyway, he wants us to go as soon as possible, but nobody, not a soul, has to know what we're doing. The lads from the group know, and they've all agreed to keep quiet until after we've gone, at least, I think they have."

"Oh come on, Marie. You're trying to keep a secret and you've let your brothers and Phil Oxley into it already. Why don't you just tell half of Liverpool and then mention, "Oh, by the way, please don't tell me Mam and Dad. And what's to say your precious Brendan won't take you over there and then dump you if things don't go well for him and he runs out of money or meets some rich yank bird or whatever?"

"He won't do that, Clemmy. He's asked me to marry him. I'm going to be Mrs. Brendan Kane."

"God, no wonder you've been all edgy lately. Just when is all this going to happen?"

"As soon he's made all the arrangements. And my brothers won't say a word. They've known me and Brendan have been sweet on each other for a long time, so it seems, and they just want me to be happy."

"You know your Dad'll go bloody mad if he finds out, don't you?"

"But he won't Clemmy. None of the boys will say anything and I'm telling you because you're my best friend and I just felt I needed to tell, well, someone, or I'd have burst, you know?"

Clemmy fell silent for a few seconds, and after contemplating her friend's revelation, finally spoke again.

"Well, there's not much I can say, is there? You know I love you and want you to be happy too, but, by God, I'll miss having you around. Who'll I go shoppin' with on a Saturday now, or go dancing with?"

Marie's face fell for a second, as though she hadn't really considered not seeing her best friend again once she and Brendan left the country, then said,

"Look here, once we get settled over there, maybe you can come and see us, like, for a visit now and then."

"Don't be daft, Marie Doyle. When would I ever get the money to pay for a holiday in bloody America? I only work for B.I. you know; I don't friggin' own the place."

Marie reached a hand across the table, and took Clemmy's hand in hers.

"We can write to each other, Clemmy, can't we? We don't have to forget each other. I'll never have a better friend than you, I know I won't."

A small tear formed and slowly ran down Clemmy's face and she quickly wiped it away.

"Aw, give over, look what you're doing. You'll have me crying like a baby in a minute. Look, we'd better hurry up or we'll be late back from lunch and we don't want to get a tongue lashing from bloody Mrs. Marley do we?"

* * *

"You did what, Marie?"

"I told Clemmy what me and Brendan are going to do. She's my best friend, Mickey. She won't tell anyone. She promised."

"Are you crazy? Clemmy De Souza is a total airhead. She couldn't keep a secret if her life depended on it. Half of bloody Liverpool will know all about you and Brendan going to America by this time next week."

Mickey could scarcely believe his sister had told Clemmy about her and Brendan's plans. Since the meeting at Brendan's flat, he and Ronnie had carefully avoided saying anything about America to Marie when their parents were around. They restricted any discussion on the subject to the times when their parents were out of the house or when they might meet Marie for a drink in the pub or to share a coffee in the local café.

"She's not an airhead, Mickey. She promised not to tell and I believe her."

"Look, Marie, me and Ronnie's gone out on a limb for you, girl, helping you and Brendan and keeping everything quiet as far as Mam and Dad are concerned. Last thing we need is big mouth Clemmy lettin' the world know about everything. How d'you think Dad would carry on if he found out all three of us have been keeping secrets from him, especially one as big as this? I'm going to tell Ronnie and we'll see what he thinks about it."

"Go ahead, Mickey, but what do you expect Ronnie to do? Whether you like it or not, I've told me best friend, and she's promised not to tell anyone, and that's all there is to it."

Three hours later, after coming home from work to find a worried and irritable Mickey waiting for him, and having placated his fretting brother somewhat, Ronnie Doyle took a walk to the phone box at the end of the street, where he first made sure no one was around, and then lifted the phone and rang Brendan's number. The conversation that followed was short and sweet. Ronnie explained his and Mickey's worries but Brendan simply replied, "Don't make a big fuss about it, Ronnie. Marie should know if she can trust her best friend or not. If Clemmy says she'll keep the secret then that's good enough for me."

"You're sure, Brendan? There could be big bother for all of us if Dad finds out what you and Marie are planning."

"I'm sure. Biggest problem right now is this green card thing the Americans are talking about."

"Eh?"

"Something to do with their immigration rules. I don't get it myself. I'm trying to work something out even if it's just a tourist visa to get us into the country to begin with."

"Listen, Brendan, don't you go letting our little sister down, you hear me?"

"There's no way I'd do that, mate. You should know that. Look, Ronnie, I've gotta go, man. I'm doing a gig in Southport and I need to get on the road."

"Well, okay, but be careful, Brendan, you hear me?"

"I hear you, see you, Ronnie."

With those few words, Brendan ended the conversation, Ronnie finding himself left holding a silent phone in his right hand. Replacing the phone on its cradle, he pushed the door of the phone box open, made his way home, and on seeing his father in the sitting room, watching the television with his brother, he simply nodded to Mickey to indicate he'd dealt with the matter in hand. They'd talk later when they had a degree of privacy. Marie, it transpired, was out, enjoying a night at the cinema with Clemmy, the two girls excitedly having ventured to The Odeon to see the newly released *Alfie*, starring Marie's favourite actor, Michael Caine. Both girls had bought the single of the theme song sung by Cilla Black and released earlier in the year, and had been mortified when they found the title theme for the movie had been sung by Cher, rather than local girl, Cilla.

Ronnie walked through the hallway and entered the kitchen, where his mother sat in her fireside chair near the small coal fire, darning her husband's work socks, and listening and laughing along to a repeated episode of *The Clitheroe Kid* on the radio. Hot as the kitchen felt, it was necessary to keep a small fire burning in order to provide heat to the boiler which in turn ensured they had hot water provision in the house. Winter or summer, the fire would be kept burning and the kitchen at all times stood out as the warmest room in the home, uncomfortable as it might feel in the heat of high summer. Ronnie leaned down, giving her a brief hug where she sat, then lit the gas on the stove and put the kettle on. A cup of tea would be just the thing to settle his nerves, he thought.

"Hope you're making me one, too," his Mum said softly, without looking up from her darning.

"Of course I am, Mam," he replied as he waited for the kettle to boil. In a couple of minutes, the kettle began to whistle, Ronnie set about the time-honoured English ritual of first warming the pot, then brewing the tea, his Dad's favourite, PG Tips, and, to all intents and purposes, life in the Doyle household appeared a picture of domestic normality. Future events would soon prove otherwise.

CHAPTER 20

A DEAD END?

"That's it? That's all the contact you had with Brendan after the time you'd met at the flat?"

Andy Ross had hoped Ronnie's recollection of the last contact between the Doyle brothers and Brendan Kane might prove to be a little more revealing. In truth, he found it rather odd that the brothers appeared to have had minimal contact in the run-up to their little sister's perceived departure for the New World. He said as much to Ronnie, who replied,

"Honest, Inspector, that's all, right Mickey?" his elder brother nodded in confirmation and added to his brother's words. "We wanted to go and see him again. We were a bit worried by these 'problems' he was supposedly having with the whole emigration thing. We thought we might be able to help him, but Marie said it was best not to keep going round there, to his flat that is, in case someone saw him and Ronnie going there a lot and maybe word got back to Dad. She told us she'd pass on any messages between us and Brendan, and that Phil Oxley was doing what he could to help. He was good at paperwork, filling in forms and stuff like that, was Phil."

Ross shook his head and fell silent. He found it hard to accept some of the Doyle brothers' story, but then remembered that back in the nineteen sixties the world, and Liverpool in particular was a very different place to today's fast-paced, technology driven metropolis. There had been a naiveté, a sense of being involved in the beginnings of a brave new world, almost, as the rapid rise of the British pop music industry walked side-by-side with the technological and lifestyle revolutions that went along with it.

For people like the Doyle brothers and Brendan Kane, all children of the immediate post-war years, a set of old-fashioned values and standards, alien in many ways to those of a similar age as the millennium dawned, were the norm, and despite their claim to the contrary, the teenagers and young adults of those days were in fact far less 'street-wise' than their modern-day counterparts. Perhaps the current familiarity of the music and the groups who made the Liverpool of the sixties such a throbbing, vibrant environment in which to grow up somehow masked some of the realities of those times. Andy Ross just couldn't imagine the kids of today being quite so 'unworldly' as the boys from Brendan Kane and The Planets appeared to have been back then. Today, a few minutes on the internet, a few calls on the phone, and today's youth would have all the information they needed at their fingertips.

"Sir? Do you have any more questions?"

Izzie Drake broke into Ross's reverie. The inspector hadn't realized he'd allowed himself to drift away from the conversation and he quickly pulled himself together again and faced Ronnie Doyle.

"Yes, sorry Sergeant, sorry gentlemen. I was lost in thought for a minute there. Thinking about what you've told me so far. So, Ronnie, I'm presuming things went along quite normally from that time until Brendan and Marie suddenly disappeared, right?"

"Yeah, well, no, not really 'normal', Inspector. Over the next couple of weeks, we could see Marie was getting edgy, nervous, like. I tried to get her to tell me exactly what Brendan had arranged but she was a bit…what's the word? Evasive, that's it."

"In what way?" Ross asked.

"She just kept saying that Brendan was taking care of things and we'd know about it all when the time was right. I know Mickey tried as well, to get her to talk to us, but she just clammed up and we both thought things weren't going just as they were supposed to. Tell you the truth, we, that's me and Mickey, we thought perhaps the whole plan had fallen through, didn't we, Mickey?"

"Yeah, we did," the elder brother agreed. "I phoned Phil Oxley the next day, and he said he'd been in touch with Brendan, helping him to get things sorted out. He said he didn't think Brendan's plans were workable but he was trying to help Brendan get tourist visas for him and Marie. Brendan thought he might still find a record company or producer to represent him even if he was only there for a short time. If he succeeded, according to Phil, a U.S record company would be able to help him get whatever permits he needed to live and work over there. A couple of weeks later, me and Ronnie knew something was in the offing. Marie was definitely acting odd, like, and I waited outside her work one day and met her when she knocked off. I told her I wasn't going to just leave things as they were, and that even Mam and Dad had mentioned she was acting weird.

Dad even wondered if she'd got herself pregnant by 'some scally' as he put it. She just laughed and told me not to worry about things, that she and Brendan wouldn't be around much longer, and then, just a week after that, she went out late one afternoon, a Saturday, I remember, and that was it. We never saw our little sister again after that day."

Mickey fell silent, looked at his brother, and the two men seemed to be sharing an intense sadness as the recollection of the last time they'd seen their sister came flooding back to haunt their collective memories. To Andy Ross, none of this seemed to add up, however. Even back in the nineteen sixties, people rarely just vanished without leaving a single piece of trace evidence behind them. How could Marie Doyle and Brendan Kane simply disappear from the face of the earth? Of course, Ross now felt sure he knew what had happened to Brendan, but what the hell had happened to Marie, and why hadn't the police at the time of their disappearance done more to try and find them? It was time to move on. Despite his interest in the saga that the Doyle brothers had laid out before him, he needed more if he was going to solve the murder of Brendan Kane and the disappearance and perhaps also the murder of Marie Doyle. For now, he didn't want to raise that spectre too highly in the two Doyle's minds. He turned to Ronnie again, and decided to move on to the alleged lack of investigation by the old Liverpool City Police.

* * *

"Ronnie, I want you to tell me why you first became suspicious that something was wrong, and why you went to the police, and then, please try to recall exactly what happened when the police became involved. Take your time. Gather your thoughts. I know it all took place a long time ago, but anything you can tell us could be important, even now."

Ronnie Doyle nodded and pursed his lips as he once again allowed his mind to wander back in time. Ross waited patiently as Ronnie's brow furrowed as he concentrated hard, doing his best to dredge up even more details of events that took place over thirty years previously. At last, after an interminable pause, and after taking a deep breath, he began.

"Well, Inspector Ross, you need to understand that when Marie didn't come home that night, me and Mickey didn't think she'd run off with Brendan, not at first. We thought she'd maybe been with a friend, and missed the last bus home or something, and maybe stayed overnight at the friend's house, didn't we, Mickey?"

Mickey nodded his agreement but remained silent.

"So, Marie didn't come home, and Mam and Dad were going frantic. They were convinced she'd been raped or murdered by a nutter or something, you know? Anyway, they wanted me and Mickey to go look for her, so we did. We went to Clemmy's house first, on Huyton Road. Marie hadn't told either of us where she'd been going that night, no hint that she wouldn't be coming home, or that she'd be seeing Brendan, anything like that. Looking back, that's what she must have done of course, but we didn't know it then. Clemmy said she hadn't seen her all day, but said that when she'd seen her the day before, Marie had seemed excited and on edge at the same time. Clemmy asked her if she and Brendan had made their plans but Marie clammed up. We knocked on a couple more doors of friends of hers, but no one had seen her that day.

We found a phone box and called Phil, but he hadn't seen either Marie or Brendan that day. He admitted he'd been a bit worried about Brendan lately, that he didn't seem to accept that going to America wasn't as easy as he'd thought at first. He kept telling Phil he was going to make it one way or another and Phil was getting exasperated with him. I was running out of coins so instead, agreed to meet Phil in person the next day. We couldn't do any more that night, we had no more money and so couldn't ring Brendan's number, though Phil said he'd try and make sure Marie contacted us somehow if she was with Brendan.

Our parents worried all night, and Dad was ready to call for the police right away, but we knew the police wouldn't do anything about someone who hadn't even been missing twelve hours. Next day, I went alone to see Phil, 'cause Mickey had to go to work. We met on the waterfront in the city, and sat on a bench outside The Cunard Building. I thought Phil looked uncomfortable, but that was maybe because he'd worked in that place until a few months earlier, but had been made redundant when Cunard moved their centre of operations from Liverpool to Southampton. Poor old Phil wasn't enjoying unemployment, but work wasn't easy to come by. Thank God he had the part-time job in the dance band in the evenings, or he'd have been stony broke. Anyway, we sat there for a few minutes, watching the world go by, feeling a bit uncomfortable with each other. Then, Phil sort of coughed, and then told me he'd tried ringing Brendan the previous night and received no answer, so he'd been round to the flat first thing that morning. He'd knocked, rung the doorbell and knocked again, but no one answered. He'd had to assume there was no one at home after knocking on the door of Brendan's flat, then tried the flat next door, and the woman who answered the door said she hadn't seen or heard anything of Brendan for a couple of days. Phil admitted he felt a bit guilty by that time, for helping Brendan, who he now believed had 'lost the plot' a bit. You can imagine how I felt when he said that, Inspector. My sister was, as far as I knew; with a man who Phil thought might be so obsessed with his American dream that he'd maybe lost touch with reality."

Ronnie paused at that point, and appeared to Ross to be struggling to control his emotions. Ross asked a question at that point, in an effort to take some of the pressure off Ronnie and give him a break from his retelling of his sister's disappearance.

"Mickey, tell me, do you know if Phil Oxley is still living in Liverpool? Are either of you still in contact with him?"

"Haven't seen or heard from him for years, Inspector Ross. Last I heard, he was living in Fazakerley somewhere. Don't know if Ronnie's heard from him."

"Not for a long time. I saw him in town about five years ago, as he was leaving the main post office. I tried to cross over and say hello but by the time I got there, he'd disappeared into the crowd of shoppers and pedestrians," said Ronnie.

"You're sure it was Oxley?" said Ross.

"You don't forget someone you've known since you were about six years old, Inspector Ross. He'd lost a lot of hair over the years, but his face hadn't altered much at all, and he had a way of walking that was pretty unmistakable. I think it was something to do with the way he used to sit at his drum kit. He walks kind of bow-legged. It was Phil alright, I'm sure of it."

"Right," said Ross, "we've established that Phil Oxley is still somewhere in the local area. Sergeant Drake?"

"I'll get someone on it as soon as we're done here, sir." Drake replied. Izzie knew McLennan would soon be able to find an address for Oxley, probably from the local electoral roll.

"Ronnie, go on with what happened next, please," Ross prompted Ronnie to continue his story.

"We waited two days, Inspector," Ronnie quickly went on, eager to get things out in the open. "Two full days and not a bloody word from her. Mam and Dad were going out of their minds with worry and us two were mad at Marie and Brendan for just taking off without a word after we'd kept their secret for them. In the end, me Da insisted on going to the police station to report our Marie as missing, and it was Mickey, not me who went with him. Tell the inspector about it, Mickey, what happened at the cop shop."

"Yes, Mickey, and please, try to remember everything that was said to you at the time, and what action, if any, the police took at the time," said Ross.

A little like his brother before him, Mickey took a couple of seconds to compose himself, his mind working on recalling the events that had transpired over thirty years in the past. Before he began, Izzie Drake interrupted the flow of the interview with a question of her own.

"Just one question before you carry on, Mickey. Do either of you know if Brendan's parents are still alive, or if he has any other family in the area? If I'm going to try and locate Phil Oxley, I can search for Brendan's family at the same time."

"Good idea, Sergeant," Ross added. "Anything you can tell us, lads?

Mickey replied instantly.

"Brendan's Dad was already ill at the time he left Liverpool, Inspector. We heard it was cancer, and he died about a year after Brendan disappeared. His Mum never got over Brendan leaving home and then losing her husband within a year and I saw her death notice in the Echo one night about five years after that. When we were growing up together, Brendan always told us he had no other family in the city. His grandparents died during the war in an air raid, and he apparently had an Uncle Michael in the Royal Navy who died when H.M.S. Hood was sunk by the Bismarck. Me and Ronnie spent quite some time with his Mum and Dad after Brendan and Marie disappeared. They were as worried as we were, and I think his Dad died sooner than he should have from the worry of it all. Honest, nobody could understand why Brendan and Marie never got in touch with anybody."

Ross nodded as Mickey fell silent again.

"Right then, Sergeant, just Oxley to locate if you can."

"Yes, sir," Izzie replied. "Sorry for the interruption Mickey, please carry on with what you were about to tell us."

"Oh yeah, right, the police back in sixty-six. There was a big row at home before we went to the police. Me and Ronnie couldn't keep the secret any longer and we came clean to Mam and Dad. I thought Da was going to explode when he realized we'd misled and deceived him, as he put it. Me Mam cried and cried, and told me and Ronnie she was ashamed of us, that we couldn't be trusted any more. We couldn't blame them, deceiving them like that and all. We only meant to help Marie, Inspector, we never thought it through properly, I suppose. We sure as hell never meant to hurt our Mam and Dad. Anyway, they calmed down eventually and we were surprised that Da seemed to be the first to accept what we'd done, but he told us that there was now no alternative to going to the police. He said it was obvious that Marie had run off and something had to be done to find her. I can remember he went upstairs to the bathroom and a few minutes later he came back down to the kitchen. He'd changed into his best suit, his only suit to tell the truth and had his best white Sunday shirt and tie on, that he normally only wore to church, or maybe for weddings and funerals. Not that we got invited to many weddings, and we certainly didn't go to many funerals in those days, not at our ages, anyway. He'd shaved and even used some of Ronnie's after shave, a bit too much as I remember. When he walked in the room the smell of Old Spice nearly knocked us out.

I remember going to the police station with me Dad on the bus. I think it was on St Annes Road or something like that. They kept us waiting ages, even though Da told 'em we were reporting a missing person. Eventually a sergeant came out and saw us and took us into an interview room."

"Was this a detective or a uniformed officer?" Ross asked.

"He was in uniform. Big bloke, name was Carson. I remember he had a mustache, looked a bit like a bloody RAF Wing Commander in a war movie. He asked us a few questions, well, he asked Dad mostly. I felt bad for Dad. He hardly said a word."

"Okay then, Mickey, in your own words, try to tell me everything you remember about that interview with Sergeant Carson and what subsequently took place following the day you and your father made the initial report."

"Eh?" Mickey sounded a little nonplussed by Ross's terminology. Ronnie decided to help his brother out.

"He means, tell him what happened when you and Dad met with Carson and then as much as you can remember about everything the cops did from that day onwards, for what it was worth."

"Oh, yeah, right. Got it. I were never right impressed with Sergeant bloody Carson, inspector, right from the start. Sorry, I know he was one of your lot, but that's the plain truth of the matter. The bloke was friggin' useless, so he was."

Ross simply nodded in response to Mickey's remark and replied

"Don't apologise, Mickey. If the investigation wasn't carried out properly back then, I need to know about it. Try and recall any details that come into your mind, however small and insignificant you think they might be. It could be important today in helping us ascertain what happened to your sister and to Brendan Kane."

Ross turned to Izzie Drake.

"Could you please organise some more tea and coffee please, Sergeant, and maybe some biscuits? I think we could all do with a little refreshment before we continue."

Drake nodded and closed her notebook, placing it on Ross's desk as she moved to the door.

"Right sir, won't be long." She smiled at Mickey Doyle, having decided there was something rather likeable about the elder Doyle brother. Despite his rough and ready exterior she sensed a vulnerability about Mickey, a fragility of temperament his brother Ronnie certainly didn't suffer from. From the moment the brothers had begun relating their story to Ross and herself, Izzie had been using her intuitive prowess to weigh up and analyze the two men. Both she and Ross were aware that it wouldn't be the first time a potentially psychotic murderer had walked into the hands of the police, often with a view to taunting the law by appearing to help the investigation, inserting themselves into the case as willing witnesses while at the same time using their inside connection to discover how much the police knew, and often being able to deflect the investigation from the truth. After over an hour spent in the company of Ronnie and Mickey Doyle she felt reasonably certain that neither of the brothers had been involved in the murder of their friend, Brendan Kane, or the subsequent disappearance of their sister. If anything, she thought they'd been naïve and a little too trusting of their friend and of the so far unknown quantity that was Phil Oxley, but she could feel no malignant hostility coming from either brother. Returning to Ross's office soon afterwards with a tray containing the requested beverages and a packet of chocolate digestive biscuits, Ross's favourites, Izzie poured drinks for all of them, and pulled a stool from under the computer desk in the corner of Ross's office and sat down, her feet growing tired of standing as she listened to the men's story. Izzie took up her notebook from where she'd left it on the desk, looked up and out of the window, where the earlier clouds had given way to heavy rain, falling in almost horizontal sheets, driven by a strong wind blowing in from the Irish Sea. She felt the weather suited the mood of the interview they were conducting. Ross took a drink of his coffee allowing the hot liquid to refresh his throat before speaking again.

"Right Mickey, I apologise this is taking so long, but I'm sure you both realize by now how important your information is proving to be. Please, take your time, clear your mind again and then, do your best to take me back to the interview with Sergeant Carson."

Mickey Doyle nodded, coughed once and cleared his throat, and allowed his mind to once more return to nineteen sixty-six, as Ross and Drake listened intently to the next installment of the story of Brendan and Marie.

CHAPTER 21

MISSING PERSONS, 1966

Sergeant Robert Carson sat quietly observing the two men, father and son, who'd just spent half an hour relating an almost unbelievable tale to him. Now, he had to decide just what, if anything, he intended to do in relation to their story. Looking at the notes he'd made on the form that sat on the table in front of him, he decided to first of all recap the details of what they'd told him.

"So, Mr. Doyle, and Michael, you insist Marie had every intention of leaving the city with her boyfriend, this Brendan Kane character, correct?"

James, (Jimmy) Doyle replied with exasperation in his voice.

"That's what we've been telling you for the last thirty minutes. And I told you I knew nothing about Marie wanting to run off with the lad until just before we left home, when Mickey and Ronnie told me and their Mother all about it."

"Ah yes," said Carson, "quite a little conspiracy of secrecy, wouldn't you say?"

"What the fuck d'you mean by that? What conspiracy?" young Mickey snapped at the sergeant.

Carson puffed his chest out, a visible display of his own self-importance. Aged fifty-three, and close to retirement, the dapper sergeant, with his knife edge creases in his uniform, and crisply starched collar, firmly believed in his own ability to tell truth from lies, or to know when his time was being wasted on trivia when there were more serious crimes out there waiting to be solved. Sadly, even his own superiors saw another side to him, that of a man too set in his ways and unable to accept change readily, thereby holding him back and being among the reasons he'd never managed to pass his inspector's exams. Carson had held the rank of sergeant for fifteen years, and would remain in his rank until the day of his retirement. The Doyles, of course knew none of this. To them he was 'The Police' the man they'd been introduced to by the desk sergeant as being the officer available to help in their search for their daughter and sister. He now responded to Mickey's angry comment. Maybe he'd used the wrong word?

"Whoa there, young fellow," he said to Mickey." I meant nothing sinister by my use of the word. Just that it seems to me you and your brother and your mate Oxley seemed to be the only ones in on the secret of this planned move to America. You all played it very close to the chest to ensure your Dad here, and your Mother, knew nothing about it."

"Hang on a minute," said Mickey, "Clemmy knew too."

"Clemmy?"

"Marie's best friend, Clemency De Souza. Marie told me and Ronnie she'd told Clemmy about it, a while ago. She swore her to secrecy."

"Ah, right, I see," Carson nodded his head in mock understanding at Mickey's explanation. "Tell me, has it ever entered your head that Marie and this boyfriend of hers might have been spinning you a line?"

"How d'you mean?" Mickey asked the apparently all-knowing experienced officer sitting looking sternly at him.

"Well, in my experience, I've often found that when young folks want to do a disappearing act, they often tell people one thing, and then up and do something totally different. Have you considered the fact that your sister and her fella might have told you they were planning to go to America, while they secretly made plans to go somewhere different entirely?"

Carson leaned back in his chair with a self-satisfied smile on his face as he watched his words take effect.

"But, why would they do that?" Mickey asked, incredulously. "She knew me and Ronnie were on her side," he said, rather sheepishly as he felt his father's eyes boring into him, his and Ronnie's earlier deception rising high in Jimmy's thoughts once again.

"And you fell for it, didn't you?" Carson went on. "You believed every word. They even got this Oxley lad to go along with their plans, have him make all sorts of inquiries about how to go about getting to America, as you've told me. What better way to throw everyone off their true scent than by creating a clever fantasy that you all fell for? You told me, Mr. Doyle, that Marie is almost twenty one, and there's no law that says a couple can't up sticks and move away from home without telling their parents about it, you know. Also, from what you and your son here have told me, it seems you'd have been none too pleased if you'd known they were planning to run off and elope together."

Both Doyles, senior and junior, appeared quite nonplussed by Carson's theory. Jimmy Doyle appeared lost and unable to respond to Carson, but eventually replied,

"Yeah, well, that's true enough. I don't hold with mixed marriages."

Now it was Carson's turn to look nonplussed, not quite able to grasp Doyle senior's meaning at first.

"Mixed marriages? Are you telling me Brendan Kane is foreign, Asian, or West Indian or something? Is it because you wouldn't want your daughter marrying a coloured person?"

"Colour's got nothing to do with it," said Jimmy Doyle, forcefully. "Brendan Kane is a bloody proddie, a protestant, Sergeant. We're good Catholics, so we are, and I'll not have my daughter marrying a bloody proddie."

Carson almost choked at the man's bigoted words, unable to really grasp such feelings.

"Mr. Doyle," he said. "This is the nineteen sixties. Surely you can see such ideas and attitudes are out of date? If you must know, I happen to be Catholic myself, and I've been happily married to my wife, a 'proddie' as you'd call her, for over thirty years. This is England, Mr. Doyle, not Northern Ireland, though I suspect from your name and your attitude you may have connections over the water."

"I do indeed, Sergeant. I have many cousins and uncles and aunts in Belfast and Derry. As for you and your wife, that's your business. I've no interest in you and your marriage. Like I said, I'd not let any child of mine marry outside our own faith. It's not right and that's all there is to it."

Carson was almost lost for words. He was well aware of the problems that existed across the Irish Sea in Northern Ireland, but had never seen or heard such a display of outright bigotry here in his home town. He could see from the look on Mickey's face that the younger man felt totally embarrassed by his father's outburst and tried to reach out to the father again.

"If you feel so strongly about it, Mr. Doyle, how come you let your sons appear in the pop group with Kane, and let your daughter help them?"

"Aye, well, we don't have a lot of choice in this day and age, do we? We might have to work with people of the other side, but that doesn't mean we marry them and raise kids who don't know the true faith."

Carson had just about had enough of Jimmy Doyle, and any sympathy he felt towards the family's plight now switched entirely to the worried-looking Mickey, who now looked totally uncomfortable in response to his father's outburst.

"Look, here's what I propose. I'll make some inquiries among their friends and social circle. I'll speak to Mr. Oxley, and go along to Brendan Kane's flat, and speak to his parents. Like I said, this whole America thing may have been a total red herring, concocted to make sure you and anyone else couldn't follow them or find them wherever it is they've really gone."

Jimmy and Mickey Doyle left the police station a few minutes later, arriving home half an hour later, soaked to the skin after a very wet walk to the house from the nearest bus stop. Marie's mother, Connie, waiting impatiently in the kitchen, was anxious to hear the outcome of their visit to the police, but became very angry and agitated when Mickey told her about his father's religious outburst to the sergeant. She'd been baptized forty four years earlier as Concepta O'Malley, a good, old-fashioned Irish Catholic name, but one she'd hated since childhood, always preferring the more modern and as far as she was concerned, secular name of Connie. Unlike Jimmy, who was Liverpool born and bred, Connie had actually been born in Lisburn on the outskirts of Belfast, her parents having moved to Liverpool when she was ten years old, themselves sick and tired of what her father referred to as the 'medieval' attitudes towards alternative religions that existed in the Northern Irish community. She'd met and fallen in love with a young, handsome Jimmy Doyle when she was eighteen and he'd been a year older, and they were married a year later. The football loving, weekend fisherman she'd fallen for hadn't displayed his latent tendencies towards religious intolerance until some years later, and she certainly didn't share her husband's religious bigotry, and often found it embarrassing to hear his outdated views on religious affiliations.

"In the name of God and the Holy Virgin, James Doyle, why'd you have to behave in that way in front of the police? Marie's missing, and a young man too, and all you can do is turn it into a speech on marriage between Catholics and Protestants. You're a disgrace, man, so you are."

"D'you think I care what happens to a little scally like Brendan Kane? He's probably already had his way with our Marie and spoiled her for a proper marriage in the future. Then he's enticed her away from her home and family and our two stupid sons went so far as to help them keep it all under wraps. They knew what I'd say if I found out, and so did Marie. That Oxley boy's just as bad, conspiring with them to deceive us."

"He's not a boy, he's a young man, same as Mickey and Ronnie, and he didn't conspire against us, as you put it. He just helped his friends, Jimmy, same as you probably would have done at their age."

"That's where you're wrong, woman. There's no way I'd have disrespected my parents like that."

"Of, for crying out loud, Jimmy, hush your mouth for a minute. I want to know what they said at the police station. You tell me, Mickey. You'll make more sense than your father, to be sure."

Jimmy Doyle gave a kind of growl from deep in his throat, but at least he fell silent and walked across the kitchen, where he took up residence in Connie's comfortable fireside chair, knowing it would irritate his wife as he did so. Connie chose to ignore him as Mickey quickly filled his mother in on their conversation with Sergeant Carson.

"That's all he'd say for now, Ma," Mickey said as he came to the end of relating the story of their interview to his mother. "The sergeant did say he'd be in touch with us after he's made some inquiries and asked around a bit, but I don't think he was really all that interested in what we had to say."

Mickey's back was to his father as he spoke and he managed to gesture with a sideways glance that his mother correctly interpreted as him indicating that his father definitely hadn't helped matters.

Connie Doyle managed to hide her simmering anger towards her husband over the following days, though the atmosphere in the Doyle household deteriorated until it was almost possible to cut it with a knife. Jimmy spent every spare minute at the pub, drowning his sorrows in beer, while Mickey and Ronnie did their best to avoid both their parents. Instead of joining their father at the Red Rose as they would normally have done, they found a haven of relative peace at the local billiard hall, where they did their best to work off their anxiety and frustrations over endless games of snooker and billiards. John Pullman had successfully defended his World Championship status in a series of challenge matches with Fred Davis at the City Hall in Liverpool, and the two brothers had developed a love for the game from watching some of the matches on television. Days passed almost interminably, with no word from Marie or Brendan as to their whereabouts. When the loud knocking that could only be that of a police officer interrupted the family's early evening six days later, it almost came as a form of relief when Connie opened the door and admitted Sergeant Carson to her home, showing him into the sitting room, where she invited him to sit down, introduced him to her younger son, Ronnie, and then together with her husband and sons, nervously awaited his news. Carson sat in one of the two armchairs in the room and politely refused Connie's offer of a cup of tea. Having developed a dislike for Jimmy Doyle at their first meeting, he wanted to keep his visit to the Doyle home as short as possible. Opening his notebook, the sergeant began his report to the expectant Doyle family, delivering his words towards Jimmy Doyle, as the head of the family.

"As I attempted to explain to you when you visited me at the station, Mr. Doyle, bearing in mind the circumstances surrounding this matter, there isn't an awful lot the police can effectively do…"

"So what the fuck do we pay your bloody wages for?" Jimmy Doyle almost exploded at the sergeant.

"For crying out loud, Jimmy, will you just let the man speak?" Connie snapped at her husband, instantly winning the respect of Sergeant Carson. In a quieter voice she continued, "Please go on Sergeant, and forgive my husband's rude and uncouth outburst."

For once, Jimmy Doyle found himself on the receiving end of a tongue lashing, and he made a gruff sound in his throat, stood up and walked across the room to the fireplace, where he stood leaning against the mantelpiece as Carson continued. Even Mickey and Ronnie appeared impressed as their mother at long last appeared to have found the courage to assert herself over her domineering husband.

"Yes, right, thank you, Mrs. Doyle. As I was saying, we don't have many options open to us, I'm sorry to say. I have visited Mr. Kane's parents, your friend, Mr. Phillip Oxley and your daughter's friend, Clemency De Souza, and obtained statements from each of them. I followed this up by reporting the case as you yourselves, Mr. Doyle and Mickey presented it to me, to my boss, and it is Inspector Ledden's opinion that none of the people interviewed, and this includes yourselves, have been able to show that any threat existed against the couple. In other words, nobody has been able to say with even a hint of certainty that they believed Marie and her boyfriend to be in any imminent danger, either from each other or from any other person or persons, known or unknown. There is absolutely no evidence to suggest that this is anything other then a case of two young people, both over and above the age of consent, and of legal voting age, deciding to leave their homes and make a fresh start somewhere else."

"That's a load of bollocks, Sergeant Carson," Mickey cut in. "Me Dad and me only came to see you because we were worried about them disappearing without leaving word. It was totally not like them to do that, especially after making their plans to go to America."

Connie Doyle shot a glance at Mickey that he instantly recognized and responded to.

"Er, sorry about the bad language, Sergeant, sorry, Mam."

"Yes, well, where was I?" Carson almost smiled at the tiny domestic cameo that had just played out before his eyes. "Oh, yes, so, we have a situation where Marie and Brendan Kane appear to have produced an elaborate plan to run away to America, but as your mate Phillip Oxley told us, Brendan Kane knew he couldn't just waltz into the United States without going through a lengthy immigration process, so my boss concluded that they must have got tired of waiting, and have gone somewhere else entirely. There are lots of places in the world that don't have such strict rules about who they allow into their countries. I take it Marie has a passport?"

"Yes, she does," Connie replied.

"Listen, Mrs. Doyle, it's been my experience over the years that most missing adults go missing because they want to do so, whatever the reason or the rights and wrongs of the matter, that's a simple fact. If they don't want to be found, there are many ways for them to remain hidden, often in plain sight in another town or country, but by the same token, many of them will simply turn up after a few days, or weeks perhaps, when things don't go quite the way they expect them to. You know, the old 'grass isn't greener on the other side' thing. If there had been any evidence of foul play here, rest assured we would have thrown the weight of the force behind a search for them, but as it stands, no one can substantiate the merest hint of a threat to their safety. No crime has been committed and the inspector simply won't sanction the number of man hours required for an extensive country-wide search for a couple who everyone admits had planned to leave town anyway."

A pall of desperation hung heavy in the Doyle's living room as the sergeant's words struck home to each member of the family. Jimmy Doyle at last found his voice once again.

"So that's it? That's all the police can do for us? What about that scally's flat? Did you even bother going round there?"

"I did go there, as a matter of fact, Mr. Doyle. There was nobody at home, and I looked up the landlords of the building, and they told me they received a letter from Kane just two days ago, saying he was leaving town, and enclosing a month's rent in the envelope, along with instruction to sell his things, as he wouldn't be coming back to Liverpool."

"But, that's rubbish," Ronnie said in response to the news of the letter. "He'd never do that, not leave all his things behind, not Brendan. I mean, there was his new record player, his guitar, all that kind of stuff. Did you ask if his guitar was gone or still in the flat?"

"Ronnie, love, I know you're upset. We all are, but you mustn't badger the sergeant like that, really you mustn't," Connie Doyle said to her son. Connie retained a good old-fashioned healthy respect for the police and didn't like to see and hear her son acting in a belligerent manner towards a member of the force.

Ronnie shook his head in exasperation.

"Yeah, right, sorry Mam, sorry Sergeant," he apologised.

With great dignity, Connie Doyle rose from her chair by the fire and walked slowly to the polished wooden sideboard at the opposite side of the room, and picked up a small, yellow plastic transistor radio from behind a large school photograph of Marie, taken when she was fourteen. Holding it as though it were an item of inestimable value she held it up so Carson could see it clearly.

"This, Sergeant Carson, is my daughter's most treasured possession. It cost her two shillings on Kirkby Market. Expensive? No, but valuable beyond words to Marie. She loves music, Sergeant, and if she was going anywhere important, or for any length of time, this little radio would have gone with her. That's why I know something's very wrong, and that my little girl is in trouble of some kind."

"Look," said Carson, "I've personally distributed your daughter and Brendan Kane's descriptions to other police forces in the country. If any officer sees and recognizes them they will report it back to us here in Liverpool and I promise to let you know if that happens. The case file will remain open, but for now, there's not much more I can do for you. I'm sorry."

"Yeah, I just bet you are," said Jimmy Doyle, his voice heavy with sarcasm.

"I have to go, I'm afraid," Carson said, now in a hurry to be gone from the Doyle house. "If I hear anything, I'll be in touch."

Connie Doyle saw the sergeant out and as he disappeared down the street to the spot where he'd parked his sleek, white, Ford Zephyr 6 patrol car, she slowly closed the front door, somehow knowing in her heart of hearts that she would probably never see her little girl again.

CHAPTER 22

CONFIRMATION

"That was it, Inspector Ross" said Ronnie Doyle with a look of intense sadness on his face. "The police did virtually sod all to try and find Marie or Brendan for that matter."

"Are you telling me you never heard from the police again after the visit from Sergeant Carson?" Ross asked Ronnie.

"Well, we did get another visit a few weeks later. Sergeant Carson came to the house one morning. Me and Mickey were at work and Dad was out, I can't remember where. Me Mam told us later that Carson had done a routine follow-up on our report of Marie's disappearance and that there'd been no word from any of the flyers he'd sent to other forces and there'd also been no reports of any 'victims of violence' as he put it, being found anywhere in the country. That was his nice way of saying murder, I reckon, and not wanting to upset me Mam. He told her he'd checked with the airports and docks and found no reference to either Brendan or Marie attempting to leave the country. I think, by that time, me Mam had resigned herself to Marie not coming back, but I remember her sitting crying very quietly to herself that night. I left her to her own thoughts, because I didn't want to upset her even more and to be honest, I wouldn't have known what to say to her, Inspector. She cried a lot after that, usually when she thought no one could hear her, but we did, often."

Andy Ross sat, deep in thought for a few seconds after Ronnie finished his story. He could understand why the Doyles felt less than satisfied with the response of the old Liverpool City Police in nineteen sixty-six, but knew that Sergeant Carson, by all accounts, though not sounding like the most dynamic officer he'd ever experienced, had probably done his best under the circumstances. In addition, Carson was only human and his reaction to James Doyle's outburst of blatant religious bigotry had probably been entirely justified, bearing in mind his own personal circumstances. Favouritism was frowned upon in the police service but no one could be blamed for not being entirely sympathetic to someone like the elder Doyle. Without doing his best to make some attempt to look into the investigation that took place at the time of Marie's original disappearance, he certainly wasn't going to buy into the Doyle brothers' account of the rights or wrong of the way the police handled their complaint at the time, or make any criticism of Carson or anyone else involved. Based on what they'd just told him, Ross knew something the brothers weren't aware of, something that might add a little sensitivity to the way he approached his research into the past, but now wasn't the right time to mention it. He needed to try and communicate that to them in a way that wouldn't alienate his best, in fact his only witnesses to the final days of Brendan Kane. He quickly decided on his next move and after allowing Ronnie a brief respite, Ross said,

"Look, Ronnie, you too Mickey. It's been a long interview and you've both been very helpful. I know today hasn't gone exactly as you expected when you walked into the station earlier but you really have given me a lot to work with. We now know with reasonable certainty that the remains found at Coles' Wharf are those of your friend, Brendan Kane and thanks to you, we now know about the disappearance of your sister, which I assure you, I'm going to follow up on, as I feel both cases are closely connected. We'll speak to everyone we can find from those days, Phil Oxley, Clemmy De Souza and whoever has a good recollection of either of the two. I forgot to ask if your mother and father are still alive?"

"Yes, they are," Ronnie replied. "Dad is eighty now, but still fit as a fiddle, Inspector. Hardly had a day's illness in his life. Our Mother is only about a year behind him but not as well as she was. She has severe arthritis and has coronary heart disease, but still lives in hope that one day she'll find out just what happened to our Marie."

"Okay, that's good to know. I will of course need to speak to both your parents in due course. I hope their powers of recollection are as good as yours."

"I wouldn't count on it, Inspector. They are getting on a bit, you know," said Mickey. "I know they're great for their age, but Mam especially is a bit forgetful these days."

"Understood," Ross replied, "but whatever they can remember may prove useful. Please make sure you give Sergeant Drake both of your telephone numbers and that of your parents before you leave, so we can get in touch with you quickly if we need to."

Both men provided Izzie Drake with the required numbers and Izzie herself showed the Doyles from the premises a few minutes later, then returning to Ross's office where the inspector and his sergeant sat quietly and began to confer on the events and the information they'd received in what had been a rather long two hour interview with the brothers.

* * *

"Wow, that was a bit of a marathon session, sir," Drake commented.

"It was indeed, Izzie," Ross replied, "and totally unexpected. Who'd have expected those two to walk in off the streets and give us the vital link we needed to identify our victim?"

"You're sure the remains are those of Brendan Kane, then, sir?"

"Everything they told us seems to fit with what we already have, which admittedly wasn't much up until now."

"But what about the missing sister, sir? Where do we go with that one?"

"I must say, Izzie, I'm not too sure at the moment. It adds another, highly sinister element to the case we already have. I'm going to have to talk to the boss. D.C.I Porteous will have to allow us a little extra manpower I think. I want a few uniforms available to help us with the foot-work that I envisage we'll need to go deeper into the affairs of nineteen sixty-six."

"Do you believe everything the brothers told us, sir?"

"They came here believing we may have found the remains of their sister. They had no reason to lie to us and I believe they were genuinely shocked when we suggested the bones could be those of their friend. I think they both firmly believe Marie is dead, and in light of what they've told us, I must admit I tend to subscribe to that theory too."

"But why, sir? Why would anyone want to murder a young couple who, as far as we can ascertain, hurt no-one and whose only fault appears to have been the fact they fell in love and wanted to start a new life some-where else?"

"Well, according to the brothers, their father was certainly bigoted enough to want Brendan Kane out of the way, but, would he have harboured sufficient hatred to murder his own daughter too? Somehow, I just don't see that happening. He seems to have been a hundred percent family orientated, though we'll know more about him when we interview the man. Plus, if Marie Doyle was murdered at the same time as her boyfriend, how come her body has never been found?"

"It's taken over thirty years for Brendan's remains to turn up, with all due respect sir."

"Yes, of course it has, Izzie. Thanks for reminding me." Ross smiled at Drake as he accepted his sergeant's mild rebuke. "It's always possible they were killed together and Marie's body simply got carried away by the tide, and ended up as fish food somewhere between Liverpool and the Irish Sea."

As the two detectives continued bouncing ideas back and forth between them, the afternoon began to grow darker, as the overhead storm clouds grew in intensity and the view outside Ross's window became even more depressing than it had been during the visit of the Doyle brothers. Ross stood, pushed his chair back and walked to the window, peering out into the sheets of almost horizontal rain that were lashing down, presenting a grim picture of the world outside to go with the grim task he and Drake were involved in.

He walked across the room and flicked the light switch. A few clicks from overhead heralded the coming of the light from the long fluorescent tubes, which burst into full life after a few hesitant seconds of flickering. Andy Ross re-took his seat, and just as he was about to continue his discourse with Izzie Drake, the telephone on his desk began ringing. Ross lifted the receiver.

"D.I. Ross," he announced to the caller, and then, "McLennan, why are you phoning me from the other end of the office?" He listened to the young detective constable for a few seconds, and then with an amused look on his face, he replied, "Oh yes, right, I see, the door was closed and you thought it best not to disturb me by knocking on my door, so I presume you thought it best to disturb me by phoning me instead?"

Before Derek McLennan could say any more, Ross said, "If you have news for us, better get yourself in here now, McLennan. Don't keep me waiting, there's a good lad."

"You can be a cruel sod, sir, if you don't mind me saying so. He's a good lad, and trying to impress you whenever he can, you know?"

"I know, Izzie. Can't help winding the lad up sometimes. In a way he reminds me of me at his age, intense and doing everything by the book, trying to please the boss, until one day I realized the way to get on was just to be myself, do my best and sod the consequences. He'll get there one day. He's got the makings of a first class detective and…"

A knock on the door interrupted Ross's words and as the door opened, Derek McLennan strode into the room, a very big smile on his face, and a sheet of A4 paper in his hand.

"From the look on your face, I'd say you come bearing tidings of great joy, Constable McLennan", said Ross, returning the smile.

"Yes sir, very good news, I'd say. We have a positive I.D on the dental records of our skeletal remains. A firm of dentists in town, Ledger and Crowe, they've been in business for donkey's years, and the current Mr. Ledger is the grandson of the original owner. Seems dentistry runs in the family and anyway, they were able to put a name to the remains from the photographs Doctor Nugent and his people gave us."

Ross couldn't stop himself.

"Brendan Kane, unless I'm very much mistaken, eh, young Derek?"

McLennan's jaw dropped, surprise clearly evident on his face at Ross's apparent wizardry in coming out with the name on his sheet of paper.

"Well, yes, that's right, sir, but how the heck did you know that? I've only had the confirmation myself for ten minutes."

"Don't fret yourself, lad. Believe it or not, Sergeant Drake and I have just finished a grueling two hour interview with two brothers who gave us the name in connection with the disappearance of their sister around the same time. I took a chance on asking if their friend had broken his leg as a boy, they said yes, and the rest just fell into place."

"Oh, I see, sir. That's great then, isn't it?"

"Yes, and well done on tracking the dental records down too. I'm not stealing your thunder, because if the Doyle brothers hadn't come in to see me today, the dental evidence would be the only identifying evidence we have, which in reality it still is. You've done well."

"Thank you, sir," said McLennan, holding out the sheet of paper and passing it to the D.I. Here's the faxed confirmation from Ledger and Crowe, absolute one hundred percent certainty that the teeth are those of Brendan Kane."

"Right then, here's what I want you to do next. Sergeant Drake has some things to check while I go and have a word with the D.C.I. In the meantime, I'd like you to run a criminal records check on these two men," and he passed a piece of paper bearing the names and addresses of the two Doyle brothers to McLennan. "It doesn't hurt to be thorough, and this case has just expanded greatly, so I want to be sure our two witnesses are all they appear to be."

McLennan grasped the piece of paper and was gone in a few seconds, eager to play his part in the gathering intensity of the case.

"Er, before we go our separate ways, sir, just one question, if I may?" said Drake after they were alone again.

"Go on, Izzie, what's on your mind?"

"You said there was something you'd tell me later, sir, when we were with the brothers. Well, is this 'later' enough?"

"Oh yes," Ross smiled at her. "You remember the Doyles mentioned an inspector, Sergeant Carson's boss by all accounts?"

Quickly flicking back through her notes, Drake replied,

"Inspector Ledden; that was the name, sir."

"Yes, that's right. I didn't want to appear too hasty in any condemnation of the previous investigation into Marie Doyle's disappearance, because, if I'm right, the Inspector Ledden they were speaking of is now Detective Chief Superintendent Bernard Ledden, head of the Regional Drug Squad. If so, I don't want to go treading on toes that can be avoided if you know what I mean, at least, not at this stage of our investigation."

Drake nodded her head in agreement.

"Oh yes, sir, I see very well indeed. I'd best be getting on with looking for these addresses for now then hadn't I?"

"Yes, you do that, Izzie. I'll be with the boss for a while, please fix up a mini-conference for the two of us, McLennan and Paul Ferris for eight o'clock in the morning. Then tell them to finish what they're doing and go home. I won't be out of the boss's office for at least an hour, so we can't do much more today, but I want everyone bright and fresh in the morning. We're going to have a lot of work to do in the next few days. We can then discuss where we go from here after I've spoken with the D.C.I. See you when I get back," and with that, he rushed out of the office to report the new developments to D.C.I. Porteous. Izzie tidied Ross's desk, and left to do her own assigned tasks before talking to the team and leaving for home. Tomorrow promised to be an interesting day.

CHAPTER 23

CASE CONFERENCE, LIVERPOOL, 1999

Although he'd told Izzie Drake to arrange the operational conference for eight a.m. Andy Ross made sure he arrived at the station a half hour earlier. The two reasons for his early arrival followed him into the conference room soon after, and were closely followed by Drake, Ferris and McLennan, who may have been surprised to see two new faces in their midst, but waited for Ross to explain. After inviting all those present to be seated, Ross took up a position at the head of the grandly sounding, but actually quite functional and cheap wooden conference table, this being the city of Liverpool after all, not a gentlemen's club in Mayfair. Various nods and quiet hellos were spoken and then, Ross gave a polite cough to catch everyone's attention before speaking.

"Good morning, everyone," he began. "As you can see, we have two new faces with us this morning. After my meeting with D.C.I. Porteous yesterday afternoon, and after he agreed that, as the local bad boys are not giving us too hard a time at present, he generously allotted us a little extra manpower. Let me introduce you to Detective Constables Nick Dodds and Samantha Gable."

Another series of more formal welcomes and hellos followed and as silence fell once more, Ross continued.

"Nick comes to us from the burglary squad, and Sam has just completed a year working the vice squad. Both are experienced officers and I have to stress that, following my talk with the gaffer yesterday, he agrees there is more depth to this case than the original discovery of the skeletal remains suggested."

Ross gave a brief resumé of the initial discovery of the remains at the wharf, mostly for the benefit of the newcomers, followed by a detailed run through on the interview he and Drake had conducted with Mickey and Ronnie Drake the previous day, ending with the confirmation of Brendan Kane's identity from his dental records, miraculously still available after over thirty years, a lucky break if ever they needed one.

A soft knock at the conference room door followed, and the door opened to admit a well-dressed man in a grey pin-stripe suit, sporting a blue silk tie, aged somewhere in his forties. The man issued a brief apology for being late, and Ross quickly introduced the newcomer.

"Ah yes, no problem, George. Everyone, I'd like you all to meet George Thompson. George is the Headquarters' Press Liaison Officer. D.C.I. Porteous wants us to keep George in the loop on the case, now that it's expanded beyond its original parameters. Seems there's likely to be a fair bit of local interest in this one, with young Brendan Kane having been something of a relatively minor local celebrity among the growing rock and pop music fraternity in the early days of the sixties. Add in a young girl, his sweetheart, missing for over thirty years, and the boss wants George to be able to keep any press interest on track and avoid the force coming under any unduly harsh criticism for its handling of the case either then or now. Anything you'd like to add, George?"

Clearing his throat, George Thompson moved round the table to sit at the opposite end of the table to Ross.

"Just that it's good to meet you all. I promise you that despite what you may hear sometimes, as PLO I'm here to act as a back up to the work you do, not to do anything that might hinder your investigation. I want to portray the force in a good light of course, but I also want to make sure that I can help the case wherever possible by passing sound bites or articles to the local and if necessary, the national press that might assist in your inquiries. Any appeals you guys want out there, I'll be happy to put them together in a way that they look and sound good and reach the target audience. So please, don't see me as a hindrance, but rather, use me and my expertise in my field as a useable asset in your approach to solving the case. As D.I. Ross just said, there is likely to be some media interest and it's my job to deal with it, and to protect your backs from any mud slinging that might begin when the facts of the case come out. I'll be putting out a press release in the next day or two, detailing the identification of Kane's remains and the connection with the long-forgotten disappearance of a girl called Marie Doyle. Hopefully, it might jog a few memories and maybe bring in one or two pieces of useful information. That's all for now, everyone, and thanks for listening to me."

Ross in turn thanked Thompson for his time and invited him to remain in the meeting until its conclusion, so he could understand just what Ross and his team was initially trying to achieve. George Thompson sat listening as Ross brought the team planning conference towards its conclusion.

"There's one other thing that arose as a result of the visit by the Doyle brothers yesterday. They still feel the police at the time of their original complaint failed to take the disappearance of Marie Doyle seriously enough and didn't do enough to find her, and it would appear the officer in charge at the time was an Inspector Bernard Ledden, who just happens to still be with the force and is now a Detective Chief Superintendent, in charge of the Regional Drug Squad."

After a few murmurs from those around the table, Ross continued.

"Yes, a potentially sensitive issue, as I'm sure you can appreciate. I can't exactly go marching in to the office of a D.C.S and accuse him of failing in his duty thirty three years ago. The D.C.I has given me the go ahead to go and talk to Ledden, with the proviso I tread carefully and avoid making any unsubstantiated allegations of dereliction of duty towards him or his team at the time. I phoned yesterday and I've an appointment with D.C.S. Ledden later this morning. In the meantime, Sergeant Drake has obtained certain addresses of those people I need interviewing in connection with the two cases, which I now want us to regard as part and parcel of one, wider reaching case. I agree that coincidences happen, but the fact that Marie Doyle and Brendan Kane disappeared from sight at the same time all those years ago is just stretching coincidence too far. Ferris, you're a good man on computers so I want you to be our case coordinator and collator, any and all information you all obtain comes back to Ferris who will keep me updated at all times. Spend an hour or so this morning setting up your case files while we're out, okay?"

Nods of agreement from Ferris and the others followed and Ross then proceeded to hand out individual assignments.

"Sergeant Drake will visit Phillip Oxley this morning. Sam, I'd like to you visit the last known address we have for Marie's former best friend, Clemency De Souza, and Nick, I want you to accompany Sergeant Drake and after interviewing Oxley, I want you to pay a call on James and Connie Doyle. I'd like to meet this old man myself but at present, it's important we move swiftly to try and get a handle on exactly what we're dealing with. If these two young people were simply a pair of runaways, I fail to see how Brendan Kane ended up with two bullet wounds in his knees and his head bashed in, and then, what the hell happened to Marie? We have questions that require answers, and I don't care how long ago this all took place, as far as I'm concerned it's an open murder inquiry, and we're going to work hard at finding those answers. Everybody got that?"

Everyone gave more nods and words of agreement as Ross brought the case conference to a close. After sending his now expanded team off to deal with their allotted tasks, Ross made his way to conduct his interview with Detective Chief Constable Ledden.

* * *

"Detective Inspector Ross, pleased to meet you," said D.C.S. Bernard Ledden, rising from behind his large, highly polished mahogany desk after Ross had been shown in to his office by Claire, his secretary. He offered an outstretched hand as he reached across his desk and the two men shook hands. Ross was impressed by his first impressions of the man. Tall, just over six feet, his uniform immaculately pressed and a face that seemed to exude a look of confidence born of many years experience in the job. There appeared to be no pomposity about the man, something Ross had seen in all too many officers of senior rank over the years.

"Please, sit," said Ledden, gesturing to a large, comfortable looking leather upholstered chair to the left of his desk. Ross sat as requested, and realized the layout of the office; the positioning of the chair he sat in was intended not to intimidate Ledden's visitors, but to put them more at ease with man. Sitting directly opposite from the Chief Superintendent would have increased any junior officer's tension at such a meeting. As it was, Ledden was making Ross feel welcome, on a more equal footing than he actually occupied.

"D.C.I. Porteous spoke very highly of you when he phoned me yesterday. Apparently you have some questions to put to me about a case I may have been involved in back in my days as an inspector?"

"That's correct, sir. It's about a missing persons case from thirty three years ago, one that we've only just tied to the murder of a young man whose remains were recently discovered in a dried up part of the river bed beside an old wharf undergoing redevelopment."

"Ah, yes, I saw something about that case in the Echo, and then caught something about it in a recent newsletter that landed on my desk. Please, tell me how you believe I can be of help in your investigation."

With Porteous's words about being diplomatic and non-confrontational ringing in his ears, Ross first passed the Chief Superintendent a file containing the pertinent facts of both cases and then tried, in the best way he could, to lay out the case before the D.C.S as briefly as possible, knowing that senior officers such as Ledden appreciated brevity and keeping to the point. When he'd finished, he breathed a sigh of relief and waited as Ledden assimilated the information Ross had presented to him, both verbally and in print.

After what felt like an age, but was only about a minute, during which Ross barely drew a breath, Chief Superintendent Ledden looked up, closed the file on his desk, and delivered his reply.

"Well, you've certainly painted quite a picture here, Inspector. From a pile of old bones barely two weeks ago to an unsolved murder, an identified victim and a girl missing for over thirty years, really quite something. You and your team have done well."

"Thank you sir. My team will be pleased to hear that."

"It's true. A lot of officers wouldn't have put such effort into a case like this and would have left it on the unsolved pile rather than go digging like this, but that shows what a diligent police officer you are. Now, as for the Marie Doyle case, there's not a lot I can really tell you. Yes, Bob Carson was a sergeant under my command, and he was a good man in his younger days, though he did kind of let things slide a bit as he moved towards retirement, as I recall. He was tenacious in his own way though, and from what these two brothers have told you, he appears to have ticked all the boxes, without going too far beyond the basics. I won't knock him for that, Inspector, as I don't honestly recall the case, but if he'd thought there was a case to investigate at the time, and he'd recommended further investigation to me, I would have given the go-ahead, I can assure you. My God, there were so many cases that fell under my purview in those days, and if I had any knowledge of this Marie Doyle, I'd share it with you, please have no doubt about that, but thirty three years is a long time, Inspector."

"Yes, sir, I do understand that. I wasn't expecting miracles but I hope you understand why I needed to at least ask if you had any memory of the case?"

"Of course, and credit to you for making the effort. Anything else I can help you with, while you're here, Inspector?"

"One question, sir. Would you happen to know if Sergeant Carson is still alive? It might help if I could talk to him, maybe jog his memory and see if he can remember something that might help me."

Ledden slowly shook his head and a grave look crossed his face before he replied.

"I'm sorry, Ross, but Carson died about three years after he retired. Bloody tragic. Just beginning to enjoy some quality time with his wife and they took a holiday in Thailand, I think it was and he picked up some heinous tropical disease. Poor chap died within two weeks of returning to the UK. I attended his funeral. Poor Emma, his wife was totally devastated I can tell you."

"Well, sir, thank you for being honest with me and for giving up your time. I know you're a very busy man."

"Not a problem, Inspector Ross. Listen, let me tell you something. I've been a police officer in this city almost all my working life. I joined the old Liverpool City Police as a probationary constable when I was twenty years old, and by the time the force was amalgamated with the Bootle Borough Police in nineteen sixty-seven, I'd made it to Inspector. Liverpool and Bootle didn't last long, Ross, and in nineteen seventy-four, the powers that be decided to change things again, and took large slices of the old Cheshire and Lancashire Constabularies to form what we have now, under this grand title we have of Merseyside Police. You probably know the history of the force from your own time with the force, but my point is that over all those years, and through all the reorganizations and amalgamations, I've seen a lot of good coppers come and go and known a few bent ones in my time. I have never allowed a bent copper to escape if it was in my power to do something about it and the same thing goes for any officer who didn't apply due diligence and professionalism to any inquiry. Bob Carson was neither bent, nor unprofessional, despite what these two brothers have intimated in their statement. The worst accusation you could have made against him was that he slowed down a little as retirement approached, and that is something that applies to many long-serving uniformed officers, as I'm sure you're aware. Now, having said that, I'm only sorry I couldn't be of more help to you, but I do wish you good luck in your efforts to try and solve this one. It would be quite a feather in your cap if you could solve a thirty-three year old murder and disappearance at the same time. I'll keep a watching brief on your progress, and wish you the best of luck."

Knowing the meeting had reached its natural ending, Ross stood and prepared to leave the Chief Superintendent's office. Ledden also stood and walked around the large mahogany desk, and stood facing Ross as he first shook his hand warmly and then passed the file Ross had brought, back to him, adding a few parting words before allowing Ross to depart.

"I know you probably thought you'd find evidence of a failed or botched investigation, Ross, but believe me, Bob Carson might not have been 'Columbo', but he wouldn't have let the case of a missing girl slip past him if he'd thought there was anything sinister going on. He was a husband and father himself you know, and he must have genuinely believed this girl had simply run off with her boyfriend. Have you found anything that suggests otherwise in your new investigation, so far?"

"No, sir, we haven't, and I wasn't insinuating anything untoward had taken place in the original investigation. But, I did want to know if everything that could have been done, was done. I hope you understand my reasoning."

"I do, Inspector, and I appreciate you being candid with me. Your honesty is refreshing. There are too many 'yes men' around nowadays. Now, go catch yourself a murderer, if you can after all this time, and if you do find what happened to the girl, as it was my case once upon a time, please do me the courtesy of letting me know."

"I will, sir, and thanks again for seeing me," said Ross as he took his leave of the Detective Chief Superintendent.

* * *

A sense of relief washed over Andy Ross as he sat behind his desk, back in his own office once again. Being in the rarefied atmosphere of the office of one of the upper echelon of the city's senior officers had made Ross slightly uncomfortable. D.C.S. Ledden had come across as far more 'human' than Ross had expected and had seemed to be open and honest with him. Yes, it had been over thirty years since the Marie Doyle investigation, and it was true that Ledden must have overseen thousands of cases in his years on the force, so Ross agreed in his mind that it had been impractical to expect the man to remember each and every one that landed on his desk. However, he did feel that more could have been done on the original inquiry and that Ledden himself, as the inspector in charge at the time, could have pushed Carson to take his inquiries further. Perhaps, he surmised, they had other, more pressing cases on their books at the time, cases with identifiable victims and perpetrators, or with more at stake either personally or financially for those involved. Whether that excused a slight lack of application to the Doyle case, he couldn't truly decide. After all, he'd have had to be there at the time to make such a judgement. For now, he knew he had to accept Ledden's word for things, and press on with his own inquiry.

Knowing his own ineptitude at remembering important family dates, he immediately picked up the phone, making a call to Maria's favourite restaurant and reserving a table for two for the night of her special day. A second call to the florists also ensured a delivery of red roses in the late afternoon of her birthday. He'd already checked and knew she'd be working the early shift at the surgery that day. The similarity in Christian names drew his thoughts back to Marie Doyle. Somehow, the two Doyle brothers and their story had touched Ross in a way he'd never have expected. Over thirty years had passed and yet her brothers had never given up hope of finding out what had happened to their little sister. Such loyalty, Ross had inwardly decided, deserved rewarding and if he hadn't already done so, he now made himself a mental promise that, one way or another, he'd do everything possible to achieve a result, to find not only the murderer of the young Brendan Kane, but also to discover exactly what fate had befallen Marie Doyle.

His reverie was interrupted by a knock on his half open door, followed by the appearance of the Press Liaison Officer, George Thompson, who entered the office, briefcase in hand.

"Got a minute, Andy?" Thompson asked.

"Sure, George. What can I do for you?" Ross replied.

"I've composed a new press release, and wanted to let you read and comment on it and suggest any changes you feel may be appropriate before I let it out to the newshounds,"

Having worked with Thompson on a couple of previous occasions, one of the things Ross liked about the man was that, unlike some P.L.Os, George Thompson never lost sight of the fact he was part of a team, and whatever he did could have a major bearing on the results of any inquiry he became involved with. The man was devoid of what Ross saw as the curse of many a Press Officer, that being a sense of self-importance that could lead to conflict with the investigating officers. In short, he rather liked the man.

"Thanks, George. I appreciate that. Let's see what you've got for me then."

George Thompson opened his slim leather briefcase, slowly removed a sheet of A4 sized paper and passed the printed, proposed Press Release to Ross.

"Sit down for a minute, won't you, while I read through it, George?"

Thompson sat in the chair in front of Ross's desk and remained silent as Ross read:

'Skeleton Identified, - Police Seek Missing Woman!'

Following the recent discovery of the skeletal remains of a young man in the river bed adjacent to a dried up, disused warehouse in the old docklands area of the city, Merseyside Police have now been able to positively identify the remains as being those of twenty one year old Brendan Kane, a one-time musician and book store worker in the city. It is known that Mr. Kane, once the lead singer and a guitarist with the early sixties pop group, Brendan Kane and the Planets, had planned to leave the city together with his girlfriend, twenty year old Marie Doyle, in the summer or autumn of nineteen sixty-six. Pathologists have determined that Mr. Kane was the victim of a vicious attack prior to his body being deposited in what, at the time would have been a watery grave in the Mersey, close to the disused Coles' Wharf, in the old docklands area of the city. Miss Doyle is reported as having disappeared either simultaneously with the murder of Mr. Kane or at some time close to his death and has not been seen or heard from since that time. Anyone with information they feel might assist the police in this inquiry should contact Merseyside Police on… (phone numbers).

"Looks good to me, George," said Ross. "One small point though. Shouldn't we be a little more specific regarding approximate dates and times etc? You know, try to get people to focus on what they were doing right about the time both people disappeared?"

"In my experience, Andy, it's usually best not to be too date-specific with this type of appeal. If you try to pin people down to, for example, 'between the dates of 10th-20th August, you tend to find they will mentally ignore anything that might have occurred before or after that time, but that may still be relevant to the inquiry. Better to be deliberately vague so that anyone who thinks they might have seen or heard something prior to, or after the time of the double disappearance, won't be put off contacting us because they fear their information may not be relevant or important."

"I see what you mean, George," Ross replied, impressed with the Press

Officer's thought processes. "I'd never have thought of it like that. I'm glad we've got a real professional on the job."

Thompson accepted the compliment gracefully.

"Just doing my job, Andy. I only hope it produces results for you and your team, though, after over thirty years, I wouldn't be too optimistic. A lot of folks who may have been around then with any knowledge of your case could well be dead and buried by now."

Ross nodded his head slowly, almost ruefully.

"I know," he said. "That's my biggest fear, too. We could be chasing ghosts in this case, people who just aren't around any longer to help us."

"Well, good luck with it, anyway. I'll get this to *The Echo* today, and copy it to all the nationals by tomorrow. It might help to have full coverage in the dailies as well as the local press. People move around a lot more these days. We may find witnesses in other areas who lived here way back when."

"Thanks again, George," said Ross as Thompson closed his briefcase and got up to leave, the copy of the press release left on the desk for Ross to show to his team later.

"My pleasure, Andy," said Thompson, who closed the door quietly as he left, leaving Ross alone with his thoughts once more.

CHAPTER 24

A STEP IN TIME

Izzie Drake pulled up on the street about five doors away from the home of James and Connie Doyle. An earlier visit to the address Izzie had found for Phil Oxley had proved fruitless, with no reply to their knocking at the door and ringing the doorbell, so she'd decided to try the Doyle home first and return to Oxley's later. The two detectives exited the car, and as Drake pointed the remote at the vehicle, activating the central locking system, Nick Dodds looked up and down the street and commented on his first impressions.

"My God, Sarge, this place looks as if it's hardly altered since the nineteen-sixties, at least from pictures I've seen of those days, me being a bit young to have been around then."

"Oh, the wisdom of youth, what are you, a child of the seventies?" Drake quipped, and then, also looking at their immediate surroundings, "But yes, you're right. Red brick terraces, back to back gardens, all we need is a bomb site at the end of the street with dirty-kneed kids in short pants kicking a ball around among the rubble and we could be in another time, Nick, for sure."

Grafton Street, where Mickey and Ronnie Doyle had grown up and spent their early adult years had indeed retained much of the way it must have looked thirty to forty years ago. Though many owner-residents had invested their money in improving their properties, with new, uPVC double glazing, and new front doors, others, perhaps those still owned by absent landlords and rented out as cheap, low income housing, seemed to bravely

139

carry the scars of years of at least partial neglect, with peeling paintwork on window ledges and doors, and faulty pointing in brickwork and the occasional missing roof tile. It really did represent a place out of time, a throwback to another age, and a million light years away from some of the ultra-modern apartment complexes and other new developments taking place in various, more desirable parts of the city. In place of the bomb site Drake had joked about, at the end of the street stood a nineteen-eighties built community centre and library, perhaps the local council's attempt to help create some sense of belonging and identity among residents, most of whom had probably lived in the surrounding streets for much shorter durations than older families like the Doyles. The graffiti-covered walls of the community centre were perhaps a measure of the project's success.

As the two officers arrived at the door to number 26, the sound of loud reggae music could be clearly heard from an upstairs bedroom of the house next door. Having heard about James Doyle from his two sons, Izzie had a feeling he might not be too enamoured of his current next-door neighbours. She nodded to Nick Dodds and the constable knocked firmly on the front door, which Drake could swear she saw shaking on its hinges as he did so. A few seconds later the door opened, just a crack, and a voice, female and frail-sounding asked, "Yes, who's there?"

"Mrs. Doyle?" Izzie asked.

"Yes, and who are you?" the old lady asked.

"My name is Detective Sergeant Clarissa Drake, Merseyside Police, and this is Detective Constable Dodds. We'd like to talk to you about your daughter, Marie, Mrs. Doyle."

The door opened fully as the old woman gasped and almost fell forward into Izzie's arms. Izzie reached out to steady the woman, not having prepared herself for such a reaction.

"Oh my, what is it? Have you found my little girl after all this time?" gasped Connie Doyle, pulling herself upright as she recovered from her initial shock.

"No, not exactly, but look, can we come in, please, Mrs. Doyle? I'm sure you don't want to talk about this on your front doorstep?"

"Oh, sorry, of course. Please, come in. You must excuse the place. I haven't finished the housework yet you see and…"

"Please don't apologise, we didn't exactly make an appointment did we?" said Izzie, feeling a little sorry for the woman, who looked as frail as she sounded.

Connie Doyle looked ill, thought Izzie, her skin having a rather dull, lifeless pallor, though the woman's blonde hair retained much of its life and was well-styled. Mrs. Doyle cared about her appearance and probably paid regular visits to her hairdresser. Her floral patterned dress looked clean and ironed and her pale yellow cardigan was of good quality and hung unfastened on her shoulders.

"Would you like to come into the kitchen?" Connie asked the officers. "I was just making some tea when you knocked on the door."

"That would be nice, thank you." said Drake as she and Dodds followed Connie Doyle along the hallway and into the small but surprisingly clean and well appointed kitchen, the centerpiece of which appeared to be an old, but beautifully maintained sideboard, the wood polished to a high gloss and the brass handles on the drawers and doors gleaming like new. Izzie couldn't help noticing a photograph subtly placed to the rear of the sideboard, quite clearly the photo of Marie she'd heard about the previous day. She'd wait a little while before asking to see it.

As Connie busied herself boiling the kettle and brewing the tea, Drake and Dodds used their eyes to take in every aspect of the room. The kitchen table and chairs were, like the sideboard, definitely from a previous age, but again superbly looked after. By contrast, all the major appliances, washing machine, gas cooker, fridge freezer and microwave oven all looked quite new. Drake quickly noticed that the fireplace which would once have burned brightly with a welcoming coal fire now contained a 'living flame' gas fire, eminently practical but somehow an indictment on modernisation in Drake's mind.

Tea made, and the three of them seated at the kitchen table, Drake asked Connie, "Is your husband at home, Mrs. Doyle? We'd like to speak to both of you at the same time, if possible."

"Oh, sorry, yes of course, silly me," said Connie with an almost girlish giggle that Drake found particularly engaging. "He's in the garden. Seems he's always in the garden nowadays, so he is. The Holy Virgin herself must know what he does out there, all day. It's no bigger than a postage stamp."

Connie's accent betrayed her Irish upbringing, now intermingled with a liberal dose of the local Scouse dialect. Izzie thought it quite endearing.

Rising from her seat at the table, Connie walked to the back door, opened it and called to the unseen James Doyle. "Jimmy Doyle, get yerself in here this minute. There's two bobbies here wanting to have a wee word with you."

Drake smiled to herself. It had been a long time since she'd heard anyone refer to her as a 'bobby', a term of endearment for a policeman that, like Connie Doyle, belonged to a happier, previous age. A few seconds passed before the back door opened and James, (Jimmy) Doyle walked in, only as far as the large Hessian door mat that awaited anyone entering the house, where he stood and removed a pair of mud-stained brown boots, turned round and placed them outside the door on the doorstep, turned again and closed the door. Only now did the large man with thinning grey hair bother to look at and acknowledge the two police officers who sat drinking tea in his kitchen.

"I know why youse are here," said Doyle, looking at Dodds. "Your lot did fuck all about finding Marie thirty three years ago, so what chance d'you think you have now? I don't know why those idiot sons of mine had to go running to the police just because a few bones got dug up."

Izzie felt an instant dislike for Doyle. She'd already heard him described as a religious bigot, and a possible racist. Now, his immediate direction of his words to Nick Dodds indicated an in-built sexism too. A woman couldn't possibly be in charge, could she?

"I'm Detective Sergeant Drake, Mr. Doyle, and this is Detective Constable Dodds. Those 'few bones' you mention happen to be the mortal remains of Brendan Kane, your daughter's boyfriend at the time of her disappearance. I'd have thought you might show a little concern that he's been found dead after all this time, particularly as his death may bear a strong connection to what happened to Marie all those years ago."

"Hmm, sergeant eh?" Doyle pronounced the word with a heavy hint of sarcasm. "Well, in the first place, I'll shed no tears for the man who took my daughter away from me and secondly, why should you finding his bones have anything to do with my Marie?"

"Mr. Doyle," Izzie replied, "You can't seriously think it was a pure coincidence that Marie and Brendan disappeared at the same time? They'd made plans to run away and start a new life together, as you well know."

"Aye, thanks to my sons helping her to deceive her poor Mam and Dad."

Nick Dodds stepped in with a question of his own before Izzie could speak again, part of a strategy they'd agreed on earlier.

"And why do you think they did that, Mr. Doyle? I presume you felt they should have shown loyalty to you and told you their secret long before the couple disappeared."

"So they should have," Doyle snapped back at Dodds.

"Could it have had anything to do with your dislike of Brendan Kane?" Dodds pressed his point home.

"I'd no particular liking or dislike of the man."

"But you didn't like a protestant, a 'proddie' being so romantically involved with your daughter, did you?"

"Bah," Doyle mumbled. "All he wanted was to get in her knickers and have his way with her, turn her into his tart."

Connie Doyle now exploded at her husband. Frail or not, Connie possessed a temper worthy of her Irish roots.

"James Doyle, how can you say that about your own daughter? Marie was a good girl, you know she was. And Phil Oxley told us a long time ago that they truly loved and cared for each other."

"Oxley? Another scally like his pal, Kane, if you ask me. I heard he helped them plan it all,"

"He helped his friends, Mr. Doyle. Isn't that what friends do?"

Izzie Drake now came back into the conversation as Doyle blustered and hesitated.

"You didn't seem to have any objections to your sons and daughter being involved in the pop group though, did you?"

"Look, Sergeant, playing music together is one thing, marrying someone outside your faith is different to my mind, okay?"

"Faith, Mr. Doyle? I thought Protestants and Catholics were all of the Christian faith, or is that wrong?"

Doyle again fell silent, not wanting to be drawn by Drake's line of questioning. Izzie instead turned to Connie Doyle.

"Is that a photo of Marie on your sideboard, Mrs. Doyle? May I see it?"

Connie proudly walked across to the sideboard, picked up the framed photo and passed it to Izzie.

"She was a very pretty girl, wasn't she, Sergeant?" Connie said, proudly.

"She certainly was," Izzie replied.

"Do you think she's dead?" Connie asked suddenly, with tears beginning to form in her eyes.

"I'm being honest when I say I just don't know, Mrs. Doyle. Until a couple of days ago we knew nothing about Marie or her involvement with the case. We were focused on identifying the remains that have turned out to be those of Brendan Kane and thanks to your sons, we've been able to confirm that identification and we now know about Marie so we'll be treating the whole affair as one case. Trust me; we'll do all we can to discover what happened to your daughter."

Connie pulled a small lady's hanky from the sleeve of her cardigan and dabbed at her eyes, as she placed a hand on Izzie's arm and sniffed, "thank you."

Izzie's eyes caught sight of another object on the sideboard, previously hidden by the photograph. Connie saw her looking and picked up the small, yellow plastic, nineteen sixties transistor radio.

"It was Marie's," she said. "She used to take it almost everywhere with her. She loved music, Sergeant. That's how she got involved with Brendan and the group in the first place. She had a driving licence and used to help out by driving them to and from their performances sometimes. Mr. Oxley, Phil's dad would lend them his van until his business went bust."

Connie turned a dial on the side of the radio and Izzie was surprised to hear the sounds of Radio One coming from the tiny speaker.

"I make sure it always has new batteries in it, you know, just in case Marie ever…"

Connie let her words hang and Izzie nodded and took the old lady's hand in her own. Words failed her for a few seconds, but eventually she looked across the room at Nick Dodds, who nodded back at her and she brought the interview to an end.

"Thank you both for your time. We wanted you to know that we're seriously looking into Marie's case and would appreciate you getting in touch with us if you can think of anything that might help us with our inquiries."

Passing a card bearing her phone number at the station to Connie, she turned to Jimmy Doyle.

"Thank you for your time, Mr. Doyle. We'll be in touch."

"Yeah, sometime never, I'll bet," Doyle replied.

"Manners, Jimmy, please," Connie pleaded, but Doyle simply stood his ground and maintained a silent pose, by the back door.

Connie saw the two detectives to the front door and just before they took their leave of her, said,

"Please don't think too badly of my husband, Sergeant. He's getting on in years and he's very set in his ways. He talks tough, but he's never got over Marie leaving as she did. He's not half as bad as he sounds."

"Yes, well, thanks, Mrs. Doyle. Like I said, we'll be in touch."

As the front door closed behind them, the pair walked briskly to their car and were soon motoring back in the direction of the last known address of Phil Oxley, Nick Dodds at the wheel.

"Any thoughts, Nick?" she asked the constable as the streets of the city sped past the car windows.

"Nice old lady, bitter and twisted old man," Nick Dodds replied without hesitation.

"My thoughts exactly," Izzie concurred.

"Why the hell does someone stay with a bloke like him for all those years?"

"That's an easy one to answer, Nick," she replied. "First of all, they're from a generation where husbands and wives stuck together through thick and thin, the 'for better and for worse' bit of the marriage vows, I suppose, but, more importantly to them at any rate, is the fact that they're obviously staunch Roman Catholics, and for them, divorce is one massive taboo, a great big no-no."

"But couldn't she just have left him, gone somewhere else and lived on her own, without getting a divorce?"

"And gone where, Nick? She probably couldn't have managed financially or emotionally without her family around her. A case of 'better the devil you know,' I think. But, do you think either of them knows more than they're telling us about Marie's disappearance?"

"I doubt the mother knows anything, and though he seems a right old bastard to me, I can't see her father doing anything to hurt his own kids, especially if, as you say, the whole concept of family means so much to them."

"I tend to agree. We'll see what the boss thinks when we meet up later."

"Yeah," said Dodds. "I wonder if this Oxley chap can tell us anything new, once we get hold of him?"

"We'll soon find out," Drake replied as Nick turned into Phil Oxley's street for the second time that day.

CHAPTER 25

SURPRISE, SURPRISE!

As Dodds pulled up a couple of doors away from Phil Oxley's address they saw a couple unloading bags of shopping from the rear of a Vauxhall Astra hatchback, parked directly in front of the Oxley address. In contrast with the home of James and Connie Doyle, this street, though composed of similarly aged terraced homes, had a far greater upmarket feel to it. All the houses were in excellent repair, with much modernisation having been applied to virtually every property in the street. Obviously no absent land-lords here, and lots of middle earning blue collar types in residence, Izzie thought to herself.

Izzie exited the car and left Dodds to lock up as she approached the middle–aged couple who were intent on their unloading and who hadn't noticed the car pull up not far from their own.

"Excuse me? Are you by any chance Mr. Phillip Oxley?" she asked the man, who had turned instinctively towards her as she'd got closer to the couple.

"And who wants to know?" the man replied.

Izzie flashed her warrant card and introduced herself and Nick Dodds, who'd joined her by now.

"Oh, I see. Hello, Sergeant, Constable. How can I help you?"

"Could we go inside, please, Mr. Oxley? We have a few questions we'd like to ask about something that happened a long time ago, and we think you may be able to fill in a few gaps for us."

A knowing look appeared on Oxley's face and he nodded slowly.

"Well, yes, of course, do come in. I don't know how I can help you, but you can tell me inside."

"Let me help you with these bags," Dodds said, as he moved to take a couple of obviously heavy bags from the woman accompanying Phil Oxley. "Mrs. Oxley is it?"

"Yes, I'm Phil's wife, and thank you," the woman replied, allowing Nick Dodds to help with the laden shopping bags.

Minutes later, Phil Oxley was seated in his favourite armchair in his and his wife's beautifully decorated and clean living room. The two detectives sat side by side on the sofa, and the three managed to make small talk for a minute or two until Mrs. Oxley entered the room with a tray, loaded with cups of coffee and a selection of biscuits. Although she must have been around fifty years old, Mrs. Oxley looked and dressed at least ten years younger. She was very pretty, with long, dark, wavy hair that framed her face perfectly, with a figure some twenty year olds would kill for, and now that she'd divested herself of her coat, was dressed in a cream, pleated blouse and a navy pleated skirt that ended just above the knee. After ensuring everyone was served with drinks and had helped themselves to biscuits, the petite and well dressed wife of Phil Oxley seated herself in the room's remaining armchair and her husband said, "Now, Sergeant, you have our full attention. Please tell me how we can help you."

Izzie Drake wanted to complete the introductions first.

"Yes, of course, Mr. Oxley…"

"Please call me Phil," Oxley interrupted.

"Right, thanks. Can I please just ask your full name, Mrs. Oxley, for the record?"

"Yes, Sergeant. It's Clemency Anna Oxley."

Izzie Drake was stunned as Phil Oxley's wife gave her name, and even Nick Dodds' pencil seemed to hover in shock over his notebook. Drake was the first to react.

"Clemency, as in Clemmy De Souza?"

"Why, yes," Clemmy replied, equally surprised that the police sergeant knew both her nickname and her maiden name. "But, how did you know?"

"Perhaps I'd better explain exactly why we're here," Drake said to the couple.

"Might be a good idea, Sergeant Drake," said Phil Oxley.

Izzie Drake spent the next ten minutes bringing the couple up to date on everything, from the original discovery of the skeletal remains at the old wharf, through the process of attempting to identify the bones, and the visit of the Doyle brothers to the police station, where they provided information that not only helped to identify Brendan Kane as a murder victim, but also brought the name of Marie Doyle into the investigation for the first time. Obviously, she explained, both Phil and Clemmy had been

147

mentioned in the course of Mickey and Ronnie's statement to the police about events surrounding the eventual disappearance of the couple. When she finished telling the Oxleys the story so far, she waited for a response, Clemmy looked on the verge of tears, but Phil Oxley didn't hesitate.

"My God! We read the story in the Echo about the bones being found during a regeneration project. We'd no idea it could have been poor Brendan. All these years, I believed he and Marie had gone off somewhere together and were living a happy ever life far away from here, and now here you are, telling me poor Brendan never left Liverpool, and that someone actually murdered him. Who the hell could have hated him so much that they'd shoot him, beat him and throw him into the river?"

With his final words, Clemmy couldn't hold the tears back any longer, and her shoulders drooped and her face became a mask of tears. Phil quickly moved to comfort his wife, sitting on the arm of her chair and placing a comforting arm around her shoulder.

"I'm sorry to have had to break it to you like this," said Drake, "but there's never an easy way to communicate these things."

"It's alright, Sergeant," Phil replied. "I think deep down, we maybe knew we'd never see him again. It was always odd that he never got in touch after he left, especially after all I did to help them get away in the first place, but I can't believe he was murdered. Who ever'd do such a thing? He was only a young man. We all were, little more than kids, really."

Nick Dodds changed tack a little to allow them to recover their composure.

"And you two fell in love and got married? Brendan's best friend and Marie's best friend. That's nice for you, isn't it, Sarge?"

"Yes, very romantic," Izzie agreed. "How did that come about, if you don't mind telling us?"

Clemmy had managed to control her tears, and though she appeared pale and shocked, she replied to the question before her husband could say anything.

"It was romantic, really. When everyone first realised that Brendan and Marie had gone missing, I think either Mickey or Ronnie went to the police with Mr. Doyle to report Marie as a missing person. The two lads had been to my house, to see if I'd heard from Marie, which I hadn't, and then a couple of days later, Mr. Doyle came round to talk to me and started to get a bit angry, saying I was her best friend and that if anyone knew where she was, it should be me. My Dad got mad at him for bullying me, Sergeant, and my Dad was a big man, and he got tough with Mr. Doyle and virtually threw him out of our house. I didn't like him at all, and don't know how Marie put up with living with him for so long, but he was her Dad, after all, so I suppose she loved him in her own way, and didn't know any other way of life, until she met Brendan, of course.

Anyway, after Mr. Doyle's visit to our house, I was really worried about Marie and I knew from what she'd told me that Phil was doing his best to help Brendan find a way to get to America, so I went to see him a few days later and we got talking about everything. We started meeting in coffee shops and for the odd drink in the pub and gradually we became closer and closer.

Anyway, the longer Marie and Brendan were gone, the more we felt they'd finally got sick of waiting and Brendan had somehow found a place for them to go while he got things sorted properly. I know Marie would've followed him to the ends of the earth, Sergeant. She loved him so much. Me and Phil dated for a few months, and then, like young people do, we sort of drifted apart, and we split up and went our separate ways. We didn't see each other again until about ten years later, when Phil walked into the record shop where I was working. We got talking, and Phil asked me to meet him for a drink after work. To cut a long story short, we started seeing each other regularly again and this time, one thing led to another, we fell for each other big time and we were married a year after meeting up for the second time. Two years later we had a child, our daughter, Carrie Anne. She pointed to a framed school photograph of a young girl, probably about the age of Marie in the photo her mother kept on the side-board of their home. She goes to the same school where Phil teaches music, Our Lady of Sorrows. It's a private Catholic School for Girls in Walton."

"I know the school," said Izzie Drake. "I remember playing hockey against them when I was at school. So you're still involved with music, Phil?"

"Yes, I became a teacher when Carrie Anne was still a toddler. Clemmy was a big fan of The Hollies in the sixties, in case you're wondering," Phil explained. "She named our baby after one of their hit records." The detectives nodded and smiled and Clemmy continued from where she was before Phil's interruption.

"In the early days we'd talk about those days with Brendan and Marie and wondered what might have happened to them, but over the years they faded into the background of our lives, and now, well, I'm so sorry and upset to hear about poor Brendan. I don't suppose you know what happened to Marie, do you?"

"Not at present, Clemmy," Drake answered her honestly." We hoped Phil might be able to help us, and we'd planned to seek you out next to talk to you too. Finding you here together has been a lucky break for us, really."

Talking to Drake had produced the effect of calming Clemmy down and Phil now took his arm from her shoulder, rose and took a seat in his previous armchair. Scratching his head in thought for a few seconds, he seemed to be weighing up what he might or might not know that could be helpful and then said, "I'm not sure how I can help much after all these years. Is there anything specific I can tell you?"

"According to Mickey and Ronnie Doyle, you did a lot of the research for Brendan in finding ways to emigrate to America, is that correct? Drake asked.

"Yes, quite true. Brendan was useless at anything like that. I think he had a bit of a mental block when it came to dealing with forms and official documents. I can even remember him getting flustered when he first applied for a provisional driving licence. Anyway, I eventually told him it would take a couple of years at least for him to fill the requirements for immigration into the USA, and he couldn't work over there without a Green Card. You have to understand, Sergeant, that Brendan really was quite talented and it was a shame we didn't make the breakthrough over here, but he just might have made it in The States, which is why I was happy to help him as much as I could."

"We'd heard something about that from Ronnie and Mickey," said Drake. "How did your attempts to help end up?"

"Well, after a lot of research and some phone calls, I managed to convince Brendan of the most practical option left open to him if he was serious about making a new start in the music business in America."

"Which was?"

"First of all, we contacted several music producers and record companies in the States, giving them information about Brendan and his career so far, and also sent copies of the demo disc we'd made as a group. I contacted the U.S. Immigration Service on advice from someone at the embassy in London, who told me that if, while on a holiday in the USA, Brendan received an offer of work or a contract with a U.S. recording company, they would view an application for residence favourably. A couple of the recording companies and music producers got back to us saying they would be happy to audition Brendan if he contacted them once he arrived Stateside. It was the best, and probably the only chance he would ever have, and he seemed to accept that. One night, I sat with him and Marie at his flat and together we completed applications for tourist visas for them both. He'd saved enough money to allow them to spend at least four weeks over there, and we applied for the visas to take effect from late October, I think. It's a long time ago, I can't be sure of dates and things, you know?

"That's alright, Phil. Thanks for that information. We weren't aware of any such applications being made. Tell me, did they receive their visas?"

"Yes, they did. I remember Marie being excited when she and Brendan showed them to me on another evening visit to his flat."

"And she told me about it too," added Clemmy. "They had passports, too, Sergeant."

"That's right," said Phil. "All the lads in the group had passports of course, from when we first started out, in case we got any bookings on the continent, you know? Like The Beatles used to do Hamburg and that in the early days?"

Clemmy added, "Yeah, and people used to joke that Marie had never been out of Liverpool, but she had, once. A couple of years earlier, their parents took her and the boys on a self-catering holiday in Benidorm, so they all had their own passports."

Nick Dodds quickly added their observations to his notes and now asked, "Did you tell the police about this at the time they talked to you after Marie had been reported missing?"

"Yes," Phil replied. "A Sergeant came round in a big Ford Zephyr police car, like they had on *Z Cars* on TV. He seemed to think my information just confirmed his thoughts that they'd done a runner, left town and gone off to start a new life together."

Drake took over again, turning to Clemmy.

"Clemmy, one of the brothers told us he thought Marie was a little preoccupied, or on edge in the week or two before she disappeared. He assumed it was because she and Brendan were planning their sudden getaway from Liverpool. Can you think of any other reason why she might have felt worried or preoccupied?"

Clemmy Oxley thought about the question for a few seconds before replying.

"Now you come to mention it, she was a bit edgy around that time. I think it was mostly to do with her uncle."

"What uncle would that be?" Drake asked.

"Well, he wasn't really her uncle, he was her Dad's cousin from Ireland, so strictly speaking I suppose that made him her second cousin, but because he was a lot older than Marie and the lads, they all called him Uncle Patrick. His name was Price or Bryce I think. Marie didn't like him. She said he was bit of a bully, and really full of himself and what she called his 'silly tales' about what he called 'the old country'. Marie was just happy he wasn't staying at their house. He had a room at a B & B somewhere but was round at their house a lot she said, talking about all sorts of stuff she didn't understand with her father."

Drake was more than interested in this piece of information, as it placed another, previously unknown name into the mix, and could maybe open up another line of inquiry. She couldn't help but wonder why one of James Doyle's Irish cousins had suddenly appeared on the scene prior to the double disappearance. Coincidence? Maybe. Relevance? Quite possibly. She was certain this was something Ross would find of interest.

Another ten minutes passed by, with the Oxleys merely seeming to reinforce what the police already knew, until, just as Izzie was about to bring the interview to an end, she had a thought, like a light bulb flashing on in her mind.

"Just one more question, Phil," she began.

"Yes, Sergeant?"

"We've been told that Brendan had a car, is that correct?"

"Yes he did, an old Hillman or Humber, something like that. I'm not too sure after all this time."

"That's okay. My question is, do you have any idea what happened to it? I mean, when he disappeared, was the car left parked near his flat, or at his work, or whatever? You see, he must have either used the car to get to the docks, if he was meeting someone there, or else he caught a bus into town. Now, if you had a car, would you bother using a bus if you could get to where you where going in the comfort of your own vehicle?"

"Good point, Sergeant, and I'm sorry I can't give you an answer," Oxley replied. "I'm sure the police must have spoken to Brendan's parents and probably asked about the car, but after they'd interviewed me at the time, they didn't come again or tell me anything about any other lines of inquiry they were following. Confidentiality I suppose."

"Yes, of course, thank you Phil. I just thought I'd ask. Oh yes, another thought just sprang to mind. Clemmy, you worked with Marie, didn't you?"

"Yes, in the typing pool at BICC."

"Do you know if Marie gave her employers any notice she was about to leave?"

"No, I don't know for sure, but if she had, I'm sure she'd have told me. You see, Sergeant, a lot of her Dad's mates worked at B.I. too, and she wouldn't have wanted to risk one of them finding out what she was planning and then telling her Dad, would she?"

"That's true, thank you, Clemmy. Do you have anything else you'd like to ask, Constable?" Izzie said, thinking Nick Dodds may have also thought of something she could have omitted. Dodds thought for a second or two, and then his brow furrowed and he said,

"Well yes. We have on record that Brendan Kane apparently left his landlord a typewritten note saying he'd left the flat, and that he wouldn't be coming back and saying the landlord could sell off anything he'd left behind. Now, knowing him as you did, would you say that was typical of the man, and do you know if Brendan owned a typewriter?"

"D'you know? I heard about the letter, and always thought it a bit weird at the time," Phil replied. "First of all, in all the time I spent at his flat, I never saw a typewriter, and I doubt very much whether he could type anyway. I sort of thought that if it was a typewritten note then Marie must have typed it for him. That was her job after all."

"Yes, that makes sense," said Dodds. "Do either of you know the name of Brendan's landlord back then?

"No, sorry," said Phil and Clemmy shook her head. "But I can give you the address of the flat. If they haven't bulldozed the place to make way for more urban redevelopment the place might still be standing and maybe someone in the area might be able to help you."

"That might be helpful. Thank you," said Dodds and the two officers waited while Phil Oxley wrote Brendan Kane's old address on a yellow post-it from a pad by the phone, which he gave to Dodds.

Taking their leave of the couple, Drake and Dodds were soon motoring back across the city to headquarters. "First impressions of our lovebirds?" Drake asked Dodds as he drove.

"Well, Sarge, bit of a shock to find two of our persons of interest together like that. Saves us some time for sure. I liked them both though. I got the feeling they were both incredibly shocked to hear about Kane's murder, and in Mrs. Oxley's case, I think that knowledge only served to heightened her fears that Marie Doyle is probably also long dead. I don't think they could tell us any more than they did. It all happened so long ago that I doubt anyone has a really accurate recollection of what took place at the time. You know how people's memories degrade over time."

"And there lies the crux of the problem with this case, Nick. Time, or rather the passage of time, has created so many barriers that we have to overcome if we're ever going to solve this one, but I tell you now, D.I. Ross is determined to solve this case and if know him, together with the rest of us, that's just what he'll do, despite whatever obstacles we might come up against."

"Is he really that good, Sarge? I've heard he's like a dog with a bone when he gets his teeth into an inquiry. Do you think we can solve the case, even after all these years?"

"Short answer, Nick? Yes, he is that good, and yes, I really think with him in charge of the investigation, we'll solve this case, and find justice for Brendan Kane at the very least."

"And Marie Doyle?"

"You've got me there, Nick, I'm afraid. I just don't know how to answer that one, at least, not yet."

CHAPTER 26

BITS AND PIECES

"Okay everyone, gather round. I want us to take a long, hard look at where we are with this case. Let's see if we can start to add some of the pieces together."

Detective Inspector Andy Ross and his team were assembled in the small murder squad conference room. The team had spent three days assembling and collating every scrap of information they could find on both Brendan Kane and Marie Doyle. As Izzie Drake had pointed out to her boss shortly before the team meeting, trying to 'join the dots' as she put it, to a case so old, with no witnesses and with those involved at the time not necessarily able to trust their memories, they really were chasing shadows, with little hope of being able to pull the whole thing together.

"I'm well aware of that, Izzie," Ross had replied in response to her quite valid point. "The thing is, I feel as if we're missing something, something that may be so simple we just don't recognize it yet. When we do, I think the case will open up before us and we'll be able to put together all these small bits and pieces to form a complete picture of what took place thirty three years ago."

"You know, sir, if there's one thing I hate, it's a bloody mystery without clues to follow."

"Ah, but that's just it," said Ross. "The clues are there, Izzie. It's just that we don't see them yet."

"Oh, very cryptic, sir. You been doing the Daily Telegraph crossword again?"

They both laughed, the mood lightening for a few vital moments before they returned to the serious business of unsolved murder and a young woman missing for over thirty years.

Now, they stood either side of a large white board, with Nick Dodds, Sam Gable, Paul Ferris and Derek McLennan seated in the uncomfortable plastic chairs around the white-topped table which occupied the centre of the room. At the back of the room, Press Liaison Officer, George Thompson stood, nonchalantly leaning against the pale green painted wall, his briefcase positioned at his feet, resembling an obedient puppy, waiting for its master's next instruction.

On the left hand side of the white board, Izzie had taped a large blown up photograph of Brendan Kane. Paul Ferris had worked hard, managing to find an old and faded photo of Brendan Kane and the Planets in a now ancient copy of the *Echo*, taken when they'd won a talent contest in their early days. He'd used computer technology to isolate the head of Kane, and had blown it up as large as was possible without losing too much definition. At least the picture gave Brendan a more 'human' face than the photo displayed side by side with it, of the skeletal remains that were all that remained of the one-time pop singer and guitarist. Displayed on the opposite side of the board was a photo that depicted an eighteen-year old Marie Doyle, pictured in a happy pose with her best friend, Clemmy De Souza, now of course known to be the wife of Phil Oxley. Sam Gable had borrowed the photo from Clemmy's parents during her abortive trip to find and talk to Marie's best friend. Clemmy's Mother had explained that it was taken on the occasion of her eighteenth birthday, when the two girls celebrated by visiting their local Berni Inn Steak House, where Clemmy enjoyed her first legal alcoholic drink. Apart from growing her hair an inch or so longer, Marie hardly changed at all over the next two years, Clemmy had explained, so the photo was a good representation of how she would have looked at the time of her disappearance.

Beneath the photos, Paul Ferris had noted down all the relevant facts relating to each of the couple in one column and items of conjecture or open questions in another. Unfortunately, for the moment, the conjecture column contained a lot more than the factual one.

Ross surveyed the faces in the room as they waited expectantly for his next words. He knew from past experience that this was the type of case that could soon breed frustration, due mostly to the age of the case, the lack of direct witnesses, few clues as to motive for murder and even fewer clues relating to the disappearance of a young woman who seemed to have everything to live for. He'd admitted to himself that in all probability, Marie Doyle was dead, quite possibly murdered and her body disposed of at the same time as Brendan Kane met his death. He was loath to voice that thought to his team, however. Better that, for now, they kept an open mind and worked on the very faint possibility that the girl had survived, but, if she did, then what the hell had become of her? Choosing his words carefully, he began the morning briefing.

"Good morning," he began, receiving in turn various acknowledgements and greetings from the members of his team. "As you can see, our collator has been hard at work. Well done, Ferris. You've done well here, given us a good background to both victims, if indeed we want to view Marie Doyle as a victim. For now, I'd prefer we did just that, until we know otherwise. How's that boy of yours by the way?"

"He's doing okay, thank you, sir," Ferris replied, grateful that his boss had taken a few seconds to think of him and his son, still waiting patiently for the kidney transplant that might never come. "I tried to put as much relevant info on the board as I could find, without muddying the waters with pure speculations."

"Yes, like I said, good job. I like the fact you've got a photo representation of Brendan up there. I want you all to look hard at that picture, and remember this was a young man, healthy and ambitious at the time of his death, who was brutally murdered, and not just a pile of bones as he was when the builders dug up his remains."

"Sam," he said next, looking directly at D.C Gable, "I'm sorry you had a wasted trip to try to find Clemmy De Souza, but at least Sergeant Drake and D.C. Dodds got lucky, finding her married to Phil Oxley. And, you did get the photo of her and Marie from Clemmy's parents, plus a little more background information on the girls."

"Thank you, sir. Yes, I must say I was shocked when Mrs. De Souza told me her daughter was married to Phillip Oxley, but she was very helpful in answering my questions, not that her information will go far towards helping us find a solution to the mystery. She did say that Marie was a very pretty girl, with a sweet and trusting nature. She added that Marie could be a little naïve at times, easily taken in, and could understand how she'd be enthusiastic about Brendan's plans to go to America. Clemmy had told her that Marie was besotted with Brendan, and would go along with whatever he suggested. Clemmy was disappointed that her best friend was planning to leave Liverpool, so she said, and was even more crestfallen when it appeared Marie had left without even saying goodbye. Mrs. De Souza's enduring memory was that for weeks after Marie's disappearance, Clemmy moped around the house, both worried she hadn't heard from Marie, and angry that Marie might have run off without a word."

"Okay, Sam, try following up with Mrs. Oxley. See if she or Marie had any other close friends, someone either of them might have confided in. Also, ask if there were any particular places that meant something special to her or Marie, somewhere Marie might have run to if she was in trouble or needed to get away from home for a while."

"Okay, sir," Gable replied.

Ross moved on to the information gathered by Drake and Dodds so far.

"You two seem to have made some progress in your talk with Marie's parents."

"We do?" Drake said, surprised her boss thought that way.

"Yes," Ross replied. "I've been thinking through everything you were told, and it strikes me that the mother was very close to the girl, but the father was more of an old fashioned patriarchal figure, and liked to rule the household with something approaching a rod of iron, pushing his own principles and beliefs onto his children. The two boys, Mickey and Ronnie appear to have been tough enough to live their lives around their father's code of discipline, but I believe Marie may have retreated into a kind of fantasy world of her own as a kind of coping mechanism. Hence her love of music, the fact she carried her transistor radio almost everywhere, and also, perhaps why she fell for Brendan's almost impossible scheme to emigrate to the USA and become a huge rock star. That fits with what Sam heard from Mrs. De Souza, and is probably the first piece of tangible and substantiated evidence we've received about her state of mind at the time."

"There's something else about old James Doyle that's bugging me, sir," Drake said.

"Go on, Sergeant. Let's hear it."

"Well, I think D.C. Dodds will agree that James Doyle is not a particularly nice person," Izzie said, and Nick Dodds immediately agreed, saying, "You can say that again. What a bigoted and objectionable bastard he is, for sure."

"Yes, but sadly we can't arrest the man for being a bigot, at least not yet," Ross laughed. "Tell me what it is you find unsettling about the man, Izzie."

"Well, he obviously didn't give a damn about what happened to Brendan Kane, even though he was his daughter's boyfriend, and in all likelihood Marie suffered the same fate as Kane. If it was me in his place, I'd want to know just what happened to young Brendan, but all he seemed bothered about was his daughter being romantically involved with a protestant. The man's a real religious dinosaur. He belongs in the middle ages."

"Or on the Falls Road in Belfast," Dodds quipped, referring to one of the notorious areas of sectarian violence in Northern Ireland.

"Funny you should say that," Drake went on. "Clemmy De Souza, sorry, Oxley, told us one of Doyle's Irish cousins, who Marie referred to as 'Uncle Patrick' came to Liverpool a week or two before Clemmy's disappearance. Clemmy told us Marie didn't like the man and was glad he wasn't staying at the house with them. Patrick stayed in a B & B or hotel as far as she knew. The thought just struck me, I wonder if this 'Uncle Patrick' could have had anything to do with both the murder and Marie's disappearance?"

Ross suddenly realized that Drake and Dodds might have stumbled on an important clue.

"Did Clemmy have a surname for this 'Uncle Patrick' character?" he asked.

"Yes, sir," Dodds spoke up, as he referred to his notebook. "Mrs. De Souza thinks it might have been Price, or Bryce, something like that."

"Ferris," said Ross, and Paul Ferris looked up expectantly, "when we're done here, I'd like you to run a full criminal records check on anyone with the names Patrick Price or Bryce, or any similar sounding names you can think of, probably from the Belfast area. Let's just see what comes up when we go looking for Uncle Patrick."

"Right you are, sir. I'll get on to it as soon as we're finished here."

"Good man," said Ross, who now turned his attention to young D.C. McLennan.

"I've got a tricky little job for you, McLennan. I want you to do your best to go back in time and find out if any cars, possibly Hillman or Vauxhalls, were either reported abandoned, or were picked up and impounded by the old City Police between August and September in sixty-six. It means wading through lots of old records and you might not find anything, but Brendan Kane owned a vehicle that, as far as anyone knows, simply disappeared along with its owner on the night of his murder. That car must have ended up somewhere. See if you can find it."

"Okay, sir," McLennan replied. "Er, sir?"

"Yes?"

"What's a Hillman, sir?"

Ross laughed and said, "A bit before your time. Great cars, My Dad had one once, a Hillman Hunter, I think. Try the Hillman Minx. That was a popular model back then. Look it up, Derek."

"Right, sir"

"If you need help with all that, ask D.C. Ferris. He'll probably know exactly where you should be looking for the information we need, isn't that right, Ferris?"

Paul Ferris nodded and said, "I'm here if you need me, Derek."

McLennan thanked him as Ross carried on,

"Dodds, I want you to look into the backgrounds of both Mickey and Ronnie Doyle. They're not out of the woods yet, in my book."

"But sir, they'd hardly have walked in here saying they thought the skeletal remains were Marie's if they'd killed Kane and left him there, would they?"

"Think about it for a minute," said Ross. "It's possible one of them is guilty and the other innocent. Let's say the innocent brother sees the newspaper article and wants to come and see us because he thinks it might be Marie. Now, if you're the other, guilty brother, what do you do?"

Dodds hardly hesitated before replying:

"Go along with the innocent one, sir. Pretend you're as innocent as he is, and play it clever. That way, you not only make yourself look innocent, you also find out how much the police know, if you're lucky."

"Good. I see you're thinking, that's great. Check 'em out, make sure neither of them's hiding any skeletons of their own in their cupboards, okay?"

"I've got it sir."

"Izzie, you're with me," he said to Drake. "We're going to see your friend, James Doyle. I have a feeling the time has come for me to meet this cantankerous, bigoted old man. There's something 'off' about him from what everyone's telling me. And don't forget the kneecapping. Maybe, just maybe, Doyle and his Irish connection had something to do with all this."

"You have anything to say, George?" he asked, as all eyes in the room turned to look in the direction of George Thompson.

"Not at present, thanks Andy. I just wanted to keep up to date myself. I only hope the press releases bring you something useful eventually."

"Me too, George, me too," said Ross, bringing the briefing to a close. When the others had left the room he said to Drake, "Well, Izzie, we've got a real mix of unrelated odds and ends, bits and pieces here, and we have to pull them all together. When we do, we're going to find a killer, I mean it."

"I hope you're right, sir," she replied. "It would be a pity for Brendan Kane's remains to resurface after all this time and still fail to find justice."

"That's where we come in, Izzie. We're going to be the instrument of that justice, I promise you. I intend to do what I can to find out if those visas issued to Brendan and Marie were ever used. I know it's a long shot, but the Americans may have records that go back that far."

"But, why, sir? We know Kane never got to the USA, so what's the point?" Drake asked.

"Because, it's possible someone killed the pair and then faked their own identities, became Brendan and Marie, and used those visas to effect a very clever getaway."

Drake looked impressed at her boss's line of thought, and said so.

"I'd never have thought of that, sir. Rather an inspired piece of thinking."

"Thanks, but it is just a long shot, though we seem restricted to those at present."

"What about me, sir? Anything specific you want me to follow up?"

"Yes, Izzie. Gretna Green has been mentioned more than once. I'd like you to check back and find out if a marriage was recorded at any time during nineteen sixty six, between our couple. I haven't had time to check on the actual residence period required back then. It's possible they intended to go to Scotland and get married before doing a runner, and maybe they did or did not make it."

"Will do, sir. I'll get started then, if there's nothing else?"

"Carry on, Sergeant," said Ross. "I'm going to get on the phone to our American cousins and try out my long shot, or maybe should I call it my *very* long shot."

CHAPTER 27

HELPING HANDS

"Inspector Ross? Good morning to you. My name is Ethan Tiffen. The lady on the switchboard tells me you're seeking some information on Visa applications?"

The voice on the telephone immediately reminded Ross of New York, having spent a holiday there himself a couple of years previously with Maria. It was rare for them both to be able to secure a week away from work at the same time, so their brief time in The Big Apple remained firmly embedded in his mind, as did the unmistakable accent of a native New Yorker.

"Yes, well, something like that, Mr. Tiffen," said Ross in reply to Tiffen's cheerful voice.

"Hey, please call me Ethan, Inspector, and tell me exactly how the United States Immigration Service can help the police up there in Liverpool, I think Deirdre said?"

"My name's Andy, and yes, I'm in Liverpool, with Merseyside Police," said Ross. "I'm not sure if or how you can help…"

"Try me, Andy," Tiffen interrupted.

"Okay, here goes. I need to know if a pair of tourist visas issued to two British citizens were ever used in order to gain entry into the USA."

"Sounds doable," Tiffen replied. "When exactly were these visas issued, Andy"

Andy Ross paused, took a deep breath, and then allowed the words to pour out.

"That's the thing, Ethan," he said. "These visas were originally issued sometime in nineteen sixty-six."

"Whoa, there, buddy," a rather shocked-sounding Tiffen responded. "You're talking about another world, another time, another place, Vietnam, Civil Rights marches, Peter, Paul and Mary protest songs, and long haired hippies. I guess this request of yours is important, but then, I doubt you'd be asking such a question if it wasn't, am I right?"

"Yes, it's very important," Ross said. "I'm investigating a murder that took place in sixty-six, together with the disappearance of a young woman at the same time. The skeleton of the murder victim, a young man, a musician with a local band, a pop group, was only recently discovered by a contractor carrying out an urban redevelopment project, and the missing girl, his girlfriend, hasn't been seen or heard of since the time of his own disappearance."

"Hell, that's a long time to be missing. How old was the girl when she went missing?"

"Nearly twenty-one, and the boyfriend was almost twenty-two."

"Andy, I have a daughter almost the same age. I can't imagine losing her like that, not knowing where she is, or what happened to her."

"Look, I know it's a very, very long shot, and your records may not go back that far, and I'll understand if you can't do anything to help, but anything you can do will be greatly appreciated."

"Now, just hold up there, Andy, my new friend. I never said I couldn't help, did I? Just let me think a minute, okay?"

The line fell silent for what seemed an interminably long few seconds and Andy Ross wondered if he'd been cut off, when the sound of the phone being picked up at the other end rattled his eardrum.

"Sorry to be so long," Tiffen apologised. "Just needed a quick word with one of my people here. Seems we do keep records going back a long, long time, to well before the advent of computers, in fact. Thing is, it might take some time to track down the original issue of the visas and then it'll need another search to find out if those visas were ever used, or cancelled, or just disappeared."

"Did that happen often, visas just not being used and disappearing, never to be heard of again?"

"Hell, yes, more than you'd imagine. People would apply for a visa, then change their minds or their holiday plans at the last minute and just throw the darned things in the trash. Still happens today, Andy."

"But you might be able to help me, is that what you're saying?"

"That's what I'm saying, Andy, sure. Now, what I need from you is all the details you can give me. I need the names of your couple, including middle names if they had any, addresses at the time of application, dates of birth, and, if you have them, photographs of each of them. A good written description would be good also. I know this is pushing it, but if you

162

or their families have their passports, then the passport numbers would be a big help too. Probably be a good idea if you can fax them to me so I can get the ball rolling here at my end, and then maybe mail me copies of the documentation as soon as you can."

"I don't know what to say, Ethan. I wasn't expecting such a helpful response to an old case like this. I'm grateful to you, I really am."

"Hey, better save your thanks until we see if I come up with anything helpful. I can't give you any guarantees, like I said. Oh, yes, and please be sure and send me an official request so I can reconcile this with our people here at the embassy."

"Consider it done, Ethan, and thank you. I'll have all the relevant information with you within the next hour or two, as soon as I can get my collator to pull it all together for you."

The two men exchanged their direct line telephone numbers and fax numbers as well as, in Ross's case, the number for the main switchboard at Merseyside Police Headquarters. He gave Tiffen the names of Izzie Drake and D.C. Paul Ferris, telling the Immigration Officer he could be reached through either of them if he wasn't at his desk if the American needed to speak to him again.

Ross knew he'd just played a very unlikely long shot, but even a negative response to his inquiry might serve useful in terms of eliminating other theories, no matter how improbable or outlandish they might seem. As he explained to Paul Ferris while outlining the information and documentation he needed collating and sending to Tiffen, the whole frustrating part of investigating a mystery was in not knowing what information may or may not bear relevance to the case. Every avenue, no matter how vague, had to be investigated and followed to its conclusion, with the majority of such investigations almost inevitably leading to dead ends. What he fervently hoped of course, was that by following each and every blind alley, they would eventually hit on the one course of action that would suddenly unlock the whole case and lead him to its eventual solution.

Leaving Paul Ferris to do what he did best; Ross went looking for Izzie Drake, wondering how she'd got on in her attempts to track down marriage records from Gretna Green. He found her in the canteen, doing her best to look as if she was enjoying a limp-looking cheese and ham sandwich and a cup of something that he thought vaguely resembled coffee.

* * *

"Looks almost edible," Ross quipped as he pulled up a chair and seated himself opposite his sergeant.

"Almost, being the operative word," Drake replied, a wry smile on her face. "They ought to make it a criminal offence you know, trying to slowly poison police officers through the administering of noxious sandwiches."

"Couldn't agree more," Ross agreed. "Give me a bag of nice, greasy chips, liberally doused with salt and vinegar from Rothwell's Fish Bar over the road, any day. Any luck with Gretna Green?"

Swallowing a chunk of plastic-looking cheese, almost choking in the process, Drake cleared her throat before replying. "Well, we can forget any romantic runaway wedding for a start, sir. Just didn't happen. A nice, kind old lady, well, she sounded old, up at the Gretna Register office kindly looked it up for me. No Brendan Kane, and no Marie Doyle, at any time in sixty-six. She was very thorough, old Mrs. Burns, checked every month that year. She also informed me that there was a fifteen day residency rule, before anyone could get married at Gretna so, with the timeline we have, our couple just couldn't have done it anyway, unless they'd gone after leaving Liverpool, which, with Brendan lying dead in the water was impossible. Dead end, I'm afraid, sir."

"That's alright, Izzie. I really didn't expect there would be any marriage in Gretna, but we had to check. It's all adding up to something less than we might have expected, and as much as someone might want us to think the answer lies in some transatlantic musical dream, I think we'll find our answers much closer to home."

"You do, sir? Want to share your thinking with me?"

"Sure. Look, we have lots of conjecture surrounding the fact that Brendan and Marie wanted to go to America. Phil Oxley did his best to help Brendan in his quest for a means of entry to the States. I've got a U.S Immigration Service official checking, even now, to see if the visas issued to the couple were ever used. I doubt he'll find anything. We have no real evidence to link anyone with the murder of Brendan Kane, but a few of the people we've come across in recent days could have had a vague motive for wanting him dead."

"Okay, sir, I'm hooked. Go on, please."

"We know there was bad blood between the group members and Brendan when he decided to go solo, so any one, or combination of two or three of the band members might have felt aggrieved enough to take out a form of revenge, especially if they thought Kane was going to America and stood a chance of real stardom, after they'd all struggled along on the local circuit for years. Then, there's Marie's father. James Doyle would have gone mad if he knew his daughter planned to run off with a protestant lad. Mickey and Ronnie Doyle told us they broke the news to their parents about Brendan and Marie just before going to the police station to report her missing. That puts their father in the clear, on paper, but what if he already knew about the couple?"

"How, sir?"

"I don't know. I'm just brainstorming, speculating. You'll just have to humour me, Izzie, okay?"

"Okay," Drake replied. "So, that makes four potential suspects. Any more to add to the list?"

"Ah, that's just it, isn't it? We're assuming this is all to do with the group in some way. We know so little about the lives of both Kane and Marie. If this was a fresh murder case, we'd be interviewing families, friends, everyone who knew the couple. Because it took place so long ago, we're denied that luxury, so we are kind of left with a very narrow track to follow, hoping it'll lead us somewhere."

"And is it, sir? Leading anywhere, I mean?"

"I have a feeling it's about to, Izzie. For now, I want you to drive me over to James Doyle's house. I really want to meet, and talk to this cantankerous old bastard myself. A real charmer, according to you and Dodds, and also it would seem, in the memory of Clemmy Oxley."

"You want to go now, sir? I can't take any more of this bloody sandwich anyway."

Ross laughed as he and Drake rose and left the canteen, casting mock salutes at poor old Doris, the canteen supervisor who stood behind the servery, a look of confusion on her face.

CHAPTER 28

COMING TOGETHER

Before Ross and Drake left headquarters, they were called over by D.C. Ferris, sitting as usual at his desk, his fingers dancing over the keys of his computer keyboard.

"You have anything for me, yet, Ferris?"

"I do indeed, sir. I was about to come and find you. You asked me to look into this relative of James Doyle?"

"That's right, Bryce, or Price, wasn't it?"

"It was Bryce actually, sir. Patrick Bryce. Born in Belfast in 1941. Lots of petty crime in his teens, four arrests, three convictions and was first suspected of being a member of the Provisional IRA in nineteen sixty three. Like a lot of those suspected of involvement in the troubles over there, the Royal Ulster Constabulary could never pin a thing on him. He was thought to be involved in at least a dozen sectarian murders but fell off the authorities' radar in the early nineties."

"Well, well, well," said Ross, slowly and deliberately as the gears of his investigative brain kicked in. "Looks like our friend James Doyle has a few questions to answer."

Izzie Drake added, "I should say so, sir. The man has a potential IRA man in his family and Bryce was apparently in Liverpool just before Marie went missing."

"And more importantly, just before Brendan Kane was killed, if the timeline holds firm," said Ross.

"Makes the kneecap shootings fall into place, sir," Ferris added.

"It does, Ferris. And it also possibly reveals just why Doyle is such a religious bigot. If his philosophy is the same as the IRA's, it's bloody easy to see why he was so set against Brendan Kane and his daughter Marie being romantically involved."

"But James Doyle was born here in Liverpool, sir. Why the hell would he subscribe to such sectarian rubbish when he'd never lived in Ireland in his life?"

"Because his family is rooted in Ireland, Ferris. I don't know why, but it seems Liverpool in the sixties was still quite a divided city in terms of religion. Most folk couldn't care less, but in certain areas of the city people still clung to the old divisions. You're too young to remember Scottie Road in its heyday. Loads of Irish Catholics settled there in the eighteenth century and it almost became a city within a city. Even later generations kept up the old religious divides well into the sixties, when modernisation gradually dragged Scotland Road kicking and screaming into the twentieth century, over half a century too late. The place you see today is nothing like it once was, with all the old red brick terraces stretching for miles along the A59. Did you know, Cilla Black was raised on Scottie Road?"

"No, I didn't know that, sir," said Ferris. "So in a way, it's hardly surprising there are people like James Doyle around, even today. His ancestors probably came over and possible lived in the Scottie Road area over a hundred years ago, and a few of them have obviously perpetuated the old hatreds. It's almost unbelievable."

Ross nodded and replied, "Sounds crazy, I know, but it was there, just under the surface. It was never extreme though, as far as I know, and certainly the nineteen sixties helped bring all that sort of nonsense to an end. You've done well, Ferris. Any word from the others?"

"Yes, sir. Derek McLennan has had no luck trying to determine what happened to Brendan Kane's car. It was a pretty thankless exercise really, given that we had no registration number for the vehicle. He even tried DVLA in Swansea but they couldn't do a thing without either a registration number or a vin number."

"Well, he tried, and I didn't expect much after all these years, but it was worth a go. How about D.C. Gable?"

"Still out sir, probably talking to the Oxleys again as you ordered."

"Good, we'll see what, if anything she comes up with when we meet up later. If the boss or anyone wants to know where we are, Sergeant Drake and I are going to talk with James Doyle again. It's time for him to be a little more honest with us, I think."

As Ross and Drake motored across town to the home of James and Connie Doyle, the inspector confided his private thoughts to Drake.

"Right from the beginning, something has bugged me about the kneecapping of Brendan Kane. It was typical IRA justice, but we could find no connection at all between Kane and the terrorists. It was never something that criminals on this side of the water went in for, not even the

London gangs, so there had to be something, somewhere, even though no evidence existed to confirm it. I think we dismissed it all too easily after the anti-terrorist boys told us they had no information relating to IRA activity in the city at that time. Even Porteous virtually told me to leave that avenue of investigation alone, not wanting to add a political angle to the case."

"And you think there may have been such a connection, now, sir, is that it?"

"Not quite, Izzie. I've said all along that I thought the solution to this case lay much closer to home than we all thought. I don't think Brendan Kane had any links to terrorism or the IRA or any so-called 'Loyalist' organization, but I do think that we might just have uncovered a personal reason for what happened on that wharf. I'm speculating now, but let's say, knowing James Doyle's bigotry towards the prospect of Protestants having anything to do with his daughter on a romantic level, that he brought his cousin Patrick over here to 'sort' Kane out, scare him off, or give him a warning."

"But, isn't shooting a young man in the kneecaps a bit of an extreme way of warning him off, sir, especially as it would probably lead to someone making an instant connection to IRA involvement?"

"But it didn't, did it, Izzie, because we never found Kane's body, at least until now? Maybe killing him was an accident, I don't know, but I'm sure as hell going to put some pressure on bloody James Doyle, until we get the truth out of the old bastard."

"But, even if you're right, it doesn't do anything to explain Marie's disappearance, does it, sir?"

"No, it doesn't, Izzie. You're quite right, and that's the side of the puzzle that's confounding me a bit. I'm pretty sure Doyle wouldn't have hurt his own daughter, so we're still in the dark there. Maybe when we talk to him, we'll find a clue or two to what happened to that poor girl."

"We're here, sir," said Drake, as she pulled over and parked as close to the Doyle's house as she could.

"Right," said Ross, his face set in an impassive mask. "Let's see if we can get some truth out of Mr. James Bloody Doyle, shall we?"

CHAPTER 29

JIMMY DOYLE

Sister Mary Dominique stood quietly on the corner of Jubilee Street and St. Michael's Road, where they formed a three-way junction with Grafton Street. She'd seen the black Ford Mondeo arrive some minutes earlier, and seen the two police officers alight from the vehicle and make their way to the house in the centre of the terrace on the opposite side of the street. She knew they were police officers. Their bearing, the way they walked, even the way the younger of the two officers, the woman, held the thin file folder spoke to the world and announced them as officers of the law. If that wasn't enough, the way the light fell on the car it was possible to make out the red and blue flashing lights, situated behind the radiator grille, which clearly identified the Mondeo as an unmarked police car.

Mary Dominique had waited for some time in her position on the corner, before the arrival of the police car and its occupants. She was warm, too warm, and Mary Dominique let up a prayer of gratitude to The Lord Jesus and to The Holy Virgin, for the fact that the order she belonged to, The Sisters of The Virgin, Blessed, had long ago eschewed the use of the old, heavy, black cloth habits, so typical of Orders all over the world. Instead, Mary Dominique wore a neat, white blouse, with a high collar and a fairly lightweight grey pinafore dress with a hem that fell chastely just below the knee, and a grey and white half-wimple that complimented the rest of the habit. Her shoes were of plain black leather, functional but not too heavy, but still, she felt overdressed for the purposes of standing on a street corner in the heat of the day.

Seeing the two police officers being granted entry to the house halfway along the street on the opposite side of the road from her vantage point, she debated what to do next. Should she stay, and wait to see what happened next, or should she simply leave, and come back later, or perhaps another day, or then again, maybe not return at all? After all, if she hadn't seen the article in the Daily Mail during a recent visit to her local library, she wouldn't be here at all. The things she knew, the things she'd seen, surely could result in her knowledge of the past hurting the innocent as much as the guilty. It all happened such a long time ago. At first, she'd been all fired up with the thought that she ought to tell someone what she knew, maybe the police, or someone at the newspaper, she wasn't sure, and so, here she stood, in the heat of the day, watching and wondering, unable to decide her next move. The thought crossed her mind that maybe she'd never be believed anyway. Then again, would anyone have the temerity to accuse a nun of lying?

* * *

"You, Mr. Doyle, are a liar."

Ross had decided to take an aggressive stance with James Doyle from the moment he walked into the man's house. Despite his age, James Doyle appeared to be well capable of putting up stern resistance to Ross's line of questioning.

"What right do you have to come into a man's house and call him a liar?" Doyle snapped back at the inspector.

"The law gives me that right," Ross replied. "As I've already stated, I don't believe your story that your cousin, Patrick Bryce, visited you in nineteen sixty-six purely to look for work in Liverpool. It's also my belief that you have always been aware of his connections to the Provisional IRA and that in fact you are a wholehearted supporter of their beliefs."

"That's nonsense," Doyle replied. "You're talking as if I'm some sort of terrorist. Connie, tell them, in the name of God, that I'm no terrorist." He directed his plea at his wife, seated in the opposite armchair to himself.

Connie Doyle had listened patiently as her husband had conducted his verbal sparring session with the inspector, but suddenly, the old lady seemed to snap, as though some long pent up frustrations couldn't be held in any longer.

"In the name of God Almighty, James Doyle, why don't you grow up at last, before you're too old to do so? I'll tell the inspector the truth, if you won't."

"You'll shut your mouth, woman, that's what you'll do."

"No, Jimmy, no I won't. No more. Inspector, let me tell you, that damned cousin of his was never anything but trouble. I don't know how or why my husband ever grew so close to him, but I'll tell you this, he wishes he never had. When Patrick came over here in sixty-six, my husband was afraid of him, Inspector Ross. You only had to see them together to know that. My husband wouldn't say no to him. It was me that told Patrick he wasn't welcome in my home. I couldn't stand him near me, and neither could Marie. I made him find a room in a bed and breakfast place. What he and Jimmy got up to when they met up in the evenings I can't say, but I will say this, my husband is a bigoted old fool, and he acts like he's a big, tough guy, but he isn't. There's no way he would have allowed himself to be dragged into anything to do with the IRA, I'm sure of it."

"I'm not necessarily saying he had anything to do with the IRA, at least, not intentionally, Mrs. Doyle." Ross said, quietly.

"Then what do you…oh, in the name of Heaven, please don't say you think he had something to do with Marie's disappearance? He loved her, Inspector. Marie was his pride and joy. He'd never have hurt her."

Izzie Drake was the one who replied, "Not Marie, Mrs. Doyle."

She allowed the words to hang for a second, and then, Connie Doyles eyes seemed to fill first with realization and then with tears as she gasped,

"No, you can't mean you think he had something to do with Brendan's death?"

"That's precisely what I do mean, Mrs. Doyle," said Ross, forcefully. "Why don't you own up, Jimmy? Come on, be a man for once, tell us the truth, like your poor wife here asked you to."

Jimmy Doyle had turned red in the face as the others talked around and about him for those few seconds. He was fighting to control the rage that was building up inside him.

"For cryin' out loud," he screamed at Ross, "I've bloody told you I had nothin' to do with that lad's death, I didn't. How many times do I have to tell you?"

"You can keep telling me until Hell freezes over," said Ross, his anger barely under control. He truly believed he was now face to face with a potential murderer. He had to forget James Doyle was an old man in his eighth decade, and remember that at the time of Brendan Kane's death, he'd have been a strong and fit forty-something, and easily motivated enough by hatred to carry out the evil task of cold-blooded murder. "Come on, out with it, Jimmy. Did you ask your IRA hitman cousin to help you get rid of your daughter's 'proddie' boyfriend? Or, maybe you just wanted Bryce to put the fear of god into young Brendan, to scare him off, keep him away from Marie. I'll bet he'd have loved that, wouldn't he? Is that why he was over here in the first place, Jimmy? Did you invite him to do you the favour because maybe you didn't have the guts to do it yourself? It's not that easy to kill a man in cold blood, is it, Jimmy?"

"I didn't do it," Doyle shouted at Ross, and now, for the first time, the two detectives could see tears forming in the old man's eyes. "Please, listen to me. I didn't do it. I didn't."

"I'm sorry we have caused you upset in your home, Mrs. Doyle," said

Ross, quickly rising from his seat. Izzie Drake followed his lead and stood at the same time.

Connie Doyle looked shocked at the abrupt move and Jimmy Doyle, equally surprised gazed almost robotically at Ross and half spluttered, half gasped, "That's it? You believe me, then, you're leaving?"

"We're leaving, for now, Jimmy, and no, I don't believe you, and I certainly haven't finished with you, so don't think for one minute you're off the hook. Next time we meet, you'll probably be under arrest and in an interview room at Merseyside Police Headquarters."

Doyle looked on, speechless, as the two detectives walked from the room, closely followed by Connie Doyle. As they stood at the front door and prepared to leave, as part of their pre-arranged strategy, Drake opened the file she'd carried with her all this time and took out a photograph, which she handed to Connie for her to look at. Connie Doyle peered closely at the black and white print, gasped and said, "Holy Mother of God. Is that all that was left of that poor boy?"

"That's it, Connie," said Drake, gently removing the photo of the remains of Brendan Kane as they'd first been found at the old disused wharf. "All that's left to testify to the life of a young man, a man who loved your daughter, and may have paid for that love with his life."

"And Marie? What about my little girl? Do you still have no clues at what happened to her?" Connie sniffed as the tears slowly dripped from her eyes.

Andy Ross placed a hand on her arm, and softly said, "Not yet, Mrs. Doyle, but I'm going to find out for you, that's a promise."

No further words were spoken as Ross and Drake left the house, leaving Connie with her thoughts, and Jimmy Doyle, hopefully, panicked enough to do something that would give himself away in the next day or two. Ross would have Dodds and McLennan shadow the man in one shift, with Ferris and Gable taking over in watching over the old man, who, Ross firmly believed, was still a potentially dangerous and slippery character.

As they climbed back into the car, satisfied with their strategy so far, Drake turned to her boss and said, "You do know we were being watched when we walked from the car to the house, don't you, sir?"

"We were?"

"Yes, by a nun. I saw her on the street corner as we pulled into the street."

"And you think she was watching us?"

"Well, she looked towards us as we walked from the car."

"Probably thought we were interfering with her door to door work, you know, selling copies of the War Cry or something."

"Oh, sir, the War Cry is The Salvation Army, not the Catholic Church, I thought you knew that."

Ross laughed. "Of course I know that, Izzie, just joking, that's all.

Anyway, I wouldn't have thought we'd be of much interest to a nun, would we? She was probably waiting for someone and we were probably the only moving thing to catch her eye in the street when we parked up and walked to the Doyle's house."

"Yes, you're probably right sir. Just thought I'd mention it, that's all."

"Right, let's get back to base then, and we'll set up the surveillance on Jimmy Doyle. I don't trust that old bastard as far as I can throw him."

"Okay, sir. I think you did a good job in there, if you don't mind me saying so."

"Why, thank you, Sergeant. Yes, we put the fear of God Almighty into Jimmy, I hope, and with luck, Connie will work on him in the home. Now she knows our suspicions, she'll want the truth from her husband, if it has anything to do with the disappearance of Marie. Connie Doyle could be our best bet for obtaining the truth in this case, if we play our cards right."

As they drove round the corner at the end of the street, Sister Mary Dominique stepped out of the small café on the next street after enjoying a nice cup of tea and a Bakewell tart, and watched as the police car disappeared from sight, lost in the general rush of traffic heading towards the city centre. She was still far too warm and headed away from the area towards her next port of call at a slow but steady pace, the pain from her arthritic knees forcing her to pace herself carefully as she walked.

CHAPTER 30

CLOSING IN

D.C. Paul Ferris, having added all the latest information to the white board in the squad's small conference room, and having heard Ross's plan for surveillance on James Doyle, took advantage of Ross's "Any questions?" to ask,

"So you really do think James Doyle is our man, sir, especially in the murder of Brendan Kane?"

"I certainly think he's involved, yes," Ross replied. "At the very least, even if he didn't pull the trigger, or bludgeon Kane about the head, I'm pretty sure Doyle was, in some way, complicit in the murder."

Sam Gable produced the next question.

"But what about Marie, sir? Do you really think James Doyle would have been so foolish or so filled with sectarian hatred that he'd put his own daughter at risk, or, worse still, do something to harm her?"

"That's the part of the puzzle that's evading me. He seemed genuinely affronted that I'd had the temerity to suggest he may have had something to with his daughter's disappearance. That's the problem with mysteries, I'm afraid, especially one this old. I have to be honest and say we've all done bloody well so far to piece together what we've achieved so far, with no real evidence, witnesses or solid clues to go on. Did your fishing expedition with Marie's old friends throw up anything of interest?" he asked as he finished his speech, knowing in advance the probable answer. If Sam Gable had found anything relevant, she'd have reported it to him by now, he was certain.

"No, sir. I'm sorry. Those I was able to trace and speak to mostly came up with the same kind of answers, you know the sort of things I mean, *"I can't remember back that far,"* or *"I didn't know her that well"*, and *"Wasn't it a shame? Have you found her then?"* If you ask me, most of Marie's so-called friends probably forgot all about the poor girl about a month after she'd gone. Apart from Clemency De Souza, no-one really admitted to being that close to her."

"Nothing less than I expected, but thanks for trying," said Ross. "I want to let James Doyle stew for a day or two before we have another crack at him. I'm hoping his wife puts a heap of pressure on him to come clean about whatever he's hiding, and I'm certain he *is* hiding something."

"So, what do we do in the meantime, sir?" Drake asked.

"We still have to do what we can to try and discover what became of Marie Doyle. If, as he insists, James Doyle had nothing to do with his daughter's disappearance, it leaves us still pretty much in the dark where she's concerned. We need to push for information on Marie. Sam has done her best, but while we wait to interview Doyle senior, I want us to try and tap in to the only other sources of information we have on the girl. Dodds and McLennan, I'd like you to go and talk to each of the Doyle brothers, individually and see if they can give us something, anything that they may have forgotten previously. Can they suggest a favourite place, for example, where she might have felt safe if she did escape the same fate as her boyfriend? We need a trail to follow, but unless we can come up with a starting point, we're just running around chasing our tails, and getting nowhere. Sam, I'd like you to go and do the same with Clemmy Oxley and her husband. Perhaps, Clemmy, of all people might know if Marie had, or maybe the two of them shared a secret place, or dreamed of visiting a place, like, oh, I don't know, like London, or the wilds of Cornwall. You'd probably know more about the way young girls and women think and you might be able to jog some sort of memory from Clemmy."

With the team briefed, they sat down with Paul Ferris, who, as collator had worked out just how they could fit their new assignments in with the task of shadowing James Doyle over the next couple of days. As he pointed out, the interviews of the Doyle brothers and Clemmy and Phil Oxley wouldn't take too long so could be fitted in around the surveillance operation. As the detectives left the room, Ross turned to Ferris. He had something else in mind for his collator. Ross had come to realize over the last few days just how much he valued the quiet, but highly intelligent D.C. Ferris. If anyone could be counted on to give maximum attention to a particular problem, it was Ferris. Ross appreciated how much strain the young detective must be under at home, with the worry about the health of his son always lurking at the back of his mind. Ross found himself sincerely hoping it wouldn't be long before the health service found a kidney donor for the lad. His wife, Maria, had told Ross just how difficult it was to find donors for a patient so young, and she'd expressed her own admiration for the medical staff who worked on such cases, where quite often the end result could have tragic consequences for a family. She was glad she was, as she put it, 'just an ordinary doctor' and not one specializing in such a high risk area. For now, though, Ross put such thoughts aside and stood in front of the white board as Paul Ferris updated it with the latest assignments and information, such as it was.

"When you did that check on Patrick Bryce, you said he'd dropped off the R.U.C's radar a while ago, but, I'm guessing that whoever you spoke to was only looking into known or suspected criminal activity, right?

"Yes, that's right, sir," Ferris replied.

"Okay, here's what I want you to do. Get back in touch with our friends in the R.U.C. and ask them to look for Bryce's last known address, and also try and see if they can find any legitimate references to him. He'll be getting on in years too, now, like Doyle, so maybe he really is legit these days. He may appear on an electoral register somewhere, or even had or still has a business of some kind. Somebody, somewhere in bloody Northern Ireland must know where Patrick Bryce is. Wherever he is, I want to speak with him, sooner rather than later."

"Right sir. I'll contact the R.U.C. but there may be an easier route."

"Go on, I'm listening," said Ross.

"If he's over sixty-five, there's a good chance the guy is drawing his old-age pension sir. If he is, the pensions people will have him on record, his address, where he collects his pension and so on. Could be just a matter of calling them and seeing if he's registered for his pension, sir."

Ross smiled a broad expansive smile.

"You're a genius, Ferris. Go to it, lad. See what you can dig up for me."

"Consider it done, sir," Ferris replied, as he began tapping keys on his computer keyboard.

Confident that he was close to a solution to the case, and that solving the murder of Brendan Kane would lead to the solution of the mystery surrounding Marie Doyle's disappearance, he left Ferris to his task as he made his way to the office of D.C.I. Porteous. It was time to update the boss.

CHAPTER 31

PROOF, WHAT PROOF?

Sister Mary Dominique stood just where she'd stood yesterday and the day before that, and the day before that, when the police officers had visited the house halfway down the street. She could see more police officers today, though, like yesterday, these two officers made no attempt to enter the house. Sister Mary knew they were police officers. Who else would sit for hours on end in a car, drinking tea or coffee from a flask occasionally, and trying not to look obvious each time the door of the house opened? It appeared to the nun that the police were only interested in the man in the house. They'd made no attempt to follow the lady of the house on the occasions she'd left the house alone. But, she felt sure the two men in the car would soon be on their way if the man left alone or in the company of his wife.

Mary Dominique decided to move from the street corner. If she stayed there too long, she felt sure the police officers would be certain to notice her, and in fact, was surprised they hadn't noticed her as yet. Then again, with their attention focused on the house occupied by Mr. and Mrs. James Doyle, they probably wouldn't notice her if she walked past their car half naked.

Carefully looking both ways, she ensured the road was free of traffic, then crossed the street, walking close to but behind the police car, and then made her way along the small passageway that led to the alley that ran the length of the rear of the houses in the street. She walked the full length of the street along the rear alley, coming out at the other end, where she found a new position, close to a betting shop built in a converted terraced house at the end of the street. Just like the street she'd grown up in as a girl. She chuckled to herself, as she thought of the effect her dress would have on some of the regulars at the bookies. Nuns and horse racing just didn't quite go together.

At that moment, Jimmy and Connie Doyle exited from the front door of their home and climbed into their Vauxhall Astra, parked immediately outside the house. Connie carried a collection of carrier bags under her arm, and this was obviously a shopping trip. The officers in the police car saw Jimmy Doyle say something to his wife, who appeared to answer him with a stony gaze. Even from a distance, it was easy to pick up the coldness of the atmosphere emanating from Connie towards her husband.

"Looks like things are a bit frosty in the Doyle household," Nick Dodds commented, as Derek McLennan started the unmarked police car and readied himself to follow the Doyles at a subtle distance.

"Yeah," McLennan replied. "Even from here, I'd say you could cut the atmosphere between them with a knife. Looks like the inspector's ploy to set the old lady against her husband is working. Where d'you think we're headed, Nick?"

"Tesco or Sainsbury's, I'd guess, looking at the bags she's carrying," Dodds replied. "Well, will you look at that?" he commented as they turned the corner at the end of the street, McLennan keeping a respectful distance between the two cars.

"Eh, what?" said McLennan.

"A bloody nun, Derek, right outside the bookies on the corner. She's just standing there, like she's waiting for someone. I'd place a bet of my own she'll be doing a great job of driving the punters away from that little den of iniquity."

McLennan, focusing his attention on the car they were following caught the merest of glimpses of the nun in his rear view mirror and then she was lost from his sight as they followed the bend in the road towards their destination, wherever that maybe.

* * *

Ross was at his desk, sipping coffee and reviewing his files on the case, when he was interrupted by the telephone on his desk, ringing loudly and demanding his attention. Knowing there was no escape, he picked up the receiver.

"D.I. Ross," he spoke into the phone.

"Well, hi there, Andy." The cheerful sound of the unmistakable Ethan Tiffen of the U.S. immigration Service assaulted his eardrum and he found himself holding the phone slightly away from his ear. "Didn't I tell you I'd get back to you real soon?"

178

"Hello, Ethan. Yes, you did. How are you, and how have your inquiries gone?"

"I'm fine buddy, just fine, thanks, and hope the same goes for you and your guys up there in little old Liverpool. Now, as for my inquiry into your visas from long ago, there's not really what you could call good news, I'm sad to say."

"That's what I was afraid of, Ethan, so look, don't worry about it. I didn't really expect you to find anything, to be brutally honest with you."

"Well, let me just tell you what I did find," said Tiffen, and Ross listened.

"I was able to track back all those years, and found the records of the original visa applications and the eventual issue of three month tourist visas to your Brendan Kane and Marie Doyle. I'll not go into dates on the phone as I'm having everything faxed to you when we get off the phone. It was as you suspected, Andy, we have no record of those visas ever being used, and certainly no record of anyone with either of those two names entering the States legally through any of the major ports or airports during that year. If your couple, or even just one of them, did find their way over to Uncle Sam, they did so as ghosts."

"Ghosts?"

"Yeah, ghosts, illegals, under the radar, you with me? You get your fair share of illegal immigrants over here too, don't you?"

"Yes of course we do, as you must read of from time to time in the news, Ethan."

Ethan Tiffen let out a quiet, diplomatic cough.

"Sure do, Andy, sure do. It's a shame your government can't seem to control the influx of immigrants into your great little country, and I don't mean that as an insult. This here is an island nation you live in, buddy, and it surely can only hold a finite number of people. If things go on like this, one day soon you guys are going to have to hang a 'full up' sign at all your points of entry. Your whole island might just fall into the sea if it gets too overcrowded."

There was little more Tiffen could say that would help Ross's investigation. At least he'd kicked into touch the idea, slim though it had been anyway, that someone had stolen the visas and used them to enter the USA, though, as Tiffen had pointed out, it didn't preclude anyone entering the States illegally. Ross knew Brendan hadn't done so, his body had been lying at the bottom of the river, but could Marie, perhaps with help, have joined the many thousands of illegal immigrants who flood into the United States every year?

Ross and Tiffen exchanged pleasantries for a minute, with Ross thanking the American for his attempts to assist his investigation, and expressing his admiration for Tiffen's dogged determination in seeking and resurrecting the records of those visa applications from thirty three years ago. Tiffen, in return, issued a well meant and genuine invitation for Andy and his wife, Maria, to join Tiffen and his wife for dinner, maybe spend a weekend as their guests in London, one day soon. Ross thanked him profusely, whilst doubting such a time would feasibly come up in the foreseeable future.

Hanging up the phone, Ross sat and shuffled the papers on his desk aimlessly for a few seconds, as he allowed his thoughts free rein. He was fairly sure Marie Doyle died at the time of Brendan Kane's murder, but whether her father James had been a party to her death, he still couldn't decide. Either way, he felt he and his team were on the cusp of identifying the murderer, or murderers, of Brendan Kane. The problem, as he knew only too well, was that knowing who did it, and being able to prove it sufficiently well to present to a court of law, were two very different things. He thought he knew who'd done it, but did he have any evidence that would convince the Crown Prosecution Service to launch a prosecution against those responsible? No! He knew it only too well, and the thought caused him to slam his fist down hard on the desk, so hard that he actually issued a cry of pain.

"Damn!" he exclaimed and then again, "Damn, damn, damn."

CHAPTER 32

THE TAPE

Just as he was about to leave his office, and take Sergeant Izzie Drake for a well-deserved coffee, a knock on his door signalled the arrival of Press Liaison Officer, George Thompson, accompanied by another man, who, without introduction, Ross immediately sensed was a member of the fourth estate, a reporter. The newcomer wore a well-used brown check jacket, with leather reinforcements on the elbows and his pale grey trousers looked as if they'd last been ironed around the time of the Queen's silver jubilee. His dark brown hair was neat but a little long over his collar, and he simply smelled of 'press' to Ross, who guessed the man's age at around fifty to fifty-five.

"Hello, George. Come on in," Ross said, wondering what information, if any, George and the newcomer might be bearing for him.

"Andy, hello," Thompson replied. "This is Terry Wallace, from the *Echo*. He received a phone call earlier today and thought it best to get in touch with us right away. We've known each other for quite some years and he thought contacting me would be the quickest way to get to you and be taken seriously."

"Looks like he was right," Ross smiled and gestured for the two men to take a seat. As they did, he spoke his first words to Wallace. "Mr. Wallace, good to meet you. I've read one or two of your pieces in the past. I must say they're a bit better than the usual standard of crime reporting found in local, provincial newspapers. I'm presuming you feel what you have to tell me is of some importance, or you wouldn't have gone to the trouble of going through George to get to see me so quickly."

"Nice to meet you too, Inspector Ross. George has told me good things about you, too, and thanks for the compliment. I'm not here to discuss my credentials, but suffice it to say, I used to work for a couple of London dailies in the past. I moved up to Liverpool for my wife's sake, when her father had a long illness and well, I liked it so much we stayed. Anyway, to business."

Ross immediately liked this man, with his businesslike approach and lack of the usual self-importance so often seen in members of the press corps.

"Yes, please, go on, Mr. Wallace."

"Okay. Well, as you know, we ran George's press release a few days ago and to be honest, I doubted you'd get much from it. Thirty three years is a long time, and most people's memories tend to dim after thirty-three days, never mind years. So, anyway, when a woman was put through to my desk this morning, I wondered first of all why she hadn't done as the press release asked and contacted Merseyside Police directly."

As he spoke, Wallace removed a small, miniature tape recorder from the inside pocket of his jacket, explaining as he did so,

"I often use this little gadget to tape interviews, to make sure I'm reporting facts accurately, and sadly, I was already about a minute into my conversation with this woman before I realized the potential significance of what she was telling me. At that point, I grabbed my recorder, turned it on and held it as close to the phone as I could. I had the phone resting on my shoulder, under my chin, and was holding the recorder as close to it as I could, while trying to make notes with my other hand on a notepad, so the quality is pretty awful, but we can still make out what the woman was saying. I'm sorry it couldn't be any better, but as I said, I was hardly expecting a call like this, and I hope you don't think I'm wasting your time in bringing it to you."

"We'd better hear it then, hadn't we?" said Ross, as Terry Wallace laid the recorder on Ross's desk and switched it to 'play'.

As Wallace had said, the quality of the recording was poor, with plenty of additional background noise from the various activities taking place in the newsroom, and lots of scratching sounds as Wallace had attempted to keep the recorder close to the phone, but he'd been able to hear the woman's words by listening carefully, his head cocked to the side as he tried to blot out the surrounding white noise of his office. Now, as Ross listened, he could almost feel the events of thirty three years ago taking place in his mind. As Wallace had warned him, the conversation was already under way before the recording commenced, but he could hear enough as the woman's voice, slightly distorted by the surrounding noises, spoke from the recorder's tiny speaker in the middle of his desk.

* * *

"…and I saw it all. I was lucky they couldn't see me, or I'd probably have suffered the same fate as Brendan Kane."

Next, Wallace's voice was heard, clearer, asking the mystery caller, "But tell me, why have you waited until now to come forward with this information? Please, just tell me your name, and if you want, I'll meet you somewhere, a place of your choice, and I'll even go to the police station with you, if you're afraid to go on your own. This is too important to just pass on to me, you do know that, don't you? And the police will ask for corroborating evidence, as well."

"Look, I'm telling you what happened. Never mind my name, at least for now. Why have I waited so long? Fear, Mr. Wallace. Fear and a mind that found it hard to reconcile what I saw take place that night in Liverpool all those years ago with supposed civilized human behaviour. Tell the police and I'm sure they'll be able to corroborate what I'm telling you by adding together what they've probably already discovered for themselves."

Obviously not wanting to lose the woman, just in case she was a valid witness, Wallace was heard encouraging her to continue her story, and her voice was heard again.

"I saw them walking towards the old warehouse, and heard the two of them bullying Brendan Kane as they pushed him towards the far side of the building, where it was darker than it had been at the front. The smaller man looked to be in charge of what was happening, but the taller one, with the Irish accent, he was the one who was pushing and shoving and swearing at Brendan. They obviously had no idea anyone was watching them, and they didn't even make any effort to keep their voices down, so they must have known the place was deserted and didn't expect anyone to show up and see what was happening. The Irishman hit Brendan a couple of times, once across the face and another blow to the back of his head. I heard him tell Brendan he was scum and not fit to be near honest and pure Christian women. He kicked Brendan at the back of his legs and he fell to the ground. As he lifted himself up, on to his knees, the Irishman pulled a gun from the waistband of his trousers. The other man, the older one, suddenly took a step back, with a look of horror on his face. "What are you doing?" he said to the Irishman. "I didn't say anything about guns. We're just supposed to scare the shit out of the little bastard." The Irishman didn't reply, and the …………..(here, her voice broke up too much to hear clearly), I heard the sound of two shots from the gun. They were so loud, it was like a cannon going off, and then poor Brendan fell forward, screaming. I thought the Irishman had killed him when he fell silent, but then I heard him sobbing and realized he must be in shock. He just lay there, on the ground, bleeding, in the darkness. I could see enough from the light of the moon to make out what had happened, before you ask. Next thing I knew the Irishman was making the other, older man help him to drag Brendan towards the edge of the wharf. I wanted to call out, to stop them from what they were doing, but I was paralysed with fear. Even if I had called out to them, I was sure I'd end up being shot too. Before I knew what was happening, the Irishman pulled something from a pocket in his trousers. It was a hammer, Mr. Wallace, and without even hesitating he started to hit Brendan over the head with it. The sound of that hammer hitting Brendan's head has stayed with me a long time, and when the two men then pushed him off the edge of the wharf into the water, I heard a splash and then everything seemed to fall silent. It only lasted a few seconds, that awful silence and then the older man turned on the Irishman, calling him a crazy, mad fucker, those were his words. I was rooted to the spot on the corner of that warehouse, hidden from them by the darkness that shielded me from their view. I couldn't move, and my legs felt like they were going to collapse from under me, but I knew if they did, those two men would find me and kill me too. They carried on arguing for a minute or two, and then there was another splash. I think one of them had thrown the hammer in the water. The older man said, "What about the gun?" and the Irishman replied, "That goes with me, Jimmy boy. You never know when I'll be needing it again."

The one called Jimmy looked as though he was on the verge of panicking, he couldn't keep still, his feet all a-fidget, and then I heard him say, "What about Marie? What the hell do I tell my little girl when she wants to know where her fella is?"

The Irishman said, "You say nothing, you idiot. You know nothing. You were never here. How can you know where her filthy proddie boyfriend has run off to? As far as anyone knows, he's probably gone off somewhere with some proddie bitch who'll open her legs for him whenever he wants a good shag."

There's not much more to tell. I waited until they'd gone, and then stayed put for at least another twenty minutes in case they came back and found me, and then I ran. I just ran and ran and never looked back. I'd never thought to see such horror. I thought maybe I was dreaming, that it was all a nightmare, but of course, it wasn't. I knew who they were, you see. Both men. I knew who they were."

At that point, the woman's voice seemed to choke up, as though overwhelmed by the strain of reliving her nightmare. Wallace's voice was heard again,

"Please, tell me your name. Are you Marie Doyle? And the name of the men you say you saw carrying out the killing. Who were they?"

After a pause, with just a hissing sound on the line, the woman's voice finally returned, as she said, very quietly, "Marie Doyle died a long time ago, Mr. Wallace. As for the men who did it, the police will find out their names soon enough, though I believe they know one of them already."

"What do you mean about Marie Doyle dying? Who are you?" Wallace persisted.

"You can call me Jones, and I saw Marie die, too," the woman said, eventually.

"And Marie died too? When? Where? Did you know her?"

"I knew her," the woman said as her voice changed in tone, almost as though she was in a dreamlike state.

"And why were you there that night?"

"I was just walking, just walking, and I saw them and followed them."

"Listen, Miss Jones, you should go to the police. Tell them what you've told me," they heard Wallace say, but then came the sound of the phone being hung up. She'd gone, and all that now played on Wallace's recorder was the sound of static.

* * *

"I'm sorry I couldn't get any more, Inspector," said Wallace.

"Don't apologise, Mr. Wallace. You did well to keep her on the line that long and get that much from her," Ross said in reply, his face showing deep thought and worry.

"You look concerned, Andy," George Thompson ventured, seeing the frown on Ross's face.

"I'm very concerned, George. If this woman saw all that, why didn't she report it to the police right away? Where did she go and why suddenly crawl out of the woodwork and tell you this story, Mr. Wallace? If she was afraid for her life thirty three years ago, she must feel confident that nothing's going to harm her now, or, she's got no reason to be afraid any longer. Thanks for bringing the tape in. I hope we can count on your help in not letting this information out to the public until we've had an opportunity to check the truth of her story, Mr. Wallace?"

"Don't worry, Inspector. We won't print a word until you give the go-ahead. We don't want to jeopardise an ongoing investigation. In fact, you can keep the tape, in case you need to copy it, as long as we get it back at the Echo when you've done with it."

Ross thanked Wallace for his public-spiritedness and the loan of the tape, and quickly called Izzie Drake to his office and played the tape for her.

"Bloody hell, sir, who the hell is this woman?"

"Who indeed, Izzie, and what about this assertion of hers that Marie Doyle died a long time ago? What do you make of that?"

"Maybe she was a friend of Marie's? She may have seen the killing and may even know where Marie went afterwards. In fact sir, she might have been hiding Marie for years, maybe until her death, and now the case has made the papers again, she's decided to tell us what really happened."

"Sounds feasible, Sergeant, but, it still doesn't quite add up. She mentions Jimmy, and an Irishman, so that puts both Jimmy Doyle and

Patrick Bryce in the frame, as far as I'm concerned. But why was this mystery woman out there, on the docks, at night, as she describes it, just conveniently around the time Doyle and Bryce show up with a captive Brendan Kane?"

"I don't know sir, but surely, everything she said on that tape fits with what we either know or have surmised so far?"

"Yes, it does, with a few gaps here and there." Ross fell into deep thought for a minute or so, then, making up his mind on his next step, spoke once more. "I want Jimmy Doyle brought in, as soon as possible. And we need to try and find this woman. She could be a genuine eye-witness."

"Could she be lying, sir? Could it be Marie, resurfacing after all these years?"

"But why, Izzie? If it is, why now? What can she hope to achieve?"

Before they could continue their conversation there came a knock on the door, quickly followed by the entry of Detective Constable Ferris, who almost fell into the room in his haste to reach Ross. The young detective's face was flushed. Something had obviously brought him to Ross's office in a hurry.

"Blimey, Ferris," said Ross, observing the state of his detective, "Where's the fire, lad? Slow down, take a breath, and then tell us what's got you so fired up."

Hardly able to contain himself, Paul Ferris thrust a sheet of paper into Ross's hand, and stood back from the desk. Ross looked at the paper, and his face assumed a look of shock.

"What is it?" asked Izzie Drake, and when no one replied immediately, again asked, "Paul, *what* is it?"

"Tell her, Ferris," Ross instructed him.

"Right sir. Well, you asked me to look deeper into Patrick Bryce, and I put in a further request to the R.U.C. for any additional background information they might possess on the man, and, well, this just arrived. He picked up the sheet of paper that Ross had now placed on his desk. Patrick Bryce is dead, murdered, Sarge."

"My God, when? How recently?" Drake asked, as both she and Ross felt their senses suddenly switch to red alert status.

"Just a week ago. His body was discovered floating in a restored canal lock near Lisburn, near Belfast, and get this…" Ferris paused for effect, and then announced, "he was shot in both kneecaps and then bludgeoned over the head with a heavy object, more than once, and his body dumped in the canal lock."

"Revenge," said Ross. "Someone has decided the time has come to avenge what happened to Brendan Kane and Marie Doyle."

"The mysterious Miss Jones?" Izzie Drake postulated.

"What have I missed?" asked Ferris, "and who the hell is Miss Jones?"

"You could be right, Izzie," said Ross, and then he passed the tape Wallace had loaned him to Ferris. "Take this, listen to it, then get me the best quality copy you can. It'll tell you all we know about Miss Jones. Get back to your friend at the R.U.C, Paul and get me all you can on Bryce's death, circumstances, witnesses, bloody hell man, anything and everything they have. We need to get the team together for a meeting, and fast. Arrange it will you, Izzie?"

"Yes, sir. What about the surveillance on James Doyle?"

"Tell McLennan and Dodds to pick up our friend, Jimmy Doyle, and bring him in. I want a nice long chat in an uncomfortable interview room with Mr. James Doyle."

* * *

Two hours later, old Jimmy Doyle was sitting at a table in interview room two at police headquarters, waiting to be interviewed by Andy Ross and Izzie Drake. Ross had deliberately kept Doyle waiting in an attempt to ratchet up the man's tension levels. He hoped Doyle would finally crack when faced with some of the information on the tape. Once he became aware that the police knew so many intimate details about the murder of Brendan Kane, Ross felt they just might manage to squeeze the full story and secure a confession from Doyle, always supposing of course, that the story told by 'Miss Jones' was as truthful as Ross hoped it was. For now, that was a gamble he was prepared to take in order to elicit Doyle's confession.

Before commencing the interview, he'd first had to spend an uncomfortable few minutes attempting to mollify Mickey and Ronnie Doyle, who Connie had called as soon as Doyle had been taken from their home under police caution. The brothers had both made their way to their parents' home, and at her insistence, had then taken Connie to headquarters, where they currently stood facing Andy Ross.

"We came to see you in an effort to help, because we mistakenly thought the remains were those of our sister, Inspector and in the end, you turn round and arrest our Dad," said Mickey Doyle. "Are you sure he had something to do with Brendan's murder?"

"Look Mickey, I'm afraid I can't go into details with you. The investigation has gone too far now, and as an ongoing murder investigation, even though you and Ronnie have been very helpful, there are protocols I must follow, one of which is not discussing those details with anyone not authorized to be privy to them."

"It's alright boys, really," said their mother, at long last saying something after maintaining a dignified silence since she'd arrived at headquarters and been placed in a waiting room with her sons. "The inspector has a job to do and I just wanted to be here, and have a word with him before he interrogates your father."

"What can I do for you, Mrs. Doyle, bearing in mind what I just told Mickey?" Ross asked Connie Doyle, who seemed to have shrunk since the last time he'd seen her, ageing at least ten years in the process.

"It's more a case of what I can do for you, Inspector," she replied. "I wanted you boys to be here, too," she said to both sons, "because you deserve to know what I'm going to tell the Inspector."

"Bloody hell, Ma, that sounds ominously serious," said Ronnie, and Mickey said, "Christ, Mam, what is it?"

"No need to take our Lord's name in vain, Mickey," Connie reprimanded her eldest son, who mumbled an apology, and then she turned to Ross once more and said to him, her voice small but filled with dignity, "After you called the other day, Inspector, you can guess, I think, that things between my husband and me deteriorated rather quickly after the things you accused him of. When you'd gone, I demanded that Jimmy come clean, at least with me. I told him that if he'd had anything at all, no matter how small a contribution, to Marie's disappearance, and poor Brendan's murder, he owed it to me, his wife, to be truthful with me. I knew he'd been evasive with you. I've been married to the man long enough to know when he's not being truthful. He continued to deny everything, even though I now knew he was lying with every word that came from his mouth. Your father is not a good man, boys, and I hope you can get him to confess his sins, Inspector. This is about his own daughter, in the name of God, and he still can't be man enough to tell me, his wife, what happened to her, or how he helped to murder Brendan."

Both Mickey and Ronnie blanched visibly at her last words, and she ended by saying, "Tell him he needs to look for God's forgiveness, Inspector, for I'm sure I don't know if I can find it in my heart to grant him mine. Please, take me home now, boys, and let the inspector do his job. We'll hear soon enough what he decides to do about your father."

With that, Connie Doyle and her sons left the room, Connie's arms linked with her sons, and Andy Ross prepared to begin his interview with Jimmy Doyle.

* * *

"Before we go in, there's one thing we need to remember," Ross said quietly to Izzie Drake as they stood outside the door to interview room two.

"What's that, sir?" she asked.

"We've all worked hard to try and solve this case, Izzie, and now it looks as if we've finally got our hands on one of the two perpetrators. The other, Patrick Bryce, is sadly beyond the reach of earthly justice, as we've recently learned. You and I know that the man we're about to interview is guilty as hell, but, and this is the sticky point about this bloody case, we have no hard and fast evidence to confront him with. With what we have at present, a good solicitor would have him out of here in a couple of hours."

"So, what exactly are you saying, sir?"

"I'm saying we go in there and do all we can to wring some form of admission of guilt from him. We use the accusations 'Miss Jones' made on the tape and see if he caves in when faced with the fact he was seen on that wharf when Brendan was killed. If he does, we might be able to hit him with a conspiracy charge, and even then, the C.P.S. might say we have little realistic chance of a conviction."

Drake's face revealed her understanding of her boss's words, and she certainly didn't like the implications of what he'd just said. She knew only too well that if the Crown Prosecution Service felt a case had little chance of obtaining a conviction, they wouldn't go ahead with the prosecution. The police needed to produce hard evidence, proof of a person's guilt before they'd go ahead.

"You're telling me that no matter what we do in there, that old bastard is likely to walk, aren't you?" she said.

"That's exactly what I'm saying, Izzie, unless we can unearth some physical evidence, or unless the mysterious 'Miss Jones' comes forward and agrees to be a witness, which might at least see Doyle having to answer in court for his crimes. Just be warned, don't be surprised by anything I say in there, and back me up as though we have a cast iron case against Doyle, okay?"

With a tinge of apprehension mingled with disappointment in her voice, Drake simply replied, "Okay, sir, let's do it."

Jimmy Doyle looked up as the two detectives walked confidently into the room and seated themselves in the two chairs on the opposite side of the table to where he sat. At first, Ross had been surprised when the man hadn't insisted on a lawyer being present while he was being questioned, but soon realized that the old man, despite his crimes, had previously had no close contact with the legal system and probably wouldn't demand a solicitor until he was faced with the severity of the potential charges against him, though, as Ross had just pointed out to Drake, the likelihood of such charges ever being laid against Doyle was pretty slim. Ross himself had been less than pleased when D.C.I. Porteous had pointed all this out to him in a brief but ultimately frustrating telephone conversation he'd had with his boss after learning the information on the tape, part of which he'd played over the phone to Porteous in an effort to save time.

Arrogant as ever, Doyle smiled a crooked smile, though without much feeling in it, as they stared at him silently for a few seconds, the atmosphere in the room one of expectancy, perhaps on both sides. Doyle's first words clearly showed what his expectancy of this interview was.

"You ready to let me go home now, Inspector?" the arrogance in his voice tempered a little by a hint of nervousness. Leaving him alone for a while in the windowless, drab and sparsely furnished interview room had at least served Ross's purpose in making Doyle a little edgy and unsure of himself.

"What on earth makes you think that, Mr. Doyle?" Ross asked. "We've only just begun here. We have received some serious allegations against you and we're duty-bound to investigate them. Ross now turned on the dual tape recorders on the other table in the room, used to tape all such interviews, and quickly identified himself, Drake and the suspect, giving the time and date of the interview. Undeterred by Ross's actions, Doyle simply carried on as before, replying to the inspector's previous words."

"Allegations? What bloody allegations?"

"Oh, quite simple ones really, the same ones I discussed with you at your house the other day. It is our contention, Mr. Doyle, that you were a willing party to the murder of Brendan Doyle on a date as yet unknown during the summer of nineteen sixty-six, and that you acted in partnership with your cousin Patrick Bryce, a known member of the Provisional I.R.A. who you invited to Liverpool in order to carry out the act of murder. Also, we need to discuss the subsequent disappearance of your daughter, Marie Doyle, who, according to all known information, was last seen around the time of Brendan Kane's death, and who has never been seen or heard from since then."

As with the interview they'd carried out at his home, mere mention of his daughter's name served to galvanise Jimmy Doyle, who immediately raised his voice in indignation at Ross's insinuation.

"I've already told you, I know nothing about Marie's disappearance. Do you seriously believe I'd ever do anything to hurt my own daughter? What kind of man d'you take me for, Inspector Ross?"

Privately, Ross now believed that as a result of Doyle's vociferous and agitated denials of involvement in Marie's disappearance, he might possibly be telling the truth about that side of the case, but he wasn't going to let Doyle know that, at least, not yet. Instead, he replied to Doyle's outburst.

"A very bad man, is the simple answer to that, Mr. Doyle. I take you for a narrow-minded religious bigot who would stoop to murder before letting his daughter become romantically involved with a member of the protestant faith, even though, from what we've learned, neither Marie, nor Brendan Kane gave a fiddler's kiss for any form of religion. They were just two young people in love with each other, with music and the sheer joy that living in those early years of the nineteen sixties seemed to generate in the younger generation of that era. You masked your feelings well, making a pretence of not caring that your sons and daughter were having the time of their lives as part of a pop group that included a protestant. How soon after they began hanging around together did you develop your hatred of Brendan? Was it when they formed the group, or maybe earlier, going all the way back to infant or junior school? You're a man who has probably spent your entire married life imposing your will and your outdated religious intolerance on your wife and family, all of whom, I must say, appear to have inured themselves against your attitudes and even your wife has now decided to stand up and be counted, because, Jimmy Doyle, she's quite simply had enough of you."

"And I've had enough of you and your questions," said Doyle, still a hint of arrogance in his voice. "I've told you before that Patrick came here to look for work. Why don't you find him and ask him?"

"As it happens, we have found Patrick Bryce, or rather, the Royal Ulster Constabulary have, but we won't be able to ask him anything. Your cousin's body was found in a renovated lock on a canal near Belfast, with his head bashed in and two bullet wounds in his kneecaps. Does that sound familiar to you, Mr. Doyle?"

Ross's words stunned Doyle into silence. Deep down, he could feel his by now tenuous grip on reality, and on his freedom, beginning to slip away. Not knowing what to say or how to react to Ross's news without incriminating himself any further, Jimmy Doyle simply sat shaking his head, the beginnings of tears appearing to form at the corners of his eyes. He could be heard mumbling under his breath, over and again, the one word, "No, no, no."

Becoming irritated by the verbal sparring that appeared to be leading nowhere, and wanting to press home the advantage he felt the shock news about Bryce may have gained him, Ross now nodded at Drake, and on the prearranged signal, the sergeant opened the brown manila folder which she'd placed on the desk and made a pretense of reading something within the file, before looking Doyle in the eye, clearing her throat and at length, continuing the interrogation.

"What would you say, Mr. Doyle, if I told you a witness has come forward to tell us you were seen on the night of Brendan Kane's murder, acting in unison with your cousin, Patrick Bryce in the killing of that young man?"

"What? You're lying, that's what you're doing, lying to try to get a confession out of me, to something I didn't do. I know about these things. You read about the police trying to trick innocent people into false confessions all the time."

"Is that so, Mr. Doyle?" Izzie asked as she proceeded to repeat to him the words as spoken by 'Miss Jones' on the tape, with Doyle arguing with his cousin about the severity of what Bryce had done. Ferris had made a quick copy of the tape and Drake had made notes of the most important sections, those she felt could best be used in the interview with Jimmy Doyle. She fell silent and waited as both she and Ross watched and waited for Doyle's reaction.

Jimmy Doyle's face immediately paled and the man swallowed hard, both visually and audibly. After giving him time to answer, and receiving no response, Ross stepped in to the conversation again.

"Well, Jimmy, don't you have anything to say to us?"

A further pause followed, and then, speaking very slowly and deliberately, as if the gravity of his situation had finally hit home, Doyle said just four words;

"I want a lawyer."

With that, Ross had no choice but to bring the interview to an end. Under normal circumstances, he would send his suspect to the cells while a solicitor could be found to represent the man, but, knowing he was on pretty thin ice, and that a half-decent solicitor would take one look at the police case as it stood and have Doyle released in no time, he took the unusual step of releasing Jimmy Doyle on police bail, with instructions to return to the police station in forty eight hours in company with his solicitor. He offered to contact the duty solicitor to represent Jimmy, but Doyle insisted he could find a solicitor himself.

Before Doyle could leave headquarters, however, as the paperwork for his release was being completed, D.C. Ferris came looking for Ross.

"Sir, I'm glad you've finished the interview. While you were in there with Doyle we received a phone call from Ronnie Doyle. It seems that, while the whole family was here just after Doyle was brought in for questioning, someone broke into Jimmy and Connie's house."

"Bloody hell, what's next in this twisted case of ours Ferris? Did Ronnie say what, if anything, had been stolen, presuming it was a case of theft?"

"Not exactly, sir. He said someone had broken the small window next to the back door and reached in to open it using the key that was left in the lock. I said we'd get someone round there as soon as possible, and asked him to get his mother to make a list of anything she thought had been taken. I thought that was the best thing to do, sir. I hope I did right?"

"Yes, of course you did, Ferris. Well, as we have to visit the Doyle's home again, we might as well give Jimmy a ride home. You can ride along with him in the back, and help Sergeant Drake and me at the house, presuming that both sons will still be there as well as Connie. The more of us to take statements, the better. You'd better go and inform Sergeant Drake and then go and find Jimmy, before they finish processing his bail release and make sure he waits for us. I don't want him going home on his own."

Twenty minutes later, Ross, Drake and Ferris, accompanied by a surly and silent James Doyle were in a police car, heading once again to the Doyle's house. Ross may not have realized it at the time, but this strange case, and the mysterious and baffling disappearance of Marie Doyle, was about to take another and on this occasion, final twist.

CHAPTER 33

ANGEL!

"Looks like someone waited for you to leave and then took advantage of the situation to effect a quick break-in," said Izzie Drake as she surveyed the broken pane of glass beside the front door. She'd checked for blood, in case the thief had cut themselves on the broken glass, perhaps conveniently leaving them a potential DNA sample, but nothing was evident around or beneath the shards of glass that littered the kitchen floor.

Ross and Ferris had taken a quick look around the kitchen and the neat, tidy living room, and could see little evidence of anything looking out of place, never mind any visible signs of anything having been taken from the rooms.

The family members obviously hadn't expected Jimmy Doyle to be home so soon, and certainly not in the company of three police officers. Ross had explained to Ronnie the circumstances surrounding his father's release on bail, but Ronnie totally ignored the old man, who, seeming to be in a trance and without attempting to help with the inquiry into the break in, took himself out to the garden, where he began his usual pottering about among his small assortment of flowers.

Ronnie explained that Mickey had taken his mother upstairs to lie down. The poor woman had suffered enough shocks and upheaval for one day, Ross thought to himself as he mounted the narrow staircase, knowing he had to speak to Connie. She would be the one to tell him what, if anything, had gone from her home.

Knocking on the door to what he guessed was the master bedroom of the immaculately clean terraced home, Ross gently pushed the door inwards to reveal Mickey sitting on the side of his parents' bed, his mother lying flat on her back, covered by a blanket that Mickey had probably taken from the floral patterned ottoman that stood at the bottom of the bed.

"I'm sorry to disturb you, Mrs. Doyle," Ross said quietly, stepping tentatively into the bedroom.

"It's alright, Mickey," said Connie, placing a hand on his arm as she sensed her son was about to protest at Ross's intrusion. "The inspector has to ask his questions, or he'll not know who's done this to us. Please, come in, Inspector. I'm okay, really, just a little tired, that's all. Things have been rather hectic today, as you know, and I'm afraid I'm not getting any younger, you know."

The smile that Connie directed at Andy Ross could have melted any man's heart, and in that short second or two before it faded, he could see the once beautiful woman she must have been in her younger days, much as her daughter Marie must have been when she disappeared thirty three years ago. Smiling back at her, Ross also saw for the first time since he'd met him, just how kind and gentle Mickey Doyle could be. Any pretence at being a big, tough guy simply faded away as he sat at his mother's side, care and concern the two emotions prevalent on his face. If only his father had been blessed with such a personality, Ross thought to himself, instead of his mean and bigoted, cruel way of living. Shaking himself from such thoughts, Ross replied to Connie in a soft and kindly voice, knowing the poor woman had suffered enough in her life, and not wanting to add to her troubles.

"Mrs. Doyle, Connie, I'm sorry, I know it's an awful time, but none of us expected this. It may have something to do with Jimmy's arrest, or it may have just been kids, or an opportunist burglar who did this. That's why we need to know what was taken. Have you had an opportunity to look around and perhaps make us a list of missing items?"

"I'm sorry, Inspector. I was about to look around and see if anything was missing, when I came over all 'funny' and dizzy, like, and Mickey insisted I come up here for a lie down."

"That's alright, Connie, and I'm sure Mickey was justly concerned for you and did the right thing in making you come up here for a lie down and a rest. Mickey, would you know what was missing if you came and took a look round with Ronnie?"

"What about him, the old man?" Mickey asked. "I saw you pull up in the car with him. It's his house, Inspector, not mine. I wouldn't really know if anything important was gone, but I can say that nothing obvious was missing when we walked in, you know, the telly, video player, stereo system are all still here. They're the usual things thieves go for, aren't they?"

"Yes, they are," Ross agreed. "If you don't mind, if you feel well enough, Connie, I really would appreciate it if you'd come down and have a look around for me."

Connie Doyle pushed herself up into a sitting position.

"Mickey, help me up, will you? There's a good boy. I'll come and have a look Inspector, if you think it'll help."

"I'm sure it will, Connie, and thank you."

Ross led the way down the narrow staircase, Mickey supporting his mother at the rear. Halfway down, the sound of a small explosion reverberated in the narrow passage that formed the stairway. Mickey thought the sound was that of a firework being let off by neighbourhood kids. They seemed to let them off all year round nowadays, not just to celebrate Guy Fawkes night. Andy Ross, however, immediately recognized the sound of a gunshot, fired from a small calibre weapon.

"What the hell…?" Ross exclaimed and took the last few stairs in two leaps, running through to the kitchen, the sound having come from the rear of the property.

The kitchen stood deserted, the back door hanging open, and as he carefully walked towards the door, Ross realised that Mickey and his mother had entered the kitchen and were attempting to follow him. He quickly held up two hands in a 'stop' gesture, and said to the pair,

"Please, stay here, until I'm sure it's safe out there. Look after your mother Mickey. I won't be long."

Ross stepped to the back door, and before stepping outside, called to his sergeant.

"Sergeant Drake, D.C. Ferris, are you both okay?"

"Sir, we're okay, but you need to come out here, now," came the reply from Izzie Drake.

Ross stepped out into the garden, where he quickly took in the scene that awaited him. Drake and Ferris were standing over the body of Jimmy Doyle, who lay across one of his prized flower beds, blood seeping through his shirt from a gunshot wound to the chest. His youngest son, Ronnie knelt beside his father, cradling his head in his hands.

"What the hell happened here?" Ross shouted at his detectives, just as Connie and Mickey Doyle appeared in the doorway and saw the scene being played out in the garden. Connie gasped audibly and as Ross turned at the sound, the old lady's legs gave way as she fainted, thankfully being caught and supported by Mickey.

"Mickey, take your mother indoors and stay with her," Ross ordered and Mickey, stunned, meekly obeyed, lifting his mother tenderly in his arms and carrying her into the house, as Ross moved closer to the scene of the shooting.

"Now, will someone tell me what happened?" he asked again.

Izzie Drake provided him with the answer.

"You were upstairs with Connie and Mickey, sir, and Ronnie was

checking around in the kitchen with me and Ferris, to see if he could identify anything that might be missing, and Doyle was out here, tending his
flowers. We heard a noise, obviously the gunshot, and by the time we got
out here, Doyle was on his knees, almost as though he was praying, and as
we got to him, he keeled over, and Ronnie's been with him until now."

"Is he dead?" Ross asked.

"No, sir, at least, not yet. I radioed in for back up and an ambulance
just before you came through the back door."

Ross moved to where Ronnie knelt beside his father, and placed a hand
on his shoulder.

"Ronnie, has your father said anything at all about what happened?"

Ronnie looked up at Ross. Despite his loathing for what his father had
possibly done in the past, he was, after all, still his Dad, and he couldn't
help being upset and confused by the events of the last couple of minutes.

"He…he…tried to say…something," Ronnie almost choked on his
words. "It, well, it sounded like, "An angel, an angel came for me." It
doesn't make sense. Why would he think an angel had come for him when
whoever it was bloody shot him? Dad, hang on, you hear me? The ambulance will be here in a minute."

Bending down, D.C. Ferris placed two fingers to Doyle's neck, then
looked up and shook his head.

Izzie touched Ronnie gently on his right arm, and said, sadly,

"I'm sorry, Ronnie. He's gone."

"Ronnie, please, you should go inside and be with your Mum and
Mickey," Ross said, and he gently but firmly helped Ronnie to his feet, and
motioned to Ferris, who slowly walked Ronnie towards the house, leaving
Ross and Drake together with the body.

Ross turned to his sergeant.

"And nobody saw or heard anything, right?"

"Not a thing, sir. One minute all was peaceful, then we heard the shot,
we came out, I ran to the back gate and looked both ways along the back
alley, but saw nobody."

"So whoever shot Jimmy Doyle, came and went quietly, and moved
pretty fast too. Pity we never had someone out front at the time, in case the
killer had a car waiting on the street."

"We never expected someone would take a pop at him in his own back
yard though, did we, sir?"

"No, Izzie, we didn't, but maybe we should have, after what happened
to Patrick Bryce."

"But that was in Northern Ireland, sir."

"Which is only a ferry ride across the Irish Sea away, and so easy for a
killer bent on revenge to slip over here to finish what they started with
Bryce."

The sound of sirens interrupted their conversation, and seconds later,

Paul Ferris was escorting a pair of paramedics, their skills now redundant to the situation, through the back door, where they quickly confirmed the fact that Jimmy Doyle had indeed gone to meet his maker. They were closely followed by Detective Constables Dodds, Gable and McLennan, who gazed almost unbelievingly at the death scene in the otherwise peaceful street. Jimmy Doyle's body was quickly and professionally removed from the flower bed, the blooms around him crushed and broken from his fall, and placed on a wheeled stretcher, and, to save the family unnecessary grief, taken through the back gate, and along the rear alley and round to the waiting ambulance on the street. As the ambulance pulled away, en route for the hospital mortuary, Ross gathered his team around him.

"Right, we have to move fast. As I was just saying to Sergeant Drake, this is all about revenge. Someone, and I believe it to be the mysterious 'Miss Jones', has carried out the murders of Patrick Bryce and Jimmy Doyle in revenge for the killing of Brendan Kane. We need to find her quickly, before she disappears back into the obscurity she's been hiding in for a long time."

"But, why revenge now, sir?" asked Derek McLennan. "It's over thirty years since Kane was killed. Why didn't she, if it is this Jones woman, take action against Bryce and Doyle years ago? Why wait until now?"

"I don't know, Constable. We can ask her that if and when we catch her," Ross replied.

"Sir?" said Drake. "What about what Doyle tried to say to Ronnie as he lay dying? What did he mean by 'an angel' coming to him? Was he just delirious or was he trying to tell Ronnie something about the killer?"

"I really don't know the answer to that one, either Izzie, not yet. Listen, we still haven't determined if anything was taken during the earlier break-in. We need to know whether that was the work of our killer, or a separate, unrelated crime of opportunity by someone taking advantage of the Doyle's absence."

A thought struck Ross, and he said to his sergeant, "You spent quite a while here a few days ago, Izzie. Please, it's a long shot, I know, but go inside, take a look around the downstairs rooms and see if anything looks different or out of place compared with your last visit. Ferris, go and talk to the family. They've had a few minutes grace to pull themselves together. I know it's a bad time for them, but we need to know if Connie, especially, has seen or heard anything lately that she might have viewed as suspicious. Be gentle with them, they've had a shock, but we need a statement from Ronnie too, he was one of the first on the scene. Find out if his father said anything else as he lay there. The family may not have liked Jimmy Doyle much at the end, but I doubt they would want his killer to escape justice."

Drake and Ferris were soon indoors carrying out Ross's instructions. Now, he directed Dodds and Gable to begin house to house inquiries in the street, in case any of the Doyle's neighbours saw or heard the killer, either before or after the shooting. Unfortunately, being the middle of the day, most of the residents would probably be out at work, and the chances of finding any useful witnesses were slim. Even the sound of the gunshot would probably have been mistaken for the sound of a firework being let off. The youth of today seemed able to obtain them all year round and Bonfire Night, the 5th November held little exclusivity any more when it came to the firework trade. He ordered Derek McLennan to assist him in examining the garden and the rear alley, for any signs the killer may have left behind, and was about to begin his search when, first of all the Scenes of Crime people arrived to carry out their own investigation of the crime scene, and they were closely followed by a slightly breathless Izzie Drake.

"Sir, I may have something significant to report," she said.

"Go ahead, Sergeant," Ross urged, "I could do with some good news amidst this god-awful mess."

Drake took a deep breath and said, "Well, sir, I just ran up and down stairs to check something with Connie, hence my breathless state, because when we were here the other day, she showed me a couple of things she keeps as reminders of Marie. One of them was Marie's little yellow transistor radio. She keeps it behind a photograph of Marie on the sideboard in the kitchen. When I looked around as you asked me to a few minutes ago, I looked at the photo and was about to move on when something made me look behind it. The radio's gone, sir, missing. I ran upstairs to where Mickey had made his Mother go and lie down. She was still in shock but I just had to know if she'd moved the radio, maybe while cleaning, or to put batteries in it, as she'd told me she still kept fresh batteries in it at all times. Anyway, she said she hadn't touched the radio since I was here the other day, sir. What kind of thief breaks in to a home with modern appliances in all the rooms, but only takes a thirty something year old transistor radio?"

Ross thought about it for a moment, before replying.

"The kind of thief who was here for one thing and one thing alone, Izzie. Listen, when Doyle was gasping out his final breaths, did you hear his exact words to Ronnie?"

"Well mostly, sir, yes, but he wasn't speaking clearly, coughing up blood and everything."

"Right, so, when he spoke about the 'angel', did he actually say, 'an angel, or could it have been, 'my angel'?"

"I'm not entirely sure, sir. I heard angel quite clearly but the rest was pretty garbled."

Overhearing their conversation, Derek McLennan made a comment that suddenly made Ross's hackles rise.

"Doyle talked about an angel at the end did he? Maybe he was visited by that nun me and Nick saw hanging around the other day."

"Nun? Did you say you saw a nun, McLennan?"

"Yes, sir. When we were watching Doyle the other day, and when him and Mrs. Doyle set off in the car to go shopping, as we followed them and turned at the end of the street we saw a nun standing outside the betting shop on the corner. She looked as if she was standing there, waiting for someone. We joked about it not being good for the bookie's business, having a nun loitering about outside their front door."

"That's it, Izzie," Ross shouted excitedly. "Remember, we, or rather you saw a nun hanging around on the street when we first came round to interview James Doyle?"

"Yes, sir, I remember," Drake replied. "What exactly are you thinking about her?"

"Don't you get it, Izzie? The nun, for God's sake. The nun, Miss bloody Jones, they're one and the same person, and under that habit, if I'm not mistaken is the answer to the other half of our mystery. Marie Doyle isn't dead, and for reasons known only to herself, she's resurfaced after all this time, to exact revenge for her dead boyfriend. It all makes sense now, apart from the question of where she's been for thirty three bloody years."

"My god, sir. Marie Doyle!"

"Yes, Sergeant, Marie Doyle. You, young Derek, are a bloody genius, well done lad."

D.C. Derek McLennan beamed with pride as Ross clapped him on the shoulder.

"I am, sir? Thank you, sir."

"Yes, Derek, you are. If you hadn't mentioned the nun just now, I'd not have worked it out as quickly. That's what Jimmy Doyle was trying to tell Ronnie at the end. He'd been visited by *his* angel, his missing daughter, back after all those years, except she wasn't his loving little girl, his angel any more, was she? Marie Doyle has become an avenging angel and we have to find her and end this now. The question is, where would she go? Did she have a special place locally, maybe somewhere she and Brendan treated as their own secret meeting place or something? Izzie, go and ask Connie, quickly, but for God's sake, don't tell her we think Marie's alive and is the killer of two people."

Izzie quickly disappeared back into the house, returning a few minutes later.

"Sir, Connie just remembered that something else went missing a few days ago. It may be significant. Marie keep a five-year diary, you know, one of those thick ones with a lock and key that people used to keep years ago. It was kept in a drawer in the sideboard, and the day we first called, Connie found it missing in the afternoon. If that nun was Marie, she might have slipped in to the house through the back door, which the Doyle's always left open by habit when someone was at home, though they'd locked it today when they all set off for police headquarters, and rifled through the sideboard, found it and taken it. She wouldn't have known her mother took it out regularly, just to hold it, feel it and feel a closeness with her missing daughter. But the thing is, she must have taken a hell of a risk, walking in like that, if the couple were at home at the time."

"Unless she knew they were both out, like the day they went shopping. There must have been other opportunities for her to sneak in and have a good look around," said Ross. "What about a special place?"

"Connie couldn't help us with that sir. She said, if anyone would know any of Marie and Brendan's special or secret meeting places it would be Clemmy De Souza, Clemmy Oxley as we now know her, of course."

"Right, Izzie, get on the phone right now. Try the Oxley's home number. If she's not there, but Phillip is, get her work number. Tell him it's important, but don't mention the murder, okay?"

"Right, sir, but just why the urgency? What do you see happening here?" Izzie asked her boss, who seemed galvanized by the need to move with all speed.

"Okay, Izzie, hear me out for a minute, okay? For the sake of argument, and based on the bits of information we've picked up from her friends and family, let's say that Marie left home one evening to meet up with her boyfriend. She didn't take her beloved transistor radio, which we're led to believe went everywhere with her, either because she forgot it, or, I suspect, she didn't expect to be out very long, or maybe the batteries were dead. Anyway, off she goes, but before she can meet up with her boyfriend, he's intercepted by her father and Patrick Bryce. Somehow, she sees them together, and follows them, unsure what's going on. When she sees Bryce and her father murder Brendan, well, here my theory is admittedly a little fuzzy, but maybe her brain switches off, or she is just too terrified to say or do anything, so she runs. God knows where or with whom she ended up, but somehow she managed to stay out of sight for over thirty years, until word surfaced in the newspapers about the discovery of Kane's remains. Maybe that acted as a trigger and set her on this course of revenge for what took place thirty three years ago. If we catch her, we can ask her."

"Sir, it's a good theory, but when you say if…?"

"Look, Izzie, she's obviously unstable in some way, and she's accomplished what she set out to do, and she still has a gun. Do I have to spell it out for you?"

Instant enlightenment flashed across Drake's face. She knew what Ross was intimating, and could understand his reasoning. "I'll make that phone call right away, sir."

Ross could only stand and wait for what seemed an interminable few minutes as Drake made her call from inside the Doyle's home. Meanwhile he tried to take an interest in watching the crime scene technicians at work, but without much success. It wasn't as if they would find much that would add to his case, after all.

Eventually, Drake returned, and free from the burden of waiting, Ross's nerves relaxed a little as he listened to what she'd learned.

"Thankfully, Clemmy was at home, sir. She was obviously very curious about the urgency of my request, but I told her we'd fill her in later. She thought about the question for a minute and then remembered that Marie and Brendan loved to visit New Brighton. Brendan sneaked her over there for a long weekend on a couple of occasions. She'd lied to her parents and told them she was going to stay with friends. They had of course, no reason to suspect her of lying at that time, so, off they went. Marie told Clemmy she actually lost her virginity to Brendan one afternoon in a caravan he'd rented for the weekend."

She handed a piece of paper to McLennan. "Contact headquarters, Derek. See if this place still exists."

McLennan nodded and moved closer to the back gate to check the address via headquarters, as Drake continued speaking to Ross.

"I also took the liberty of asking if the name, 'Miss Jones' meant anything to her, just in case there is a second woman out there, maybe working with Marie. She laughed and told me that 'Miss Jones' was her own mother, sir. Apparently, when her father, the Portuguese sailor met her mother, her maiden name was Victoria Jones. Her father, Luis, was a big fan of Ava Gardner in those days, and took Clemmy's Mum, who he always said resembled Gardner, to the cinema to see the film, *Bhowani Junction*, which featured Ava Gardner and Stewart Granger. Luis was tickled pink that Ava Gardner's character was called Victoria Jones and would often refer to his wife as 'Miss Jones' as a term of endearment. Marie knew all about it, sir, it was just the kind of romantic story best friends would share, so I think you're right on all counts."

"That was good thinking, Izzie, well done. Any word, Derek?" he called to McLennan, who quickly finished speaking into his police radio and ran across the garden to where Ross and Drake stood.

"It's still there, sir, the holiday park. Modernised and upgraded, with chalets and things for those with a richer pocket, and it still has the same beach front and the wooded area for walks and so on, apparently. One of the guys at headquarters overheard me talking to Mackie on the phone and came across to give me that extra info. Told me he often spends weekends in a chalet with his wife and kids there, in the school holidays."

"Great work, Derek. Okay, here's the plan. We'll leave D.C. Gable here, and let Dodds carry on with the house to house. Derek, I want you and D.C. Ferris in a separate car. You can follow me and Sergeant Drake. Come on, let's hurry it up. We're going to the seaside!"

* * *

The road to New Brighton was relatively clear. Using the modern Kingsway Tunnel a mere one and a half mile trip under the River Mersey made the trip easier and faster than having to catch a ferry in the 'good old days', and the two police vehicles made good time to the town of Wallasey, and thence to its seaside partner, the once grand, but now slightly faded, New Brighton.

Following directions provided by D.C. Mackie at headquarters, they arrived at the aptly named Seaview Holiday Park a mere five minutes after arriving on the south side of the river. Pulling up at a gated entrance, Ross jumped from the car, allowing Drake to ease the car through, followed by Ferris and McLennan in the second car. Ross followed the polite instruction to drivers to 'Please close the gate, help keep our children safe' and ran across to the reception building ten yards from the gate, also adorned with a message, 'All visitors please report to reception'.

Ross virtually burst through the door to the reception office, built to resemble a log cabin such as might be found in the wilderness parks of Canada or the USA, taking the young woman behind the reception counter by total surprise, closely followed by Drake who had pulled up outside the door, leaving the police car's engine running.

Acting quickly to allay her fears, Ross shouted one word, "Police" to her, producing his warrant card in an instant as though by sleight of hand.

"H…How can I help you?" the trembling young woman, who looked no more than eighteen or nineteen asked, still unsure what was happening. Ross read the name badge pinned above her left breast.

"Kylie," he said, "I can't take time to explain right now, but we need directions to your woodland walk and the beach area, and we don't have time to waste."

Quickly attempting to pull herself together after the initial shock of Ross's unorthodox entry, Kylie picked up a copy of one of the holiday park's glossy introductory leaflets for those holidaying at the park. Opening it out fully on the counter she pointed to a map of the park, conveniently spread across the two centre pages of the leaflet.

"Just follow the main road through the park," she said, "then follow the green signs for the woodland walk and beach where the road forks off to the various chalets and static caravans. It's a much narrower road, more a wide path really, and it comes to a dead end about half a mile from the actual beach, and I'm afraid you have to walk from there. Cars aren't allowed. Please, can't you tell me what's going on? My manager will want to know."

"We don't have time to explain, Kylie. We'll tell your manager all about it later. Thanks for your help"

With that he made for the door, Izzie Drake in his wake. It took no more than a minute for the two police cars, easily exceeding the park's five m.p.h speed limit, to arrive at the blocked-off entrance to the path that would lead them through the small wooded area to the beach.

The four officers gathered together and Ross quickly issued his instructions.

"Listen carefully," he began. "I want you all to stay close to me until we come out of the woodland walk, which, according to the map opens out about a hundred yards from the beach. These fuzzy little tufts on the park's map seem to indicate an area of long grass between the trees and the beach, so we'll stop there and assess the situation before deciding how to carry out the search for the woman."

"Are you certain she'll be here, sir?" Ferris asked.

"No, Paul, I'm not a hundred percent sure, but all my instincts tell me this is where she'd want to be after completing what she sees as her work. When we do split up to search, I want absolute silence maintained. I don't want anyone doing anything to spook her into doing something stupid. Got that?"

Receiving nods of acknowledgement from his three officers, Ross took a deep breath, said "Let's go," and slowly led his small team through the narrow entrance to the woodland walk path.

* * *

Standing in the long, waving strands of sea grass that formed a natural border between the woodland and the beach, Sister Mary Dominique looked out at the gently undulating waves as they seemed to lazily approach the shore, small white caps forming as they broke upon the beach. She smiled as her mind began to drift, and in seconds, she'd ceased to be Sister Mary Dominique, the nun, dressed in her drab grey and white habit. Now, she saw herself as she'd once been, a young woman, just twenty years old again, and as she looked down, she admired the pretty yellow sundress with its gaily decorated floral print pattern. She giggled as the sand tickled her bare feet, and she peered out across the beach, watching the tide roll in. In her mind, she reached in to her long-handled beach bag; in reality, she was reaching into the large pouch-like pocket in the front of her habit, from which she extricated her treasured transistor radio and her diary. She looked across the beach, out to sea, as though expecting to see someone. Somehow, she knew he wouldn't be coming. Marie Doyle turned on the little radio, turning the tuning dial until she found a station playing the latest chart sounds. Listening hard to the music that seemed to have to fight its way past the tiny and well-worn speaker in her radio, she realised that this music was all wrong. This wasn't the sound that she and Brendan had grown up with, and she sighed as she turned the dial again, finally finding a station that played a constant stream of 'golden oldies,' the sounds of the sixties, hers and Brendan's sounds. She began to tap her bare foot and smiled as the sound of The Searchers' *When You Walk in the Room* played through the tiny speaker, just as it had done so many times, so many years earlier.

The sound of The Searchers was just fading out as Ross and his small team of detectives emerged from the tree line and stepped on to the path leading to the beach. The radio began to produce another golden oldie, The Cascades singing, *Rhythm of the Rain*, and as the sound drifted across the open space between the police officers and Marie, she turned to look at them as if she'd sensed their presence from the second they'd appeared on the path.

Marie smiled in Ross's direction, and then turned once more, staring out towards the incoming tide, her face a mask of concentration. She tensed for a second, and a slight breeze blew up, carrying the sound of the music from her radio clearly towards Ross and his officers. Ross stared at the woman, the nun, standing mere yards away from him, though he felt somehow as if he was watching a surreal tableau, something real and yet not real, as Marie reached a hand into the pocket in the front of her dress/habit and slowly pulled what could only be her old five year diary from within. She turned towards Ross once more, holding the diary out towards him as if in invitation, and then she slowly and deliberately placed the diary on the ground, beside her treasured transistor radio.

She turned around once more, facing the incoming tide, and reached once more into the pocket of her dress. Ross suddenly went cold, knowing exactly what she was about to remove from the voluminous folds of her habit. Time appeared to stand still, the whole surreal tableau playing out before the detectives in slow motion as Marie slowly retrieved from her pocket the menacing shape of a small handgun. Knowing it was the weapon used to kill both Patrick Bryce and Marie's father, Ross now had no doubts as to what Marie intended to do next, yet he inexplicably felt rooted to the spot, frozen in that moment in time as Marie half-turned towards him one last time.

She smiled once more and looked out across the waves again, before turning to face Ross and saying, quite clearly, her voice carried by the breeze, "He's waiting for me."

In the next few, confused and terrifying seconds, as the detectives appeared to regain control of their faculties, Marie raised the weapon, placing it against her right temple as Ross shouted "Marie, no, don't do it," and the sound of the gunshot resonated across the sands, Marie falling to her left as the gun fell from her lifeless fingers to fall with a soft thud on the sands of New Brighton.

Beside the now lifeless body of Marie Doyle, no longer a missing person, her small, insignificant yellow transistor radio played Herman's Hermits' *No Milk Today*.

Ross bent down, picked up the radio, turned it off and placed it in his pocket.

EPILOGUE

In the days following the death of Marie Doyle, Ross and Drake were able to piece together much of the mystery surrounding her disappearance and subsequent years in obscurity.

Before ending her life on the beach at New Brighton, Marie had, as Ross suspected, left a few detailed notes in the back of her old five year diary that contributed greatly towards filling in the blanks.

It transpired that Marie Doyle was a genuine nun. Sister Mary Dominique had come into being soon after the death of Brendan Kane. On her way to meet him on that fateful night thirty three years previously, Marie had missed her bus and was subsequently delayed. When she finally arrived in town, she hurried to meet Brendan near the docks, where they usually called in to a small cafe there, that provided privacy and ice cold Coca Cola. As she was about to turn into the street where the café stood, she heard raised voices, immediately recognizing those of Brendan, and to her surprise, her father, Jimmy Doyle. Marie had sensed something was not right and she pulled back into a shop doorway where she heard her father telling Brendan he'd been seen, by a friend of Doyle's, with her, coming out of the caravan park in New Brighton on their last visit there. Doyle had quickly put two and two together and rightly surmised the reason for the couple hiring a caravan in the holiday park. She saw Patrick Bryce, her so-called Uncle Patrick step from the shadows and push Brendan in the back.

Her diary went on to describe the events on the wharf, exonerating her father from directly committing violence against Brendan, but not from instigating what happened next. It was all there in those last, sad pages, the beating, the kneecapping, her father's protestations and Brendan being hit with the hammer and tossed unceremoniously into the Mersey at Cole & Sons wharf.

Horrified by what she'd seen, frozen by fear, Marie heard Bryce telling her father to go and get rid of Brendan's car, and her father had rushed off to where Brendan had parked his car, and she never knew what he did with the car, though she wrote that she suspected her father had hidden it for a day or two and then sold it for scrap to one of the city's many shady scrap metal dealers who would ask no questions and pay a decent price.

She couldn't go home, not after what she'd witnessed, and she'd walked for miles until she'd arrived at the gates of a convent where she'd been taken in unquestioningly by the sisters who dwelt within its safe and solid walls.

Ross had visited the convent, where the Mother Superior, Sister Mary Angela, had filled in more of the blanks for him. They'd never known Marie's real name. She'd simply called herself Clemency when she arrived, borrowing the name of her best friend, Clemmy De Souza. The previous Mother Superior who'd been in charge at the time of Marie's arrival, respected her need for privacy, realizing that the girl had been the subject of some terrible tragedy, and Marie was never asked about what had brought her to the doors of the convent, and Marie certainly never volunteered any information about whatever had befallen her, and eventually she had taken holy orders and become a valued member of their convent, though shunning the many opportunities she was given to become involved in work in local schools and on various projects in the community, preferring instead to stay within the sanctuary of the convent, tending the gardens where the nuns grew vegetables and also some very impressive flower beds. Ross thought her father might have been proud of his daughter for that.

The years that followed had proved uneventful, though Mary Dominique, as Marie became known after her ordination, always seemed to be weighed down with some great sadness, and her eyes would sometimes betray a hint of fear, as though, even in the safe haven provided by the convent, she felt threatened or unsure of herself. She'd possessed a beautiful voice and had been a valued member of the convent's choir.

Things had taken a turn for the worst around six months before the murder of Patrick Bryce, when, after a short illness, Sister Mary Dominique had been diagnosed as suffering from an inoperable brain tumour. Her personality changed, and she suddenly decided to become involved with an outreach project that helped former convicts in their rehabilitation into the community. Ross guessed she obtained the gun, which had proved impossible to identify, from one of her new-found friends in the criminal fraternity. She certainly wouldn't have known how to file off the serial number of the weapon, or where to obtain the correct ammunition for it. Most recently, she'd taken a short holiday from the convent, which Ross presumed would coincide with her visit to Northern Ireland where she'd meted out her own version of poetic justice to Patrick Doyle.

As her condition deteriorated, she'd spent more and more time away from the convent, and most of her fellow nuns merely thought she was perhaps visiting places and people she'd once known before the tumour led to the inevitable conclusion. Little did they suspect what was really happening to her mind, as her illness finally led her to seek a terrible revenge for the wrongs done to her and Brendan so many years earlier.

There wasn't much more to tell, and the police were satisfied no-one else had been involved in Marie's plot to kill Bryce and her father. Some-one, probably a friend of James Doyle who worked at BICC had probably typed the fake letter for him to send to Brendan's landlord, but nothing would be gained by pursuing a new inquiry into that one detail of the case. Ross had stamped 'Case Closed' across the file he'd opened on Brendan Kane and latterly, the long-time missing Marie Doyle.

* * *

Dr. William, (Fat Willy), Nugent had carried out the obligatory post mortem examination of Marie Doyle's body, confirming the presence of the brain tumour that he estimated would have killed her in less than three months. Apart from arthritis, present in her hands and feet, nothing else of significance showed up in his examination.

A hastily convened coroner's inquest recorded Marie's cause of death as 'suicide while the balance of her mind was disturbed' and the body was released for burial.

A leading psychiatrist had confirmed to Ross that the human mind, complex and at times unfathomable, had the capacity to 'switch-off' when faced with events or sights that were simply too terrible to bear, and this was in all probability what had happened in Marie's case. Unable to cope with what she'd seen that night when Brendan had been murdered, she'd blocked it out, withdrawing into herself, and remaining in a new, safe world of her own until the news of the recovery of Brendan's remains had reached her and set in motion the tragic recall of those events that had led to such a tragic conclusion.

With the cooperation of the police and the coroner's office, the Doyle family decided to hold a joint funeral for Marie and Brendan Kane, whose mortal remains would be finally laid to rest alongside those of the woman he'd loved, his beautiful Marie.

By contrast with the previously held funeral of Jimmy Doyle, attended only by Connie and his sons, and even then only because they felt an obligation to be present, the funeral of Marie and Brendan became something of a media circus. Despite the fact that Marie had murdered Patrick Bryce and Jimmy Doyle, her story, and that of her doomed love affair with Brendan Kane and the part played in the young man's murder by Bryce and her father had become national news, and with a little help from the media, Marie had become something of a celebrity in death.

All of a sudden, Brendan Kane and the Planets achieved a level of fame they had perhaps only dreamed of back in the early nineteen sixties, when, as young men, they'd tried and failed to make it in the ruthless world of the pop music industry. A record company even went to the trouble of contacting Mickey, Ronnie and Phil Oxley in an attempt to persuade them to accept a recording contract to produce an album based on some of the songs penned by Brendan Kane back in their early days. To a man, all three declined the offer. They'd grown up, life was different now, and they would never have withstood the glare of the modern media, even if the songs had been successful in the current charts, something they all privately doubted would happen.

The joint funeral was massively well attended, with even a few of today's crop of chart toppers present to pay their own tributes to one of the forerunners of the modern pop industry, a description that Brendan Kane would have loved. Connie Doyle and her sons paid glowing tributes to the beautiful but ultimately damaged daughter and sister, who time and circumstances had taken from them, not as a result of her recent death, but due to the evil that lurked in the hearts of men who should have known better over thirty years previously. They each paid additional tributes to Brendan, to the love he shared with Marie, and to the fact that what they were robbed of in life, they would now share forever in death.

Ross and his team were there, only Paul Ferris being absent, as he and his wife attended the Children's Hospital with their young son Aaron after being notified that a kidney had become available following the death of an eight year old boy in a road traffic accident.

Dr. William Nugent and Hannah Lewin, who had worked so hard to identify Brendan's remains, attended to pay their respects, as did Ethan Tiffen, who'd made the journey from London, having been touched by the story of the two lovers whose impossible dream had been to live and work in his country,

Phil Oxley was there of course and he spoke succinctly of his old friend Brendan, and of Marie, always happy, always smiling, and always accompanied by the music from her radio. Perhaps the final word went to Marie's former best friend, Clemmy, now Mrs. Phil Oxley, who wept as she recalled their days together, as they grew up in what she called, "A different world, a cleaner, happier world, and one those of us who grew up in will never forget. Wherever you are now, girl," she said, "One thing's for sure. You'll make sure the music never dies."

As Marie's coffin slowly disappeared into the ground, the sound of Neil Diamond's 'America' played from a nearby sound system, installed specially for the day. It was, Connie Doyle said, after asking that Marie's transistor radio be buried with her, suitably fitting for the occasion.

Connie, of course made sure the little yellow radio was fitted with new batteries before it joined Marie in her final resting place.

ALL SAINTS, MURDER ON THE MERSEY

MERSEY MURDER MYSTERIES
BOOK 2

Former Karting and lawn mower racing champion John Gill was the husband of a dear friend. Just two weeks before his sudden and tragic death, John wrote a glowing review of the first book in this series, *A Mersey Killing*. It turned out to be the last review the book received before his untimely death. With the permission of his widow, Carole, I have dedicated All Saints, Murder on the Mersey to John's memory, in the firm belief he would have enjoyed this second instalment of the Mersey Mysteries series.

John's review of *A Mersey Killing:*
A MERSEY KILLING IS FAB

A Mersey Killing, as well as being a great story, succeeded in taking me back to the days of my own youth. The hopes, dreams and aspirations of a generation were perfectly summed up here by young Brendan Kane who simply wanted 'something more than his Mum and Dad had, maybe one of those new colour television sets'. Few of us had them back then unless you had plenty of money. Nothing too grand in his ambitions then, and that's the great thing about the book. It recreates the sixties just as it was for those of us who lived through those heady days of The Beatles, Gerry and the Pacemakers, et al. The author's descriptions of sixties life were bang on, right down to the washing drying on the old wooden clothes horse in front of the coal fire, which had to be kept going in the summer to heat the water!

As we moved to the nineties, the investigation into the skeletal remains found in the old disused Cole Brothers wharf sets in train an investigation that leads the detectives right back to those early years of the Merseybeat, with murder, betrayal and a missing woman thrown into the equation. As D.I. Ross and Sergeant Drake delve into the past, we eventually learn the tragic secret of A Mersey Killing… simply fab!

ACKNOWLEDGMENTS

All Saints, Murder on the Mersey is the second book in my Mersey Mysteries series and owes its existence to a number of people who were invaluable to me in bringing the book to life.

First and foremost, my thanks must go to Miika Hannila at Next Chapter Publishing, whose faith in, and enthusiasm for the first book in this series, A Mersey Killing, inspired me to decide to create a series of books based on the cases of Detective Inspector Andy Ross and Sergeant Clarissa, (Izzie) Drake.

Thanks also to Debbie Poole of Liverpool, who so enjoyed A Mersey Killing that she contacted me to volunteer her services as a beta reader for All Saints. She has done a fantastic job and she has earned my gratitude for her diligence and attention to detail, not to mention the laughter we've enjoyed along the way at one or two hilarious typos she's picked up during the process, e.g. 'hysterical window,' where I of course meant 'hysterical widow'. Thank you, Debbie.

As always I have to thank my dear wife for her patience and her patient checking of each chapter as it was written, and also a big thank you to fellow author, Carole Gill, who helped me enormously during a potentially catastrophic computer breakdown, and provided her usual support at times when my muse threatened to desert me.

Finally, my thanks go to the members of my family, mostly and very sadly no longer with us, in the great city of Liverpool, upon whom many of the characters in the book are based. I should also say a thank you to the people of Liverpool, my ancestral home town. It took me many years to finally get around to setting one of my books in the city, but since writing A Mersey Killing, I've received so much wonderful feedback from the people of Liverpool by way of reviews and messages that I wish I'd done it years ago.

INTRODUCTION

All Saints, Murder on the Mersey is the second book in my Mersey Mysteries series, featuring Detective Inspector Andy Ross, Sergeant Izzie Drake and the fictional Merseyside Police Murder Investigation Team, following on from the so far successful, *A Mersey Killing*.

Though set in my ancestral home of the city of Liverpool, this is a work of fiction and though many of the places mentioned in the book are of necessity, real locations in the city, many of the places are in fact fictitious, the creations of my own mind. This is particularly true of the churches mentioned in the book. Liverpool is blessed with many churches of differing faiths, but it would not have been fair or respectful to use any of them as locations for this story. The churches mentioned in *All Saints, Murder on the Mersey* should therefore not be assumed to bear any reference to actual churches in the city that bear the same names.

Look out for the forthcoming books in the series, *A Mersey Maiden, A Mersey Mariner, and A Mersey Ferry Tale.*

PROLOGUE

SPEKE HILL ORPHANAGE, LIVERPOOL

Strictly speaking, Speke Hill Orphanage was something of a conundrum. First of all, it wasn't in Speke, the area of Liverpool that today is possibly best known as the location of Liverpool's John Lennon airport. Secondly, there wasn't a hill in sight, and in point of fact it had never been designed to be used for its current purpose. There probably wasn't a living soul who could rightly recall how or why the former Mental Asylum had been given its original name other than those who assumed it was perhaps an attempt to give the old place a touch of the grandiose with a name bearing a similarity to Speke Hall, the Tudor mansion once owned by the wealthy Norris family, and now in the care of The National Trust, a few miles away. Though, bearing in mind the 'clientele' of the old asylum, it would have been debatable whether any of the inmates would have appreciated the pleasant rural-sounding name of their place of incarceration.

For most of those held within the grim walls of the old Victorian buildings that comprised the asylum, Speke Hill would have been the last place on earth they wanted to be, and for the worst afflicted, it may also have been the last place on earth they would see, many being confined without limit of time behind the locked doors and corridors of the bleak, forbidding red-brick buildings.

Set back from Woolton Road, in its own deceptively pleasant landscaped grounds, a sweeping, curved gravel driveway, bordered by an avenue of fir trees, the asylum employed all the horrors of early Victorian psychiatric 'treatments' to those in its care, including dousing with freezing cold water from high-pressured hoses, to beatings, long periods of solitary confinement and worst of all, the enforced use of frontal lobotomy in a madly useless attempt to cure the sufferers of perceived insanity.

Thankfully, the suffering of those held behind the walls of Speke Hill ended when the asylum was closed in the 1930s, and its inhabitants transferred to other establishments, though whether their treatment improved or deteriorated in their new 'homes' was hardly a subject considered worthy of recording by the chroniclers of the time.

After standing empty for five years, it was decided that, rather than the council going to the expense of demolishing the three buildings that comprised Speke Hill, the old place could be utilised, following a cheap and cheerful programme of renovation, as an orphanage, there being an ever growing proliferation of parentless children in the city and its environs during the austere and barren industrially sterile years following the Great War of 1914-18. Often, children whose fathers were away at sea and whose mothers simply couldn't cope would be placed in orphanages. Hunger, general deprivation and homelessness had taken a bitter toll on the great port city.

The project gained more popularity with cost-conscious councillors when the local diocese of the Roman Catholic Church offered to contribute a sizeable portion of the cost of renovation, provided they were given the rights to run the orphanage, placing a strong emphasis on discipline and religious instruction, with the stated aim of turning out useful members of society by the time their charges were old enough to leave full time education, usually at the age of fifteen, which would be provided in the school which would be run in one of the three old asylum buildings. There had been some opposition in the council chamber at this development.

It was felt by some that the orphanage should be run on secular lines, as not all the children who would populate the orphanage would be of the Catholic faith, but the voices of dissent were over-ridden, probably for reasons more to do with cost than matters of faith. It was, however, written into the constitution of the new Speke Hill Orphanage that no child should be forced to follow the Catholic faith if they held strong beliefs of an opposite faith. Of course, this tended to be easier to say than to execute, as most children of tender years would find it difficult to argue such a point with those in charge of their everyday lives, and so catholic or protestant, the children who first moved into the dormitories of the newly renovated buildings found themselves being taught as though they were all of the Roman Catholic faith. Most of them, being children of the poorer inner city areas and rather wise to such things, tended to take the religious instruction with a pinch of salt, and most people thought at the time that the new orphanage was initially a great success. What many failed to realise at the time was that by allowing Speke Hill to effectively become a closed community, many of the children accommodated in the new orphanage felt as though they were in an environment that almost amounted to being incarcerated in much the same way as the previous inhabitants of the old asylum must have felt.

The well-meaning diocese of the church provided plenty of areas within the grounds for the children's recreational needs, a football pitch and netball court, two separate playground areas containing various implements of play, slides, swings, etc, and the children were allowed out of the grounds on certain days so they could interact with the local population, but those youngsters who were forced to call Speke Hill home found they would never be fully integrated or accepted by those who lived in the surrounding areas along Woolton Road.

And so, life went on at the new orphanage, the old wards gradually being modernised and the large open dormitories eventually becoming partitioned so that groups of four children could have their own shared 'rooms' and a modicum of privacy. The school, taught by well qualified Catholic priests, and at first thought of as providing nothing more than basic education to the children of Speke Hill, surprised everyone by establishing a good reputation for turning out young teenagers with a higher than average standard of education for the time, and even bred a little resentment among the children and parents of some children at other schools in the area.

With the coming of World War Two, things changed at Speke Hill, as they did almost everywhere in the country. Though those in charge attempted to carry on normally, by the time the blitz arrived, with regular bombing of the city of Liverpool, the docks being seen as a prime target by the Luftwaffe, it had become apparent that even one stray bomb, dropped on the buildings of Speke Hill, could result in devastating loss of life, and the children were added to those who would be evacuated out of the cities to temporary homes well out of reach of the Luftwaffe's bombs.

Speke Hill closed temporarily, and didn't reopen its doors, unscathed by the attentions of the Luftwaffe, until after the end of hostilities in 1946. Most of the staff who had worked hard to build the reputation of the orphanage and its school, both ecclesiastical and civilian, in its early days had moved on to other things during the war years, and indeed, many of the children who had been evacuated had reached an age where they were ready to leave school and begin their working lives, and for the most part, Speke Hill was virtually reborn in the post war years with new staff and a mostly new population of poor and needy children from the poorest housing estates of Liverpool.

* * *

The nineteen sixties arrived with little having changed in the running of Speke Hill during the post-war years, apart from the fact that the new Local Education Authority exercised more control over the educational standards required of pupils in the United Kingdom than in pre-war years. As such the school at Speke Hill was overseen in greater detail than before and the priests charged with the children's education were now all required to hold relevant teaching qualifications in the subjects they taught. For the most part the orphanage had grown to be a reasonably happy place for those living there, with educational standards once again rising, and very little trouble caused by those very children who might at one time have been deemed 'troublemakers' if left to roam the streets from whence they originated.

In an effort to add a touch of 'class' to the educational side of things, the teaching staff copied the 'house' system, as used in many secondary schools at the time, to help instil a sense of pride, belonging and competition among the children, and so Molyneux, Norris, Stanley and Sefton, all names historically associated with the city, were chosen by a Diocesan committee as the names for the four Houses of the Speke Hill School.

By the time the 'Swinging Sixties' hit the United Kingdom in general and the city of Liverpool in particular, Speke Hill had expanded its sports facilities to include a second football pitch, a rugby pitch, the netball court remained of course, and the school now boasted an indoor gymnasium, with sport and recreation having been deemed as being good not only for the body, but for the soul as well, by those with responsibility for the youngsters in care in the orphanage.

As Cilla Black's *You're My World* became her second UK number one chart hit at the end of May, 1964, the staff and children of Speke Hill prepared for their forthcoming school sports day with all the usual enthusiasm that went hand-in-hand with a day spent out of the classrooms and buildings of the orphanage. An air of excitement spread through the halls and dorms of the orphanage, and the children felt a slight lessening in the usual strictness of the regime enforced by the priests and nuns who held control over their everyday lives. An extra hour was allowed for all the boys and girls in the communal TV room, a privilege extended to allow a similar additional allowance to radio time, for those lucky enough to possess a transistor radio and the batteries to power it. Only a few lucky children owned such treasures, saved for out of their meagre weekly allowances, pocket money that most would quickly spend in a few days at the local sweet shop or on cheap throwaway toys, perhaps from Woolworths, on rare visits to town, under supervision by an ever watchful priest and nun.

And of course, in case you were wondering, due to its former incarnation as an asylum it was almost inevitable that over the years certain stories of a more fanciful nature began to attach themselves to the orphanage, spread no doubt by boys or girls with lively imaginations and too much time on their hands in their spare time to allow such thoughts to manifest themselves, and so, as with many such institutions, Speke Hill is reputed to possess its very own resident ghost…

CHAPTER 1

HOMECOMING, LIVERPOOL, 2002

Gerald Byrne stood at the ship's railing, his eyes stinging slightly, his hair damp from the salt spray of the voyage across the Irish Sea. He would not, however, have missed the sight of the ferry's arrival in Liverpool for the entire world. As the ship neared the great sea port, the city of his birth, he smiled as the iconic view of the world-famous Liverpool waterfront came into view, dominated by the three majestic buildings that had come to be known as 'The Three Graces'. The Royal Liver Building, The Cunard Building and the Port of Liverpool Building had dominated the Liverpool waterfront for almost a century, defining the city's skyline for locals and visitors alike. The sun was already quite high and played upon the waterfront buildings, making them gleam and reflect almost perfectly in the waters of the River Mersey. Byrne could make out movement on shore as the people of the city went about their daily business, pedestrians, buses and cars clearly visible from his ship-board vantage point as the ferry drew nearer and nearer to Liverpool's ferry port.

The priest sighed as the ship swung towards the ferry terminal, and his view was temporarily obscured by the change in the ferry's orientation. The eight hour crossing had been boring and uneventful, the Irish Sea not too violent in its treatment of the ship and its passengers. Father Byrne had spent most of the trip in one of the aircraft-like seats that P &O Ferries supplied in lieu of cabins on the service, his mind alternating between his reading of the Bible and thoughts of returning to the city of his childhood after so many years.

Life had been good to Gerald Byrne over the years. Born in a back-to-back terraced house on Scotland Road, one of the poorest areas of the city in nineteen fifty four, he and his sister ended up in Speke Hill after their mother died of pneumonia in nineteen sixty-one, their father having died four years earlier, having eventually succumbed to ill health as a result of disease and deprivation suffered during his time as a prisoner-of-war, working on the notorious 'railway of death' in Burma under the brutal regime of the Japanese guards.

Against all odds, young Gerald thrived in his new environment and impressed his teachers and the caring staff at the orphanage with his capacity for learning and exemplary behaviour. He developed a deep interest in theology and the Catholic Church and from an early age, he knew the direction he expected his future to take.

Following his chosen path by living his life in the Roman Catholic Church, he'd left Liverpool in nineteen seventy five, at the age of twenty-one, and following his eventual ordination in Rome, of all places, he'd led a good life, serving the church in various locales around the world, expanding his knowledge of the diverse people and races that went to make up the vast worldwide congregation of Catholicism. Gerald had witnessed life and death in all its forms, having served in war zones, areas of famine relief, and in disease-ridden areas of some of the poorest nations of the world, ministering to the poor and the sick. He'd managed to learn to speak four languages, apart from English, quite fluently, and had learned from his experiences that quite often the rich were in as much spiritual need, if not more in some cases, than the downtrodden masses of the third-world nations so often in the news headlines around the world.

Now at the age of forty-eight, the church had agreed to his request to return to his home town, following a diagnosis of severe unstable angina by his doctor. If anything were to happen to bring him ever closer to his eventual meeting with his maker, Byrne wanted to be in his home city when it occurred. Five feet ten, hair still a dark brown with only a few flecks of grey, Byrne looked far fitter then he really was, his physique built over many years of enjoying various sporting activities.

Having spent five years teaching at a seminary just outside the village of Enniskerry in County Wicklow, Byrne had moved on to become a parish priest once again, and now, his congregation at the small church of St Clement in a small town in County Cork had been upset and saddened to see their priest of these past ten years leave them. Gerald Byrne had become part of the fabric of their lives, a fixture in their religious and devotional faith, and in truth, it saddened him to be leaving them also, but, as he explained to a full church at the end of his final mass at St. Clement's, God, his conscience, and the lure of his home meant it was time to leave, to go back to his roots, and to be at peace with God, with himself and with his past before finally leaving this earthly plane.

Father Byrne found himself jolted out of his reverie by the sound of the ship's hooter as the *Port Erin* swung beam-on to the dockside and crewmen ran to the port side of the ship, where they heaved the thick hawsers over the side to be caught by the dock workers on shore, who proceeded to wrap the ropes around the capstans on the dock, until the ship was made fast and the throbbing of the powerful diesel engines died away, and the vibration of the deck beneath the passengers' feet ceased as the eight hour voyage came to its end. For a few seconds, the silence was palpable until, as if as one, passengers and crew seemed to come to life and there began a mass exodus from the ship, as the city of Liverpool beckoned those on board.

Within a short time, Father Byrne found himself being carried along in a wave of humanity down the gangplank, and he said a silent prayer of thanks as his feet touched the ground on the dockside. He was home again.

Carrying his single suitcase into the ferry terminal building, and wearing his charcoal grey suit, black shirt and white clerical collar, Gerald Byrne's calling was evident to anyone who cared to look at the tall hand-some man with the dark brown hair, only slightly greying at the edges. Within seconds of his arrival in the terminal, a diminutive figure, at least six inches shorter in height, and dressed in similar fashion to the priest, came scurrying up to him, addressing Byrne in a breathless voice as he held out his right hand in greeting.

"You must be Father Byrne," said the new arrival. "Please say you are. I'd hate to be speaking to the wrong priest after being delayed in a traffic jam on the way and then finding hardly a space to park the car."

Gerald Byrne smiled as he shook hands with the little priest, whose words spilled out in a hurry, as though he was recently qualified in speed-speaking.

"I am indeed Father Byrne, have no worries, and you, I presume, are Father Willis?"

"Yes, yes, that's right, Father. David Willis, your Deacon, praise God, and pleased to be so."

Still grinning, Byrne placed a hand on the young priest's shoulder as he spoke again.

"Father Willis, David, if I may?" Willis nodded emphatically. "Good, now David, calm yourself, dear boy. There's no harm done. The Good Lord saw fit to aid you through the traffic jam and the car park just in time to meet me here, without you having to wait for ages and perhaps having to sit and drink some terrible potion masquerading as tea or coffee out of that infernal machine over there."

Willis looked behind him to where Byrne indicated a hot drinks machine, beloved of railway stations, ferry terminals and bus stations the world over

"Well of course, Father Byrne, you're quite correct in that respect. I was just so afraid you'd arrive and there'd be no-one here to meet you and you'd have thought me so terribly remiss."

"So, there's no harm done, now, is there?"

"No, Father, as you say, no harm done at all."

"In which case, I suggest you take a moment to calm yourself and then we'll take a walk to your car and you can drive me to my new church, and my new home, and we can become better acquainted along the way, eh, David?"

"Oh, yes, of course. The car park's not far away and we'll soon have you at St. Luke's, Father."

Byrne placed another steadying hand on Willis's shoulder.

"And tell me, David, do you always speak so quickly, as if the words are likely to go out of fashion if you don't get them out fast enough?"

"Oh dear, that is a rather bad habit of mine, when I'm stressed or nervous. Father O'Hanlon used to say the same thing to me, you know, bless his soul."

"Well, please, David, there's no call for you to be stressed or nervous around me, that's for sure. Did you work under Father O'Hanlon for long?"

"I came to St. Luke's exactly a year ago this month, Father. It was a real shock when poor Father O'Hanlon passed away so suddenly."

"I'm sure it was, David. A heart attack I believe?"

"Yes, indeed it was, Father."

"Well, he's with our Lord in Heaven now, David and it's my job, and yours, to ensure we carry on the Lord's work at St. Luke's, and so, let's go."

David Willis nodded, took up Byrne's suitcase, and led Gerald Byrne to the car park, where the older priest couldn't help but smile as Willis stopped at a rather battered looking Ford Escort, that had obviously seen better days, opened the boot and deposited the suitcase within. The young priest then rushed to open the passenger door for the new parish priest of St. Luke's, Woolton, and within minutes they were clear of the ferry terminal and heading to Byrne's new parish, and new home.

CHAPTER 2

NORRIS GREEN, LIVERPOOL, 3 MONTHS LATER

Detective Inspector Andy Ross pulled the unmarked police Mondeo to a halt, its right side wheels pulled up on the pavement outside St. Matthew's Church in Norris Green in an effort to avoid restricting the traffic flow along Brewer Street. The Norris Green housing estate, built on land donated to the council by the Norris family, was unusual in that the original bequest of the land included the stipulation that no public house be built on the land. To this day, that instruction has been adhered to, meaning residents of Norris Green have to venture further afield to obtain whatever alcoholic stimulation they require.

There were already two police patrol cars parked on the street, together with another pool car identical to his own which he knew would have brought his assistant, Sergeant Clarissa, (Izzie) Drake and Detective Constable Derek McLennan to the scene as well as an ambulance and the green Volvo he recognised as that belonging to Dr. William (Fat Willy, but don't tell him that) Nugent, the overly rotund but eminently brilliant pathologist who served as the city's senior medical examiner. Blue and white police crime scene tape had already been strategically placed across the wide double gated entrance to the churchyard, with an attendant uniformed constable on guard to prevent unwanted sightseers trying to gatecrash the crime scene.

Ross silently cursed the court case that had demanded his appearance at nine a.m that morning. The trial of a serial mugger who had almost killed his twelfth and last victim before being almost comically apprehended by the off-duty Andy Ross had been suddenly curtailed when the accused changed his plea from not-guilty to guilty, thus relieving Ross of the need to hang around the court building waiting to give evidence. As soon as he exited the court and turned on his mobile phone, Ross received word of the 'incident' involving a body being discovered in St. Matthew's churchyard from his squad's collator, D.C Paul Ferris. The fact that he would now probably be the last to arrive on the scene did little to improve his humour after what he considered a wasted and fruitless start to his day.

Luckily for him, the uniformed constable on duty at the gates recognised the detective inspector and with a brief, "Good morning, sir," waved Ross through after lifting the crime scene tape for the detective to pass beneath. Ross had no need to ask the constable where to go. He simply followed his nose along the path that led around the church itself, in the direction of the noise of voices and activity in the graveyard that stood to the rear of the church.

As he neared the scene, Ross could see Dr. Nugent on his knees, his assistant, Francis Lees beside him, both men obviously intent on carrying out their initial examination of the body of the unfortunate victim. Sergeant Drake and Constable McLennan were in attendance, standing just behind the doctor and Lees, while three uniformed constables stood further back from the scene, each man bearing what Ross could only describe as a disturbed look upon their faces.

Seeing him drawing near, Izzie Drake broke away from her position and walked briskly towards him.

"Morning, sir. I'm afraid we've got a bad one today."

"Hmm, well, there are never any good ones when it comes to murder, are there, Sergeant?"

"I know sir, I'm sorry, I just meant..."

"Forget it, Izzie. My apologies. I'm just in a foul temper after wasting my time at the damn court this morning."

"I know, sir. Ferris told me when he called to let me know you were on the way. Damn shame, wasting your time like that, but, at least Phillip Downes won't be troubling the courts again for a few years after he's sentenced."

"Very true," Ross replied. "Now, come on, what have we got here?"

"It's bloody gruesome, sir, and that's the truth. Poor Derek threw up almost as soon as we got here, as well as one of the uniformed lads. Bet they both wish they hadn't eaten a hearty breakfast this morning. Come on, sir, best you see for yourself."

Ross nodded and the two detectives walked slowly towards the location of the body that had necessitated the appearance of the Murder Investigation Team at the scene.

Sensing their approach, William Nugent turned and looked up from his kneeling position as he greeted Ross in his variable Glaswegian accent. Ross always thought of the word 'variable' when it came to Nugent's speech as the more upset or irate he became, the more guttural and broad his accent became, even after spending most of his working life in the city of Liverpool.

"A late start this morning, eh, Detective Inspector?" he chided, though Ross knew the pathologist would have been made well aware of the circumstances surrounding his delay in attending the death scene. Ignoring Nugent's obvious attempt at a witty remark, Ross replied, in a total business-like tone.

"Yes, indeed, Doctor. I take it you've been here long enough to carry out at least a cursory examination of the victim?"

"Aye, well, you could say that, I suppose. Ye'd best come and take a look for yourself, but I'm warning ye, it's not a pretty site. Francis, please step away and allow the Inspector and the Sergeant to get a good look at the poor soul, would ye?" he said to his tall, thin assistant, whom many of Ross's team though of as being almost as cadaverous in his appearance as some of the bodies they were forced to deal with in the commission of their jobs.

"Oh, my God," Ross exclaimed as he drew closer to the scene, Drake slightly behind and to the side of him.

"I told you, sir," his sergeant said, quietly.

"Yes, but this…this is, well, nothing short of bloody monstrous. What the hell happened to the poor bastard?"

William Nugent spoke up in reply from behind the inspector.

"Well, at first glance," he spoke almost reverently, "the victim, a man I'd put in his mid-to late fifties by the way, has been almost totally eviscerated. As you can see, the poor sod's intestines have been removed and draped across the headstone of the grave on which his body lies, and his other major organs, liver, kidneys, spleen and heart are neatly arranged around the body, almost as though the killer had laid them out for us in readiness for a post-mortem examination. But, and if you look closely, you'll see the worst part of all this, Inspector, your killer removed the victim's penis, and then stuffed it down the poor bugger's throat. Oh yes, one more thing, he also removed the victim's tongue, though I cannae find it anywhere up to this point in time. The killer may have taken it with him, a trophy of his handiwork, perhaps. Of course, that's more in your pervue than mine, I'm simply surmising."

Ross couldn't help himself. He visibly gagged as he took in the blood-drenched scene that lay before him. The naked body of the unfortunate victim lay across the gravelled top of a grave, and as Nugent had indicated, the intestines had been draped across the headstone that stood at the head of the grave, the internal organs dripping blood as they lay in the gradually warming sunshine around the sides of the grave. From what he could make out, the look on the dead man's face was one of total fear and horror.

Ross gulped hard, and turned his face from the scene. Hardened detective he may have been, but this definitely was 'a bad one', as Izzie Drake had called it, and he was hardly surprised that the uniformed constable and his own detective constable had felt the urge to be sick at the sight that they'd stumbled onto when they'd arrived at the scene.

"Tell me Doctor, can you say whether these…er, these mutilations were carried out while the victim was alive or dead, and what may have been the actual cause of death? I know that sounds stupid, but would one particular injury the victim sustained have been enough to cause death, or was this a prolonged and sadistic attack by some kind of pervert, perhaps?"

"Ah wish I could tell ye, Inspector, but, it's too early for me to say and you know I dinna like to speculate on these matters. We'll have to wait until we get what's left of yon laddie to the morgue and I can carry out a detailed examination. For now, I think we can say without much doubt that the cause of death was exsanguination, though which wound, or wounds were the fatal blow, well, I just cannae say."

"Any identification, his clothes, any personal items, were they found?"

"Not a thing," Nugent replied. "As far as I can tell, he was left here naked as he is now. Whoever did this, and he's a sadistic bastard I can tell you for free, made sure he took the poor man's clothes and any identification he was carrying with him when he dumped the poor sod here."

"Thank you Doc," said Ross, turning to his sergeant who was by now visibly pale at being in close proximity to the remains of the victim for so long.

"Who found him, Izzie?"

"The poor bloody priest, Father Michael Donovan. He entered the churchyard through the rear gate and was making his way along the path towards the church when he almost literally stumbled over the body. Apparently, he threw up too, over there."

Izzie pointed to a grave two places along from where the victim lay. At least the priest hadn't contaminated the crime scene.

"I'm not surprised," Ross grimaced. "And where is the good Father now, may I ask?"

"Last seen in his church, praying as though his life depended upon it, sir"

"Right then, let's go and have a word with Father Donovan."

* * *

"Terrible, simply terrible, that poor, poor man," Father Donovan wept openly, his head in his hands as he sat in one of the pews at the front of his church, five minutes later, speaking to Ross and Drake who sat either side of the visibly shaking priest.

"It must have been an awful shock for you, Father," said Ross, sympathetically.

"It was indeed, Detective Inspector. I mean, there I was, enjoying this beautiful sunny morning, whistling to myself, *All Things Bright and Beautiful* of all things, and then, all of a sudden he was there, lying on that grave, virtually in pieces, I tell you, in pieces."

Izzie Drake placed a comforting hand on the priest's right arm in an effort to calm him.

"Father, you need to calm down a little," she said, quietly.

"Just take your time and try to recall everything that happened as you walked along the path from the time you passed through the gate until the moment you found the victim."

"Please, Father, it's very important," Ross added, grateful to his sergeant for using her feminine compassion to reach out to the shaking priest.

Michael Donovan took a couple of deep breaths, closing his eyes as he attempted to compose himself and recall the terrible events of earlier that morning. Finally, opening his eyes, he spoke in a faltering voice.

"Well, Inspector, it was just after eight o'clock. I'm sure of the time because I always leave the manse which is just behind the church, at eight precisely. I like to come to church when it's peaceful and quiet and pray for a while in solitude. I hold a morning mass at nine, you see, and, oh, it was just awful seeing your officers turning my parishioners away as they arrived for the service," he rambled for a moment.

"It's alright, Father. I know you're in shock, so just take your time. Now, it was just gone eight o'clock, you say?"

The priest gathered himself together again and went on with his statement.

"The sun was shining and it was already quite warm. I heard a black-bird singing and looked up and saw him perched on the wall that runs along the north side of the churchyard. I remember smiling to my self and began whistling the tune of *All things bright and beautiful*. I didn't stop to watch the bird as I wanted those few precious minutes of contemplative prayer to myself, you see."

Ross nodded but didn't interrupt.

"The path winds its way around the church as you've probably seen, in a sort of S pattern, I suppose you'd call it and as I came round the corner of the church onto the straightish part of the path that leads to the main doors, I saw something ahead of me on one of the graves. At first I thought it might be the work of vandals, the Lord knows we get enough of that sort of thing round here, or maybe someone had dumped a load of old rubbish on the grave, in an act of blatant sacrilege. I slowed down as I got closer and it was then, when I was just a couple of yards away that I realised what I was seeing. I know it sounds stupid, but the first thing I did was wonder if I might be of some help to the man but when I got even closer I saw the terrible, monstrous things that had been done to him and

I'm ashamed to say I…I…well, I'd just finished breakfast before I came out, you see, and I couldn't help myself. I staggered over to one of the adjacent graves and was awfully sick, I'm afraid. I've never in all my life seen anything like it, you see, and I pray to God I'll never see the likes again as long as I live."

"You've nothing to apologise for, Father," said Ross. "Two experienced police officers have been sick out there as well. We're all human and none of us should ever have to see such things."

"But sadly, you do, don't you Inspector Ross?"

Ross nodded, but still remained silent, allowing the priest to speak and hopefully recall any small details he may have noticed when he discovered the body.

"There was blood everywhere, Inspector, so much blood. And then, I saw the other things, you know the, the…"

"It's alright, Father, I know what you saw, but tell me, from the time you entered the churchyard until you found the victim, did you see or hear anything else, or any other people, perhaps?"

"Not a soul, no. To be honest, if there had been anyone lurking around, I might not have seen them. I was so focussed on the sunny morning and the birdsong. But I'm still pretty certain there was nobody else around."

"Now, and perhaps most importantly, I know you probably only got a quick look at the victim, Father, but did you recognise him? Is he known to you at all, either as a parishioner or maybe just someone you've seen in the area at all?"

"Yes, it was only a quick look, Inspector. Nobody could possibly have stood staring at that poor man, but I saw enough to know he wasn't anyone I know. I'm sorry. I can't help you there."

Father Donovan's face paled again at the thought of the sight he'd witnessed in his churchyard and he fell silent for a few seconds. Izzie Drake spoke in her quiet voice again.

"I know this is pretty much a rhetorical question, Father, but we have to ask…er, you didn't touch anything at all before calling the police did you?"

Donovan looked aghast at the mere thought of having done so as he replied.

"Sergeant, I most certainly did not. What kind of man do you think I am? A person would have to be very sick in the head to want to mess around with what I saw out there. I simply tried to compose myself and then ran as fast as I could into the church where I rang 999 from my little office in there. Then I waited at the church gates for the police to arrive and to keep anyone from entering the grounds until your people got here."

"And a very good thing you did, Father," said Ross. "It wouldn't have done for anyone else to come wandering in and be confronted with the sight of the poor man out there."

There being little else the priest could tell them, the two detectives left the church, with Father Donovan again on his knees praying before the altar, and moved back into the daylight, where by now the forensic experts of the Crime Scenes Unit had arrived and were busy searching and examining the crime scene and surrounding area.

Ross spoke briefly with Constables Knight and Riley, the first officers to respond to the emergency call, who confirmed they'd arrived on the scene, assessed the situation and immediately called for C.I.D. assistance, and a second squad car of officers to help secure the area, realising the gravity of the situation they'd found. Ross commended both men and then returned to speak to William Nugent, who, together with his assistant, Lees, was packing up his instruments and accoutrements as the body and associated parts were being carefully loaded into a body bag ready for transportation to the morgue, having been fingerprinted where it lay in the hope of identifying the victim, and once at the morgue, he'd carry out a full post-mortem in an effort to determine exactly what had happened to the deceased.

"Anything else to report, Doc?" Ross asked as he drew closer to the pathologist.

"Nothing that I can tell you at present, Inspector. Ye'll get ma full report as soon as possible, like always. Let me get back to the mortuary with the poor man and I can get on with ma job."

There was that strange and for some, disconcerting comingling of accents again, part Glaswegian, part Liverpudlian, that always rather amused Ross.

"A preliminary report will suffice for now, Doc, as soon as you can. This case is likely to generate some nasty headlines if the press gets hold of it, so I'd like to move as fast as I can to find the sick bastard who did this."

"Aye, well, I'll give you a call later today, if I can, and if you and your sergeant care to come along in the morning, I'll schedule the full post mortem examination for nine a.m. if that'll suit you, Inspector?"

"Perfect, thank you Doc." Ross replied, standing aside to let the Doctor and his assistant pass. Ross next spent five minutes talking to Miles Booker, the senior Crime Scenes Officer who was leading the examination of the area around the body. Booker would ensure his team combed every blade of overgrown grass, every sliver of granite chips, every nook or cranny where a minute piece of trace evidence might have been deposited. As he broke away from Booker, Detective Constable McLennan walked up to Ross. McLennan shared the same post-vomiting complexion as the uniformed constable and Father Donovan.

"You alright, Derek?" asked Ross.

"Yes, thank you sir," McLennan replied. "It was just a bit more then my stomach could stand, seeing what the killer did to that poor man."

"No need to apologise, Derek. We're all human, after all. None of us should have to see things like that. Sadly, it's our job when some bastard decides to make a mess of someone in that way. Now, do you have anything for me, anything we can use?"

"Not really, sir. I've spoken at length to the two constables who were the first attenders. They're both adamant there was no one around in the churchyard when they arrived, and neither of them saw anyone acting furtively or suspicious out on the streets as they arrived in response to the emergency call from Father Donovan."

"Alright Derek, Sergeant Drake and I will be heading back to head-quarters soon. I'll arrange for Sam to join you out here in a minute. Then I want the two of you to take charge of the scene, until the crime scene boys have done their thing, and then, make a quick sweep of the area, talk to some of the nearest residents in the hope someone may have seen or heard something. I'm going to organise a team of uniforms to carry out a house to house inquiry in a half-mile radius of the church, but something tells me we're going to come up empty handed. And, Derek?"

"Sir?"

"Get one of those constables at the gate to arrange to seal off the back gate too. We're lucky nobody's blundered through there so far."

"Right, sir. I'll get on it right away."

As they spoke, Miles Booker walked up to the detectives with a small cellophane evidence bag in his hand.

"Got something for me, Miles? Ross asked.

"Not sure," said the Crime Scene Investigator. "One of my lads came up with this," and he held the bag up, close enough for Ross and Drake to see a small silver coloured key inside.

"A key," said Drake.

"Hey, ten out of ten, Sergeant," Booker grinned.

"But a key to what?" Drake persisted, "and how do we know it belonged to the victim?"

"That's just it, you see," said the C.S.I. "We don't, at least not yet. Maybe, once we have his fingerprints, we may get lucky and find they match the print we found on the key." He smiled.

"Ah, so you do have a print?" Ross asked.

"Yes, and a pretty good one, looks like most of a thumb print, you know, from when someone held the key to insert it into a lock."

"Looks like the sort of key that fits a safety deposit box, or maybe an airport or railway left luggage locker," said Drake.

"Can I see it, please?" asked Derek McLennan. Booker passed the bag containing the key to the detective constable who scrutinised it carefully for a few seconds before passing it back to him.

"Sir," said McLennan, turning to Ross, "I think we'll find that it is a locker key but not for a left luggage locker at the airport or from a station."

"Alright Derek, let's have it. What's your theory?"

"I think it's from the Halewood Plant, sir."

"The car factory? What makes you think that?"

"Well sir, the cellophane makes it hard to see, but there are a series of four numbers on one side of the key. My brother-in-law works at Halewood, sir and he has a key just like that on his car key ring. The anglar shape is quite distinctive. I've seen it when he's let me use his car once or twice. The way the numbers are etched into the key looks just like this one."

"So, we may have a clue after all. Well done, young Derek," said Ross.

"Thanks, sir," McLennan replied.

"Yes, well, that's assuming the key belonged to the victim, isn't it?" said Miles Booker.

"Very true, Miles," Ross agreed. "Any way you can tell us more that might help?"

"Sorry, Andy, not a thing. If the fingerprint matches your man over there, okay; if not, you're going to be hard pressed to discover if it belonged to him or not."

"We can show his photo to employees at Halewood, see if anyone recognises him," said Izzie Drake.

"Yes, well, bearing in mind what he's got stuffed in his mouth, I wish you luck with that one."

"I'm sure Doctor Nugent can make him look presentable enough for us to get a photo likeness we can show around," Drake responded.

"Of course, just me joking around, Sergeant."

"Could be easier than that, sir, Sarge," McLennan interjected again.

"How's that, then Derek?" asked Drake.

"The numbers on the key," he replied. If it is from Halewood, they'll refer to a specific numbered locker, and that locker will be allocated to an equally specific employee. Simple logic really."

"Yes, of course, well done Derek," said Ross.

Andy Ross had learned to come to rely on young Derek McLennan in the three years he'd served with him. The young man had developed from a hesitant, awkward young D.C. into a clever, confident and reliable member of Ross's team, with a quick mind and an even temperament when working under pressure, not a bad thing when faced with some of the cases the team was called upon to handle. Ross recalled the first major case the young detective had worked on with him, when the skeleton of a long time dead pop guitarist had surfaced in the mud of an old dried up dock in the city, sparking one of Ross's strangest and perhaps most tragic cases to date, which resulted in the ultimate suicide of a woman who'd spent over thirty years of her life officially listed as 'missing'. That case had been the foundation on which Derek McLennan had gradually forged his career and now, Ross knew he could rely on the man's intuitive skills as well as his quick, intelligent mind.

Ross and Drake left soon afterwards, and made their way to the city mortuary, where they knew William Nugent would by now be carrying out an initial examination of the victim's remains. Ross had questions that needed answers and for the moment the only man who could help him was the rather obese but professionally superb pathologist.

CHAPTER 3

SPEKE HILL ORPHANAGE, WOOLTON

Charles Hopkirk, Senior Child-Care Officer in charge of the latter-day orphanage rose from his leather chair and stepped out from behind his desk to greet the newcomer to his office. Five feet nine, already turned grey, and with a slight stoop as he stood, Hopkirk looked every bit as worn down as his slightly crumpled dark blue suit with its shiny elbows, and his black shoes with attendant scuff marks, betrayed the lack of a Mrs. Hopkirk. No one would believe a good wife would allow her husband to leave home each day looking quite so dishevelled. Doing his best to look the opposite of his actual appearance and putting on an air of assumed authority, he held his hand out as he spoke and shook hands with his visitor.

"Father Byrne, welcome to Speke Hill. We're delighted to have you here as our new chaplain to the pupils."

"It's a pleasure, Mr. Hopkirk, I assure you, and you must call me Gerald, please, unless we're in formal circumstances, of course."

"Well in that case, you must call me Charles. I insist. And, it seems rather appropriate to have you here as part of our community, don't you agree?"

"It does?"

"Oh come now, you must know we'd soon find out you were once one of our boys here at Speke Hill, and to have you return as the Parish Priest at St. Luke's and our chaplain here is wonderful, a great example to hold up before the children."

"I wouldn't go so far as to say that, Charles. It's a tradition that the priest at St. Luke's takes the role of chaplain here at Speke Hill, and yes, I may have been an orphan myself, raised here, as you say, but I wouldn't want to be held up as an example of something I'm not. Not everyone at Speke Hill aspires to grow up to be a Roman Catholic Priest."

"You're too modest, Father, er, sorry, Gerald, I'm sure, but let's not dwell on it. I imagine you'd like a quick tour? Many things have changed since the days when the Catholic Church ran the place. Now that Liverpool Council, together with the Local Education Authority have control over Speke Hill, there've been many improvements and changes to the place, as you'll see."

"And some things never change, eh, Charles?"

"I'm sorry?"

"The entrance gates and the driveway, with those rowan trees and elms lining the gravel drive. It still gives the false impression of arriving at some old Victoria country mansion. It was just the same when I was a boy here"

"Oh, I see," said Hopkirk, who'd wondered for a moment just where Father Byrne was heading with his previous remark.

"Yes, I suppose like the original incumbents of Speke Hill, those in authority long ago decided to maintain the sweeping curve of the driveway and the grandly ornate gates at the entrance. It does after all give the place a touch of the grandiose, don't you think? Nice for those who live here, Father, I think. Not just some grey concrete monstrosity in the middle of an inner city sink estate. At least the boys and girls who live here and are schooled here can feel proud of the place, which does of course, have an excellent academic record and a long list of former pupils at the school who have gone on to achieve good things in life. Rather like yourself, Father Byrne."

"Yes, well thank you, Charles, and please, my name, again is Gerald. I did well, as have quite a few former orphans and pupils from here. It's a pleasure to be able to come back and perhaps contribute a little to the spiritual welfare of the boys and girls."

"I looked you up, Gerald," said Hopkirk, looking pleased with himself.

"Did you now?" asked the priest. "And just what did you discover, I wonder?"

"Only that you arrived here, together with your ten year old sister, Angela, as a seven year old after your mother died, in nineteen sixty-one, with no other relatives left to look after you. Your father had died a few years earlier, finally succumbing to illness following years of ill treatment during the war in a Japanese Prisoner-of-War Camp and the two of you then lived in the orphanage and attended the church school here until you were both old enough to leave and make your way in the world. One particular note on your records really stood out, Gerald."

"And what, I wonder, would that be?"

"Well, it was two things really. It said you were an outstanding sportsman, having represented the school, and Stanley House, at football, rugby and cricket, and that you also, even then, possessed a strong sense of spirituality, and had professed your intention of entering the priesthood as soon as you were old enough. It's nice to know you were successful in your ambition, Gerald."

"Thank you, Charles. My life has indeed been one of enrichment and service to God, and I'm happy to be home again after so many years away."

"And your sister, Angela? How has she fared in the big wide world since leaving us?"

A cloud momentarily seemed to pass before the priest's eyes and his shoulders appeared to droop as his demeanour changed for a few seconds, until he pulled himself together before replying.

"I'm afraid Angela died at a young age, Charles. I'd prefer it if we don't discuss the details. It was a painful time for me and remains so to this day."

A look of genuine concern appeared on Charles Hopkirk's face. He'd looked up the original records of their new priest as soon as he'd heard that he was an 'old boy' of Speke Hill. Those records showed his sister Angela to have been a resident of the orphanage at the same time as Gerald Byrne, but obviously, those records ended when each of the children reached the age of maturity and passed out of the local council's care. He now felt he may have committed something of a 'faux pas' in mentioning what was obviously a painful subject for the priest.

"I'm so sorry, Father Byrne," he said, returning to a veneer of formality. "I didn't mean to upset you."

"It's okay, Charles, really. It's just that it all happened a long time ago and isn't something I care to talk about any more. My sister dwells with the Lord now, and I'd like to leave it at that, and, my name is Gerald, remember?"

Byrne smiled now, and Charles Hopkirk felt an instant forgiveness in that smile. Here indeed, he thought, is a good man.

"Right, well, I suppose you'd like to take a brief look around the old place eh?"

"That would be nice, thank you."

"I hope you won't mind, Gerald, but, knowing you were coming today, I asked one of our teachers to give you a guided tour of the modern version of Speke Hill. A lot of things have changed since you were here, as I've said, but many things are still the same. It just so happens that we have another 'old boy' on our staff at the senior school, another lad from your own age group during your time here. You might remember Mark Proctor?"

Byrne's face almost betrayed an emotion he wouldn't have wanted the senior care officer to witness at the mention of Proctor's name. Mark Proctor, who the other children back then used to call 'Garibaldi' due to his lack of hair, even at such a tender age, had never been a particular friend to

Gerald Byrne, who recalled him as something of a bully, always picking on those younger or smaller than himself and unable to defend themselves against his aggressive tendencies. He'd always felt that Mr. Pugh, the senior housemaster for Stanley House knew just what Proctor was like, but could never actually catch him in the act of bullying, so had tried to channel some of his aggression into boxing training, a sport at which Proctor excelled and in due course won a number of trophies for the school in local competitions. Byrne doubted very much that boxing would feature on the modern day sports curriculum, far too violent for today's passive and non-confrontational educational system. Keeping his dislike of the man, well, in fact the boy he'd known decades earlier, hidden for now, he replied politely to Hopkirk's minor bombshell of information.

"Mark Proctor? Yes, I do kind of remember the boy, Charles. What subject is he teaching?"

"Physical Education."

"That makes sense. Proctor the boy was always involved in all things physical."

Byrne tried hard not to let the sarcasm of his words transmit themselves to Hopkirk, who barely seemed to register the priest's reply as a knock on the door heralded the arrival of the former bully, now respected teacher of P.E at Speke Hill, and Byrne's thoughts turned to buried memories.

CHAPTER 4

MORTUARY MATTERS

Andy Ross exited the car, leaving Izzie Drake to lock up and he was first to the entrance to the mortuary building. He'd just pressed the intercom button as Drake arrived at his side, and a familiar voice came through the little box on the wall.

"Please identify yourself and state your business today."

"Peter, it's D.I. Ross and Sergeant Drake. Dr. Nugent is expecting us."

"Ah, hello Inspector. You know the routine, please come in."

The speaker pressed a button inside the building and Ross waited until he heard a 'click' and then pushed and the door swung open to admit the detectives. Ross and Drake soon arrived at the office, (Ross thought it more of a cubicle really, but politeness precluded him mentioning it), where Peter Foster, the senior mortuary receptionist was seated behind a small desk, protected by plate glass. A circular speaking outlet allowed visitors to speak through the glass, and a small slot at the bottom allowed Foster to pass the appropriate 'Visitor' badges to those authorised to progress into the main mortuary building. Ross could clearly remember when a younger Peter Foster had first begun working here, just before a complex case relating to the long deceased singer, Brendan Kane had reared its head some three years earlier. Foster had become a real asset to the department and had been promoted to the senior position some months earlier, much to the delight of Izzie Drake, who Ross had been surprised to discover had been dating the younger man for a few months by then.

"Good morning, Inspector, Izzie," Foster said as the detectives smiled in greeting.

"Everything okay, Peter?" Ross asked.

"Fine, thanks," Foster replied.

"Hello, Peter," said Izzie Drake,

"You're looking good, Izzie," he replied.

"Considering what we've seen this morning, I'll assume you're being very nice to me, Peter. I feel like shit after being in that churchyard."

"Oh well, you know me. I know nothing about the cases when they first come in so I have to assume it was a bad one?"

"Very bad, Peter," Ross interrupted, "and if you two lovebirds don't mind, I'd rather we didn't keep Dr. Nugent waiting while you discuss my sergeant's appearance."

"Oh God, yeah, sorry, Inspector, he's in Autopsy One," a flustered Peter Foster responded, pushing two visitor badges through the slot at the base of the window and pressing the entry button that allowed the detectives into the main corridor. Ross grinned at the man, who smiled sheepishly back at him. Ross still found it strange that his sergeant had found herself attracted to the younger man, though only by a couple of years, and he'd been surprised when she'd told him in his office one day that she'd met Foster in a pub one night, quite accidentally, and that they'd shared a drink or two and found they shared a number of common interests. Soon after, they'd begun dating on a regular basis and six months down the line, it seemed the couple were growing closer with the passage of time. Ross was pleased for Izzie who'd always seemed to be beset by bad luck in her personal relationships in the past. Perhaps Peter Foster might be her 'Mr. Right' at last.

Izzie blew Foster a kiss as she and Ross disappeared along the corridor, and a minute later they found themselves in Autopsy Room Number One, in the company of William Nugent and his assistant, the ever-present Francis Lees.

* * *

The cadaver on the stainless steel autopsy table bore little resemblance to the living, breathing human being he had been up until a few short hours ago. By the time Ross and Drake had arrived, Dr. Nugent had already made a start, the customary Y incision not really necessary after the killer had virtually opened up the entire upper torso of the victim and he and Lees had clearly been hard at work on the remains of the as yet unidentified victim.

"Ah, Inspector Ross and Sergeant Drake, welcome. As ye can see, Mr. Lees and I have made a start without you. I thought you'd appreciate not having to watch the really grisly parts, as usual."

The pathologist had a wry and at times wicked sense of humour. He'd long ago learned of Ross's aversion to the procedures of a post-mortem examination and he loved to occasionally wind-up the inspector a little. It was all part of a strange but mutual admiration that existed between the doctor and the policeman; not quite friends, but respected colleagues would be an apt description.

"Your thoughtfulness is amazing, Doc," said Ross, a smile on his face. "Anything to tell me yet?"

"Quite a bit to tell the truth, Inspector. Look here," he indicated the deceased's throat, and now, with the blood washed away, it was clear to Ross and Drake that the killer had not only cut the throat of the victim but had done it so viciously that the cut had almost gone through to the man's spinal cord.

"Bloody hell, sir," Drake exclaimed.

"Bloody hell indeed, Sergeant," Ross agreed.

"Cause of death, I presume, Doc?"

"In all likelihood, yes," Nugent replied. "However, I have to admit that with the massive amount of 'work' your killer has carried out on this poor soul, any of the wounds to his lower abdomen could have led to death from shock and blood loss. If I had to hazard an informed opinion though, I'd say he cut the victim's throat first and then swiftly got to work on the evisceration of the body."

"I thought the heart stopped pumping blood at the moment of death, Doctor," said Drake. "So why was there so much blood at the scene if the first cut to the throat led to the man's death?"

"Quite simply, ma dear girl, because the killer didn't just stab or inflict wounds on the body he literally cut the man open, gutting him, to all intents and purposes, so all the blood contained in the abdomen and chest cavity simply flowed out onto the ground around the body. You and the inspector have attended enough autopsies here to know how much blood leaks from a body when cut open, hence the channels in the tables here for the blood to drain from. Don't forget, he also cut out virtually every major organ from the torso too, leading to even more blood being dumped rather than bleeding out onto the ground."

"Yes, of course, sorry Doctor. I should have known that."

"Don't you go beating yourself up about it, Sergeant. You had a real shock seeing that murder site this morning. Police officer or not, it had to have an effect on you, so it's no surprise if you're nae thinking straight right now."

Drake nodded her thanks to the pathologist, though inwardly cursing herself. She'd seen enough bodies and attended enough post-mortems over the years and she really did think she should have been a little more 'on the ball' over the subject of the blood loss. It was Ross's turn to question Nugent.

"Doc, the other, er…mutilations? Can you tell us if they were carried out using the same weapon as the killer used on the man's throat? If not, we have to assume our killer used more than one weapon and as yet, we haven't located any weapons at or near the graveyard. I'm presuming at this stage that the murderer took the weapons away with him."

William Nugent, used to seeing some of the worst that man can inflict on his fellow being over his many years as a pathologist, shook his head slowly before replying to Ross's question. He looked across the room to where his assistant, Francis Lees, was busily weighing the various organs removed from the victim by the killer, before placing them in sealed jars of preservative.

"Francis," Nugent said, and Lees turned and waited for his boss to speak again. Bring me your clipboard will you, please?"

Lees nodded, and stepped across the room and handed the clipboard, containing various sheets of paper, including the notes he was making on the victim's organs, to the senior pathologist, who flicked Lees' notes over until he arrived at what he was looking for.

"Right, Inspector," he began, "all I can say is that whoever perpetrated this damnable atrocity on the victim certainly wasn't medically trained. The poor man was systematically hacked open by what I estimate to be an extremely sharp blade of around nine to ten inches in length, almost certainly the same implement used to cut the poor man's throat. There are enough tell-tale signs on the body to show where he literally chopped at the torso in order to open the man up, almost using the blade like a saw, but, without a serrated blade, it got very messy. Look at the abdomen."

Ross and Drake leaned over to see what Nugent was indicating.

"See, the flesh is hanging in shards around the cuts, and from the depth of penetration, I think you can assume great rage existed within the mind of your killer. There was no need to go as deep as he did to reach the organs, which were then almost chopped out of the body cavity."

"Sounds as if this was very personal Doc."

"Aye, well, that's for you and your people to determine, I'm pleased to say. My job is simply to tell you what killed the poor chap and I still have to determine that for certain."

Izzie Drake rejoined the conversation.

"But, I thought you said the wound to the throat…"

"Aye, Sergeant, but I did qualify that statement by adding the words, 'in all probability' ye may recall."

"So you're not certain?"

"Look, detectives, with the massive amount of damage the killer inflicted on this poor man, it's safe to say that any one of the wounds inflicted on the body could have been fatal, but in my opinion, I am leaning towards the belief that it would have been easier for the killer to ensure the man was dead by slitting his throat first before carrying out his series of atrocities upon the body."

"So you don't think the poor sod was alive while he was being disembowelled?" Ross asked.

"Correct, Inspector," said Nugent, who then hesitated before going on, "but, there is a possibility that one of the injuries was inflicted antemortem."

Ross had a feeling he knew what the pathologist was about to say, and he felt a sinking feeling in his stomach as he waited for Nugent to continue.

"With the amount of trauma, and copious blood loss in the genital region, I have to hypothesise that your killer removed the victim's penis while he was still alive."

"Oh, God," said Drake,

"That's fucking sick," Ross added.

"Indeed it is," Nugent agreed, "but it is highly likely."

"And that would almost certainly confirm a highly personal motive," said Ross.

"Aye well, that's your job to determine, not mine, as I said," Nugent replied, "but one thing's pretty certain. You are, without doubt, seeking an individual filled with severe rage and also with sufficient strength to have somehow overpowered and subdued the victim in order to carry out this heinous attack."

"Would he have placed it, his, penis I mean, in the mouth before or after killing the man?" Drake asked.

"I cannae be sure, Sergeant, but I'd say after if you wanted to pin me down. The way it was located so far down the throat, I doubt he'd have managed that with a living, struggling victim, as this poor bugger must have been doing at the time."

"Right, I see. Thanks, Doc. I think we'll leave you to conclude your examination in peace," said Ross. "If you find anything else you think may be helpful…"

"I'll let you know, right away, Inspector, as always. Hopefully, that clever young detective of yours at headquarters may have a name for you by the time you get back."

"You mean D.C. Ferris?"

"Yes, that's him. I had Mr. Lees here send a copy of the victim's fingerprints over there as soon as we'd taken them. I remembered the detective constable was your team's collator and you'd be anxious to try and make a rapid identification, so yes, he has them and if the victim is in the system, you may have a name for him very soon."

"That's great, Doc, thanks" said Ross as he and Drake prepared to head back to police headquarters. Ross wouldn't wait to get back before contacting Ferris though. Once outside the building, he'd turn his phone on again and call Paul Ferris to ascertain what, if any progress he'd made with the fingerprints.

"I'll be in touch if I find anything else of interest," Nugent called, as the two detectives were just about to exit the autopsy room, adding, as Ross's hand closed on the handle to open the door, "Oh yes, and how's your love life, Sergeant Drake?"

Izzie Drake blushed; having been unaware that word of her relationship with Peter Foster had reached the ears of the city's chief pathologist"

"It's, erm, it's fine. Thank you, Doctor," she said, quietly.

"Aye well, I'm glad to hear it. Just go gentle on my poor receptionist, you hear me, Sergeant"

Nugent had a grin like a Cheshire cat on his face, enjoying his small moment of managing to embarrass Izzie in such a jocular way.

"Goodbye, Doctor," she said, as she and Ross exited the room, her boss also grinning at her momentary discomfiture.

CHAPTER 5

MEMORIES

In the few seconds it took for the door to Charles Hopkirk's office to open, admitting Mark Proctor, Gerald Byrne experienced one of those strange, almost out-of-body experiences, whereby his memory took him back in time and an entire scene seemed to play out in his mind, a reminder of one particular episode from his youth.

The sun was shining, and an air of excitement permeated every dormitory and school classroom of Speke Hill. As was the custom, classes had been suspended and all thoughts, of both pupils/residents and staff turned to the afternoon's events. Sports Day had arrived and each House wanted to emerge victorious from the proceedings. The winning House Captain would then assume the honour of receiving the 'Bishops Cup,' a beautiful engraved silver trophy awarded each year to the victorious House.

The morning had begun like any other, with breakfast, followed by prayers in the school chapel. Prayers over, normal routine was suspended as everyone returned to their dormitories to prepare for the big event. One of the responsibilities of the senior girls in the school was to make sure all sports kit was clean and ironed. All pupils had chores to perform, from juniors to seniors, and this was one of the tasks never allotted to junior school members due to the dangers of using a hot iron. In fact, the words 'senior' and 'junior' were rarely used at Speke Hill as the younger children attended what was termed the 'lower' school and seniors the 'upper' school. So they became 'lowers' and 'uppers' within the terminology of the school.

Gerald Byrne made sure his kit was ready for use. His shirt, like all the sports shirts at the school was reversible. The fronts of the shirts were green with cream coloured collars and cuffs, while the reverse side was the same green with a large, broad hoop across the chest area in the various house colours, yellow for Molyneux, red for Norris, blue for Stanley and white for Sefton.

Most of the boys thought the shirts would make people think they were playing for Liverpool Corporation Transport, whose buses were a similar green to the school's. Gerald's shirt had a blue hoop, showing he represented Stanley house, and he laid it out, together with his white shorts and green socks, on his bed and made sure his running plimsolls were clean of mud before placing them under his bed, ready to change into soon before the afternoon's events began. Gerald excelled at most sports, but athletics, track and field were far from his favourite sporting activities. He preferred football, rugby and cricket, team games, rather than the individual competition he'd be involved in today. He'd been selected to run in the 100 yard sprint for his year group, and later in the afternoon, he'd take part in the relay race at the same distance. Between the two events, he had an hour and a half of free time to watch the rest of the day's events or just do whatever he liked if he chose not to watch his fellow school mates toiling in the afternoon heat, and anyway, he hardly knew any of the uppers who'd be competing in their events in the latter half of the day's events, apart from his sister, Angela, who was taking part in the upper girls' long jump competition, not the most riveting of events to watch for a spirited ten year old boy.

As the other boys in his dorm also prepared themselves for later in the day, Peter Forester, a friend of Gerald's, switched on his little transistor radio, and the sounds of Radio Caroline filled the room. The pirate radio station had begun broadcasting in March of that year from a ship anchored just outside British territorial waters off the coast of Felixstowe. The kids of Speke Hill thought the idea of a 'pirate' radio station was great fun and loved tuning in at every opportunity they got. Thanks to the relaxing of the usual school regime for the day, they were able to listen to the radio while they enjoyed the morning's relief from the usual routine of their lessons.

They all wanted to hear the Beatles of course, as only that month, the group's movie, *A Hard Day's Night* had been released in cinemas, and though most of the children would eventually get to see their idols at the cinema, only a few lucky ones had so far saved up enough pocket money to see the film. Some of the boys and girls from Speke Hill had asked the teachers if they could go into the city on the day the Beatles returned in triumph from their latest tour, but wisely the staff refused, as over three hundred people were hurt in the crush that accompanied their return. As Father O'Reardon, headmaster of the school had said, "School not scream is the order of the day," a reference to the screaming fans who always accompanied any public appearance by the Fab Four.

Gerald, known to his school friends and fellow orphans as Gerry, meanwhile teamed up with his two friends, Tim Gregson and Frank Jessop to complete the one task they had to carry out that morning. Usually, the lower school pupils had certain chores that would be carried out between the close of school at three-thirty p.m and their evening meal at five p.m but today, due to the extended time taken up by the sorting activities the pupils were instructed to carry out such tasks during their free time in the morning.

So, the three boys set about cleaning the dormitory's shower room and toilets, while others attended to such jobs as cleaning windows, polishing the tiled floor and vacuuming and dusting, all designed to engender not only a sense of cleanliness and domesticity in the boys, but to foster a spirit of teamwork,

With the job finished the boys returned to the main dormitory, where it took Gerry no more than a minute to realise something was wrong. His plimsolls were missing from their place under his bed. Someone was quite clearly playing a prank on young Gerry and he wasn't in the least bit amused by it.

"Okay, you bunch of scallys, who's taken my plimsolls?" he called at the top of his voice to the room in general.

All eyes turned to look at him, but not one reply was forthcoming.

"I said, who's taken them?" he tried again, receiving the same negative result.

"One of youse lot has had me pumps," he shouted, getting louder as his frustration boiled over, "and whoever it is had better own up and give' em back, right now."

As silence pervaded the room once more, Gerry Byrne looked intently at each of the boys in turn. Most looked genuinely innocent but one or two seemed to be doing their best not to break out into mischievous grins.

"Well, ain't any of you got owt to say?" he asked yet again.

"Gerry, honest, none of us saw anyone take 'em. If we had, we'd tell you, wouldn't we?" said Billy Ryan as he joined Gerry in trying to look for the missing footwear.

"Some of you would, and some wouldn't," Gerry replied in an accusing tone.

There weren't many places in the dorm where a pair of shoes might be hidden and Gerry and Billy had soon checked under all the beds in the room, the broom closet, where Gerry, Tim and Frank had already returned the cleaning materials from their shower cleaning, making it an unlikely place to find them, and behind all the boys' individual lockers and small wardrobes that stood either side of each bed. Leaving the main dormitory, and being joined by Tim and Frank, the small group now went from dormitory to dormitory, checking and asking all the other boys in their accommodation about the missing plimsolls.

Almost on the verge of tears, and knowing he wouldn't be able to compete that afternoon without his pumps, Gerry now realised that whoever had taken them must have them hidden in his own bedside locker or wardrobe.

"If someone doesn't tell me where me pumps are in one minute, I'm going to report it to Father Mullaney," said Gerry, referring to the priest in charge of the orphan boys' accommodation blocks.

As he spoke he looked around at the others in the room once again and this time he saw that one boy just couldn't seem to hide a knowing smirk from appearing on his face.

Gerry Byrne now fixed a look of realisation on young Mark Proctor. As he did so, Proctor tried to switch off the tell tale look, covering his mouth with one hand and affecting a false cough to hide the knowing grin that now began to appear on his face. Proctor was taller and heavier than Gerry and already earning something of a reputation as a minor bully amongst the lower school boys, but, not one to back down in the face of what he now felt sure of, young Gerry Byrne now stomped across the room to where Bolton sat on his own bed, obviously enjoying the smaller boy's discomfiture.

"It was you, Mark Proctor. Give 'em back, right now, you rotten thief," he shouted at the other boy.

"Aw, listen to little Gerry," Mark Proctor smirked. "Lost yer pumps, 'ave yer, little boy?"

"Give 'em to me, you thieving little git," said Byrne. "You've got 'em in your locker. I know you have"

"Yeah, right, if you say so, and who's going to make me open up my own private locker, eh, Gerry boy?"

"I'll tell Father Mullaney, and he'll make you open it and then you'll be in real trouble, you scally, Proctor."

"Watch who you're calling a scally, you little bastard, Byrne"

"I'm no bastard, Proctor, not like you. You don't even know who your dad is."

"Liar! My Dad was a famous American soldier."

"Famous my arse," Gerry Byrne laughed. "Everyone knows he was an American soldier alright, one of them stationed out at Haydock after the war, until they all went home and he left your Mam with a snivelling little brat to look after. No wonder she killed herself, Mark Proctor. Who'd want to look after you for the rest of their life?"

Quite clearly, the piety of his later calling had not yet had time to mature in the young Gerald Byrne and his telling remarks now led to Mark Proctor springing up from his bed and the fight that ensued saw both boys throwing punches at each other's face, and letting loose with a few well-aimed kicks. Mark Proctor landed the most telling punches, his future success in the boxing ring giving him the upper hand in close combat, while young Gerry Byrne, the footballer, was ahead on points in the kicking department as the other boys in the room cheered the fight on, until a loud voice boomed out from the doorway.

"And what in the name of all that's Holy is going on here, might I ask?"

The look on the face of Father Mullaney was enough to halt the cheering in less than a second and as the hubbub surrounding them died a death, so the two combatants sensed more than saw the six foot three inch priest as he marched down the centre aisle of the dormitory, and grabbing both boys by their shirt collars and dragging them apart, feet off the floor, he slowly deposited them back on the ground.

"I want the truth, now, no lies, and I'm only asking once. Who started this unholy scene?"

"He stole my pumps, Father, and then he attacked me when I told the truth about his Dad," said Gerry Byrne.

"Is this true, Mark?" asked the priest, and Mark Proctor's face turned even redder than it was already from his exertions in the fight. He remained silent however, forcing Father Mullaney to ask again, "I said, did you steal this boy's plimsolls?"

Shamefacedly, Mark Proctor looked up at the towering figure of the priest and, trying his best to sound contrite and innocent, replied,

"It was a joke, Father, just a prank. I was going to let him have them back before Sports Day started."

"I see, and just where are they now, young Proctor?"

"In my locker, Father."

"Go and get them and return them to young Mr. Byrne, right now, if you please."

Mark Proctor ran the few feet to his locker, and quickly opened it and removed Gerry Byrne's plimsolls, and quickly handed them over.

"Here they are, Gerry. Sorry, honest. It won't happen again."

Gerry Byrne scowled at his adversary, saying nothing as he grabbed his plimsolls and gathered them against his chest.

Father Mullaney next turned to Gerry.

"And as for you, Byrne, what gave you the right to insult this boy's dead father, if that is indeed what you did?"

"Because he wouldn't give them back, Father and he called me a bastard, too."

The priest sighed, before speaking again.

"I can see that you two boys have a lot to learn about the ways of the world and about learning to get along together. Now, you'll shake hands with each other and as it's Sports Day and things have been allowed to be a little too relaxed, to my way of thinking, I'll be lenient with the pair of you. You, Mark Proctor, for stealing the plimsolls in the first place, and for compounding your crime by then starting a fight, will be confined to the dormitory after evening meal for one month, and you will attend chapel both morning and evening every day during that time, where you will pray on your knees to our Lord Jesus Christ for forgiveness for your sins, for one hour in the evening session, and for ten minutes in the morning, which should leave you time to get back to your dorm after chapel and gather your books in time for school."

Mark Proctor gulped, looking totally crestfallen as he saw his freedom being seriously restricted for the coming four weeks. Father Mullaney next turned to Gerry Byrne.

"Now, as for you, Gerald Byrne. I thought better of you than this. Fighting in the dorm, indeed, and making accusations against another boy's father is not the Christian way of handling a dispute. You are all unfortunate enough to be without your parents, which is why you have all ended up at Speke Hill Orphanage, and no matter the reason for your loss of your parents, I will not have you using the circumstances surrounding that loss to be used in such a way. You'll be confined to the orphanage grounds for the next four weekends. No walks into the village or trips to town with Father Hunter, do you understand?"

"Yes, Father. I'm sorry, Father, it won't ever happen again."

"And, you'll say ten Hail Mary's before and after every lesson in school for the next week, is that clear?"

"Very clear, Father," Gerry said, quietly.

"Very well," the priest went on, "I've a mind to stop you both taking part in this afternoon's events but that would unfairly penalise your fellow house-members, so I suggest you both stay well away from each other until this afternoon, and don't you ever let me see or hear of such behaviour taking place ever again, or, in the name of our Lord, I'll personally take my cane to the pair of you, and you'll not be able to sit down for a week. Is that clear?"

Both boys nodded and looked totally abashed at Father Mullaney's words. As the priest turned on his heel and stormed out of the dormitory, the two of them shared a look of pure hatred at each other, and an enmity was born that would last far beyond Sports Day, until both boys were well into their teens.

* * *

Mark Proctor walked confidently in to the room, his hand extended in friendship.

"Gerry Byrne, as I live and breathe, it *is* you. I'm sorry, it's Father Byrne now of course, isn't it? Welcome home, Father, it's good to see you again after so many years. How are you?"

Gerald Byrne was almost taken aback by Mark Proctor's effusive welcome, but he thought the P.E. teacher could do nothing else under the

252

circumstances. It would hardly be fitting for his old adversary to greet the new chaplain of the orphanage and school with a roundhouse punch to the head, now would it?

Quickly recovering his composure, Byrne reached out and took the proffered hand, and the two men shook hands vigorously, like two old friends, reunited after so many long years.

"I'm well, thank you, Mark. It's good to see you again, too. I see the wheel has turned full circle for you too, ending up back here again. I take it you haven't always taught here?"

"Quite right, Father Byrne. I've taught at a few schools over the years, but when I heard of the vacancy for this job, I just felt I had to apply for it, and, well, as you can see, here I am."

"Yes, indeed, and I hear you're to be my guide around the 'new' Speke Hill, too."

"Yes, that's right. When he realised we were both old boys from the same year at Speke Hill, Charles here asked if I'd be happy to show you the changes that have taken place since you last saw the old place. I was delighted to be able to help."

I'll just bet you were, Byrne thought to himself, sarcastically, but kept such uncharitable thoughts to himself and instead replied, "Excellent. So, I've taken up enough of Mr. Hopkirk's time this morning, shall we get on with the guided tour?"

"It's nice to have met you and had our little talk," Hopkirk said as Father Byrne stood, and the two men shook hands.

"Yes, indeed Charles," Byrne replied as he moved to follow Bolton out of the office. "We'll doubtless meet in the future, I'm sure."

"Oh yes, I look forward to it. I don't attend the services in the chapel as a rule but we'll bump into each other during your visits, without doubt," Hopkirk said as the two former residents of the orphanage left the room and the door closed behind them.

Mark Proctor appeared not to harbour any ill-will towards Gerald Byrne as he took pleasure in showing the priest around. Whether his attitude was a true reflection of his thoughts, or a clever cover-up, Father Byrne couldn't ascertain at that point.

Surely he can't believe the past is totally buried, that all his bullying and cruelty towards those weaker than himself can be put down to childish pranks as he used to call them, thought Byrne, as he followed Bolton around, trying to be polite and showing interest where he felt it was called for.

In truth, there hadn't been too many drastic changes to the old place. The trees lining the approach drive had grown substantially of course, and the dormitories had undergone quite a radical upgrading, with those living at Speke Hill now being housed in rooms that held just four people, rather than the open dorms of the past which held up to thirty boys or girls. Such a change had inevitably meant that overall numbers had been reduced, with Speke Hill now being 'home' to twenty-five percent fewer boys and girls than in Byrne's days as an orphan.

The biggest changes had been effected in the school, with the class-rooms having been totally modernised. Gone were the old chemistry lab, and art room, both being replaced by modern versions of the same, which bore little resemblance to the originals. Each classroom now had state of the art computers installed to enable the children to be taught about, and using, the latest technology. Gerald Byrne managed to keep conversation to a minimum, for the most part managing to make the appropriate noises and speak the expected words in response to Proctor's enthusiastic showing off of the facilities.

Quite naturally, he lingered for a little longer than necessary in the chapel, kneeling in prayer for a couple of minutes, during which time he prayed for forgiveness for his feelings of antipathy towards his old nemesis and Mark Proctor waited patiently in the doorway, not intruding upon the priest's solitude while at prayer.

A visit to the staff room followed where Proctor introduced him to the few teachers who were present at the time, and then he was led to the headmaster's office where, unfortunately, Mrs. Davis, the head's secretary informed them that Mr. Machin was teaching and wouldn't be free until after lunch, and would be sad to have missed Father Byrne, but she was sure he'd look forward to seeing him on his next visit. Gerald Byrne replied that he understood how busy the head must be and he too would look forward to a future meeting, though inwardly he felt the headmaster might have made time to meet him, as he'd known in advance of his visit. He concluded this was a sign of the times, the church no longer wielding the strings of power at Speke Hill as it used to, and his part, therefore, in the overall scheme of school life, would be far less than he'd perhaps imagined.

Not until they exited the main school building towards the end of his visit did the two men find themselves speaking of anything attached to their joint past at Speke Hill.

As they walked down the sweeping arc of steps that led from the main doors down into what was now a much larger car park than used to exist there, Proctor suddenly stopped and pointed to a point to the left of the low wall that stood along the length of the steps.

"Do you remember when old Father Loony used to park his old motor cycle just there every day?"

Gerald Byrne couldn't help but smile at the sudden recollection.

'Father Loony' had in reality been Father Rooney, who taught both geography and history. The name 'Loony' had been affectionately applied to him by pupils who found it quite incongruous that a priest of the Roman Catholic Church, and a serious teacher of stuffy old geography and history would finish teaching for the day and then change into full motorcycle 'leathers' before mounting his gleaming, powerful Norton

Commando motorcycle, revving the engine in a display of power, and then zooming off, in a cloud of exhaust smoke, down the drive and out onto Woolton Road, destination unknown.

The boys who'd drooled over Father William Rooney's superb Norton machine would have been surprised to know the priest was a member of the Liverpool Motor club, a long established group catering for both motorcycles and motor car enthusiasts, and often rode his bike in various road trials and shows. Likewise, many of the club members would have been astounded to know that the rider of the red and black Norton was a Roman Catholic Priest, and not a rather well-turned out 'rocker'.

Gerald Byrne smiled as he recalled the motorcycling priest.

"Yes, I remember him well. He used to help me quite often with history projects, and he also helped to fuel my thirst for knowledge of life in the priesthood. He made me realise you could be a Catholic priest and still have a life that included outside interests, as he had with his motor bike. He was a great Rugby League fan too, and used to travel to watch Wigan's matches whenever he could."

"I didn't know that, about the Rugby, I mean," Proctor replied.

"He told me he used to play the game himself for an amateur club in his teens, and even had trials for Liverpool City, at the old Knotty Ash Stadium but never quite made it. Most people have forgotten them now of course. They moved and changed their name to Huyton and then slowly slid into oblivion I seem to recall."

"I remember them," said Proctor. "Never very good, were they?"

"Maybe not, but they played the game because they loved it, a bit like Doncaster and Batley in those days, always bottom of the league but still turned out every week and their small band of supporters would follow them around the North of England in the hope of an occasional win to talk about."

"You played rugger for the school, didn't you, Gerry?"

"That was Rugby Union," Byrne nodded in reply. "The good Fathers of Speke Hill preferred us to play according to the amateur code, which most schools did in those days."

"Who'd have thought you'd have ended up as a rugby player though? You were a bit weedy as a lower, if you don't mind me saying."

Gerald Byrne inwardly seethed at Proctor's obvious reference to their days in the lower school, when he'd been small enough to be on the receiving end of Proctor's 'pranks'. It was only when he'd attained his teens that his muscular development had kicked in and Gerry Byrne had grown into a strapping rugby winger and footballer. Not wanting to rise to the bait, he instead took a deep breath before replying, diplomatically,

"We all developed at different times and in different ways in those days, Mark. I recall you suddenly putting a few pounds on in your teens, after all that boxing you did."

This was a clear reference to the fact that Mark Proctor gradually went from well built to rather flabby, and by the time he reached school leaving age, his boxing days were already behind him.

"Yes, well, I managed to lose some of that weight in later years so I could qualify as a P.E teacher," Proctor responded.

It was now becoming clear that the atmosphere between the two men was growing strained and Father Gerald Byrne quickly made his excuses and walked away from Mark Proctor, wishing in a very non-Christian way for God to send a thunderbolt to strike the man down, to the car where young Father Willis had patiently waited for him while he'd 'enjoyed' his visit to Speke Hill. Willis turned the car radio off as Byrne opened the car door and they were soon on their way, back to the sanctuary of St. Luke's, where Byrne later insisted on Father Willis hearing his confession

What the young priest thought when he heard Father Byrne confess to wishing Mark Proctor some kind of harm, only he could know, thanks to the sanctity of the confessional, but, on hearing Byrne's words, Father Willis couldn't help raising an eyebrow in surprise at the thought that the new Parish Priest might not be as pure and Godly as he'd initially thought him to be. But then, he comforted himself with the thought that it was only a silly wish, brought about by some reference to an event that had taken place a long time ago…wasn't it?

CHAPTER 6

'RAZOR'

"Any luck with the victim's fingerprints, Paul?" Ross spoke into his mobile phone as soon as he and Drake walked out of the doors of the mortuary building. Detective Constable Paul Ferris, his team's collator and expert on all things of a computer based nature had received the prints only an hour or so earlier but had achieved success already.

"Got a hit right away, sir. The victim is in the system. His name's Matthew Remington, aged forty-eight, known to his friends as 'Razor', for obvious reasons. Not very original I must say, naming someone after a brand of shaving products. Seems our Matthew had a record going back quite a few years, mostly minor stuff, petty theft, taking a vehicle without consent, a couple of assault charges, but, get this, sir, his most recent conviction though it was a few years ago, was for a sexual assault offence."

At that, Ross's mind immediately switched on to the hacking off of the victim's sexual organ. Could this murder be a simple case of revenge by someone connected to Remington's victim?

"Good work, Paul. We'll be back in a few minutes. Get me all the information you can on this 'Razor' Remington. Let's see if someone decided to exact a brutal revenge for his last offence."

"I'm on it already, sir," Ferris replied, as Ross pressed the red 'end call' button on his phone.

"I take it Ferris came through quickly," said Drake as she drove towards headquarters.

"He did, Izzie. The guy was a sex offender by the name of Matthew Remington"

"A ha," Drake replied, her thoughts immediately echoing those of the inspector. One of the reasons the two worked so well together was their uncanny way of thinking along parallel lines at times.

"Exactly," said Ross. "It looked bad, but the solution may be simpler than we thought."

Drake fell silent for a few seconds, and Andy Ross knew her brain was ticking over, an idea forming in his sergeant's thoughts.

"You're thinking of something, Sergeant, I can tell. Come on, out with it."

"Well, it might be nothing, but I wonder if there's any significance in the fact that the victim's name was Matthew and his body was found in St. Matthew's churchyard?"

"Good point," Ross conceded. "Let's see what Ferris has got for us when we get back before we begin jumping to any conclusions, though"

An hour later, having taken time to study the information D.C. Ferris had unearthed on the victim, Andy Ross and Izzie Drake sat in the small 'murder room', a small conference room used by the murder investigation team for the purpose of team meetings and where Ferris had already begun composing his 'murder board', a large whiteboard that would hold all the information on the case, and where all the team's planning and strategy meeting were held.

As well as Ross, Drake and Ferris, also present were D.C's Samantha Gable and Lennie Curtis, the newest member of the team. For some reason, despite his real name being Leonard, his colleagues had chosen to address the young D.C. as 'Tony', naming him after the famed American Film Actor. Ross guessed it was probably due to Curtis and the actor having similar looks and hairstyles that made the detective look like the actor in his *Vikings* days. Sam Gable had initially been seconded to Ross's team three years previously and had since been made a permanent member of the murder squad, after spending years working in vice. Gable and Derek McLennan had only just returned from their initial sweep of the vicinity of St. Matthew's, with none of the residents having reported seeing or hearing anything out of the ordinary in the hours preceding the discovery of Matthew Remington's body. McLennan was conspicuous by his absence, a fact not unnoticed by Andy Ross.

"Where's Derek, Sam?" he asked Gable.

"He won't be long, sir. He was rather embarrassed about throwing up at the murder scene, and felt a bit, well, you know, unclean. He's in the gents now, changing into a shirt he managed to borrow from one of the uniform boys who had a spare in his locker."

As though on cue, the door to the conference room opened and Derek McLennan walked in, looking a darn sight better than when Ross had last seen him at the murder scene, or body dump. Ross still wasn't certain which description could be best applied to the churchyard. Dr. Nugent thought the man had been killed on site, there being enough blood to qualify the churchyard as the location of the murder, but, there was still a chance the man had his throat cut elsewhere and the blood at the scene was a result of the multiple mutilations carried out on the victim.

"Sorry I'm a bit late, sir," said McLennan as he ran his fingers through his tousled hair, still wet from his attempts to tidy himself up in the gents' toilets. His borrowed shirt hung on him a little, being at least a size too big for him, but at least he'd regained some of his natural colour again. "I was…you know, just…"

"Don't worry about it, Derek. We know it was bloody awful back at the churchyard. You're only human, so nobody's going to hold it against you. Come on in and sit down, while Paul brings us up to date regarding our victim. All yours, Paul."

D.C. Ferris stood and moved to stand in front of the whiteboard. He'd already appended photos of Matthew Remington's body, provided in double-quick time by the forensics team as well as a copy of his prison mugshot which had already caused one or two raised eyebrows as the team members realised their victim was an ex-con. Ferris had also added comprehensive crime scene photos, a picture of the Parish Priest, Father Donovan, where he got it from, Ross wondered in admiration, and finally a photograph of a young woman, who looked to be in her early twenties, and as yet unknown to anyone other than Ferris himself. As the rest of the team fell silent, Paul Ferris began.

"Thank you, sir. Okay everyone, it's confirmed that our victim is one Matthew 'Razor' Remington. I'm sure I don't need to explain the source of his nickname."

A short chorus of laughs and groans followed, before Ferris continued.

"Remington was 58 years old, locally born, lived on Hazel Avenue in Norris Green and worked at the Motor Vehicle Factory at Halewood."

"I knew it," exclaimed Derek McLennan, now feeling a little more like his usual self.

"Eh, what's that, Derek?" Ferris sounded a little annoyed at the early interruption.

"Oh, sorry Paul. It's just that we found a key at the scene that I thought looked like a locker key from Halewood. I've seen one before."

"Right, okay, thanks, Derek. Now, where was I? Yes, right, looks like our victim was a bit of a scally in his youth, always in trouble for one thing and another. Nothing serious, just a long string of petty crimes, though he gradually worked his way up to a couple of assault charges in his thirties. He was married for a short time, God bless the poor woman who fell for his particular charms, and his wife, Margaret, known as Maggie, left him after he was jailed for the second assault charge. The marriage had lasted eight years apparently, but only because he spent four of those years in prison. She still lives locally, in Norris Green.

Anyway, our friend would probably have remained under the radar if he'd stuck to the petty stuff, but not long after his wife did a runner on him, he really messed up. A young woman called Claire Morris," he pointed at the picture of the young woman on the whiteboard, "was raped after leaving a pub in Croxteth. I'm not going to go into all the details, as they're all in the files I'll pass out before we leave the room, but her assailant grabbed her from behind, dragged her onto a building site, and made her strip her skirt and underwear off in front of him before raping and sodomizing the poor girl."

"So he was a right bloody sadist as well," said Izzie Drake.

"Sounds like it," Ferris replied, "Claire stated later that she felt he wanted to humiliate her, as well as doing what he did. When he'd done with her, he gave her the skirt back but kept her underwear."

"The bastard wanted a trophy," Lennie 'Tony' Curtis snapped. "Sounds to me as if the low-life scumbag got what he deserved."

Ross felt it wise to interject at that point.

"D.C. Curtis. I'd be grateful if you kept those thoughts to yourself. Whoever or whatever he may have been, Remington was a human being, and one who's been murdered in a particularly brutal way. It's our job to catch his killer, and we'll do our job to the best of our ability. I will not have anyone in this city taking the law into their own hands, besides which, whatever we may think of Matthew Remington, he was caught, tried and convicted and served his sentence, so technically, he'd paid his debt to society. He didn't deserve to die like that. If any of you are uncomfortable investigating his death, speak up now and I'll have you removed from the case."

A deathly silence filled the room for a few seconds. Although Ross felt pretty much the same as his young detective constable, he had to maintain his own position as head of the unit and at the same time make sure his team didn't lose sight of their duty to uphold the law. After what seemed an interminable silence, Curtis spoke up.

"I'm sorry, boss. I spoke without thinking. It won't happen again."

"Good," Ross replied. "Anyone else got anything to say?"

Silence.

"Right then, please continue with the briefing, Paul."

Paul Ferris cleared his throat loudly, and took up the reins of the briefing again.

"Right, sir. Where was I? Oh yes, Claire Morris managed to stagger a few hundred yards until, as luck would have it, she spotted a passing patrol car and literally stepped out into the road right in front of it. The driver only just managed to stop in time without hitting her. The two officers in the car ascertained what had happened and called the incident in. One of them stayed in the car with Claire, waiting for the ambulance and back-up while the other officer made an examination of the building site in a search for clues.

Thanks to them coming on the scene so quickly, forensics were on the scene in no time and Claire was examined at the hospital within an hour of the rape taking place.

Remington was soon picked up and Claire picked him out of an identity parade, and the case became what the Americans call a 'slam dunk.' He got eight years, was released in five, placed on the sex offenders register, and nothing more was heard of him until his body was found this morning. Seems he'd kept his head down and had been working at Halewood for the last three years. That's it, folks."

Ross took over once again.

"Thanks, Paul. Now listen up everyone. I want this killer caught quickly. Don't ask me why, but I've got a bad feeling about this case. The way Remington was killed was so brutal that I feel we haven't heard the last of this killer. Whether he's someone seeking revenge for what happened to Claire, or some kind of vigilante, he's got to be found before he does anything else."

"You think he could strike again, sir?" asked Derek McLennan.

"I don't know, Derek, but he virtually butchered Matthew Remington and I sure as hell don't want to think he might do the same to someone else. Sergeant Drake has a short list of assignments for you. Listen carefully, and let's move fast, people, but also, let's not miss a thing. Be professional, understand?"

Murmurs of assent circulated round the room as Izzie Drake stood up.

"Okay, everyone, here goes," she began. "Derek and Sam, I want you to take the Claire Morris file and go through it with a fine tooth comb. Then, go and talk to everyone involved, her family, friends, whoever gave statements at the time. If they're in that file, talk to them, got it?"

"Okay, Sarge," said Sam Gable. "What about Claire Morris? Do you want us to speak to her as well?"

"No Sam, you two stick to the other witnesses and family members. The boss and I will talk to Claire. She'll need very careful handling. Tony", she said, referring to Lennie Curtis, "I want you to go out to the factory at Halewood. Talk to Remington's boss, supervisor, co-workers. See if anyone knows if he had anything on his mind recently, whether he told anyone about any threats he might have received, you know the type of things to ask."

"Right, Sarge," Curtis replied.

"Anything else you want me to do?" Paul Ferris asked.

Before Drake could reply, a knock at the door heralded the arrival of George Thompson, the force's senior Press Liaison Officer. Unlike some P.L.Os from other constabularies, Thomson was held in pretty high regard by the officer of the Merseyside Police. He always consulted with the officers in charge of a case before releasing any information to the media, and was quite happy to allow those officers to work with him on ensuring the accuracy of the information released to the news hounds. As he walked quietly into the room, dressed as he always seemed to be in a grey pin-striped suit, blue silk tie and pristine white shirt, Ross groaned inwardly. It was obvious to the inspector that Thompson's presence meant the press had got hold of the story and would be clamouring for the details of the gruesome killing of Matthew Remington. Ross also allowed himself a moment to wonder why George Thompson never appeared to look any older. In the years he'd known him, Thompson managed to look no older than about thirty-five or there-abouts, though he must be in his late forties by now. One day, he'd ask him how he kept looking so youthful, but now wasn't the time for such thoughts.

"Am I interrupting your briefing, Andy?" asked the PLO, knowing full well that he was.

"Hello, George. Yes, you are, but don't let that worry you. Your presence here makes me think that news of the murder has somehow leaked to the press?"

"I'm afraid so, Andy. D.C.I Porteous just called me into his office and asked me to come and see you and your people. Seems someone tipped the press off about the murder. Whether it was the priest at St. Matthew's or one of the uniforms on the scene perhaps, I don't know, but the Chief wants me to try and cap the lid on the story before the sensationalist element of the media takes over and blows it up into something like the modern embodiment of bloody Jack the Ripper."

Detective Chief Inspector Harry Porteous was Ross's immediate superior and the overall head of the Murder Investigation Unit. An old-school police officer, Porteous was happy to leave the day to day running of the unit's investigations in the capable hands of his officers, while at the same time maintaining close contact and overall control of the team.

"It sounds as if it might be a bit late for that," Ross said, ruefully. "I'm sure the press hounds will already be making up their own sensationalist stories before you've breathed a word to them."

"Yes, well, that's precisely why I'm here. I know you're incredibly busy with the investigation and need to be out in the field pursuing leads and so on, so whatever you can give me to help put a short statement together will do for now, as long as I can give them something that will allow you and your team a little breathing space."

Ross fell quiet as he thought of the best way to give Thompson what he needed without compromising the need to get out and track down a particularly vicious killer.

"Tell you what, George. We need to hit the streets, as you rightly point out, so why don't you sit down with D.C. Ferris and he can fill you in on

262

what new have so far, little though it may be. I presume you'll want to give the local press in particular something to make the evening edition?"

"That's what I'm hoping for," said Thompson, referring to the *Liverpool Echo*, the major local newspaper.

"Right, Paul, you make sure George gets what he needs, and then you can go to St. Matthew's. I want you to talk to the priest, Father Donovan. Now that we have a name, address and place of work for the victim, it might mean something to him. He only got a quick look at the dead man this morning and went into shock almost immediately so he might have remembered something that could be helpful by now."

Ferris nodded.

"Okay, sir."

Ross turned to Thompson again.

"George, I hope that helps and I'd like you to run anything you intend to release to the press by me before you give it to them."

"No problem, Andy. Where will you be if I need to contact you?"

"Sergeant Drake and me are going to talk to the girl Remington was convicted of raping, either at home or at work, if we can track her down quickly. Then we'll be back here in time for any press briefing I hope. If we're delayed, you can call me on my mobile."

"Okay," Thompson replied. "Shall we get to work, D.C. Ferris?"

With that, Ross and the rest of the team left them to it as they left the conference room, each detective intent on playing their part in the hunt for Matthew Remington's Killer.

CHAPTER 7

CLAIRE MORRIS

"Did you really mean all that crap you said in there about Remington being a human being, paid his debt to society etc. etc? Sorry if I'm speaking out of turn, sir, but well, it wasn't like you to sound so conciliatory about a low-life like Remington obviously was."

Izzie Drake was talking as she drove Ross and herself to Claire Morris's home. Information obtained by Paul Ferris had told them that the rape victim had moved from her address at the time of the attack, understandably in everyone's mind, and that she now lived in a terraced house in Seaforth, which she apparently shared with her boyfriend. She knew how her boss thought, the pair usually sharing an almost telepathic understanding of each other's thought patterns, and she'd been a little taken aback by Ross's words to young D.C Curtis back at headquarters.

"Course I didn't really mean it, Izzie. What d'you take me for? But, young Curtis had to be put in his place. It's okay to think these things, and believe me I sympathized with the lad's feelings, but we have to make sure everyone is focussed on the job. If they thought for one minute that I endorsed what he said, we'd have the whole team thinking it was okay for some bastard to do what he did to Remington. I thought you'd have realised that."

"Yes, I suppose I did really, but just wanted to hear you say it. Didn't want to think you were suddenly going soft in your old age," she said with a grin on her face.

"We'll have less of that, Sergeant Drake," Ross said, grinning back at her. "Old age indeed! I'm not quite in my dotage yet, young lady"

"No, I must say you're not looking bad for your age, sir. Maria looks after you well, I'd say," Izzie replied, referring to Ross's wife.

"What makes you think it's all Maria's doing? I know how to take care of myself, you know."

"Of course you do, sir," Drake said with a hint of sarcasm. "Last I heard, Maria had banned you from all those juicy burgers you enjoy so much when we're out on a job."

"Oh yeah, and who told you that?"

"You did, as a matter of fact, sir, about a month ago."

"Oh, right, well, she may have a little to do with it, I agree."

The pair continued their cheerful and relaxed banter as the Mondeo ate up the final couple of miles to Seaforth, one of the older parts of the city, mostly made up of old Victorian terraced houses, and home to Seaforth Dock, the largest dock facility in the modern port of Liverpool. Drake took her foot off the peal as they slowly drove along Garstang Road, looking for the home of Claire Morris.

"There it is, sir, number twenty-four," she said as she pulled in to park the car behind a battered looking old Ford Transit van. "What do we do if there's nobody home? Don't you think we should have got her phone number and checked first to se if she was at work or at home?"

"I didn't want to phone in advance and give her the opportunity to decline to talk to us, Izzie. Rape is such a delicate subject and she may have done her best to put it all behind her. I know it'll be difficult for her to talk to us, but at least just showing up like this will make it harder for her to refuse to speak to us. It's also why I wanted you with me, a woman's touch and all that, you know? We may have to have a rethink if she's not at home, of course, but we'll soon find out."

Drake and Ross exited and locked the unmarked pool car, and walked the few yards to number twenty-four, where Ross stood back and allowed Drake to knock on what appeared to be the recently painted dark green front door. He wanted the first face Claire Morris saw on opening her door to be that of a woman, rather than of a man totally unknown to her.

A few seconds later the door opened, and the detectives were surprised to find themselves confronted not by the woman they were expecting, but a man, whom Ross estimated to be in his late twenties, wearing a white shirt and black trousers, somewhat reminiscent of a uniform of some kind.

"Hello, can I help you?" the man asked with a puzzled expression on his face.

"I'm Detective Inspector Ross and this is Sergeant Drake, from Merseyside Police," said the inspector, as he and Drake both held up their warrant cards to identify themselves. "We're looking for a Miss Claire Morris and we were led to understand this is her home?"

"Claire? Well, yes, it is, but she's not at home right now. I'm her fiancé. Won't you come in, please? She'll be home very soon."

A minute later the two of them were seated in a neat sitting room, furnished in a modern style, with a two-seater sofa, a single matching armchair, and a large wall-mounted television above the old original Victorian fireplace. In one corner of the room stood a state of the art hi-fi system and a new looking laptop computer sat in the middle of a glass topped coffee table in front of the armchair. In truth, there wasn't room for much more in the room and Ross found himself wondering whether the couple ate their meals on trays on their laps, or perhaps had another downstairs room, an old-fashioned dining room maybe. These old Victorian terraced homes could, he knew, be deceptively large inside.

"I'm Lee Denton," the man said, introducing himself. "Can I ask why you're here, Inspector?"

"Well, we'd rather discuss that with Miss Morris, if you don't mind?"

"Is it connected with the rape?" Denton asked, bluntly.

"As I said, it's a private matter, Mr. Denton. You said Miss Morris would be home soon?"

Denton smiled.

"Yes, in the next few minutes, I'd say. She finished work not long ago, and is usually home within half an hour. She works as an input clerk for a computer services company not far away."

"And you, Mr. Denton, what do you do for a living?" asked Ross, still feeling the man had an air of authoritative confidence about him.

"Me? I'm a customs officer, Inspector Ross."

Ross smiled to himself. He knew it had to be something like that.

"I see, at the port?"

"No, at John Lennon," he replied, referring to John Lennon Airport, renamed after the former Beatle from the original name of Speke Airport. "I'm home because I'm on night shift this week. We don't get many flights late at night but we have to maintain a customs presence on the site twenty four hours a day. Listen, can I get you both some tea or coffee while you wait for Claire?"

"I'd love a coffee," Izzie spoke up, before Ross could refuse.

"Right, well, yes please, Mr. Denton. Coffee would be nice, thank you."

"Great," said Denton as he rose from his chair, and moved to the door, quickly making his way to the kitchen from where he called loudly.

"Milk and sugar for everyone, is it?"

"Milk and no sugar for both of us, please," Drake called back.

"Oy, I like a spoon of sugar in my coffee if you don't mind," he complained quietly to his sergeant.

"Think of your waistline, sir, and your cholesterol levels. I could be adding years onto your life."

"Yeah, or driving me into a mental home," he laughed.

Almost simultaneously, Lee Denton walked back into the living room, carrying a tray loaded with three mugs of steaming coffee, a sugar bowl, much to Ross's delight, and a plate of digestive biscuits, and the front door opened and Claire Morris arrived home.

"Hi, Lee, you there?" she called as the front door closed and before Denton could reply, she walked into the room, just as he placed the tray on the coffee table. Claire stood looking at the two visitors, smiling tentatively at the unknown newcomers to her home, The attractive young woman was smartly dressed in a dark blue pantsuit with low heeled black shoes, her shoulder length blonde hair cut in a fashionable bob, exuding an air of professional respectability.

"Oh, you've got visitors," she said, making an obvious assumption.

Andy Ross rose from his seat and took out his warrant card as he identified himself and Izzie Drake. After he'd corrected her assumption, informing her it was herself he and Drake wanted to talk to, she sat down and asked him the obvious question.

"And how can I help you, Inspector Ross?" she asked as Lee Denton hurried out to the kitchen again to make another coffee, this time for his fiancée. Before Ross could answer her question, Denton returned with Claire's coffee and asked if the detectives would rather speak to Claire on her own but she insisted he stay with her. He sat on the arm of the sofa next to her and Ross began.

"I'm sorry to have to bring this up after all this time, Miss Morris, but we need to speak to you about the man who raped you."

"Matthew Remington?" she snapped the name out as if it was a swear word. "Why, Inspector? Has he done it again to some other poor girl? I always said his sentence was too bloody short, and please, call me Claire. Miss Morris makes me feel like some middle-aged school teacher."

"No, Claire, he hasn't re-offended," Ross replied, instantly feeling stupid at his use of the police jargon, "he's dead. Matthew Pennington was murdered sometime in the early hours of this morning."

A look of what Ross saw as genuine shock appeared on the young woman's face on hearing the news of Remington's demise.

"Murdered? How? Where?"

"He was found in a churchyard. I'm not at liberty to reveal any details yet, I'm afraid."

"I see," Claire responded and then, as realisation struck her she said, "But, what has it to do with me? I can't pretend I feel sorry for him, Inspector Ross, but you can't think I had anything to so with his murder, surely?"

"Not directly, no, Claire. But it's theoretically possible that someone may have attacked Remington in revenge for what he did to you."

"You can't be serious, Inspector. I know that Remington was released from prison years ago. Don't you think if I, or someone I know was going to do something like that, it would have happened back then?"

Izzie Drake spoke before Ross could answer.

"Ever hear the phrase, 'revenge is a dish best served cold', Claire? In other words, wait until your target is least expecting it and then strike."

Claire Morris, far from becoming angry, looked aghast at Drake and then burst out laughing.

"Sergeant, that's funny. Really, it is. All the revenge in the world could never make me feel better about what that man did to me. Do you know how I felt when I was in the hospital, being examined after the rape?"

"No, Claire. I can't begin to know how you felt," Drake answered honestly.

"Then let me tell you," said Claire." First of all, I was scared in case my rapist had given me AIDS. Secondly, I was afraid of being pregnant. The thought of carrying a rapist's child filled me with more dread than you can imagine. I'm Catholic, Sergeant, so the possibility of abortion could never have been an option if I was expecting, and then thirdly, I was afraid in case the man came back and did it again. I only relaxed a little bit eventually when first the AIDS test came back negative, then I found out I wasn't pregnant, and eventually my rapist was sent to prison. When I saw him in court at his trial, I suddenly realised he was nothing to be afraid of. He was such an insignificant and pathetic excuse for a human being. I knew I'd be ready for him if he came back again after his release, and I took martial arts classes until I graduated with a black belt in Tai Kwan Do, and also in Judo, so slowly the fears went away. No amount of revenge in the world could pay me back for what he put me through that night. Listen, when I was told how rapists got treated in prison, that made me feel good, and then I knew he'd have to go through his life always looking over his shoulder just in case someone did go after him, just like what's happened, and that was better than any thoughts of actually harming him, just knowing he'd never really be free, even though he'd been let out."

"Wow, that was some speech, Claire," said Ross. "I admire your resilience and your strength in getting your life back together, but we do have to investigate Remington's murder and find his killer. Whoever did this, they had a powerful motive, I can tell you that much."

Ross turned to Lee Denton.

"How long have you and Claire been together, Lee?"

Lee looked a little surprised that Ross had addressed him directly.

"Oh, must be about three years, Inspector. We got engaged when we bought this place together two years ago."

"I assume you were aware of what happened to Claire?"

"She told me all about it once we found ourselves growing close. I admired her for the way she'd fought to put her life back together after such a terrible experience. As it happens, my own sister was the victim of an indecent assault some years ago, so I found I could relate in a small way with Claire's emotional turmoil. Anyway, don't look at me for your killer, Inspector. I have too much respect for the law in the first place, and in the second place, you said the murder tool place in the early hours of the morning, right?"

"That's right, and you were on duty all night I presume?"

"From ten last night until eight this morning, Inspector. I should have finished work at six, but we were short staffed as usual so I ended up doing a couple of hours of overtime. By the time I got out of work and drove home, it was about nine fifteen when I got home. I put my feet up and watched the breakfast news programmes for a while, had some breakfast and then dozed off for a while. I was about to go up for a shower and a shave when you and the sergeant came knocking on the door."

"And you, Claire?" Drake asked.

"Me? I left for work just before eight, after Lee phoned to say he'd be late home, started at eight thirty and finished about an hour ago. I stopped for a few bits of shopping at Khan's Deli on the corner before coming home. The bags are still in the hall. I dropped them when I came in. I should get them and put the stuff in the fridge."

"We won't keep you much longer, Claire," said Ross. "Just tell me, honestly, if you think anyone in your family or circle of friends could have hated Matthew Remington enough to kill him?"

Claire laughed again, then replied.

"All of them, Inspector, obviously. They all had a motive, didn't they? But I doubt either me Mam or Dad would have the strength or the real inclination to do it, and as for my brother Steve, I doubt he made a trip up here last night to knock Remington off and then zoomed back down to Devon in time for lectures. As for my friends, they're all female, but as much as the ones who know about my rape might have wanted Remington dead, I doubt they'd have gone so far as to murder him. You still haven't told me how he was killed, Inspector. Was he shot, stabbed?"

"As the inspector said, Claire," Izzie stepped in, "we can't reveal that, yet, but believe me, it wasn't something you'd care to think about, unless you feel like having nightmares for a month."

Claire Morris seemed to stop in her tracks, drawing a deep breath and then said just the one word, "Oh."

"That bad, was it?" Lee Denton asked.

"That bad, yes," said Drake.

The mood in the room seemed to deteriorate further at that point, and Ross felt it was time he and Drake made their exit. He could always come back if he needed to talk to Claire Morris again.

"Right, well thanks for your time, Claire," he said, rising from his seat as he spoke. Drake followed his lead and stood also.

"We'll be in touch if we need any further information."

Claire and Lee both stood also and Lee Denton shook hands with both detectives as he saw them out at the front door, Claire remaining in the sitting room.

"I know you had to come and talk to her, Inspector," Denton spoke very quietly, "but believe me, Claire's spent her time since that man was jailed doing all she can to put the rape behind her as best she can and has built a new life for herself, happily with me, She would never have had anything to do with something like this. It's not in her nature."

"I understand what you're saying, Lee," said Ross, "but we have to explore every possibility in a case like this. The chance that someone saw a chance for some kind of retribution against Matthew Remington has to be investigated, and…"

"Lee," Claire called from the sitting room. "Are you coming in or what?"

"I'd better get back inside," said Denton, quietly.

"We'll be in touch again if we need to," Ross replied and the two men shook hands, before the two detectives walked away and the front door of Claire Morris's home closed almost silently behind them.

* * *

"Well, what d'you think of her?" Ross asked Izzie Drake as they motored back across the city towards headquarters.

"I think she's done remarkably well to rebuild her life, sir," Drake responded. "A lot of rape victims tend to withdraw into themselves after such experiences, at least from what I've heard and read. Claire Morris seems to have been something of an exception, not letting it ruin her life and trying to just get on with things as normally as possible. Having Lee Denton around obviously helps."

"Yes, I liked him, too" said Ross. "He's the stability, the rock she probably needed to enable her to rebuild her life. I also think he's in the clear as far as the murder goes. I know he could have been part of some sort of conspiracy to get rid of Remington, but this crime feels more like a personal one, a single perpetrator with a strong motive for doing away with Remington."

"I agree," Drake concurred. "What do you think the others will find when they interview Claire's family?"

"We'll find out soon enough, Izzie. The others should be back around the same time as us, I think, but I doubt they'll find anything."

"Are you saying you don't think her family or friends are involved at all, sir?"

"It's too early to say, but we have to consider the possibility this case has nothing at all to do with Claire and what happened to her. Who's to say that Remington hasn't had other victims, and they've not reported the attacks and then taken their own revenge on him, without ever bringing us on board?"

"Good God, I never even thought of that," Drake exclaimed. "But you're right sir, a large proportion of rapes do go unreported. Remington could have carried out any number of attacks since his release."

"But we have no proof, Izzie, and we also need to keep an open mind. This could have absolutely nothing to do with his crime, or crimes. What if he upset someone during his time in prison, someone who's only recently been released and who saved up a whole lot of rage while he was inside?"

"You want me to look into that angle, sir?"

"No, but get Ferris on it. Tell him to contact the prison, find out who Remington was paired with, if at all. He'd probably have been on a segregated wing, being a sex offender, so he'd either have been kept in solitary or banged up with another rapist or molester of some kind. We need to know if he managed to upset anyone during his time inside, and if so, who."

"OK, sir. Looks like this case could turn out to be a bloody complicated one, doesn't it?"

"With the amount of rage the killer displayed in the way he killed Remington, I think you're right, Izzie. I've got a bad feeling in my gut about this one."

* * *

Back at headquarters, the rest of the team had indeed returned from their various assignments and were gathered around the incident board in the conference room as Paul Ferris updated it with the results of their findings when Ross and Drake walked in to the room.

"Hello, boss," said Ferris as he turned to greet the pair.

"Paul, everyone," Ross acknowledged the team collectively.

"Do we have anything useful?"

"Not really, sir," Ferris replied on behalf of the team. "I'm just listing the fact that we've visited and to a degree, eliminated the family of Claire Morris from the list of potential suspects. How about you and Sergeant Drake, anything for me to add here?"

"Just another elimination, I'd say, Paul," Ross replied. "Claire Morris has a new life, a new fiancé, and was genuinely surprised to hear of Remington's death, not that she shed any tears for him, mind."

"Same here sir," said Sam Gable. "Her parents were positively delighted that Remington had finally got his 'comeuppance' as they called it. When Derek here said he thought murder was a bit over the top in terms of a comeuppance they were quite vehement about it, saying they were glad it had happened, and that they could never forgive Remington for what he did to their daughter. Having said that, I don't think either of them has the gall or the strength to have murdered Remington. The mother is about five feet nothing and has arthritis in her hands and feet and anyway, together, she and the father have a solid alibi. He was at the hospital most of the night. He suffered a serious angina attack yesterday evening, was taken in by ambulance and then was kept in overnight for observation. Lots of nurses and so on to confirm he was on the observation ward until Mrs. Morris came to pick him up at about nine thirty this morning"

"And the son?" Drake asked.

Derek McLennan took up the reins as he answered Izzie's question.

"He's in the clear too. Steven Andrew Morris, aged twenty, currently studying computer sciences at Exeter University. We contacted the uni, and asked the administrator to check if Morris was on campus today. Turns out he was in a lecture at the time we called, so we asked the administrator to get someone to interrupt the lecture and bring him to a phone. The lady," he consulted his notes at that point, "er…a Mrs. Davenport, wasn't too happy about helping us out there, but relented when I told her it was a murder inquiry, involving his sister. Whether she thought his sister had been murdered, I can't say, but she suddenly seemed very helpful."

"You can be as sly as a Scottie Road scally when you want to be, Derek McLennan," Drake grinned as she spoke. "You worded that so that she'd think just that, you clever little detective, you. Well done."

The rest of the team, Ross included, laughed aloud at McLennan's display of resourcefulness, a display of initiative that would have been beyond the rather green and ineffectual McLennan who'd first joined the team three years previously.

"Yes, very well done, Derek," Ross agreed, as the young detective blushed at the unexpected praise.

"Yeah, well, I've been learning from the best, haven't I, sir?"

"Well said, Derek. Please go on," Drake encouraged him.

"Oh yes, where was I? Right, of course, so a few minutes went by and I thought the old bag, I mean, Mrs. Davenport, had left me in the lurch, but then she picked up the phone again. She said she'd sent a messenger to the lecture theatre where Morris should be and said she'd summoned him as a matter of urgency to her office. Due to the urgency, she asked for my mobile number and said she'd get him to call me back as soon as he got there. So, about fifteen minutes later he called me, and confirmed the fact that he'd been in the halls of residence all night, and his room-mate would confirm it if we needed him to. Either way, there's no way he could have got from Exeter to Liverpool and back in time to have killed Remington some time this morning and been back there in time for his first lecture. He was right relieved though when I told him his sister hadn't been murdered."

Spontaneous laughter broke out once again among the team, everyone grateful for the brief moment of levity in the midst of a horrific murder investigation.

"Oh yes, he's turning into a right good joker is our Derek," Sam Gable giggled, with a broad smile on her face.

"Alright, you two, calm down a bit," said Ross. "Anything from Claire's friends, if you managed to contact them after all that?"

"Nothing at all, sorry, sir," said Gable. "There were two witnesses, if you could call them that, listed in the file. One was Lisa Owen, a friend of Claire's. She wasn't at home, but her mother directed us to the florist's shop where she works. She confirmed her original statement, that she'd been with Claire in the pub that night and got into a taxi and said goodnight to Claire at the end of the night. She said Claire wanted to walk home to clear her head, it wasn't too far, and the next she heard, was when the police came to her door the next day, and she learned about the rape. She said she hasn't seen or heard from Claire since around the time she moved into her new house with her boyfriend. Told us Claire's built a new life and let most of her old friends and reminders of the past behind her."

"Yes, that last bit gels with what Claire told us herself," said Ross. "Anything else?"

D.C. McLennan looked up from his notebook, his composure fully returned after the previous levity.

"The only other witness was Martin Riley, sir. He was the neighbour who told of Remington coming home late that night. He told us again what he'd told the police at the time: that he was letting his dog out for a wee last thing at night, when he saw Remington arrive home, looking dishevelled and 'aggravated' as he put it. There's a street light right outside their houses and he clearly saw scratch marks down the left side of Remington's face and neck. He asked Remington if he was okay but Remington just grunted something at him that sounded like "stupid bitch," and almost staggered into his home. He wasn't surprised when the police came knocking at his door and he heard of his neighbour's arrest. Of course, the scratches he testified to matched exactly with what Claire Morris said she'd done as she fought with her attacker. He said he never much liked Remington who kept himself to himself but was never very friendly with anyone in the street. I can't see him as being involved, sir. He's almost sixty, and lives alone with his dog, Rex, and uses a walking stick to get around. There's no way he could have overpowered a man like Remington, even if he'd wanted to. Oh, yes, he also told us he hoped Remington's soul would burn in hell for all eternity after what he'd done to Claire Morris."

"Humph," said Izzie Drake. "Sounds like the only person so far not to have wished him dead was Lisa Owen."

"Oh but she did, Sarge," Sam Gable piped up. "She actually said she'd often wished him dead, and, get this for a coincidence, she said she'd often wished that someone would cut 'that bastards cock off and turn him into a fucking eunuch, so he couldn't hurt any more innocent young girls or

273

women,' and I promise you we never said a word about what had happened to Remington. I was going to add that bit at the end, when Derek finished."

"Oh right, saving the best till last, eh?" said Drake, while Ross added,

"But you didn't think she could have been involved, Sam?"

"Oh, no sir, She was just spouting the kind of rhetoric that women often do when talking about scumbag rapists like Remington, erm, sorry, like our victim, sir."

"Yes, right, I think we all know the team's estimations of Mr. Remington's character, thanks Sam, but remember everyone, a crime has been committed, a bloody brutal and vicious murder, and whatever we may think of the victim, I'm reiterating for you all, our job is to catch his killer, so do not lose sight of that objective, not even for a second."

Grunts of assent and agreement mumbled their way from the lips of those in the room.

"Right then, how about you Tony?" Drake said, turning to D.C. Curtis, who'd been sent to speak with Remington's employers.

"Drew a blank there as well, Sarge. None of his co-workers knew of his past. The personnel department, who, by the way, they like to call 'Human Resources' now, knew about it, but their records are confidential, and his line supervisor knew, but that was all. Seems they have a policy of employing a limited number of 'rehabilitated' offenders at Halewood, only a small quota of the total workforce. Anyway, unless someone found out about his record from somebody outside work there's little chance any of his fellow workers would have known he was a convicted rapist. Makes you feel sick really, when you think of the women who work there, not knowing who they were sitting with in the canteen at lunchtime, for example."

"Yes, well, we've been through all that before, Curtis," said Ross, so let's all drop the references to what we'd all have liked to do with Matthew Remington, or what we think should have been done with him."

A few more low frequency grumbles ran round the room as Ross turned finally to Paul Ferris.

"What about you, Paul? Did the good Reverend Donovan have anything else to tell us?"

"No sir. He was still in a state of shock if you ask me. I took a picture of Remington as he was in life to show him and he said he'd never seen him before. He might have come to his church at some time for all he knew, but he certainly wasn't a regular. If you ask me, sir, the churchyard was our killer's choice for the murder and had nothing to do with Remington, or whether he attended St. Matthew's or not."

"I think you're right, Paul," Ross agreed. "And listen, everybody. I want this bastard caught sooner rather than later, because, if what you've all told me today, backed up by what Sergeant Drake and I learned from talking to Claire Morris is correct, then it's my strong suspicion that Matthew

Remington's murder had nothing to do with the rape of Claire Morris. If that's the case we're not only back to square one, but we now have a crime without an apparent motive. That, as we all know, is bollocks. A crime as violent as this had to have been caused by a very strong motive, and we have to start again and try to find out just what that motive is.

I want everyone to start digging into Mathew Remington's past. Go back to his childhood if you have to. Someone in this city hated him enough to virtually butcher him and then cut off his manhood and stick it down his throat. It takes real hatred, and real rage to do all that to a man. I want to know what Remington did, no matter how long ago to make someone feel they had to do what we saw the results of today. Any questions?"

Silence filled the room, accompanied by a chorus of shaking heads.

"Okay, listen, people, it's too late to do much more today. Go home, all of you, get some rest and be here bright and early in the morning. I'll be holding the morning briefing at eight a.m. sharp.

With that, the working day ended for Ross's team, and within minutes, all were on their way to their homes. Ross couldn't wait to see his wife, Maria. He felt somehow soiled and sullied by the day's events and he needed to feel a semblance of normality and humdrum home life, even if only for a few hours. His neat suburban detached home in Prescot might only be a few miles from the city, but right now, as he left the headquarters building, it felt like it was a million miles from the smells of blood and death that had followed him around all day.

CHAPTER 8

RESPITE

"You look absolutely shattered," Maria Ross exclaimed as she looked at her husband, who'd just walked in to the kitchen, his sagging shoulders and downcast expression betraying the effects of a stressful day at work. Andy always used the back door as a rule when coming home from work. Nine times out of ten, his shoes would be dirty and soiled from his exposure to the 'wild side of life, as Maria described his job. Today was no exception.

"Been a rough day, sweetheart," he replied as he dropped exhaustedly into an armchair that looked out of place in its surroundings. The old, blue velour upholstered fireside chair had moved with them from their previous house and had previously belonged to Ross's father, where it had held pride of place in his parents' kitchen. It was probably the most comfortable chair Ross had ever sat in and Maria would never dream of asking her husband to get rid of it.

"Want to talk about it?" she asked.

"You won't like it," he replied.

"Try me."

"We had a bad one, Maria. A man's body was found in a churchyard in Woolton. He'd been virtually butchered and..." he hesitated.

"Go on, Andy, and what?"

"Well, the killer opened up his body and cut out and sort of scattered all his major organs around the grave he'd been dumped on, but the worst part was the other thing he did. He cut off the guy's bloody penis, Maria, and stuffed it down his throat."

"Before or after he was killed?" Maria asked, calmly.

"Doc Nugent thinks the mutilations were all carried out post-mortem, apart from the penis, maybe. The man's throat had been slashed, cut almost through to the spine, and he was almost definitely dead before the killer hacked him to bits."

Maria's face registered a mixture of shock and sympathy at Ross's gruesome revelation.

"That must have been a terrible thing to see, my darling. I'm sorry you had to be there."

"That's my job, isn't it? Clearing up the mess the criminal fraternity leave behind themselves. It then turned out the victim was a convicted rapist. We thought at first he might have been killed by someone connected to his victim but we moved fast to interview her and her friends and relatives and there's no way I can see them being involved. So, we're back to square one."

Maria moved to her husband and, standing behind him, placed her hands on the back of his neck and slowly began to massage his tense and taut muscles. It was something she always did when he was stressed from a hard day at work and gradually, he began to relax a little.

"I love you, Maria Ross," he spoke quietly as her hands gently eased away the tension in his neck muscles.

"I love you too, Andy Ross," she whispered as she bent down and kissed the top of his head gently.

"Better stop before I nod off," Ross said as he felt his eyes beginning to droop.

"Why don't you go and take a shower and freshen up while I cook us something?"

"Good idea," he agreed, as he heaved himself up from his chair, kissed Maria tenderly on the lips he loved so much and walked from the room. As she heard him walk up the stairs to the bathroom, Maria thought, not for the first time, of how lucky she considered herself to have Andy Ross as a husband. She'd fallen for him almost from the first time she'd met him, and that love had never diminished. She loved his olive tinted skin, the result of his distant Anglo-Indian-Portuguese ancestry, and his intense dark brown eyes, with a head of luxuriant dark brown hair that was only just beginning to show a hint of grey as he approached his late forties. Equally, she knew Andy cared just as much for her. He never ceased to compliment her on her long, blonde hair, blue eyes, and her lips, always a prime target for his kisses. She'd kept herself in shape and still had a figure that many women half her age would have craved.

Daydream over, Maria set to work and quickly prepared a meal of spaghetti bolognaise for the two of them. After dinner, the pair snuggled up together on the large four-seater sofa in their lounge, her head resting on his chest as they relaxed together, watching TV for a while, and then listening to music for an hour until tiredness began to summon them both to bed.

"Doctor Ross prescribes an early night, Inspector," she whispered quietly in his ear.

"I'm happy to go along with your prescription, Doctor," he replied.

"You lock up down here, then go and get into bed, Andy. I'll grab a quick shower and be with you in ten minutes. If you're a good boy, the doctor might prescribe a spot of intimate massage, if you follow my meaning," she grinned at him.

"Mmm, sounds good to me. Don't be long in the shower. I'll be waiting."

They rose from the sofa, Maria quickly heading upstairs for her shower. Andy went round each room ensuring all the windows were locked, and then finally making sure the front and back doors were locked and the security alarm switched on, finally following his wife up the stairs.

"Don't be long, darling," he shouted, as he quickly undressed and jumped into bed.

"Two minutes," Maria shouted from the en-suite bathroom. Shower over; Maria quickly removed the shower cap that had kept her hair dry, shaking her hair loose, allowing to cascade down, creating a look of wilful abandon. *Pefect,* she thought. Now wasn't the time for washing her hair and spending fifteen minutes with the hair dryer, certainly not for what she had in mind. Although she and Andy slept in the nude, she reached up and took a slinky, narrow strapped satin negligee from a hook behind the bathroom door. She knew her husband enjoyed the feel of the satin against her skin and removing it was one of his special sensual pleasures. A quick look in the mirror, a brush through her hair and Maria was ready. After the kind of day he'd endured, Andy deserved a little pleasure, and she was intent on providing it.

She exited the bathroom and softly padded, barefoot across the bedroom to where Andy lay, on his side, facing away from her. She smoothed the chemise down as she moved closer and lifted the edge of the duvet. Sliding in beside and behind him, Maria softly whispered in his ear, "I've got something special for you, big boy"

Receiving no reply and no response, she reached her right arm across her husband's body, allowing her hand to gently stroke his manhood.

"Are you kidding me?" she asked, and then realised he wasn't. Andy Ross was fast asleep.

* * *

"Don't stop, Oh god, please, don't stop."

Izzie Drake lay beneath Peter Foster, her legs apart and wrapped tightly round him as he approached his own climax. Izzie could feel the beginnings of her own orgasm as she urged him on, until he gasped, grunted and cried out a loud "*Yes,*" as he spilled his seed deep within her. Feeling his penis throb and swell within her as he came, Izzie's own orgasm burst through the barriers of her own expectant passion and she herself cried out in ecstasy as the strength of the orgasm overwhelmed her, shutting out all other feelings and sensations until, slowly, as Peter sighed loudly, she released him from the intense leg lock she held his body in and allowed her legs to fall languidly and lewdly apart, knees slightly raised, as the lovers allowed themselves a few moments of breathless respite.

"Bloody hell, Izzie. You're amazing!" Peter exclaimed, having finally got his breath back enough to speak.

"You're not so bad yourself," she grinned up at him, before pulling his face down and planting a long, lingering kiss on his lips.

The pair had spent the evening at Peter's two-bedroomed apartment in a fairly new mid-priced development overlooking the docks. He'd bought it the previous year after inheriting a reasonably generous legacy from his always doting grandmother, who'd brought him up herself after his parents had died in a car crash when the young Paul Foster was ten years old. Her death from liver disease had hit him hard at the time, and his relationship with the pretty police sergeant had helped him greatly in his recovery from the initial grief at her passing. He and Izzie had enjoyed a takeaway from the local Indian restaurant before falling into bed together, Izzie virtually ripping his clothes off as she pulled him into the bedroom.

"You're not usually quite so…intense," he observed, tactfully, as Izzie eventually eased herself out from beneath him, pulling herself up to a sitting position beside him.

"Not complaining, are you?"

"Hey, no way. Just wondering what I've done to deserve such a treat, that's all."

Izzie sighed before replying.

"I think it was just such a shit day at work today, Paul. I've never seen a body mutilated in that way. I mean, come on, you might not have seen it when it was brought in, but you must have heard what the killer did to Remington."

"Oh, yes, it was quite the talk of the office when we heard the details. I was glad I'm only employed on the admin side of things, so I can imagine a little bit of what you're getting at. I don't know how you can look at stuff like that every day and not be physically sick," he said.

"I felt like being sick, for sure, but I held on, I'm glad to say. We don't get to see that kind of thing often to be honest. Most murders are nothing like that, maybe a simple gunshot, or sometimes a stabbing or strangulation, but this was different, and to be honest, when we found out just what

Remington had done in the past, I found it hard to feel too much sympathy for him."

"That's only natural, Izzie. You're only human, after all, and a gorgeous young woman too. You must feel a certain empathy with the girl he attacked."

"That's true, and Peter?"

"Yes?"

"Thanks for being so kind and understanding."

"Come here," he said and as she turned to face him, he kissed her long and hard, the kiss carrying a welter of emotion that carried Izzie back from her thoughts of work and once again turned her on to the romantic and erotic feelings they'd been sharing up until a few moments ago.

"Peter?" she gasped as she pulled her lips away long enough to talk.

"Uh huh?"

"Take me to the moon again."

"My pleasure," he grinned, pushing her down onto her back once more.

Izzie Drake needed no prompting as she opened her legs to welcome her lover into her body and into her very soul once again. As Peter Foster began to make love to her for the second time, a thought entered her mind, and for the first time, she realised…she was in love.

The couple soon fell asleep, though they woke twice in the night and indulged in repeats of their earlier lovemaking. Whatever the following day might bring, for now, at least, Izzie Drake was at peace with herself and with the world, the Matthew Remingtons of the world banished to the tiniest corner of her consciousness.

* * *

Sweat poured from every pore of Father Gerald Byrne's body. The sight of Mark Proctor, screaming in terror, and the sight of his blood, flowing in a torrent from a vicious head wound filled his mind until he thought his brain would swell and burst from his skull. Even then, his arm acted as though independent of his body, rising and falling in an arc of destruction as he wielded the heavy sword, one of two that usually hung in a display at the bishop's palace, the crossed swords being relics from the days of the crusades, so it was said. If this was indeed a crusader's weapon, it was enjoying a vicious renaissance in the hands of this twenty-first century warrior-priest.

As his arm finally tired, and the weight of the sword caused it to fall limply at his side, the bloodied blade pointing at the blood-soaked ground, Byrne finally allowed himself to stop, his chest heaving, and he surveyed his work. Little remained of Proctor's skull, his chest a gaping maw and the blood seeping from under the corpse until it appeared to be floating on a miniature lake of deep crimson.

That Proctor was dead, there could be no doubt, so, when the cadaver suddenly sat up, the bloodied, shattered head turning towards him, Gerald Byrne recoiled in abject fear. The hideously torn lips, the toothless mouth began to move and Proctor, impossibly, spoke,

"Gerry, oh Gerry, what on earth have you done? You'll be in trouble for this, you know you will."

Byrne screamed, a scream so loud it reverberated from the walls of his bedroom, so loud in fact that it woke him from his dream, or was it a nightmare? He really was sweating as he sat upright in bed, looked around him, recognising the familiar fixtures and fittings of his own bedroom, the dressing table, the wardrobe, the paisley-patterned quilt on his bed. Gerald Byrne forced himself out of the bed, and padded across the room to the dressing table, where he paused to view his reflection in the mirror. "Holy Mother of God, Gerald," he spoke to himself, "you truly look like shit, my friend."

Byrne almost staggered from his bedroom, making his way to the bathroom at the end of the landing, where he splashed cold water on his face and neck until he began to feel less wretched and more like his self again.

As he prepared to walk out of the bathroom, he became aware of an urgent knocking on his bedroom door, and he heard David Willis's voice calling out to him.

"Father Byrne, are you alright in there? Father, please open the door."

"I'm here, David," he said as he exited the bathroom, stepping out onto the landing. He realised his shouting must have woken the young priest, whose own bedroom was just along the landing from his own.

"Oh, thank the good Lord," Willis exclaimed, standing at the bedroom door in his red tartan dressing gown and matching carpet slippers, his blue striped pyjama bottoms protruding from the hem of the robe. "Was it a nightmare, Father? I was worried when I woke to hear you screaming so loudly. At first I thought someone had broken in and was attacking you."

Byrne walked up to Willis and placed a reassuring hand on the younger man's shoulder.

"Yes, David, it was just a nightmare, nothing to worry about. I probably shouldn't have enjoyed the biscuits and cheese so much after dinner. I've often heard that cheese can be the cause of bad dreams if eaten in excess before bedtime."

"Well, if you're sure you're alright, Father?"

"I'm fine, really, David. I'm sorry to have disturbed your sleep. You go and get yourself back to bed."

"Right, okay then, Father. I'll say good night again, then."

"Yes, goodnight, David, sleep well, and I'm sorry, once again."

Father Willis smiled a slightly worried smile as he headed back to his room, and turned round just before entering the bedroom but Father Byrne had already disappeared into his own bedroom, closing the door virtually silently.

Back in bed again a few minutes later, Gerald Byrne laid his head back on his pillows, closing his eyes, and allowed himself to slowly drift back to sleep. Just before sleep claimed him however, he found himself thinking,

Couldn't have happened to a more deserving case.

CHAPTER 9

ESCALATION

Every member of the investigation team was on time for the morning briefing, so much so that Andy Ross was the last to arrive, and he was ten minutes early! Acknowledging the greetings of his fellow officers, Ross felt good about himself this morning. Although he'd fallen into a deep sleep the previous night, depriving himself of the immense pleasure of a steamy lovemaking session with Maria, she'd made sure he was wide awake at five-thirty a.m. as Ross felt himself being gently coaxed into the mood by the tender ministrations of his wife's nimble fingers. What he'd missed last night, Maria was determined to make up for that morning. The sex was steamy alright, as his wife made sure they both extracted maximum plea-sure from the thirty minutes they dared devote to each other before rising to begin the day. He hoped he could hide the self-satisfied grin that he felt was a sure giveaway to his team, but nobody appeared to notice, he thought.

Izzie Drake was at the front of the room, in conversation with collator, Paul Ferris, the pair of them standing in front of the whiteboard.

"Morning, sir," Izzie said as she turned to him. *My God, she looks like the cat that got the cream,* Ross thought as he looked at his sergeant's face and recognised the gleam in her eye as a sure-fire tell-tale sign.

"Good night, last night, Izzie?" he asked, looking straight in the eye, and Izzie instantly knew that he knew exactly what she and Peter Foster were doing the previous night.

"Very good, sir, thank you. And you?"

"Oh yes, very good, thank you, Sergeant. Very good indeed."

That was enough. The almost telepathic connection between Ross and his Sergeant meant that he realised she could read him as well as he read her. Seems like both master and apprentice had found the ideal outlet to release the tension and the stress of the previous day's gruesome discovery.

"Right then, that's good, so, let's get this show on the road, shall we?"

Within five minutes, Ross had summarised the efforts of the previous day, ending by thanking everyone for their hard work and professionalism in managing to complete a major slice of investigative procedure in one day. He praised Paul Ferris for helping George Thompson put together a Press Release that said very little, just enough to keep the press hounds at bay for a day or two while they attempted to press forward with the investigation, and then moved on to the orders for the day.

"We might not have unearthed a viable suspect as yet, but I think it's safe to say we've eliminated any connection between Remington's murder and the rape of Claire Morris. So, as I said yesterday, we go back into his past, and we dig, dig deep into anything and everything that man did in his life that might have some bearing on what happened yesterday. Someone held a pathological hatred for Mathew Remington. They must have done to have killed him and mutilated him as they did. We have to find out what he did to bring about such hatred."

"Any ideas where to start, sir?" asked 'Tony' Curtis.

"At the beginning of course, Tony," Ross replied. "D.C. Ferris will start the ball rolling by digging up his birth certificate. Paul, I want you to trace his early years, find out where he went to school, if he had any reported problems with other kids, or his teachers, that kind of thing."

"Okay, sir. I'll get to work right away, though I do know from the file on his arrest that he was an orphan with no known relatives, so we can eliminate the family angle right away," Ferris replied.

"Fair enough," said Ross, "concentrate on the rest. Sam, Derek, you two work together and go back to Remington's time in the nick. Speak to the prison governor, any of the prison offices who were there at the time. Bear in mind I don't know what we're looking for, but it's possible he upset someone badly while he was banged up. We know he was segregated from the general prison population because of the nature of his offence, but we haven't yet considered the fact he may have done something to upset someone who wasn't a prisoner."

"Bloody hell, sir. You think a prison officer might have done it?"

"I don't know, Derek, but I'm not discounting anything at this time."

What about me, sir?" Izzie asked.

Before Ross could reply, the door of the conference room was opened and the figure of D.C.I. Harry Porteous stood there, framed by the doorway. His words sent an immediate chill down the spine of everyone in the room.

"We've had another one, and it's even worse than Remington."

Andy Ross's mouth fell open in shock, Izzie Drake looked as though someone had smacked her across the face and rest of the team froze where they sat or stood, unable to quite comprehend this latest shocking news.

The detective chief inspector strode to the front of the room and stood beside Ross before speaking again.

"I just received a call to say a body's been discovered in the church-yard at St. Mark's in Croxteth. It's another shocking mutilation scenario I'm afraid. According to the officers who responded to the 999 call, they've never seen anything this bad in their lives, and Sergeant Donaldson has been on the force for over twenty years and has seen most things it's possible to come across in that time. If he says it's bad, believe me, it is. He's aware of the Remington murder but he assured me, when he was put through to me, that this is much worse. I want you there as soon as possible Andy. Take as many of the team as you can spare from here, if they're not actively pursuing any leads on the Remington case."

"Right, sir. Paul, you stay here and work on those records. With any luck, we may find a connection between Remington and the latest victim once we know who it is. Did the sergeant tell you if he'd managed to I.D the victim, sir?"

"No, he didn't. There was too much confusion at the scene he said, and he didn't want to disturb anything before C.I.D arrived on site. He's had the wherewithal to ask for forensic back-up and the duty pathologist is already on his way to Croxteth. You'll be pleased to hear it's your old friend, Dr. Nugent," Porteous informed them.

"It would be," said Ross, "but at least Fat Willy knows what he's doing and understands the urgency of what we need."

"Right then, you'd better get going, Andy," Porteous urged him.

"Consider us gone, sir," Ross replied as he motioned for the team to follow him and Drake as they led the way from the conference room.

* * *

Located virtually next door to Norris Green, Croxteth, 'Crocky' to most of its inhabitants is a fairly modern addition to the suburbs of Liverpool, despite being located close to Croxteth Hall and Country Park, once the home of the Earls of Sefton. Just prior to World War Two, large areas of housing were built there to house skilled workers from the English Electric and Napier factories who had moved to the area from the towns of Slough and Rugby. Later, families who had lost their homes during the bombings of the second world war moved into the area, which gradually grew over the years until it became what it is today, a large urban housing estate, which together with its neighbour, Norris Green, is one of Europe's largest housing developments.

St. Mark's church stood on the edge of the estate, close to the road leading to the country park, making it slightly isolated from the main housing areas of Croxteth. It was a small church, with a graveyard to the rear, and a small and continually dwindling congregation. The events of that morning would surely serve to reduce it still further.

Sergeant Vince Donaldson had taken charge of the situation as soon as he'd realised the importance of the crime scene. His partner, Constable Tim Mallory had quickly surrounded the entire church grounds with crime scene tape, making the whole of St. Marks an island of police and forensic activity. Donaldson had also requested additional uniformed officers from the local station and a total of six constables now stood ready to assist the detectives in any way necessary.

Ross and Drake led the way into the churchyard, where they were met by Donaldson, who'd had Constable Mallory on lookout for their arrival. Followed by Sam Gable, Derek McLennan and 'Tony' Curtis, they followed the sergeant along the narrow path that led round the church itself to the graveyard at the rear.

As soon as they turned the corner that gave them visual access to the graveyard, Ross saw just why Porteous had said this was worse than the previous day's crime scene.

"Bloody hell," he exclaimed.

"Oh…my…God," Izzie Drake choked the words out.

"Holy Mother of God," came from Sam Gable, who held her hand to her mouth in shock.

"Oh, fuck," was D.C Curtis's reaction, and whatever Derek McLennan was about to say never actually came out as he lurched off the path into the grassed area between two graves and for the second time in two days, was violently sick.

The scene before them was, Ross thought, surely something from a 'B' grade Hollywood slasher movie. About twenty yards ahead stood a grave, decorated as graves often are with the statue of a winged angel that Ross estimated to be around six to seven feet tall, the deceased obviously having been from a family able to afford an expensive funeral and the aforementioned grave statuary.

Far from appearing as a symbol of God's love, or of peace and benevolence, the angel instead presented them with a vision straight from hell. Tied to the outstretched wings of the angel with what looked like barbed wire, were the arms of the victim, crucifixion-style. The man's naked body hung in place across the front of the angel, his waist again secured by more wire, with his feet tied similarly, his legs bent unnaturally backwards to bring them into contact with the base of the statue.

Even without the benefit of Dr. Nugent's examination, Ross felt sure the victim had been alive when his murderer had fastened him to the angel. The amount of blood that had fallen to the ground from the man's wrists, his torso and feet surely indicated he'd been breathing at the time and must have endured interminable agony. Far worse however, were the additional wounds inflicted on the naked man. Whoever had perpetrated this horror had literally slashed the man's lower torso wide open and the detectives were faced with the horror of seeing the man's intestines and entrails literally dripping from the open gut. The victim's blood obscenely stained the consecrated ground red, both the grass and the once white surface of the grave stone itself. As with Matthew Remington, once again the man's penis was missing, a bloody void in its place and Ross held no illusions as to where they'd find it. Again, at first glance Ross could see no sign of the victim's clothes or belongings

"Who the hell could do this to another human being?" Izzie Drake was the first to break the shocked silence that had befallen the group.

Before anyone could proffer an answer, the sound of horrified gasps and exclamations from behind them announced the arrival of medical examiner William Nugent and his assistant, Francis Lees, accompanied by two obviously unnecessary paramedics. They were closely followed by Miles Booker and his team of four Crime Scenes Officers who had arrived simultaneously with the M.E.

"Och, man, ye've really got a doozy for me this morning, Inspector Ross. The poor soul. Ah cannae imagine any human being doing this to his fellow man."

"Sergeant Drake said virtually the same thing just as you arrived, Doc. This is just about the worst thing I've seen in all my years as a copper."

"Aye, well, standing here talking about it isn't going to help us find his killer is it? Come on, Francis, we've work to do."

Francis Lees followed the doctor, and as they began their initial examination of the body, to establish that the victim was in fact dead, though no one could be in any doubt as to the fact, Miles Booker walked up beside Ross.

"Jesus Christ, Andy. This is bloody grotesque."

"Tell me about it, Miles. I'm not sure my team can take much more of sights like this."

"Yeah, I can see young McLennan has lost his breakfast again."

Both men looked towards the death scene as Nugent beckoned to them. He and Lees, dressed in their white forensic suits and matching boots, resembled a pair of rather deformed wingless angels themselves as they tentatively examined the corpse.

Ross and Booker walked slowly towards the two men, stopping a few yards away, conscious not to disturb any trace evidence.

"Got something, Doc?" Ross called to him.

"Just confirmation your man is dead, Inspector. Mr Booker, does your team have a ladder in your van? I need to get up there and take a closer look at the victim. It's a good six feet to the top. We've tried not to disturb anything in the immediate vicinity, but I need to examine him in place before we take him down."

"Sure, Doc, give me a minute."

Booker sent a member of his team to fetch the ladder and in the mean-time, Ross made an observation.

"Miles, I don't understand how the killer got him up there, or how he's overpowering his victims. Remington was no weakling, by appearances, and this poor sod looks quite well-built and muscular."

"Have you had the toxicology report back on number one yet? Maybe he's drugging them first"

"Ha, give the Doc a chance, Miles. Even Nugent can't quite work mira-cles. You know as well as I do it can take up to forty-eight hours to get the tox report, and let's face it, he didn't have a whole body to work with did he?"

Just then, one of Booker's crime scene techs arrived with a lightweight collapsible aluminium ladder and within a minute, despite his bulk, Nugent had ascended the angel and was carrying out a close-up examination of the victim. Meanwhile, one of Booker's men had identified a number of unidentified footprints in the immediate vicinity of the grave on which the victim had been displayed and was taking casts of the imprints, being careful to eliminate the prints left by Nugent and Lees in their need to carry out their initial examination. As everyone carried out their allotted tasks and with Ross's team pretty much idle for the moment, he sent Izzie to bring Sergeant Donaldson to him.

"Who found the body, Sergeant?"

"The vicar, sir, a Reverend Blake."

"Shouldn't that be Father Blake?"

"No sir, this is a Church of England church."

"So, our killer isn't just targeting Catholic churches as his kill sites. Either he doesn't really care about the religious aspect or he wants to take it out on all religions by leaving his victims in churchyards. Hard to fathom really. Ross looked at the gravestone again and at the incumbent angel, noting the family name on the long, horizontal slab of marble. I doubt the Seagrove family ever envisaged anything like this taking place on their last resting place," he mused, and turned to Drake. "Make a note of the family name, Izzie. We may find some significance in the killer's choice of grave-stones by the time we're done with this bloody case. We might even have to investigate the families buried here and at St. Matthew's"

Drake nodded and dutifully noted the Seagrove name in her notebook.

William Nugent, his initial examination concluded, had descended from his position on the ladder and now walked across to Ross and Booker.

"Right then, Mr. Booker. Your people can carry on and do whatever needs to be done. As for your victim, Inspector, I believe your murderer has escalated his level of violence in terms of his means of execution."

"In what way, Doc?"

"Once we get him back to the mortuary I'll be able to tell you more, but for now, I think I can safely say that this poor man was still alive when he was hauled up and secured to the statue."

"Hauled?" Ross asked.

"Yes. There are marks under his arms and around his chest to suggest the killer tied a rope of some sort around the body and then literally hauled him up there. I found footprints some yards to the rear of the statue where he probably stood and heaved on the rope to slowly lift the body into place. You can see the indents where he dug his heels into the ground to gain purchase. Also, the amount of blood loss around the wrists, torso and ankles indicate he bled profusely from those wounds, which he wouldn't have done if he'd been dead at the time he received them. I can see numerous scratches all over the back too, where the dead weight of the body has caused it to sag forward, where he scraped against the angel as he was hauled up."

This information confirmed what Ross had initially thought.

"So, he knew what he was going to do before he got here and came prepared."

"I think so," said Nugent.

"There's not much more I can do here. Let's get him back to the mortuary and I can get to work," said Nugent, beckoning to the para-medics who would have the unenviable task of transporting the body, and its associated entrails and organs to Nugent's own domain, where a full post-mortem examination could be conducted.

"Perhaps, if they've got all the photos they need and your initial search for trace evidence is completed, Mr. Booker, you can get your crime scene people to take the body down and bag the organs so the ambulance crew can move everything back to the morgue for me?"

Booker nodded and moved off to organise his crime scene team.

"Oh, one more point, Inspector."

"Go on, Doc. What is it?"

"You're going to have the unenviable task of notifying a widow, I believe. Yonder laddie is wearing a wedding ring, so either he's married, or divorced and just hasn't bothered removing the ring. Some men do that, don't they?"

"Yes, they do, Doc, thanks. Don't suppose you took it off to see if there's any engraving inside the ring?"

"Perched on a ladder? Do me a favour, Inspector Ross. I'm nae stupid enough to try that. I'll make it a priority when I get him to the lab."

"Right, thanks Doc."

* * *

Leaving the specialists to handle the removal of the body, Ross and Drake stood looking at each other for a few seconds as they contemplated what they'd seen in the last hour or so. It was Drake who broke the silence.

"Sir? Are you with me? We need to move on this. What do you want the others to do?

"Yes, sorry, Izzie. I was just trying to think this through. There seems no way the two killings can be connected to Claire Morris so it's now totally safe to conclude her rape isn't part of our killer's overall scenario."

"Unless this victim is connected to Claire, sir?"

Ross nodded, thoughtful.

"A possibility, Izzie but somehow I doubt that. We do need to identify this man though, the sooner the better. Come on, we'd better go talk to the priest, sorry, the vicar. Get the others to start an immediate search of the area. Have Donaldson leave two men on duty here to secure the scene along with McLennan, if he's stopped throwing his guts up all over the churchyard and then team his officers up with our people. There aren't many houses in the immediate vicinity of the church so it's possible someone may have noticed something out of the ordinary."

"Such as?"

"I don't know, Izzie, but this bastard came prepared. I suspect he brought the victim here in a van or truck of some kind. He'd have needed a vehicle that could carry a ladder and whatever tools he needed to pull this off. He had to have had a roll of barbed wire with him and some pretty heavy duty gloves with which to apply it to the poor sod. He'd have needed cutters, God knows what else. This took time to execute, Izzie. If he did this in the dark or half-light of dawn, he'd have needed a powerful torch. He must have been supremely confident he wasn't going to be disturbed while he did this. Once we get an approximate time of death from Doctor Nugent we'll have a better idea of the timeline. I want to know exactly what time sunrise occurred. He needed light to see what he was doing, so may have strung the victim up to the statue and completed his killing ritual as the sun rose."

"Right, sir. When you said ritual, does that mean you think…?

"I don't know what to think yet, Izzie. Let's not discount anything until we know more."

"I understand, sir," she replied as another thought struck the D.I.

"And another thing. If he was awake, the victim must have screamed

290

his head off. Someone in one of those nearby houses just might have heard something."

With the team quickly allocated to their various tasks, Ross and Drake prepared themselves for an interview with the Reverend Blake, whom Donaldson had sent back to the vicarage, accompanied by one of his uniformed officers, to await the arrival of the C.I.D detectives.

CHAPTER 10

CONFESSION

The fourth confession of the morning at St. Luke's Parish Church sent shivers down the spine of Father Gerald Byrne. As the voice, quite clearly that of a young woman, a teenager perhaps, on the other side of the confessional screen described her inner torment, it brought back memories to the priest, painful memories that he'd rather remain locked away in the deepest part of his soul. But, even as the young woman divested herself of sin before God, hoping for an absolution, Byrne knew that those memories, now resurfaced, could never be put back in the convenient mental box where he'd managed to store them for so many years.

As the woman/girl eventually fell silent, waiting for his response, a new and terrible burden came to rest on the shoulders of the Catholic priest. Bound as he was by the sanctity of the confessional, Byrne knew he could never reveal any of what the young woman had just imparted to him, no matter what the eventual outcome may be, a fact that troubled him deeply, far more than it should do, given his priestly status.

Byrne rushed through the next stage of the confessional, the young woman probably being surprised at the priest's response and lenient penitence he demanded of her. As he heard her footsteps recede towards the church exit, Byrne slumped against the wall of his side of the confessional, his head resting on the cold, hard wood as his mind filled with recollections of those things and events he'd much rather remain locked away.

"Forgive me, Father, for I have sinned. It has been one week since my last confession."

Byrne was suddenly brought back to reality by the voice of the next occupant of the confessional box. For now, he needed to concentrate on the here and now, put the past aside, and yet, the priest knew now that the past could never be totally put to one side, locked away out of harm's way, and, after hearing the previous occupant of the confessional's story, Father Gerald Byrne was now a worried man, afraid the past and the present were about to collide, and there was little, if anything he could do to prevent the events that were to unfold.

Confession finally over, Byrne virtually staggered from the church and on arrival at the manse, he almost collapsed into a softly upholstered, welcoming armchair in the living room. Hearing his entry through the front door, David Willis, who'd been carrying out visits to sick parishioners that morning came into the room, ready to offer Father Byrne a refreshing cup of tea. One look at the Father's face however, made Willis stop in his tracks, a worried look upon his face.

"Father, are you alright? You look pale. Are you ill?"

Byrne failed to answer right away, and Willis would swear to it that the priest looked as though his mind was a million miles away at that moment, his eyes seemingly focussed on a point in time and space that had little to do with the here and now.

Willis now walked up to Byrne and placed a hand on his shoulder as he said again,

"Father, are you alright?"

Byrne suddenly appeared to return to life, as though he had indeed been in another time and place. He looked up and seemed surprised to see the worried face of David Willis staring down at him, his face a mask of concern. Byrne quickly attempted to pull himself together.

"Oh dear, David, hello. I'm sorry if I frightened you, but I must have been miles away. I'm afraid daydreaming is almost a pastime of mine these days. So many faces, so many events over the years. Sometimes I remember and recall those events through harmless little daydreams, especially on warm sunny days like this. I'm sure you understand me, David, yes?"

Although he didn't really understand what Byrne meant, and though he honestly believed something was deeply troubling Father Byrne, Willis just smiled and replied,

"Of course Father. You've had a long and interesting life within the church and must have many happy memories. It's nice to be able to recall them I'm sure."

"Happy memories? Yes, David, I suppose most of them are."

Byrne said no more and David Willis diplomatically felt he should press no further, though he was certain something was on the older man's mind.

"I'll go and make us a nice cup of tea, shall I Father?" he said instead and Byrne smiled up at him from his chair.

293

"Yes, David, you do that. That would be nice. Yes, a cup of tea, very nice indeed."

* * *

Lisa Kelly alighted from the bus and stood watching as it pulled away and disappeared into the distance. She began walking slowly but determinedly, knowing exactly where she was going. Soon afterwards, she arrived at her destination, the dunes at Formby Beach. Lisa had always loved coming here. Her mother had been taking her to the beach at Formby since she was a little girl, often taking a picnic with them and enjoying afternoons together walking along the beach, watching the red squirrels that frequented the 'squirrel walk', before catching the bus home as evening fell. After visiting the church that morning, Lisa had sat on a bench in the churchyard for ten minutes, contemplating her next move. Finally, knowing there was no other way, she checked her purse, making sure she had enough change for the bus fare, and set off for Formby. Lisa sat for a while, listening to the sound of the breeze as it played a soft concerto among and around the dunes. Taking her mobile phone from her purse, she turned it on, and over the next two minutes, recorded a message on its voice recorder that she hoped would explain her actions to her Mum and her priest, the nice new man, Father Byrne. Satisfied, she rose and began walking towards the beach. Being a weekday, there weren't too many people around and Lisa made sure she headed for the most isolated section of beach she could find.

Arriving at the water's edge, she kicked off her shoes, and without hesitation, began slowly walking into the cold water, her eyes filled with tears as the waves grew taller the further out she walked, until her feet began to lose their purchase on the soft sand beneath. A sudden shout from behind her came from a man walking his dog, obviously aware of what she was doing, but Lisa simply ignored him and allowed the waves to take her, finally succumbing to the power of wind and wave as she sank below the waves, the weight of her clothes helping to carry her down, until finally, her head disappeared as the man and his dog stood helplessly looking on as witnesses to the final living moments of Lisa Kelly, just seventeen years old.

CHAPTER 11

TEA AT THE VICARAGE

"Please come in, Inspector Ross, Sergeant Drake. I'm Simon, Simon Blake."

Ross and Drake followed the Vicar of St. Mark's church into a neat and tidy parlour, furnished as Ross would have expected a churchman's home to be, with a red leather three-piece suite taking centre stage in the room, a mahogany coffee table strategically placed in the middle of the room. Beneath the bay window, which overlooked an expansive lawn, planted with well established shrubs and trees of varying species, stood a desk, also in mahogany, on which stood a modern laptop computer and printer, an open invitation to a thief, Drake thought to herself, but also typical of the trusting nature of a man of the cloth. Along the adjacent wall a bookcase held a fairly eclectic collection of reading material, from religious tomes to crime thrillers and romantic fiction, quite clearly the reading material of the vicar's wife, Ross presumed. What immediately caught Ross's interest however, was a photograph of the man who stood before him in the typical dress of a Church of England Priest, black shirt and white 'dog collar,' that stood to one side of the mantlepiece across the rather old-fashioned granite fireplace. The photograph showed the Reverend Simon Blake, some years younger dressed in the uniform of a British Army officer. Ross would ask about that in due course.

For now, he and Drake sat side by side on the sofa, at the vicar's invitation. Before Ross could ask anything, Blake took the initiative and asked the first and perhaps predictable question,

"Would you both like a cup of tea? I imagine you could both use one after seeing that poor man out there."

"Yes please, Vicar," Ross replied. I think you're right, that's kind of you."

"Just a moment and I'll ask my wife to prepare the tea, and then I'll answer whatever questions you may have for me."

"Right, yes, thank you," said Ross, who noticed Izzie Drake smiling at him in a way he took to mean she was amused at seeing the vicar apparently taking charge. It was usually the other way round, and she knew Ross well enough to know he'd feel a little strange, being 'organised' by the man in the clerical collar.

Blake walked to the door and called to his wife, who Ross assumed must be in the kitchen or dining room perhaps.

"Darling, would you mind popping in here for a moment please?"

"Be right there, Simon," a disembodied voice replied from another room, followed seconds later by the entry into the parlour of a striking brunette, probably in her late thirties, with a figure that wouldn't have looked out of place on a woman half her age. Her hair was neatly styled in a fashionable bob, and her skirt fell invitingly just above the knee. Ross found himself thinking that if all vicars' wives looked like Mrs. Blake, the churches might be a little fuller each week.

Blake immediately crossed the room and stood beside his wife as he made the introductions.

"Darling, this is Detective Inspector Ross and Detective Sergeant Drake. Inspector, may I introduce my wife, Cilla?"

Both detectives looked at one another with a shared look. Ross was glad when Drake spoke first.

"Er, Cilla Blake?" she asked with a hint of levity in her voice.

"I'm afraid so," Mrs. Blake replied, smiling as she spoke. "It's quite alright to react as you have. You must remember though, that Blake is my married name. I was born Cilla Marianne Prentice, Inspector. My Dad, bless his soul, was a fanatical fan of 60s pop music and loved Cilla Black and Marianne Faithfull. He had all their records, and so when I came along he named me after them. It was a big decision to make for me, when Simon proposed as I realised right away how people would react to my married name."

"Hey," Simon Blake began, but Cilla intervened.

"Of course, he knows I'm only joking, don't you darling?" She reached up and kissed her husband on the cheek. "After all, it's only a name isn't it? Now, I suppose you'll be wanting me to make the tea, Simon, while you discuss the awful business outside?"

"Would you, please, darling?"

"Of course. Won't be long, and do make yourselves at home, Inspector,

Sergeant. You've both had a terrible experience, I imagine. I haven't seen that poor man of course, but from what Simon has told me…"

She left it there and quickly withdrew to carry out what she obviously saw as her duty as a good vicar's wife.

"Your wife seems a very capable woman, Reverend Blake," Ross observed, after Cilla had left the room."

"Oh yes, she certainly is, and please, Inspector, call me Simon."

"Very well, Simon. Now, you found the body, I believe?"

"Yes, I did. Terrible, just terrible."

"Tell me how it came about, please."

"Well, as you can see, the vicarage is immediately across the road from the church. Every morning, I cross the road and make a quick tour of the church, whether we have a service or not that day, just to make sure everything's alright, if you know what I mean?"

Ross knew only too well what Blake meant. So many churches had become easy targets for thieves, either for the lead from their roofs, or the communion plate or other valuable items stored within church buildings.

"Anyway, I came through the front gate, walked up the path, unlocked the church and spent five minutes making sure everything was okay. I left through the front door, locked up and then noticed the side gate on the north side was open. I always make sure it's closed at night, and I thought perhaps we'd had vandals in the graveyard again. It wouldn't be the first time we've had graves desecrated, Inspector. No criticism intended but I'm afraid the police have been singularly impotent when it comes to catching whoever is committing such acts."

"I'm sorry we…"

"No, please, forget it. It's not important right now. Of course, I followed the path round the church and saw…well, you know what I saw, Inspector. That poor man was just hanging, sort of suspended, I'd call it, from the statue of the angel on the Renton's family grave. What suffering he went through, I'd hate to imagine, and I've seen a few appalling acts of cruelty in my time, I can tell you."

Ross looked again at the photograph.

"You were in the Army?" he asked.

"I was in the Army Chaplain's Branch, Inspector. I held the honorary rank of Captain, but was universally known by all and sundry as 'Padre' as I'm sure you're aware if you know anything about the military.

"Yes, of course," Ross nodded. "I was wondering about the photo on your mantelpiece."

"Yes, you were probably wondering how a soldier became a vicar. Most people who don't know my past ask that same question. It's not always possible to make out the crosses on the uniform unless you look closely at the photo, and even then, some folk probably wouldn't know what they signify. Anyway, I served in a few trouble spots, ministering to the troops, and saw the results of men being blown apart by land mines, gunfire, air-to-ground missiles and cannon fire. All of it was horrendous, but to be honest, what happened out there in my churchyard this morning is on a par with the worst excesses I've witnessed of man's ability to cause pain and suffering to his fellow beings, Inspector."

The door was pushed open and Cilla Blake walked into the room carrying a tray, complete with teapot, cups and saucers and the almost obligatory plate of assorted biscuits. Izzie Drake jumped up to help her and held the door back as the vicar's wife placed the tray on the coffee table in the centre of the room.

"Thanks, darling," Blake smiled at her.

"You're welcome. Would you like me to stay and pour, or would you rather speak to my husband on his own, Inspector?"

Ross smiled warmly at Cilla Blake.

"Please stay, Mrs. Blake. You may be able to help us."

"Oh, I doubt that very much," she replied. "I was at home here while Simon was making his gruesome discovery."

"Even so, please stay," said Ross. "You may help your husband in remembering something."

Cilla nodded her agreement and sat on the arm of her husband's chair, smoothing her skirt in an attempt to appear demure as she did so. Ross thought it made her look even more attractive.

"So," Ross went on, "You saw the body and, then what, Simon?"

Blake paused for thought before replying.

"The first thing I did on seeing the man on the angel, realising he was dead, was to offer up a prayer to God. Then I approached the grave and stood some yards away. I knew the police wouldn't want anyone disturbing the scene, but I felt I needed to get a closer look, to see if perhaps I recognised the poor man."

"And did you recognise him?"

"No, Inspector. I did not."

"Could he have visited your church, perhaps as a member of the congregation?" Drake added.

"If he did, I can honestly say he never made himself known to me, Sergeant. As I said, I didn't recognise him at all."

Blake's reaction was just the same as Father Donovan's the previous day. Again, an unknown man had been murdered and left on display in his churchyard. Why? Ross needed to solve that one before he could go further.

"Okay, now please think carefully, you too Mrs. Blake."

"Oh, please call me Cilla, inspector."

"Right, yes, well, you too Cilla. As I said, take your time, think very carefully. Have either of you seen any strangers hanging around the church or its grounds in recent days, or weeks even? Whoever did this must have had a reason for choosing your church. It's possible they reconnoitred the area first, before picking St. Mark's. Maybe you noticed a strange van or car that was parked nearby more then once perhaps, or someone on foot watching the church, that kind of thing."

"I'm sorry, Inspector," Blake replied. "If I'm not sitting here writing my next sermon on the laptop over by the window, I'm usually out and about taking care of the work of the parish. I don't exactly spend all my time at the church. If I'd noticed anything out of the ordinary I'd tell you about it, without a doubt."

Izzie Drake suddenly noticed an odd look on the face of the vicar's wife.

"Cilla, you saw something didn't you?" she hazarded a guess.

"Well, now I come to think of it, yes. Last week I was dusting in here when a van pulled up just outside the church gates. I half expected it to be a delivery for Simon. He often receives parcels of books or garden plants that are usually delivered by courier. Then I dismissed that thought because there was no writing on the van."

"What colour was it?" Drake prompted her.

"White, definitely white," she answered.

"Did you see the driver at all, "Ross asked.

"I'm afraid not. I did hear a door slam as though someone had got out of the van but I never saw who it was."

Ross thought of something.

"Do you recall which way the van was pointing?"

"Oh yes, it was on the correct side of the road, so it would have been pointing that way," she pointed in the direction she was indicating, which would have placed the vehicle on the far side of the road from the vicarage, with the passenger door closest to the gate into the churchyard.

"Clever bugger," said Ross, then, "Sorry about the language, Simon."

"No problem, Inspector. I'm a vicar, not a member of the language police. We all slip up now and then, even me, and you have good reason today, I think."

"What are you getting at, sir?" Drake asked.

"Well, if he was pointing that way, in order not to be seen from here, he'd get out of the passenger door. That way, Cilla here would have heard the van door shut, but even if she'd tried she'd not have seen him and he'd have been through the gate and into the churchyard in a couple of seconds."

"So you think that van contained the killer?" Cilla Blake asked. "Oh, my, that's positively scary."

"I'm sure he wouldn't have bothered you, Darling," said Simon Blake, reassuring his wife. "If he really was reconnoitring the church and church-yard he'd have remained as unobtrusive as possible. Even if you'd walked out there to him, he'd probably have made up some valid excuse for being there."

"Your husband is quite right, Cilla," Drake said to the worried-looking woman. "He'd probably have just said he was looking for the grave of a dead relative of friend and I would think you'd have been quite satisfied with an answer like that. After all, you would have had no reason to suspect anything, would you?"

Cilla Blake looked a little relieved as she realised her husband and the sergeant were both, in all probability quite correct in their assumption. She felt a little better as she picked up her willow-pattern tea cup, sipping the contents, and then reaching out to the still warm teapot to pour herself a refill, automatically doing the same for everyone else.

"So, if we assume that the occupant of that van *was* the killer," Ross re-entered the conversation, "we know that he owns, or perhaps borrowed or rented a white van in advance of the murders, though I'd plump for it being his own van. It would be difficult to erase any forensic trace evidence as it is, and he wouldn't want to risk a rental company or even a friend coming across anything incriminating if he'd slipped up somewhere."

"Er, Inspector Ross, can I say something, please?"

"Of course, Simon," Ross replied as the vicar looked at him with a look of deep intensity on his face.

"I'm not a police officer of course, and far be it from me to tell you or Sergeant Drake your jobs, but, well a thought just came to me and I hope you won't me mentioning it."

"If it's a helpful thought, I don't mind in the slightest," Ross replied, wondering just what Blake might have thought of that he could have missed. The answer that followed really did stop him in his tracks, making him wonder why he hadn't thought of it in the first place.

Simon Blake paused before replying, sipping from his cup, much as his wife had just done. The great British stress reliever at work before his eyes, Ross thought to himself. When all else fails, *'Put the kettle on, Mother.'*

"Well, Inspector, if you don't mind me saying, and I don't mean to sound critical, but you and the sergeant are both talking as if you believe you're only dealing with an individual killer here. Believe me, having been in the Army, the Royal Engineers in particular, I've witnessed plenty of scenes where it was necessary to haul heavy objects around and it's not always a simple task. Heaving that poor man out there up and into position on the statue of the angel took some doing, is all I'm saying. My question therefore is this. Have you at any time, since that poor man turned up yesterday at St. Matthew's which was on the news this morning, and that I knew about through the ecclesiastical grapevine within hours yesterday by the way, considered the fact that there could be two people involved in these murders?"

Andy Ross could have slapped himself across the face. When the vicar, of all people, albeit one with a military background, put it like that, it almost became obvious. Two killers, or at the very least one killer and a helper, would have been able to haul the current victim up and fastened him to the statue of the angel with far greater ease than a single perpetrator.

"Vicar, you're a bloody genius," Ross said, oblivious to his language, which only served to make Blake smile. "Why the heck didn't we think of that, Izzie?"

Blake answered before Izzie could reply.

"Don't beat yourself up, Inspector. I could be wrong anyway, and from what I hear, yesterday's attack could have been the work of one man, or woman, God forbid, and you've only just got here and your mind hasn't had a chance to process all the information yet."

"Maybe not, but you have, Simon."

"Only because I've been thinking about it since I first saw the body, over an hour before you did, and because my time with the military taught me to look at things a little differently, that's all. I may have only been a padre, but I learned a lot about the ways of the world, Inspector."

"Even so, we may owe you one, for this theory. It's worthy of serious consideration, wouldn't you agree, Sergeant?"

"It certainly is, sir," Drake replied, knowing her boss well enough to know he'd never reject positive or practical suggestions regarding a case, no matter what the source.

After asking a few more routine questions, similar to those they'd directed at Father Donovan the previous day, they ascertained that regular services took place at St. Mark's twice on Sundays, and just once during the week, on Wednesday mornings. Weddings, funerals and baptisms were different of course and could be arranged to suit individual requirements. A final check that Blake had never seen the victim before and with a promise that they may be back to show a photo of the dead man to Cilla Blake to see if she recognised him from anywhere, which didn't seem to faze her at all, and the two detectives said their farewells to the couple for the time being and rejoined those still working the scene in the graveyard.

* * *

Miles Booker's team was hard at work by the time Ross and Drake returned to the scene of human carnage in the graveyard. The victim's body had been slowly and very carefully removed from its position adorning the angel, and was now being respectfully placed in a black body bag, almost ready for transport to the morgue. William Nugent had completed his initial examination of the remains to the best of his ability, considering it still had yards of barbed wire wrapped round it, and was packing up his own instruments as he and Lees prepared to follow the ambulance back to the mortuary where they could commence a full and proper examination. Even Fat Willy was aware how urgent this matter had now become. Two gruesome murders in two days were enough to move this case to the top of everyone's priority list.

"The reverend gentleman should have been a detective, sir. That was a quick piece of incisive thinking back there, don't you think?" said Izzie Drake as they walked towards Derek McLennan, who looked pale, but brighter than when they'd last seen him.

"I have to agree, Izzie. Wish I'd thought of it first though."

"You would have done soon enough, sir. We'd only been here a few minutes, and first thing we did really was go talk to the vicar. He's very sharp though, thinking of that the way he did."

"It opens up a whole new ball game though, Izzie. Yesterday we thought we were looking for a lone killer, and today it looks like we may possibly be seeking a pair working together."

"What about the footprints, sir?"

"Eh?"

"There were footprints behind the angel, where it looks like someone hauled the dead man up but shouldn't there be footprints in front too if there were two of them?"

"Bloody hell, you're right. Let's go have that talk with Booker."

"You okay now, Derek?" Drake asked as they drew level with D.C. McLennan.

Derek McLennan looked shamefacedly at the inspector and sergeant as he replied.

"I think so, thanks, Sarge. Sorry, sir. Did it again, didn't I? Can't believe it, two days running."

"Not your fault, Derek. I felt like throwing up myself to be truthful," Ross answered with a sympathetic look towards the young detective.

"Really sir?"

"Really, Derek, I'm only human too you know. Now come with us. We need a word with the SOCO."

Miles Booker, the Scene of Crimes Officer waved as he saw them approaching, then held a hand up to prevent them approaching any closer to the blood soaked grave and its accompanying angelic statuary.

"Stay there, would you, please Andy? We might have something here."

"It wouldn't by any chance be a set of footprints would it, Miles?"

"Fucking hell, Andy, you turned psychic all of a sudden? How did you know we were going to find them?"

"To be honest, I didn't until the vicar suggested the possibility."

"The vicar suggested it? What is he, a modern day Brother Cadfael or something?"

"No, but he's ex-Army, a padre in the Royal Engineers and understands the business of heavy lifting better than most. He thought it unlikely anyone would be able to haul the body up single-handedly from the rear as we thought at first."

"Clever man, eh? Well, you'd better come and take a look. Just walk carefully and follow my footsteps, keeping to this side of the gravestone."

"They're small," Izzie Drake observed as Miles Booker indicated the indentations in the blood pools that had gathered at the base of the statue. Almost like…"

"A woman's," said Ross.

"I concur," Booker agreed. "We didn't see the prints right away because they'd been partially filled in by the blood that had pooled around the base of the statue and on the stone itself, and with this side of the churchyard being in deep shade until the sun rose fully, it was almost impossible to make them out. As the blood settled and began to dry and the sun rose higher and the shadows lifted, well, there they were."

"So, it is a pair," Drake exclaimed.

"Looks like it, "said Ross. "That means our job just got a damn sight more difficult, and do *not* tell me to mind my bloody language. I'm well aware we're in a churchyard, but doubt that the inhabitants are likely to complain, are they?"

"Sir?" Derek McLennan spoke up from his position behind Ross and Drake.

"Yes, Derek, what is it?"

"Just a thought, sir. If the second perpetrator is a woman, do you think it means this victim could also be a sex offender and that we are looking for someone seeking revenge? I know we decided that Remington's murder wasn't about Claire Morris, but what if we have a pair of vigilantes at work, targeting known sex offenders who've been released from prison. Maybe they think the rapists or whatever they are haven't been punished enough by the courts."

"You could be on to something, Derek, well done lad. We're going to have our work cut out with this case if you're correct though. Where the bloody hell are we going to start looking, and who the heck is this second guy? We need to I.D. him, and fast."

As the ambulance carrying victim number two rolled away, taking the bloody corpse towards its appointment with the scalpels and bone saws of Doctor William Nugent, Ross left McLennan to co-ordinate the police presence at the scene until the others returned from their house to house inquiries, with instructions to bring everyone back to headquarters as soon as they reassembled at the churchyard. Miles Booker's forensic team would complete the examination of the death scene and report back to him as soon as they had something to tell.

The inspector and Izzie Drake meanwhile, motored as fast as they could to headquarters, where Ross wanted Paul Ferris to begin setting up the murder room to include this latest victim, start the identification process and to report to D.C.I Porteous on the latest developments. Ross felt he might need more help on this case, and Porteous was the only one who could authorise the additional officers and resources he felt the case deserved.

CHAPTER 12

MISPERS

"I want to know who he is, and fast"

D.C.I. Porteous rarely raised his voice when speaking to his own officers, but the frustration caused by the team's inability to identify the second
victim with two days having passed since the discovery of the bloodied
corpse in the churchyard of St. Mark's was clearly evident as his voice now
reached hitherto unheard of decibel levels, causing those in the murder
team's conference room to visibly wince, as he addressed their morning
briefing.

"We're doing all we can to i.d. the victim sir," Ross replied in an
attempt to placate his boss."

"Then all you're doing just isn't good enough, Detective Inspector.
We've had two killings in two days, and so far you and your team don't
appear to have made any progress whatsoever."

Allowing his voice to descend an octave or two, Porteous now opted for
a less aggressive tone.

"Andy, you're the best we have in this kind of investigation. Please tell
me you have something, anything, that I can report to the Chief Superintendent, who, I can tell you, is getting his ears burned by some very senior
officers, not to mention the fact that the press are sniffing around, sensing a
real sensationalist story. Word has somehow reached the *Echo* that the
second victim was even more horribly mutilated than Remington. Only the
fact that the editor is a good friend of the Chief Super is keeping them
quiet for the moment, but they aren't going to fall for any weak and non-

committal press release from George Thompson this time. They can sense blood, like sharks round a shipwreck. Now, talk to me, for God's sake."

Andy Ross knew things were bad when his boss adopted such a stance as this. Admittedly, they had made little progress since the discovery of the second body, but he knew also that no case could ever be as simple as the top brass might like. He took a deep breath before responding to Porteous, as his team waited with baited breath, wondering just what he could say to placate the boss.

"Sir, we're doing all we can to identify victim number two. So far, D.C. Ferris has been able to ascertain that the man's fingerprints do not show up in any relation to any criminal activity. That leads me to assume he either has no criminal record, or, if he has, he's never been apprehended for any of his crimes. Even if he'd been fingerprinted in relation to any investigation and later eliminated, as you well know, those prints would have been destroyed thanks to current legislation regarding storing such prints. I've asked all police stations in our own force and all neighbouring forces to inform us instantly if they receive any mispers reports of anyone fitting our victim's general description, but you know as well as I do, sir, that missing persons reports will generally only be accepted once someone has been gone for forty-eight hours. If our man was taken immediately prior to his murder, any such report may not even have been accepted by one of the smaller police stations in the area. They have enough to deal with in terms of everyday policing, as we all know. However, I have sent a flyer out to all stations that any report of anyone remotely resembling the victim must be reported to me, whether an official report has been filed or not. In other words, if anyone walks into any Merseyside Police station to try to report a missing person from now on, if it's a male and fits our victim's description, we're going to know about it."

"What about releasing a photograph?" Porteous asked.

Before Ross could answer, Izzie Drake, a horrified look on her face, took it upon herself to interject.

"Sir, you've seen what the victim looked like after the killer finished with him. D.C. Ferris has sent facial close-ups to the other forces and circulated them to other stations in the area, but I'm sure you'll agree it wouldn't be a good idea to allow the press access to such a gruesome sight. Can you imagine how that poor man's wife or family would feel if they saw that picture in the Echo or in a national daily? Bad enough for any family to know their loved one is missing, but I'd hate to think they found out about his death by seeing such a bloody gruesome picture plastered across a front page."

Porteous seemed to come down from his high horse in reaction to Izzie's words.

"Ah, yes, you're right of course, Sergeant Drake. Look, D.I. Ross, I'm not telling you how to run your investigation, but the pressure from on high is already building and it's going to get a damn sight worse before we solve this bloody case. You said the wife of the vicar at St. Mark's saw a van lurking around outside the church. Any chance of a lead arising from the sighting?"

"Yes, she did, sir, but you know what it's like, people see something briefly but they never quite see the whole picture. It's possible she might have noticed something but not been able to recall it yet."

"Hmm," Porteous mused. "I'm not interfering here, but I want to call in a spot of specialist help for you, Andy."

"What sort of help, sir" Ross wondered what was coming next.

"I've been instructed by the brass on high to bring in a profiler, and she's arriving later today."

"A profiler? What do we need a profiler for, sir?" Ross asked, having always been sceptical about the modern trend of using psychological aids to criminal detection.

"Because the Chief Super says so, and I say so, which gives you two powerful reasons to co-operate with her when she arrives."

"She?" Ross asked.

"Yes, 'she', unless you have some objections to bringing in a female to assist you."

"Not at all, sir. It's just that I didn't think we had any female profilers, or male ones come to that, employed on Merseyside."

"Quite correct," Porteous agreed. "We don't. Christine Bland is employed by the Home Office as a sort of roving profiler, going where she's needed, when she's needed. The Chief assures me she's one of the best there is and she may just be able to help us by pointing us in the right direction towards the type of people our killers might be, if indeed there are two of them operating together, and what their motives might be, and therefore where we might begin looking for them. Any objections, D.I. Ross?"

Faced with the inevitable, Ross shook his head.

"None at all, sir. If she can help us pinpoint what to look for it can only be helpful, I suppose."

"Good," said Porteous, forcefully. "In the meantime, I'll leave you to it. For crying out loud, try to find out at least who the second victim is before she arrives, and that means all of you."

Before anyone could reply, the D.C.I. performed a smart, almost military about-turn, and marched out of the room, leaving Ross and the team almost speechless. Andy Ross gathered his wits quickly, turned to the assembled team and said,

"Right you lot, you heard the boss, let's get to it!"

CHAPTER 13

BRIEF ENCOUNTER

Lime Street Station, Liverpool, is a main line terminus station, originally opened to the general public in 1836. In keeping with the grand designs being applied to their station buildings by the early railway companies, the station was fronted by a magnificent reproduction of a French Château, formerly the North Western Hotel and now serving as accommodation for students at Liverpool's John Moores University. The whole station edifice stands as a magnificent testament to the ingenuity and design of the Victorian age, with its vast iron and glass roofs sweeping in a graceful arch over the station's nine platforms.

Two days after the murders however, the Burger King on the station concourse found itself playing host to a couple with no thoughts whatsoever for the beauty of the architectural history that surrounded them. Sitting opposite each other at a table near a window looking out onto the main concourse of the station, slowly sipping coffee from Styrofoam mugs, the man and woman hunched over the table, selected by the man as being the most isolated from the numerous travellers seeking refreshment before during or after their journeys. Keeping their voices low, but not too afraid of being overheard against the general hubbub of the comings and goings around them, their conversation continued as another train thundered into the station with a squeal of brakes as it slowed to a halt against the buffers at the end of the platform, easily heard from where they sat.

"We have to wait a few days before the next one. The police aren't entirely stupid and we need to pull back, let them run around chasing their tails for a while before we carry on," the man said, glancing around at regular intervals surreptitiously in an effort to remain anonymous. His nondescript olive green padded waterproof jacket, dark blue faded jeans and cheap chain store trainers, topped off with a Liverpool F.C. baseball cap already made him appear as nondescript as any typical walker heading up to the Lake District for a weekend in the hills and lakes. His partner, a few years younger and similarly dressed, with a black cotton tracksuit under her hiking jacket, and a red woollen cap on her head, with her shoulder length hair tucked up underneath, almost exuding a masculine appearance. At her feet, sat a weather-worn rucksack, a recent purchase from a charity shop, blending perfectly with her weekend hiker image, but which in fact contained a single change of clothes and her make-up bag.

"But we planned to hit them fast, get it done and fade away into the background again," she replied. "Why stop now?"

"Because I say so, for one thing, and secondly, number three is away on holiday in Greece until next week."

"Oh, well, we don't have much choice do we?"

"No, we don't. Did you get rid of the clothes from this morning like I told you to?"

"Yes, I burned everything, including my trainers, like you said. Bloody shame that was. They cost me a lot of money."

"Sod the money. The bizzies aren't stupid you know. They're bound to have found mine and your footprints around the grave, and too many people have been caught over the years through stupidly hanging on to things like shoes and clothes that the cops can use to link them to whatever offence they're investigating."

"Okay, okay, I get the picture. So, what do we do in the meantime?"

"Go to work, carry on as normal. Express your horror when people talk about the murders. They're bound to feature number two on the news tonight, and it'll be in the evening edition of the *Echo*, for sure, and it's bound to make the national dailies too."

The woman nodded in agreement, sipping from her coffee mug, then grimacing as she realised the contents had gone cold as they'd sat talking.

"Ugh" she spluttered. "Stone cold. I need a refill. Want one?"

"Yes, please," the man answered politely.

She rose from the table and walked across to the servery, looking back once and smiling at her partner. To any casual observer they looked as innocent as any other travellers waiting for the arrival of their train. As he waited for her to return with the fresh drinks, the man drummed his fingers on the table top, a random tattoo that he performed in order to stop his hands from shaking. He'd felt repulsed by the sight of their latest victim's innards spilling out from his guts after he'd slit him open, and he hadn't been prepared for the immense gush of blood that had accompanied the outpouring of intestines and bodily fluids, not to mention the smell as the man's life ebbed away in front of him. He knew they were doing what had to be done, but that didn't mean to say he had to like it, though it wouldn't be wise to share that with the woman who now came striding back to the table, a plastic tray in her hands, bearing two fresh disposable mugs of steaming hot coffee.

"You look a bit pale. Are you alright?" she asked as she placed the tray in the centre of the table before taking each mug and placing one in front of him, the other on her side of the table, then placing the tray on the floor beside them, propped up against the table leg.

"I'm fine," he replied, forcing a smile on his face. "Just daydreaming for a minute, that's all."

"About number two?" she asked, receiving a non-committal nod in return. "Did you see the look of panic on that bastard's face when he realised what was about to happen? It was priceless, and then the look of pure terror and shock on his face when you slit his guts open? I just wish he'd have lasted a bit longer, suffered even more, before going to hell."

"Keep your voice down," the man ordered. "Someone might overhear you."

"Right, yeah, sorry," she whispered across the table. "Just can't believe it was so easy, and so bloody satisfying to see his blood pouring out onto the ground like that."

"Come on," the man replied. "Enough of that. We're doing what has to be done. Let's not revel in it too much, ok?"

He felt he had to say something, if only to shut her up, before she blabbed too loud and someone heard her and called the police.

"Drink your coffee and we'd better go."

"When will I hear from you again?" she asked.

"Not until I've got things sorted and in place for the next one," he replied. "Best if we're not see together too often. That way nobody will think of connecting the two of us. It has to be bloody obvious to the bizzies that there were two people involved in the last one by now. They'll know one person couldn't have got him up on the angel by himself and the foot-prints we must have left in the blood and on the ground will confirm there were two of us as well. Hopefully, they'll think they're looking for two men, which will also work to our advantage. They probably won't dream a woman could be involved in such gruesome killings."

"Ha," she exclaimed, being careful to keep her voice to a bare whisper. "That just shows how wrong they are, doesn't it?"

A few minutes later, the pair rose from the table, the woman picking up the tray and depositing it in the used tray rack at the end of the counter, then walked casually from the fast food restaurant and out of the station onto Lime Street.

The pair quickly separated, the man walking to the station car park where his own transport was parked waiting for him. He looked back just once, to see his partner in crime walking briskly away from the station in the direction of the city centre, where, he knew, she'd soon find a store with a ladies changing room where she'd quickly transform herself back to her usual everyday appearance. The 'hiker' from the railway station would disappear, never to be seen again.

As he pulled away and began the drive back to home and work, he allowed his mind to drift back in time, and to a reminder of just why he was following his current course of action. The mind pictures that played in his thoughts reassured him and he knew that despite what the police and the law might think, his actions were entirely justified. Soon, it would be time to venture out once more, and the hunt would begin anew.

CHAPTER 14

ALL I HAVE TO DO IS DREAM

Sunday evening Mass completed, Gerald Byrne was looking forward to a meal, a hot bath and perhaps relaxing in front of the television for a couple of hours, followed by a cup of cocoa and a little light reading in bed before sleep claimed him for the night. Father Willis was in his room, reading before dinner, and would join him when their housekeeper/cook, Mrs. Redding, informed them their evening meal was ready. Byrne enjoyed the company of the younger priest and had soon began to feel at home in his new parish, feeling particularly pampered by the wonderful cooking of Iris Redding, who kept the house spotless and seemed to enjoy mothering the two priests. Aged sixty-two, but trim and sprightly for her age, Iris had kept house for the priests of St. Luke's for almost twenty years, and couldn't imagine her life without the daily tasks of 'doing for' the Fathers, as she described her work. Her husband, Tom, younger than Iris at fifty-eight, had worked as a landscape gardener until a heart attack had restricted his activity, and now kept his hand in by taking care of the quite substantial gardens at the manse, as well as tending to the not insubstantial task of looking after the grounds of the church, keeping the grass cut and tending to the graves, keeping St. Luke's churchyard a neat and tidy oasis of calm for the relatives and friends of those buried there, and who came to pay their respects at their loved ones' gravesides. Tom worked in the church-yard three mornings a week, though what he'd think when he saw the blood-stained grave and desecrated angel statue of the Seagrove's joint grave on his next scheduled gardening visit the following day, Iris Redding didn't dare to imagine.

Mouth-watering smells were already emanating from the kitchen and wafting through the house by the time Byrne had changed into a comfortable pair of jeans and his favourite brown polo-neck sweater. He seated himself in one of the room's two armchairs and reached across to the nearby magazine rack to pick up the latest edition of the *Liverpool Echo*, delivered each day to the manse.

The local newspaper's banner headline read, GRUESOME DISOVERY – SECOND MUTILATED BODY IN CITY CHURCHYARD.

Byrne had heard of a second murder via the bishop's office earlier that afternoon but the way it was reported in the *Echo* was sensationalist to say the least. Byrne guessed that the reporter had made light of the truth in a lot of his article, the priest doubting the police would have provided the press with some of the more lurid details contained on the front page.

As he read, Mrs. Redding knocked quietly on the parlour door and walked in to the room to announce that dinner would be ready in five minutes, but seeing the priest reading the article she felt she had to say something.

"Oh, Father, that poor man. What could he have done to make someone do those terrible things to him?"

"Now, now, Mrs. Redding," Byrne replied, "We mustn't necessarily believe all we read in the newspapers. I'm pretty sure the journalist who wrote this article used an awful lot of speculation and half-truths in his composition. The police certainly don't usually give information like this to the press, especially as it says near the bottom that the police will be releasing further details when the victim has been identified and next-of-kin informed. The police would never release some of this stuff in the newspaper article if the nearest and dearest hadn't been informed yet. They're not that insensitive."

"Perhaps you're right, Father, but it does sound as if it's a horrific killing, doesn't it? And just a day after the other one, and both victims left on holy ground, in churchyards. What is the world coming to?"

"Indeed, Mrs. Redding. It makes one think, for sure."

"Does young Father Willis know," she asked.

"Oh yes, I spoke with him when I arrived home this afternoon. He was shocked of course and we both prayed for the victim together."

"That was kind of you," said the housekeeper, and then, satisfied that she'd fulfilled the need to show concern for the victim of the latest brutal murder to hit the city, she went on, "Anyway, Father, dinner will be ready in five minutes. Liver and bacon, with onions, served with mashed potatoes, carrots and peas. And gravy, of course. Perhaps you'd be kind enough to let Father Willis know while I'm serving it out, and you can both enjoy it and take your minds off horrible things like murder and mutilation."

"Yes, of course I'll tell him, Mrs. Redding. Five minutes in the dining room, right?"

"Right Father. Five minutes," and then almost as an afterthought, "and there's one of those 'Stop Press' boxes at the bottom of page three, Father. Some young girl, nothing more than a teenager apparently, drowned herself off the dunes at Formby. All it says is a man walking his dog witnessed it and police are investigating."

"Ah, poor, tortured soul," Gerald Byrne said, sadness evident in his voice.

"But suicide's a sin, Father, isn't it?" Iris Redding said, as though in condemnation of the girl's action.

"So the good book tells us, Mrs. Redding, but that doesn't preclude us praying for the poor girl's soul, now, does it? For one so young to take such drastic action must mean she was under intolerable pressure of some kind to have pushed her into making such a terrible decision. We mustn't be too quick to condemn in such cases. Perhaps, like I will, you'll say a prayer for that poor girl's immortal soul before going to bed tonight."

Feeling a little guilty, Iris Redding replied,

"Yes, of course, Father. I didn't mean anything bad about the girl, just well, you know, it does say in the Bible that…"

"Yes, I know, Mrs. Redding, but also, the Bible tells us it is not the pure in heart that Jesus came to save, but the sinners, who he called upon to repent and accept the love of God, does it not?"

"Yes of course, Father, you're right of course."

Gerald Byrne smiled at his well-meaning housekeeper as the tantalising smell of his evening meal assailed his nostrils as it wafted through the door.

"Always remember, Mrs. Redding, that without sinners, people like me and Father Willis would technically be redundant. Now, about that excellent meal you've prepared for us?"

"Of course, Father, forgive me waffling on like this when you must be starving hungry. I'll be away and getting it now for you."

With that, Mrs. Redding walked swiftly from the room to begin plating up the two priest's evening meal as Byrne quickly glanced at the Stop Press article before placing the paper back in the magazine rack, walking into the hall and calling upstairs to his young assistant priest.

"David, Father Willis, dinner will be on the table in five minutes. Are you coming to join me?"

A muffled reply was just audible as Willis acknowledged Byrne's call from his bedroom, and five minutes later joined Byrne in the dining room as Mrs. Redding, in a display of perfect timing, followed within seconds, a smile on her face, with two tantalising tasty meals steaming on their plates as she approached the dining table with her serving tray.

"That smells delicious," David Willis said as Iris Redding placed the dinner plates down in front of the two priests.

314

"Mmm, looks it too," Gerald Byrne agreed. "You always do us proud, Mrs. Redding, thank you."

Smiling, Iris Redding stepped back and tucked the now empty tray under her arm.

"Enjoy it Fathers," she urged, "and there's my home-made treacle sponge pudding for afters, too."

"Oh, she's spoiling us to death, David," Byrne enthused. "You treat us too well, Mrs. Redding."

"Nonsense, Father," she replied. "You deserve a good meal at the end of the day. Now, go ahead and eat. I'll be back in a while to see if you're ready for pudding."

The two priests tucked in to their meal with gusto, finishing off with the promised sponge pudding, with home-made custard, after which Mrs. Redding cleared the table, stacked the pots and cutlery in the dishwasher ready to attend to the next morning, said goodnight to the priests and then headed off home to her husband, who would be eagerly awaiting his own evening meal when she got there.

* * *

After a quiet and peaceful evening in the company of his younger assistant, having enjoyed watching the television together and spending a short time discussing the day's news, including the horrific murder at St. Mark's, both men expressing their disgust and horror, not just at the gruesome nature and cruelty of the murders, but also the acts of sacrilege committed on holy ground, Byrne and Willis bade one another goodnight and headed upstairs. Byrne made for the bathroom where he kept his earlier promise to himself and spent a half hour luxuriating in a hot bath, before towelling himself dry and heading off to bed, calling out his goodnight to Father Willis as he passed the younger priest's bedroom door. Receiving no reply, he assumed Willis was already asleep and was soon tucked up in his own bed where he first spent ten minutes at prayer before picking up his book from the nightstand beside the bed. Less than ten minutes later, with his eyes growing heavy and the words of the pages beginning to swim in front of them, he placed the book down, plumped up his pillows and fell into a deep sleep in seconds, the sleep that carries the mind far inside itself, leading the sleeper into dreams so vivid they become, for a time, the sleeping brain's reality…

Speke Hill Orphanage and School's Sports Day, 1964, proved to be a great success. Teachers, carers and pupils alike had all entered into the relaxed spirit of the day, with much cheering and applause greeting the winners, and indeed the losers of each event. The ethos of the Catholic priests and nuns in charge of the event was simple, taking part was ultimately its own reward and though prizes were awarded to the winning house, everyone was to be congratulated on giving their all in the cause of their team.

Earlier in the afternoon, young Gerry Byrne had received great applause as he finished first in the 100 yard sprint, the blue hoop on his shirt flashing past the finish line a good two yards ahead of the white hooped shirt worn by Mark Proctor, who finished second for Sefton House. Alan Prosser, a school prefect and the Upper's House Captain of Stanley House, even came across to young Byrne and slapped him on the back in congratulations as another ten points for first place were added to Stanley House's total for the day, taking them into a sizeable lead. Mark Proctor was angry with himself for failing to beat the smaller Gerry, who he'd fully expected to defeat in the race, and he promised himself there'd be no repeat of his defeat when the pair faced each other again later in the 4 X 100 yards relay race.

Gerry's sister Angela, meanwhile, did her bit for Stanley House by winning her long jump event and as proceedings drew to a close, only the two boys 100 yards relays remained, with Stanley being three points ahead of Sefton, the other two houses trailing some way behind. The Lower School race was first, and Proctor saw his chance. As the pair took up the baton within a half-second of each other both having been picked to run the last leg of the relay, he surreptitiously tripped Gerry Byrne with a sneaky tap on the ankle, enough to make Byrne stumble and lose enough ground to be unable to make up over such a short race distance. Mark Proctor snapped the finish tape ahead of Molyneux and Norris with Stanley, in the shape of Gerry Byrne in fourth place. Thinking his triumph complete, and that he'd put his house into the lead with one race to go, Proctor was ecstatic until Master of Ceremonies, Father Rooney, announced an inquiry into the running of the Lower Boys relay. As the Upper boys relay race took place, with a win for Stanley, Sefton finishing a distant third, Stanley House was once more just in the lead in the race for the Bishops Cup. Everything now depended on the result of the inquiry into the earlier race. Mark Proctor's trip on Gerry Byrne had been seen and he was disqualified and Sefton House placed last, with the other houses all being promoted a place. Stanley House were the winners of the Bishop's Cup for 1964, and Sefton were runners-up, with Molyneux third and Norris fourth.

Gerry Byrne's disappointment at being cheated out of the chance of a win in the relay was slightly assuaged by the sight of Proctor's fellow relay team members kicking and thumping and slapping him in disgust at his behaviour, out of sight of the priests of course, that had cost their house the opportunity of winning the Bishop's Cup.

* * *

Angela's screams broke into his dreams. Young Gerry was fast asleep, his mind reliving his win in the relay, and the later sight of Proctor being knocked about by his own team members, when the shrill sound of his sister's voice, in obvious distress brought him to full wakefulness in an instant. Jumping up from his bed, Gerry leapt to his feet, oblivious to the cold of the lino floor against his skin, and ran to the window. There, on the grassed area outside, he saw Mark Proctor and three other boys holding his sister down on the ground. Gerry didn't know what they were doing to his sister, but the fact she was screaming and trying to fight them off and in obvious distress spurred him to action. Gerry clambered through the window and ran the few yards to the group on the ground, leaping at Mark Proctor, who was immediately on top of his sister, trying it seemed to Gerry, to force her to open her legs by forcing a knee between them. Whatever it was he was doing, Gerry knew it was wrong and he flung himself on to Proctor's back shouting as many obscenities as he knew at his tender age, while lashing out with his fists and bare feet, scratching Proctor's face as his nails clawed down the other's cheek, until the other three boys grabbed hold of Gerry and began pummelling him with their fists, until he fell back on to the grass, blood pouring from multiple cuts on his face and legs. As he lay there, sore and bleeding, he heard his sister scream again, and saw a look of terror on her face as Mark Proctor began to remove his trousers, and Gerry wondered why none of the boys, Proctor included, had spoken a word, why nobody else had heard her screams and why no-one had come to help, and even as his mind pondered these questions, everything turned black.

* * *

"Wake up, Father Byrne. Father, Gerald, please, wake up."

The voice of Father David Willis eventually penetrated into the dark world of Gerald Byrne's dream state and he felt himself being pulled back to reality. Slowly opening his eyes, Byrne felt the strong arms of David Willis on his shoulders, shaking him as the younger priest's words continued to implore him to escape the nightmare in which he'd become entrapped.

Byrne looked up and there was David Willis, his countenance one of deep concern, his words soft and soothing.

"Father Byrne, are you okay? I was so worried. You were screaming fit to bring the roof down, and woke me from a deep sleep, not an easy thing to do, I assure you."

"Screaming? I was screaming, David? I was…I saw…I was young again and…it's a bit hazy."

"Get off her. Leave her alone, you bastards. That's what you were screaming in your sleep, Father. Well, that and more, but all in similar vein."

"Oh, Holy Mother of God forgive me, David, for disturbing your sleep and frightening you half to death, I'm sure."

"It's alright, really. Here, take a drink of this," Willis lifted a glass of water from the bedside table and handed it to Byrne, who sipped from it gratefully, then gulped down the second half of the glassful.

"No, really, I apologise, David. I don't know what came over me."

"A nightmare, Father, for sure. Who were you trying to defend? Do you recall the details? Who was the girl? Was it something that maybe happened to you in the past?"

"A nightmare, yes, of course it was. No, I don't recall the details," he lied, "and I don't remember a girl in the dream," another lie, "but I guess I ought to thank you and let you get back to your bed, Father Willis. I'm certain I'll be okay now, really."

Willis thought Father Byrne was being evasive, but why would he lie about a dream of all things?

"God save me," Byrne prayed once Willis had been placated sufficiently and had returned to his own room. The truth was, he recalled every detail of his dream, winning the race, being tripped in the relay, Proctor's subsequent disqualification, all real-life events, but the attack by Proctor and his friends on Angela, his sister? Fact and fiction were somehow merging in his mind and if he wasn't careful, he was in danger of losing his grip on reality. That attack by Mark Proctor was just a terrible, nightmarish distortion of reality...wasn't it?

Sleep was a long time coming again for David Willis that night. Something, he felt, was seriously troubling the new parish priest. This was the second time Byrne's nightmares had encroached upon his sleep. Could Father Byrne be ill, perhaps some dread, nameless terror from the past had reared its head and was torturing the older priest? Willis knew something of the background of Gerald Byrne as told to him by the bishop when he'd told Willis of Byrne's appointment to St. Luke's, but was there something more, something no-one was telling him? David Willis eventually drifted off into a fitful sleep after first deciding to try and find out more about the new parish priest of St. Luke's.

CHAPTER 15

ALL IN THE MIND

Andy Ross had grown tired of waiting for the Home Office Profiler to arrive. A visit to the mortuary had brought little new in the way of information that would help them find the killer or killers of the two graveyard victims. The 'immediate' post-mortem promised two days ago had been delayed as William Nugent had cut his hand badly on his return to the mortuary and had required medical attention himself, leading to the postponement of the examination for just over twenty four hours.

Doctor Nugent and Francis Lees had at last carried out the post-mortem on the 'angel of death' victim, a name given to the unfortunate man by one of Miles Booker's crime scene technicians. Nugent had, at length, given Ross a tentative cause of death.

Standing over the autopsy table, his left hand heavily stitched where the knife blade had slipped and bitten deep into his flesh, Nugent looked up from the cadaver and looked at Ross.

"This one seems a little different, Inspector. The throat has been cut, as before, but not as deeply and it's my professional opinion that this poor bugger was killed by disembowelment. The massive trauma to this area," he indicated the lower abdomen with a flourish of his right hand, "is massive and the blood loss would have been tremendous. I believe yon laddie was opened up and bled to death as he hung, attached to that bloody stone angel. The blood pooled on the grave back at the churchyard indicated such a massive blood loss and my examination confirms it."

Ross rarely felt ill during post-mortems or autopsies but found himself feeling quite nauseous as he looked at the dead man's remains on the table in front of him. Izzie Drake also felt her legs going weak as she looked at the butchered remains of what, not long ago had been a living, breathing human being. Both officers had seen the scene at St. Mark's, which had been bad enough, but to now stand over the remains as Nugent picked over them in his hunt for clues they might use to find the killer or killers, was almost too much for them.

"I'm also pretty sure now that ye'll be looking for two killers, Inspector. It's my opinion that the slash across the throat was inflicted by a different hand than the wound on Remington's throat. It's not so deep, and there's evidence that whoever did it almost used their blade in a sawing motion, totally different to the first murder. The two sets of footprints help to confirm it. I think you might be seeking a woman, and a man, who prob-ably was the one who opened up the man's abdomen, letting the innards spill out as he died. Oh yes, and the tongue's missing as with the first case, so that gives you your confirmation that this murder was comitted by the same killer or killers as Matthew Remington?""

"A woman?" said Drake, surprised, who, since talking with Miles Booker, had denied to herself that a member of her sex could have been responsible for such savagery. Are you sure?"

"Aye, Sergeant, a woman. The Crime Scenes Officers will confirm it, but those footprints in the blood in front of the angel looked too small to be those of a man, and that neck wound would be consistent with a woman's hand being at work."

"That puts a new slant on things," Ross commented. "A man and woman working together would be unusual but not unheard of. If there's nothing else you can tell us right now, Doc, we'd better get back to Head-quarters. We're expecting the arrival of a profiler."

"Och, a profiler is it now? Your bosses think you need some help, I take it?"

"I'll take any help I can get right now, Doc," Ross acknowledged as he and Drake took their leave of the autopsy room, Drake lingering in recep-tion for a brief conversation with Peter Foster before joining Ross outside as he stood by the car.

"Lover boy alright, is he?" Ross asked as Drake unlocked the Mondeo and the pair climbed into the vehicle.

""Peter's fine thank you, sir," Drake replied.

Ross smiled as Drake squirmed a little at his 'lover boy remark'.

* * *

The squad room at headquarters was unusually quiet on their return. Most of the team were out pursuing inquiries to try to establish the identity of the latest victim, with Gable also trying to find more on the life and rela-tionships involved in the life of Matthew 'Razor' Remington.

Paul Ferris looked a forlorn lone figure among the desks and computers of the room but he quickly rose to his feet as Ross and Drake walked in.

"Everything okay, Paul?" Ross asked.

"Yes, sir. I'm still working on the tracking the life of Matthew Remington, while Sam is on the streets trying to find anyone who can give us more intel on his recent activities. I'll have it all up on the murder board as soon as I can, and by the way, sir, you have a visitor."

"The profiler?"

"Yes, sir, waiting in your office."

"Been here long?"

"About half an hour sir. I wanted to call you at the mortuary but she told me not to, that she was happy to wait and didn't want to interrupt you in mid-investigation."

"Very considerate of her, I must say. Come on Izzie, let's go meet the woman who'd supposed to help us solve the case."

With that, Ross walked off towards his office, Drake following closely in his wake. As he opened the door to his inner sanctum, he caught his first sight of the Home Office Criminal Profiler.

Doctor Christine Bland rose from the visitor's chair in his office as he and Drake entered the office, immediately holding her hand out towards Ross. He took it and as they shook hands, she spoke first.

"Pleased to meet you, Inspector Ross. I'm Christine Bland. Sorry I'm late. I know you were expecting me hours ago, but there'd been a mega pile up on the M62, and the traffic delays were horrendous."

Ross looked at the woman standing before him. Christine Bland was, he guessed somewhere in her late thirties. Her long blonde hair was tied in a pony tail and the two piece black skirt suit accentuated a well formed figure and the pencil skirt helped to accentuate her slim legs, She was about as far from the look of a profiler as he could imagine, but then, she wouldn't be here if she couldn't to the job, he supposed.

"No apologies needed, Doctor. Bland," he replied. "We've had plenty to do in keeping the investigation moving forward." He nodded in the direction of Izzie Drake. "This is Sergeant Clarissa Drake, by the way. Anything I know about the case, she knows, so you can speak freely in front of her."

"Pleased to meet you, Doctor," Drake said to the profiler, "and most people call me Izzie. Clarissa sounds so formal."

"Hello, Sergeant, good to meet you too."

The woman turned again to face Ross.

"Inspector Ross, I'm aware you might be a little dubious about the value of what I do. A lot of officers are the first time they work with a profiler, but believe me when I say that there are many ways in which I can maybe help you identify the type of person or persons you may be seeking in this case. D.C. I. Porteous already told me it looks like you're looking for a man and woman team now."

Ross, trying to be welcoming despite his doubts about the value of Bland's potential help, smiled as he replied.

"Look, Doctor Bland, I have no doubts that you're good at what you do, but it's not as if we have a serial killer at work with a string of murders behind them already. I know the top brass feel you can help and on that basis I'm happy to work with you, but just don't see how much you can possibly read into what's taken place in the last few days."

"Perhaps you'll change your mind after I've had an opportunity to review the case files, Inspector?"

"What? Oh, yes, of course."

Turning to Izzie Drake, he asked her to go and bring all the case files and notes they had amassed to date for the profiler to look at. Two minutes later, she returned, with Paul Ferris in tow, the team's collator looking agitated and somehow excited at the same time.

"Sir, you need to listen to Paul, right now," Drake informed him.

"Okay, Paul, what have you got for us?"

Ferris looked at Christine Bland, a questioning look on his face. Ross reassured him.

"It's okay, Paul. Doctor Bland is here to help us."

"Oh, right sir. I just had a call from an Inspector Woodruff out at Bootle. He thinks he might have identified our second victim."

Ross's senses jumped to full alert.

"Go on Paul. Don't keep us in suspense."

Looking at a sheet of paper he held in his hand, Ferris read from the notes he'd made of his conversation with Inspector Woodruff.

"Well sir, seems they had a report of a missing person from a lady whose husband hadn't come home from work the previous day. She'd called the station the previous night and of course they'd told her to call back if he didn't turn up by morning, and anyway, he didn't come home and when she called his work, they told her he hadn't shown up that morning either. She called the station at Bootle immediately and they sent someone out to see her, a D.C Collins. Anyway, Collins seems to be a bright chap, and he took notes, and obtained a photograph of the husband.

When he returned to the station, Collins remembered seeing the flyer with our inquiry the previous day and when he compared it to the photo of the missing man he went straight in to report to his boss, Inspector Woodruff, who took one look and called us."

Ross, becoming impatient, urged Ferris on

"Alright Paul, come on, who the hell is he?"

"Well sir, this is where things begin to come together a bit, I think. The dead man appears to be Mark Proctor, a P.E. teacher. The thing is, sir, he taught at Speke Hill School."

"That place with the orphanage combined, out on Woolton Road?" Drake asked.

"That's right, the old loony bin they turned into an orphanage and school years ago. Anyway, what made my brain cells go into overdrive sir is that Matthew Remington, victim number one, was a resident of the orphanage and pupil at Speke Hill when he was a boy. There has to be a connection, sir, surely."

"Bloody hell, Paul. You might be on to something. It has to be too much of a coincidence for an ex-pupil and a current teacher from the same place to meet with similar violent deaths like this," Ross replied.

"How old was Proctor?" Drake asked.

"Fifty seven," Ferris replied.

"Similar ages," said Ross. "Paul, I think we may have our connection, as you say. Please start a background check on this Mark Proctor. Let's find out how far back the two dead men could have been connected to each other."

"Consider it done sir. Anything else?"

"Not for the moment. Give it your highest priority, Paul. I want to know all there is to know about Mark Bolton. I'd better speak to Inspector Woodruff and then go and talk to the widow, if we're sure of the identification. Did Woodruff give you any indication of what they're doing about that?"

"He said he thought you'd want to see her yourself sir, and arrange for her to identify the body."

"Of course he did," Ross said with a wry smile. "Pass the buck as soon as possible. No one wants the task of dealing with a potentially hysterical widow at the best of times, and certainly not one with a victim as badly mutilated as this one. Do we have a copy of Mrs. Bolton's statement yet?"

"Bootle are emailing it to me as we speak, sir. I'll have a copy printed out for you by the time you're ready to go and see her."

Ferris left the office and the two detectives and the profiler looked at one another. It was Christine Bland who broke the silence.

"Looks like you might have something I can work with here, Inspector Ross. Do you mind if I accompany you and Sergeant Drake when you go to speak to the widow?"

"Not at all, Doctor. As you say, you may be able to offer some helpful insights."

"How will you proceed without a formal identification?"

"At this point, I want to talk to Inspector Woodruff, see how much he can tell me, then we'll go and talk to the widow, and show her a photo of the dead man. She'll see enough to be able to tell us if it's her husband, I'm sure."

"Even the touched up versions of the photos, taken at the morgue, are pretty awful to look at sir," Drake pointed out to her boss.

"I know, but if we're to move fast in trying to find his killers, we have little choice, and anyway, a photo will be far less painful than the formal identification she'll have to make at the mortuary tomorrow. Sorry Izzie, you'll have to put off seeing lover boy tonight. Looks like we might be in for a spot of overtime. I'll phone Woodruff then let Maria know I'll be late home too.

Why don't you take Doctor Bland for a quick coffee while I'm talking to Woodruff then we'll head off to Bootle as soon as I'm finished in here. Is that okay with you, Doctor?"

"Coffee sounds good, Inspector, and please as we're going to be working together, don't you think Doctor Bland is a little cumbersome every time you talk to me? Chris will do fine as far as I'm concerned. It's what most people call me."

"Fine, Chris it is then," Ross replied. "Now, you two ladies go grab a coffee, let me talk to Woodruff and Maria."

The switchboard connected Ross to the police station at Copy Lane in Bootle. Ross had visited that station maybe once or twice over the years, the only memorable fact he could bring to mind about the place was the fact that it was located not far from a McDonalds on the nearby leisure park. He'd heard of, but never met Inspector Bob Woodruff, nothing bad, a sensible, level-headed copper as far as he knew.

"Woodruff here," a rather gruff voice answered after a couple of rings of the internal phone system.

"Inspector Woodruff, Andy Ross here from the Major Crimes Squad."

"Hello there, the specialist murder team, eh? Call me Bob. You must have got my message about Mark Proctor."

"Yes, thanks, Bob. Sounds as if you're pretty sure this Proctor chap is our victim?"

"Sure sounds like it. The photo his wife gave us looks very close to the one you guys circulated, minus the facial wounds of course. It's too close a match to be anyone else, really."

"Did you tell her you think we may have found him?"

"Er, no. I didn't think it wise at that point. Thought you guys might prefer to handle it, being as it's your case and all that."

And saved you the problem of dealing with a hysterical newly-widowed wife of a murder victim, Ross thought.

"Thanks a lot, Bob," he voiced instead.

"Hey, never say I don't leave all the fun to the big boys," Woodruff laughed down the phone.

"Okay, but thanks for getting in touch so quickly. Can you give me the Proctor's address?"

"Sure," said Woodruff, reading off the address, which Ross duly noted down on a pad of post-its on his desk. "You can't miss it," he added, "It's just off the main road, about a mile from the station, about a hundred yards past the Shell filling station."

After thanking Woodruff, Ross made his way out of his office to find Izzie Drake and Christine Bland, coming to the end of their coffees, talking with Sam Gable.

"Meeting of the Women's Institute?" he joked as he drew near.

"Ha-ha, very funny, Boss," Drake replied. "Sam here was just telling us she used to live not far from Speke Hill."

"Really?" Ross said, quizzically. "What's it like, Sam?"

"Creepy, sir," she answered. "Well, it was when I was eight years old. It used to be a mental asylum back in Victorian times, and was converted to an orphanage and school sometime in the early part of the twentieth century. It was a real old gothic pile, at least, that's how it looked to us kids when we were growing up, you know, a real haunted house look to it. In fact, there were lots of stories around at the time about the place having a resident ghost."

"Ah, well, it would have to have a ghost wouldn't it?" Ross laughed.

"The thing is, sir," Gable went on, "lots of the kids who lived there used to get out at weekends and hit the local shops and villages or the older ones could catch the bus into town, and me and my friends often knocked about with some of the girls from there. They used to tell us about strange goings on in the orphanage at night."

"What kind of 'goings on' were they talking about, Sam"

"They said that sometimes they'd hear screams in the night, like a child in pain, a girl, they thought, and some of them said they'd seen a dark figure prowling the corridors in the dead of night, moving silently as though it was floating along, not touching the floor."

"Oh, come on Sam. You don't expect me to believe in some ghost wandering around scaring girls shitless in the night do you?"

"I'm only telling you what they told us, sir. Oh yes, and they did say that girls sometimes disappeared and were never seen again."

Now Ross's interest was aroused.

"Do you remember the names of any of those girls you talked to," he asked.

"Oh God, no sir, sorry. It was years ago and they were only kids we met up with now and then at weekends. I don't think we even knew some of their names."

"Okay, well, try to think of anything you can while we're out. Write down any memories you have that might help give us some additional background on the place. We're going to have to visit Speke Hill very soon. You might as well join us when we head over there. Your knowledge might be useful."

"Right you are, sir," said Gable, pleased to have the opportunity to work alongside Ross and Drake when the time came.

CHAPTER 16

MELANIE

Crossing the car park to reach the pool car, Ross noticed Christine Bland casting a long look at a gleaming maroon Vauxhall Carlton, parked in one of the visitor spaces.

"Yours?" he asked, pointing to the pristine looking car, the Registration plate indicating the car to be around ten years old.

"Yes, it is," Bland replied

"I thought you'd have owned something bang up to date and trendier than the Carlton," he observed.

"Sentimental value, Inspector," the profiler replied. "It belonged to my late father. He bought it brand new and it was his pride and joy. He looked after it as though it was his baby. When he died five years ago, I asked Mum if I could have it, and I've done my best to keep it as he'd have liked. Vauxhall ceased production of the Carlton a few years ago but the parts, if needed, are still cheap enough and in plentiful supply."

"Nice," Ross said. "Sorry about your Dad."

"Thanks," Bland responded. "He was a lovely man, my Dad. Supported me in everything I did as a girl, through uni, the lot. I miss him a lot."

A companionable silence fell over the small group as they entered the car, and Drake drove out of the car park and headed for Bootle. On the way, Izzie decided to try and find out more about the new temporary addition to the team.

"If you don't mind me asking, Doctor," she began, "but how did you get into the business of criminal profiling? We didn't get much chance to talk back there, thanks to Paul Ferris and his new information."

"I don't mind at all, Sergeant. I always wanted to by a psychologist, from around the age of twelve or thirteen anyway. I was lucky, got the grades I needed to get into medical school, got my M.D. and then went up to Oxford and got a degree in Psychology, followed by another in Criminology. When I was suitably qualified, I applied to the Home Office to be included in their list of Criminal Psychologists, able to assist the police in difficult cases. I became fascinated by the actual science of exactly what made certain criminals tick, why they did the things they do and so on. An opportunity came along to spend a year studying with the F.B.I's specialist Criminal Behavioural Analysis Unit at their H.Q at Quantico in Virginia. I applied and was accepted, and the rest, as they say, is history. I came back and was employed as one of a small number of profilers working directly for the Home Office, on a full time basis, basically going wherever I'm needed when a force such as yours specifically asks for help with cases like this one."

Drake was impressed and said so in no uncertain terms.

"Wow. That's fascinating. You must have been really determined to have gone through all that studying and training."

"I wanted to make my parents proud of me," Bland replied. "I'm pleased to say I think I succeeded."

Ross, who'd listened intently to her reply to Drake's question, added.

"Well, Christine, with all that training and your obvious qualifications for the job in hand, I have to say I'm pleased you're here to give us the benefit of your expertise."

"Thanks," she replied. "I'm developing a few thoughts already. I'll know more after we've seen this poor lady and when I finally get to finish reading the case notes you gave me back at headquarters. I might need to talk to the pathologist too, a Doctor Nugent, I believe?"

"No problem. Maybe you can take Doctor Bland to meet our friend at the mortuary tomorrow, Sam, after she's had a chance to read up on the case?"

"Be glad to sir," Sam Gable replied from her place in the back of the car, seated next to Christine.

* * *

"This is it, number forty-five," Drake announced as she pulled the car to a halt on the street outside a fairly modern detached three bedroom house with a well kept lawn to the front, liberally planted with various hybrid tea roses in well kept borders. An almost new Toyota Corolla, in a fiery red, stood on the drive in front of a closed up-and-over garage door.

Ross hated the task that lay ahead of them in the next few minutes.

Informing a loved one of the death of a spouse or other relative was about the worst job a police officer had to attend to in his career, and in a case like this, the thought of how the man's widow might react was almost too terrible to contemplate, but knowing there was no way to avoid what had to be done, he took a deep breath before grasping the door handle, ready to open the door, and then...

"Okay, let's get this over with. Izzie, in the front with me. You at the back with the Doctor, please, Sam."

The woman who answered the door in response to the ringing of the doorbell looked to be in her mid-fifties, slightly overweight though not obese, with auburn hair that fell to her shoulders and looked in need of washing and brushing. Ross assumed worry about her husband had brought about the temporary neglect of her otherwise neat and well turned out appearance. She wore a cream blouse, and brown trousers that ended at a pair of brown house shoes of a similar colour.

"You must be the police," she immediately stated as she took in the rather large contingent of people standing on her doorstep.

"Yes, and you must be Mrs. Melanie Proctor," Ross said as he held up his warrant card to identify himself, and sought confirmation they had the right woman in front of them.

"Yes, please come in. Do you have any news of Mark?"

"Let's go inside and sit down, Mrs. Proctor," Drake urged as the woman seemed to hesitate for a second before moving aside and admitting the four of them. "We can talk better indoors rather than on the doorstep."

"Oh yes, of course, I'm sorry, please come in."

Melanie led them into a spacious living room, neatly furnished with three-piece suite in deep red leather, good quality carpet with a soft, deep pile in a dark grey shadow design, and a large screen television in one corner. A bookcase stood against one wall and a standard lamp stood in the corner opposite the television. A chest of drawers stood under the window and Ross couldn't help but notice the wedding photograph proudly displayed on top of the chest, a younger and slightly slimmer version of Melanie Proctor smiling with happiness beside her husband, Mark.

"Sit down, please," she invited, and Drake, Gable and Christine Bland did as she suggested while Ross remained standing behind Drake's chair, while Melanie stood looking nervously at the officers from a position standing in front of the cream marble fireplace.

"Do you have any news of Mark, then?" she now asked again after Ross had introduced the others. "Has he been involved in an accident? It must be that. I told him not to buy that bloody Subaru, it was too fast for him, but I think he wanted to show off in front of the boys at school. Is he

329

in the hospital, Inspector? Was someone else hurt? Is that why you're here?"

Ross knew she was babbling, her words flying from her mouth from a nervousness born of fear. He'd witnessed this type of behaviour previously over the years as a kind of 'advance denial' reflex that kicked in to protect the speaker from potentially hearing bad news. He tapped Izzie Drake on the shoulder, and the sergeant spoke.

"Mrs. Proctor, Melanie, please, calm down. Inspector Ross needs to tell you something."

It worked. Melanie Proctor fell silent for a few seconds, and then spoke once more.

"Forgive me Inspector, I'm sorry. It's just that I've been so worried. Please tell me if my husband's alright or has he been hurt in some way?

Andy Ross took a deep breath and then said, as sympathetically as he could.

"Mrs. Proctor, I'm sorry to inform you that we believe your husband was the victim of a vicious assault that took place in St. Mark's churchyard…"

"What? Wait a minute, I heard about that on the news on Radio Merseyside. But, that poor man, was…he was…"

"Dead, I know, Mrs. Proctor. I'm sorry to tell you we have good reason to believe the body currently in the mortuary is that of your husband, Mark Proctor."

Melanie Proctor didn't shout, she didn't scream or become in any way hysterical. She stood staring directly into Ross's eyes for about twenty seconds as his words seemed to bore their way into the deepest recesses of her consciousness, and then, as all the colour in her face drained away, leaving her looking paler than a ghost, she simply fell to the floor in a dead faint, so fast, none of the officers could move to try and catch the poor woman.

"Oh shit," said Ross.

"She'll be fine sir," said Drake. "Sam, go and find the kitchen, bring her some water, and if you can find a towel or something, wet it and bring that too."

"Right you are, Sarge," said Gable, heading for the door.

"Can I help?" Christine Bland asked.

"She's only fainted," Ross replied. "We'll bring her round in a minute."

Eventually, they did just that and Drake and Gable gently laid Melanie Proctor on the sofa as she seemed to struggle for breath.

"Do you want us to call a doctor?" Ross asked, or maybe someone to come round and be with you?"

"No, thank you. Why do you think it's my Mark?"

"We sent a photo of the victim to all police stations in the area, Mrs. Proctor. Inspector Woodruff at Copy Lane recognised the man from the photo you'd given them at the station. I'm afraid I don't have much doubt that the victim in the churchyard is Mark."

Tears were now flowing copiously from the woman's eyes, which were becoming redder by the second. Ross hated moments like this. There was just no way to make such moments any easier for the bereaved.

"I'm so sorry, Mrs. Proctor, but if we're to find who did this we need to ask you a few questions, and eventually, we'll need you to come and identify the body officially."

"Oh my god, no. It can't be Mark, Inspector. Who could possibly have wanted to hurt him?"

"That's one of the questions we need to ask you. Do you know anyone who might have held a grudge of any kind against Mark, or perhaps someone he'd upset at work recently?"

"No, nobody at all. Mark is a teacher, Inspector. As far as I know he doesn't have an enemy in the world. He teaches P.E. at Speke Hill"

Melanie continued to speak of her husband in the present tense. Ross knew it might be a while before she used the past tense, accepting he'd gone.

"Alright, and I know this is hard for you, but we have to ask these things. When did you last see Mark, Mrs. Proctor?"

Melanie suddenly began shaking and her body almost convulsed as it became wracked with sobs and tears of pure grief.

Ross spoke quietly to Izzie Drake.

"I think we should give her some time. Izzie, you know what we need to find out from her. You and Sam stay here with Mrs. Proctor. Try and question her again when she's recovered slightly. I'll call Copy Lane, see if they can spare a patrol car to run me and the Doc here back to Headquarters, and also get them to send out a Families Liaison Officer to sit with Mrs. Proctor after you leave. Hopefully by then she'll have given us the name of someone, a friend or relative who can be with her. She shouldn't be on her own at a time like this. Before you leave, fix a time for her to come and identify her husband's body."

"Okay, sir."

"And Izzie?"

"Sir?"

"Don't be all day about it, know what I mean?"

"I know exactly what you mean sir," Drake replied.

Ross turned again to Melanie Proctor.

"Mrs. Proctor, this is terrible news for you, I do appreciate that, but anything you can tell us may be helpful in finding whoever did this to your husband."

"I understand, Inspector," she sobbed.

"Let's make a nice fresh pot of tea, Melanie," Izzie said. "We'll talk again in a few minutes when Inspector Ross and Doctor Bland have gone, okay?"

Melanie Proctor nodded and allowed Sam Gable to lead her into the kitchen, leaving Izzie Drake to talk privately with Ross for a minute.

"She's in shock, Izzie, so go easy on her, but try to find out anything you can about her husband's day to day life and activities. We need to establish whatever links him and Matthew Remington as well, which is vital if we're to move this case forward."

"No problem sir. We'll use the gentle touch with her, see what we can prise out of her."

"I thought you'd be talking to her yourself," Bland said to Ross.

"Izzie knows exactly what she's doing, and she and D.C. Gable will probably get more from her than I will, being women and perhaps more empathic with Melanie."

"Ah, so you do employ a little psychology in your methodology," Bland smiled at him.

"Well yes, I'm not a total dinosaur, Doctor. We do try to be sensitive to victim's families as well."

A knock on the door was answered by Izzie, who admitted a uniformed constable to the hallway.

"Constable Holland, sir. I'm supposed to drive you to headquarters," the young man said to Ross.

"Excellent, let's go, then, constable."

On the way back to town, Ross took advantage of their time together to find out a little more about Christine Bland.

"So, where are staying while you're in Liverpool?" he asked.

"The Marriott," she replied.

"Very nice," said Ross.

"Yes, it is. The room's excellent and I can work in it if I need to."

"So, what do you think so far?"

"It's too early to draw any conclusions yet, but you've already established that there must be a link between the victims. Once I read through the case files I may be in a position to offer a suggestion or two."

"Well, I hope you can offer something that will help us identify who or what we should be looking for, and soon."

"I'll do my best, Inspector. I don't offer miracles, but if I can at least point you in the right direction, establish a motive, anything to help, I will."

* * *

Meanwhile, Izzie Drake, having questioned Melanie Proctor about her husband's friends, regular routine and more now sat back and allowed D.C. Sam Gable to ask the widow of Mark Proctor a number of questions based on Gable's own knowledge of Speke Hill, gleaned from her own friends who'd lived and been educated in the orphanage and school.

"So, Melanie, Mark was a P.E, teacher, right?"

"Yes, he was actually recently promoted to head of the P.E Department at the school. It made him very proud."

"I'm sure it did. Tell me, did Mark teach just the Upper or Lower School pupils, or did his job entail teaching both groups?"

"Oh, the whole age range, not just the younger or older children."

"Thanks, and did he teach just boys, or the girls as well?"

"Both. Speke Hill is a co-ed school, with mixed classes, although the children are accommodated separately of course."

"Yes, I see. Melanie, do you think any of the other teachers in the P.E. department might have been jealous of Mark's promotion?"

"Oh no. that's preposterous. The staff members are all very friendly. Mark said they were a great team to work with."

"Okay, but we have to ask these questions, you do understand?"

Melanie nodded, her eyes puffy and red with tears as she reached for another tissue from the box Gable had found in the downstairs bathroom not long ago.

"Did Mark ever become involved with the orphanage's weekend shopping trips into town?"

"Oh, you know about those?" Melanie sounded surprised. "No, he didn't. He was a teacher at the school, and the activities of the orphanage were organised and run by the care staff. Most of them are what Mark laughingly called 'civilians' though there are still couple of nuns teaching there. Once upon a time they were all priests and nuns you know, both the teachers and orphanage staff."

"Yes, until the place came under Council control," Gable replied.

"And was Mark particularly close to any of the other teachers, any of them special friends, maybe came round to dinner or you went to their homes?"

"No, I'm sorry, nothing like that. He just went to work and came home after school."

Another bout of crying took over at that point and Drake signalled with a sweep of her hand to Gable to bring things to an end.

"Well, I think that's all for now, Melanie. You've been really helpful, thank you."

The woman was clearly close to the verge of cracking up at that point and the two detectives where grateful when a knock on the front door heralded the arrival of the Families Liaison Officer promised by Andy Ross.

Police Constable Sally Akeroyd quickly introduced herself to the two detectives and Melanie Proctor. Sally seemed to form an immediate bond with Melanie and Drake thought how well suited she was to the role of

Families Liaison Officer. The time was appropriate to take their leave and Izzie informed Melanie they would send someone at ten the following morning to collect her and take her to perform the official identification of Mark's body, and bring her home afterwards. Just as Izzie and Sam were about to leave, Melanie made a final comment that brought them up short.

"It's so unfair," she said. "Mark spent almost his whole life at Speke Hill, first as a child and then as a teacher. They'll miss him almost as much as I will."

"What do you mean, child *and* teacher, Melanie?" Drake asked her. "Are you telling us Mark was a resident of the orphanage when he was a boy?"

"Yes, didn't you know that?"

Drake shook her head.

"He told me all about it. His Mum died when he was young. His Dad, an American soldier, was sent back to the States when he was nothing but a baby. Don't ask me why his Mum didn't go with him. I've no idea. I do know that Mark never knew him or his name. Proctor was his Mum's name. Mark was sent to the orphanage because his Mum had no relatives that could or would take a baby into their homes."

Drake knew there and then that they'd found the connection between the two victims. Both had been orphans at Speke Hill, and from their ages, almost certainly at the same time. She knew they had to get back to headquarters as soon as possible to report the information to Ross.

Placing a comforting hand on Melanie Proctor's arm, she thanked the still gently sobbing woman and called to Sally Akeroyd.

"Take good care of her, Constable," she said.

"I will, Sergeant Drake, don't worry. I've done this for two years. She'll be fine with me."

Drake and Gable were soon motoring back across the city towards headquarters. From the passenger seat, Sam Gable turned and spoke to Drake.

"Bloody hell, Sarge. That was a real turn up, finding out about Proctor's childhood like that."

"Wasn't it just?" Drake agreed. "The way it just came out like that. We knew he was a teacher there. We'd never have thought to ask if he'd been an orphan in the home as well. The boss will be bloody gobsmacked. We've definitely found the link between the two dead men. You did well in there as well, Sam. I wouldn't have known what questions to ask about the way things worked at the school or kids home or whatever they want to call the damn place."

"Thanks, Sarge, I appreciate that."

A few minutes later, Izzie pulled into the car park at headquarters and she and Sam Gable almost ran from the car, into the building, and up the stairs, ignoring the lifts as they rushed to inform Ross of the latest development. Things were moving at last. Perhaps now they could begin to find a reason for the appalling murders in the churchyards, and if they had a reason, they might just have a chance of identifying and tracking down the killers.

A few minutes later, the two breathless women burst into Ross's office, as he sat talking with Christine Bland.

"Sir, we need to talk, right now!" Drake gasped as she almost collapsed into a visitor chair beside the profiler, and Gable stood panting against the office door.

"Er, sit down, Sergeant, why don't you?" Ross laughed. "Come on then. What's so important? Out with it, Izzie. I know that look, like the cat that got the cream. You've got something, I know you too well."

So she told him everything she and Sam Gable had learned from Melanie Proctor.

CHAPTER 17

PROFILE

Following the report from Izzie Drake and Sam Gable, revealing that Matthew Remington and Mark Proctor had attended Speke Hill Orphanage and School at what they believed to be the same time, Andy Ross knew they had the connection they were seeking. Now, he felt that if they could just 'join up the dots' of how the two men were connected together by their pasts, he'd be well on the way to solving the gruesome murders. Christine Bland also felt the new information would be helpful to her in producing at least a preliminary profile of the killers once she'd read the case files, which she'd taken back to her hotel room the previous night to study. Word had gone out for all officers to be on the lookout for Mark Proctor's silver Subaru. If they could locate the car, it might give them a clue as to where Proctor had been abducted, unless the killers had moved it from the abduction site and dumped it miles away. It would certainly give them the opportunity for locating any forensic trace evidence the killers may have left behind.

Now, as the early morning sun shone through the plate glass window of the murder room, highlighting Paul Ferris's murder board as well as illuminating rows of dust motes floating in streams across the room, Ross felt as if the case was about to witness a new beginning.

After a brief up-date from each of the team, with the only significant information being a report from 'Tony' Curtis that included the news that Remington had been to all intents and purposes a model prisoner during his incarceration for the rape of Claire Morris, but despite being kept on the isolation wing for his own safety, had nonetheless been the victim of two serious assaults during his time in prison.

"Maybe he was so weird even the other nonces couldn't stand him," said Derek McLennan.

"The impression I got from the governor was that Remington had something of a reputation on the wing for talking about what he called 'fantasies' though he wasn't able to tell me exactly what those fantasises were," Curtis went on.

"Hmm, wasn't or wouldn't maybe?" Drake interjected.

"But why would the governor stand up for a fucker like Remington?" asked Curtis.

"I don't know," Drake replied. "But you know what some of these modern prison governors can be like, glorified social workers who think it's their job to rehabilitate the offenders in their jails rather than punish them, so if he had no proof of Remington's fantasies actually taking place, he'd rather keep them quiet instead of telling us about them and sullying the dead man's reputation even more than it already has been."

"Are you serious, Sarge?" asked Curtis.

"Yep, she is," Ross spoke up. "You've a lot to learn yet, Tony."

"Fucking hell," said Curtis, not too loudly.

"Maybe we need to speak to the governor at Walton again," Ross added, ignoring Curtis's profanity. "We'll come back to that later. First, for those who didn't meet her yesterday, this is Doctor Christine Bland, a profiler from the Home Office, sent to try and help us identify the type of people we should be looking for if we're to stop these murders."

A murmur of greetings rippled through the assembled officers.

"Doctor Bland has formulated a preliminary profile overnight and she'd like to share it with us. It's all yours, Doc," he said, handing over to the profiler, dressed this morning in an immaculate grey pantsuit, with low heeled patent leather black shoes, her hair still tied in the same style as the previous day, obviously her working style, Ross decided.

Bland stood and faced the team, smiling as she did so.

"Good morning, everyone," she began. "I met some of you yesterday, and hope to get the chance to talk to you all individually later. I'm here to help and together, hopefully, we'll bring these vicious killers to justice. Please don't stand on ceremony with me. My name is Christine, forget the Doctor Bland bit. We're all on the same team, and now, if I may, I'll give you what I've got so far. I spent yesterday afternoon with Inspector Ross, visiting Melanie Proctor, then was present in his office when Sergeant Drake and D.C, Gable came back to tell us that Mark Proctor and Matthew Remington were both orphans and lived at Speke Hill Orphanage at the same time."

A general murmuring encompassed the room at this latest information. Derek McLennan spoke up.

"Er, Christine?" I'm D.C. Derek McLennan. "So you're telling us that as well as living and obviously studying there as a boy, he then went on to become a teacher there?"

"Exactly. Looks like his whole life, apart from a few years spent studying was tied up with Speke Hill. That place is going to bear some very close scrutiny in the next few days. I'm sure Inspector Ross will have more to say about that when I've finished."

She turned towards the desk behind her for a moment and picked up one of the case files, holding it up as she turned back to address the team.

"I spent last night going through every word of these files. From these, added to what Sergeant Drake and D.C. Gable learned yesterday and the minimal forensic evidence at the murder scenes, my immediate thoughts are as follows. We're looking for a team, a man and a woman working together who have implicit trust in one another. It's likely that the woman is older than the man by quite some years, as it's unlikely a younger female would have built up the type of rage we're seeing displayed here. Dr. Nugent has carried out a minute study of the wound patterns on both bodies and it's probable that the woman was responsible for most if not all of the shallower stab and slash wounds found on both victims. As to the man, he's younger, fit and strong enough to subdue the victims and carry out the actual killings. The grass behind the angel memorial at St. Mark's was quite long, so ascertaining his shoe size from the prints found in the grass is an approximation only, as many of the indentations came from the time he was obviously leaning back and pulling the body of Mark Proctor upward to harness him to the angel, so those prints are not perfect as they show greater heel indentations and less of the tread from normal walking. It's Doctor Nugent's belief that the man wears size 9 to 11 shoes and the tread marks at the scene indicated some kind of heavy-duty boots, perhaps hiking boots. Forget the woman's shoe size as the prints in the blood on the marble slab of the grave stone were so blurred as to be useless, but they were narrow enough to indicate a woman's foot. Any questions so far?"

She paused and D.C. Curtis raised a hand.

"Yes, detective?"

"Curtis, Tony, ma'am."

"Please, not ma'am, D.C. Curtis. Christine will do."

"Yeah, right, well, Christine, why can't they possibly be the same age? A younger woman might also be capable of making those shallow wounds, right?"

"It's possible, yes. Profiling isn't an exact science, but from previous experience of similar recorded partnerships, one side of the killing team is usually older than the other. You usually find that one of them will be the dominant side and the other more of a submissive partner. In this case it's not yet clear who the dominant one is, but my money at this point would be on the male."

"Why's that?" Curtis asked.

"The sheer savagery of these attacks indicates a hugely narcissistic personality, someone who has total belief in his own ability to carry out these killings, without showing any sign of mercy to his victims. The fact that there were no hesitation marks on the victims, and I'm talking about the major wounds now, indicates a confident and well ordered mind. He knew what he was doing and he wanted to do it. This indicates a leader rather than a follower."

Moving on to the sexual mutilation, there are a couple of ways to look at this. One, the killer may be exacting revenge for an incident related to the victims' own sexual activity, either against his partner or some other perceived victim or, it may be connected with killer's own sexuality. Believe me, as gruesome as it seems, I've seen similar mutilations in the past in cases of homosexual killings."

Various comments swept the room as the gathered detectives speculated on the fact they now had to consider other motives for the murders.

Derek McLennan raised a hand.

"Go ahead, please," said Christine.

"Okay, if we accept what you're saying, why do you think the woman is involved with this man? Could she be a relative, his wife, or what?"

"I said there's trust between them so it is possible they are related, or, as seems likely, the large age difference, if I'm right in my estimation, means this case is probably rooted in something that happened a long time ago. The woman may herself have been involved in whatever has been allowed to lie dormant for years. How and why the younger man came to be involved, it's too early for me to hazard a guess, but there will be something that connects them."

"Thanks," said McLennan. "So, you think Speke Hill is connected to the killings?"

"No, I didn't say that exactly. What I did say is there is something at Speke Hill, or an event at Speke Hill that connects the victims. That's not quite the same thing."

"Er, right, thanks," said Derek, still a little unsure of exactly what Bland was inferring.

"Finally," said Bland, "it's likely that the male drives a car. He'd need to be mobile in order to track and locate his victims. Mark Proctor had a car and it's missing. Our man could have arranged an accident or immobilised Proctor's car and then ferried him to the murder scene in his own vehicle, which might turn out to be a treasure trove of forensic and trace evidence if we can locate it."

Ross took control of the meeting again.

"Right you lot. You've heard what Doctor Bland has had to say. It may not be much at this point but it does give us some pointers to be going on with. Last chance for final questions, anyone?"

"Sir, one for the doctor, erm, Christine," said Sam Gable.

"Go ahead, Sam."

"Well, Christine says we're looking for a younger man and an older woman, but my question is, just how young is the man supposed to be? Are we looking for a teenager, a man in his twenties, thirties or what?"

Christine Bland was quick to reply.

"These murders have been carried out in a cold and clinical manner, which suggests a high level of sophistication and intelligence. They were obviously well planned and executed, so my belief is that we're looking for someone in his early to late thirties, physically fit, his partner probably being in her later forties or fifties. It wouldn't surprise me if she has some degree of influence over him, in that he perhaps sees her as either a mother figure or maybe even a surrogate for someone who has undergone a trauma that he associates with these men. We have to consider the fact that the woman may herself be a victim of an experience connected to the two victims."

"Thank you," said Gable.

Derek McLennan now added another question.

"Yes, Derek?" Ross said, becoming a little impatient to be moving on.

"Do you think the killers are finished? I mean, are the two victims so far the extent of their 'mission', as they see it?"

This time, Ross provided the answer.

"Doctor Bland and I discussed this at length yesterday. It's hard to anticipate what they intend from now on. It may be that Remington and Proctor were the only targets, or, they may be lying low, waiting to strike again. If one or both of them have any ideas of the way the police work, they'll know we usually scale down an investigation after a period of time if we have nothing to show for our efforts. They may be waiting for that moment to arrive, after which they could crawl out of the woodwork and strike again. Right, anything else?"

"Just one thing, sir," said Paul Ferris, who went on to say, "I was wondering if there might be some significance in the fact that Matthew Remington was killed in St. Matthew's churchyard and Mark Proctor in St. Mark's?"

"May I answer that one, Inspector?" Bland asked.

Ross nodded.

"We don't know, D.C. Ferris. It might be planned, it could be coincidence. I hate to say it, but unless we get another murder, there just isn't enough at this point to indicate anything other than the fact the churches concerned may have simply been convenient for the killers. Or, they're using the names to throw us a red herring, something to make us look for a connection that doesn't exist."

"Now that's bloody clever," said Ferris.

"That's what I meant about sophistication," Bland replied.

"Right you are, everyone," Ross said, bring the meeting to a close. "We've got work to do. Derek, I want you and Sam on Remington. I know we've checked him out already, but we need more, and concentrate on his early life. Let's look for some connection or cross-over with Mark Proctor. I'm going to Speke Hill with Izzie and Doctor Bland. Sam, you'll need to postpone taking Christine to talk to Dr. Nugent until later."

Sam Gable nodded, as did Christine Bland, both in agreement with Ross.

" Everything we've learned so far tells us that Mark Proctor was Mr. Squeaky Clean, little orphan boy made good. Well, it's plain to see that someone thought otherwise. While we're gone, let's hope his car turns up. Tony," he said, turning to D.C Curtis, "get on to Traffic Division. Make them understand I want a priority on locating that Subaru."

"Okay sir," Curtis replied.

"And you Paul," he said to Ferris, "start going through those computer records of yours or whatever it is you do. Look for anything to do with Speke Hill that might tell us what may have taken place there during Remington and Proctor's youth."

"I'm on it sir," Ferris confirmed.

"Okay everyone. What are we waiting for?"

There followed a scraping of chairs on the floor as everyone rose to go about their allotted tasks, a hubbub of voices accompanying the departure of the murder team as Ross led Drake and Bland out of the building to the car park, ready to begin their investigation into Speke Hill.

CHAPTER 18

ST LUKE'S

Iris Redding had done the priests proud. Breakfast had been a wonderful concoction of bacon, sausages, fried eggs, tomatoes and hash browns, sufficient, both priests agreed, to feed the two of them and probably half the church choir too. Mrs. Redding, her face bright and cheerful, simply ordered the Fathers to eat as much as they wanted. She'd make up some sandwiches for her husband from the leftovers. Tom Redding would soon be arriving to tend to the gardens and trim the grass around the graves in the churchyard, and bacon and sausage sandwiches would suit him down to the ground for a lunchtime snack.

After she'd cleared away the breakfast pots, she dusted the living room, vacuumed the carpets and then left the priests with a cup of coffee and the morning newspapers as she went about the business of cleaning the rest of the house.

"We'd be lost without that woman," Byrne observed after hearing the dulcet tones of her footsteps as she made her way upstairs and out of their hearing.

"We would indeed, Father," Willis agreed. "Not only that, but she probably thinks we'd starve too, if she didn't ply us with mountains of food every morning for breakfast."

Both men laughed, the pair in relaxed mood, enjoying a rare quiet morning with no services to conduct and no pressing engagements until the afternoon.

"Can I ask you something, Father Byrne?" Willis asked, the question coming at Byrne completely unexpectedly.

"But of course, Father," Byrne replied.

"You've been having the nightmares again, haven't you? I'm concerned for you Father. They're coming frequently aren't they? You'll never tell me what they are about, but they disturb you greatly, that much I do know."

Gerald Byrne didn't reply at once. He hadn't been aware that his continued nightmares were becoming a regular disturbance to the other priest's sleep.

"I'm sorry, David. I really am. I assure you there's nothing for you to worry about, though I'm upset if I'm causing you loss of sleep as a result of the dreams."

"But, Father, they're not just dreams, are they? I've heard some of the things you shout in your sleep. You seem to be describing some terrible event from your past. Forgive me for intruding, but on the couple of occasions when I've gone in to attend to you, you have indeed sounded quite terrified at what you were seeing in your mind."

"David, listen to me please. When you've been in the priesthood as long as I have, been to some of the countries I've been to, and witnessed man's inhumanity to man to the degree that I have, then you might just begin to understand that the human mind is like a great repository of memories, not all of them good ones, and that sometimes, the only way the mind can deal with those memories is to replay them in a man's dreams, for I believe if we did not dream of such things and bring them to mind in such a way, those memories just might become all consuming. In his wisdom, our Good Lord allows us to relive them in a way that makes us realise they were once real, not to be forgotten, but not to be confined to the deepest recesses of the mind, where they may fester and turn us bitter and twisted. I have walked in places in this world, David, where God was truly forsaken by those who inhabited such lands and where the sights would truly have given you nightmares had you seen them."

David Willis heard the older priest's words, all of which made sense, so why, he wondered, didn't he wholeheartedly believe Gerald Byrne? Not wanting to press the matter, however, he merely replied,

"I understand Father, I think, but if such things are troubling you, do you not think it wise to seek help, perhaps a talk with the bishop, or maybe even medical help if the dreams are causing you such mental anguish?"

"I'm fine, David, really. I appreciate your concern, honestly, I do, but there's nothing for you to worry about. I pray to the Lord every day for his help in reconciling what I've seen with the words of our Father in Heaven. Perhaps you'll join me in prayer right now and then we can move on with our day."

Byrne had cleverly backed the younger priest into a corner. Unable to refuse his offer to join him in prayer, Willis felt obliged to let the matter drop, for now.

After ten minutes of prayer, a short silence followed between the two men, broken by Gerald Byrne.

"And how is your work going David? You devote much of your time to the sick and the needy of the parish. I feel remiss at times for not joining you for an occasional morning as you do your rounds. I know you must find it hard sometimes, being up early and out before the crows have taken their breakfasts."

"Oh, it's all going well, Father, and I know you have enough to do here without having to join me out there. I enjoy what I do, and feel I'm achieving a great deal."

"Well, there you are then, David. We're both happy, aren't we?"

"Yes, Father Byrne," Willis replied. "I suppose we are."

"Well then, let's have no more talk of dreams, nightmares or whatever. I must go and begin work on preparing my next sermon. You, I take it, have places to go and people to see, so I'll see you at lunchtime, when Mrs. Redding will, I'm sure, make certain we don't feel the pangs of hunger during our afternoon's labours."

Byrne rose from his chair, placing the newspaper he'd been reading on the coffee table in front of him, and strode from the room. David Willis watched him go and picked up the paper he'd been reading. It lay open at the latest report on 'The Churchyard Murders' as they'd been dubbed by the local press. Father Byrne had discussed the killings at length with Willis the previous evening, and appeared to be very interested in the subject of the murders, so it seemed to David Willis.

CHAPTER 19

ORPHANS & DEMONS

The journey from headquarters to Speke Hill would, under normal circumstances, take no more than fifteen minutes, but the traffic was heavy all over the city, thanks to the sudden descent of thick fog, that had made its way inexorably inland from the Irish Sea, enveloping the city in the muffled calm generated by a thick old-fashioned pea-souper.

Izzie Drake behind the wheel, the Mondeo almost seemed to groan at the forced lack of speed as the fog presented motorists with an almost impenetrable grey cloud-like barrier. Small golden-yellow haloes appeared around each of the normally bright street lights, adding a surreal feel to the vista that presented itself to those brave or foolhardy enough to attempt to drive in such weather conditions.

Ross felt an almost imperceptible increase in speed as the unmarked police vehicle began to close the distance between it and the car in front, an old Ford Fiesta that even in the thick fog appeared to be well past its best, with rust and scratches to the paintwork evident to Ross's keen eyes. He knew Izzie was growing impatient and even though his trusted sergeant had passed the police force's own advanced driving course, clearing her to participate in high-speed car chases if necessary, he didn't fancy their chances if she got too close and the old Fiesta suddenly slammed on the anchors.

"Izzie?"

"Sir?"

Please get us there intact. You can't even tell if that old bucket in front of us has got working brake lights. Before you know it we could be wrapped round his rear bumper."

"I know, sorry, sir, it's just so bloody frustrating, crawling along like this. We should have been there by now."

"It's the same for everyone, Izzie, and let's not give our guest in the back heart failure while we're at it."

"Oh, don't worry about me," Christine Bland piped up from the back seat. "I'm keeping my eyes shut, so I won't know anything until we get there or hit the car in front."

Ross and Drake both broke into spontaneous laughter, relieving the tension and boredom of the snail's pace journey. Ross's mobile began ringing, the unmistakable sound of the theme from The Great Escape emanating from the depths of his jacket pocket. He quickly fished around the pocket, retrieving it just before it switched to voicemail. The screen identified the caller as Paul Ferris.

"Paul, hello, I take it this is important? We're stuck in traffic in this bloody fog. Not even got to Speke Hill yet."

"Yes sir, I think you'll consider it very important."

"Well, don't keep me in suspense, Detective Constable. Let's have it."

"The car's turned up, sir, Proctor's Subaru, and we have two suspects in custody, and listen to this, they're a man and a woman."

Forgetting for a moment that Christine was in the back seat, Ross exclaimed, "Fucking hell, Paul. That was quick."

Remembering Christine he turned and quickly said sorry but she waved his apology away and he asked Ferris for the details.

"The car was found in Southport, sir, parked on the promenade, in plain view for the entire world to see. Two enterprising traffic cops were making a routine sweep of the seafront and thankfully they'd had the foresight and intelligence to read their alerts and bulletins and recognised the car as being sought in connection with the murders here in Liverpool. Seems they kept an eye on the vehicle under orders from their sergeant back at Southport Nick, and while they waited for the plain clothes guys to turn up, a man and woman came sauntering along the sea front carrying fish and chips and got into the car. Not wanting to risk them driving away and losing them, the two constables left their patrol car where they'd parked up to watch the Subaru, and quietly approached the vehicle and took the pair inside totally by surprise. They had the cuffs on them before you could say 'Cod 'n Chips twice please', apparently. That's the way it was related to me not more than five minutes ago by Sergeant Reeves in Southport."

"I presume we're getting them back to Liverpool post-haste?"

"We are, sir. I let D.C.I Porteous know of course and he grabbed Tony Curtis and seconded our old mate Nick Dodds who was walking past his office at the time to drive up and bring them back for interview."

"We have names yet, Paul?"

"No, sir, not yet. Anything special you want us to do with them if they arrive before you and Sergeant Drake return?"

"Just put them in separate interview rooms with a uniformed constable to watch over them. We should be back in a couple of hours, if we ever get to Speke Hill in this bloody fog. It'll give them both time to stew and they should be ripe for questioning when we get back."

"Right sir, good luck up at the school. Hope you find something that might help us nail these two, that's if they're our killers of course."

Drake and Bland had heard Ross's end of the conversation and he quickly filled them in on Ferris's input.

"Seems too easy, sir," said Drake.

"I agree," said Christine Bland. "So far your killers have shown resourcefulness, care and meticulous planning. It doesn't seem plausible that they'd slip up so blatantly as this."

"I tend to agree also," said Ross, "but the pair in Southport were found with Proctor's car, so they are involved in some way, but we won't know anything more until we question them."

"Well, anyway, we're here at last, sir," said Drake with relief as she turned off the road and through the entrance gates to Speke Hill, gravel crunching under the tyres as they motored up the sweeping drive, through the arch of trees until the main buildings hove into view. The fog had lifted slightly, enough to give them a decent view of the gothic-style buildings as they pulled into the parking area in front of the largest, central building, a large sign outside listing the various departments inside, including Administration and most importantly, Visitor Reception.

"Creepy," said Drake as she looked up at the old Victorian walls, and the crenulated roof, giving the place the look of a typical haunted mansion, she thought.

"Very Gothic," Christine Bland agreed.

"Still looks like an asylum to me," Ross commented as he led the way through the main entrance doors.

Inside, they followed an arrow on the wall that led to reception, where a cheerful young woman reacted with surprise when they identified themselves and asked to see the Chief Administrator or Headmaster, whoever was available. Five minutes later a rather severe looking woman, no more than five feet three in height, but well proportioned and in good physical shape, wearing a plain grey skirt suit, her hair, greying at the ends tied in a bun at the back, arrived and introduced herself as Vera Manvers, the School Secretary. As soon as Ross informed her of the reason for their visit she led them to her office where she asked them to sit down while she contacted Charles Hopkirk, the Chief Care Officer, and Alan Machin, the Headmaster, as she assumed they'd need to speak to both men.

A short time later, Vera answered the phone on her desk, listened for a

347

minute, then replied, "Right away, Charles," and turned to the detectives and the profiler.

"Mr. Hopkirk has got Mr. Machin with him in his office, Inspector. If you'll come with me I'll take you there now. It's a terrible business, isn't it? Such a shame about poor Mr. Proctor, and him being such a popular teacher too."

Ross thought it odd that she hadn't spoken a word to them until that point, but put it down to her rather abrasive and uncooperative demeanour, despite her efforts to appear affable. He was a good judge of people, usually and he simply couldn't find himself liking Vera Manvers.

"Thank you, Mrs. Manvers," Ross replied, "and yes, a very nasty business indeed. You knew the dead man of course, so we may need to speak to you too after we've spoken to the Headmaster and Mr. Hopkirk."

"I'll be here in my office, if you need me, Inspector, and it's Ms Manvers, actually."

She emphasised the *Ms*, as though Ross had insulted her by inferring she was married.

That's it, she's probably a closet lesbian, hates all men, Ross thought, as he moved to follow her.

"Right, my apologies, Ms Manvers."

She led them from her office, along a short corridor where she knocked and walked straight into the larger and airy office of Charles Hopkirk. The Chief Care Officer and the Headmaster were both standing waiting to greet them and after a round of introductions and hand shaking, they all sat, chairs having been provided to accommodate everyone.

"So, Inspector, we've been expecting you, of course, haven't we, Alan?"

"Indeed," the headmaster replied. "As soon as we heard about poor Mark, it was only a matter of time before you arrived, wasn't it?"

"Yes," said Ross. "How did you hear about Mr. Proctor, by the way?"

He knew the press hadn't released the name of the second victim as yet so it would be interesting to know where the school had got their information from.

"We had a call from poor Melanie Proctor, Mark's wife, Inspector. She was beside herself as you can imagine. She'd contacted us on the morning after his last day at school, telling us he hadn't come home. It was Alan, Mr. Machin, who advised her to go to the police, wasn't it, Alan?" said Hopkirk.

"Yes, I did. It was totally out of character for Mark to simply disappear, Inspector. He was devoted to Melanie and I was sure he must have been in an accident or something. He'd never have made her worry like that, not deliberately"

"Right, okay," Ross was thinking as he replied. He needed to move as swiftly as possible into the youth of Proctor and Remington but wanted the two men to feel at their ease first. Truth be told, Ross felt rather intimi-

348

dated by the old asylum, despite its current mode of use. The sooner he could get back to headquarters the better.

"Well, gentlemen," he began, "I need to ask a few questions. I'll try not to take up too much of your time, but it's important you tell me all you know about Mark Proctor. How long had he worked here as a teacher?"

"About five years," Machin replied. "He was recently appointed as head of the P.E. Department as a reward for his hard work with the pupils. He was a popular and efficient teacher."

"And did that popularity extend to both the boys and girls he taught?"

"Yes, of course. What an odd question, Inspector."

"I just want to learn as much as I can about the man, that's all, Mr. Machin. That means asking some questions you may find strange, but I assure you they're all relevant. Did you ever feel there was any animosity shown towards him by any other of the staff members?"

"Never," said Machin. "Like I said, he was a popular teacher."

Ross looked at Drake, a signal for her to enter into the interview. She didn't hesitate, sticking to their pre-arranged plan.

"Mr. Hopkirk, as you are responsible for maintaining all the records of Speke Hill as I understand it, I believe that Mark Proctor was an orphan himself and actually lived here and attended the school?"

"Well, yes, that's quite correct, Sergeant. Mark was very proud of that fact, having been a student here and ending up as head of department."

"And is it also correct that at the same time as Mark was at school and living here, you also had a pupil by the name of Matthew Remington?"

"I don't know, I'd have to check the records. The name sounds familiar though."

"Matthew Remington was the first murder victim, Mr. Hopkirk. His body was found in the churchyard of St. Matthew's church."

"Oh, God," Hopkirk exclaimed. "And you think there may be some connection between the two men?"

"Yes, I do, sir. How long would it take for you to check your old records and confirm that both men were in residence and in education here at the same time?"

"Oh, well, the old archives are still on hard copy. They are planned to be put onto computer but we've never got round to it, yet."

"How long, Mr. Hopkirk, please?"

"If I enlist the help of Vera, our secretary, I may be able to find what you need by tomorrow at the latest, Inspector. I do have other work I have to do, you know."

"This is a murder investigation, sir," Drake stepped in quickly. "I think that's slightly more important than the mundane everyday task of running the orphanage, don't you?"

"Well, yes, of course, I only meant…well, yes, I'll give it top priority."

"One more question, gentlemen," Ross added. "In the last few weeks or say, the last three months, have you employed any new members of staff; teachers, orphanage carers, even gardeners or odd job people, anyone at all?"

"No, nobody," said Hopkirk. "Oh well, not unless you count the new chaplain."

"You have a new chaplain?" Ross's interest was immediately engaged. Anything connected to the church had to be of significance.

"Yes," said Hopkirk. "You know we were once a wholly run Catholic Church endeavour?"

Ross nodded in the affirmative.

"Well in those days the orphanage and school were both run by the church, most of the teachers were priests and the school's church of worship was St. Luke's down the road at Woolton. After the local authority assumed control of Speke Hill we maintained the link with St. Luke's and the parish priest became traditionally the chaplain to the school and orphanage. Just a few months ago the previous priest passed away and was replaced by Father Byrne. He's not employed by us of course, but he's the only newcomer to the routine of Speke Hill in recent times. That's was another happy coincidence for us, because it turned out that Gerald Byrne was also a Speke Hill 'old boy' and attended here at the same time as Mark."

"He did?" said Ross, almost incredulously.

"Oh yes, and in fact they remembered each other well, and Mark showed Father Byrne around when he first came to see me, just to show off our modern facilities etc. Things have changed considerably since he was here as a boy."

By now, Andy Ross's senses were on high alert. A brief glance at his two companions and the looks on their faces told him they shared his thoughts. This was too much of a coincidence. A new priest arrives on the scene, an ex-Speke Hill resident and scholar and within weeks two of his former peers are found horrible murdered.

"Mr. Hopkirk, Mr. Machin, I appreciate the fact that these men were all here many years before your time at Speke Hill, but it may be there is some connection, a thread of circumstances that may point to the motive for these brutal murders. I hope I can count on your discretion to say nothing of this matter outside these four walls, and certainly not a word to Father Byrne until we've had a chance to talk to him."

"You can't seriously imagine Father Byrne has anything to do with these terrible murders," a shocked looking Alan Machin said in reply.

"I'm not saying he's directly involved, Mr. Machin," Ross replied, "but it does appear he may have known both victims when they were all boys together and he may be able to give us important information relating to events at Speke Hill during those days of their youth."

"Ah, of course. I see what you mean," Machin said with a hint of relief in his voice. "As a matter of fact, Father Byrne isn't due to visit us in the next couple of days anyway, is he, Charles?" he delivered the question to Hopkirk.

"That's right, Alan. We won't see him to speak to until you've had a chance to speak to Father Byrne, Inspector."

"Good, thank you. We won't keep you any longer for now, gentlemen, but we will have a quick word with Ms Manvers on the way out if you don't mind."

"Feel free Inspector," said Hopkirk. "We're happy to help in any way we can, if it will help bring Mark's killer to justice."

Machin agreed and Ross, Drake and Bland took their leave of the two men and stopped at the office of Vera Manvers on their way out.

"Hello again," the school secretary said as Ross led the way through her door, the three investigators standing in line before her like three naughty schoolchildren, Ross felt.

"Ms Manvers, Mr. Hopkirk will be enlisting your help in a search of the school archives later, but in the meantime, I just want to ask you if you personally know of anyone, either staff or pupils, who may have had any reason, no matter how trivial you may have thought, to feel a sense of grievance or ill-will against Mark Proctor?"

Vera Manvers was silent for a few seconds as she appeared to be delving into her own personal memory archives. Just when Ross began to think she'd forgotten they were waiting for her response, she seemed to return to the present and finally replied to his question.

"To be perfectly frank with you, Inspector, I knew very little about Mark Proctor, apart from his reputation within the school, which was of a very high standard. I met him socially twice, I think, at staff functions, when he was accompanied by his wife of course. I have very little day to day contact with the school itself or the orphanage. My role, as you can see, is purely an administrative one. I make it my business never to listen to rumours, or unsubstantiated facts that may sometimes be bandied around the staff room."

"So, are you saying there were rumours, Ms Manvers?"

"No, I'm not saying that at all. Just that if there were, I wouldn't have listened to them."

Ross felt the woman was being evasive, but he wanted desperately to return to headquarters and speak to the man and woman they had in custody there. Ms Vera Manvers and her rumours could wait for a little while.

"I see. Well, thank you, Ms Manvers. Just so you have advance notice, a couple of my detectives will also be arriving later and they will want to speak in turn to all the teaching and care staff, and any ancillary workers who may be present today. If they have to, they'll return tomorrow to complete the interviews."

"Very well, I'll make sure they have a suitable room allocated where they can speak to the staff, Inspector. I'm sure everyone will want to help find Mr. Proctor's killer."

* * *

"Bloody irritating woman, that Ms Manvers," he said to his two companions as Drake drove them back towards headquarters in bright sunshine, the fog having lifted during their time at Speke Hill.

"My thoughts, exactly," Drake concurred, "almost as if she knew something, but wasn't prepared to divulge it for some reason."

"I though they were all rather elusive and hardly totally forthcoming," Bland added. "I felt they weren't exactly lying, but were perhaps being a little economical with the information they were prepared to give us."

"I agree," said Ross. "Maybe they're being defensive of the establishment and its reputation but that doesn't help when we have a couple of killers running around out there. And there's this Father Byrne. We need to talk to him, Izzie. If we have time, I want to visit him later today."

"I'm with you, sir, whatever you decide."

"I just have a feeling we're on the cusp of discovering something, but whatever it is, I can almost feel a wall being thrown up to keep us out. Does that make sense to you, Doctor Bland?"

"Actually, it does, Inspector. I know my job is simply to provide you with a profile but I must admit my instincts all tell me the same as yours. Someone knows something, but they just aren't telling."

"Well, we're here now. Let's go see what Southport have dug up for us, and before we speak to them, I want you to arrange for Ferris and Gable to go out to Speke Hill, Izzie. Sam's good with women and Ferris has a certain instinct, as well as an understanding of the way such places operate I think."

"Right, sir," said Drake as she parked the Mondeo and switched the engine off.

As he marched ahead into the building, Ross couldn't wait to begin interviewing the two suspects apprehended in possession of Proctor's car.

CHAPTER 20

"BILLY RUFFIAN"

Pausing only long enough to grab a quick coffee and an update from D.C. Ferris, Ross and Drake prepared to interview the couple found in possession of Mark Proctor's silver Subaru. Ferris had made sure the couple had been kept apart in separate interview rooms as instructed, and informed Ross of the names they'd provided, Archie Pitt, and Carrie Evans, aged twenty-six and twenty-two respectively. Neither one had requested or been offered legal representation. After all, they hadn't been charged with anything as yet, and had been told that for the moment they were 'assisting with inquiries'. Ross felt instinctively that this young couple were not the killers, but the fact they'd been in possession of Proctor's car put them, quite possibly, at the scene of the victim's abduction, and maybe even made them witnesses to what had taken place on the night of the teacher's disappearance.

Ross and Drake spent a few minutes peering at the pair through the one way mirrors that gave them views into both interview rooms from the viewing area that served to separate the rooms. Christine Bland and D.C.I. Porteous were with them and would observe the interviews from there. Ross decided to take the young man, with Ferris as back-up, Drake would interview the woman, with Nick Dodds, who'd helped collect the couple from Southport as her number two, the other team members being out and about carrying out their own allocated inquiries. Dodds had worked with the team before and was well respected by Ross and the others, and was only too pleased to help out.

"Archie Pitt, that your real name?" Ross asked the scruffy twenty-something young man sitting opposite him.

"Aye, course it is. Why should you think otherwise?"

"Archie, that's a Scottish name."

"So, me Dad liked the name. Told me he named me after a character in that old war film, *The Great Escape*."

"Ah, right, *Archibald 'Archie' Ives*, known as *The Mole*, I believe," said Ross. I rather like that film too. The name suits you. You look like a little mole to me. Now, Archie, are you going to tell me how you came to be caught in possession of a car that belonged to a man who was murdered in a particularly nasty fashion? Just what part did you and your girlfriend have to play in all this?"

Archie Pitt's face fell at the mention of the word 'murder'.

"Whoa, hold your horses there, Mr. Policeman. I ain't had nothin' to do with no murder, like, you know?"

"That's just it, Archie, I don't know. You tell me. I want to know exactly how you came to be driving that Subaru, where and when you found it and why you took it."

"Okay, okay, as long as you know we didn't do no murder, you know?"

"So talk to me."

* * *

"I've only known him a couple of weeks," Carrie Evans bleated in a rather irritating high-pitched voice. "We met up one night in town in a club and sort of got along, like, you know?"

"So tell me about the car, Carrie," said Drake.

"Yeah, right. Well, we was in the Billy Ruffian that night, early doors you know? Archie said it was a good place to score."

"What was it you were after, Carrie, cocaine, heroin?"

"God no, nothing like that. I'm not into the hard stuff, just a bit of grass, you know?"

"Okay, calm down, Carrie and tell me the whole story."

Behind the mirror, Bland looked questioningly at D.C.I. Porteous, and asked, "Billy Ruffian?"

"A pub near the old Clarence Graving Dock, used to be popular with seamen. Its real name is *The Belerophon*, named after one of Nelson's warships at the Battle of Trafalgar. The pub sign shows the old ship, all guns blazing, quite impressive."

"I see, thanks for the history lesson," Bland replied, smiling as they turned back to the interviews in progress.

"Archie saw the guy he was looking for, and went to talk to him, while I sat at the table next to the window."

"Who was this man, Carrie? Do you have a name for me?"

"Shit, I don't know. I'd only been in there once, the week before with Archie. I don't know the name of his supplier if that's what you want?"

"I'm not interested in a bit of cannabis, Carrie. I just want someone who can confirm your story, someone who can make me believe you're not involved in two murders."

"Murders? I'm not into anything like that, honest, and I'm telling the truth. I don't know who the man was. You've got to believe me."

"What did he look like, then? Describe him to me."

"I only saw him from the back, while Archie talked to him at the bar. He was just some scally, thin, with long black hair and he was wearing an old donkey jacket, black with leather across the shoulders, you know what I mean?"

"Yes, I know what a donkey jacket looks like, Carrie. Anything else, jeans, trousers?"

"Jeans, I think."

* * *

"What's his name, Archie?" Ross asked as Archie Pitt told a similar story in the next room.

"Er, I don't know."

"Yes, you do. You don't expect me to believe you regularly buy cannabis from a man and don't even know his first name."

"It's Mac, and honest, Inspector, that's the only name I've ever known him by. Everyone just knows him as Mac."

That, at least, was believable.

"So you bought your drugs, then what?"

"I bought us a drink, a pint for me and a gin and tonic for Carrie, then went and sat back down with her."

"Where were you sitting?

"Next to the window that looked out on to the car park. That's when I saw the car."

Now he had Ross's attention. By careful questioning, Ross had brought Archie round to what he really wanted to know. Now, perhaps Archie would reveal something of real relevance to the case.

"Go on, Archie. I'm listening."

* * *

"Archie saw this car pull up," Carrie Evans said. "It was a silver one. He said the guy who got out of it was a pillock because he didn't lock it. He could tell he said, 'cause the idiot just got out and walked away without pointing the keys at it, you know, like, to lock it. Archie said we'd leave it a

355

few minutes and if the guy didn't come back, we could maybe take it and go for a ride."

* * *

"This man, Archie. Did he come into the pub?"

"No, that was the weird thing, like. He just got out of the car and walked away. Then, I saw him standing by the side of the main road, like he was waiting for someone. Another car pulled up and he looked around as if he was looking to see if he was being watched, then jumped into the car and it sort of sped off. I knew he'd left the Subaru unlocked so me and Carrie finished our drinks, and walked out, casual, like, and I checked no one was watching and told her to get in. I, er, well, sort of hot wired it and we were away before you knew it."

"Done it before, have you, Archie, car theft?"

"Yeah, alright, once or twice, but you said…"

"I know, just tell me the truth, Archie."

"That's about it, really. I had a few quid in me pocket, you know, so I said to Carrie it'd be nice to go to the seaside for a day or two. Less chance of the car being spotted too, I thought, so I drove to Southport and that's where we stayed until those two coppers picked us up."

"Did you get a good look at the man who left the car in the pub car park?"

"Well, no, I didn't. When he got out of the car, he had his back to us, and didn't even turn round to look at the pub. He was tallish, maybe five foot nine or ten, had a dark blue hoody on with the hood up and it was pulled tight if you ask me so it covered a lot of his head and face. He had gloves on too, black ones if it helps."

"Could you tell if he was black or white?"

"No, not that I was taking notice. I was more interested in the car."

* * *

"What about the car that picked him up, Carrie?" Drake asked. "Do you know what kind of car it was?"

"It was red, I think," Carrie replied. "I don't know nothin' about cars."

"What about the driver. Could you see if it was a man or a woman?"

"Too far away to tell," said the girl. "Soon as he got in they were away like the wind. We went out, got in the car and Archie did something to it and it started and he drove us to Southport for a little holiday, he said."

* * *

"Come on, Archie, you've nicked cars before so you must know what type of car picked him up." Ross was hoping for a real clue, depending on Archie Pitt's answer."

"Look, Inspector, I'd smoked a couple of joints that afternoon, and I was kinda focussed on the Subaru, so I wasn't paying much attention to the friggin' car that picked the jerk up."

"Think, Archie, come on, for God's sake man, you must have seen it for at least a few seconds."

Archie Pitt closed his eyes, trying to recall those few seconds when the driver of the Subaru climbed into the other car. He shook his head and replied,

"I'm real sorry, honest, but I just don't know. It was red, I think, that bright pillar box red, you know, the bloody default colour the dealers offer to everyone when they can't supply the colour of choice to customers. Fuck me, Inspector, every bloody car maker on the planet makes cars that colour. But listen, I think I remember it was a hatchback, not too big, maybe a Ford or Vauxhall, or then again it could have been a Honda or even a Citroen. I just don't know. It's not like I thought I'd ever have to bloody well remember the damn car is it?"

Archie threw his hands up in a gesture of despair and somehow, Ross felt he'd got all he was going to get from the young cannabis smoking car thief.

* * *

Izzie Drake passed a box of tissues across to Carrie Evans, as the young woman sat quietly sobbing. Carrie had finally broken down when Drake told her the potential trouble she could be in, and was now in fear of having to tell her parents about the mess she'd got herself into. Unlike Archie Pitt, who appeared to live on his wits and rented a poky little flat in one of the city's few remaining high rise blocks, Carrie lived in Huyton in a modern three bedroom house with her stockbroker father, stay-at-home mum, and younger brother, all of whom would be in shock at the trouble the young rebel of the family had got herself into.

"You're going to have to face up to it, Carrie. You'll probably end up in court over this little mess so your parents are bound to find out. Best to tell them now and get it over with. You might find they'll forgive you and stand by you, but my advice would be to dump your asshole loser of a boyfriend before you tell them," Izzie Drake advised.

"They'll go ballistic when they know about the drugs," the girl cried into a tissue.

"Can't help you there, Carrie," Drake continued, but maybe you'll see this as a lesson and stay away from cannabis or any drugs in future. I don't care what scallys like Archie Pitt and his kind tell you, there's no such thing as a safe drug, Carrie. Even long term use of cannabis can harm your brain, believe me."

* * *

"What's going to happen to me now, then?" Archie Pitt asked Andy Ross.

"You're going into a nice warm cell for a little while until we check out your story, Archie. If you're lucky, you'll be charged with taking away a vehicle without consent, and with being in possession of a controlled substance. Bit stupid of you to be caught with that cannabis in your pocket wasn't it old son?"

"Yeah, but I thought you said you'd turn a blind eye if I helped you?"

"And that's what I'm doing, Archie. If I wanted to really drop you in it, I'd send a team down to the Beleraphon and raid the place. I bet we'll find more than just your mate Mac dealing in that place, and they'd all be really interested to know who tipped us off about them doing business there, don't you? So I'm turning a blind eye on this one occasion, but don't be surprised if a couple of plain clothes coppers drop in there one night soon and find a couple of dealers at work, know what I mean, Archie?"

Archie Pitt nodded slowly.

"You're telling me stay away from the place, right?"

"Sounds like a good idea to me, Archie. Oh, and one other thing."

"What?"

"Our boys are going over the Subaru even now, as we speak and if they find any more drugs in there, enough to suggest to me you're dealing as well as using…"

"They won't, I'm not, I told you, I just smoke a bit of dope now and then."

"Now and then? You've admitted you were half stoned when you stole the car, Archie. How responsible was that, eh? You could have knocked a child down, caused a serious accident, anything. Driving under the influence of drugs is as bad as drunk driving as far as I'm concerned so you'd better hope our paths don't cross again in the near future. Take him away, Paul, lock him up and give our friend here a chance to think of the error of his ways until we've checked the car out."

"Right sir," said Paul Ferris as he placed a hand on Archie's shoulder and the young man rose to his feet. "Come on sunshine, let's get you settled. You never know, we might even treat you to nice cup of tea."

"Yeah, can't wait. I'm bloody ecstatic," Pitt quipped, trying to sound tough.

"Oh, get him out of here, Paul," said Ross as the pair exited the room, followed a few seconds later by Ross who instead of taking the same route, stopped and entered the viewing room where Porteous and Bland were watching Izzie Drake bringing her interview with Carrie Evans to a close.

358

"Well, that was almost a total waste of time," Ross blasted the words out, frustration in his voice. "They're not our killers, not that I thought they would be. Whoever killed Remington and Proctor had more brains in their little fingers than our friend Archie bloody Pitt. He doesn't have the brains or the sophistication to have planned something like this. No, he's just a thieving little scally who saw a chance of a free ride to the seaside with his girlfriend and grabbed it with both hands. We'll show Proctor's photo around in *The Belerophon* but it's likely the murderer just picked it as a random location to dump the car."

"It certainly wasn't as productive as we'd hoped, Andy," Porteous agreed.

"No sir, it bloody well wasn't."

"But we know the accomplice drives a red hatchback, at least," Christine Bland added, trying to sound positive."

"Yes, but have you any idea how many red hatchbacks there are on the roads of Liverpool and the surrounding area? Probably around two thousand at a guess," said Ross, "and bloody Archie in there couldn't even tell his Fords from his Nissans, he was so toked up at the time. And, the red car could have been nicked like the Subaru, so we're really no further forward, unless there's any trace evidence in the car."

"Miles Booker is working on it himself," Porteous informed him. "If there's anything to find, he'll find it."

Ross turned to look through the one way mirror as Izzie was closing her interview with Carrie Evans.

"Anything from the girl?"

"Useless," said Porteous. "She saw even less than Pitt. She's more worried about what her parents are going to say when they find out about her being picked up by the police."

"I wonder why neither of them asked for a solicitor," said Bland

"They weren't under caution yet and were simply helping with enquiries," said Ross. "Once we finish the forensic examination of the car, we'll have them in again, caution them and offer them legal representation. Then we'll take formal statements from them and they'll be charged and released on police bail. When we catch our killers, and we *are* going to catch these murderous bastards, I'll want them both to give witness statements, no matter how vague they may seem, so I want them in the system where we can find them at the right time."

"What now, then, Andy?" Porteous asked.

"First, I want to talk to this Father Byrne, the ex-Speke Hill pupil who recently became Parish Priest at St. Luke's, Woolton, and then when I get the reports from the interviews with the staff at Speke Hill, we're going to have to go back there and dig deeper. Whatever triggered this killing spree, I'm certain it has its roots in something that happened there in the past."

"I agree," Christine concurred. "From a profiling point of view, I have to say that there is usually a trigger to these types of killings, something that activates a long dead, or dormant memory. The F.B.I. profilers call it a 'stresser,' but I prefer trigger. I'd like to visit Father Byrne with you if you don't mind. My own gut feeling is that the arrival of this man, another Speke Hill old boy, may have provided the trigger for these killers to start their murders. It's almost too coincidental that he arrived back in the area just before the killing began."

"You're welcome to join me," said Ross, "but there's another option you haven't considered here."

"Which is?"

"Well, as you just said, he arrived here just before the killings started, so we also have to take into consideration that this Father Byrne could be one of our murderers."

"Oh, shit," she replied, quickly throwing a hand over her mouth, just as the door opened to admit Izzie Drake, young Carrie Fisher being escorted to the cells by Nick Dodds.

"Have I missed something?" Drake asked, seeing the shocked look on Christine's face.

"Only that your boss just hypothesized that one of the killers could be a bloody Roman Catholic Priest," Porteous said, with an almost comical grin on his face.

"It couldn't be, surely," said Bland.

"Why not?" said Ross. "Stranger things have happened. There've been numerous murderous doctors over the years, so why not a priest?"

"Even so," Bland remonstrated with him. "It's a big stretch to think a Catholic Priest could have done this."

"Not if he's lost his marbles," Izzie pointed out. "And don't forget, the Inquisition was wholly run and executed by the Catholic Church. They killed thousands in the name of God in the Middle Ages."

"True," Christine agreed. "I suppose in my job I shouldn't exclude any possibilities, though I still think it's unlikely."

"We'll get a better idea when we speak to him," Ross went on. "Let's go home, get some rest and turn off for a few hours. We'll hold the morning briefing as usual tomorrow, catch up with the rest of the team and then head for St. Luke's and see what we can make of Father Gerald Byrne."

Ross spent five minutes tidying his desk, rose from behind his desk and was about to head off for home when the telephone on his desk rang. Debating whether to ignore it and walk away, he thought better of it and reached across to answer the offending, jangling instrument.

"Andy Ross, you old reprobate, how are you?" came the hale and hearty voice of his old friend and former partner, now Detective Inspector Oscar Agostini.

The two men had worked together some years before as sergeants, and had become firm friends, though Agostini's promotion had taken him a little out of town and he now worked out of the police station at Church road in Sefton, serving the town of Formby. Six feet tall, his dark brown wavy hair a giveaway to his Italian ancestry, Agostini had always been something of a magnet for members of the opposite sex and Ross had been surprised but delighted when his friend announced his intention to marry, and had been best man at Oscar's marriage to Fern, some ten years previously.

"Oscar! I'm harassed, hungry and in a hurry to go home. Apart from that, I'm fine. How's yourself, and the beautiful Fern?"

"Ah, nothing's changed then eh? I'm okay my friend, Fern too, and she sends her love, but listen, we're not exactly a million miles away and I still keep up with the news there in big-city-land. I think we may have a case here that somehow connects to those churchyard murders of yours we keep hearing about."

"Go on, Oscar, I'm all ears."

"Right. A few days ago, we attended a suicide by drowning off Formby Dunes, a young girl, only seventeen, called Lisa Kelly."

"Yes, I saw the news of that one, tragic by the sounds of it."

"Yes it was, poor kid was obviously seriously depressed. But here's the thing, Andy. She had one of those new-fangled mobile phones with a mini-recording device built in to it. Her Mum said it was her pride and joy, that phone. She'd saved up for it from her wages from the day she started working at Woolworths on South Road in Waterloo. Anyway, it turns out Lisa left a kind of suicide note cum confession on her phone, Andy, and it mentions one of your victims."

Agostini had Ross's full attention by this point.

"I'm intrigued Oscar, please go on, mate."

"Sure, so, it seems young Lisa was a confirmed member of the Catholic faith, and as a result of events in the last year, she was so wracked with guilt that the poor kid ended up topping herself. On the recording she mentioned being raped, and then finding she was pregnant a short time later. Her mother was supportive of her, don't get me wrong, but there was so much religious feeling in that house, Andy, that when she decided to have a termination, her mother was supportive but horrified at the 'sin' involved in going so strongly against the church's teachings. Lisa had gone ahead with the abortion anyway, but since then, the girl had grown progressively more and more depressed, and found she couldn't live with what she'd done in 'killing her baby' as she put it. For God's sake, Andy, I'm a Catholic, but I'd like to think I wouldn't pour all that religious fervour and guilt onto a child of mine if she was in that situation. Sorry, I'm digressing. Anyway, on the tape she says she wished she'd reported that man Remington when he'd raped her. Seems her Mum talked her out of going to the police at the time because of the 'shame' she thought it would bring on the family, for fuck's sake."

"My God, Oscar. What kind of Mother would do that? Didn't she want to see her kid's rapist locked up and put away?"

"I know, Andy. It fucking beggars belief doesn't it? Anyway, she'd read about the murder in the papers and once you'd released his name she knew it was the man who'd ruined her life, and in her mind, he'd cheated justice. There was no way she could ever absolve herself from what he'd done to her, as she put it."

"Hang on Oscar. How did she know her rapist was Matthew Remington? Wasn't he masked or anything when he raped her?"

"Oh, it's worse than that, my friend. Seems he'd known the family for years and she thought she'd be okay when she bumped into him in town after work one evening, and he offered to walk her to the bus station."

"Bloody Hell, Oscar. Didn't her mother warn her to stay away from him?"

Agostini seemed to hesitate and take a deep breath at the other end of the phone.

"You won't believe this, Andy, but her mother, good Catholic that she is, told her that Remington had done wrong in the past, but had paid his debt to society, and because he'd apparently repented his sins, God would have forgiven him and he was entitled to begin a new life, without his past sins being held against him."

"Jesus, Mary and Joseph!" Ross exclaimed, disbelief clear in his voice. "How bloody naïve can that woman be? Look, Oscar, I know you're Catholic, my friend, but surely not everyone is as gullible as this woman appears to have been."

"She damn well knows it now Andy. In fact she's now on the world's biggest guilt trip. Seems she was always telling Lisa her skirts were too short, her make-up too thick, all that kind of stuff, but then allowed her to think a man like that was reformed because she'd met him at church one day soon after his release and he'd told her that whole crock of shit about repentance."

"Remington went to church?"

"For a short time, apparently. Long enough to pick out his next target if you ask me."

A thought occurred to Andy Ross, another possible connection?

"Oscar, did the mother tell you what church she attends?"

"Yes, The Church of St. John the Baptist. It's only about half a mile from her home, but that's all Remington needed to push young Lisa into an alleyway and do the business with her, leaving her bleeding, crying and bloody pregnant."

"I just don't understand why the bloody mother didn't report it. I mean, her own daughter had been raped, for fuck's sake, Oscar, and she rationalised it by saying it would bring shame on the family? That's not good religion, mate, that's fucking crazy, religious fanaticism maybe, but not religious realism."

"I know, mate, and she knows it now it's cost her a daughter. Anyway, I hope the intel helps, old buddy."

"It might, Oscar, thanks a lot. It gives me another avenue to explore for sure. And now, I'm going home to my gorgeous wife, where I expect a hot meal, a couple of hours vegetating in front of the telly, then bed, and who knows what might happen?"

"Dirty bugger," Agostini laughed. "And give the beautiful Maria a kiss from me while you're at it."

"You should be so lucky, Agostini." Now it was Ross who laughed and the two men said their goodbyes and for the second time in the last half hour, Andy Ross rose from his desk, this time managing to make it out of his office and the building and was soon on his way home to Maria.

CHAPTER 21

GOODNIGHT SWEETHEART

"You haven't heard a word I've said, Andy Ross." Maria. said, as they sat across from each other at the dining table, supposedly enjoying the beef bourguignon she'd prepared for the two of them.

"Eh, what, oh, sorry darling. What were you saying?"

"Only that Alice and Ray have invited us over for dinner next Saturday night. Alice was on the phone today, telling me Ray's a lot better since his heart bypass."

"That's good to hear. I'm sorry if I'm a little pre-occupied this evening."

"A little? Andy, I've known you long enough to know when a case is really getting to you, and this one is, isn't it?"

"Big time, Maria. I don't know why, but I feel as if I'm on the cusp of discovering something vital, but I just can't put my finger on it. After talking to Oscar earlier, I'm sure something he said triggered something in my brain, but whatever it was refused to surface properly. It was nothing concrete, just a hint of something that was there, and then it was gone, if you know what I mean."

"I think I do. Like when something's on the tip of your tongue and then simply disappears, but in this case, it wasn't a word, but a thought."

"Yes, that's it exactly. Not only that, but I can't understand the mentality of that girl's mother."

He'd talked to Maria as she'd prepared dinner and brought her up to date on the case. His wife had tried, unsuccessfully to get him to talk about something else, but it was evident to Maria that her husband was totally immersed in his need to apprehend the killers of the two men.

"You've been in the job long enough by now to know you can't argue with the religious fervour that drives some people, Andy. The mother was probably brought up in a family where everything revolved around the church and God. Old-fashioned hellfire and damnation stuff, every small transgression treated like a major sin, you know the type."

"Yes, mores the pity," he agreed. "Anyway, dinner's great, thanks, and you can phone Alice in the morning and tell her we'll be glad to go for dinner."

After dinner, Andy and Maria curled up together on the sofa, and watched Andy's favourite movie, *Independence Day*, Maria having bought him the DVD for his birthday. Maria always enjoyed watching it with her husband who she thought would have made a good stand-in for the actor playing the President of the USA, whose name she could never remember.

Before they knew it, eleven o'clock had arrived and Andy locked up the house while Maria went up stairs to get ready for bed. Andy's mind had at last relaxed and when he walked in to the bedroom to find Maria sitting on the bed, wearing a very short, very sheer pink nightie, her legs crossed suggestively, his eyes lit up. With a gleam in her eye, a smile on her face and affecting her best 'vamp' voice, his wife said, huskily, "Well, hello there, big boy. Wanna play?"

This time, he didn't fall asleep!

* * *

Peter Foster lay on his back, smoking a cigarette as a naked Izzie Drake lay beside him, twirling the hairs on his chest between her fingers.

"That was amazing," Izzie gasped as she attempted to bring her breathing back to normal after a highly passionate session of love-making.

"You were great," Peter said, turning to look at her with a satisfied smile on his face.

"I wish we could do this every night, Peter," Izzie said, dreamily.

"Well, there's one way we could do it every night, mornings too if you wanted to," he replied.

Izzie sat up straight and looked him in the eye.

"Peter Foster, you bad, bad boy. Are you asking me, a police sergeant of all people, to move in with you and live in sin?"

"No." was all he said and fell silent.

"What then? What exactly do you mean?"

Peter stubbed out his cigarette in the large glass ashtray on top of the bedside cabinet and quietly opened the top drawer of his bedside cabinet, removing a small, blue velvet box. He slowly turned towards Izzie, whose eyes began to glisten with tears of emotion as he opened the box to reveal a sparkling diamond solitaire ring."

"Marry me, Izzie, please."

"Oh God, Peter. Are you serious?"

"Deadly, if you'll excuse the word, considering my job," he replied, slipping the ring slowly onto the third finger of her left hand. It was a perfect fit.

"How did you know my size?"

"I guessed."

"Wow."

"Well?"

"Eh?"

"What's your answer you daft girl?"

Izzie fell silent, looked Peter Foster in the eyes, and then, after keeping him waiting for an agonising fifteen seconds, she threw her hands round his neck, kissed him passionately on the lips, whispered the one word, "Yes," and lay back, pulling Peter on top of her as they took up from where they'd left off half an hour ago.

CHAPTER 22

A QUESTION OF FAITH

A few minutes after Andy Ross had climbed out of bed, feeling great after his night of unbridled passion with Maria, the telephone rang. Surprised to hear the voice of D.C.I. Porteous so early in the morning, Andy neverthe-less came instantly alert as his boss asked him to arrive a quarter of an hour early and meet him in his office before commencing the morning briefing with the team. All would be explained when he got there, Porteous informed him.

Intrigued, Ross quickly showered and dressed and popped a couple of slices of bread in the toaster as he made coffee for himself and Maria, who arrived in the kitchen as the kettle boiled.

"Who was that on the phone?" she asked, smiling at Ross, her eyes a little bleary from lack of sleep.

"The boss. He wants to see me before the briefing."

"Did he say why?"

"Nope, all very mysterious if you ask me. I tried not to wake you, but failed by the look of it. You look tired, darling."

"Hardly surprising is it? You wore me out last night, Mr. Super Stud," she laughed and Ross grinned back at her.

"Your fault," he laughed in return, as the toast popped up. "You shouldn't have worn that incredibly sexy little number should you? But I'm bloody glad you did."

Maria giggled, grabbing the two rounds of toast, buttering them and placing them on a plate on the table for him, placing two more slices in the toaster for herself.

"Ha, it didn't stay on very long once you got going, did it, you sex maniac?"

"Yes, well, if I'm not totally knackered tonight, how do you fancy a rematch?"

"Now, that sounds like an offer a girl can't possibly turn down," she said as Ross hurriedly swallowed the last piece of toast and grabbed his jacket from the back of the chair where he'd left it the previous night. A quick kiss, and Ross was out the door, climbing into his car and on his way to work.

* * *

"You're not serious, sir, surely?" Ross asked as he sat across from Harry Porteous in the D.C.I's office, the door closed to prevent anyone hearing their conversation.

"But I am, Andy," Porteous insisted. "I'm taking early retirement and I'll be leaving at the end of the month. That's why I'd really like to finish on a high and get this bloody churchyard case closed with a couple of arrests before I go."

"May I ask why you're retiring, sir. I mean, you're still relatively young?"

"Exactly, Andy, and that's one compelling reason to go now, while I'm young enough to enjoy life with Sarah. And no, before you ask, she hasn't pressured me into it. I've been a copper for over thirty years, Andy, and I'll get a full pension and we can enjoy some quality years together, maybe do a round the world cruise or two, who knows"

"I take it Jake and Laura are happy for you too?"

Porteous's two children were both grown up and married, Jake, the eldest, now a successful architect, and Laura was happily married to an airline pilot, had two children of her own, and lived down south, not far from Heathrow airport, where Geoff, her husband was based.

"They're delighted for us both, Andy. Geoff thought it was about time I treated his Mum to some good times, and Laura says it might mean we'll see more of the grandkids, and can go and visit her down in Hounslow more often, stay a while from time to time and so on."

"Well," Ross sighed, "I guess we'd better pull out all the stops and catch these murderous bastards for you, sir, hadn't we?"

"Yes, please," Porteous smiled. "There's one other thing, Andy, a small matter of my replacement."

Ross's stomach lurched, knowing Porteous might want him to accept a promotion and take over his job when he departed.

"Sir, I hope you don't want me to take over from you. I know I've passed the exams and everything, but you know as well as I do that I'm not cut out to direct investigations from behind a desk. I'm a field investigator, always have been and always will be."

"I thought you'd say that, and I admit I tend to agree with you. You'd be like a fish out of water stuck in this office most of the day, every day, but I want you to know the promotion and the job's yours if you want it. The Chief Super has agreed to it if you decide that way but he also knows how you'd feel and to be honest you'd be a loss to the team if we took you out of the field of everyday investigative work. Thing is, if you do turn the promotion down, it might be a long time, if ever, before you get another chance at senior rank."

"I don't mind, sir. Maria already earns more than me as a G.P. and we're not exactly hard-up. She knows I'd never want to be a desk jockey as well, so she won't mind me turning the job down."

"Well, that's that, then. You'd better get off and get on with the briefing. We've got two killers to catch. My replacement will be announced in due course, but I'll make sure you're informed of the appointment before anyone else knows. I'm sure once the jungle drums start spreading the news of my imminent departure the chief will receive more than one or two calls with suitable, and maybe unsuitable candidates putting themselves forward for my job. You can inform the team but please ask them not to broadcast it too far and wide just yet."

A handshake later and Ross exited the room, arriving in the squad's conference room just as the last of his team, in this case, D.C. Curtis was entering the room, the young detective holding the door open for Ross.

"Morning sir."

"Morning Tony."

Within five minutes, Ross had informed the team about Porteous's impending retirement, ending with the news that the Chief Superintendent wanted the D.C.I.'s replacement in place at least a week before his departure to give the new man a settling in period, working together with Porteous, so they should expect an announcement at any time on the name of their new boss.

Ross allowed a further ten minutes for the rest of the team to update him with mostly negative progress reports, before he informed them of the phone call from D.I Agostini the previous afternoon.

"Bloody hell, sir," Izzie Drake said. "That throws a new light on everything, surely."

"It must do," Paul Ferris agreed. "It could mean the case has nothing to do with the past, or with Speke Hill, but could be rooted right here in the present."

"Possibly," said Ross, "but this Kelly girl was raped by Remington, not by Proctor. We have no evidence as yet to give us a concrete link between the two men, yet something has to put them in the frame together for something, sometime. We have to look at another possibility too. If Remington raped Lisa Kelly, it's highly likely he raped or assaulted others too. We all know a lot of women refuse to report rape or other sexual assaults for a variety of reasons, one of which we've seen in the Kelly case, with all too tragic results. I also want us to look into rapes and assaults that have been reported but remain unsolved for, say, the last three years, to begin with, and while we're at it, let's look a lot deeper into Mark Proctor's life. Izzie and I are going to talk with Father Byrne this morning. Christine, please join us. I'd like your thoughts on the good Father. The rest of you, get to it, people. Tony, take Sam and pay a visit to *The Belerophon*. Knock the landlord up out of bed if you have to. Show him the photo of Proctor, maybe also the one of Remington. Let's see if either man used the pub regularly or at least any time recently, assuming the landlord takes notice of who's drinking in his pub."

"But isn't it more likely the killers chose the pub sir, rather than it being a hang out for the victims?" Curtis asked.

"Yes, it is, Tony," Ross replied, "but we're clutching at straws a little. It may be our killers first encountered one or both of the dead men in *The Belerophon* and identified them as targets from there. We have to explore all possibilities."

"Understood, sir."

"Good. As interviews with the staff at Speke Hill produced nothing we have to assume if anything linked the dead men it was either something that happened there a long time ago, which is where Father Gerald Byrne could be helpful, or as we now suspect, something much more current in time, so we need to look very deeply into every and I mean *every*, aspect of these men's lives."

"Any good talking to the mother of the dead girl, sir?" Derek McLennan asked.

"Maybe, Derek. Go and see her. I wouldn't trust myself near that woman right now. I hate to say it but she's right, her daughter would probably be alive today if she'd handled things differently. Show her Proctor's photo as well. See if you get a reaction."

"Right sir," said McLennan, pleased to have his suggestion acted upon.

"While you're at it, see if there's anyone at the Church of St. John the Baptist near her home. Remington went there a few times apparently. The priest there might remember him, and Derek?"

"I know sir, show him the photo of Mark Proctor, too."

"Good man, you're learning." Ross smiled at the young detective.

* * *

"Are you alright sir?" Izzie asked Ross as they drove across town en-route to St. Luke's to speak to Gerald Byrne. "You're very quiet. Is it D.C.I. Porteous?"

"No, Izzie, nothing like that. I've had something eating away at the back of my mind since I talked with D.I. Agostini yesterday. Something, a buried thought almost broke through as he said something, I don't know what, but it came and went before my conscious mind could grasp it."

"I might be able to help with that," said Christine Bland from her seat in the back of the car."

"Really?" Ross asked. "How?"

"It's a technique for helping witnesses remember long buried thoughts. The Americans have used it with some success. I studied the method while I was at Quantico. Maybe we can try when we get back to your office later. We need peace and quiet and no distractions, hardly the thing we can do in a moving car."

"I'll think about it, thanks," said Ross as Drake slowed the car down as she pulled up outside St. Luke's Church.

* * *

The two detectives, plus Christie Bland, had been greeted like old friends by the redoubtable Mrs. Redding and were shown into the sitting room and invited to sit. Ross and Drake took up positions on one of the two large, comfortable sofas in the room, the profiler taking up one of the two velour upholstered armchairs. Mrs. Redding scurried away to summon Father Byrne, who, she informed the inspector, was taking a breath of fresh air in the garden. Before the priest arrived, Ross spoke quietly to Izzie Drake.

"Usual strategy, Izzie, OK?"

"OK sir."

In reply to Bland's quizzical look, Ross explained.

"We each take a different tack. I go one way, and Izzie will step in with questions that deviate from the main point. It tends to throw a suspect off and often leads to them slipping up."

"So Father Byrne is a suspect?" Bland asked.

"Only until we can definitely eliminate him, Christine. Your opinions on him may help us in that respect, which is why I wanted you along today. He's closely connected with the victims, albeit historically, and the orphanage, and he arrived on the scene just a short time before the murders began."

Byrne joined them a couple of minutes later and, introductions over, took a seat in the remaining armchair.

Ross was impressed by the physical appearance and overall demeanour of the priest, who certainly looked as if he could handle himself in a barroom brawl if needs be. The man exuded an overall sense of athleticism,

371

perfect for hauling a body up and suspend it from an angel memorial, the inspector thought.

"So, how can I help you, Detective Inspector?" Byrne addressed his question directly to Ross, who appreciated the fact that Byrne used his correct title. So many people simply called him 'inspector' and he hadn't the heart to correct them most of the time.

"I'm sure you're aware of the recent murders that have taken place in two local churchyards?"

"Only too aware, Detective Inspector. Horrific, truly horrific."

"The thing is, I've been made aware by the staff at Speke Hill that you were actually acquainted with both victims."

"Ah, I see. Yes, Inspector, I knew Mark Proctor, quite well at one time, but the first victim…er?"

"Matthew Remington, Father."

"Yes, right, thank you. You must understand, Detective Inspector Ross, that at the time I was at Speke Hill as a boy there were probably around a thousand children resident and being educated there. I'm perhaps exaggerating slightly, but it was certainly well over five hundred, I'm sure. I'm not sure how well you've been informed on the set-up back then, but the boys were of course segregated from the girls in respect of their living accommodation, and we were further split up into various dormitories usually up to thirty boys per dorm. We would all have known the boys in our own dormitory rather well as we lived with them on a day to day basis, but, unless our paths crossed during lessons at school, or if we played together in one of the various school sports teams, we could go through our entire time at Speke Hill without making the acquaintance of some of the boys or girls who lived separately from our own dorm, which in many ways was like our own private world within the orphanage."

"So you're saying you didn't know Matthew Remington at all, Father?"

"To be honest, Inspector, what I'm saying is I don't remember a boy of that name. Our paths may have crossed but I know for sure he wasn't in my dorm and I don't remember him from any sports teams. I was quite good at various sports in those days, played football for the school, rugby too."

"Would a photo help, Father?" Izzie Drake asked. "We had a couple of detectives over there to talk to the staff about Mark Proctor and Miss Manvers loaned these to us," she said, opening a large brown envelope and withdrawing a small handful of black and white photographs, each one a different year photograph of boys and girls, all posed in what Ross now assumed to be individual dormitory groups.

"Ah, yes, the redoubtable Miss Manvers," Byrne replied, smiling knowingly at the sergeant. "I hope she was helpful, Sergeant. I shouldn't say this, but that lady is a bit of a dragon at times."

Drake smiled back at the priest, warming to the man.

"We've noticed, Father, yes. Now, please take a look at these for me."

"Perhaps if you could point out the boy you're referring to, it might be helpful, or I could sit here all day and not realise I'm looking at him."

Ross, agreeing that was a fair point if Byrne was being truthful, nodded at Drake, and she leaned across and pointed a finger at a thin and gangling boy, aged about twelve or thirteen, who stood at the end of the tiered ranks of boys in the picture. The photographer had arranged the boys, smallest in front, tallest at the back, with the medium height lads in the centre row, with Remington and another taller boy acting as 'book ends' at each end.

"That's the young Matthew Remington, Father," said Drake. "Ring any bells?"

Byrne studied the photograph intently for a while. His brow furrowed as he allowed his mind to drift back in time, recognition slowly beginning to dawn as he peered at the boy in the picture.

"That's Plug," he suddenly said, his brain eventually plucking the name from his memories of the past.

"Plug?" Ross asked

"As in the Bash Street Kids, Inspector, in the comic, *The Beano*."

"Yes, I remember it," Ross nodded his head, as he reached across, took the photo from Byrne and glanced at it.

"Oh, I see what you mean," he smiled at the priest. The young Matthew Remington did bear an uncanny and unfortunate resemblance to the character in *The Beano*.

"So you did know him, Father?" Drake now asked.

"Well, yes and no, Sergeant. He wasn't a friend or anything like that, and he tended to be the butt of quite a few jokes and taunts because of his looks. It wasn't his fault of course, but, well, boys will be boys, and especially back then, when there was less, shall we say, tolerance, he got a lot of grief because of his teeth especially. I can only assume he eventually had them fixed when he grew up."

"Yes, he must have done," Drake agreed. "They definitely weren't as bad as they were back then, anyway. So, what exactly was your relationship with him, Father?"

"I didn't have a relationship with him, Sergeant. I suppose all the lads knew him as Plug of course, and we all indulged in our own fair share of teasing him, I'm ashamed to say. He most definitely wasn't in any of my classes, or sports teams. I do recall he wasn't too bright, and I was in the top stream for most subjects, so our paths wouldn't have crossed much. You must understand I was just a child, not a priest at that time, no different to any other boy of my age really, so might easily have been involved in a bit of name-calling and so on, but I never really knew him, and wouldn't have known him at all if you hadn't shown me that photograph. I'm not even sure if I would have known his real first name in those days, let alone his surname. He was just Plug to me. I do seem to recall him being something of a troublemaker, a bit like Mark Proctor. I think every dorm had one or two boys like that."

"Proctor was a troublemaker?" Ross asked. "So far everyone has told us what a great teacher he was and that he was a really lovely man."

"People change, Inspector. When I came back to Speke Hill, Mark volunteered to show me around, showing off all the new stuff they'd incorporated over the years. We swapped a few stories from our time as kids there, and I think I only saw him a couple of times in passing during my occasional visits after that first day. As a child, Mark Proctor was a bit of a bully to be honest and would often hang around with the older boys, and got involved in a few scrapes in his time. He was a useful junior boxer but as he grew older he started to put on weight in the wrong places, lost his fitness and ended up having to quit the ring. I'm not surprised nobody told you or your detectives about him. You have to remember that all of today's staff have only been there a few years at most. They wouldn't have known Mark's record as a child unless they'd deliberately looked up his records. I'd have thought Miss Manvers and Charles Hopkirk and probably the headmaster would know though. Surely they'd have checked back on his time at Speke Hill before he was accepted on to the teaching staff."

"Yes, you'd think so, wouldn't you?" Ross mused. "I wonder why nobody mentioned it."

"Respect for the deceased? Not wanting to sully his name because of some childhood misdemeanours?"

"You're probably right Father, thank you."

Ross decided to take a chance and think out of the box for a minute.

"Father, I'm sure you heard about a young girl's suicide at Formby soon after Matthew Remington's death?"

"I saw something in *The Echo*, yes, such a tragedy. It didn't say much really."

"Show Father Byrne the photo, please Izzie."

"Oh, no," Byrne exclaimed as he looked at the photograph of Lisa Kelly.

"So, you did know her?"

"Yes, that's Kelly. She started coming here not long after I arrived. She told me she wasn't happy attending her Mother's church any longer. I never knew her surname. The newspaper didn't identify her and I'd no reason to think it was poor Kelly. That poor dear child."

"Her real name was Lisa Kelly, Father. She obviously kept her real name from you. She was raped by Matthew Remington, found she was pregnant afterwards and then had a termination. She simply couldn't live with the feeling she'd committed some terrible sin and became deeply depressed. You know the rest."

"That's just terrible news. I now realise I only took the poor girl's confession that very morning, not that I knew it was her when I read about the suicide of course."

"I'm afraid the mother didn't help the situation" Ross said rather accusingly.

"I'm guessing from your attitude she was something of what we might call a religious zealot?"

"Exactly. She made her own daughter feel dirty, rammed it home to her she was an unworthy sinner and had the nerve to say that because Remington had started going to her church and had repented his sins, he should be forgiven, and Lisa just couldn't handle it."

Byrne looked genuinely horrified at Ross's short summary of Lisa Kelly's last days on earth.

"I'm only guessing, but from the way you tell it, I assume Remington wasn't prosecuted for his attack on Kelly, sorry, I mean Lisa?"

"That's right Father. Her mother virtually accused her of inviting the rape by wearing short skirts and provocative make-up. I suspect Remington may have got away with more than just the rape of Lisa Kelly."

"Oh, in the name of all that's Holy. She was little more than a child, experimenting with her own feelings of growing up. I can see why she left her church and came here. She must have been looking for help. I just wish she'd trusted me enough to tell me about it. I may have been able to help her."

"Without judging her, Father?"

"I don't judge anyone, Inspector," Byrne stated firmly, having now dropped the 'Detective Inspector' and reverting to the usual shortened version most people used when speaking to Ross. "That's a privilege reserved for our Lord in Heaven. I promise you, I'd have done all I could to help the poor girl, and I'm saddened that I will never have that opportunity. I don't mean to pry, Inspector, but if it's not confidential information, may I ask what church she originally attended?"

Ross saw no harm arising from giving Byrne the answer.

"It was The Church of St. John the Baptist."

"Ah, that would be Father Joe, real name Father Giuseppe Albani. I've met him a few times since I arrived, at the regular monthly meeting held at the Bishop's Palace. I know now why the mother was so committed to the old-time faith. Although many of us in the Catholic church have embraced a certain degree of liberalism in the last few years, I'm afraid Father Joe is very much of the old school. His way could almost be described as being deeply entrenched in Catholic fundamentalism. Sin is sin, and redemption can only be achieved by total acceptance of the literal word of The Bible."

"And you don't believe in the literal word?"

"We live in a world where we are all, priests included, allowed to question certain things in the good book, Inspector. Perhaps the hottest potato at present is the subject of the Creation. Do we accept it as being literally as told in Genesis, or is it in fact a wonderful but stylised rendition of the story of how our world began?"

"And the Catholic Church is actually debating the subject?"

"Indeed it is."

Ross found this all very interesting but he realised the conversation had drifted off course and he heeded to return to the reason for being here.

"Tell me Father Byrne, do you feel that all is well at Speke Hill?"

"How do you mean, Inspector?"

"Look, cards on the table, Father. You're new in terms of how long you've been there as a priest. Has anything struck you as odd, or has anyone behaved in a way that has given you any cause for concern on any of your visits?"

Byrne looked shocked at the question.

"Well, no, I can't say it has, Inspector. Everyone has been quite normal as far as I've been able to discern, but then I don't spend much time there, I hope you realise that."

Ross found himself unable to really voice his thoughts without revealing exactly what was on his mind. He tried another approach.

"Father, when you were boys, do you recall whether Remington and Proctor were ever involved in any sort of trouble?"

"What kind of trouble?"

"The kind of trouble that might cause someone to harbour a grudge over the years, something bad enough to cause someone to want to murder both men."

"Oh," said the priest.

Ross's instincts sensed that Byrne might know more then he was saying.

"Father Byrne, please, if you know something that could be relevant to these killings, I need to know about it."

Rather then reply to Ross, Byrne turned to look at Christine Bland.

"Doctor Bland," he said, hesitancy in his voice. "You're a profiler, but also, due to your title, I assume you're a doctor of psychology or similar, am I correct?"

"Yes, Father, I hold doctorates in both Clinical Psychology and Criminal Psychology."

"Look, this is difficult and I'm not sure how to say this without sounding ridiculous, but lately I've been having a recurring dream."

"Please, go on, Father."

"I had a sister, Angela. We were at Speke Hill together. She was older than me, and lived in the girl's home, obviously but we were still close. Angela died at the age of twenty-three, running away from a man who had tried to assault her, much in the way Matthew Remington assaulted his victims."

"He tried to rape her, in other words?"

"Yes, that's right. The thing is, Angela got away from her attacker but as she ran away, she ran into the street and was hit by a car. It wasn't the driver's fault. He didn't have time to react as she appeared in front of his car."

"I'm so sorry, Father, that must have been awful for you."

"It was, Doctor. I was at the seminary by then, training for the priesthood and for a time, I admit to questioning my faith, and wondered if I'd ever make a good priest, but that's irrelevant now. The thing is, the dream that's kept me awake for so many nights is a warped, surreal nightmare. I'm a boy again, it's the night after Sports Day, and I'm wakened by a scream. Next thing I know, I'm outside the building on the grass and I can see Angela being held down by Mark Proctor and three other boys. Mark is on top of Angela, trying to force her legs apart. I was too young to understand what rape was at that time, Doctor, so I didn't really understand what was happening, but knew it was something bad. Angela is screaming, and yet there's not a sound coming from any of the boys, or from me, like I'm somewhere else, looking on but not being a part of what's taking place. I try to get closer, but something is stopping me and then, just before I wake up screaming myself, one of the other boys turns and grins at me. Until this morning, I didn't know who that boy was, but since the sergeant showed me that photograph, I now know that boy was Matthew Remington."

As Byrne paused, Ross asked,

"Father Byrne, are you telling us that Mark Proctor and Matthew Remington raped your sister?"

"No, no, not at all, please hear me out. You see, they were the same age as me, and I certainly wasn't sexually mature at that age, so I doubt they were. And believe me, if anything even remotely resembling a sexual assault had taken place on Angela at Speke Hill, she'd have told me and the staff, and anyway, she was quite capable of taking care of herself and would have put up one heck of a fight against four boys so much younger than herself. My point is this, Doctor," Byrne again turned to look almost pleadingly at Christine Bland, "no such thing ever happened, and yet the dream is so real. I apparently scream so loudly that it wakes young Father Willis up and a couple of times he's come into my bedroom to make sure I'm alright."

"Who's Father Willis?" Drake asked.

"Oh, sorry, he's my assistant, my deputy priest. He lives here too. You're not Catholic, any of you?"

They all shook their heads.

"Well, in the Church of England, I think you'd call him a rector, you know, he assists the priest in services, and helps with community work and the general running of the church. He's out doing visits to the sick right now as a matter of fact."

"I see. Thank you for the explanation, Father. Please go on."

"Yes, of course," Byrne appeared lost in thought for a moment or two. "Doctor Bland, the thing that's been torturing me at night and increasingly in the daytime too, as a result of the dream is, could I, as a young boy, have seen something that didn't register logically in my mind and then blocked it out for years?"

"Yes, it is" said Bland. "You were young, and it's quite possible you saw something, maybe only a second or two of whatever was happening, and your mind then either ignored it as irrelevant to your young mind's way of thinking, or you knew it was bad, and your mind blanked it out, as you've suggested. Something must have happened in recent weeks or months to trigger the old memories and the dream has been your mind's way of processing the information by mixing it up with the facts surrounding Angela's tragic death."

"I see, thank you. I thought I was going crazy."

"Far from it, Father. Such events are quite normal, I assure you, and happen more frequently than you imagine."

The wild theory that had sprung into Ross's mind earlier now seemed less fanciful to him.

"Now, that's the kind of trouble I was talking about. It's possible Remington and Proctor were involved in some kind of assault or deviant behaviour as youngsters, maybe in their teens and you saw or heard something, as Doctor Bland suggests. If that's the truth, I want to know why there's no record of it at Speke Hill, or if there is, why nobody there mentioned it when we talked to the Headmaster, Chief Carer and that irritating school secretary."

"I can't help you there, Inspector," said Byrne.

"No, but there might be a way to help you remember the facts, the truth about what you saw as a child," Christine Bland said suddenly.

"There is?" Byrne asked.

"If you're willing, I could organise a session of hypnotism. If you're suffering from a form of retrograde amnesia caused by a mental trauma as a child, it's possible we can unlock those memories under carefully controlled conditions."

"Hypnosis? I'm not sure, Doctor."

"It may help us both, Father, by revealing to the inspector something that could help his case, and in your own case, it may help put an end to the dreams."

Byrne thought long and hard before replying.

"I'm a man of God, Doctor," he said. "I can't say I'm comfortable with this. Please can I think about it?"

"Yes, Father." It was Ross who answered. "But please don't think for too long. We've got two murderers to catch."

"I'll be quick, I promise you, Inspector."

"Then I think we're done for now, thank you Father," said Ross, who rose from his chair.

Drake and Bland took his movement as a signal for them to follow his lead and were soon out the door and on their way back to headquarters with the priest's promise to give them an answer later the same day on Bland's hypnotism proposal.

Ross remained relatively quiet on the journey as his latest theory formulated in his mind, becoming more tangible by the second.

CHAPTER 23

BRENDA

Helmdale Lodge Psychiatric Nursing Home stood in its own extensive grounds, on the outskirts of the seaside resort of Rhyl in the county of Denbighshire in North Wales, some forty three miles from Liverpool. A private facility, the Lodge was a small and self-contained unit, with views over the Irish Sea, that catered for no more than thirty patients at any given time, most of them on a long-term basis.

A hundred years ago, Helmdale would perhaps have been described as a private mental asylum, but modern day enlightenment had removed such stigma from the treatment of mental illness and there was nothing of the Speke Hill style Victorian Gothic about its appearance, or in the way its inmates were treated; private rooms with television, comfortable beds and furnishings replacing such Victorian niceties as rubber coshes, water cannon, straight jackets and padded walls.

Built a mere thirty years previously, Helmdale appeared no different to the majority of onlookers than any run-of-the mill residential care home, with the obvious exception of a tall, eight feet high fence that encircled the entire property, complete with closed circuit television cameras mounted at strategic points on the fence, giving staff a constant video stream of the Lodge's perimeter.

Not that anyone had ever attempted to escape from the home. With all the patients being private, only those regarded as 'non-risk' patients were admitted to Helmdale Lodge. Fees were usually paid for by family members grateful to find a place where their mentally disturbed loved ones could be cared for in a pleasant and non-institutionalised environment. Everything about Helmdale Lodge was designed to make patients feel at home and comfortable and the doctors and nursing staff employed by the home's owners were of the highest calibre imaginable. Even the general care workers and ancillary staff were carefully selected, ensuring a sense of harmony prevailed at all times within the walls of the unit.

* * *

The man slowly pushed the wheelchair along the smooth black tarmac path that wound its way through a pretty, tree-lined avenue of poplars and firs, all kept neatly trimmed and at a height that wouldn't cut off the sunshine from those who felt like the walk that led to the extensive gardens beyond the trees. Here, the path opened up to reveal well-lawned, perfectly mown areas to both sides, and as the man arrived at the gleaming, silver painted ornate double gates that opened into the garden, his female companion walked ahead of him to open the gates, closing them after he'd wheeled his charge into the garden area.

The woman in the wheelchair stared straight ahead. If she saw the profusion of summer blooms that nodded their heads in the soft sea breeze that wafted through the garden, she made no acknowledgement of the fact. Peonies, Roses, Gladioli, Sweet Williams and so many more cast their heady scents into the air, in particular a bower of climbing roses in alternate red and yellow gave the garden the appearance of a place of peace and tranquillity, occasionally enhanced by the buzzing of a visiting bee, gathering nectar at its leisure, to the accompanying twittering of small birds, seeking seeds from various hanging feeders strategically placed so residents could watch the sparrows, greenfinches and other wild birds that regularly visited the garden.

"It's so beautiful here, isn't it, Brenda?" the woman asked, not expecting nor receiving an answer from the occupant of the chair, some ten years younger than herself, though the years spent locked away in her own mind, never mind behind the tall fences of the home had not been kind to her. A casual observer might have put them at the same age, such were the ravages of body and soul that time had wreaked on the younger woman.

It was important to try and engage in conversation with her sister, though, so the staff had always told her, and she never gave up hope that one day Brenda just might show some sign of recognition, might remember who she was and the life they'd once enjoyed as sisters.

"Look at those roses, they're so pretty. You always loved roses didn't you? You knew most of their names too. I just liked to look at them, but you were cleverer then me and used to tell me all about them."

She pointed at one particular hybrid tea rose bush as the little trio slowly passed it by, the smoothly oiled wheels of the chair virtually silent as they rolled along the smooth tarmac path.

"I do know that one, though, Bren. It's called Blue Moon isn't it? You used to tell me it wasn't really blue, more a sort of pale mauve really, but it was the nearest that growers had ever come to growing a real blue rose. I've never forgotten that."

"You know she's never going to answer us, don't you?" the man finally spoke as he carefully, lovingly, used his fingertips to push a lock of hair away from the patient's face, where it had been blown by the wind, slightly obscuring her view of the garden. Whether she acknowledged them or not, he did nevertheless feel, or rather hoped that she knew where she was, and could see and perhaps deep down in her subconscious mind, still take some pleasure from her surroundings.

"You never know. They said there's always a chance she might just snap out of it one day. Something might just shock her back to reality. We can't give up hope."

"That was over fifteen years ago. For crying out loud, you have to be realistic. Yes, there may have been a chance she'd suddenly snap out of it back then, maybe in the first year or two, but I've long ago accepted reality, even if you haven't. This is Brenda, as she is today, and will be every day for the rest of her life."

As he spoke, tears ran down his face, and he knelt down in front of the woman in the wheelchair, his hands gently stroking her hair and then tenderly touching her cheek as his body shook with emotion.

"Oh my darling, Bren," he sobbed. "You're still as beautiful to me as you were back then. I've never stopped loving you, and never will. If only we'd married as we planned. We'd at least have had some time together, time to love each other before…before…"

The words dried up, choked by his emotions and the woman in the chair continued sitting there, her face a blank canvas, devoid of emotion, as he poured his heart out knelt there on the hard tarmac, surrounded by the beauty of the garden and with sunshine pouring down on them, with a warmth he couldn't even be sure she could feel any more.

A hand on his shoulder snatched him back to reality.

"We should be getting back," said his companion. "You know they don't like her being out too long."

"We've only been here for ten minutes, at least let her have a little more time in the garden before we go."

"Okay," she replied. "You see, you do hold out hope, don't you? You might not admit it, but you do still hope she'll come back to us."

"Don't be fooled by my tears. Oh, yes, they're real alright, but like I said, I'm a realist. I know she's never coming back to us and that's exactly why we're doing what we're doing, isn't it? It's time they paid the price for their actions, and we're the ones to exact that payment, that retribution from them."

The woman took a step or two back from the wheelchair, as if not wanting the other woman to hear her words.

"So, when do we start again?"

"Soon, number three returns from holiday in a day or two and I want him to establish his routine again before we strike. I don't want to get caught out by him making changes to his previous routine after the holiday. Let's be sure he's sticking to everything as before."

"Alright, though I can't wait to finish what we've started. I must say, my nerves were on edge when the police were crawling all over the school and orphanage the other day. I thought they could see right through me, and knew exactly what I was thinking."

"Of course you did. That's only natural, but you have to stay strong, remember they have no real idea what it's all about. They have no way of connecting us together and are probably still working on all sorts of wrong theories, connected with religion, the Catholic Church versus the Church of England. Using a Catholic and a Protestant churchyard for the first two should act as a good smokescreen. As long as they keep working the religious angle they'll never work out what we're really doing."

"You're sure about that?"

"Yes, of course. Trust me. We've waited all this time. I'm not going to allow the prospect of vengeance slip by now we've started."

He turned to the woman in the wheelchair once again, this time taking her left hand in his own.

"Brenda, beautiful, gentle Brenda, you'd never hurt a fly would you? Those bastards did this to you, and now, at last, they're going to pay the price. I know you don't know what I'm talking about, but in God's name, the others will suffer as the first two did before we've finished with them."

He stared into her face, her eyes, eyes that once sparkled with the love and energy of life, but now stared out blankly at the world, stripped of every sign of emotion and feeling. A single tear now ran from his right eye, down his cheek and dripped on to their joined hands. He slowly drew his hand back and took a handkerchief from his trouser pocket, using it to gently wipe Brenda's hand.

"I think it's time," he said, and slowly he turned the wheelchair around and began a slow walk back though the garden, out of the decorative gates, retracing their path through the tree-lined arbour, returning Brenda to her room some ten minutes later.

"How was she today?" asked a nurse, as the pair walked along the corridor towards reception after getting Brenda settled comfortably in the armchair in her room before leaving her.

"Oh, you know, the same as always," the man said.

"I thought maybe she might give us a sign today," the woman added. "You know, like the doctor said, one day, if we hope and pray?"

"Yes, of course," said the nurse, whose name badge identified her as Registered Psychiatric Nurse Paula Dale. "You should never give up hope."

"I won't," said the woman. "Is Doctor Feldman here today? I'd like a word with him if at all possible."

"Oh, no, I'm sorry. Dr. Feldman is consulting at the Royal today," said Paula Dale, referring to the Royal Alexandra Hospital in Rhyl. "He'll be there until around four o'clock but he will be checking in here afterwards. He always comes back here before going home, to check on his patients after a day at the Royal. If you like, you could come back a little later. I'm sure he'd be happy to talk with you about Brenda."

The man reached out and placed a restraining hand on her arm. He spoke quietly but firmly as he addressed the nurse.

"I don't think we can hang around that long, but thank you Nurse Dale. Perhaps you can tell Doctor Feldman we were here today, and we'll try and catch him next week?"

"Oh, right, I see. Yes, I'll do that."

"It's time we were going now. Thanks again for all you're doing for Brenda."

"You're welcome, I'm sure," Paula Dale replied as the man turned and began to walk away towards the exit doors. The woman appeared to hesitate for a second or two, as though unable or unwilling to leave her sister, until the man looked around, saw her lagging behind, and called to her.

"Vera, are you coming? *Vera…*

CHAPTER 24

MYKONOS

The sun was just reaching its zenith on the tiny Greek island of Mykonos, one of the brightest jewels in the Aegean Sea. Poolside speakers at the small but well-appointed Hotel Sunbird played a continuous loop of music, alternating between traditional Greek and the ubiquitous and at times annoying Europop sounds. For those relaxing on the hotel's sun-loungers, strategically placed around all four sides of the pool, the hotel owners thankfully kept the volume at a manageable level, so it was never overly intrusive.

Back home in Liverpool, where it would just be approaching nine a.m. the temperature was a comfortable sixty degrees Fahrenheit, but on the sun-drenched island the mercury had just passed eighty five degrees and was steadily rising. The island itself seemed to bask in the sunshine, it's white-walled houses, set against the backdrop of surprisingly lush and verdant trees, shrubs and olive groves reflecting the glare of the sun and appearing as tiny, pristine jewels to anyone approaching the island from the stunningly azure blue waters of the Aegean. The little island's idyllic charm was disturbed only by the influx of summer visitors who might provide a good source of income for the locals, but whose presence was still resented by a few.

The ever popular *Cotton Eye Joe* by Swedish group Rednex, had just begun a new round of Europop emanating from the speakers as one guest tried his best to ignore the sound of his mobile phone, which began to ring from its place in his poolside bag, containing the phone, his cigarettes and lighter, and just in case he ever got the opportunity to use it, his personal

CD player and a small selection of discs he'd brought from home to keep him entertained. So far, he'd only used it while lounging on the beach, no chance of being able to hear anything properly over the constant throb from the hotel's sound system.

The ubiquitous sound of the Nokia ringtone finally died away and the man closed his eyes and let his mind take him back to the previous night. One of hotel's young maids had succumbed to three days of careful 'grooming' and an offer of one hundred dollars in American Express travellers cheques and joined him in his room late at night, where she participated in what he described to her as his 'rape fantasy,' nothing nasty he'd said, and he'd kept to this promise, for the most part. He smiled to himself at the still fresh memory of seeing the girl, hands tied to the metal bedhead, her ankles secured to the legs of the bed, her legs spread invitingly. Her only complaint had come when he'd begun to take photographs of her in her spread-eagled position. Whether she thought he'd show them around at the hotel and that word would reach her parents of what she'd done, he didn't know, but her shouts had become dangerously loud and he'd given her a quick slap across the face, the only thing that marred the evening. He'd taken the girl three times and then released her from her bonds, apologised for the slap, not wanting to draw attention to himself in the last days of his holiday and handed her an extra fifty dollars in travellers cheques to ensure her silence. In truth, he shouldn't have done it, and should have simply concentrated on improving his tan and enjoying the last couple of days of his time on the island, but his sexual urges had got the better of him. In the end, no harm had been done, he decided, and turned his attention to trying to decide what to have for lunch. The Sunbird's poolside bar did a mean cheeseburger with fresh salad, and just as he was about to rise from his lounger and look for a waiter to call and order his burger, the phone in his bag began ringing once again. Irritated, but deciding he should answer it in case the caller kept up a barrage of calls through the day; he reached into his bag, pulling the phone out just in time, before it rang off automatically. With little or no time to look at the number of the incoming call, he pressed the green button to accept the call.

"Hello?" he said.

"It's me," an instantly recognisable voice came though the phone's speaker.

"I can hear that," he replied, anger evident in his voice. "What the fuck are you calling me for? I'm on holiday, trying to get some relaxation, and this call will be costing you a bomb."

"Look, I know you are, and I didn't want to spoil your holiday, but there's something you need to know and it can't wait any longer."

"What the hell is it, then? It had better be friggin' important."

"There's no way to put it any other way. Someone's on to us, they know about the club."

"Don't talk soft, man. What the fuck do you mean? Have the bizzies been sniffing around?"

"No, it's not the cops. I almost wish it was."

"Well, what the fuck are you talking about?"

The caller took a deep breath, clearly audible over the phone and then said, his voice dropping to a quieter tone.

"Razor and Mark are dead."

"What?" How the hell…?"

"They've been murdered, man, both of them. Whoever did it slashed their throats and mutilated their bodies, really badly, including sexual mutilation, according to *The Echo*."

He didn't mention the sexual mutilation in detail because the press had been asked not to reveal the exact nature of that side of the killings. The term, 'sexual mutilation' could mean anything and for now, the press were content to use the all-encompassing term that gave their stories on the killings sufficient sensationalism and dramatic effect.

"Fucking hell!" the man on the lounger exclaimed. "Have the bizzies caught the murdering bastard who did it yet?"

"No man, they haven't. Don't you see, whoever did it must know about us? Some bastard's decided to take revenge on us, man. We could be next."

"You need to stop panicking. Their murders might have nothing to do with us. You know as well as I do that they've both got up to enough tricks of their own over the years. Mark was lucky. No one ever fingered him to the cops so how the hell could someone suddenly crawl out of the woodwork and start killing any of us?"

"I don't know, but I'm scared, looking over my shoulder all the time. I'm thinking of leaving town for a while. Maybe for good, you know? Even if I have to live rough, change my name, just do what it takes, like, if it means staying alive. Maybe you should just stay out there in Greece for a while. They can't get to you there."

"Are you totally stupid?" said the man on the lounger, trying to keep his voice as low as possible. "I'm on a fucking package holiday, you moron. I have to leave my hotel in less than two days time and fly home. You can't just extend your stay when you're on a package. And what the hell would I do out here? Do you seriously think I could just hide away on a Greek island for the rest of my life, just in case some nutter comes looking for me? I'll tell you now; it won't pay anyone to try it on with me. I can look after myself. I'll kill any bastard who thinks they can take me down. If you want to run, you run, but don't expect me to do the same. Listen, we'll get together and talk about this when I get back, okay?"

"Yeah, right, okay, if you think that's best."

"I do, and try to stay bloody calm until I get home, and one more thing."

"Yeah, man anything you say."

"Don't ever let me here you mention the club over an open telephone line again, you got that?"

"Yeah, right, sorry man. I was just kinda panicking, you know?"

"The only people who call it that are you, me and the others. It's just our own little in-joke name for it, isn't it?"

"Of course, like I said, I'm sorry."

"Okay. Now, are you going to let me enjoy the last couple of days of my holiday? I'll call you when I get home. Don't worry. We'll get it sorted. No one's going to get you or me, Johnny boy, got that?"

"If you say so," said the worried man back home in Liverpool. "Sorry about spoiling your day. I'd better go. Need to get to work, but I don't feel like going to be honest, you know, just to be on the safe side."

"Go to work, Johnny. It'll look suspicious if you suddenly stop turning up."

"Yeah, right, I suppose so."

"I'm going now, get off to work and stop your worrying."

With that, the man on the sun-lounger pressed the 'end' button on his phone, cutting his friend off. Despite what he'd said to Johnny, the news from home was indeed seriously perturbing. There was no way he was going to derive much enjoyment from the next two days on Mykonos. If indeed someone had uncovered his secret life and embarked on a mission to eliminate the members of his very special, very private and exclusive 'club' he knew there was only one way to stop them. He'd have to identify and eliminate them first.

CHAPTER 25

A GOOD NEWS DAY

"Come in, Izzie," Ross called from within his office, recognising her distinctive knock on his door.

Izzie Drake walked in and closed the door behind her.

"Something wrong?" he asked her. "What happened to your usual knock and walk right in?"

"Well, it's more personal than business, sir, so I thought it best to wait and see if you were free."

"Oh, for God's sake, Izzie, what is it? You look like a cat on hot bricks, and your face is red as a beetroot. Don't make me guess at whatever it is."

Izzie Drake took a deep breath, and blurted out her news before she changed her mind about telling her boss.

"I'm getting married," she said, "Peter proposed, and I said yes."

"Oh, is that all?" Ross replied with a smile on his face. "I had an idea something like that was coming from the way you've been acting for the last day or two."

"You knew all along then?"

"I'm a detective, remember? I guessed." Ross grinned from ear to ear.

"And here's me, getting all worked up about telling you."

"Why, Izzie? You don't me permission to get married, and Peter's a great guy. Congratulations to you both."

"Thanks, sir, that's a bloody relief," and the two of them laughed together.

"Listen," Ross said. "I'll have a word with Maria and the two of you can come over and we'll have a bit of a celebration dinner for you."

"Wow, yeah, that'd be great sir, thank you."

"Right then, that's sorted. Now, Sergeant, do you think we can get back to the business of catching killers?"

"But of course sir, any time you say," she smiled at her boss, breathing a big sigh of relief at the same time. She didn't know why she'd got so worked up about telling Ross about Peter's proposal. After all, the two of them had worked together long enough for her to have known her boss would be pleased for her. Anyway, it was done now, and he was pleased, she was happy, and it was time to get back to work.

She didn't get off quite so easily however, as Andy Ross began the morning briefing with an announcement of her engagement. Five minutes of celebration followed with one or two ribald comments thrown in for fun.

"Did he propose, before, during or after, Sarge?" Curtis asked, grinning like a Cheshire cat.

"Bollocks, Tony," Izzie laughed, picking up a pencil from the nearest desk and throwing it at the grinning Curtis.

As the laughter and congratulations flowed, Ross felt grateful for the distraction brought about by Drake's news. It had, temporarily at least, given the team a chance to release some of the tension that was gripping them all with each day that passed without an arrest. The door to the conference room opened and D.C.I. Porteous walked in to see the team engaged in their light-hearted banter.

"Am I missing something?" he asked. "I hope this isn't a celebration of me leaving the team, by any chance?"

"Not at all, sir," said Ross. "Sergeant Drake has just announced her engagement.

"Oh, yes, the young man from the mortuary. I'd heard about that. Congratulations, Sergeant."

"Thank you, sir, but, wait a minute. Where did you hear about it?"

"Doctor Nugent at the lab was talking to me yesterday. Seems your young man had already told him the news."

"Is there anyone on the Merseyside Police force who doesn't know about it?" Izzie groaned, still smiling.

"Okay, everyone. That's enough, I think," said Ross. "Can we do something for you sir?" he enquired of the D.C.I.

"Just thought I'd sit in and see where we're at, if that's okay with you," Porteous replied.

"Of course, sir. Take a seat. Right, everyone, let's get to it."

The earlier frivolity quickly forgotten, the small group of detectives took their seats and all attention focussed on D.I. Ross as he cleared his throat and instead of his usual request for updates, which he knew in his heart would all be negatives, he decided on a new tack, having been awake for much of the night, allowing the theory that had been forming in his mind the previous day to percolate and take shape.

With Drake seated to his right and Christine Bland to the left, he began.

"First, I want to say that I know we've all been working bloody hard on this case, with very little to show for it. That's nobody's fault, because the clues just haven't been there, we have no witnesses and so far, we're only guessing at a motive, though we're all pretty much agreed on revenge, some kind of vengeance or retribution as the number one possibility. The question we have to answer is exactly what the killers feel they are avenging."

"It has to be a rape, sir, surely," said Derek McLennan.

"I agree, Derek, but a rape that took place years ago when Remington and Proctor were young men, or one that took place very recently? Also, we have to remember that Mark Proctor had no criminal record, had never been arrested on suspicion of committing any crime whatsoever, and not so much as a parking ticket against his name. I'll come back to him later."

"So, how do we find out which it is, sir?"

"Exactly, Derek, and if we find the answer to that question, we could be one step from identifying the murderers. Doctor Bland's original profile still holds good as far as I'm concerned. We know the type of people we're looking for, but unless we can pin down the crime that links our victims to them, we're still blundering around in the dark."

"So, what do we do next sir?" came a question from Sam Gable.

This was it. Ross prepared to test his theory. He'd outlined it very briefly to Maria over breakfast. His wife, always a willing sounding board for his more outlandish ideas, agreed it had merit and urged him to put it to the team.

"I have an idea, and I want you all to listen very carefully. I've had a theory taking shape in my mind over the last two days, and it's time you all heard it, so here goes.

Let's assume for one minute that this case has its roots in events that took place back in the nineteen-sixties at Speke Hill. Just remember that what I'm about to say is just an idea, a conjecture, a wild speculation on my part of what may have taken place, so bear with me as I outline it to you, and we can discuss it when I've finished.

Matthew Remington, known as 'Plug' apparently because of some resemblance he bore to a character in *The Beano*, a popular kid's comic of the day for those who don't know it, was obviously not the best looking kid on the block. Mark Proctor, however, was good looking, a talented boxer, at least until he passed through puberty and piled a few pounds on, and had a reputation for being a bit of a bully. Knowing how kids minds work, let's suppose young

Proctor took Remington under his wing, and young 'Plug' became dependent on Proctor for protection, and in gratitude, became a devoted follower of the better looking and by all accounts, more intelligent boy. As they grow older, Proctor and Remington indulge in typical acts of schoolboy bullying, nothing overtly serious, but then, that word puberty raises its head again.

They begin to experience the beginnings of sexual urges. Whether they managed to experiment with any of the girls at Speke Hill, I can't say, but, and here's a wild card, the priest at St. Luke's in Woolton, Father Gerald Byrne, admits to suffering a recurring nightmare that makes no sense, as though his mind is mixing up a pot-pourri of fact and fiction. In it, he sees Proctor, Remington and two other lads, as yet unknown, attacking his sister, Angela. In this dream he sees Proctor trying to force his sister's legs apart, an obvious reference to sexual assault, but Father Byrne assures us that no such attack took place while he and his sister were at Speke Hill. However, years later, Angela was attacked by persons unknown in an attempted sexual assault, managed to break away from her assailant and in the course of running away, the poor girl ran across a road and into the path of an oncoming car, which knocked her down, the young woman eventually dying from her injuries."

A low buzz of sympathetic noises quickly went round the conference room like a Mexican wave.

"Yes, I know, bloody horrible set of circumstances, I agree, but, that's how it happened. Now, Christine, Doctor Bland, assured Father Byrne that such nightmares are quite common, where fact and fiction become distorted, particularly where childhood memories are concerned. She's offered to try and probe his memories through hypnosis, and just before Sergeant Drake came to see me with her happy news, the good Father called me to say he'd thought it over and he's agreed to allow Doctor Bland one session only in which to try and unlock his memories. The thing is, this dream, nightmare call it what you will is in fact the first suggestion we've had of Mark Proctor being involved in any overtly sexually deviant behaviour, and I think the young Gerald Byrne actually did see or hear something all those years ago, something his mind has blanked out, which has then become entangled with the terrible memories of what happened to his sister. Doctor Bland agrees and hopes to untangle those memories. If we can find one tiny clue as to what took place at Speke Hill, and who the other boys in Byrne's dream are, we may actually and surprisingly have our first tangible clue.

Now, my theory gets a little more outside the box here. Let's suppose that the four boys involved in whatever took place at Speke Hill, assuming Byrne's dream to have its basis in fact, which again, Doctor Bland thinks is highly probable, not only got up to some kind of sexual activity in their teens, but then carried on their aberrant behaviour into adulthood. The four of them remain in touch and go on to carry out a series of rapes and sexual assaults over a period of time. We know Remington was convicted of the rape of Claire Morris, and we've since learned of his unreported attack on the unfortunate Lisa Kelly, so who's to say there weren't more attacks over the years? As for Proctor, Mr. Squeaky Clean is obviously far from that, but we have no evidence to prove it, as yet. I want a full scale probe launched into every aspect of Proctor's life. His wife clearly has no idea what her husband was getting up to, but he must have been going somewhere from time to time and giving her a load of bullshit about what he was up to. Maybe she thought he was doing extra curricular teaching, coaching some fictitious sports team, I don't know. Maybe she thought he was having an affair and didn't dare ask him about it in case she was right and her 'perfect' marriage collapsed like a house of cards around her ears.

Izzie, I want you in charge of a comprehensive probe into Proctor's life, and I mean every aspect of it. Sam," he said, turning to look at D.C. Gable, "you'll work with Sergeant Drake on this, as you at least have a little knowledge of how Speke Hill worked a few years ago through your child-hood friends and you worked Vice for a time so you have some idea how the whole sex crime thing works."

"Yes sir," Gable replied.

"Paul," he said next, addressing D.C. Ferris, "I want you to give them all the back-up you can from whatever records you can access on that super computer of yours, and anything Sergeant Drake needs, she gets, understood?"

"No problem, sir."

"Right, now, where was I? Oh yes, back to the subject of Speke Hill. Something is 'off' about that place. I know all the staff there today are new compared to the time period we're looking at, apart from Father Byrne of course, who was there as a boy, but he's only their visiting chaplain, and not there on a full time basis. The thing is, they have records, and I would have thought they would show up any incidents of potentially serious aber-rant behaviour in any of their pupils, even all those years ago, but according to the secretary, there's no mention of anything like that in any school or orphanage records."

"Sir," came an interruption from Derek McLennan.

"Yes, Derek, what is it?"

"Sorry for interrupting, but I can think of two reasons why the secre-tary came up with nothing."

"Go on, Derek, we're listening."

"Well sir, back in the sixties, the orphanage and the school were still very much under the control of the Catholic Church. I know that the council had assumed overall control of the place, but from what we've discovered so far about the place, it wasn't like any other Council-run home or school I've ever known. Most of the teachers were still Catholic priest and nuns, with a smattering of 'civilian' teaching staff, for want of a better word. The same applies to the actual orphanage where the Church retained most of the control over the place until well into the seventies. Anyway, sir, my point is this: if such incidents took place under the auspices of the Roman Catholic Church, as stupid as it may sound to us today, it's possible the priest in charge of those boys might have known about it and dealt with it internally. We're talking Catholic Church, remember, sir. If the boys were caught and knew they were in a lot of bother, it's possible they admitted their transgressions to the priests and were given the opportunity to repent their sins in return for forgiveness, or, they admitted their crimes under the absolute secrecy of the confessional, in which case the priest who heard their confession could never reveal what he'd heard to another soul."

Ross was impressed by the thought that McLennan had put into his own theory, and said so.

"Well done, Derek, good thinking. The whole sanctity of the confessional could be covering up a multitude of sins here and we can't do a thing about it unless we can find out the truth some other way. I just hope Father Byrne provides us with some names if there really are two more possible rapists out there. Anyway, you said you had a couple of ideas concerning the records?"

"Oh yes, sir. The second idea is that just possibly the bloody secretary is quite simply lying to us."

"You know, Derek, that same thought had struck me too, though I don't know why the woman would want to protect them."

"Ah, but it wouldn't be them she's protecting, Inspector." D.C.I. Porteous rarely spoke at these morning conferences, but for once he decided to add a little input.

"Sir?"

"She sounds like a few women I've come across over the years. Middle-aged spinster, no love life to speak of, married to the job and fiercely loyal to her employers. If she was going through those records and found something she thought might be potentially embarrassing or detrimental to those who pay her wages and give her a focus in her life, I certainly wouldn't put it past a woman like that to lie to protect their name and reputation. Then again, you also have the possibility she's lying to protect the killers themselves due to her having some connection with them. Perhaps she was in love with Mark Proctor, even to the extent of having an affair with him. What you need is a search warrant and or a court order to open up those old records, and I'll see that you get them."

"I see what you mean sir, and thank you. Even the old bat who seems to be jealously guarding those records can't turn us away now. Sounds as if we need to look a little more closely at the secretary. What's her name again, Derek?"

"Manvers, sir, Vera Manvers."

"Right, that's a job for you, please, Derek. Find her home address. Visit her away from school. I'd put money on the fact that her office at Speke Hill is her ultimate comfort zone, a place where she feels in total control. Maybe you turning up on her doorstep will succeed in rattling her cage a bit."

"Right sir, I'll see to it."

Porteous now raised a hand and Ross gave the D.C.I. his full attention.

"You want to say something else, sir?"

"Yes, Andy. Please don't think I'm interfering but let me say this. I've listened to this briefing and I'm impressed by your theory. It has a ring of credibility about it, but as you say, we've no actual evidence yet to even suggest Proctor's involvement in any crimes at all. Can I make a suggestion?"

"Please do, sir. You know I'm always ready to hear your thoughts. You're the boss after all."

"Yes, but we all know who the brains of this squad is, Detective Inspector. Anyway, compliments aside, I think what you're suggesting beneath the thinly veiled exterior of your theory, is that Remington, Proctor and two other, as yet unidentified men met as boys at Speke Hill and grew up to form some hideous gang of rapists, possibly helping each other to target and select their victims, maybe even helping in the actual rapes themselves. I'm going to second D.C. Dodds to the squad again for the duration of this case and he and young Curtis can work on listing every unsolved rape case, and indeed, attempted rapes, for the last twenty years in Liverpool and the surrounding area. Obviously, when such cases occurred they'd normally have been investigated as single cases but suspecting what we do now, we may find that a pattern emerges, something that will link a number of them together and may point us in the direction of these bastards. I think we definitely have a pair of vigilantes at work, and it's almost certain they're reacting to an unsolved case where they feel the rapists got away with it, or perhaps were arrested but never came to trial, another angle we should look at, so we need to work fast to try and bring the other two rapists in to custody before our killers can strike again. We may also find a study of those unsolved cases will identify the vigilantes' motive for this sudden spree of killings."

"Yes, sir, thank you sir," said Ross, impressed by his boss's immediate grasp and acceptance of his theory, and for throwing his weight behind it by the addition of Nick Dodds to the squad for the duration. He felt he needed to add one thing, though.

"Can I suggest that in addition to the unsolved rapes, we also have Dodds and Curtis include unsolved serious sexual assaults for the period, too? We all know there's often a fine dividing line between the two."

"Of course, Andy, you see to it. Now, I'll leave you to it, and good luck everybody."

A short series of "Thank you sirs," emanated from the assembled detectives as D.C.I. Porteous exited the room, closing the door quietly as he left.

"Bloody hell, sir, that was a turn up," said Curtis.

"Yes, it was, rather, Curtis," Ross agreed. "Thankfully the boss agreed with my theory. So, let's get to work. You all know what you need to do, so come on people, let's find ourselves a couple of killers, not to mention a possible pair of serial rapists while we're at it."

The sound of chair legs grating once again on the conference room floor not only put Ross's teeth on edge, but signalled the end of the meeting as everyone set off to work on their allotted tasks. Izzie Drake stopped at Ross's office door on her way to begin the in-depth investigation into the life of Mark Proctor, beginning, she'd decided with a visit to Melanie, his widow, who she knew wouldn't be pleased with the questions she'd already decided needed to be asked. But first, a word with Ross was her priority.

"Sir, a quick word?" She stood framed by the doorway. Ross sat behind his desk, making notes on a pad.

"Go on, Izzie, what is it?"

Drake was grinning as she said, her face deadly serious,

"Well sir, I just wanted to make sure you're going to be alright going out and about in the big wide world without me there by your side, holding your hand, so to speak."

Thankfully, Izzie possessed good reactions, as she just managed to dodge the folded-up copy of the previous night's *Echo* that sailed across the office in her direction.

She was already halfway across the squad room laughing to herself as Ross's voice boomed out of his office and followed her to the door,

"I'll see you later, *Sergeant* Clarissa Drake…"

CHAPTER 26

TOO GOOD TO BE TRUE

"I don't know what you're getting at. I've already told you, Mark was just a lovely man. Ask anyone. They'll all tell you the same."

Melanie Proctor had been surprised to see the two detectives standing on her front doorstep when she answered the ringing of the doorbell. After recovering her composure she then asked Drake if she'd come with news regarding the capture of her husband's killers. She'd then found herself being interrogated on the most intimate details of her life with Mark and was becoming more upset by the minute, but Izzie wasn't about to give up on her line of questioning.

"Melanie, I'm sorry, but I just don't believe you. You're basically asking us to believe that Mark went to work in the morning, came home in the afternoon and never went out at all, even at weekends. That's just too far-fetched for anyone to believe."

"Well, you know, he did go out sometimes, just not very often."

"That's better. Now we're getting somewhere. So, come on, Melanie, where did he go on these rare occasions?"

"I'm not really sure."

Sam Gable joined in the questioning. It was time for 'good cop, bad cop' with Gable assuming the good cop role.

"Listen, please Melanie. We know you're grieving for Mark. He was your husband and you loved him, but we are trying to find out who killed him, and stop them before they do anything like this to someone else's husband. Whatever Mark may have done isn't going to hurt him now, is it?"

"I suppose not," Melanie agreed with a degree of hesitation in her voice.

"Listen, Melanie, we're not accusing you of anything. If Mark did have any secrets from you, it's hardly your fault is it? But if he was up to anything that wasn't strictly legal, it could have provided the motive for someone to have killed him, do you see?"

"He played poker," Melanie just blurted out, without replying directly to Gable's question.

"Poker?" Gable asked. "Who with, and where and how often?"

"I honestly don't know," Melanie sniffed as she began to cry, quietly. "He went out once, sometimes twice a week to meet his friends. He said they met at a pub in Crosby, I don't know the name. In the early days, I asked him who his friends were, but he just said they were some old school mates, and the only name I ever heard was one time when he answered the phone and he mentioned the name Johnny. I think that was probably one of his poker playing pals because once I overheard him say something about having a 'full house' next time. That's a poker term, isn't it?"

"Yes, it is," Gable agreed, but thought it could also have been some kind of private code for something entirely different. "And you say you don't know the name of the pub where they met? You never heard any mention of the name, ever?"

"No, sorry, I've no idea."

"Didn't you think it strange, Melanie, that your husband never told you where he was going or exactly who he'd be with?" Izzie Drake asked her. "What if there'd been some sort of emergency at home? How would you have been able to reach him? That really wasn't very thoughtful of him was it?"

Melanie Proctor's sobs had turned to serious tears now and Sam Gable reached across to the coffee table and passed the box of tissues that stood there to the weeping woman.

"Melanie, please be open with us. Nothing's going to bring him back is it? We need to know everything about Mark's life if we're to put a stop to these killings and find whoever did this to him. You don't really think he was playing poker do you?"

Sam Gable had spent three years working vice before joining Ross's team. She'd seen plenty of prostitutes who'd been subjected to vicious assaults and rape, and she couldn't help but feel a certain degree of empathy for Melanie Proctor. Somehow, the woman presented a similar vulnerability as those girls, trapped in a situation they had no control over, and having no one to turn to when things went bad.

Melanie slowly regained control of herself, and as she brought the tears to a halt, she looked up at Sam, and shook her head.

"I thought he was seeing someone else," she said. "I loved him, but there was a too good to be true element about Mark. Do you know, he even went out on a Saturday morning to do the weekly shopping at the supermarket? I wanted to go with him but he always said I worked hard enough all week in the home and deserved to put my feet up for a couple of hours at the weekend. But he was gone too long. I would have done the shopping in about an hour at most, but he'd take at least two hours, sometimes longer. He'd joke about it if I asked him why he'd been so long and say he had a lousy sense of direction in supermarkets and ended up going down the same aisle time and again, and that he couldn't find certain things but he went every week so he should have known where most things were shouldn't he?"

Izzie understood the woman now. She must have spent years in denial, suspecting her husband of having an affair but believing excuse after excuse from him because she didn't want to believe him capable of such a thing. In fact, Izzie was now fairly certain he'd been guilty of so much more than marital infidelity.

"Listen, Melanie, I can't go into details with you at this time, but we don't believe Mark was having an affair."

The woman looked at Izzie Drake, and as their eyes met and locked, realisation dawned on Melanie Proctor.

"You think he did something bad, Sergeant Drake, don't you?

What is it you think he did when he was supposed to be playing poker with his mates?"

"I'm sorry, I'm not at liberty to tell you, as I said earlier, but we do need to find his killers and you can help by telling us everything you can about Mark, right back to the time you first met him."

Melanie had passed the point of no return. Her desire to protect the outward appearance of a happy marriage and a loving husband crumbled to nothing as she took another tissue from the box, blew her nose and placed the crumpled tissue in the pocket of her jeans, and with a steel-like resolve said,

"Tell me what you want to know."

CHAPTER 27

UNDER THE INFLUENCE

Gerald Byrne looked slightly incongruous as Ross greeted him in his office. Having agreed to the suggestion by Christine Bland, he was dressed casually, as she'd suggested, in a simple t-shirt emblazoned with the words, *Jesus Loves You* in bright red against a black background, a pair of blue denim jeans and black trainers that made him look anything but a Catholic priest. Ross led him to the office of D.C.I. Porteous, who had given up the use of his own inner sanctum when Bland had expressed a need for somewhere private and relatively comfortable in which to carry out the session. The profiler had asked that she be allowed a few minutes in private to prepare Byrne and to 'put him under' and Ross reluctantly agreed to wait outside the door, having wanted to see exactly how Bland achieved the act of hypnotising her subject.

"You can come in now, Inspector," she said as she opened the door ten minutes after she and Byrne had disappeared into Porteous's office. Ross found what followed engrossing. Unlike various TV dramatisations, Gerald Byrne didn't regress to talking in a childish voice or give any outward indication he was under hypnosis at all. However, what he revealed was illuminating to the detective. First of all, Christine Bland asked him to recall his days as a junior in the Lower School at Speke Hill. Most of the information that came from the priest was routine and irrelevant but certain passages of his memories struck a chord with Andy Ross.

"Nineteen sixty-four? Oh yes, the year of the Moors Murders, Hindley and Brady. We were being constantly reminded of the dangers to children at morning assembly in school and during services in the chapel. At first the children were reported as missing and the bodies weren't found until later, upon Saddleworth Moor.

Father Mullaney was especially concerned that those children who were allowed out of the grounds to go to the local shops or on Saturday trips to town were chaperoned at all times. There were always a couple of adults, usually priests or nuns to accompany the children, but if a couple of kids wanted to visit a store to buy something with their pocket money, well, the adults couldn't be everywhere at once, so it was made a new rule that we could only be apart from the grown-ups for a maximum of twenty minutes and there had to be at least four children together, two Uppers and two Lowers, so that the older boys or girls could take care of the young ones. That was around the time poor Keith Bennett went missing. Of course, nobody knew he was a victim of Hindley and Brady until they confessed to his killing in the nineteen eighties. The poor boy's body has never been found, you know, even after so many years."

"Do you remember Matthew Remington and Mark Proctor being together on any of those trips to town, Gerald?"

"Oh yes, they were usually together from when we got off the bus until we returned to Speke Hill."

"And they had two older boys with them if they went off on their own, away from the adult staff?"

"Yes, that's right."

"The older boys, Gerald, do you remember their names?"

"No, sorry, I don't."

Damn, Ross thought. He now had an idea that the two boys who took Remington and Proctor under their protection all those years ago could well be the two senior members of whatever weird, perverted association that eventually led to them eventually becoming serial rapists, if his theory held up.

Christine Bland, however, carried on, unfazed by Byrne's inability at this stage to identify the two elder boys.

"Tell me about Angela, Gerald. How did she feel about the awful case of the missing children?"

"Angela was three years older than me, of course so she probably understood a lot more than me about it. She didn't say much about it, as far as I remember, except to say that the children who'd gone missing were all from around Manchester and she didn't think we were in real danger in Liverpool. I remember the two of us going into a record shop, with two older girls. Angela bought *Have I The Right* by the Honeycombs. They were her favourite group at the time. She loved the fact they had a girl drummer and said one day she wanted to be just like Honey Lantree and play the drums in a pop group. It was just a childish dream, of course. I think I wanted to be like Billy J Kramer when I was seven years old. The girls in Angela's dorm had saved their pocket money for ages and clubbed together to buy a second-hand Dansette record player at the market in town. Sister Thomasina was the nun in charge of their dorm and was a dab hand at fixing things, and she made sure the record player worked properly for the girls. Anyway, a lot of the older boys were jealous because at that time, I think only one of the Upper boy's dorms had a record player, so sometimes, in the evening, a group of boys could be seen gathered on the grass outside Angela's dorm. The girls would place the record player as near to an open window as they could, and play the latest records for the boys to listen to. Funny really, when you think about it, all those lads jigging about on the grass and the girls dancing to the music inside the dorm."

"And did Angela ever have any problems with the boys at that time, Gerald? You know, did she ever tell you about any of them bothering her or making unwanted suggestions to her about doing things she knew were wrong or indecent?"

"No."

"So, you never heard Angela screaming in the night, or found her being pinned down on the grass by Matthew Remington, Plug you called him, and Mark Proctor?"

"Oh no, nothing like that."

Convinced by now that nothing untoward had taken place in the time frame suggested by Byrne's nightmare, he used hand signals to indicate to Christine Bland, urging her to move forward in time. She now asked Byrne to fast forward to his teenage years. She asked him the same question regarding any form of assault on Angela.

This time, the answer varied slightly.

"Nothing ever happened to Angela, no."

Something in those words alerted both Bland and Ross's

instincts. Both profiler and detective knew from the way Gerald Byrne spoke of nothing happening to Angela, that he was in effect saying 'but' as though somewhere in his mind lurked a memory of an incident relating to another girl, one that had become subconsciously entangled in his mind along with other recollections of his sister to form the basis for his current nightmares.

"Did something bad happen to another girl, Gerald? One of Angela's friends perhaps? Try and think. Let your mind take you back, you saw something, didn't you, or maybe it was Angela who saw it and told you, her little brother, all about it?"

Christine Bland waited, as the priest drifted away once again on a tide of buried memories, and all she, and Andy Ross could do, was wait to see where, and at what point in time Byrne's mental rewind stopped. Gerald's breathing intensified for a few seconds and then very slowly returned to what appeared to be a normal rhythm. His eyes, previously cast downwards, now shone brightly as he appeared to be focussing on something, an event from the past?

"What is it Gerald? Where are you? What do you see?"

Without hesitation, Byrne replied to Christine Bland's questions.

"I was walking across to the girl's dormitories. I'd arranged to meet Angela after tea, just to go for a walk around the grounds. We often did that, so we could talk in peace and privacy. Before I got there, where Angela would be waiting outside as usual, Father Rooney called to me from the doorway to the Admin block as I passed it."

"Okay Gerald, that's good. Describe what happened next. How old were you at this time?"

"Not sure, but I remember we all loved a song that was in the charts that year. It was called *Nobody's Child* and was about a blind orphan boy who nobody wanted to adopt. All us kids thought it was kind of like us being stuck here in Speke Hill. I must have been about twelve, thirteen perhaps. There was another song I liked, *Bad Moon Rising*."

Ross knew that one. *Creedence Clearwater Revival* was one of his favourite groups from the sixties, having discovered them much later, when he was in his own teens, having heard the song when it was featured during a very scary werewolf transformation scene in the film *American Werewolf in London*. It would be easy to pinpoint the exact year Byrne was talking about as long as he was talking about the time both songs were current in the U.K charts.

"Alright, Gerald. So, Father Rooney called to you. What happened next?"

Now it was as though Byrne had slipped through a time warp in to the past as he relived the next few minutes of his youth.

* * *

"Gerald Byrne, please, wait a moment," the voice of Father Rooney halted the young Gerald in his tracks. He turned to see the priest calling to him from the Administration Building.

"Hello Father," he called in return.

Father Rooney walked down the three shallow steps from the building entrance to the path and approached Byrne who waited for the priest to catch him up.

Slightly out of breath, Father Rooney smiled as he stopped in front of the young lad.

"Thanks for waiting, Gerald," he said. "How would you like to earn yourself a shilling?"

"A shilling, Father? All for me?"

"All for you, Gerald, and just for doing me a small favour."

"Okay, Father. What do I have to do?"

"Nothing arduous young Gerald. I collected the first fifteen rugby kits from the laundry today and dropped them off at the pavilion, ready for tomorrow's match with The Blue Coat School. I've a meeting to go to later and I just realised I must have left my motorcycle gauntlets in the pavilion. I have some important marking to do and can't spare the time to run down there right now. Would you be a good boy and run down and get them for me and bring them back here?"

"I was just going to meet my sister, Father."

"That's alright, go and meet her and she can keep you company. Tell her there's sixpence in it for her too. That won't interrupt your plans too much will it?"

"Oh no, Father. We just meet and go for walks around the grounds some evenings, that's all. We can easily go down to the sports field and the pavilion to get your gloves."

Rooney smiled.

"Gauntlets, Gerald. They're called gauntlets. You know what they look like, don't you?"

"I think so, Father, big black things with like, kind of flap things that stick out and cover your wrists when you're riding your motor bike?"

"Yes, I suppose that's a decent enough description, young Gerald. At least you know what you're looking for. They should be in the changing room where I unpacked the clean shirts and hung them up on the team hooks ready for tomorrow. Here's the key to the pavilion." Father Rooney tossed the key to young Gerry Byrne who deftly caught it in his right hand.

"Okay, Father," Byrne said to the motorcycling priest, probably his favourite among the ecclesiastical members of staff at Speke Hill. Father Rooney, probably because of his love of motorcycling, seemed more 'with it' than the other priests and nuns, Gerald thought.

Leaving Father Rooney to return to his marking, Byrne skipped off happily to meet Angela who was waiting patiently outside her dormitory building, one of two large buildings allocated to the girls of Speke Hill. She was sitting on the grass, her knees tucked beneath her as she waited, a small book in her hand.

"What kept you?" she asked as Gerald arrived, slightly breathless from running the last few yards.

"Father Rooney," he replied, and explained Rooney's request to his sister.

"Okay, come on then," said Angela, holding a hand up so her brother could help her to her feet."

"What's the book?" Byrne asked his sister as they walked.

She handed it to him.

"*The Observer's Book of Birds*," he read from the cover.

"I borrowed it from Maggie Miller," Angela said. "I love birds, Gerry, and thought it might be nice if I could identify them when I see them. We might see some down on the sports field, looking for worms and things."

"But we only get sparrows and blackbirds round here, Angie."

"Don't be daft. I've seen greenfinches, robins and lots of birds I don't know the names of."

"Oh well, if it makes you happy, that's okay."

It was quite a walk from the accommodation block to the far side of the sports field, where the grandly named 'pavilion' stood. It was a small, wooden building, with two cramped changing rooms for opposing teams, whether it be for cricket, football, rugby or whatever, and a small central area where a small refreshment table could be set up when entertaining visiting teams from other schools as would be the case the following day. Though the school had considered installing showers for the players the cost of installing the necessary plumbing had been prohibitive and so the pavilion retained a rather dated air, with its overhanging roof that provided cover over the small raised outside wooden terrace and steps that led down to the field.

As brother and sister drew closer, Angela suddenly spotted a flurry of avian activity in the bushes that formed the border between the playing field and the adjoining field belonging to a local farmer and currently lying fallow.

"Oh, Gerry, look," she enthused. "Maybe there are some birds I haven't seen before. Do you mind if I go and creep up quietly and see what they are while you go in and get the Father's things?"

"Go ahead, Angie," Byrne replied. "I'll only be a minute though, so don't go far."

"Okay, I'm only going over there," she pointed.

"Angela quickly skipped away, book in hand, and Gerry Byrne strode up the steps, unlocked the door and entered the pavilion. He moved automatically into the changing room to the left, knowing it was used as the 'home' changing room. Sure enough, as soon as he walked in he saw Father Rooney's gauntlets where he'd left them on one of the wooden bench seats that ran along the wall under the hooks that held each freshly ironed rugby kit, ready for the Upper's big match the next day.

As he was about to turn and leave, a noise from somewhere behind the pavilion reached his ears. Instinct told him it was the sound of someone, a girl, in some distress.

Louder, male voices could be heard, too, and Gerry Byrne, sensing something wasn't quite right about what he was hearing, padded almost on tiptoe to the small window, covered by steel mesh, that was fitted high up into the outside wall of the home changing room. Not being very tall, Gerry had to stand on the wooden bench seat and even then, reach up on tiptoes to gain a very restricted view of what was happening behind the pavilion.

Four boys were out there, on the grass and they had a girl with them. From the sounds the girl was making, she wasn't enjoying or encouraging whatever they were doing.

"Go on Plug, get her skirt off," a voice Byrne didn't recognise ordered as a boy he recognised as Matthew Remington slapped the girl across the face, causing her not to scream but to cry, her tears only serving to fuel the boys' cruelty.

"Shut up, you little bitch or it'll be a punch in the face next time," Remington leered at her, as he tried to force the poor girl's legs apart.

"Oh, move over, Plug, let me have a go at her," said the unmistakable voice of Mark Proctor, much to Gerry Byrne's horror. He couldn't get high enough to see the girl's face, so he wasn't able to see who it was the boys had pinned down on the ground, but whoever it was, it was plainly obvious that what the boys were doing to her was very wrong. Gerry Byrne, still innocent in the ways of the world was in a quandary. He didn't know who the other boys were, but something in their voices told him they were older than Plug and Mark. He knew he had to do something to stop them from hurting the girl, but what could he, one young lad do against four of them, without probably getting badly hurt himself if they retaliated against any attempt he made to help her? He didn't have time to run back to Father Rooney and he suddenly thought of Angela. What would happen if she walked in to the situation now, and saw and heard what was happening? Dare he risk his sister being caught by the older boys and suffering the same fate as the girl on the grass?

"Please don't do this," the girl pleaded.

"Shut it, bitch," one of the older boys snapped at her. "For God's sake, Mark, if you can't the fucking skirt off, just lift it up and get on with it."

"She's struggling too much," said Proctor.

"So fucking slap her again," said the unknown voice.

As Gerry Byrne tried to think of a way to help the girl without ending up being beaten or worse by the four thugs outside the pavilion, fate, or maybe the God he would end up serving through the church, took a hand in proceedings.

Some four hundred yards away, Angela was scurrying about under a clump of trees and bushes, seeking bird life, when she inadvertently disturbed a family of crows, roosting peacefully in one of the trees. The birds took to the air in a flurry of flapping wings, accompanied by a cacophony of screeching bird calls, and by chance flew directly in the direction of the ongoing assault, flying directly over the scene, forcing the girl's assailants to suddenly look up in surprise. Simultaneously, a man walking his dog in the fallow field just beyond the boundary of the school playing field began calling his dog, which had run off in pursuit of the birds that had caught his attention with their flapping and screeching. The dog found a small hole in the boundary fence and slithered through into the school field, and within seconds the four boys were surprised to see a muscular, black Doberman pinscher bounding across the field in their direction. The dog's owner's face appeared at the fence as he shouted, "Paddy, where are you boy?"

"Bloody hell, lads, fucking leave her and leg it, quickly; don't you dare say a word, bitch or we'll be back," said one of the older boys, and in less than a second the four boys abandoned the attack on the girl and ran off in the opposite direction to the dog's approach. Luckily for them, the dog stopped as it reached the distressed, crying girl, and began licking her face affectionately. From his position at the window, Byrne was able to witness the arrival of the man who had climbed the fence to follow his runaway dog.

The man quickly ascertained that the girl was alright and amazingly accepted her claim that she'd fallen and hurt herself. *Didn't he hear her screams?* The thought ran through Gerry Byrne's mind. He seemed more concerned about his dog, Paddy, who's back bore a long, angry looking red scratch where he'd cut it as he'd wriggled under the seven foot high chain metal fence between the playing field and the narrow path that ran along the side of the adjoining farmer's field.

Feeling it was safe to exit his hiding place in the changing room, Gerry stepped out and quickly ran round to the rear of the wooden structure to where the man was on his knees, his attention seemingly divided between the girl on the ground and Paddy the dog. When she saw him approaching, at first the girl's eyes registered fear, obviously thinking he was one of her attackers, perhaps returning to ensure her silence, but then she seemed to realise he was a newcomer to the scene.

"Are you okay?" Gerry asked the girl, who looked up at him as though he were a being from another planet.

"Seems the young lady fell down and hurt herself," the man said to Gerry before the girl had a chance to reply, and at that moment, Angela arrived, and took one look at the girl and somehow, in the way that only a female possibly could, she seemed to know exactly what had happened.

"What the heck's going on?" she asked.

Gerry looked at his sister, as if to say, *"don't say anything until he's gone."*

As if on cue, satisfied that the girl was safe in the hands of her two 'friends' as he called them, the man clipped Paddy's lead to his collar and left the scene, leaving Gerry and Angela to attend to the girl.

"Right, is someone going to tell me what happened here?" Angela asked again.

"Four boys tried to do things to her," Gerry said. "I could hear them and see some of it through the little window in the changing room, but I didn't know what to do to help her."

"Is that right?" Angela asked the girl, taking hold of one trembling hand.

"Yes," the girl said, trying hard not to burst into tears.

"What's your name?" Angela asked her.

407

"Elizabeth Dunne," she replied. "They call me Lizzie."

"You're not from Speke Hill, Lizzie, are you?"

"No, I met this boy, and arranged to meet him here, and he sneaked me in through the gate at the far end of the path along the field. I thought he fancied me, you know, and he was good looking and a bit older than me so I was flattered when he asked me to meet him. Anyway, when we got here, he changed completely, and there were three other boys waiting behind the building, and they tried to…to…you know?"

"Bastards," said Angela through clenched teeth.

"What was this lad's name, Lizzie, and where did you meet him?"

"He called himself Johnny, and I met him in a coffee bar in town last Saturday."

"Did you see him, Gerry?" Angela asked her brother.

"Not properly, no," Byrne replied. "But I know who two of them were."

"Who were they, Gerry?"

"Mark Proctor and Plug, you know, Remington?"

"Bloody hell."

Gerry had never heard his sister swear before, and the vehemence in her voice took him by surprise.

"We've got to tell someone," Angela quickly decided.

"Oh please, I don't want to get into trouble," Lizzie pleaded. "If my parents find out I've been hanging around with boys they'll kill me."

"But, they tried to rape you, Lizzie. That's what happened, isn't it?" said Angela, far more forcefully than Gerry would have thought possible at her age.

"Yes, but they didn't actually do it in the end, did they?" said Lizzie.

Ten minutes of discussion ended when Angela told Gerry he'd better take Father Rooney's gauntlets to him and think of an excuse for being late, while she walked Angela safely out of the grounds. Unfortunately for the little group, Father Rooney, worried at Gerry's long absence, appeared at that very moment, and unused to lying to a priest, the children soon revealed all to the shocked looking Father.

Lizzie refused point blank however, to reveal her surname or her address to Rooney, insisting she wanted to forget the whole episode. Knowing he couldn't force the girl to talk to him, Father Rooney stood silently for a minute as he tried to decide his next course of action. Reaching his decision, he ordered Angela and Gerry to go about their business as though nothing had happened.

"Carry on with your walk, as you normally would, and I'll walk young Lizzie here safely out of school grounds. As for the boys responsible for this appalling act of savagery, you leave them to me. I don't want you two involved, do you understand?"

"But Father," an incensed Angela said, "we don't even know who the other boys are, and they're just going to get away with it, aren't they?"

"No, they most certainly are not, Angela, and as for the other two boys, I can promise you that Proctor and Remington will reveal all to me. I'll make sure of it. But listen, if they know you two have talked to me and are involved in me finding out what's taken place here today, they could make things very difficult for you both for the remainder of your time at Speke Hill, do you understand that?"

Gerry and Angela simultaneously chorused "Yes, Father."

Angela then asked, "But how will you say you found out, Father?"

"Oh, you leave that to me, Angela. For one thing, I can say I came here to get my forgotten gauntlets and found this young girl, and she told me what had taken place. I can assure you they'll be terrified at the prospect of what may happen to them next, and they know she heard the names, Mark and Plug, and Johnny, so it won't seem too strange to them that I was able to identify them. Now, do as I've told you while I see Lizzie off the premises."

Feeling shaken and a little unsure of themselves, Angela and Gerry nevertheless did as Father Rooney asked and went back to their walk, though neither found any pleasure in their remaining time together. Gerry noticed that, despite her earlier enthusiasm, Angela never looked at *The Observer's Book of Birds* once during the rest of their walk. Brother and sister hugged each other as they parted a while later at the entrance to Angela's dormitory, having promised each other never to mention what had happened in front of a living soul, as long as they had to live at Speke Hill, trusting Father Rooney to make sure the guilty boys were punished.

* * *

Andy Ross now felt he had not only the explanation for Father Gerald Byrne's rather mixed-up nightmare, but more importantly, confirmation of what he guessed had been the beginning of an evil partnership of four young men who would go on to commit further acts of evil as they achieved maturity. Now, if only Christine Bland could extract the names of the two older boys from the depths of Gerald Byrne's memory. She now tried to do just that.

"Tell me please, Gerald, what happened after that evening. Did you hear what happened to the boys who'd perpetrated the attack?"

"We never heard a word. Father Rooney called me aside one day and told me the matter had been dealt with privately, *within the orphanage* as he put it. Though we'd promised never to talk about it, Angela and I discussed it years later when we'd both left the orphanage and our promise no longer held firm. We both agreed there had to have been some kind of cover-up.

Speke Hill had closed ranks to protect its own. Maybe they did punish the boys in some way, but it was never made public, as far as we knew."

"And do you recall the names of those other boys, Gerald, the older ones who seemed to be egging on the two younger ones?"

"I only know one of them was called Johnny, because I heard the other older boy say his name one time. I never saw his face because if I had done, I might have seen him with the other boy in the following days and been able to find out the other boy's name, but it never happened."

Christine Bland drew the session to a close and told the priest, "I'm going to count to five, now, Gerald. When I reach five, you'll wake up and your mind will recall what you've told me, not as a nightmare, but as a distant memory from long ago, and it will no longer disturb you. You were a child when what you've told me took place and you will no longer carry the burden of what you saw all those years ago"

Ross said to her, before she began counting, "don't they usually tell people they *won't* remember what they've revealed under hypnosis?"

"This isn't a stage act or a movie, Inspector. This is supposed to be a cathartic process for Father Byrne, a way to help him put the past to bed, so to speak, to banish the nightmare. He can only do that if he remembers the truth about the past, and not some twisted subconscious version of reality."

"I think I understand, and thank you for doing this."

"It's time to bring him back," she said as she slowly began counting to five.

CHAPTER 28

BACK TO 'BILLY RUFFIAN

Randolph Newman stood head and shoulders above Detective Constable 'Tony' Curtis. At six foot four inches, he was a good six inches taller than Curtis, and his black, tightly curled hair, dark good looks that betrayed his Caribbean heritage and powerful physique had the effect of intimidating the young D.C. before they'd exchanged a word. Newman hadn't exactly looked pleased when Curtis kept up an incessant knocking on the front doors of *The Belerophon* at nine thirty in the morning. As landlord of the pub, he'd fallen into bed some time after one a.m. after closing the pub, making sure all was secure, and balancing the day's takings before locking them in the safe. He'd been in the cellar, changing a barrel of lager when the knocking began and made sure he finished the task in hand before climbing the stairs, crossing the floor of the pub and opening one of the double doors, just a crack, to identify the cause of the disturbance to his morning.

"Yes?" he snapped at the sight of the young man in blue jeans and a leather jacket standing at his door.

Curtis, forced to look up to face the man directly, took one look at Newman and gulped internally, before pulling his warrant card from the inside pocket of his jacket and holding it up for the landlord to examine.

"Police," he announced. "Detective Constable Curtis, Merseyside Police. I'd like a word, sir, if I may?"

"Humph," Newman shrugged. "I hardly thought you'd be from the Met, would you?"

Curtis looked a little nonplussed by the remark.

"Oh, never mind. Come on in, Detective. I was just about to put the kettle on. Tea or coffee?"

"Er, right, thank you, sir. Coffee for me please."

Five minutes later the two men faced each other across a well used wooden topped table in the lounge bar of the pub.

"How long have you been the landlord here, Mr. Newman?"

"Oh, must be around ten years now, since I left the Royal Navy."

"I see, so you'd remember most of the regulars over that period?"

"Well, maybe not all, but most of them, sure," Newman replied. "What's this all about, Constable?"

Curtis quickly filled Newman in on the reason for his visit and then reached into the inside pocket of his leather jacket and removed photographs of both Matthew Remington and Mark Proctor. The landlord gazed at them for a few seconds, and then nodded.

"Yes, I've seen them in here a few times. Two of the four apostles."

"Eh? What do you mean, Mr. Newman?"

"The four apostles is what I called them, 'cos of their names, right?"

"I'm sorry, I'm not with you."

"When we was very little kids, Constable, me and me brothers, well, our Mam taught us this simple little bedtime prayer. It went like this. *Matthew, Mark, Luke and John, Bless the bed that I lie on. God bless Mam and Dad, Samuel, Levi, and Gary.* Of course, me brothers would insert my name instead of their own, but we could also add anyone else we wanted to the prayer, like grandparents, friends, cousins here and in Jamaica and so on. It was just easy for a little child to remember you see, based on the four gospels of the New Testament, the books of Matthew, Mark, Luke and John, so when these four fellas stars coming in here, and I gradually over-heard their names, I thought of them as being all saints' names, like the four apostles of my childish prayer, and I always thought of 'em that way, whenever I saw 'em in here."

Curtis was elated. They had a name for the fourth man. Though saint was the last name he'd apply to the men Newman just described."

"I heard about the murders on Radio Merseyside and on Mersey Radio. One of them said that one of the dead men had a record of serious sexual offences but they didn't give any details."

"We believe all four men were involved in a number of offences, Mr. Newman, but I can't go into details, I'm afraid."

"I understand, Constable," Newman replied. "Need to know basis and all that, eh?"

"Exactly," said Curtis. "You'd have come across stuff like that in the Navy, I suppose."

"All the time. You can count on me to keep my mouth shut. I won't even tell my wife why you were here. She's upstairs and will be wondering where her cup of tea is," he grinned. "I'll tell her you came about a fracas in the vicinity or something and asked if we'd heard anything."

"Mr. Newman, you don't know how helpful you've been. One last thing, did you ever overhear any of them mention any surnames?"

"No, sorry Constable. It weren't even very often I overheard a first name. It probably took me three months of them coming in here before I gave 'em the four apostles name, it took that long to hear all their names."

"How about hearing any of their conversations?"

"I'm a good landlord, Constable Curtis. That means I stay out of the faces and the business of my regulars. It wouldn't do to be eavesdropping on conversations, especially in an area like this, if you know what I mean."

"I see, yes, I get your point, but that's still great. How long have they been coming in to the pub, can you remember?"

"Oh, I'd say at least for the last four or five years. They'd sit at a corner table in the bar. I'll show you their regular spot when we go through there again on your way out. If that table was taken they'd sometimes come in the lounge bar and take pot luck on a table."

Curtis was delighted with the result of his interview with the landlord of *The Belerophon* and felt sure D.I. Ross would be, too. He thanked Newman who duly showed him where the four men usually sat in the bar, and then duly departed and made his way back to headquarters, a sense of satisfaction overtaking his earlier trepidation at the sight of the very tall, heavily built ex-seaman, now the jolly 'mine host' of *The Belerophon*. Curtis made a mental note to try not to judge people quite so quickly based on nothing but their appearance. The tall and powerful Jamaican-born former seaman had just taught the young detective an important lesson that would serve him well in future investigations.

CHAPTER 29

A WOMAN OF MANY FACES

Having spent most of the day in the office with Nick Dodds, pulling the required records of past rape, attempted rape and serious sexual cases as Ross had requested, Derek McLennan looked at his watch, stood up from his computer screen and stretched to loosen the stiff and aching muscles in his back and neck.

"Had enough, Derek?" Dodds asked as Derek almost slumped into his chair again.

"For now, yes. Listen, Nick, school's out now. Why don't we nip down to the canteen, grab a sandwich and give the Manvers woman time to get home? I pulled her address earlier, and it'll only take about twenty minutes to get there, traffic permitting. I don't think the boss will mind if you join me in going along to talk to her and two heads is better than one anytime. You might think of something I don't while interviewing her, unless you want to just head off home. It's been a long day, after all."

"What's to go home for?" Dodds replied. Since his divorce a few months earlier, Nick had left the marital home and now lived in a small rented flat above a Chinese restaurant in the city centre, not far from work. His evenings tended to be, long, lonely and monotonous, so he was in no hurry to finish work for the day.

* * *

Vera Manvers stepped from the shower, dried her body and then padded barefoot into her bedroom, where she quickly blow-dried her hair, and allowed it to fall into its natural wavy shoulder-length tresses. After sitting before her dressing table and applying her make-up, she dressed in a pair of comfortable, slim-fitting black slacks, topped with a lightweight cream coloured polo-neck sweater, then sat back on her dressing table stool to admire the transformation. She smiled at her reflection in the mirror, knowing that the staff at Speke Hill would be hard-pressed to recognise the attractive, well manicured woman who stared back at her from the mirror from the dowdy spinster who arrived at work with hair tied in a bun, dressed in sensible skirts and blouses or sweaters depending on the weather with her low heeled, sensible shoes, and pale, make-up free face.

She thought how surprised they'd be if they could see the real woman in her off duty garb, the above the knee skirts showing off a well formed pair of legs, her high heels and general appearance taking at least ten years off her apparent age.

Vera Manvers was in fact much younger than she appeared to her colleagues at work. Even her name was a fabrication. Some five years earlier she'd scoured local churchyards, slowly building a list of names of children, mostly babies, who'd died in the first few months of life. With the help of her partner, she'd gradually completed extensive checks on her final short list of four names, finally selecting the one with not one single living relative, and therefore no chance of her new identity being acciden-tally revealed by some suspicious cousin, grandparent or whatever. Vera Manvers, who had died at the age of just two months in a tragic house fire, along with her parents and two siblings had been tailor-made for her plans. From there, it had been a simple matter of obtaining a copy of the dead child's birth certificate and, through the contacts her partner had estab-lished, obtaining enough fake documentation to quickly establish herself in her new identity. To ensure she would be able to continue to work legally and receive any state benefits she was entitled to, she quit her previous job, changed her name by Deed Poll to Vera Manvers, dropped out of circula-tion for nearly a year, and then returned to every day life in her new guise, ready to avenge her sister. Vera's plan for revenge had built up over a number of years, and she and Brenda's still devoted fiancé had decided the time was ripe for their plans to be put into fruition when 'number three' on their list rose to the verge of success in his chosen profession, one that would be a gross travesty in light of his 'other life' activities. He would be the next to feel the wrath of vengeance and by the time they got to him, he'd know the true meaning of fear, because by then he would know they were coming for him. They'd wanted to save him till last but circumstances had altered things drastically and they needed to move him up the list.

Her sister had retained just enough of her wits and sanity to tell her the details of her attack before the full horror of what had befallen her had sent her into the state of semi-catatonia she now lived in. The next thing 'Vera' and Brenda's fiancé had done had been to follow their target for months, with Vera gradually finding a talent for disguise, being able to change her appearance almost at will, able to watch the man who'd been the prime mover in the attack on her sister with almost total impunity. Brenda had known the man slightly, but couldn't tell Vera much about the other three men who'd gang raped her as she and her so-called 'friend' Matthew Remington, had walked home from a date.

Her surveillance of Matthew Remington, beginning from the time of his release from prison had instantly enabled her to identify Mark Proctor as another of the men involved. Using her new found skill as a mistress of disguise, she'd 'accidentally' bumped into the repulsive Remington in a pub one night and plied him with enough drink to discover he'd been brought up at Speke Hill Orphanage, a link to Mark Proctor who she'd learned was a teacher at the school there. It now became a possibility that all four of Brenda's assailants had a connection to Speke Hill, but the problem was, how could she and Brenda's fiancé confirm their suspicions? The answer soon presented itself. Brenda's fiancé had visited Speke Hill under the guise of a visiting child care official and discovered that the school secretary was on the verge of retirement. Now there only remained the problem of guaranteeing Vera got the job.

They soon found that Charles Hopkirk, who would be responsible for interviewing and hiring the new secretary was something of a ladies man, who enjoyed trawling the city's clubs on Friday and Saturday nights, often managing to fall into bed with numerous one-night stands, probably all the worse for drink and or recreational drugs. Wearing a blonde wig, party clothes and heavily made up, a totally changed Vera, going under the name of 'Poppy Gillespie' followed Hopkirk to the Red Pelican club one night, waiting until he'd drunk enough to be slightly inebriated before making her move.

Later that night, lying on her back with Hopkirk grunting above her, she'd pushed aside her revulsion long enough to get him to tell her about the vacancy at his workplace. Saying she had a friend who'd love to work at the orphanage, she'd allowed him to use her body again and promised to meet him the following week if he'd agree to consider her friend for the job.

Five days later, 'Vera' arrived at Speke Hill for an interview and was promptly hired by Charles Hopkirk. He never once suspected that the prim and proper, dowdy spinster with a rather 'plummy'accent sitting across from him at the interview was the sexy and very gorgeous 'Poppy' he'd met at the club.

The following Saturday night, 'Poppy' had met Hopkirk again as arranged. She needed to be certain he wasn't about to go back on their deal and found herself once again in his bed, promising herself this would be the last time. As he groaned and grunted his satisfaction for the last time, she lay back, thinking she'd never have to do this again, after he'd told her how impressed he'd been with her 'friend' Vera Manvers.

She was in! As much as it had disgusted her to virtually prostitute herself in such a way, she considered that opening her legs for Charles Hopkirk had been nothing more than a means to an end, a giant step in the quest for revenge for her sister's life having been effectively ended by Remington, Proctor and two more, as yet unidentified men. At least she was on the pill and there was no chance of Hopkirk's seed producing anything more than a short inconvenience as she washed herself in the bathroom after what would be her last 'date' with the odious little man.

In the coming days, as Vera settled into her new job, Charles Hopkirk, puzzled that he hadn't seen Poppy in the club as usual, asked her 'friend' Vera if she was alright.

When she informed Hopkirk that 'Poppy' had developed a rather nasty sexually transmitted disease and had retired from the social scene while undergoing treatment at the local STD clinic, the look on his face had been pure gold for Vera. He visibly paled and began to sweat as Vera informed him she was sure Poppy would look him up as soon as she was cured and 'back on the scene' ready to go clubbing again.

"Are you alright, Mr. Hopkirk?" she'd asked, trying so hard to maintain a sweet and innocent demeanour. "You look a little pale."

"Oh, yes, of course, Vera, thank you. Please tell Poppy I'll look forward to seeing her soon," said Hopkirk, deciding there and then to never set foot in the Red Pelican again. The next few weeks and months would be a continual source of worry for him as he checked and re-checked himself for any sign of scabs or lesions that might indicate him having contracted some dreaded sexual disease.

Let the fat bastard suffer, Vera thought as she revelled in his misery.

It took her quite a while in her new position to systematically scour the old records of Speke Hill in her search for any connections between Remington, Proctor and any other boys who may have been involved in any kind of illegal activity, either individually or as a group.

She'd only conducted her search a small piece at a time, not wanting to draw attention to the fact she was searching past records of the school and orphanage, none of which bore any reference to her current employment so it took a little longer than she'd at first anticipated.

Boys being boys, there had been a number of instances of lads from Speke Hill having been in trouble at various times, mostly for trivial and non-criminal offences.

Eventually, her senses were alerted by a sealed envelope that carried the pencilled names, now a little faded, of Proctor, Remington and two others she'd never heard of before. With a shaking hand, she took her letter opener and without further hesitation, sliced the envelope open. She'd hit pay dirt! The whole incident relating to the attempted assault on the girl behind the pavilion was revealed to her, and now, at long last, she felt able to prepare, along with Brenda's fiancé, to exact revenge for her sister's treatment at the hands of the monsters who defiled her for life and so it began.

* * *

Her thoughts were suddenly interrupted by an unexpected knocking on her front door. Annoyed, as she rarely had visitors of any description, and certainly not unannounced ones, Vera walked to the door, pulled it open, expecting to find a couple of Jehovah's Witnesses or perhaps a double glazing salesman at her door and was instead surprised to find two police detectives, warrant cards already held up on display, standing on her doorstep.

"Miss Vera Manvers?" the older of the two detectives asked.

Struggling, and just managing to maintain her composure, Vera replied, "It's *Ms* Manvers, if you don't mind."

"Right, okay, Ms. Manvers," said Nick Dodds. "Can we come in please?"

"What's this about?" Vera asked.

"Just a few more questions about Speke Hill," Derek McLennan said in response to her question.

"Well, yes, I suppose so, but I hope this won't take long, I have to go out soon."

"I can see that," McLennan replied. His look at his fellow detective said it all. They'd both expected a dowdy spinsterish woman in her fifties to answer the door. Instead, they were both a little taken aback to see the very attractive, well dressed woman standing before them, who couldn't have been more than forty-five at the outside.

They followed Vera into her tidy living room, and seated themselves in opposite armchairs. Vera sat on the sofa, and the act of crossing her legs made her already short skirt ride up, revealing even more of her well tanned and shapely legs.

"Well?" she asked, aware that the two men were staring at her, particularly her legs.

Derek McLennan spoke first.

"Ms. Manvers…"

"Oh, do call me Vera, dearie," she interrupted, almost coquettishly. She'd decided the best way to deal with the two young detectives was to try and thrown them off guard a little and so far she felt it was working.

"Okay, Vera," McLennan went on, "we need to inquire a little more into the subject of the records of Speke Hill, going back to the fifties and sixties."

"Yes? What about them? How can I help you?"

Nick Dodds joined the questioning.

"Our colleagues previously visited you at work, Vera, looking for information relating to both Matthew Remington and Mark Proctor."

"Yes, that's correct."

"You're aware that we're involved in the investigation into their murders, Vera?"

"Yes of course I know. I did what I could to help the police, but the information you were requesting went back to a long time ago and the old paper records are not exactly easily available or necessarily filed in proper date sequence, a failing of the previous person to hold my position, I'm afraid," she replied, attempting to divert any blame or suspicion from herself.

"That's as maybe," McLennan said, "but our boss, D.I. Ross feels you may have been holding something back from us, Vera."

Vera looked shocked. In truth, she was afraid they may be onto her, but McLennan's next words gave her cause for hope.

"He thinks you may be going out of your way to protect Remington and Proctor by withholding information about them that might assist us in our inquiries into their murders."

Emboldened, Vera replied, "Now, why on earth would I do such a thing, Detective Constable? In the first place, I never knew Matthew Remington, and I only met Mark Proctor when I went to work at Speke Hill, and that was only a passing working relationship."

McLennan was thrown off kilter by the logic of her answer, and Dodds came to his rescue.

"We think you may be trying to protect the reputation of Speke Hill, Ms. Manvers. If the place has certain skeletons in the cupboard, so to speak, as secretary, you have access to all past records and would be in a position to withhold anything that might throw a bad light on your employers."

Vera relaxed a little at Dodds's words. They actually thought she was trying to protect those vicious perverts. Surely, if that was the case, they had no inkling she was in fact responsible for the murders.

With new confidence born from that thought, she replied to Dodds confidently.

"I can assure you, Constable that I have never tried to withhold any information from the police, certainly nothing that would interfere with your inquiries into the murders of two men, one of whom was a respected teacher at my place of work."

"I hope not," Dodds continued, "because we will be obtaining a court order to grant us access to all of Speke Hill's records, both for the orphanage and the school, and we will without a doubt soon discover if you're being evasive with us."

"I'm sure that won't be necessary," Vera replied. "The headmaster has already given his permission for you to access the records and I provided your people with all the help I could on your previous visit."

"Yes, I'm sure you did," said Derek McLennan, "but you may have overlooked some detail that we may think important, even though you may not have been aware of its significance."

"Of course. I understand," said Vera, a little perturbed again as she thought of the police trawling through the records and finding the envelope containing the details of the four boys who'd attacked the girl behind the pavilion. Would they become suspicious at seeing what should have been a sealed envelope opened as she'd left it? Depending on circumstances, she knew she'd need to access the file room and place the documents in a new sealed envelope as she should have done when she'd found it, only to leave it in her excitement at her discovery of the contents.

McLennan and Dodds, despite sharing a belief that there was something 'off' about Vera Manvers, realised there was little point in pushing the interview any further. Yes, they'd confronted her at home and been very surprised to find her a very different woman from the one they'd expected, but that in itself wasn't reason to be particularly suspicious, but she'd seemed helpful and co-operative. If there was more to Vera Manvers, it would need further background investigation to reveal it. They certainly hadn't been able to ascertain any cause for them to think she was protecting Remington and Proctor, as D.I. Ross suspected.

CHAPTER 30

AT THE END OF THE DAY

Ross, tired and frustrated, was preparing to leave for the day. With most of the team still out pounding the streets or following up with their allotted lines of inquiry, he knew he'd catch up with everyone in the morning. He had one more thing to do however, before heading off and doing his best to switch off from work for a few hours. He'd acknowledged a phone call from D.C. Curtis a little earlier in which Curtis had given him the fourth name they'd been searching for, but there was little they could do about tracing the mystery man until the morning. A knock on his door heralded the arrival of Press Liaison Officer, George Thompson, who Ross felt might be able to assist in identifying not just the newly mentioned Luke, but also the other elder boy, Johnny.

"You look knackered," Thompson said as he took a seat in the visitor chair opposite Ross's desk. "You should go home, get some rest, carry on with all this in the morning."

"That's a pretty good assessment of my current condition, George," Ross replied with a wry grin. "You should be a detective."

"Ha, ha, very funny, Andy. I think I'll stick to what I do best, thanks. Speaking of which, how can I help you?"

"I have an idea, and you could maybe help us in identifying the two older boys who quite probably instigated everything while the boys were at Speke Hill. I still believe Remington and Proctor were nothing more than followers and the older lads were the ringleaders of this bloody horrendous perverted quartet."

"Okay, what do you want me to do?"

"Can you put out a new press release, George? I want to appeal to the public without them really knowing the extent of the crimes Remington and Proctor were involved in."

"Hang on," said Thompson. "I thought you had no evidence to suggest Proctor committed any crime?"

"We don't as yet, but I'm sure we'll find it, soon enough. Meanwhile, I want to put out a public appeal for anyone who knew Matthew Remington and Mark Proctor during their time at Speke Hill, to com forward with any information they can give us about their childhood. If anyone remembers them well, they might just be able to recall the names of the older lads they were knocking around with in their teens. If we can put surnames to Luke and John, we're well on our way to identifying two more potential victims for our killers. For all we know they're planning to hit one or both of the other men any time now, and I don't want another bloody and gutted corpse on my hands if I can avoid it."

"No problem," Thompson replied. "It's an ingenious idea actually, Andy. I can word it so that readers think they're assisting us in finding the killers, which they are of course, in a way, but mainly, they're helping you to identify two rapists and potential victims for the churchyard killers."

"You've got it, George. Can you do it by tomorrow?"

"Of course. I'll have it ready by the morning briefing for you if that's okay."

"You don't mind? It means I'm asking to stay and work while I'm swanning off home for the evening."

"Don't be silly, Andy. I can compose the new release while I'm sitting watching TV with my wife. She doesn't like me to talk and interrupt her while *Coronation Street's* on the box, anyway."

"You're a star, George. Tell Liz thanks for me for butting in on your evening."

"Thanks for what? I just said, she'll welcome the silence emanating from my armchair, so you're doing her the favour, not the other way round. She should be thanking you for giving her a completely George free half hour while she watches *The Street*."

Andy Ross laughed, and after Thompson said goodnight and left his office, the D. I. rose from his desk, stretched his tired limbs and was soon following the Press Officer out of the building, looking forward to spending some quality time with Maria.

* * *

A few miles away, on a small estate of industrial units in the Garston area of the city, work had also come to an end for the day. Situated to the south of the city centre, Garston was in the midst of much urban redevelopment, with large areas of its old Victorian terraced housing being redeveloped and improved and modern housing replacing much of the old red brick back-to-backs. The area's claims to fame lay in having been the home at one time of singer Billy Fury and of Ray McFall, owner of the Cavern Club, who first booked *The Beatles*.

Garston also stands as a huge container port, independent of the Port of Liverpool, and is regarded as a separate port altogether. It was close to the container port that the small gathering of units stood not more than a quarter mile from the main complex.

John Selden pulled his rather battered old Audi 100 to a halt in the car park, outside one of the larger units on the estate. Most of the businesses had closed for the day and the only lights visible as evening drew closer and a slight mist crept in from the Mersey, were in the unit whose name was picked out in bright red lettering, against the corrugated grey metal walls of the building.

Selden looked up at the name, *A. J. Devereux & Son, Ships Chandlers, (Wholesale Only)*, killed the engine of the Audi, switched off his sidelights and exited the car, being sure to lock it before walking the few yards to the door that was marked 'Office' and knocking firmly, the sound of his knocking seeming to echo and reverberate from within. Second later the door was opened from within and a hand reached through the smallest of gaps and Selden felt himself being pulled bodily into the building. Before he could speak a word, the door slammed shut and a hand reached past him and turned the key in the lock, trapping Selden inside the building.

"Bloody hell, Lucas, you almost scared me to death," he protested when he was released by the grasping hand and turned to see the man he'd been summoned to meet standing before him. Lucas, (Luke) Devereux, the 'son' in the company name, was the sole proprietor of the business. There'd never been an A.J. Devereux of course, the name being nothing more than a fabrication by Lucas aimed at giving his business an air of additional credibility, longevity and respectability. If anyone queried his ancestry, Lucas would play on his true past as an orphan made good, and sentiment always brought understanding at the pretence he'd set up to give his business a family feel to make up for the real family he'd been denied in his youth. Thankfully, there was nothing illegal in adopting such a practice, or his business ploy might have had a detrimental effect on his current plans to enter parliament, as Liverpool's latest political 'whizz-kid' after serving successfully on the local council for the previous five years. As things stood, Devereux had emerged as the narrow favourite to win a seat in parliament at the forthcoming by-election, brought on by the death of the sitting M.P. and now just one week away.

Business was doing well, thanks to his shrewd tactics of dealing whole-sale only, and thus being able to order, if necessary, a ship's boiler for delivery direct to the customer, without needing the massive storage space other such businesses might require. His customers ranged from the individual owner of a Fleetwood trawler to a couple of smaller container shipping lines, always on the lookout for a cheap deal or a discount, which Devereux was prepared to give in order to expand future business opportunities. The burgeoning use of the internet for marketing opportunities had also opened up whole new vistas for his business. Things could only get better!

"Come in, sit down and fucking shut up whining," Devereux said, and Selden could smell the unmistakable aroma of whisky on his breath.

"What's wrong, Lucas?" asked an already jittery Selden, who'd been waiting to hear from Devereux since his return from Mykonos.

"Read that," said Devereux, sinking into his leather office chair behind a large and almost barren desk, and passing a small A5 sheet of paper into Selden's hand as he stood next to Devereux's desk.

Selden did as he was bidden and read the few words that had been pasted to the sheet of paper, letters cut from a newspaper like some old style ransom demand in a movie.

YOU WILL NEVER SIT IN PARLIAMENT, LUKE!

"You think this is from the killer, don't you?" Selden asked, his own hand shaking as he held the offending message.

"Of course it is," Devereux replied. "It's fucking obvious isn't it? Only people who knew me as a boy would call me Luke. Everyone calls me by my real first name nowadays. They intend to do away with me before the election, Johnny boy, but I won't just sit back and be an easy target for the murdering bastard."

"When did it arrive?"

"Today, of course, you fucking dimwit. You don't think I'd have sat on it for days without letting you know, do you?"

"But Lucas, It might not be from the killer. Maybe it's from some disgruntled voter or political opponent."

"Oh, for fuck's sake, get real Johnny. I know the police would probably say that if I reported it to them. They'd say politicians are always getting hate mail and stuff like that. If it had said, 'You're next to die' or something like that, they'd perhaps have taken it seriously, but this is just ambiguous enough, at least to the cops, not to constitute what they'd see as a valid threat to my life, but I know it's from whoever killed Matt and Mark, I just know it is."

"So, what can you, we, do?"

"I'm going to hire some muscle, Johnny boy. First thing tomorrow, I'm hiring a couple of bodyguards to be with me twenty four hours a day."

"Yeah, right, but where does that leave me?"

Devereux stood, walked to the small window that overlooked the car park, and turned to face Selden. At six foot three, Devereux stood well clear of Selden's five foot nine, but with Selden seated in the chair, and Devereux's blonde hair, highlighted by the fluorescent lighting in the room adding a rugged Nordic look to the man, he appeared much taller to Selden, far more imposing.

"You, Johnny? You don't think I'd desert my old mate, do you?"

"Er, well, what do you…?"

"You're moving in with me tomorrow, Johnny boy. Whoever this crazy bastard is, he'll find it a damn sight harder to get to either of us if we're both together. He can't get to us while we're at work, we're both business-men, so if we stick together like glue outside of working hours, we should be safe, and if he dares try to come near either of us, the bodyguards will have him for sure."

"But Lucas, we can't stay together like that for the rest of our lives, man. It's okay for you. You've got people around you all day. As for being businessmen, you've got this place plus your council work. Me? Some busi-nessman, with a massive fleet of two ice cream vans. I don't think *Mr. Speedy Cream* ranks anywhere near your bloody business empire, do you? Plus, I'm on the road nearly all day. I'm fucking easy prey out there on my own. We've got to hope the cops find out who it is and arrests them before he can get to us."

"Johnny, what did I tell you? We can't tell the cops a thing without incriminating ourselves. We have to handle this on our own."

"But, how can we stop whoever it is?"

"By setting a trap and catching the bastard ourselves and then making sure he never lives to tell the tale."

"You mean, kill him?"

"It's kill or be killed now, Johnny. The cops seem to think there might be two killers working together according to the press, so we might have two to dispose of. Look, if you're that nervous, go home now, pack a bag and come back to my place tonight. We'll talk strategy and work out how we're going to sort this out when the bastard decides to make a move. It's bloody obvious he, or they, want to get to me before you, so they can screw up my election campaign."

John Selden felt that Devereux's plan, if it could even be called a plan, had more holes in it than a leaky colander, but for the time being, he could think of nothing better. Lucas had always been the brains of their group, his own work as an ice cream salesman often helping by allowing him to trawl the streets and often identify potential targets for their attacks, but Selden himself had never been a decision maker. That had always been Luke's domain. He knew his limitations, and saw himself as a faithful lieu-tenant, able to organise the two younger men at Luke's direction as and when they needed to get together for a new 'mission' as Luke always called their attacks on their unsuspecting victims.

* * *

With new-found confidence, Vera Manvers made a phone call, and after five minutes talking to her murderous partner, she felt the thrill and exhilaration of the next kill beginning to course through her veins.

"We need to move quickly, Vera," he said. He'd got used to always addressing her by the Vera Manvers name, giving him less chance of any slip ups if he revealed her true identity. "That bastard, Devereux, he really thinks he's going to win a seat in the House of Commons. If only the people in his party and all his supporters knew what he'd done, they'd want to crucify him. I'd almost like to see him live, go to jail and let the prisoners inside subject him to the type of homosexual gang rape his pretty boy looks would attract, but once they knew he's a multiple rapist, I think they'd just do him in anyway, so I'd rather we had the pleasure of that little task."

"Yes," said Vera, "and anyway, we can still give him a real pain in the arse before we slit his throat, if you know what I mean."

The laughter that erupted from the other end of the line made Vera hold the phone away from her ear for a second until it subsided.

"Why, Vera Manvers," the man said at length, "I do believe you're suggesting a little sadistic pleasure wouldn't go amiss in dealing with Mr. Lucas Devereux.

"How did you guess?" she grinned as she spoke. "Was it something I said?" and the two of them collapsed into a short, joint paroxysm of laughter.

* * *

Neither of them could be bothered to cook, so Andy and Maria Ross settled for a Cantonese banquet meal from their local Chinese Takeaway, while Izzie Drake and Peter Foster decided against visiting the cinema to see Toby McGuire starring in Spider Man, and enjoyed an evening of steamy sex at Foster's flat instead.

As the opening credits of *Coronation Street* rolled on the television in the home of P.L.O. George Thompson, his wife's attention riveted to the screen, Thompson instead sat making notes in preparation for his new press release as requested by Ross.

The lights in the office of A. J. Devereux & Son finally went off around the time the credits of *'The Street'* faded and Lucas Devereux stepped from the now darkened building, walking briskly across the car park to the space reserved for his sleek, black, classic, Jaguar XJ6. He'd sent Johnny Selden home a half hour earlier, and arranged to meet up with him at his city flat, overlooking Albert Dock, a little after eight.

With none of the other businesses on the estate working at night, the car park possessed a slightly eerie, ghost-like quality as the mist of another damp evening rolled in from the Irish Sea and up the Mersey Channel.

426

Devereux shivered involuntarily and hurried to his car, which started first time, as always, and he quickly reached behind him and grabbed hold of the seat belt, pulling it forwards and clipping it into place.

As he reached the wide, double-gated entrance to the industrial estate, ready to pull out onto the encircling estate road which then led to the main road out of Garston, he checked in both directions, and seeing the road clear both ways, began to edge out onto the road. It was at that moment that Lucas Devereux felt the force of a rear-end collision that pitched him forward and just as quickly, back again as his seat belt did its job. Cursing, he looked in the rear view mirror, to see the front of a large white van which must have followed him from the car park. The driver, probably half asleep, had shunted his van smack into the gleaming rear of Devereux's pride and joy, and anger overtook his other emotions as he almost flung himself from the car and ran to the rear to assess the damage.

"What the hell were you doing?" he shouted in the direction of the van. "Couldn't you see me right there in front of you?"

Instead of receiving a reply, Devereux instead watched incredulously as the driver's door of the Transit van slowly opened and a pair of very shapely, totally feminine, stockinged legs appeared, followed by the rest of an extremely good looking woman, her blonde hair partially obscuring her face. Devereux's attention was totally fixed on the figure before him as she turned to face him and smiled an enigmatic, knowing smile at the exact instant a man stepped up behind Devereux and the last thing he felt before collapsing to the ground was the short, sharp jab of the hypodermic needle containing a fast acting sedative that was thrust into his neck by the man who'd crept up silently behind him from his hiding place just outside the gates, while his attention was fixed on the legs and the alluring figure of the woman from the van.

CHAPTER 31

DEVEREUX'S DEMISE

The Stygian blackness that filled the mind of Lucas Devereux slowly gave way to a feeling of general nausea and restricted movement. He felt as if he was in some kind of box, and panic gripped his fevered mind as the thought he might be in a coffin, buried alive, took hold of his thoughts, only to be dispelled a minute or two later as his senses returned sufficiently for him to ascertain that he was tied hand and foot, secured with plastic ties and his eyes, gradually focussing once more, just managed to tell him he was in a darkened room with a concrete floor on which he was lying sideways, on his right, a garage perhaps, or a warehouse of some kind? His mouth felt strange; as though his lips were prised open and he tried, but was unable to speak or scream or do anything but make strange, incoherent noises. He'd been rendered silent by a ball gag.

The realisation suddenly dawned on him that he was naked. Naked and as vulnerable as a new born baby. Waves of panic and nausea again gripped Lucas Devereux as he realised his plans for self-preservation had been laid too late. He had no doubts he was in the hands of the killer or killers of Matthew Remington and Mark Proctor. Struggling as much as he could, he attempted to free himself but quickly realised it was hopeless. Not only were his hands and feet immobilised by the plastic ties, but a long length of something, thin rope he assumed, kept him in a hog-tied position, hand behind him and legs bent backwards at a grossly uncomfortable angle.

Despite the ball gag, Lucas attempted to shout, scream, make any kind of sound to try and call for help, all to no avail. It was useless, hopeless and as the fear of his situation took hold of his almost fully conscious mind, Devereux shivered in trepidation as he thought of the press reports on the deaths of his friends. They hadn't revealed a lot, but what they had been able to report sounded horrific enough. He had to hope his quick wits and silver tongue might still find a way out of this situation. *Money, yes,* he thought. *Maybe I can buy my way out of here.*

A strange sound reached his ears. Though clearing, his mind was still slightly befuddled and he couldn't work out what it was. Then he knew. It could only be the sound of old, rusted iron gates swinging open. The metallic grating was followed by the unmistakable sound of stiletto heels tottering down the series of steps that led to his cold, grim place of incarceration.

What he couldn't see or hear were the soft, almost silent footfalls of the man in rubber boots who followed the woman down the steps. The sound of a switch being thrown followed and the room was bathed in the soft light of a single, low wattage light bulb, suspended from a fitting in the centre of the ceiling.

"Well, hello, pretty boy," the woman spoke mockingly as she walked up to and stood directly over Lucas Devereux, who tried to look up but could do more than stare at her legs and feet, no more than twelve inches from his face.

"Oh, I don't think he looks so pretty now, do you?" said the unknown man whose voice startled Lucas, who had remained unaware of his presence until that moment. "Do you feel like a pretty boy, Luke?"

"Aw, he can't speak," the woman mocked. "He's got a big red ball gag stuck in his mouth, haven't you, Luke?"

"Bet you've used a few of those in the past eh, Lukey baby?" the man added.

Lucas struggled impotently against his bonds, and then, without warning, strong hands grabbed him by the arm and leg and rolled him over. Now, Lucas could see where he was. They had brought him to a crypt, probably underground, judging from the steps, and at least two stone coffins stood before his eyes. The man now cut the rope that joined his arms and legs, and forced him into a sitting position and the fear rose in the naked man again. Resting on one of the coffins was a selection of cutting and sawing tools whose use Lucas could only imagine at, increasing his growing terror.

"We've got such plans for you, Luke," the woman said. "You're going to be so sorry for the things you've done, Lucas. We're going to make sure you go to hell before morning, but in the meantime, you're going to suffer as you've never suffered before."

A gurgling sound came from behind the ball gag, an incoherent mumbling that did no more than produce a stream of spittle that ran down Luke's chin.

"You like causing pain and fear, don't you?" the man asked, not expecting an answer of course. "We're here to show you what it's like to be on the receiving end for a change."

"Oh look, he's wriggling with excitement," Vera said, as he struggled vainly against his bonds.

"You like scaring and raping young girls and women, don't you, you piece of scum? It's your turn now," the man added.

Suddenly, the woman reached into a handbag that stood on the nearest coffin lid and lifted out a small six by four inch photograph of a young woman, little more than a girl, that she held down to Lucas's facial level.

"Remember her?"

He shook his head, vigorously.

"No, you wouldn't would you, you bastard? Too many years ago. How many have there been since then, I wonder? You ruined her life, Lucas bloody Devereux, you and your twisted little cronies. Her name was Brenda Gillespie. You gang raped her, left her for dead and never gave her another thought, you bastards. Well, she's had to live with the results of what you did to her ever since, and so have we. She was, and still is my little sister, and he," she gestured towards the man, who Lucas couldn't see properly because of the cowled hood he wore that hid most of his face, "he was going to marry her, until you bastards caused a total mental break-down that she's still living with, every day of her fucking life, living like a vegetable in a wheelchair, unable to speak, move or do anything for herself because the horror of what you did simply destroyed her. We're here to exact revenge for my sister, his fiancé, and all the other poor girls you've terrorised over the years."

Devereux knew now that he had no chance of leaving the crypt alive. All his plans, all his dreams for the future were about to end in this cold, dank place, but, he thought, *what horrors are they going to inflict on me before they let me die?*

"Scared, are you, Devereux?" the woman asked, not requiring an answer. "You should be. Remington went quickly, too quickly really, but we hadn't refined our means of disposing of you all at that point. Proctor was a little more fun. We made him wait longer for the final release of death. He screamed his lungs out, but with the gag in place, he couldn't exactly make himself heard. Of course, the papers haven't told the whole story, because the police wouldn't tell them everything. The only thing I found unsatisfying about the two of them was that it's not a lot of fun slicing off a limp, dead penis from a corpse before stuffing it down their throats."

A look of pure terror spread across Lucas Devereux's face, and without warning, he lost control of his bladder, the fear overcoming any hope he had of arresting the flow.

"Oh, what a dirty boy you are, Luke. We'll have to punish you for that as well, won't we? And don't worry, we'll find a way to make your dick stand up before we cut it off, won't we?" she asked the man who stood a few feet behind her, who simply laughed quietly and nodded his head. "Poor Brenda can't control her bladder either. She has to wear a bloody bag to catch it in. Would you like a bag, Luke?" Vera added.

Devereux shook his head vigorously, still making incoherent sounds from behind the gag. The woman stood so close in front of him, he couldn't help looking up and all he could see was her legs, slightly apart, encased in a black mini skirt, and he could see as far as her stocking tops, and he just knew she was deliberately flaunting herself before him. She suddenly walked away and the man took her place, looking down at the shivering man, whose body was now wracked with paroxysms of fear.

"You're nothing but a waste of a heart and soul, Devereux," the man said, with a voice so flat in intonation that Devereux felt his tormentor to be completely devoid of emotion, and he knew that even if he was allowed to speak, no offer of money was likely to sway him or incite him to deviate from his intentions, which Luke knew were simply to cause him as much pain as possible before ending his life.

"I'm going to take great pleasure in watching you die and sending you to Hell, where I hope Satan decides you're too evil even to dwell there, and sends you to purgatory, where what's left of your soul will be tormented by demons for eternity. Come on Vera, we've wasted enough time on this piece of scum. Let's get started."

Lucas Devereux felt himself being lifted up by his wrists and the man suddenly spun him round and then kicked him behind he knees, causing him to pitch forward and land heavily on his knees on the concrete floor.

"In case you're wondering," the man said, his voice still flat and emotionless, you're in a crypt, Lucas, a fitting place for what we intend, don't you think? The inhabitants are long dead and the family who originally owned it have long since died out, so I doubt anyone will mind us using it. If it wasn't for the gag, you could scream the place down and no one would hear you. Do you know how long you've been out? Oh, I forgot, you don't have a watch do you? We removed it with your clothes. Time has no meaning for you any more, apart from the length of time it's going to take for you to die. Clothes, watch, money, all the trappings of wealth, they've all gone now, and you won't be needing them any longer will you?"

Devereux tried his hardest to voice the word, "please" through the gag, but if the man realised what he was saying, he took no notice whatsoever.

"Let's get him up," the man said to Vera, and Devereux couldn't help looking upwards where, to his horror, he saw what had to be a newly added butcher's hook affixed to the ceiling.

The woman joined the man in forcing Devereux to take the few steps that placed him directly under the hook. The man now walked to the side of the room, and took hold of a length of rope which he quickly attached to the butcher's hook by standing on a small, two-step stepladder. Next, a pair of manacles were attached to Devereux's wrists, replacing the plastic cable ties and together, the rope threaded through them, and the man and woman hoisted the bound man up until his feet were barely touching the floor. They were ready to begin.

* * *

Two hours later, the man and woman stepped back to examine their handiwork. Lucas Devereux was still alive, but only just. Thanks to their study of various methods of torture and of prolonging the victim's life during the process, the pair had managed to inflict such pain on the now pitiful man who hung, suspended from the butcher's hook that he had reached a point where death would come as a welcome release to him. But, they hadn't finished with him yet.

His body was bleeding in multiple places, his chest, belly and back a crazy patchwork of numerous knife wounds, all painful but designed to be non-fatal. Most painful by far had been the slicing through of Devereux's Achilles tendons, leaving his feet useless, and unable to ever support his body again, even if given the opportunity. Blood pooled all around his dangling body and his earlier attempts at screaming had reduced to a series of long, pathetic and pitiful sobs, though pity was the last thing on the minds of his tormentors.

"Do you want to know what triggered all this, at this moment in time, Luke?" Vera suddenly asked. Without waiting for an answer she knew he couldn't give, she went on:

"Your mate, Remington. He couldn't stop himself could he? Wouldn't even wait for you to come up with a new target for your perverted lust, would he? When he targeted a young teenage girl who went to a local church, and she ended up having an abortion, then couldn't live with what she'd done, and she killed herself, we decided the time had come to put our plan into operation. We'd wanted to do it for years, but it had always been theoretical, and then we snapped after that young kid died, because of you, Remington and all your kind. When you're gone, it'll be Johnny's turn, but maybe we'll just sit back and watch him fall to pieces with fear, maybe turn himself in to the police to save his miserable hide, but we all know what they'd do to him in prison, don't we? I think it best if we send him on to join you and your mates in hell, don't you?"

"You're wasting your breath," the hooded man said from somewhere to the rear of Devereux. "Let's finish this."

"Right," Vera replied, as she walked across to the stone coffin and through his tear stained eyes Devereux saw her pick up a large, black sex toy. He had an idea what she intended and tried hard to shake his head in panic.

"Rape, Lukey baby, terrible thing, isn't it? Oh, sorry, I forgot, you like

432

raping young girls and women, don't you? Forcing yourself onto them, into them, violating their most private, intimate places. Ever wondered what it feels like to suffer that kind of violation? No? Well, before you die, we want you to know a little of what it fells like."

Panic gripped Lucas Devereux as Vera walked behind him, pulled his buttocks apart and despite the gag, he screamed at last as the sex toy was rammed into him, stretching and tearing as Vera laughed at his agony and torment. The man stood back, watching dispassionately until she'd had enough of the game and walked around to face the man who'd been the prime focus of her hatred for so long.

"Had enough, Luke? I'm getting tired of this now. Oh look, he's got all excited."

Lucas couldn't help it. It had been totally involuntary, but his bleeding, weakened body was actually showing signs of arousal.

"Perfect," said Vera as she moved in closer, a long gleaming surgical knife in her right hand, at the same time as the man moved behind Luke and released the ball gag allowing hours of pent up agony to escape Luke's lips in what became little more than a loud agonised gasp, which grew to a scream once again as Vera took hold of his manhood with one hand and the blade flashed once, emasculating him in one swift brutal slashing movement.

Blood seemed to flow everywhere from the gaping wound, and now, knowing their victim couldn't last much longer, the pair exchanged a look that said the time had come.

Without further hesitation, the hooded man removed another blade from a pocket in his hooded top and grabbed hold of Luke's head, pulling it back sharply, exposing his throat. One slash, and Lucas Devereux saw the blood spurting in a fierce jet from his throat as he gurgled and began to choke on his own life-blood.

Before death took him, however he had just enough life left in him to feel the final cut as his belly was opened up, and Vera herself completed the job of disembowelment.

It was over. Lucas Devereux, parliamentary election candidate, respected local businessman and rapist of at least twenty women had been sent on his final journey to the realm of the damned.

Vera and the hooded man quickly took the body down from the butcher's hook and within half an hour, the remains of Lucas Devereux were in place, draped suggestively, naked, legs apart and bent over a randomly selected tombstone in the graveyard above. Vera herself added the final touch by pushing the amputated penis of her victim into his mouth and forcing it as far as possible into his throat. It was their 'signature' after all.

CHAPTER 32

A PLACE TO DIE

The discovery of the body of Lucas Devereux was made just after seven-thirty a.m. by Tom, the husband of Iris Redding. He'd dropped his wife at the front of the manse before driving around back, parking his car and making his way towards the graveyard's tool shed, where he stored the lawn mower and other tools needed to ensure the grassed areas, graves and pathways of St. Luke's remained as pristine as possible.

Tom Redding had the presence of mind to leave the church grounds for the few minutes it took for him to walk down the lane to the nearest public call box where he dialled 999 and summoned the emergency services. He'd not wanted to upset his wife by announcing his grim discovery and making the emergency call whilst trying to answer the barrage of questions he knew he'd face from Iris and the two priests,

Fathers Byrne and Willis.

After entering through the kitchen door, he'd asked his wife to summon the priests and he'd informed them of his discovery. Father Byrne seemed to turn almost parchment-white with shock, though the younger priest, Father Willis, appeared to Tom to be made of sterner stuff, and offered to wait outside with Tom until the police arrived.

As soon as the call was made for the duty medical examiner to attend the scene, Doctor Vicky Strauss faced a minor dilemma. The newest member of Dr. William Nugent's team, twenty-eight year old Vicky was due to finish her tour of duty at eight a.m. Her watch read seven forty, and she knew Nugent would be arriving in the next ten to fifteen minutes and would want to attend the scene, having responded to the earlier churchyard murders, but she was equally aware the police would want an immediate response from their department. Vicky gathered her bag, and on her way out, left a message for Nugent with Peter Foster, who'd just arrived to begin his day shift. She had no doubt Nugent would arrive on the scene within a few minutes of her own arrival, but guessed correctly that a prompt response was not only necessary but vital. As she climbed into her car and pulled away from the car park, she couldn't have been aware just how vital!

Mere minutes after arriving at headquarters, Ross was informed by D.C.I. Porteous of the latest murder. He'd only just reached his office and certainly hadn't been prepared for another gruesome killing to be dropped in his lap this morning.

"St. Luke's, at Woolton?"

Ross could scarcely believe it.

"Exactly," said Porteous. "Home of your friend, Father Gerald Byrne, no less."

"Oh, shit," was all Ross could say, but Porteous wasn't finished.

"It gets worse, Andy. The two uniforms who responded both recognised the victim as soon as they saw him. It's Lucas Devereux."

"The councillor?"

"Councillor and would-be local Member of Parliament. Let's not waste time. I saw Drake getting out of her car from my window. She'll doubtless be here any second. You and she get over there as fast as you can. I'll deal with things here."

"Right sir. The team…"

"I'll see to things here. Who do you want to join you over there?"

"Thanks sir. Send Gable and McLennan. He might throw up but he's a good detective. Any more is useless based on the lack of evidence at previous crime scenes. Can you send Curtis and Dodds to check out Devereux's home? I remember reading somewhere that he was single and never married."

"I'll see to it, and arrange a few uniforms to join you to conduct house-to-house inquiries and ensure the crime scene remains secure. You do realise this one is going to pull a whole load of heat down on us, don't you, Andy?"

"Yes, sir, but not as much heat as when we reveal Devereux was part of a rape gang who've escaped detection for years. We just found out the first names of the last member yesterday, and we just needed a surname. I think our killers have given it to us. The name we got was Luke, and I'll bet my pension that Lucas Devereux was known as Luke to his pals."

Drake walked in at that moment and before Porteous could say another word, Ross took her by the arm, turned her round and marched her right back out of the squad room.

"Don't ask," he said in reply to her look of shock. "I'll explain on the way."

* * *

Doctor Vicky Strauss had just conducted a preliminary examination of the body. Miles Booker's Crime Scene Unit was on the scene and Andy Ross and Izzie Drake arrived just ahead of the car containing William Nugent and Francis Lees.

The new arrivals quickly made their way to the grave where Devereux's remains were still displayed somewhat lewdly in the position he'd been found by Tom Redding.

"Fucking hell!" Ross was appalled at the sight.

"Look at the number of wounds, sir," Drake said, as yet only able to see the rear of the corpse, and still to be further shocked when she took in the frontal view.

"Inspector Ross," Strauss approached the detectives quickly, "Vicky Strauss, duty Medical Examiner."

"Hello Doctor," Ross replied. "I kind of expected Dr. Nugent to be here, somehow."

"And so I am, Laddie," came a booming voice from behind him, as William Nugent and his assistant Lees came thundering down the path towards them.

"What do we have, Victoria?" said the pathologist, ignoring the detectives at that point.

"Well, Doctor," she began. "The body was clearly dumped here. There's not enough blood present for this to be the site of the murder."

"But hang on," Ross interrupted. "The previous killings all took place in the churchyards."

"Aye, well, Victoria here says otherwise and that'll do for me."

"She's right, sir," said Miles Booker as he joined the small but growing gathering. "He's been carefully placed in that position, quite deliberately, I'd say, to make a point, or to tell us something."

"I'd agree with your last point, definitely, Miles," Ross answered as he moved closer to get a better look at the corpse. Nugent and Strauss closed in on the scene at the same time, while Izzie Drake swerved off to one side to quickly search the immediate surrounding area for any clues or trace evidence.

Despite having been witness to the appalling cruelty inflicted on the previous two victims, Ross couldn't help but feel the killers had taken things a step further with the murder of Lucas Devereux. Even at this early stage, he could see there were differences between this and the previous killings.

This was confirmed soon afterwards when Christine Bland arrived in the company of Sam Gable and Derek McLennan, the profiler having just arrived at headquarters as they were leaving to join Ross and Drake, and thereby hitching a ride to the scene with them.

"I think they're devolving," she said quietly to Ross after taking in the scene, and walking around the body which was still being scrutinised by both pathologists and Miles Booker, the senior Scenes of Crimes officer. They had raised the body sufficiently to make a quick examination of the front of Devereux's remains, and had been horrified at the proliferation of wounds present.

"Devolving?" a puzzled Ross repeated the word.

"Yes, it's a word they use a lot in the States. Basically it means our killers are now so caught up in their bloodlust that they're beginning to take risks, becoming sloppy. Whereas the first two murders gave the impression of meticulous and orderly planning, everything here hints at a level of sadism not displayed in the first two kills, and the complete change in methodology makes me believe they're essentially heading down a path of eventual self-destruction."

"Do you mean you think they're suicidal?"

"No, I'm sorry if I gave that impression. What I meant was they are now not doing things as carefully as before. Look at the facts. Previously, they left no trace evidence, and before you say you haven't found any here yet, I think you will do. The wounds on the body indicate not only a degree of sadism and, dare I say it, torture, over a period of time, and the fact that the murder took place not here in the graveyard, but elsewhere marks a distinct change in their method. There's a glaring indicator here that we're most definitely dealing with two very different personalities."

"Please, go on. What do you mean by that last remark?"

"It's like a pendulum has swung from one side to the other," she said. "Previously, I think the dominant one in this partnership, who I've always believed to be the male, was in charge, keeping them on track according to some well laid plan. This time, I think the woman somehow imposed herself on this murder and wrested control from the man, who was quite probably appalled at the way she carried out Devereux's torture and eventual murder."

"Why would he be appalled?" Ross asked. "He's already killed twice and was obviously intending that Devereux should die anyway."

"Ah yes," said Bland, "but I don't think he intended things to go this far. Did you see the damage around the man's anus?"

"Hard to miss, really," said Ross disgustedly.

"I think you'll find that was done by the woman and that could be their first big mistake."

"How so?" Ross was intrigued now.

"Because I now believe with a degree of certainty that the woman is taking a form of revenge for a very personal reason. Either she, or another female, very close to her, was the victim of an attack by your team of rapists, Inspector. It may be a daughter, a sister, maybe even a mother, but your answer lies in a previous and possibly unprosecuted rape from the past."

"Wow, that's a lot to glean from a quick glance at the scene," said Ross.

"It's my job, remember," Bland replied.

"I hope you're right, about them devolving," said Ross as he heard the voice of Izzie Drake calling to him. Looking up, he saw her standing about thirty yards away, next to an old, grotesque looking mausoleum, a crypt of some kind that looked to be as old as the church itself.

Ross summoned Sam Gable and Derek McLennan to join him. This time, McLennan had managed to control his stomach and felt rather proud of himself for not being sick at the scene.

Izzie Drake, standing close to the old crypt, waited until the three others joined her and then, without wasting a second, pointed to the old padlock on the iron gates to the crypt.

"Sir, you have to look closely, but if you get up close, you can see that this old padlock has been sawn through. It would have needed a damn good hacksaw or something similar to cut through the hasp on the old padlock, and whoever did it needed time to tackle the job. And that's not all," she said, as she bent close to the ground in the slightly overgrown grass that had sprouted up around the walls of the old crypt.

"Oh, my god, is that what I think it is?" Sam Gable asked, turning a little green at the gills as she and the others bent down to examine what Drake had indicated.

"A piece of intestine, I think, yes," said Drake as Ross waved across the graveyard for Miles Booker to join them.

"You might want to bring a couple of your team over here, Miles," said Ross as Booker carried out a tentative examination of the padlock and the small but significant piece of human remains that lay in the grass beside the entrance to the crypt.

The iron gates creaked ominously, like the entrance to the gates of hell, or maybe Castle Dracula, Derek McLennan thought. In the gloom that lay within the entrance to the crypt, Booker turned on a powerful halogen-beamed torch that instantly illuminated their surroundings. Five steps led down into the depths of the crypt, and before taking even one step into the darkness below they all smelled it, the sweet, cloying, coppery smell of blood, and Derek McLennan prayed he wouldn't let himself down by throwing up yet again.

"Oh, shit, in the name of God, look at this place," said Booker as his torch beam swung around the main body of the crypt.

The detectives stood, staring incredulously as the scene played out in the light of the torch, like a surreal and horrific old-fashioned flickering silent movie, although this one was in full colour and accompanied by the stench of death.

"Wait," said Ross as the torchlight indicated a light switch on the wall at the bottom of the old concrete steps. He quickly flicked the switch, and the crypt was illuminated by the glow from the single overhead bulb in addition to the swaying beam of Booker's torch, which he kept switched on in order to highlight the scene as they knew they were literally walking in a sea of evidence.

Derek McLennan threw a hand over his mouth as he gagged at the sight that assaulted their eyes. Ross heard the sounds emanating from Derek's throat and shouted, "Outside, Derek, right now."

McLennan turned and ran up the steps and out into the daylight, where somehow, he managed to control the gag reflex and much to his surprise, his breakfast remained in place in his stomach. Of course, he knew the boss had sent him out not just for his own benefit, but because he feared McLennan would contaminate what was now clearly the scene of Devereux's murder down there in the depths of someone's family mausoleum.

* * *

The floor of the crypt resembled that of a nineteenth century slaughterhouse. The blood from the multiple wounds inflicted on Lucas Devereux's body had stained the concrete floor a deep, dark red. The walls literally dripped with blood spatter, presumably, Ross thought, from the cutting of the man's throat, with a massive stain spreading from a lump of tissue on the floor, a large part of the man's intestines, the rest having been left attached to the corpse. The smell was terrible and it was all those present could do to prevent themselves joining Derek McLennan outside in the fresh air. Ross's eyes, and those of Drake and Booker, were drawn inexorably to the butcher's hook dangling from the ceiling. They could only imagine the suffering that must have been inflicted on Devereux as he hung from that vicious looking hook.

Sam Gable was busily taking notes, writing down the tiniest detail of everything she saw in that terrible place. It came to Ross that the fervent scratching of her pen of the paper on her notepad was probably her way of tuning out a little from the horrific sights and smells of the crypt.

"They didn't find this place by accident," Ross observed, after taking a few seconds to gather his thoughts.

"You're right," said Miles Booker. "That hook wasn't part of the original design of the crypt, that's for sure. It looks new. Someone planned this well. They were ready for him. This was their combined bloody torture and execution chamber."

Booker's two crime scene technicians were by now busily photographing the room from every angle and noting down measurements of every splash of blood, and much more.

"What about the light switch, sir?" said Drake. "Surely crypts weren't built with electric light built-in whenever this one was built."

"Not originally, but the last burial interred in here was fifteen years ago, I looked before we entered," said Booker. "It's possible the family arranged it for some reason. The switch and wiring look old enough."

"But the point remains, someone knew about this place, and I want to know who," said Ross. "I'll leave you and your lads to examine this place while we go and have a word or two with Father Byrne."

"Thanks for nothing," Booker grimaced at Ross.

"Any time, Miles," he smiled a wry smile at the Crime Scenes boss before leading Izzie out of the room of death.

CHAPTER 33

OVERKILL

"Something's not right with this one," Ross spoke quietly. "It just doesn't stack up. Don't ask me why, but I think the killers have slipped up and we just need to work out how and where."

"Your instincts are usually on the button, sir," Drake acknowledged. "What are you thinking?"

"So far, the killers have been meticulous in their planning, leaving nothing to chance. This is so sloppy, there's a sense of overkill about it. I think we're going to end up with more clues than we've had previously. It's as if they want to be caught, as if they're challenging us to work it out."

"But if what the landlord at *The Belerophon* told Curtis is correct, there's still the matter of the one called John to account for," said Drake with a slight look of puzzlement on her face.

"Maybe he's not as important to them as Devereux."

"Or maybe they knew Devereux would be harder to get to if he won a seat in parliament," Drake hypothesised.

"A very good point, Izzie," Ross agreed. "Tell you what, Izzie," Ross said in a quick change of mind, "while we go and have another chat with the pathologists up top, send Sam and Derek to begin talking to the priests and Mr. and Mrs. Redding. Make sure they talk to them one at a time. We'll catch up to them as soon as we're finished out here."

Drake left the crypt, leaving Ross, Booker and his technicians in the bone-chilling atmosphere of the murder site.

* * *

"Just awful," Nugent concluded after Ross questioned him and tried to pin him down to a preliminary determination of cause of death.

"You can't be more precise?" Ross pressed the pathologist.

"Inspector, I doubt we'll be able to be more precise even once we get the remains back to the mortuary. The wound to the neck and the one to the abdomen would both have been sufficient to cause almost instantaneous death, and it will be almost impossible to determine which came first."

"Either way, you're looking at two very sick killers," Vicky Strauss added from her place, kneeling on the ground beside the corpse, which had by now been removed from its previous obscenely grotesque position and was now laid respectfully on a black groundsheet, ready to be transferred to a body bag for transportation to the mortuary. Strauss was cataloguing the most serious injuries, as Francis Lees' camera continued to click away in the background as he photographed not only the corpse, but every inch of the scene around the grave where it had been deposited.

"We know that, already, Doctor Strauss," Ross replied, and then asked, "Any particular reason why you should say that, bearing that in mind?"

"Most of the injuries are superficial, designed to cause pain without being lethal," Strauss said. "But, as far as I'm aware, a lot of the injuries inflicted on your previous victims were inflicted post-mortem, right?"

"That's correct. So you're saying there's a significant difference here?"

"I believe so, Inspector. We should be able to determine it for sure at autopsy, and there's one other thing."

"Go on, what it is it?"

William Nugent took up the story from his junior doctor.

"The first two victims, they had their manhood cut off post-mortem before having them stuffed in their mouths. Victoria found something disturbing in this case."

Drake looked horrified as she asked, "You don't mean they…"

"Yes, they did," Nugent replied. "They must have somehow made sure Devereux was sexually turned on before they cut his penis off, Sergeant Drake."

"You can tell that from looking at it?"

"Of course we can. It's still erect, exactly as it was when they sliced it from his living, breathing body."

Drake almost turned green at the pathologist's revelation.

"They really wanted to make the poor bastard suffer, for sure," Ross said.

* * *

Devereux's body had been sealed in a body bag and removed to the mortuary by the time Ross and Drake walked the short distance to the house where Sam Gable and Derek McLennan had begun interviewing Fathers Byrne and Willis and the housekeeper and her husband.

Miles Booker's forensic team were going over the entire scene, above and below ground in a meticulous search for the smallest piece of trace evidence that could assist the investigation, while the uniformed officers promised by D.C.I. Porteous had arrived and been sent to conduct house-to-house inquiries in the area, though Ross held out little hope they'd discover anything of use.

It lurked in the back of Ross's mind that in some way, the killings were inextricably linked either to the recent arrival of Father Gerald Byrne, who never seemed far from the hub of the investigation, or to Byrne's time at Speke Hill so many years before and yet, he found it difficult to believe a direct involvement by Byrne in the horrendous series of murders. Though not an overly religious man, Andy Ross just couldn't imagine Byrne as a killer.

Meanwhile, back at headquarters, based on a vague suspicion voiced to him by Tony Curtis after his and Derek McLennan's interview the previous day, Paul Ferris and his trusty computer were on the verge of the break-through Ross had been waiting for. For now though, he was speculating, and it would take a little time to turn that speculation into facts that the inspector could use to his advantage in tracking the killers of three men.

CHAPTER 34

BEGINNING OF THE END

"Are you absolutely sure about this?" D.C. Tony Curtis could hardly contain his excitement as he read the information that Paul Ferris had just printed out.

"Of course I'm sure," Ferris replied. "Looks like you and Derek were bang on in your estimation of the Manvers woman. Nothing about her adds up at all. She's what I'd call a real enigma."

"Great," said Curtis. "This stuff is like dynamite. The boss was wrong about her motives, obviously, but he was right to be suspicious of her. You don't think he'll be mad at me and Derek for proving him wrong do you?"

"Don't be bloody stupid, Tony. If it helps the case move closer to a solution, he'll be over the bloody moon and might even recommend the pair of you for a commendation."

"You think so?"

"Well, that's maybe going a bit too far, but he'll be bloody pleased with you both, that's a certainty."

"Talk me through it one more time, Paul. Save me having to read it all again. Then I'd better call the boss."

Ferris did as Curtis asked.

Meanwhile, Ross had moved on to interviewing the residents at St. Luke's. Gable and McLennan had done well but hadn't got as far as talking to the priests yet. He'd read through Gable's notes following her talk with Iris Redding and McLennan's account of Tom Redding's rendering of his discovery of the body. While husband and wife were helpful and cooperative, neither statement threw much light on the case. Neither of them spent

444

their nights at the manse and could throw no light on how or why Devereux came to be found in the crypt. Tom Redding's statement only contained one piece of useful information. Father Byrne's predecessor, the late Father O'Hanlon, had once informed Tom that he'd installed the lighting in 'the old Greasby crypt' as he'd described it with the permission of the family's executors after the passing of the last member of the family. It appeared the crypt was the oldest of its kind in St. Luke's graveyard, and the best preserved too. With over twenty members of the Greasby family interred there, Father O'Hanlon wanted to carry out a personal investigation into the history of what he'd told Tom were an 'ordinary everyday merchant class' Liverpool family. According to O'Hanlon, the family were pretty much just a step above working class, and by no means wealthy, but their faith in God and the Church had been an example to others over the years. There were many old Latin inscriptions on the walls of the crypt itself as well as on the sides and tops of the stone coffins interred within the underground family vault. With no natural light present down there, O'Hanlon would have struggled, even with a torch, to make out some of the oldest, faded inscriptions, with which he hoped to assemble a chronicle of the family's faith and devotion through the generations. By so doing, he'd informed Tom as the gardener was working the grounds around the crypt one day; he hoped to bring some of the Greasby family values to his current day parishioners and congregation. Sadly, Tom had said in his statement, the old priest died before he could complete his task. At least, Ross thought, the mystery of the electric light in the crypt had been satisfactorily explained.

Ross and Drake were jointly interviewing Father Byrne. The man was a definite enigma. *What the hell is his connection to the murders?* Ross wondered for about the hundredth time.

"Father Byrne, don't you find it rather coincidental that you, or your name at least, appears to rise to the surface every time one of these murders takes place?" Ross asked the priest, whose face betrayed nothing but sadness and shock at what had taken place in his own churchyard, so close to his own home.

"I admit it's all rather suggestive, Inspector Ross, but, truthfully, I cannot say just why these terrible murders have begun since my return to Liverpool, or why I seem to be getting dragged into your investigation somehow. I hope you're not suggesting I may have some connection to these terrible crimes?"

"I'm suggesting nothing, Father, but I'm not a great believer in coincidences, and there do seem to be rather a lot of them springing up around your name, don't you think?"

"I'm sorry, Inspector. In this case I believe the thinking part of it is all down to you. I can offer no satisfactory explanation other than that of the one thing you appear to reject, and that is a terrible liturgy of awful coincidences. I'm shocked and appalled at what's taken place here at St. Luke's. Why my church was chosen, I really don't know."

"Oh, we can at least give you an answer to that one, Father," said Drake.

"You can, Sergeant?"

"Yes. Apparently it may be linked to a prayer."

"A prayer? But in the name of God, how?"

Drake began slowly reciting, "Matthew, Mark, Luke and John…"

Byrne took up the words, "Bless the bed that I lie on. Yes, it's an old, simple children's prayer, but what the heck has it do with these horrendous murders?"

Drake explained how the landlord at *The Belerophon* had used the four apostles names to describe the four men they assumed to be the targets of the killers. That being the case, it seemed logical that in some twisted way, the killers also thought of them in that way and were using churches bearing the men's own names as killing grounds for their victims.

"But, the man out there was Lucas, you said, not Luke," said Byrne.

"But he was apparently known as Luke to his friends, Father," Ross enlightened the priest.

"Oh, I see. So, what happens now, Inspector?"

At that point in the interview, Ross's mobile phone began to ring.

Excusing himself, Ross stood up and walked across to stand near the window, looking out onto the well-tended garden beyond the glass.

"Ross," he said into the phone, irritation in his voice at being interrupted.

"It's Curtis, sir," the voice that spoke replied.

"This had better be important," Ross said.

"Oh, I think it is, sir. It's about the Manvers woman."

"Go on then, Curtis, and make it quick."

"She's a fake sir. Vera Manvers, the real one, died as a baby in a house fire years ago, and she was the only Vera Manvers born in Liverpool in the last hundred years according to Ferris, who's looked it up. Anyway, sir, our Vera Manvers suddenly appeared about five years ago, and Ferris has traced a deed poll document which shows her birth name to have been Ruth Gillespie."

"You've got my full attention, Tony. Keep going, lad."

"Well, sir, I just can't see how she got the job at Speke Hill, because she doesn't appear to have any previous work records that we can locate, even as Ruth Gillespie."

"Okay, Tony, this is all very interesting and I must admit, a little suspicious, but I can sense you're holding something back. You and Derek have managed to connect her to the case, haven't you?"

"To be fair sir, it's more thanks to Paul Ferris's digging around in the records. Fifteen years ago, a young girl by the name of Brenda Gillespie

446

was gang raped while walking home one night with her boyfriend. She was later able to identify the boyfriend as being one of her attackers. His name was Matthew Remington."

"Bloody hell. Go on, Curtis, go on."

"Right sir. The problem arose because she reported the rape, accused Remington, but he produced a string of witnesses that said he was nowhere near the place she was raped that night. He apparently admitted taking her out that night, but said he'd dropped her at home an hour before the attack and at the time she was assaulted, he claimed to have been in a card game with a group of others who all gave him a solid alibi. He alleged she must have been so traumatised by the attack that she got confused and accused him by mistake. The police investigated thoroughly at the time, but there were no witnesses to the rape, no forensics to tie Remington to the attack and no reasons to disbelieve the men who gave him his alibi, even though there's a note on file that the senior investigating officer, a D.I. Spencer, strongly suspected the men who'd provided the alibi, who just happen to have been Mark Proctor, Lucas Devereux and a John Selden could easily have been the other three rapists, but Brenda Gillespie never saw their faces, as the three unknowns wore masks, and before the investigation could be concluded, she suffered a total mental breakdown and had to be admitted to a sanatorium of some kind, a specialist place where they treat long-term patients. The name of the institution isn't mentioned in the report, I'm afraid. I can't say for sure sir, because the case was closed due to lack of evidence, but she's probably still there if she's still alive. The thing is, she had a sister, sir."

"Don't tell me, Tony, let me guess, Ruth Gillespie?"

"Got it in one sir."

Ross fell silent for a second as he quickly processed Curtis's information. If nothing else, he now knew they had the name of one of the killers, and also of John Selden who without a doubt had to be the fourth man on Manvers and her partner's death list.

"Revenge, Tony, that's what this has always been about. I was wrong. I thought she was protecting Proctor and Remington out of some warped sense of loyalty to Speke Hill, but she used the place to access the records and managed to identify the other three rapists. The police at the time of the attack certainly wouldn't have released their names to her, they were in effect nothing more than witnesses to Remington's alibi, so she must have worked out, somehow, that the other rapists would be found amongst Remington's circle of friends. That can't have taken her forever, so she must have waited years before something set her off on the killing spree. Maybe it was her idea to start killing them now, or maybe it was the man's. She turned herself into a private investigator in order to identify and track them down. She didn't want us finding out the names of Devereux and the last man, whoever John is, before she got to them. We have to find this John Selden, and fast."

"Agreed, sir. What about Manvers? Do you want me to pick her up, sir?"

"Yes, I do, but take Paul Ferris with you. Don't forget, there's a man involved in this too. I don't want you walking into a situation where he might be with Manvers and you end up in any danger from the pair of them. God knows what they might do if they feel cornered. Dodds can check out Devereux's house with a couple of uniforms for company. I doubt they'll find anything of value and it's probably locked up but tell him to make a thorough external search and of course, if a door should have been accidentally left unlocked…"

Ross let his last words hang in the air.

Curtis acknowledged his instructions before going to find Nick Dodds to inform him of the change in plans,

"Right, sir. Consider us on our way."

"Curtis," Ross said with caution evident in his voice.

"Sir?"

"Be careful. Listen, take no chances. Go and tell D.C.I. Porteous your findings and ask him to send a couple of patrol cars along as back up when you and Ferris go to make the arrest. Also, with all the pressure we're likely to get on this latest killing, the boss should have no trouble getting a search warrant before you leave. Tell him we need the warrant to cover Vera's home and place of work. The uniforms can help with the search, and I'll ask Miles Booker to get a couple of crime scene techs to meet you at the house. She'll be at work by now I think so go there first and let Booker know when you're heading to the house, so the C.S. guys aren't hanging around waiting for you. I'd rather be with you, but I need to talk to the priests here at St. Luke's first. I'm sending D.C.'s Gable.and McLennan to meet you there as well. Don't make a move on Manvers until they get there, understood?"

"Understood sir."

"And Curtis?"

"Yes, sir?"

"Great work lad, you and Ferris."

"Thanks, sir. Don't forget, Derek was with me yesterday too."

"Of course. I'll make sure he's aware of what's happening before he leaves here with Sam. Make sure you do everything by the book when you pick her up, and keep her isolated in an interview room until we can question her."

"Okay and thanks again, sir," said Curtis, ending the call and allowing Ross to turn and fill Izzie Drake in on the call.

CHAPTER 35

HOME FROM HOME?

Detective Constable Nick Dodds, accompanied by two uniformed constables, arrived at the home of Lucas Devereux within an hour of the discovery of the body in the graveyard.

Constables Flynn and Davis were both experienced officers and Dodds felt he could rely on them to back him up in case of unforeseen problems, though he doubted they'd encounter any. He knew the dead man had been single and lived alone, so he expected the search to be nothing more than routine. In the back of his mind, however, lurked the thought that no one had told him where Devereux had been abducted from, so there was a chance he could have been taken from home, in which case, there just might be evidence at the house that would prove important. Having informed Flynn and Davis of such a possibility he decided to take the front door himself, while the two uniforms were sent round to the rear of the house, along the narrow path that ran along one side of the property.

Dodds knocked on the front door, first using his clenched fist and then, receiving no reply, by use of the heavy brass door knocker in the upper centre of the door. Continuing to receive no reply, Dodds tried the brass door handle, situated just above a keyhole. The door was securely locked. Looking up, Dodds saw a small sensor situated in the corner of the door frame, obviously part of Devereux's alarm system. Any attempt to force entry through the front door would doubtless trigger the alarm. Not knowing if it was a silent or audible alarm, Dodds decided against trying to force an entry, for fear of setting off an incessant loud alarm that might attract any number of inquisitive neighbours.

He moved to one side and, placing his hands either side of his head to obliterate glare and reflection, peered through a large bay window into what appeared to be the lounge of Devereux's home. He could make out a large television set in the far right corner of the room, a leather three-piece suite with chesterfield-style sofa, a glass topped coffee table and a tall, expensive looking hi-fi system in the opposite corner of the room. An ornate fireplace stood out from the chimney breast in between the TV and the hi-fi unit, the mantle-piece bearing a couple of framed photographs and a large anniversary clock, the balls gently twisting back and forth, oblivious of the passage of time. Nothing appeared out of place. If there had been an altercation in the house leading up to Devereux's abduction, he was fairly certain it hadn't taken place in the room he was looking into, unless Devereux had been taken by total surprise, maybe even held at gunpoint before being taken from his home, but that could mean the dead man may have let his killers in through the front door, also leading to the possibility he knew his killers and unsuspectingly let them in to his home. Nobody knew the facts of Devereux's abduction thus far and Dodds' scenario did at least fit the facts as far as he was aware at that point.

Suddenly, however, he was jolted from his thoughts and his viewing through the window by a shout that came from the rear of the house.

"Oy, you, come here you bastard," Constable Flynn shouted, followed by the voice of P.C. Davis as he joined in with a shouted warning. "Coming down the path, Nick."

Dodds quickly took three steps to his left, just in time to see a dishevelled, unkempt looking man running towards him along the path at the side of the house.

"Police, stop!" he shouted, only to be knocked to the ground by the outstretched arm of the man as he bundled his way past and onto the grassed lawn, heading for the front gate, hotly pursued by the two uniformed constables.

"I'm okay, go get him," Dodds called to the two constables as they hesitated, in case he'd been hurt.

Flynn and Davis were younger and fitter than the fleeing man, and before he managed to make it through the front gate, they were on him, an expertly timed rugby tackle by Flynn bringing him down, after which Davis quickly pinned him to the ground, wrenching the man's arms behind him and slapping the handcuffs on his wrists.

Dodds picked himself up, quickly dusted himself down and walked across to where Flynn and Davis had pulled the man to his feet, and now held him by an arm apiece as he glared from one to the other malevolently.

"Right, you," Dodds spoke with authority. "What the fuck are you doing here, on private property? And why did you run away when the constables found you?"

"They took me by surprise," the man replied. "I thought they was goin' to hurt me, like."

"And why would they do that? They're in uniform. Couldn't you see that?"

"I never took the time to stop and look, mate, honest. I was scared and just ran for it."

Dodds turned to P.C. Flynn.

"Where was he, Mike?"

"He was holed up behind the shed, Nick. As we walked round the back, he just legged it before we could say a word. Looked like the hounds of hell were on his tail."

"Right, sunshine," Dodds spoke firmly to the scruffy looking man.

"You'd better tell me what you're so afraid of and why you're hanging around in Mr. Devereux's back garden."

"I was supposed to meet Luke here last night," the man began. "I saw him at his office and he told me to go home, get some things and come and spend the night here with him, but when he never showed up, I was too scared to go home. I hope nothing's happened to him, has it?

He's not been home all night so I ended up sheltering behind the shed where no-one could see me."

Saying nothing about Devereux's murder, Dodds simply replied,

"I see, and just what is it you're so afraid of, Mr…?"

"Selden, John Selden," the man replied, and all became clear to Nick Dodds.

"Right, Mr. Selden," he said, "I think you'd better come along with us. We've some questions for you to answer and once you've warmed up and had a hot cup of tea, you're going to give us some answers, you got that?"

John Selden silently nodded his head, and as he was marched to the patrol car by the two constables, Dodds saw the man's shoulders visibly sag as if his body was acknowledging the fact he'd reached the end of the road.

As they drove back to headquarters, P.C. Davis sitting in the rear of the patrol car with Selden, Nick Dodds knew without a shadow of doubt that D.I. Ross would be eager to question the man who sat, his face a mask of fear in the back seat, staring vacantly at nothing in particular.

CHAPTER 36

ARREST

As the handcuffs snapped shut on the wrists of John Selden, a few short miles away Tony Curtis and Derek McLennan strode into the office of Vera Manvers at Speke Hill. Both officers did a quick double-take as they tried to reconcile the dowdy, matron-like woman who sat behind the secretary's desk with the vampish and sexually attractive woman they'd spoken to in her home the previous day. This Vera Manvers, with her hair scraped back, wearing a high-neck yellow sweater and long brown skirt and with nothing but a little eye shadow in terms of make-up, and reading glasses hanging from a chain round her neck could have passed as a totally different woman. The two men looked at one another before Vera herself broke the deadlock of silence.

"Good morning, detectives. You look shocked. Is it my appearance? Surely you wouldn't expect me to arrive for work in my 'off duty' clothes would you?" she smiled.

"Ms Manvers, hello," said Curtis. "Yes, I must say you do look rather different."

"Very different, in fact," said McLennan.

"Well, now that my appearance has been sorted out between you, perhaps you can tell me what I can do for you."

"Yes, Ms Manvers, or should we say Miss Ruth Gillespie? You can accompany us to police headquarters where we need to ask you some questions on an extremely serious matter."

Vera's face fell. The shocked look told the two detectives immediately that they were facing a guilty woman. If she could have turned and run away at that moment, they were both certain she would have done just that. Trapped as she was, behind her desk in the small office, there was nowhere to run. Having thought she'd outwitted the two officers the previous day, she now realised she was cornered. Somehow, they'd worked it out, or at least, some of it. She'd need to be very careful, and try to find out just how much they knew.

"Am I under arrest?" Vera asked with a faint tremor in her voice.

"I'm afraid so," said McLennan and D.C. Curtis proceeded to read Vera Manvers/Ruth Gillespie the standard police caution as McLennan helped her to her feet before snapping the handcuffs in place.

As the two men led Vera from the office, Charles Hopkirk stepped from his own office along the corridor and stared aghast at the sight that met his eyes.

"Vera?" he almost choked as he said the word. "What's going on here?"

"Ms. Manvers is accompanying us to police headquarters," McLennan said in response. "We need her to assist us with certain inquiries."

"But really, officers, are the handcuffs really necessary?"

"I'm afraid they are, Mr. Hopkirk. Now, if you'll please step out of the way?" said Curtis, taking a step towards the chief care officer, who reluctantly stepped to one side as the two men escorted his secretary from the building. He would have been less surprised if he'd been able to see through her daily disguise and recognised his one-time lover, Poppy.

In a final gesture before leaving, Curtis turned back to face Charles Hopkirk, showing him the search warrant. "A forensic team will be here soon, Mr. Hopkirk. This warrant grants us access to all the records at Speke Hill, past and present and in particular, Ms. Manvers' office."

"Oh my God, Vera, what have you done?" Hopkirk gasped.

Vera Manvers just stared ahead, blankly, as if she hadn't heard a word he'd said.

Vera remained silent in the car on the way to headquarters, only speaking give her name as Vera Manvers to the desk sergeant as she was booked into the building, before being led to an interview room, where she was asked to sit and wait, under the watchful eye of a uniformed female constable.

CHAPTER 37

A QUESTION OF ALIBIS

Sitting in the comfortable living room of the manse at St. Luke's, Ross and Drake couldn't be aware of the events that were taking place around the city as their fellow detectives gradually began piecing together the various links that would eventually lead to the final solution of their case.

Father Byrne had been as helpful as he could be, but remained mystified as to the reason the killings seemed to be in some way connected to his arrival back in Liverpool. Neither Ross nor Drake could shake his belief that his presence in the middle of all the mayhem surrounding the murders was nothing but a terrible and unfortunate coincidence, his time at Speke Hill somehow running parallel with whatever was taking place around him. Ross remained convinced in the priest's innocence in the matter, and tended to believe in Byrne's hypothesis. His instincts, usually reliable in such matters, told him the priest was telling the truth. Now, as Byrne left the room, he was replaced by Father David Willis.

Ross and Drake hadn't really had much contact with the younger priest so far, and Ross couldn't help but notice the look of tiredness and dark rings under the eyes of David Willis as he sat down in the chair opposite the inspector.

"A terrible business, Father Willis," Ross began.

"Indeed it is, Inspector," Willis agreed. "I was staggered when Tom Redding came to the door with such awful news."

"Pardon me for saying so, Father, but is everything alright? You look tired."

"Oh, I'm fine, thank you. Sleep is quite elusive sometimes, Inspector.

Since Father Byrne began having his nightmares, I must admit I tend to lie awake at night, almost expecting another one to strike him. I've attended to him once or twice when they've occurred in the past. He can get in quite a state with them."

"It's good of you to care so much for his welfare, Father."

"Yes, well, it goes with the calling, Inspector, doesn't it? And Father Byrne is such a nice man, he really is. Did you know he has a bad heart as well?"

"I didn't know that, Father Willis. So you kind of keep a watchful eye on him, is that it?"

"You could say that, yes. I was close to Father O'Hanlon, who Father Byrne replaced and was extremely upset when he passed away. I'd hate to think of something similar happening to Father Byrne. He's still a relatively young man after all."

Ross nodded his understanding before proceeding with his next question.

"Tell me, Father Willis. Were you aware of the fact that an electric light was fitted in the Greasby family crypt some years ago?"

"Of course I was, Inspector," Willis answered without hesitation. "In fact, you'll find most of the members of the congregation were aware of it. Father O'Hanlon had it installed I believe, and often regaled the congregation with little snippets of information he'd either gleaned from the inscriptions in the crypt, or that he'd learned about the Greasby family. He was quite fascinated with their history, though I never really understood why."

"I see, and you were here all night last night, I take it?"

"Yes of course, here in the manse that is, not in the crypt, carrying out heinous crimes against Mr. Devereux."

Father Willis smiled ruefully as he spoke.

"I'm sorry. I didn't mean that to sound facetious, Inspector. It's just that I've never been questioned in connection with a murder before."

"That's alright Father. People do often react in odd ways when asked to provide an alibi for a crime."

"Oh, I see. I am a suspect then, am I?"

"To be honest, everyone is, Father," Izzie Drake replied. "You have to understand we have to look at everyone who was here last night, or who had the means or opportunity to commit the murder."

"Yes, of course. I understand," said Willis.

"Can anyone vouch for the fact you were here all night?" Drake asked.

"Oh dear," Willis said, ruefully. "Well, I didn't think I'd have to account for my movements of course, but, let's see. Mrs. Redding was here until shortly after six-thirty, maybe closer to seven p.m by the time she'd got her coat on and said goodnight. I walked outside with her and saw her into the car when her husband arrived to pick her up. I went back indoors and found Father Byrne asleep in his armchair, so I took the opportunity to take a walk around the parish. I often do that if the weather's fine. I came back and went up to my room, read the Bible for half an hour, took a shower and came downstairs just as Father Byrne was waking up. I didn't think to check the time, but it must have been around eleven p.m. I made us both a mug of cocoa and we went to bed soon afterwards. That's the best I can do, I'm afraid."

"No, that's fine, thank you, Father. We do know it's hard to account for every minute of a day, and especially when you're not expecting to have to account for your time. Too many criminals out-think their situation and have a ready answer for every minute. That's not always the best thing to do."

"Oh, I see, thank you Sergeant."

Ross now asked what he hoped would be his last question, allowing him and Drake to get back to headquarters where it appeared things were moving apace in his absence.

"Do you know a woman by the name of Vera Manvers, Father?"

"The name is rather familiar, Inspector. It's an unusual name, Manvers, isn't it? Of course, she works at Speke Hill. I've met her a couple of times, I think. After Father O'Hanlon passed away, and before Father Byrne arrived, I stood in as chaplain at Speke Hill, a job that goes with the parish of St. Luke's. I'm sure I met her there, not at Sunday services, you understand, but when I had to visit Mr. Hopkirk to arrange to fulfil my temporary duties there."

"I see, well, thank you Father," Ross said, concluding the interview. "If we need to speak to you again, you'll be here?"

"But of course, Inspector Ross. Where else would I be?"

"Where indeed, Father?" said Ross as he and Drake rose to take their leave.

Outside, Miles Booker and his team were still painstakingly going over the scene where the body of Devereux had so recently been displayed, and also the actual murder site, below ground in the Greasby crypt. Booker promised to let Ross know the instant they found anything of interest.

The body of Lucas Devereux had already been removed from the scene and transported to the mortuary, where Doctor William Nugent would already be overseeing the autopsy, aided by Francis Lees and Doctor Vicky Strauss. As the first M.E. on the scene, she would want to be part of the post-mortem team for sure, and Ross knew Nugent well enough to know he'd be encouraging the young pathologist to expand her talents under his watchful gaze.

Izzie Drake was talkative in the car on the way back to headquarters.

"You seemed almost angry back there, sir, talking to the two priests."

"Did I, Izzie? Maybe I was. It's just the whole religious thing."

"How do you mean, sir?"

"Father Byrne and Father Willis, acting all nice and Godly, for want of

456

a better word. They have a man murdered in their own graveyard, in a bloody crypt for heaven's sake, and yes, they're very sorry and it's all so awful, but you just get the impression it's all in day's work for them."

"But it is, isn't it, sir?"

"Is it?"

"Well, yes, especially for Catholics I think. To a Catholic Priest, death is all part of God's great plan, I think. You know, we live, we sin, we go to church, we pray for forgiveness, confess our sins and receive absolution and then the only way we get to Heaven is by giving up our earthly bodies through the medium of death, allowing our souls to rise to Heaven where we supposedly dwell in paradise at the side of God for all eternity."

"Very profound, Sergeant, very profound indeed."

"Well, you did ask, sir," she grinned as she drove into the car park at police headquarters.

"Oh, come on," Ross said, shaking off his maudlin thoughts, "coffee first, then let's go talk to the Manvers woman."

"Right sir. You really think she's a killer?"

"It's certainly stacking up that way, Izzie. From what Curtis told me, she's got a sister somewhere. Let's get Paul Ferris working on locating her fast, unless the Manvers woman tells us right away of course, making things easy for us, but when do they ever do that, eh? And there's still the matter of her accomplice, whoever he is."

"You don't fancy either of the priests for the other killer then sir?"

"Byrne, no, Willis, maybe," he replied.

"Are you being serious?" Drake asked.

"There are holes in his alibi. He could have taken a shower to wash away the blood. He could have slipped something into Byrne's drink at dinner to knock him out for a while, allowing him to slip out and commit the murder, before arriving home in time for bed."

Drake laughed, and after a few seconds pause, Ross joined in.

Five minutes later, Ross and Drake were elated as they were informed by D.C. Dodds that John Selden had literally run into their arms and was also being held in an interview room, waiting to be questioned.

CHAPTER 38

BREAKDOWN

Ross and Drake studied the woman sitting stoically in Interview Room 1 for almost ten minutes prior to beginning the interview of Vera Manvers. Silent and motionless, she appeared to Ross to resemble one of the giant stone figures he'd seen in TV documentaries of Easter Island. Her face gave nothing away, and he wondered how hard it might prove to break her down and find a way to incite her to talk about the murders he was now almost certain she'd been a party to. More importantly, he needed to try to get Vera to reveal the identity of her partner in crime, who had so far managed to remain anonymous to the investigators, despite Vera's capture.

"She's not moved a muscle since she was placed in there, sir," said P.C. Andrews, one of the two constables who'd taken turns to stand guard over Vera in the interview room, awaiting the arrival of the inspector.

"Looks like she may be a tough nut to crack," Ross said, before an idea struck him.

Turning to Izzie Drake, he said, "Izzie, go and ask Sam Gable to start ringing round all the private sanitoriums in the area. If we can find the one in which one her sister's being cared for, it may give us some leverage."

"Right sir," said Drake, turning to leave the viewing room. Drake also added, "Another thing that's bugged me is where the money has come from to pay for the sister's care. It must cost a fortune to keep someone in one of those places for all those years."

"You're right, of course," Ross agreed. "Perhaps it's not private, after all. It's also been my experience over the years that a lot of people use the term sanitorium as a polite, socially acceptable way to refer to a psychiatric hospital. Tell Sam to check out N.H.S, long term facilities too. Tell her to ignore those designed to house the criminally insane, like Ashworth, and concentrate on what I'd call 'normal' long-term psychiatric hospitals."

"I'll tell her now sir. I agree, they'd hardly keep her in a place like Ashworth," referring to the maximum security facility where people like the notorious Moors Murderer, Ian Brady is held to this day.

Drake was gone and back in two minutes.

"Sam's on it, sir. I told her to come in and tell us if she finds the sister. It could give us some leverage."

"Excellent. Right then, let's go talk to *Ms*. Vera Manvers."

Ten minutes of futile questioning followed. Vera had obviously decided that silence was the best defence against any form of self incrimination. Ross, used to dealing with many hardened criminals over the years, marvelled at her continued stone-faced refusal to utter a single word.

Feeling the time had come to play his trump card, even though Sam Gable hadn't as yet brought them any news relating to Vera's sister, Ross made his big play.

"We know all about Brenda, Vera."

Both Ross and Drake noticed a sudden twitch of the woman's eyebrows. They'd touched a nerve.

"We know you killed them to gain revenge for what they did to Brenda. Most people would have wanted to avenge their sister after what they did to her, but most wouldn't have the courage to see it through as you have. Of course, you needed help, didn't you? We'll find him soon enough, even if you don't tell us his name, Vera."

Vera maintained her silence, but there were visible signs that Ross was reaching her. He noticed a slight tremor in her hands where they rested on the table, and her eyes had taken on a watery appearance, as if she might be on the verge of tears. He could tell it was taking all her self-control to maintain her current level of non-cooperation.

Just when he thought he was going to have to continue to bluff his way through the rest of the story, a knock on the door was followed by the entry of Sam Gable.

"Can I have a word, sir?" she asked, and Ross rose from the table, recording the suspension of the interview on the obligatory tape recorder. He returned a few minutes later, nodded to Drake from a position behind Vera Manvers, out of her line of sight, and proceeded to re-start the recorder, then he sat down again, this time looking at a sheet of A4 paper, handed to him by D.C. Gable.

"That was Detective Constable Gable, Vera. She's just been talking to Senior Psychiatric Nursing Sister Leyburn, one of the supervisors at Helm-dale Lodge."

Vera began to fidget in her chair.

"Your sister, Brenda's condition is unchanged. She thought you'd like to know. She was very surprised to hear you're in police custody. Seems she was expecting you to visit Brenda again soon. D.C. Gable pointed out to her that it may be some time before you're able to visit again, and she expressed her sadness at the fact that your sister would be reduced to only one visitor if you were 'tied up' as she diplomatically put it."

Ross fell silent for a few seconds, and Izzie Drake stepped in to the conversation.

"You can't seriously have expected to get away with it, Vera, could you? All your plans, all your meticulous planning, all for what? So you can spend the rest of your life in jail, while your sister sits there in that place, trapped in her own mind, wondering why you never come to see her any more? That's assuming she knows who you are of course."

A sound, more a whisper than anything else, suddenly emanated from the crestfallen woman.

"What was that? I couldn't hear you," said Ross.

"She knows. I said she knows I'm there and who I am. Brenda knows. I don't care what they or David says."

"David? Sister Leyburn mentioned Brenda's fiancé, David. What's his other name, Vera? He's your killing partner isn't he?"

Vera suddenly realised she'd placed David in jeopardy by her outburst, and realised they'd played on her fear of being cut off from Brenda. She fell silent again.

"Come on, Brenda. You know it's all over," Drake spoke quietly, gently, trying to coax Vera to confide in her.

"I can't," Vera sniffed as her eyes slowly filled with tears.

"Can't what, Vera? Tell us his full name? All we have to do is leave a constable at Helmdale Lodge and as soon as he turns up to see Brenda, he'll be arrested. Do you really want your sister to see her fiancé arrested in front of her?"

"Help us now, Vera, while you can. It'll help your defence if we can say you co-operated fully with us," Ross urged her, without revealing to Vera that the nursing sister had already given Sam Gable the name of Brenda's fiancé. He wanted to see if they could break through the cold and impenetrable façade that Manvers had created. The tears forming in her eyes were a sure sign that her resolve was crumbling. He passed the notes from Gable to Drake who quickly read them and saw the name of the fiancé herself, and like Ross, gave nothing away to Vera Manvers. Another knock saw Sam Gable again put her head round the door, and this time, she stepped in to the room and quickly walked across and whispered in Ross's ear before turning and walking out again. Ross knew the figurative noose was now tightening around Vera Manvers' neck.

"D.C. Gable just received word from our forensics team, Vera. They're at your house. They found your white van, parked in your garage. A very interesting collection of items in there, apparently. Bloodied clothes, surgical boots and scrubs, knives, hammers, surgical tools, and a suitcase containing changes of clothes for you and your gentleman friend. I guess you haven't had the time to dispose of the clothes and a rather expensive men's watch yet, have you, Vera? We wondered how the killers came and went so easily when they should have been covered in the blood of their victims. You and he treated it like a bloody day out at the seaside didn't you? You took a change of clothes along with you, carried out the murders, changed in the van and then burned or otherwise disposed of your old clothes and those of your victims. When Mr. Booker, our chief Crime Scenes Officer opened the suitcase containing your clothes, he found something that was a bit of a giveaway, Vera. Can you think what it was?"

"David," she said, softly.

"I know that, Vera. Tell me his other name, please."

"Willis," Vera whispered. "David Willis."

"As in Father David Willis, Vera?" Izzie Drake asked her.

Vera nodded her head.

"For the purpose of the recording, the suspect just nodded her head in response to Sergeant Drake's last question," Ross said, then went on, "Are you confirming that the man who was your partner in the murders of Matthew Remington, Mark Proctor and Lucas Devereux was Father David Willis, of St. Luke's Church, Woolton?"

"Yes," Vera spoke very quietly, just loud enough to be heard and picked up by the recording machine.

That was it. Vera's barriers had been breached and the floodgates open as she opened up and told the whole, sorry story, beginning with the rape of her sister, Brenda Gillespie. Ross's previous, almost jocular theory surrounding the killings proved to be almost one hundred percent accurate. She told how she and David Willis, then a young engineering student, planned and plotted the theoretical killing of those responsible for Brenda's condition. At the time, they'd never dreamed they'd one day put those plans into effect. It was an exercise, a means of playing out their revenge in a hypothetical scenario. She explained that Helmdale Lodge was neither private or NHS funded, but was a charitable institution, set up by a pair of wealthy philanthropists to care for special cases like Brenda's. Donations helped of course, but the wealthy owners were very much involved in the running of the home which provided the best care possible for Brenda and those like her.

Eventually, David Willis, unable to accept the love of any other woman, decided to enter the Catholic Church and was eventually ordained as a priest, whilst still harbouring his devotion to the woman he could never have, and his hatred for those who had ruined her life. He threw himself into his new life, worked hard and supported many good causes in the community. He found some comfort from working as a councillor at a rape crisis centre, where he first met a young girl by the name of Lisa Kelly. He'd introduced Lisa to Vera, who felt sorry for the girl and tried to take her under her protective wing. When she'd informed him of her pregnancy following her rape by Remington, the old anger rose in his mind again and together with Vera, began to actively plan ways to put their long-laid plans into motion. Despite his advice to Lisa not to abort her child, his Catholicism not allowing him to condone such action, she went ahead anyway, only to be consumed by guilt and eventually committing suicide at Formby Dunes.

Willis had placed no blame for her religious transgressions on young Lisa, instead laying culpability squarely on the shoulders of her rapist. The fact that she'd identified Matthew Remington, only for him to escape prosecution due to lack of corroborating evidence was the proverbial straw that broke the camel's back and set Willis and Manvers on their irrevocable course of death and destruction. Willis had indeed used sleeping tablets to ensure the new parish priest, Father Byrne, was safely out of the way on the nights when they needed to be together to carry out the killings. Willis had expressed regret to Manvers as he believed the tablets he'd crushed and administered to Byrne, either in his food or drinks had been the cause of the Father's terrible nightmares, hence his overly solicitous care of the older priest when he was present in the house to care for him after the nightmares. He'd used different medications at different times to experiment in finding an effective way of ensuring Byrne was totally unconscious during the hours he was missing from the manse.

The only regret Vera Manvers expressed was that she and Willis had been exposed before they'd finished their 'work'.

Ross omitted to tell her that John Selden was at that very moment sitting in the next room, relating everything concerning the many years of rape and sexual assault he and the others had been involved in. Derek McLennan and Tony Curtis had purposely not told Selden that the killers of his co-conspirators had been either arrested or identified. His fear of becoming a potential fourth victim of the graveyard killers as they had now become known had encouraged him to tell all. It seemed certain that the information he was providing would help the police to close the cases on a large number of unsolved rapes and sexual assaults. He told the officers that Devereux was the leader of the gang, who expressed his belief that *fear was the key* to their successful litany of crimes. If a woman felt that any one or more of four rapists was likely to come back and do her further harm, it helped to deter them from reporting the crime in the first place, thus many of their crimes would probably never be identified as they'd never been reported. McLennan and Curtis were satisfied however, that they had enough to put Selden away for many years.

At the end of their interview with Vera Manvers, Ross and Drake had her formally charged with the three murders and saw her safely locked up in the headquarters custody suite before heading out once again, this time to bring in Father David Willis.

CHAPTER 39

Ross and Drake pulled up in the driveway of St. Luke's manse for the second time that day, closely followed by constables Flynn and Davis in their patrol car. Ross stationed the two constables outside the front door to the manse, while he and Drake hoped to make a quiet arrest once they gained entry to the house. Not far away, in the graveyard, Miles Booker's forensic team were continuing their painstaking examination of the crypt and the grave site.

Iris Redding, surprised as she was to see the two detectives again so soon, nevertheless ushered them into the living room where Father Byrne stood up from his armchair where he was reading the newspaper, to greet them.

"Inspector, Sergeant," Byrne said, "is there something else you need from me?"

"It's David Willis we need, Father, as a matter of urgency, I'm afraid."

"You sound troubled, Inspector. When you say, a matter of urgency, what exactly does that signify?"

"Is he here, Father?" Ross spoke bluntly.

"He should be returning any minute now. He's been counselling at the Rape Crisis Centre. Please, can't you tell me what this is about?"

Ross saw no way of sweetening the bad news, and quickly, without going into details, informed the priest that David Willis was wanted for questioning in relation to the three recent murders. Byrne looked aghast as Ross finished delivering the shocking news.

"David? Surely not, inspector. There must be some mistake. Murder? I simply can't believe it."

"We're so sorry, Father," Izzie Drake said, softly, trying to cushion the impact of the news, knowing that Father Byrne had a heart condition and not wanting to exacerbate the problem by maybe inducing a heart attack through the shock. "It's true though. We have his collaborator, Vera Manvers in custody already and she's confessed to the crimes and implicated Father Willis."

Stunned, Gerald Byrne slumped into his armchair. Drake looked at the man and could later swear his face aged ten years in the few seconds it had taken to go from standing to sitting.

"He was even slipping drugs into your food and drink to make sure you were fast sleep so he could sneak out, commit the murders, and be back before you woke up," Ross added.

"Oh, Lord!" Byrne suddenly caught on. "So I'd fall asleep, knowing he was here, and when I woke up, he was still here as far I was concerned, so I became his perfect alibi."

"That's right, Father. The pills he was giving you were quite probably the cause of your nightmares, a side effect of the drugs. He was genuinely concerned about your health, which is why he was so solicitous, coming to your help and checking on you when you woke up screaming. If you'd had a heart attack and been admitted to hospital, they'd have likely found the drugs in your system and he'd have had a hard time explaining how they came to be there."

"Drugging me is one thing, Inspector, but the thought of him, a man of God, sworn to uphold the sanctity of life, beinga cold-blooded murderer is simply appalling and I still find it difficult to believe."

Before Ross could say anything more, the living room door flew open as P.C Flynn came hustling into the room, unannounced.

"Sir, it's Willis, he's doing a runner."

"What? Tell me man, quickly."

"He just pulled into the drive, and must have realised the game was up when he saw me and Davis guarding the door. He reversed out, burning rubber I might say and set off in the direction of the city centre."

"Are you cleared for high speed pursuit, Flynn?"

"Yes sir."

"Well, don't just stand there man. Get after him. We'll follow you out. Sorry Father, we must go."

Ross and Drake positively flew out of the house, hot on Flynn's heels. Ross shouted to Flynn as he got into the police Peugeot. "Radio headquarters and report every turn he makes. Did you get his number?"

"No sir, all happened too fast."

"Alright, now go man, quickly. Get on his tail."

"He could be a mile away by now, sir," Drake said as she drove as fast as she could in order to stay on the patrol car's tail.

"It's a straight road into town from here, Izzie, unless he turns into one of the housing estates along the way, and I doubt he's stupid enough to trap himself that way."

A minute later, the patrol car radioed that they had Willis's blue Escort in sight. The old Ford was no match for the almost brand new police patrol car and with Drake keeping close behind the Focus with its lights and siren scything a way through the city traffic they were soon gaining on the fleeing priest, who suddenly threw his car into a hard left turn.

"He's heading south. I think he's going to try to make it to the M62, sir," said Drake.

"He's going nowhere," Ross said determinedly, as he radioed in to headquarters, requesting roadblocks at all strategic entries to the motorway.

"Why is he running, sir? He must know he'll never get away."

"Simple flight or fight response, I suppose, Izzie. He must know we'll get him in the end, but his instincts have taken over."

Just ahead of their car, the patrol car driven by Flynn had closed to within a few yards of Willis's vehicle, all other traffic having pulled over at the sound of the police siren and the sight of the flashing lights. With abrupt suddenness, another police patrol car shot out of a side road a hundred yards ahead of Willis's car, the driver swinging his car to block the left hand side of the road, narrowing Willis's path of escape and the priest, not used to having to manoeuvre a car at speed, made a vain attempt to swerve past the parked car and swerved headlong onto the pavement, the few watching pedestrians scattering in panic. Willis's face contorted in horror as he realised he was heading straight for a deadly combination of a lamp post that stood immediately next to a bright red Royal Mail pillar box.

He virtually stood on the brakes, and the Escort began to fishtail as he attempted to bring the car to a halt before striking the immovable obstacles. Flynn slowed the patrol car almost to a stop, Drake doing the same with their unmarked car as they watched the scene unfold.

David Willis almost made it back onto the road, but the rear of the car struck the base of the lamp post as he tried to swerve past it and the effect of the collision caused the escort to slew round almost in a full circle, sliding into the road, losing speed, until it virtually floated into a slow collision with one of a number of cars parked at meters on the opposite side of the street.

The police were on him immediately, and after a quick check to ensure he was unhurt, Constable Davis pulled Willis from the car, and Flynn snapped the handcuffs on the would-be escapee. Ross and Drake walked up to where Willis stood between the two uniformed officers and Ross stood face to face with the second of the graveyard killers.

"Did you really think you were going to get away, Father?" he asked.

"No, of course not, Inspector Ross. To be honest, I just panicked when

I saw the constables outside the house. I'll not cause you any more trouble, I promise."

"I'm pleased to hear it," said Ross. "You know, you almost got away with it. If Vera hadn't suddenly tossed all your careful planning out of the window and gone crazy with rage, we might never have caught on to you. You were also a bit stupid using your own church to dispose of Devereux."

"Yes, well, I couldn't find another St. Luke's close enough for us to carry out the job and still allow me to get home again in time to create my alibi."

"Why did you do it, Father Willis? Couldn't you and Vera have simply gathered sufficient facts and then presented them to the police so we could have prosecuted them?"

"What? And let them walk away like they did all those years ago, after what they did to Brenda, and again the way Remington got away with raping poor Lisa Kelly? There was no way we were going to trust the police to deal with them, no disrespect to yourself intended, Inspector Ross."

Ross couldn't think of a suitable reply to Willis's statement. In fact, he privately admitted the priest had a point, though he could never openly acknowledge it. Instead, he ordered Flynn and Davis to ferry Willis to headquarters, where he and Drake would conduct their second interview of the day in Interview Room 1.

Over the following two hours, David Willis recounted virtually the identical story to that told earlier by Vera Manvers. Unlike Vera, however, the priest required no persuasion or cajoling to give a full and concise statement of the pair's murderous activities.

Standing in the viewing room, behind the glass of the one-way mirror, Doctor Christine Bland stood with D.C.I. Harry Porteous, listening to the way the priest verbally re-lived the three murders and the long years of planning that had gone into them. Christine felt her profile had been somewhat vindicated, and considered it to have been reasonably accurate, down to the fact that it had taken just one trigger event, the death of Lisa Kelly, to set Manvers and Willis on the eventual path that had led to the deaths of three men. Porteous agreed with her, and despite his many years in the job, he felt a coldness emanating from David Willis he'd never encountered before.

A third person in the viewing room took great interest in David Willis's version of events. He would after all, be replacing Harry Porteous at the end of the month and the forthcoming trials of the two killers would affect what would by then be his squad.

By the time Ross and Drake left David Willis in the care of the custody officer, the pair were both tired and elated at the same time. Stepping into the viewing room, they both looked in surprise at the additional figure in the room.

"Oscar?" said Ross. "Great to see you, but what are you doing here?"

"Perhaps, I'd better answer that," said Porteous. "D.I. Ross, Sergeant Drake, I'd like you to meet my replacement. I'm aware you two know each other quite well," he said to Ross."

"Oscar, you old dark horse," said Ross, grinning. "You got promoted?"

"I did indeed, Andy. I hope my new elevated rank won't stop us working well together, or affect our friendship outside working hours, of course?"

"Of course not…erm, sir."

"Cut out the 'sir', Andy. That'll keep for official or formal moments. We'll work better together if we keep things between us much as they are already."

"That's fine by me, and bloody hell, congratulations," said Ross who turned to Drake and said, "Izzie, meet Detective Chief Inspector Oscar Agostini. We go back a lot of years, and I know you're going to enjoy working with him."

"I'm sure I am, sir. Welcome and congratulations on your promotion sir," she added, speaking to Agostini.

"Thanks," said the new D.C.I. "That was some case you've just concluded. Must have given you a few nightmares along the way?"

"Well, the odd sleepless night, perhaps," said Ross. "The nightmares were reserved for someone else."

At the reference to Father Byrne, both Ross and Drake shared a knowing smile. Agostini noticed it and decided he'd let Andy tell him the full story another time. He could see how tired they both looked.

Christine Bland, having already said her good byes to the rest of the team, now took her leave of Ross and Drake.

"I hope I was some help in the case, Andy," she said, hoping he'd agree at least to some extent.

"Actually, I wasn't sure about you at first," he replied, "but your profile was damned good. It prevented us going off on a tangent and looking at every serial sex offender in Liverpool to begin with. Your profile effectively reduced our suspect pool and by concentrating on the events at Speke Hill and its people, we soon had it narrowed down, though we needed a large slice of luck in the end."

"Aye, well, we all need that luck from time to time, Andy, that's for sure," said Agostini.

"Thank you, Andy," Bland replied. "It's been a pleasure working with you on such an interesting case, you too Izzie," she said as she reached out to shake hands with each in turn.

"Oh, to hell with it," said Ross as he grabbed her by both arms, pulled her close and gave her a great bear hug, before releasing her to the accompanying mirth of the two D.C.I.s.

468

"Wow, thanks," was all Christine could say as she finally took a deep breath and looked at Andy Ross, surprised at his show of emotion.

"Just promise you won't tell Maria," he laughed at Agostini.

"Oh, I doubt she'd mind anyway, but your secret's safe with me," said the new head of the murder investigation unit.

Ross and Drake stood on the steps of the headquarters building, watching as Christine Bland climbed into her still pristine Vauxhall Carlton and drove away as the first grey wash of evening began to fall over the buildings of their city.

"You tired, sir?" Izzie asked.

"Bloody knackered, Sergeant. How about you?"

"The same. Fancy a pint before we go home?"

"Why, Sergeant Drake. First a hug with the profiler, and now my sergeant wants to buy me drinks. What is the force coming to?"

Izzie smiled, a devilish grin on her face as she said, "Sorry, sir, I never said anything about me paying."

Ross laughed, Izzie laughed, the tension that had built up in the two of them through the long day at last released in a moment of humour and camaraderie.

* * *

"What do you think will happen to them?" Maria Ross asked her husband as they lay in bed together later that night.

"It'll be up to the courts, of course," Andy replied, "but I can see David Willis going away for a very long time. I was surprised how cold and dispassionate he was about the whole affair when we interviewed him this afternoon. He displayed no emotion at all. I think any emotions he did possess probably died when Brenda, his fiancée was left a physical and mental cripple for the rest of her life. His own life, his hopes and dreams for their future together all died at the same time. I very much doubt whether, if she were able, Brenda Gillespie would recognise the David Willis of today. He's certainly not the man she fell in love, of that, I'm sure."

"And what about her, the woman?"

Andy Ross lay quietly thinking for a few seconds before replying.

"I'm not sure about her, Maria. She's something of an enigma, even now. She was prepared to sleep with any man she met if she felt it was necessary in the scheme of her plans to eliminate the four men. She could change her appearance like a bloody chameleon. Charles Hopkirk at Speke Hill slept with her as Poppy, but then never suspected Vera was the same woman. That was one of the most effective deceptions I've ever come across. There's a certain something, call it a madness of sorts about that woman. I don't think she'll be seeing the light of day for a long time either, but whether she'll end up in prison or a secure psychiatric unit, I just don't know."

"Well, you've done your part, darling. Come on, put the light out and let's get some sleep. You need it, and that's the doctor's orders," she said, reaching over to kiss him softly on the lips.

Just as he put the light out, Andy Ross stroked his wife's warm, bare thigh, and said, very quietly, "Oh, I forgot to tell you, I hugged a profiler today, my darling."

"Mmm, that was nice for you. Now go to sleep Andy, it's late."

* * *

Around the time Andy and Maria Ross fell asleep, wrapped in each others arms, Izzie Drake lay in the arms of her fiancé, Peter Foster.

"Wow," she gasped. "I thought I'd be too tired for that, tonight."

"So did I to be honest," Peter smiled languidly at her. "Must have been the wine and Indian takeaway that did it," he joked.

"Whatever it was, I'm glad about it. You make me feel so good, Peter."

He reached across, turned her face towards him and kissed her passionately.

"Are you glad that case is over?" he asked.

"You bet I am," Izzie replied. "So much blood and two real

whackos at the end of it. A good result"

"Yes, but you know, a lot of people might say they did the world a favour, Izzie."

"Peter, we can never condone vigilante justice, no matter what the circumstances."

"Oh, come on, Izzie, they've rid the world of three scumbags, from what you've told me. Even if they'd been caught and jailed they'd probably have been released to do it again in a few years."

"I know, Peter, and a lot of people would agree with you, but my job is to uphold the law, and that's what I do every day, to the best of my ability and the same goes for all the team. I daresay a few of them have had similar thoughts during this case, but, like I said, we have a job to do and we just get on with it."

"I know, and I'm proud of you, really. I just wonder sometimes…"

"Yeah, we all do, Peter. Now, come and give me a kiss and then, I need some sleep."

Peter Foster grinned a devilish grin.

"Sleep? Really?"

"Really."

EPILOGUE

The first of the graveyard killers to come to trial, some six months later, was David Willis. Stripped of the priesthood by the Vatican, he was described by the judge as, "One of the coldest, most calculating killers ever to stand before me. You planned these murders with malice aforethought and executed your victims in the most callous, painful and brutal manner imaginable. You have since shown no remorse for your crimes and it is the duty of this court to sentence you to life imprisonment, with a recommendation that you serve a minimum of twenty years."

Due to the fact that he'd been responsible for 'disposing' of three sex offenders, always hated by other inmates, the 'graveyard killer' became something of a celebrity among his fellow inmates. Though no longer an ordained priest, David Willis found himself in demand by many inmates who had 'found' religion whilst under lock and key, and soon made himself useful to the prison authorities by organising Bible classes for those who showed interest. Prison, it seemed, had given Willis a new lease on life.

Two months later, Vera Manvers stood trial, but escaped prison when she was found incapable of pleading, her mental health having deteriorated during her time on remand. She was now a shadow of the woman who had cold-heartedly joined in the torture and executions of their victims and her eyes displayed a haunted, other-worldly look. She was sentenced to be detained 'at her Majesty's pleasure' in a secure psychiatric hospital, and the likelihood is that she will never be released.

John Selden, having confessed to over twenty counts of rape, received a twenty year prison sentence, but, only six months into his sentence, despite being held on the isolation wing of the prison for his own protection, he was attacked and knifed to death in the showers. The 'four apostles' had all met their deaths through violence, as Willis and Manvers originally intended.

Much to everyone's surprise a relationship grew between Melanie Proctor and Charles Hopkirk, and rumour has it that wedding bells are in the air.

Brenda Gillespie, oblivious to the fate, or existence of her sister or former fiancé, continues to live her life in peace and quiet at Helmdale Lodge, where she is visited weekly by Father Gerald Byrne, who took it upon himself to take over the pastoral care of the innocent victim whose brutalisation had started the whole train of events that led to so much violence and death. Father Byrne no longer has nightmares.

A MERSEY MAIDEN

MERSEY MURDER MYSTERIES
BOOK 3

ACKNOWLEDGMENTS

A Mersey Maiden owes its existence primarily to the people of the city of Liverpool. Without them, and their influence on my younger life and without the family members, many of whom I have respectfully used as templates for many of the characters in my Mersey Mysteries I could never have begun the series. My thanks also go to my Beta reader, the indefatigable Debbie Poole in Liverpool, who painstakingly read every page of the book, correcting, suggesting and most of all; I'm pleased to say, enjoying this latest addition to the series. I send her my heartfelt gratitude.

I have to say thank you to Miika Hannila at Next Chapter Publishing for his encouragement and continued belief in the Mersey Mysteries and for helping in selecting the great cover designs for the books

My wife, Juliet is always there for me with words of support and earns my undying thanks for her faith in me and my writing.

I have to say a very BIG thank you to my friend and fellow author Mary Deal from the sunny Hawaiian Islands for giving me permission to use her name for the trawler of that name featured in the book.

Finally, my thanks go to all my readers who continue to support my work by purchasing and reading my books. You are the most important people in the worldwide chain that links authors and readers and make the publishing world go round.

INTRODUCTION

Welcome to *A Mersey Maiden*, the third book in the Mersey Mystery series, following on from the success of *A Mersey Killing* and *All Saints, Murder on the Mersey*.

Once again Detective Inspector Andy Ross, Sergeant Izzie Drake and the rest of the Merseyside Police's Murder investigation team find themselves enmeshed in a complex and at times perplexing mystery.

When an American post-graduate student at Liverpool University is found murdered with his girlfriend sleeping by his side, it begins a case that takes Ross and his team back in time to the dark days of World War Two. A British Corvette and a German U-Boat are somehow inexplicably related to the murder of young Aaron Decker, who has quickly established himself as a star cricketer for the university team.

What links the talented young sportsman to the shipwrecks that lie deep beneath the waves of the English Channel? Very soon, Ross and Drake find themselves travelling to Falmouth in Cornwall where they link up with Detective Inspector Brian Jones and Detective Sergeant Carole St. Clair of the Devon and Cornwall Constabulary to investigate the sprawling international conglomerate, the Aegis Institute and its offshoot, Aegis Oceanographic.

Secrets abound and when a dead frogman is discovered, shackled to an undersea wreck, the case soon escalates to an international level. The Royal Navy becomes involved in investigating the wreckage and the web of secrets and intrigue takes the investigators back in time to the German submarine base at Kiel, in 1945, during the final days of Hitler's Third Reich. Aided by a respected German military historian, Ross begins to piece together an intricate jigsaw puzzle of fact and rumour, slowly unravelling the mystery that has brought the past very much into the present.

Unfortunately for Ross and Drake, the body count begins to mount as more facts from the past come to light. With their new Detective Chief Inspector, Oscar Agostini behind them, they formulate a daring plan to bring the perpetrators to justice. The plan revolves around a 'bent' detective and a hired killer.

Please read on to see how things pan out in this, the most thrilling yet in the Mersey Mystery series.

Author's note: For those not familiar with the very British game of cricket, it may be worth noting that an 'over' is a passage of play consisting of six 'balls' bowled by the bowler to the batsman. If the bowler succeeds in completing an over without the batsman scoring a single run, this is known as a 'maiden over' and may give you a hint to the play on words in the title of *A Mersey Maiden*.

A SHORT GLOSSARY

Scouser/Scouse – A native of Liverpool (Scouse is also a local dish, a kind of stew made to an old Liverpudlian recipe)

Scally – a shortened version of the word 'scallywag' used extensively in Liverpool to describe a ne'er-do-well, a jack-the-lad, something of a wastrel

Made up – Another common Liverpudlian term, an expression of happiness, excitement or description of a pleasurable experience. e.g. "He'll be made up with the result of the game."

Uni – university

W.I. – The Women's Institute, a voluntary organisation that encourages women to take part in various activities within the community, originally formed in 1915 to encourage women to help in food production during World War One.

Chips - fries

Tom/prossie – a prostitute

Guvnor – short for governor, used extensively in the British police forces to describe one's boss or immediate superior.

Bent – 'A bent copper' is a term used to describe a corrupt police officer.

Dedicated to the memory of Leslie and Enid Porter
And to Juliet, my strength and number one fan

CHAPTER 1

QUINTESSENTIALLY BRITISH

"Oh, I say. Well hit sir!"

The time honoured cliché burst forth from the lips of an ageing, bespectacled gentleman, dressed in tweed jacket with leather reinforcements on the cuffs, white shirt and club tie and beige flannel trousers. Sitting in his deck chair, basking in the warmth of a sunny June afternoon, the old man could have been a contemporary of the great W.G. Grace himself, with his long, flowing beard adding to the appearance of a cricketing great from the past.

As applause rippled around the ground, the ball sailed gracefully over the boundary, the umpire duly raising both arms to signal another six runs to the university team. Nothing gave Andrew Montfort greater pleasure than spending an afternoon watching his beloved cricket; the sound of willow on cork as the batsmen amassed the best score they could being almost like music to his ears.

This particular Sunday afternoon was a little special for Montfort, as the team from The University of Liverpool was engaged in the annual Montfort Trophy match against their fierce rivals from the University of Manchester, the trophy being named for his grandfather, Sir Michael Montfort who had instituted the annual match soon after the end of the Great War in 1918.

Sir Michael had studied at the university before going on to become one of the leading industrialists of the early twentieth century. His business interests stretched from the city of Liverpool to Manchester and beyond, and the trophy was his way of encouraging the post-war youth to enjoy his favourite sport whilst studying for their futures.

Having played cricket for the university he'd also later played for the local amateur club, Liverpool Cricket Club, an old established amateur club formed in 1807 and playing at the Aigburth Cricket Ground. The ground holds a singular claim to fame in that it possesses the oldest pavilion in the country at a first class cricket ground.

Now, the bowler completed his run up and another ball sped down the wicket towards the batsman who again made a solid contact, the thwack as bat connected with ball being greeted by yet more applause. This time, the ball was successfully fielded and the batsmen completed a single run.

A tall, mustached figure dressed in cricket whites walked up and stood beside Andrew Montfort's deck chair.

"He's quite a find, young Decker, don't you think, Mr. Montfort?" asked team captain, Simon Dewar.

"Indeed he is, Simon," Montfort replied. "Who'd have thought a Yank would become one of your best batsmen in years, eh?"

"Obviously, his experience playing baseball back home in the States gave him a good grounding, and don't forget his bowling prowess too," said Dewar, a tall, rangy student of accountancy and finance.

"Yes, I heard he was something of a star for his college team."

"It was our good luck when his father was transferred to the UK, and Aaron came over with his parents. Even more so that he chose us for his post-grad studies."

"A student of modern history, I believe, Simon?"

The team captain nodded as Montfort returned the conversation to his first love.

"How many centuries did he score last season, Simon? Was it seven, or eight?"

"Eight, sir, and got out in the nineties twice."

"It's a wonder the professional county cricket clubs haven't tried to tempt him."

"Oh, but they have, sir. Lancashire tried to coax him into joining them last summer, and Durham and Worcestershire made approaches, but he was adamant he wants to remain an amateur, free to play or not play as he chooses, and, as he rightly told them all, if his father has to relocate again, he may have to leave the country at short notice."

"Well then Simon. We must make the most of young Aaron Decker while we have him, eh?"

"Definitely, sir, I couldn't agree more."

"Oh, yes, good shot, young Decker," Montfort suddenly exclaimed, applauding as he did so.

"I'd better go, sir. Soon be time to break for tea."

"Right you are, Simon. How many more do the university need to win?

My damned eyes aren't what they were, even with the specs. Can't make out the scoreboard from here."

Simon Dewar glanced across at the scoreboard.

"We need fifty five to win, sir. If Aaron can stay at the wicket, we should cruise it after tea."

"Jolly good, Simon. Be nice to see the trophy stay at the old alma mater for another year. Been a while since you chaps won it two years running."

"Ten years since we achieved that honour, sir. I wouldn't have thought it mattered to you. You have as much influence in Manchester as you do here, don't you, as your grandfather did?"

"True, Simon, but I must admit, keep it under your hat mind; I always have a slight bias for you chaps. Probably because my wife hails from the area."

"Thanks a lot, Mr. Montfort. I shan't breathe a word," Simon smiled at the old man, and then wandered off towards the pavilion as another over ended. Simon Dewar retained a quiet air of confidence that the day would end with another triumph, thanks to Aaron Decker and his uncanny eye, which seemed to guide his bat to make contact at the precise moment required to achieve maximum contact with the ball. American or not, he was a damn fine cricketer.

Following another single from Decker, and with Darren Oates now at the receiving end, the rest of the over played out without the addition of further runs, Darren being content to block the last two balls, after which the umpires signalled the tea interval and the players trooped off the field of play and into the pavilion, where refreshments awaited.

"It's going well, Aaron," Simon Dewar said as he handed Aaron Decker a refreshing glass of iced lemonade.

"Sure is, skipper," Decker replied. "Got to watch their fast bowlers though. They're not bad at all. The red-haired guy almost got me a couple of overs ago."

"Speaking of bowling, old Andrew Montfort has been watching you closely today. He was well impressed with your bowling figures earlier today. Six maiden overs from ten overs bowled is damn fine going."

"Hell, it was just good luck and poor batting," Aaron said, making light of his impressive bowling statistics. "Still, if it's giving the old guy a good afternoon, I'm real pleased."

Andrew Montfort chose that moment to walk up behind the two young men, and spent five minutes chatting to the pair, finally departing to speak to one of the lecturers he was friendly with, who'd just entered the pavilion.

"I thought he'd never leave you alone," said the beautiful long-haired blonde who walked up to the two men as Montfort walked away, wrapping her arms around Aaron's waist from behind, and reaching up to kiss the back of his neck. Dressed in a plain white, short-sleeved blouse with a fairly low cut v-neck and pale blue pleated mini skirt, her long legs bare, and with a pair of low-heeled white pumps on her feet, Sally Metcalfe exuded confidence, and Aaron spun round to take her in his arms and promptly kissed her on the lips before standing back to admire his girlfriend, who'd only just arrived at the ground, having spent the majority of the day at a family barbecue at her parents' home in Lancaster, some sixty miles north of Liverpool. Sally could have attended the university in her own town, but had chosen Liverpool in order to gain a degree of independence from her father, who she described as believing they still lived in the Victorian era.

"Hey, gorgeous," Aaron responded. "I was thinking you weren't gonna make it to see us lift that trophy again."

"I wouldn't have missed it for the world, Aaron. It's just, well you know how it is at home. I couldn't not go to the stupid barbecue; even if it was populated mostly by old farts and Daddy's cronies from the stupid transportation and pharmaceutical industries with their boring trophy wives, or worse still, their hired tarts."

"Ah, so young and yet so cynical," Aaron laughed. "I'm sure they were all perfectly charming as you English folks like to say."

"As charming as a nest of vipers, perhaps, and old man Roper, the local undertaker tried to grope my bottom too, the weasel-faced little pervert." Sally smiled back at him. "So, anyway, are we winning, darling?"

"Well, we need less than fifty to win after the interval. Roper the groper eh? Want me to go up there and challenge him to a duel?"

Sally giggled.

"You really would, I think, wouldn't you?"

"Sure thing," said Aaron. "A lady's honour and all that, eh?"

His attempt at an upper-crust British accent gave Sally another fit of the giggles. She then returned to the game.

"You're still batting?"

He grinned in the affirmative.

"Oh well, in that case they might as well start engraving Liverpool's name on the trophy now then. You're bound to win."

"Hey, this is sport, honey. Anything can happen out there, you know. I'm not invincible, not by a long chalk."

"No, but you're the very best player we have, my darling and I'm sure Simon has every faith in you to see out the game, don't you Simon?" Sally grabbed hold of Dewar's arm and pulled him close, so close he could actually see down the front of her blouse to her cleavage. Embarrassed, Simon Dewar politely extricated himself from Sally's grip as he replied, "Let's say I very much hope Aaron will do the job for us, Sally."

"Oh, I say," Sally giggled. "I've got faith, Simon's got hope, but I hope you won't show their bowlers any charity when you get started again, Aaron, darling. Get it? Faith, hope and charity?"

"Very clever, darling, and very witty. Did you also know that during the

German's siege of Malta during World War Two, the RAF used three old Gloster Gladiator biplanes to defend the island against massed attacks by the Luftwaffe and they named those airplanes Faith, Hope and Charity too?"

"Oh, really, how interesting," said Sally, who despite caring deeply for Aaron, couldn't care less about his other great passion, history. Aaron thought the world of Sally, but sometimes wished she'd realise that a working knowledge of history is, as he thought, our passport to building a better future. Still, she was great in almost every other aspect, even turning up regularly to watch him play cricket, a game he knew she barely under- stood, a fact that applied to most people outside the game. Trying to explain the intricacies of being 'in' or 'out' or the various fielding positions, including the odd sounding 'silly mid-on' or 'off,' square leg, long leg and so on, could be a baffling task, not to mention attempting to instruct someone in the difference between 'the wicket' and 'wickets' and just what the heck L.B.W. stood for, or what 'leg before wicket' actually meant was hard enough for a native, but when Aaron had tried to get the rules across to his father, Jerome Decker the third, it had turned into a session of much mirth as the elder Decker felt he was suddenly in the presence of an alien being, speaking an unknown language, rather than listening to his own son. All he said, having become totally lost as Aaron had tried to explain what the meaning of a 'maiden over' was, "Heck, son, don't tell me any more, just you go out there and enjoy yourself and show these Brits how to play their own game."

Aaron himself had known little about the game himself upon his arrival in Liverpool just over a year ago, but when team captain, Simon Dewar heard that the new American student had been something of a college star at baseball back home, he'd persuaded Aaron to try his hand at the quintessentially British game, with startling results. Aaron was a natural at both batting and bowling, and once he'd received a crash course in the rules of the game, he'd become an instant hit with players and spectators alike.

* * *

With the tea interval over, the match was resumed and with able support from Darren Oates, who was caught out with twelve to his name, and Miles Perry, Aaron was still there at the end, striking the ball cleanly for another boundary, a 'four' this time to take Liverpool past the Manchester total. Miles had added eight runs and Aaron ended with a total of fifty-five, out of the team's total of 211 for the loss of seven wickets, the last boundary taking them two runs past the opposition's quite respectable 209 all out.

The Montfort Trophy was duly presented to the winning captain by guest of honour, Andrew Montfort, and in his victory speech, Simon Dewar paid high praise to the team's star player, their superbly talented 'American cousin,' Aaron Decker, who received the man of the match award, a small silver salver, engraved with his name and the year of the award, and decorated with two crossed cricket bats overlaying a set of wickets.

As the applause died down and the crowd slowly departed, some by car, others on foot or bicycle, the two teams enjoyed a half hour of socialising in the pavilion before the coach carrying the Manchester team departed and at last, Aaron Decker relaxed as Sally sat on his knee, her crossed legs showing them off to perfection.

"Thank God that's over," Aaron whispered into her ear.

"I thought you loved it, Aaron," Sally said in quiet surprise at his comment.

"I do, honey, I do," he replied, "but I had some bad news earlier this morning and it's been on my mind all day."

"Oh, no, sweetie, what is it? Can I help?"

"Heck, no, Sally. It's just some news I'd rather not have heard. I don't really want to talk about it, if you don't mind."

"Sure, okay Aaron. Whatever you want. Listen, why don't we go to the pub, have a couple of drinks and then go back to my place?"

Aaron seemed to be deep in thought for a few seconds and then snapped out of it and replied, "Yes, why not? Sounds good to me."

"You can stay the night if you like? If we're quiet, no one will know." Sally whispered, tantalisingly. She was lucky in that her father's money had paid for her to jointly rent a house in the city with a friend and was currently considering buying her an apartment in one of the new building complexes along Liverpool's renovated waterfront. Aaron, despite his father's position at the U.S Embassy in London, had preferred to throw himself into university life in every way and currently shared a house in Wavertree with two other students. He and Sally often spent the night together, usually at his place, though he preferred the privacy of staying at her place where they couldn't be heard enjoying themselves through the walls. This was despite her landlord, prudishly in Aaron's opinion, frowning on overnight visitors of the opposite sex.

"You're on," Aaron smiled as he spoke, his earlier depression seeming to have lifted. Sally hopped from his lap and he grasped her hand firmly and led her from the pavilion, to a chorus of congratulations and 'cheerio' and 'lucky bastard' from the other remaining team members.

"Hey, don't forget this," shouted wicket-keeper Alex Dobson, as he tossed Aaron's man-of-the-match plaque across the room towards him, confident that Aaron would make the catch. He did, mouthed a thank you to Dobson as he and Sally disappeared through the pavilion door, a few drinks and a night of passion ahead of them.

CHAPTER 2

WEDDING DAY

Pedestrians passing by St. George's Hall in Liverpool's city centre might have been forgiven for thinking the police were attending a bomb threat or some other crime within the building. The presence of three police patrol cars, two rather obvious unmarked police vehicles and a dozen uniformed officers seemingly guarding the entrance to the building certainly backed up the wholly erroneous theory.

Within the famous old building, in the Sefton Room, Detective Sergeant Clarissa (Izzie) Drake and Senior Mortuary Receptionist Peter Foster gazed lovingly into each others eyes as the registrar pronounced them man and wife. Standing beside the groom, Doctor William Nugent, the city's senior pathologist and medical examiner was actually smiling for once, having been surprised but delighted when invited by Foster to be the best man at his wedding. Peter had told the rotund, overweight physician that he considered it a great honour to have him as his best man, not just as a mark of respect for the doctor, but because he was a genuinely nice man to work for.

In addition to Izzie's parents and younger sister, Astrid, also in attendance were the groom's parents, and most of the members of the city's specialist Murder Investigation team, including Detective Inspector Andy Ross and his wife, Maria, a local General Practitioner, and Detective Constables Samantha Gable, who was proud to be Izzie's maid of honour, Paul Ferris, with his wife Kareen and young son, Aaron, looking healthier than he'd ever done since a successful kidney transplant, Derek McLennan and Tony Curtis, who'd all done their sergeant proud by turning out in their best suits for the occasion. Back at police headquarters, the squad room was being manned in their absence by Detective Constable Nick Dodds, who, having worked with the squad on an ad hoc basis over the last two years, had now been assigned permanently to the team, together with their new boss, Detective Chief Inspector Oscar Agostini, who had recently replaced the outgoing and retiring D.C.I. Harry Porteous, who was present in the Sefton Room with his wife as special guests of the bride and groom. Also there from Peter's workplace was Francis Lees; Doctor Nugent's slim, pale and cadaverous but totally efficient assistant, looking cheerful for the first time in Ross's memory.

Agostini, an old friend and colleague of Ross's prior to his promotion, had offered to man the squad room with Dodds for a couple of hours, with Ross and his colleagues promising to return after the ceremony concluded. Ross had excluded Ferris from that promise, believing his senior D.C and family should represent the team at the small reception the happy couple's parents had clubbed together to pay for at the nearby Marriott Hotel. The ceremony over, the couple signed the register and left the room to the strains of the old romantic song, *No Arms Can Ever Hold You*, by the Bachelors. Izzie had fallen in love with the music of the 1960s while working on the case involving Brendan Kane and the Planets, and a missing young woman, Brendan's girlfriend Marie Doyle some four years previously. She could think of no song more romantic than this one to accompany her wedding service.

As they walked out of the building, the dozen uniformed officers who'd waited patiently outside formed a guard of honour with truncheons raised to form an arch and a beaming Izzie Drake looked towards her boss and mouthed a 'thank you' to Andy Ross for she knew it had to have been Ross who had arranged this final touch to make the ceremony complete and memorable for her.

A wedding photographer, a friend of Francis Lees, himself an expert with a camera in his hands, quickly arranged the wedding group and a series of photographs were taken in the morning sunshine, a perfect reminder of the happy day, after which he would follow the couple and guests to the reception.

Photographs over, everyone began to make a move towards transferring the celebrations to the hotel, and Ross quickly made his way to have a quiet word with his sergeant before taking his leave of the wedding party.

Pulling her to one side, Ross hugged Izzie fondly and placed a fatherly kiss on her cheek.

"Congratulations, Sergeant Drake," he said, with mock formality.

"Thanks for everything," Izzie replied. "You arranged the guard of honour didn't you?"

"But of course. No way was the best sergeant in the city getting away

486

without a proper send off. Seriously, Izzie, I hope you and Peter have a long and happy future ahead of you."

"Thanks, sir. I appreciate that. At least, Peter's under no illusions about what I do for a living or the extra hours I have to spend at work on occasions."

"That's true," said Ross. "And you see him quite a lot when we have to visit the morgue too."

"Yes, well, we try to keep that contact to a professional level, as you well know, sir."

"I know you do. I meant to ask, are you going to continue to be D.S Drake from now on, or are you changing it to Foster?"

"Peter and I agreed it's best if I carry on as Drake at work, sir. I'll get plenty of time to be Mrs. Foster in my off duty hours."

"Right, that's good to know, Izzie. At least the rest of the force won't think I've got a new sergeant working for me."

"Right, well, I'm glad we've sorted that out, sir. Oh, look, sorry, but I'm wanted."

Peter was waving to Izzie. It was time they left for the reception.

"Off you go then," said Ross, "and enjoy the honeymoon," he continued, referring to the long weekend she and her new husband had booked in London. Ross had urged them to take at least a week off work, but Izzie had insisted four days was long enough for him to survive without her and Peter had actually agreed with her, knowing just how much she loved her job and the buzz she got from working with Ross.

As the happy couple were whisked away in a gleaming silver Bentley for the short journey to the Marriott, Ross rejoined his wife and the other guests, his own detectives amongst them, who'd remained to see them off, others having already made their way to the hotel to greet them as they arrived for the reception.

Ross said goodbye to Maria, who, like him, was heading back to work at her surgery, and suddenly, standing there outside the magnificent old building on St. George's Place, he felt really alone. For the first time in as long as he could remember, Izzie wasn't there to drive him back to head-quarters, or to the next case. He and his sergeant had worked together for so long they almost thought as a single entity, being able on occasions to virtually read each other's thoughts, anticipate the other's next move in a case and so on.

"Sir?" came a voice from behind him. He turned to find D.C. Sam Gable standing there, having somehow changed from her wedding finery into her usual work outfit of plain white blouse, short black jacket and matching trousers.

"Hello, Sam. Been a good day so far, eh?"

"Yes, it has sir. Sergeant Drake looked beautiful didn't she?"

"She was positively radiant, Sam, definitely. What can I do for you?"

"More the other way round, sir. Sergeant Drake said I was to look out for you while she's away, so I thought I'd get changed in the ladies room back in the hall and then come down and give you a ride to headquarters. Izzie said your wife would probably take your car to her surgery and you'd end up stranded and having to cadge a lift with the uniform lads."

Ross couldn't help himself. He laughed out loud as he said, "Well, bloody hell, talk about a mother hen. Doesn't she think I can cope without her for a few days?"

Sam Gable cocked her head on one side, smiled a lop-sided grin at her boss and replied, "Sergeant Drake said you'd say something like that, sir, and, with all due respect, she told me to say, '*Do you really want me to answer that?*'"

Andy Ross laughed again, said, "Women, can't live with 'em, can't live without 'em," and in reply to the odd look on Gable's face, said, "Just ignore me Sam. I'm getting old, I think."

"You sir? No, not a chance," Gable replied. "Much too soon for you to be pushing up daisies or maybe retiring with pipe and slippers and a nice line in gardening tools."

"My God, Samantha, you're almost as bad as my bloody sergeant. Go and fetch my chariot, wench, before I change my mind and walk all the way back to headquarters."

Sam laughed with her boss as she almost ran round to the car park and soon had D.I. Ross seated next to her in the passenger seat of her car as she drove the short distance back to police headquarters.

Detective Chief Inspector Agostini was waiting expectantly for the team to return and was pleased to hear the wedding had gone off without a hitch. A couple of the Detective Constables had taken photos using their mobile phones and were quick to show them to Agostini and Nick Dodds.

As he sat at his desk in his office, Ross allowed himself to relax a little and take advantage of the fact that the last few days had been relatively peaceful and crime free, allowing him to catch up on the mountain of paperwork that seemed to grow exponentially with each case the squad handled. Even his team had welcomed a little peace and quiet as they also sat typing reports or preparing for forthcoming court appearances at various trials and so on.

As with all such times in the lives of the officers of law enforcement, this short lull would prove to be nothing more than the calm before a storm, and when the next storm hit, it would prove to be a damn big one!

CHAPTER 3

THE STORM CLOUDS GATHER

A hearty breakfast with Maria, followed by a smooth drive to headquarters through unusually quiet streets during his short commute from Prescot put Andy Ross in a good mood and the early morning sunshine gave the city a hint of the long hot summer that lay in wait for the inhabitants of the great sea port.

Ross made his way to the fourth floor, using the stairs as a means of exercise, and walked across the squad room, receiving morning greetings from Ferris, Gable and Dodds, already at their desks awaiting the day's developments. Placing his hand on the handle to open his office door, Ross sensed rather than saw D.C.I. Oscar Agostini enter the squad room, making his way through the mini-maze of desks to reach Ross before he'd made it into his office.

"I'm guessing you're not here to simply wish me a good morning, sir." Ross declared as he saw the look on Agostini's face, his furrowed brow a sure sign of a major problem looming for Ross and his team.

"Let's talk inside, Andy," Agostini responded, as he followed Ross in to the small office.

Ross sat at his desk as Agostini seated himself in the visitor's chair.

"I take it we have a new case?" Ross surmised.

"We do, Andy, and it might prove to be something of a hot potato."

"Come on, Oscar, it's not like you to beat about the bush. Let's have it," said Ross. Having worked together years earlier and being good friends outside of work, the two men would invariably revert to first names in private, Ross acknowledging the D.C.I.'s seniority in front of the team or in public.

"How much do you know about the United States Department of State, Andy?"

"Only that it's usually referred to as the State Department for short, and it has something to do with the USA's international political machinery."

"Right, well, we have a death on our hands that could get messy. The body of a young man was found in his bedroom in a shared house in Wavertree, yesterday. Because of his age and lack of external means of determining cause of death, pressure was apparently applied by his father for an immediate autopsy to be carried out."

"Hold on," said Ross. "Back-pedal a bit. Who is the father?"

"His name is Jerome Decker the third, and he works for the U.S Department of State, based at the U.S Embassy in London. His son Aaron was studying at the University of Liverpool and was also a bloody top class cricketer, apparently. He is reported to have gone to bed some time after ten on the night before his death, with his girlfriend and was found dead by his house-mates, the girlfriend asleep next to him when he failed to appear for breakfast yesterday morning."

"Ah," said Ross. "This sounds a bit messy. I'm presuming we're certain it's murder?"

"We are now, Andy. The friends woke the girlfriend, Sally, and she reportedly went into fits of hysterics when she realised she'd been sleeping next to her dead boyfriend without realising anything was wrong. The lads from Wavertree were on the ball, thankfully. It didn't add up to them, so they asked the paramedics to leave the body in place while they got the forensics people and medical examiner in to take a look. Doctor Strauss attended, together with Booker's team and it didn't take long for the doc to ascertain that young Decker had been suffo-cated. Obviously the boys from Wavertree thought right away of the girl-friend, but, seeing the state of disorientation of the girl, Vicky Strauss examined her on the spot and she's convinced the girl was drugged, probably to make sure she was well out of it while Aaron Decker was murdered."

"And we've been called in because the case looks like being high profile and the Chief Super wants his favourite sacrificial lambs on the job, just in case it all goes pear-shaped."

Ross's words were more a statement than a question, and Agostini had to agree with him.

"You're right, of course, Andy. If the U.S. embassy can exert pressure on the Chief Constable and he shovels the pressure down the chain of command, then sooner or later it has to reach a point where' the buck stops here," and that, unfortunately will probably be right here, Andy.

You're the best we have at this sort of case and the Chief knows it, but heaven help us if we screw up."

Andy Ross fell silent for a few seconds, apparently lost in thought.

"Everything okay, Andy?" Agostini asked.

"Mmm, yes," said Ross, thoughtfully. "Just a thought, but I have a contact at the American embassy. I might be able to find out something about this Decker character. He must carry some diplomatic weight if he's got the chief jumping through hoops already."

"Really? Tell all, Andy. It's not like you spend much of your life down South in the capital is it? Who's this contact of yours?"

"Name's Ethan Tiffen, works in Immigration. He was helpful in a case four years ago, and we've remained in sporadic contact ever since, exchanging Christmas and birthday cards and so on and Maria and I spent a weekend in London as his guests two years ago. I owe him a return of the favour to be honest. You might remember the case? We had a body found in an old disused dock and it led to a murder investigation and the case of woman missing for over thirty years."

"Brendan Kane, and Marie Doyle, right?"

"Good memory, Oscar. Yes, that was the case. I had to contact the U.S. Immigration service in the course of the investigation. Ethan Tiffen was the guy who did his best to help us out, and even came up here for the eventual joint funeral of the couple."

"That was one great piece of police work," said Agostini. "You managed to solve a thirty something year old murder and the disappearance of the woman in one felled swoop, if I remember."

"Yes, we did, so I'm thinking maybe Ethan Tiffen can fill me in on this Decker character."

"Okay, good idea, talk to him, Andy. First though, we have to take over the case. Detective Sergeant Meadows at Wavertree is waiting in my office. I asked him to come over and bring their file with him. You need to get moving on this as fast as you can, Andy."

"Right, let's go talk to Meadows," said Ross and he and Agostini quickly made their way to the D.C.I's office. As they walked through the squad room, Ross called to his team as they sat at their desks or at the coffee machine, "No one leaves the office, people. I'll be back shortly. We've got a new case, and it could be a big one."

Leaving the small team of detectives to gossip and conjecture between themselves, Ross and Agostini were soon being fully briefed by D.S. Ray Meadows on the strange case that was about to be dropped in their laps.

"As far as we can ascertain, the young guy was something of a local hero," Meadows informed them. "Went from being a star college baseball player back home to becoming a star varsity cricketer over here. Seems he almost single-handedly won the Montfort Trophy, whatever that is, for the University of Liverpool in a match with Manchester last week."

"So why would someone want to kill him?" Agostini mused.

"And why do it in such a haphazard fashion?" Ross added, "leaving the girlfriend as an obvious suspect, yet leaving her in such a state she'd be immediately eliminated from our inquiries?"

"Already asked myself that one, sir," said Meadows. "And I can't say as I'm not happy to hand the case over to you, that's for sure. Once my gaffer got the whiff of the politicos being involved, he couldn't offload it fast enough."

"Wow, thanks, Sergeant," Ross said, wryly.

"You're only too welcome," Meadows continued as he passed the thick folder containing the notes made on the case so far to D.C.I Agostini who in turn handed the file to Andy Ross.

After the sergeant had departed, Agostini said very little. Ross had read through the file and given it back to the boss to glance at. There was nothing in it that might help them in formulating a theory for the murder of Aaron Decker.

"Would someone mind telling me, just where the hell I'm supposed to start with a case that's already over twenty four hours old?" Ross asked of nobody in particular.

CHAPTER 4

AUTOPSY ROOM TWO

The drive to the city mortuary building had been a strange one for Andy Ross. It had been ages since he'd driven himself there, with Izzie Drake normally doing the driving, and visiting the place without his trusted assistant felt somehow wrong, out of place, especially as he knew her husband, Peter Foster, a familiar face on entering the mortuary building, would also be absent, and another, unknown receptionist would be on duty, ready to admit him to the antiseptic and formaldehyde-scented inner sanctum of the world of the pathologists.

Ross parked the car and waited for D.C. Paul Ferris to arrive in his own vehicle which he did a couple of minutes later. Ross's resident computer 'genius' and team collator Ferris had an incisive mind and Ross wanted him to view the body of Aaron Decker to get his 'feel' on the case. It was unusual for the team to be called into a case after the body had been removed from the murder site, so Ross felt they were playing catch-up. The old theory that the first twenty four hours of a murder investigation were the most important had definitely gone out the window on this one.

"Bet it feels strange without Sergeant Drake, sir?" said Ferris.

"I admit it does, Paul," he replied. "Still, only another couple of days and she'll be back on the job."

"Meant to ask you, is she still Sergeant Drake or Sergeant Foster now, sir?"

"Drake at work, Foster at home," Ross replied.

"Makes sense, I suppose," Ferris said as Ross pressed the buzzer beside the door that allowed entry to the mortuary building. A female voice answered, asking who required entry to the premises. After identifying himself and Ferris a click sounded and Ross pushed the door open. At the reception area usually manned by newly-wed Peter Foster, Ross was greeted by a petite brunette whose name badge gave her name as Michelle Hill.

"Inspector Ross, nice to meet you," Michelle said, after the two men had produced their warrant cards. "Peter speaks of you often."

"He does?"

"Of course. As his wife's boss your name comes up quite often in conversation."

"Hmm, I see," said Ross, wondering what Peter Foster really thought of him, but that was for another time.

"You're here to see Doctor Strauss, I presume?"

"Yes, please," Ross replied.

"Autopsy Room Two," said Michelle, "Doctor Nugent is with her I think."

"Oh, that should be fun," Ross smiled, as he thought of Doctor William Nugent, the overweight but brilliant Scottish Chief Medical Officer, not a man renowned for his sense of humour. Two minutes later, Ross and Ferris were to receive their first view of the mortal remains of Aaron Decker, just twenty two years old at the time of his death.

"Come in, Inspector Ross, come in," Nugent said in a hale and hearty voice as he and Ferris entered the autopsy room after a brief knock and wait. William Nugent stood beside Doctor Vicky Strauss, who Ross had not dealt with since her brief involvement in the horrific graveyard murders of the previous year. Ross noticed that the petite pathologist had had her brunette hair cut in a fashionable bob since the last time he'd seen her. He thought it added to her look of vulnerability, though he knew she was quite superb at her job. Anything less and she wouldn't have lasted a day working under William Nugent.

"Hello, Doctor Nugent, Doctor Strauss," Ross said as the two detectives walked slowly across the room towards the stainless steel autopsy table where the remains of Aaron Decker were already laid out, his chest cavity opened up and the majority of the internal organs already removed and weighed.

"Ah, D.C. Ferris," Nugent observed on seeing Paul Ferris at Ross's side. "I see the inspector has let you out of the office for a breath of fresh air in the absence of the newly-wed Sergeant Drake."

"Hello, Doctor," said Ferris. "Not that I'd necessarily class a visit to the mortuary as a breath of fresh air, but yes, it's good to see you again, you too, Doctor Strauss."

"Detectives," said Strauss by way of greeting. "Sorry to have to meet like this. Such a shame, tragic when we see them this young on the table," she added as the body on the table loomed larger in the view of Ross and Ferris, as they arrived at Vicky Strauss's side.

"No Lees this morning?" Ross asked, referring to Nugent's erstwhile assistant. Seeing Nugent without Lees was akin to how Ross probably appeared to those used to seeing him with Izzie Drake.

"Ah, poor Francis," Nugent replied. "Had such a good time at the wedding the other day, seems he was a little worse for the drink, and slipped on the stairs when he got home. Spent three hours at A & E, only to be diagnosed with a severely sprained wrist. He's nae good to me in that state, all wrapped up and fingers useless with the strapping, so I've told him to stay at home until he can work his hand again."

"The dangers of the demon drink, eh Doc?" Ross grinned.

"In Francis's case, aye. Silly wee boy isn't used to all that hard liquor. Seems the punch at the reception was a wee tad over-imbued with vodka, and Francis was literally bundled into a taxi by a couple of guests when he was found slumped on a staircase singing *I belong to Glasgow*."

"But he's from Fazakerley, isn't he?" Ferris observed.

"Aye, that he is," Nugent laughed. "Must have spent too much time working with me. Ma Glaswegian roots seem to have rubbed off on him and tainted the man's perception after a couple of drinks."

"Right, well, can we get to work, please Doctors? Seems this young man's father is on his way up from London. He's something to do with the U.S. State Department so the case could have political implications. The Chief Constable has apparently already been applying pressure to the Chief Super who in turn put the squeeze on D.C.I Agostini..."

"Who in turn, is putting pressure on you, I presume," Strauss observed, logically.

"Quite right Doctor Strauss. As I wasn't involved in the case until this morning, I have little to go on so far except the report from the Detective Sergeant who responded to the original emergency call, and the crime scene photos that were taken by Miles Booker's forensic team."

"Right, well, Inspector Ross, I can tell you that Sergeant Meadows was very thorough and carried out a very professional examination of the scene," said Strauss.

"I'm glad to hear it," Ross replied. "I have his report here," he added, holding up the file he'd brought from headquarters.

"Yes, in fact it was Sergeant Meadows who first suggested to me that something might be wrong with Sally Metcalfe."

"That's the girlfriend, right?"

"Yes, I was examining Mr. Decker of course, and then the sergeant asked if I'd take a look at the young lady. He thought she might be on something at first, but from her state of disorientation, he suspected she'd been deliberately drugged. I broke off from my examination of the body for a few minutes and it was clear to me that Miss Metcalfe had been drugged in some way. Her reactions didn't suggest she'd deliberately taken any kind of recreational drug, and the symptoms she displayed made me believe she'd been given something to anaesthetize her for a period of time. On close examination, I found a small needle mark on her arm that could be the site of an injection having been administered. I took blood samples at the scene, and sent them for a tox screen. We should get the results later today."

"That was good thinking, Doctor Strauss. Now, what can you tell me about this poor fellow?" Ross said as he looked at the body of Aaron Decker. Sadness showed on Ross's face, the sadness he felt at the lost life of a young man who, it appeared, had everything to live for before being cut down by the hand of a killer.

"This is where things get interesting," Strauss said, and Ross could almost swear she said it in exactly the same tone of voice that her boss, Doctor Nugent had used with him over the years. "Of course, the first thing I did was look for signs of a natural death. Even young men of Aaron's age have been known to keel over from heart failure, for example, but then, I noticed a few scraps of lint-like fibres in the nasal passages, petechial haemorrhaging around the eyes and signs of cyanosis in the face. I compared the lint fibres with the pillow cases on the bed and they provided me with a visual match. Tests are ongoing to confirm my thoughts. I made a quick examination of the body as it lay on the bed and lo and behold, I found a similar pin prick on Aaron's upper left arm. I had enough to warrant a determination of a suspicious death, and that's why we're here today."

"Seems to me you've got it all worked out, Doctor," said Ross. "I'm surprised you're going through the whole business of the autopsy if you think you've already determined cause of death."

"Ah, procedures, rules and regulations, Inspector," Nugent chimed in. "As ye well know, in cases of suspicious death we have tae carry out a full post-mortem examination, and so that's what we're about today."

"Yes, of course. I know that Doc, just seems a waste of time sometimes."

"Aye, well, I'll not disagree with you on that one, Inspector, but anyway, we were just finishing up anyway, when you and D.C. Ferris arrived."

"Okay, so, what's your verdict, Doctor Strauss?"

Ross directed the question to the younger pathologist as, strictly speaking, it was her case, despite Nugent being her supervisor.

"Death was caused by asphyxia, Inspector. But, it's possible the victim was drugged first in order to render him unconscious and therefore eliminate any chances of him struggling while he was being suffocated. It looks very much as if his girlfriend was also drugged to pacify her while the murder was being carried out."

"There is another option that you may have missed here, Doctor, if you don't mind me saying so," said the quick thinking Paul Ferris.

"Go on, please, D.C. Ferris," Strauss replied.

Ross smiled, thinking he already knew what Ferris was about to add, and as the young detective spoke he confirmed Ross's own thoughts.

"Well, what if the murderer was actually intending to kill both Aaron and Sally? He successfully knocks them both out somehow with a drug of some description, manages to complete the murder of Decker, and then before he can kill the young woman, something disturbs him, a knock on the door, a noise at the window, I don't know. It could have been anything, I'm just theorising here, but it's surely possible. The girl could still be a target."

"You're quite right, Paul," Ross agreed.

"Yes, I suppose you are," said Strauss.

After a moment's hesitation, Ross added another option to Ferris's initial supposition.

"Your theory is good, Paul, but it also opens up another possible scenario."

"Sir?"

"Yes, it's equally possible the girlfriend is a very clever and devious killer. She could have injected Decker, suffocated him while he was unconscious and then injected herself with enough of whatever the knockout drug was, just enough to make sure she was still out of it when someone came to find them in the morning. She was bound to know the housemates would come looking for Aaron when he didn't show up at breakfast time."

"I see what you mean, sir. So, Sally Metcalfe could be a potential victim or she could be the murderer. Looks like we either have to protect her, or investigate her in detail."

"Exactly," said Ross.

Having listened to the two detectives thinking 'on the hoof' Doctor William Nugent turned to his female colleague and observed,

"Aye well, that's why they're the police and we're just the old sawbones, Vicky," Nugent concluded. "It's their job to look one step beyond our findings, in order to catch the criminals. Am I correct, Inspector?"

"I suppose you are, Doctor. Yes, we rely heavily on what you can discover from the dead, but we have to take what you give us and try to build a case around the simple facts of what actually caused a person's death."

"Well, I wish you luck with this one. Such a shame, and him so young," said Nugent. "I'll have our full report on your desk as soon as humanly possible."

"Thanks to you both," said Ross, at which time the doors to the autopsy room flew open and a well-dressed figure of a man burst into the room closely followed by a red-faced and flustered-looking Michelle Hill.

CHAPTER 5

JEROME DECKER III

No one in Autopsy Room 2 needed to look further than the face of the tall man who blustered into the room to know he was the father of the young man who lay on the stainless steel autopsy table in front of them. The facial resemblance was clear for all to see. With swift presence of mind, Paul Ferris stepped quickly towards the advancing man and despite being considerably shorter and of a lesser physique, stood his ground directly in front of him, his arms spread out to form a physical barrier.

"Sir, you really don't want to some any closer. Please, just wait here a minute."

"That's my son," the man shouted, the anguish clear in his voice. "I want to see my son."

Ross quickly joined Ferris and the two of them managed to force Jerome Decker to back-pedal until he was standing with his back against the wall beside the double doors.

"Mr. Decker, I'm Detective Inspector Ross, and this is Detective Constable Ferris. You do not want to see your son at this moment, I assure you. Please allow the doctors to complete their work and then I'm sure Doctor Nugent will arrange for you to see your son."

"Aye, of course I will, Mr. Decker," said Nugent, "but the inspector is quite right about not seeing him just now. The inspector will talk to you while we finish here. Inspector Ross, you can use my office if you like. You know the way, of course."

"Yes, thank you, Doctor," Ross replied, gratefully. "Please, sir, come with me. I know you're upset and grieving, but we really do need to talk to you."

Somehow, Ross and Ferris managed to shepherd Decker senior from the room and along the corridor. Ferris opened the door to Nugent's office and Ross guided the father into the room, Ferris closing the door as he followed them inside. As soon as the door closed, without invitation, Jerome Decker slumped into one of the visitors' chairs in the office and held his head in his hands, his grief palpable as his shoulders shook and tears began to fall from his red-rimmed eyes.

"Take your time, Mr. Decker," said Ross, passing a box of tissues across the desk, obviously kept there by Nugent for just such occasions, which Ferris handed to the distraught man. Decker looked up, saw the box and took out a single tissue which he used to dab at his eyes.

"Thank you. I'm real sorry for bursting in like that. I was just … hell, I don't know what I was doing."

"You're upset, you want to lash out, and you want answers, am I correct, Mr. Decker?"

"Well, yes, you're right, Inspector. This news has devastated my wife and me, I can tell you."

"Where is your wife, sir?"

"She's still in London. I didn't want her to come here just yet, not until things are clearer. Do you have any idea exactly what happened to my son, Inspector…?"

"Ross, sir. Andrew Ross is my name."

Ross turned to Ferris and asked him to organise tea and coffee for them all. "Maybe young Michelle can help," he said as Ferris rose to leave,

With Ferris gone, Ross leaned forward and looked into the eyes of the grieving father. He decided the out and out truth was his best option in dealing with the American.

"Mr. Decker, I won't hide anything from you. All the evidence we have so far points to the fact that your son was murdered."

"Murdered? My God, we were told he'd been found dead, but nobody at the embassy said anything about murder. Please, tell me what happened. Aaron was so popular; I just can't believe anyone hated him enough to murder him."

"Your son was found dead in his bed by one of the young men who shared the house in Wavertree with him. His girlfriend, Sally Metcalfe, was still asleep beside him apparently, and when woken up, she became hysterical on finding Aaron had died in the night. We've since discovered that both Aaron and Sally were given some sort of drug intravenously to knock then both out, after which Aaron was asphyxiated with his own pillow. Toxicology tests are being carried out as we speak to determine the drug that was used to knock them out. That's about it, so far, Mr. Decker. My team were only called into this investigation this morning, though we have the file from the officers who first responded to the emergency call."

Decker looked stunned. Maybe he thought his son had died from an accident or natural causes. To be told your child has been murdered must be a terribly traumatic experience, Ross thought, glad at that moment that he and Maria had no children of their own,

"You have no suspects?" Decker asked.

"Not as yet, no sir. It's early days, yet. Tell me, do you know of anyone who might have wished Aaron harm?"

"Not a soul, Inspector Ross. Like I said, Aaron was popular, gregarious and easy to get along with. This is a nightmare, a real nightmare. What the hell am I going to tell his mother?"

"I'm sorry. I know this isn't easy for you, for we have to know as much as we can about your son if we're to find his killer."

"I understand. Ask away, Inspector Ross."

"Do you have any enemies, Mr. Decker? Could someone have tried to get at you through your son? Could killing Aaron have been meant to send you some kind of message? I understand you're something in the U.S. State Department?"

"I'm nothing special, Inspector, just a simple Cultural Attaché."

"And what exactly does that entail, Mr. Decker?"

"Nothing sensitive, I assure you," said Decker. "My job simply involves furthering positive relations between my country and yours, and any others who happen to come into contact with our embassy in London."

"So you don't have any kind of political agenda that might have made someone think that hurting Aaron could influence you in some way?"

"No, Inspector Ross, definitely not. You need to look elsewhere. What about the guys he was rooming with, or house sharing or whatever you call it over here?"

"You never met them?"

"Hell, yes, once or twice, I think, when Aaron first moved in up here. We came up to help him get settled and met the two other guys then. I never got to know them. It was just a few minutes here and there. Aaron said they were both studying at the university too, and I thought that was good enough as a recommendation."

"Okay, and the girlfriend, Sally Metcalfe?"

"Met her a few times. Seemed a nice enough girl, a little stuck-up maybe, but nice enough. Aaron said she was studying Marine Biology, and I thought that a bit odd for a girl like her, but he said she wanted to help preserve the oceans for the future, so maybe not so odd after all, huh?"

"I'd have to agree with you," said Ross. "Would Sally have any reason to harm Aaron?"

"Oh, come on, Inspector Ross. Now you're clutching at straws. You said she was knocked out too, so how could she have killed my son? And as far as I know, she adored him. Why would she hurt him? And what possible motive could she have? She came to visit us in London at least a dozen times, with Aaron. No way would that girl have hurt him."

"Okay, so, thank you for your patience, Mr. Decker," said Ross, as Ferris entered the room, carrying a tray, followed by Michelle the receptionist with a second tray. Between them, they'd made tea and coffee, and now brought them in to the inspector and the diplomat.

* * *

Ross allowed a lull in the questioning as they sipped their tea or coffee, and in those few quiet minutes, Decker seemed to relax slightly, the tension of earlier releasing itself a little.

Sensing a good moment, Ross began again.

"Do you have any other children, Mr. Decker?"

"Yes, Peter and Kelly. Peter is twenty seven and Kelly's just eighteen. She's at home with her Mom, in a totally distraught state."

"And Peter?"

"Back home in the States, Inspector. Peter's in a rock band, not quite the career choice I'd have picked for him after his years at Harvard, but then, what can we parents do nowadays, huh?"

"So, he doesn't know about Aaron yet?"

"Oh, he knows alright. I caught him between gigs when his band stopped over in Seattle last night. They've cancelled the rest of their tour and Peter is on a flight across the Atlantic right now. He's gonna check in with his Mom in London and then grab a flight up to your John Lennon airport to join me here."

"You do realise, Mr. Decker, that there's little you can do up here, unless you have information that can help the investigation? Don't you think you'd be better staying in London with your family while we do our jobs and find your son's killer?"

Decker's face seemed to change in that moment, displaying a hardness that hadn't been evident a few minutes earlier.

"Inspector Ross, if you think I'm leaving Liverpool before my son's killer is found, then you sure as hell don't know me. When Peter arrives he'll be bringing his Mom and sister up here with him and we'll be here for the duration. Any way we can help, we will, but I do promise not to get in the way of your investigation."

"I see," Ross replied. "It's a free country, Mr. Decker and you and your family will be welcome here in Liverpool. I just hope it doesn't distress your wife too much, and your daughter of course."

"They'll be fine, Inspector, just fine. Now, is there anything else I can do for you right now? I'd like to see my son, and carry out the formal identification you require, if that's okay."

"Go and see if they're ready for Mr. Decker, would you, Paul?" Ross asked Paul Ferris who went to check on the status of the remains, returning a minute later with Doctor Strauss in tow.

"We're ready for you now, Mr. Decker," Strauss said, as Decker rose from his seat, following her from the room, with Ross and Ferris close behind.

Nugent and Strauss had worked quickly to make Aaron Decker's remains suitable for viewing by his father, the Y incision having been quickly closed and the skin and hair on the skull replaced so the elder Decker wouldn't see that his son's brain had been removed for autopsy purposes.

Decker stood stoically at the viewing screen window with Straus and the two police officers as William Nugent himself performed the ritual display of the body, covered in a discreet white sheet, and Ross could almost feel the grief emanating from every pore of Decker's body as he nodded and almost in a whisper, confirmed that the body was that of his son, Aaron.

"What happens now?" Decker virtually whispered as his voice faltered.

Ross placed a hand on Decker's shoulder, slowly managing to turn him away from the viewing window as the curtains on the other side automatically slid across to block the view into the room, Ross having pressed a small button beside the glass that lit up an indicator in the laying-out room, letting the attendant know identification was complete.

"Well, for now, I think you should go back to your hotel. You've told us what you know about your son's housemates and his life over here, unless there's anything else you can add."

There were three burgundy upholstered upright chairs in the room, placed against the back wall, and Decker suddenly sat down heavily onto one of them, his face appearing even more ashen than before, having looked at the dead face of his youngest son.

"He was a good son, Inspector Ross."

"I'm sure he was," Ross replied sympathetically.

"He made friends easily, but I never knew him make any enemies."

"Well, we understand from his girlfriend's original statement to Detective Sergeant Meadows that he received some news that day that had upset him slightly. Would you have any idea what that was?"

"No idea at all, I'm sorry. Heck, it might just have been something to do with his cricketing for all I know."

"Tell me, Mr. Decker, whereabouts in the USA do you and your family live?"

"What? Oh, we live in Washington D.C. Aaron was at Georgetown University before we transferred over here. He was quite a rising star for the college baseball team and they sorely missed him when we moved, I can tell you."

"I've heard he didn't take long to make a name for himself with the University cricket team when he got here too, Mr. Decker?"

"So he did, though I can't for the hell of it figure out that crazy game of yours, Inspector."

"Neither can a lot of us, please believe me, sir."

Decker seemed to have calmed down and Ross was glad he'd been able to turn his thoughts away from the cold, lifeless cadaver in the next room with talk of his son's achievements on the sports field. He needed to press on with the investigation and for now, Jerome Decker III needed to go to his hotel, eat something and try to relax, maybe phone his wife, do anything to give Ross the chance to get on with the job of finding his son's killer.

Thankfully, Ross was able to convince Decker to return to his hotel soon after, hoping that the imminent arrival of his family might keep him occupied for a little while, and Ross had Michelle arrange for a taxi to collect Decker and ferry him to his hotel.

Ross and Decker parted with a firm handshake and soon afterwards, Ross and Ferris made their way back to headquarters, where Ross intended to step up the pace of the investigation. Something was eating away at the back of Ross's mind and he believed he knew just the man to answer his questions.

CHAPTER 6

OLD BUDDIES

"Andy Ross, well I'll be," the distinctive New York accent of U.S. Immigration Officer Ethan Tiffen bellowed into the phone when his secretary informed him who was waiting on the line to speak with him. "How are you, old buddy?"

"I'm good, Ethan, thanks. How about you and the lovely Sophie?"

"We're fine, Andy, just fine. But, I'm guessing this isn't a social call?"

"You guess correctly, Ethan. I'm looking for information about one of your compatriots, and fellow embassy employees."

"Really? Can I ask why?"

"We've got a suspicious death on our hands, a young man found dead in his bed, and his father is one of your cultural attachés."

"Got a name?"

"Decker."

"As in Jerome Decker III?"

"You know him?"

"Let's say I know of him, Andy. You say his son is dead?"

"Murdered, Ethan. Suffocated with a pillow."

"Jesus H. Christ. That's bad, real bad, Andy. I take it Decker is in Liverpool?"

"He is, and says he won't be leaving until we find Aaron's killer. I need to know if there's anything I should know about him. Seems he had the power to demand an immediate autopsy to find out what killed his son and there's some heavy pressure coming down from above for us to effect a fast resolution of the case."

Tiffen fell silent for a few seconds, and Ross could almost sense his friend being locked in thought. Ross broke the silence.

"Ethan?"

"U huh, yeah, sorry, Andy, just thinking there for a minute."

"Thinking what, Ethan? Come on my friend, I know you want to tell me something. I promise if it's of a sensitive nature, I'll keep it jut between the two of us. Just what is it about this cultural attaché of yours?"

"Look Andy, I could get canned for this, so listen up. I ain't gonna repeat it okay?"

"I'm listening, Ethan. What's going on, my friend? Just who is Decker?"

"Andy, you're not familiar with the way diplomatic missions and embassies are set up are you?"

"Never had much need of that kind of information, Ethan, but I'm guessing you're about to educate me?"

"Just a little my friend. You're obviously not aware that in diplomatic circles, a 'cultural attaché' is kind of a catch-all description for a number of different disciplines."

Ross interrupted, his initial vague suspicions already vindicated.

"He's a spook, isn't he Ethan? Some kind of spy."

"Not a spy, Andy. That would be going too far. Let's just say Jerome Decker is on the side of the angels, and looks after certain matters of our country's international security."

"C.I.A." said Ross, not a question this time, but a statement of conclusion.

"You didn't hear it from me. I never said it, Andy, you did."

"How high up is he?"

"Deputy Head of London Station, that high up, Andy."

"Right, that explains the pressure from above. Thanks Ethan."

"We never had this conversation, Andy, right?"

"What conversation?"

"Thanks, friend."

"Thanks to you, Ethan. Better go, got lots to do."

"Me too. Say hello to Maria okay?"

"Okay."

The line went dead.

CHAPTER 7

MANOR COURT, LIVERPOOL

As D.I. Ross was allowing the information Ethan Tiffen had given him to assimilate itself into his thought processes in relation to the case, Detective Constables Sam Gable and Derek McLennan were seated in the lounge of the house that Aaron Decker had shared with his two friends, both of whom sat on the sofa resembling a pair of bookends, as Gable and McLennan took up the two matching armchairs.

Tim Knight and Martin Lewis did indeed give the two detectives a book-end feeling as they sat facing the detectives, both looking nervous and apprehensive, this being almost certainly the first time their lives had been affected by such violent tragedy. McLennan expected no less and as always, was prepared to make allowances for any hesitancy, although he was aware that the two men in front of him were at present the best suspects they possessed for the murder.

The two young men were very different in appearance. Tim Knight was tall and rangy in build, with dark brown hair cut very short, and a handsome, almost aristocratic look about the face. Lewis on the other hand, was shorter, built rather more powerfully, his legs thicker around the thighs, and his chest threatening to break out of the thin t-shirt that covered his torso. His collar-length hair was pure Nordic blonde.

Of the two, Tim Knight appeared slightly more self-assured, not surprisingly as far as Sam Gable was concerned. She'd already read the initial report from Sergeant Meadows and knew that Tim was the eldest of the three house mates at twenty-five, so was perhaps a little more mature than his friend Martin Lewis, at twenty-two, the same age as the unfortunate Aaron Decker. It had been Lewis who had first found the body of Aaron, another reason for him to be in a rather greater state of shock than Knight. What privately amused Gable was that both men wore virtually the same clothing, white T-shirts, faded denim jeans and white trainers, of differing brands to be fair. *So much for the young and their aversion to uniformity*, she thought, adding to herself, *a student is a student is a student.*

"So, Martin," said Derek McLennan, "You knocked on the bedroom door and then what?"

"Well, I knew Sally had stayed over, you know? But Aaron was a real early riser, and he always said breakfast was an imperative part of the day, so when they didn't come down when they smelled the breakfast, I thought I'd better go and give 'em a shout, like. Tim was cooking, grilling bacon, tomatoes, and fried eggs with hash browns, and I left him to it, went and knocked on Aaron's bedroom door, and got no answer. I knocked again, a bit louder, and then opened the door a crack and peeped in, just in case they were…you know, doing it, like. They both looked fast asleep so I shouted, *"Hey you two, breakfast's ready. Come on, get up, it'll go cold."* Nobody moved, and I thought it odd, because Aaron is, sorry was, a very light sleeper. I moved a bit closer and something sort of spooked me. They didn't look right. I walked up to Aaron and gave him a nudge, but he just didn't react. Then I noticed his left hand was just dangling from the side of the bed. I felt his neck, like in the movies, you know, and his skin was cold as ice. I just knew he was dead. I shouted at Sally, thinking maybe she was dead too, but she moved a bit and moaned, so I went round to her side of the bed and started shaking her. After a minute or so, she began to come round a bit more and I virtually screamed at her, "For fuck's sake, wake up, Sally. I think Aaron's dead."

That got through to her and she sat bolt upright, and the duvet slipped down, and I could see was naked, so I grabbed Aaron's dressing gown from behind the door and wrapped it round her shoulders. As I did, she looked at Aaron and it was like she suddenly realised what I'd said and she started to scream. Boy, did she scream? She went from semi-conscious to hysterical in a few seconds and I ended up slapping her face to try and calm her down. When she eventually shut up, I asked her if she and Aaron had been using anything, which was a stupid question, because Aaron hated anything to do with drugs. He'd have chucked me or Tim out of he ever thought we were using anything, even a bit of weed."

Martin finally fell silent, as though he was all talked out, and had finally come up for air.

"Thanks, Martin," said Gable. "That was very precise, if you don't mind me saying so."

Breathing heavily, Martin went on, "Thanks, it's not something you forget in a hurry, finding your mate dead in his bed like that. I forgot to say, when Sally started her screaming, Tim came running up the stairs like an express train and when I sort of gasped out what I'd found, he was the one who ran downstairs to the phone and dialled 999. The police and an ambulance were here within fifteen minutes, I think. One of the paramedics confirmed Aaron was dead and the police sergeant told me and Tim to wait downstairs while he called for the Scenes of Crime people, and looked around the bedroom. We went to the kitchen, tried to eat breakfast but couldn't face it, so we just made fresh coffee and sat at the kitchen table until the sergeant came to talk to us."

Derek McLennan now joined the conversation, seeking additional background on the two housemates.

"Where are you both from originally, and what are you both studying? Tim, you sound fairly local, but your accent is definitely not Liverpudlian, Martin."

Tim Knight, the eldest of the two was the first to answer, having said little so far.

"Well spotted, detective. I'm from West Derby, originally. We moved down to Chester when I was twelve, and I thought I'd lost most of my accent over the years. Looks like I was wrong about that. I'm in the last year of doing my post doc in Molecular Biology. I could have gone to a bigger university but Liverpool is close to home, plus the labs here are great and we're lucky to have Professor Joseph Freund here, a real expert in his field."

"Thanks," said McLennan. "Your accent's not that strong, but you know what they say, you can take the lad out of Liverpool, but…"

"Yeah, right, I know," said Tim with a wry grin.

"And how about you, Martin?" McLennan asked.

"I'm from Grimsby," the younger man replied. "I'm in my second year of a post doc in English Literature."

"And how will Aaron's death affect you two with regards to the house, I mean? I presume the three of you shared the rent?"

"No problems, there," Tim Knight replied to the question. "The house is actually owned by Aaron's father. He's already been in touch to say we can stay on, same rent, as long as we find another post doctoral student to share with us."

"Isn't that unusual?" Sam Gable asked. "How come Aaron's Dad, an American embassy official, owns a house in Liverpool?"

"Oh, nothing sinister, I assure you. When we met, Aaron was looking for a place to live; he was in a hotel up until then. When we invited him to move in with us after Charlie Stone got his doctorate and moved out, Mr. Decker came up one weekend, met the two of us and the next thing we knew, he'd contacted the landlord, made him an offer he couldn't refuse, and bought the place. He said it would be a good idea for the future to have a good place for post grad students to live while they're here."

"Very altruistic of him, I must say," said McLennan.

"And did either of you share Aaron's love for cricket?" Gable asked next.

"That's how I met him," said Tim Knight. "I was the one who kind of got him hooked on the game. I was already playing for the uni team and I invited him to come and watch a game one weekend. He was fascinated by the game so I got him to come to practice one evening.

He initially thought it was a bit of a 'quaint' game but soon changed his mind after he'd been struck a couple of times on the neck and shoulder by our fast bowlers, and when he got his fingers stung trying to catch a well hit ball. Anyway, Aaron was a natural at the game and when we found out he'd played college baseball in the States, we could see why he had such great hand and eye coordination. The team captain invited him to join us and he soon learned the game and never looked back. The team's going to miss him, that's for sure."

Gable looked towards Martin Lewis, a questioning look on her face. The young man realised she was waiting for his response to the same question.

"No, sorry, I'm not a cricket player. Rugby's my game, wing three-quarter."

"Yes, I can see you're built for speed," said Gable appreciating the muscles easily discernible under the young man's T-shirt. Lewis actually blushed as he caught Sam eyeing his physique.

"I see, and did either of you mix socially with Aaron?"

"We both did," said Tim. "We were mates, for God's sake, of course we did."

"And during your nights out and so on, did you ever see Aaron get mixed up in any trouble?"

"Hell no. He was definitely a turn-around and walk the other way sort of bloke if anything started in a pub or club. Trouble just wasn't Aaron's thing, believe me, right Martin?"

"Right," Lewis confirmed. "Aaron was a real gent. He always saw himself as a guest in our country and treated everyone with great respect. He was a great guy."

"So neither of you know of anyone who may have wanted to harm him?" Derek McLennan asked the pair.

"No way," Tim replied forcefully. "He had no enemies, detective. Aaron was an all-round popular chap."

"Well," McLennan spoke in a deadpan tone, "I think it's safe to assume he had at least one, don't you?"

The two young men fell silent. There was little they could say in response to McLennan's observation, the answer being all too obvious.

CHAPTER 8

SALLY'S STORY

Andy Ross still found it a little strange walking into the office of the D.C.I. After seeing Detective Chief Inspector Harry Porteous ensconced behind the expansive desk for so many years, somehow, his old friend and Porteous's replacement, Oscar Agostini appeared somewhat incongruous in the boss's familiar leather chair.

"Still find it a bit weird seeing you in that chair, Oscar," he said as Agostini invited him to sit down.

"You'll get used to it in time, Andy," Agostini replied. "I still feel odd myself, to tell the truth, having this bloody great office all to myself. Something we both need to come to terms with. Still never mind all that. Where do we stand on the Decker case?"

Unlike Porteous, Agostini made it a point to talk to Ross immediately after the morning team briefing, in order to ensure he was always up to date with whatever his team were up to. Ross found it a good idea which took no more than ten minutes and meant he didn't have to go looking for the new boss to bring him up to speed on current cases.

"Remember I told you I had a contact at the U.S. embassy?" Ross opened the update.

"Sure I do. I take it you found something?"

"I certainly did. Our grieving father, Jerome Decker III is only the bloody Deputy Head of Station for the C.I.A. in London."

"Bloody hell, a spook," Agostini exclaimed. "Do you think it might be significant in the case?"

"At this point, Oscar, I don't know, but it does explain why he was able to bring some pressure to bear on the top brass. Whether the murder of his son has any connection to his intelligence work, I can't say, but we can't discount the possibility."

"So, this could get very messy, Andy. If there's a political motive or anything to do with the damn C.I.A's covert activities we could find ourselves chasing shadows and getting nowhere if the powers that be put the blocks up."

"I know," said Ross. "I propose to talk to Decker, let him know I'm aware of the true nature of his work, and see how he reacts."

"That's a good idea, but won't it place your source in jeopardy of exposure?"

"Hmm, you're right," Ross agreed as he contemplated ways of revealing his knowledge without compromising his friend, Ethan Tiffen.

"I don't want to go into this investigation with one hand tied behind my back, and I need to know if Decker is keeping anything from us."

"I agree. Let me make a couple of calls, see what I can do. If I can find a way to protect your source, I will. What are your immediate plans?"

"I'm going to talk to Sally Metcalfe, the girlfriend, this morning. I've given her time to grieve a little before interviewing her. She should be ready to talk to us now."

"Okay, do it and I'll see if there's a way we can 'out' our friend Decker. Izzie Drake's back at work tomorrow, isn't she?"

"Yes, and I must say I've missed having her around."

"Good sergeants are hard to find, Andy. You've worked together a long time now. You make a good team."

"I think so too."

"Well, it'll be good to have the squad back at full strength tomorrow. I'm sure you'll value her input into this one, for sure."

"I will indeed. She can be very insightful."

"So I've heard," said Agostini.

The D.C.I was well aware of the almost telepathic relationship that Ross and Drake enjoyed, and knew it was one of his team's biggest assets.

"You'd better be off then," he said, as Ross rose to leave. "Who are you taking with you?"

"I've got Ferris working with me at present. He's intelligent and also has a good insight into difficult problems. And, it's good to get him out into the field and away from his computers for once."

"Right, off you go, and check back with me when you get back and we'll compare notes."

* * *

Ross and Ferris sat opposite Sally Metcalfe, who was dressed in a 'Save the Whales' sweatshirt and a pair of expensive beige coloured jeans in the tiny living room in the small house she shared with her fellow student Megan Rose. The two-bedroomed terraced house was not far from Aaron Decker's home in Wavertree, on a street of old back-to-backs that had mostly been converted into student accommodation. The house clearly showed itself as being the domain of two young women. For one thing, Ross immediately noticed, it was clean, with the scent of air freshener hinting at housework having been completed before the arrival of the two police officers. The old fashioned sash window was slightly open, allowing fresh air into the room and there wasn't a speck of dust to be seen on the top of the television, the mantle-piece, or the glass topped coffee table positioned in the middle of the room. Ross guessed the two women probably used it as a dining table for fast food dinners or sandwiches in an evening.

The walls were decorated with old-fashioned anaglypta wallpaper, painted in a neutral magnolia finish, an obvious landlord's choice. The picture above the fireplace however, Ross surmised was purely Sally's choice, based on his knowledge of her studies in the field of marine biology. It was a superb print of an oil painting, depicting what he assumed to be a pod of dolphins leaping from the waves of, he assumed, the Antarctic Ocean, given the dramatic backdrop of what he presumed to be an ice shelf. He'd seen enough David Attenborough nature documentaries and was sufficiently well-read to feel able to comment on the dramatic scene.

"Yes, Detective Inspector," Sally confirmed. "It is Antarctica. That's the Ross Ice Shelf in the background. It could have been named for you, couldn't it?"

"Nice thought, Miss Metcalfe. Who was it actually named after, as a matter of interest?"

"It's named after Captain James Clark Ross, who discovered it in 1841. It's the largest ice-shelf in the world, and has often been used as the place to locate base camps for many Antarctic expeditions, due to it being so flat, apart from the massive coastal cliffs and ridges of course. The cliffs can reach as high as 70 metres, around 230 feet, and they are really a magnificent sight."

"You've actually been there?" Ross asked, incredulously.

"Last year," said Sally. "My parents paid for me to go on an Antarctic cruise. I flew from Punta Arenas to St George Island and then boarded an Antarctic cruise liner called the *Sea Sentinel* from there. Those Antarctic cruise ships are incredible, Inspector Ross, built to withstand the ice and the freezing temperatures while keeping the passengers warm and comfortable as long as you're not out on deck of course. For two weeks, I felt like I could be on an alien world. All the photos and TV documentaries in the world can't prepare you for the real thing, honestly"

"I'm sure they must be, that is, the ships, well protected against the ice and so on," Ross agreed, pleased that the short diversion from the true reason for his visit had seemingly put Sally Metcalfe at her ease in his company.

"My friend Megan loved the print too so she had no problem with me making it the centrepiece of the room, but you haven't come to talk to me about my Antarctic adventures, have you?"

"I'm afraid not, Miss Metcalfe."

"Call me Sally, please."

"Okay, Sally it is. Detective Constable Ferris and I have a few questions we need to ask you. I know you're possibly still in shock and grieving for Aaron, but whatever help you can give us may help us to find his killer, and the person who drugged you both."

"Ask anything you want to, Inspector. I can't believe anyone could have hated Aaron enough to want to kill him. It gave me the biggest shock of my life when Martin woke me up and I realised poor Aaron was lying dead beside me."

With those words, the realisation of the event took hold of the young woman, and tears appeared in her eyes. Ross and Ferris could see her fighting to control her emotions and both men felt a huge wave of sympathy for her.

"Wait, did you say we were *both* drugged?" Sally suddenly asked.

"Yes, it looks that way," Ferris replied. "We're awaiting the toxicology results from Aaron's autopsy and the results of your blood tests to find out what drug was used, but we think you were both drugged, and the killer then suffocated Aaron in his sleep."

"But, drugged, how?"

"Doctor Strauss found a pin prick on Aaron's arm, and there was one on you too when she examined you," Ross explained.

"But how can we have been given injections without us knowing about it?"

"You and Aaron had a few drinks before you went to bed, right?"

"Yes, why?"

"It's possible the killer gave you time to fall asleep naturally then entered the room and administered the injections as you slept. If you'd both had a few drinks you'd have been in a deep sleep in minutes."

"But wasn't that a big chance to take? I mean, what if one of us had woken up while he was doing it?"

"That's a question we've yet to answer, Sally. What were you both drinking?" Ross asked.

"Aaron had a bottle of vodka and we had maybe two or three vodka martinis. Him being American and all, he loved making exotic drinks for us."

Paul Ferris had followed Ross's reasoning perfectly.

"You think it's possible someone may have drugged the vodka to make sure they both fell asleep quickly, sir?"

"Yes, it could have happened like that," Ross replied. "How well do you know Aaron's housemates, Sally?"

"Quite well, Inspector. You can't think one of them had anything to do with it, surely?"

"I'm not eliminating anyone from our enquiries yet," he said. "They were both perfectly placed to have spiked the vodka, and would have known exactly when you went to bed and so could have calculated how long it would take for you both to be safely asleep."

"I still don't believe Tim or Martin could be involved," Sally protested. "They were both Aaron's friends, Tim especially, being on the cricket team with him and all. Before Aaron and I got together I'd gone on a couple of dates with Tim, nothing serious or anything, but I can tell you he's a very gentle and kind person, and was really happy for me and Aaron when we did become a couple."

Ross didn't press the point, feeling sure that Sally and the two men would doubtless be in touch with other and it wouldn't be prudent to give away too much at this point. Instead he rolled out the old cliché, "Do you know of anyone who may have wanted to harm Aaron or you?"

"Well no. I'd say Aaron was universally liked. As for me, I don't have any enemies that I know about either. Why do you ask if someone might have wanted to hurt me, Inspector?"

"Because Sally, and I hate to say this to you, but it is a vague possibility that whoever killed Aaron may have wanted you dead too, and that something happened to prevent them carrying out the full extent of their plan."

A look of pure shock appeared on Sally's face and she threw her right hand up to cover her mouth as she gasped, "No, surely not. Why would anyone want to harm me, Inspector?"

It was Paul Ferris who provided the answer as he said, "Why would anyone have wanted to harm Aaron Decker?"

Sally fell silent, at a loss for words.

Ross picked up the interview once again.

"You're studying marine biology, I believe, Sally?"

"Yes, that's right. You don't think this has anything to do with my studies, surely?"

"Like I said, nothing's being discounted at present. Do your studies include anything of a sensitive nature?"

"Meaning what, exactly?"

"Well, anything that might be of value to someone outside of the university?"

"Oh God, no, nothing like that. I'm currently working on a paper relating to the effect of global warming on the southern ocean and its ecology. Nothing secretive or sensitive about it, I assure you."

"And Aaron?"

"What, his historical research? Again, nothing to get anyone wound up about."

"You're sure of that?" Ferris asked.

"Honestly. He was writing a paper on the Allied invasion and liberation of Greece during World War Two. I doubt anyone could find a reason in there to want to murder him. But, listen can we get back to my question? Do you really think someone might have wanted us both dead?"

Ross replied. "Yes, Sally. We have to take it as a possibility at this time. For that reason, I'm going to assign a police officer to keep an eye on you for the next few days, to make sure you're safe."

Ross didn't say it, but such a move would also enable them to keep an eye on Sally Metcalfe's movements, just in case she was involved in the murder of her boyfriend.

"That's really going to look good, isn't it? I mean, walking around campus and going to the pub with a policeman trailing around after me like a puppy dog."

"Don't worry, Sally. The officer will be female and in plain clothes. We'll make sure she fits in with your student life as far as appearance goes, and anyone seeing her with you will just see her as another student."

Still not totally convinced, Sally acquiesced to Ross's suggestion, privately acknowledging to herself that she'd probably feel safer with a police shadow, just in case she was on a killer's hit list.

Ross nodded to Ferris who moved on to the next part of the interview.

"Tell me about your family, please Sally."

"My family? What do you want to know about them?"

"Well, just some basic background information. It helps us build a better picture of everyone involved in a case like this. We know your father is a reasonably wealthy businessman in Lancaster. What about your Mum, any brothers and sisters?"

"Okay, so you know my Dad owns a road haulage company. He started the company with one beaten up old truck and built it up to what it is today. Mum is the company secretary. She didn't have to work but hates sitting around doing nothing. My two brothers are really supportive of me even though they thought I was mad going to university."

"Why was that, Sally?" Ferris asked.

"They both went to university. Trevor, he's twenty-nine now, went to Oxford, got a degree in Applied Physics, and wanted to be a research chemist, but when he left uni, just couldn't get a job in his chosen field. Seems lots of kids got their A levels, bypassed university and got jobs with the big companies who paid for them to go to college one or two days a week. By the time Trevor left Oxford all the available jobs had gone. He got a job in a supermarket in Lancaster, stuck at it and now he's a branch manager in Sheffield, but it's not quite what he was aiming for. Ian's twenty six, and went to uni in Exeter, got his degree in biological sciences and hit the same brick wall as Trevor. There are more than two hundred people chasing every decent job for graduates, and the chances of finding what you are looking for are slim. I'm lucky, because I have a sponsor and when I leave uni, as long as I have my degree, I'm guaranteed a placement at an oceanographic institute in the U.S.A. thanks to a couple of contacts my Dad made through his business dealings."

"Lucky girl," said Ferris, and Ross couldn't help wondering if there was a connection between Sally's sponsor and Aaron's C.I.A father. He had to ask.

"Yes, very lucky. Mind if I ask who your sponsor is, Sally?"

"It's a company called Aegis Oceanographic. They're well known in the field of oceanographic exploration and it was a real surprise when I got their offer."

Ross flashed a look at Ferris that the detective constable correctly understood to mean, *Check out Aegis Oceanographic as soon as we get back to head-quarters.*

"Where are they from, Sally?"

"Oh, I think their main offices are somewhere in Maine, at The Aegis Oceanographic Institute, which is where the letter offering my sponsorship came from, but of course they own various survey ships and their people work all around the world, often working for different countries on ecological or environmental projects."

Ross was even more interested in Aegis by now.

"Does this company often sponsor students like you, Sally?"

"I should think so," she replied. "A lot of big companies work like that nowadays. I suppose it's how they target their future employees."

"Yes, I'm sure, and you say your Dad helped you get this sponsorship?"

"That's right. His company doesn't do work in the U.S.A. of course, but Aegis have a European division based in Spain and smaller research facilities all over Europe including one in Falmouth and apparently Dad had a contract to haul a load of stuff for them from the U.K. to their Spanish facility. Dad mentioned to one of their executives that I was looking to study ocean sciences and next thing I knew I received the offer from them a few weeks later. Dad said it was a gesture from Aegis because they were so pleased with the efficiency of Metcalfe Logistics. Some of the loads Dad's company carries for them are quite delicate and need special handling and he's never had any damages reported so their European director, who Dad plays golf with as well, is well pleased with the service."

"Is this European director American, Sally?"

"As far as I know, yes, but why all this interest in Aegis and my sponsorship, Inspector? What has any of this to do with what happened to me and Aaron?"

Ross hesitated for a second, unsure for a moment just what to say to Sally without tipping his hand to the way his mind was working.

"Well, with them being an American company, and Aaron being an American too, and his Dad working at the embassy in London, I just wondered if anyone from Aegis might have some connection with the Decker family, that's all, and I must say I'm fascinated by how this whole sponsorship thing works. I'm just a simple policeman, Sally; you must forgive me if I'm not quite on the ball when it comes to the academic world."

As answers go it was as bland and non-committal as Ross could have made it, but it seemed to do the trick in placating Sally Metcalfe, whose grief at the death of Aaron Decker remained the number one priority in her mind. Just as Ross was thinking of bringing the interview to a close, Ferris, who'd been unusually quite during most of the interview, intervened with a new question.

"Sally, you said Aegis have a U.K. office. Do they have any other working facilities in this country that you're aware of?"

"I think, when I looked them up after receiving the offer, I read that they have the facility in Devon, but that's the only one I seem to remember. I'm sure the webpage I read said something about Aegis being involved in some kind of research into the long-term environmental effects of decomposing shipwrecks on the marine life in the English Channel. I remember mentioning it to Aaron, who thought it was a great project, but then he would, being so interested in history. He'd have loved to go down and investigate the shipwrecks I'm sure, just for the fun of it."

"Yes, I'm sure," said Ferris. "He didn't do anything about that though, did he? And Falmouth's in Cornwall, not Devon, Sally."

"Sorry, my geography is awful isn't it? Oh no, I'm sure he didn't do anything, of course not, but he did get all excited for a couple of weeks."

"About what? Do you remember?" Ferris was on a roll.

"Yes, he said I'd inspired him to take a break from the paper he was working on and he was investigating the known shipwrecks in the Channel. He was amazed by how many recorded wrecks there are down there, a lot from the Second World War, he said, but also quite a few dating back over a hundred years or more in many cases. He seemed to have quite a bee in his bonnet about it for a few weeks, then he just stopped talking about it."

"And when was it that all this took place, Sally?"

"Oh, round about the time I was preparing for my Antarctic discovery cruise. In fact, he was still going at it when I left for the cruise but never mentioned it again after I returned. I never gave it much thought at the time. I just assumed it was one of those things he researched out of general curiosity and then lost interest after a while if it didn't give him anything that would further his post-doc studies."

"I see, thanks Sally," said Ferris as he finished jotting down her reply in his notebook. It was a good job he could read his own private shorthand which he'd developed over the last couple of years, when trying to make fast but accurate notes of witness statements and so on, because it was sure as hell that no one else would have been able to make sense of the apparent squiggles and scrawls that covered the pages of his notebook. Ross had a feeling that Paul Ferris might have hit on a new theory and would look forward to hearing his thoughts as soon as they left Sally Metcalfe's neat and tidy student accommodation.

Ross had one last question.

"Your friend, Megan. Did she know Aaron?"

"Yes, but only through me, Inspector. She's attending lectures at present but if you need to speak to her, I can ask her to call you and arrange it."

"That would be good, yes please, Sally. We just need to speak to as many people who knew Aaron, no matter how well, to dot the 'I's' and cross the 't's' so to speak."

Ross made a mental note to arrange for Sam Gable to visit Megan Rose and see if Sally's housemate could give them anything useful, and he and Ferris were soon motoring back to headquarters, where Ross called Ferris into his office for a quick two-man conference.

CHAPTER 9

NAUTICAL THEORIES

"Tell me where your thoughts are leading you, Paul," Ross said after he and Ferris had closed the door to his office, armed with mugs of hot coffee and Ferris's all important notebook.

"Well sir, it just seems to me that everything we have so far seems to be pointing across the Atlantic, so to speak. Aaron Decker was American, his father, as you told me is a fairly senior officer in the C.I.A, and then we find that Aaron's girlfriend is sponsored by an American company that could, and I stress *could*, sir, be involved in work for any number of countries around the world and so open to some kind of industrial espionage, at the very least. I thought it odd that Aaron would find it interesting when he heard about the work Aegis are doing in the English channel and then seemed to have forgotten or dismissed it in the time it took Sally Metcalfe to complete her Antarctic cruise. And didn't someone, somewhere down the line say something had upset Aaron in the days before his death, but he never told anyone what it was that had caused that upset? It all adds up to a whole load of conjecture, I know, but maybe Aaron's murder is a bit more complicated than we thought at first."

"Well done Paul, that's exactly the way I've been thinking too," Ross smiled at his detective constable. "The question is however, just what kind of complications. Any thoughts?"

Ferris went into deep thought for a few seconds, and Ross would swear he could almost hear the D.C's brain moving up a gear as he sorted through a jumble of thoughts before finally speaking.

"Suppose for a minute that Aaron Decker was digging into the past.

History was his subject, so he'd know how to research a subject thoroughly. I know that some of the wrecks around our coastline are designated war graves. What if he found that Aegis, in the course of their explorations, were disturbing or desecrating those sites? Not a great motive for murder, but worth considering. Or, maybe he found something with more tangible value to Aegis, something they would kill to protect."

"Such as? Go on, Paul, I'm fascinated by your thinking on this."

"Okay, weeell," said Ferris, drawing out the word *well*, "What if Aegis discovered one of those wrecks was carrying something when it sank, something with either significant monetary value, or maybe even military value?"

"Right," said Ross. "Now you're thinking, Paul. It would certainly interest the C.I.A. if he stumbled upon some long-lost experimental weapon or even something of substantially greater potential. A lot of work on the Atom bomb during the Second World War was shared, and maybe Decker discovered some secret he shouldn't have, or of course, as you say, maybe a previously secret cache of gold on board one of the wrecks, worth a fortune by today's standards, and it definitely wouldn't be the first time gold has served as a motive for murder."

Ferris allowed himself to take a breather and then looked almost forlornly at his boss.

"What's wrong Paul? Suddenly I get the feeling you're not totally convinced by your own theory."

"Sorry sir, don't mean to be defeatist. But if Decker did discover something and then told his father about it, surely the C.I.A would have moved on the case and Decker senior would have been a more logical target if Aegis wanted to stop any investigation into their operations. Plus, I haven't looked them up yet, but are we really going to suppose that a large company like that would resort to murder to cover up their activities?"

"If they were illegal activities, yes, they probably would and it's not necessarily Aegis as a whole that's involved here, it could just be a local thing, someone in their European division with an eye to making big money without the company being aware of it. Also, Decker would want to be certain of his information, and maybe he approached Aegis with his theory and spoke to the wrong man, from his point of view, before going to his father. That could have been what got him killed."

"Yes, that makes sense, sir, like a sort of rogue operation within the Aegis group, Decker stumbles on it, tries to check it out before telling his father, has the bad luck to speak to someone who is involved in whatever's going on, and they have to silence him before he tells his Dad, and the shit hits the fan, so to speak, pardon my French sir."

"I know it may sound a bit fanciful, Paul, but it's possible and you know what Sherlock Holmes said, don't you?"

"What's that sir, bearing in mind he was a fictional charac…oh, wait, yes, I see what you mean," Ferris smiled and went on, "When everything else has been eliminated, whatever is left, no matter how fanciful it may be, has to be the truth, or something like that, anyway."

"Exactly," said Ross. "Now, all we need to do is find out if young Decker went diving anywhere off the South coast while his girlfriend was freezing her boobs off in the Antarctic, If he did, we may just have a starting point for this case, Ferris."

Ferris saluted, sailor like as he replied, "Aye, aye sir," just as the phone on Ross's desk began to ring. Ross snatched the phone from its cradle

"Ross," he spoke into the receiver, then, "Oh hello, Doctor Strauss."

Ferris moved to rise from his chair to leave the office but Ross motioned for him to stay put, as he listened to the young pathologist's words.

"Right, I see, thank you. And there's no doubt about that?"

Ferris could hear Strauss speaking again at the other end of the line and then Ross thanked her again and slowly placed the phone back on its cradle, turning to speak to Ferris once again.

"They got the toxicology results back, Paul. It was Ketamine."

"Ketamine?" Ferris repeated. "Don't they use that on horses, sir?"

"Yes, and in other veterinary uses, though it can be used as an anaesthetic in humans too according to Dr. Strauss. The thing is, only a small dose was used on Sally Metcalfe, enough to keep her asleep for a good while, but the dose used on Aaron Decker was enough to have killed him without resorting to suffocation."

"So why the overkill, sir? Why suffocate a dying man, for God's sake?"

"That, D.C Ferris, is the burning question. Answer that one and we may just have found the key to solving the case, but do you know what I think?"

"Do tell, sir," said Ferris.

"I think the killing of Aaron Decker was personal. Yes, there may have been a greater motive that needed him out of the way, but whoever carried out the actual murder really wanted that young man dead,"

As Paul Ferris left the office to begin his online search and investigation into the Aegis Oceanographic Institute, Ross leaned back in his chair, scratched his head and said a small prayer of thanks that his team would return to full strength the next day with the return of his sergeant, Izzie Drake, the new Mrs. Foster. He had a feeling he was going to need her skills before this case was solved.

CHAPTER 10

DRAKE'S RETURN

Like many police officers, Andy Ross harboured something of the eternal optimist deep within his soul. A new day would always dawn with the possibility that this would be the day when they would crack their big case, or at least unearth the vital clue that might help bring a criminal to justice.

Today, though, Ross felt real cause for the optimism that had seen him whistling to himself while washing and shaving before work, (two shaving cuts as a result), and why he arrived at headquarters fifteen minutes before his usual time, thanks in no small part to his wife, Maria ensuring he quickly changed one of the odd socks he'd contrived to pull on while dressing, and who fully understood his enthusiasm for getting to the office. "Go on, get along now," she'd chided him as she kissed him at the door on his way out, "and be sure to ask her all about the honeymoon."

Without mentioning her name, they both knew the reason for Ross's enthusiasm. Izzie was returning to work. The night before, Ross had confessed to Maria that he sorely missed his long-time assistant, even though it had only been four days working without her. The pair were held in almost legendary regard by their fellow officers in the Merseyside Constabulary as being so tuned in to each other's thoughts and methods that they could communicate without words at times, which, though not quite true, did sum up the way their thought processes seemed to run along parallel lines at times, the two often being able to finish each other's sentences, so alike were their working mantras.

Seated behind his desk, a mug of coffee steaming on his desk, Ross heard the sound of footsteps walking across the polished squad room floor towards his office. A single polite knock on his door was followed by a small squeak of one hinge as the door creaked on opening, followed by the smiling face of Detective Sergeant Izzie Drake, or the new Mrs. Peter Foster, whichever way you wanted to look at it.

"I heard a rumour you were looking for a good detective sergeant," Izzie said by way of greeting to her boss.

"Quite right," said Ross. "Any idea where I can find one?"

"Sadistic sod," Izzie countered. "I don't have to work here you know. I could go and get a job on the drug squad."

"Of course you could, but then where else would you find a boss who brings you coffee first thing in the morning?" and he rose and carried the mug of coffee from his desk to his sergeant and handed it to her with a broad grin. "Welcome back, Sergeant Drake."

"Thank you, Inspector Ross. Aren't you having one?"

"Oh, mine's over here," Ross replied as he walked back to his desk and extricated a second, previously hidden mug of coffee from the well under his desk.

"Neat hiding place," Izzie grinned as he almost banged his head as he straightened up with the coffee mug in his hand, slopping a few drops on the office carpet.

"Only place I could think of. I knew you'd be early so thought I'd give you a treat on your first day back."

"Great," said the sergeant, taking a seat in the familiar visitor's chair.

"So, how's married life?"

"Excellent, thank you, sir. Details later. What's been happening while I've been gone?"

Ross spent the next ten minutes giving Drake a detailed summary of the Decker case, after which she whistled through her teeth before replying.

"Bloody hell. We've got a real nightmare case on our hands by the sound of it, sir. Any thoughts as to viable suspects yet?"

"Let's face it, Izzie. The two housemates are the only real prime suspects we have in the frame so far. They were both in the house at the time, and both had the opportunity to visit the couple in Aaron's bedroom at some time in the night to carry out the murders. Plus, if it wasn't one or both of them, how did the killer get in without either of them hearing anything?"

"Sounds like a slam dunk as the Yanks would say, then, doesn't it? But it also sounds too damn simple as well. Would two intelligent men, or even just one of them, commit a murder where it's bloody obvious they're going to come under immediate suspicion?"

"Precisely the way I see it, Izzie. Listen, we'd better go do the morning briefing, then when everyone's busy with their own assignments, I want you to come with me. I want another chat with Mr. Jerome Decker the bloody third, C.I.A. or not."

"What about Paul Ferris? Surely he should go with you again as he was at the first interview?"

"Paul's done a great job, but you know he's not going to take it the wrong way, you stepping in at this point. Besides, he's doing a very important job, trying to get the lowdown on this Aegis Institute. No one can work the computers like he can, and he's probably suffering from severe computer withdrawal syndrome, if such a thing exists. If there's anything dirty in their background, Paul will find it, I'm certain."

"Good point," Drake conceded. She followed with a question.

"Was Aaron Decker a diver, sir?"

"Eh, a diver? I don't know. Why?"

"Just thinking aloud here," Drake mused, "but, if as you surmise, he maybe discovered something about the activities of this Aegis lot, surely he wouldn't have simply confined his research to online searches or library records. If he thought there was something fishy, excuse the pun, about one or more of those wrecks in the Channel, it would have made sense if he'd gone to take a look for himself, or at least got someone to do it for him. Sounds as if he could afford to hire a boat and a diver if he couldn't do it himself."

"Very good point, Izzie. Ferris wondered if Aaron might have gone to Cornwall and done some diving. It's worth looking into. I'm glad to see that all the excitement of the wedding and the physical stress of the honeymoon haven't blunted your incisive thought processes."

Ross sat back, a grin on his face.

"Physical stress? What do you…oh, right. You dirty minded bugger, Inspector Ross. I'll have you know I'm a good girl, I am."

"Not what I've been hearing," he laughed as his sergeant picked up a pad of yellow post-its from his desk and playfully hurled them in his direction. Ross deftly caught the pad in his right hand, placed it back on his desk and said, "Better go or the team will think you're being unfaithful with the boss after less than week of wedded bliss."

"Yeah, right," Izzie laughed.

Glad to be working together again, Ross and Drake left the office and made their way to the briefing room, where the team was ready and waiting for the morning briefing.

A quick ripple of applause and a few risqué and ribald comments greeted the return of the newly married sergeant, and then Ross brought the meeting to order. Standing at the back of the room were six uniformed constables, assigned by Agostini to assist with the inquiry. He knew there'd be a lot of people to talk to and many statements to be taken and with the pressure from above, it was best to leave nothing to chance. The extra manpower was essential in his opinion. At Ross's request, the five men and one woman introduced themselves to the rest of the team, and Ross got to work. It was time to get serious.

* * *

"So there you have it," Ross said, bringing the update on the case to a close. As you all know, we have absolutely nothing so far. Apart from the two young men who shared the house with Decker, there are no other viable suspects at present, and up to now there doesn't appear to be any motive for either of them to have wanted him dead, and as everyone keeps pointing out, it's a bit obvious to think one or both of them would do this in their own home where they'd be bound to come under close scrutiny. I want them both brought in individually in the next day or so and we'll see how their stories hold up when they're interviewed separately. Sam," he said, looking at D.C. Gable, "I want you to track down Sally Metcalfe's housemate, Megan Rose. Get her on her own and find out what she thought about the relationship between Aaron and Sally. Any arguments or rifts between the couple, we need to know about them."

"Okay, sir," Gable replied, rapidly writing in her notebook.

Ross next turned to D.C.s Nick Dodds and Tony Curtis.

"I want you two to hit the university. Speak to Aaron's and the house-mates' professors, tutors, however they style themselves these days. Then try to talk to as many of their friends as you can pin down while you're there, and that goes for friends of the girlfriend too. I know it's a big ask and there's likely to be a lot of ground to cover and most of them will know nothing, but make use of the constables the boss has assigned to help us out with the legwork on this one. I understand from D.C.I. Agostini that you all volunteered to help with this inquiry?"

He looked at the six officers standing nervously by the wall, a couple of whom nodded in the affirmative to his question.

"That's great," he said smiling to try and put them at their ease. "I know it's probably the first time you've worked on such a big case, but don't be put off by this lot of reprobates," he laughingly motioned with his arms to encompass the rest of his team. "They're detectives, not aliens from Mars, and like me, they're grateful for your help, so work with them and do your best. It might be boring most of the time, but whatever you're asked to do will, I assure you, be pertinent to this inquiry and will help us build up a bigger picture of what and who we're dealing with. Got that?"

As the rest of them hesitated, the tallest of the men spoke up.

"Yes, sir, and thank you for having us along. We'll try not to let you down," said P.C. Will Sutton.

"You won't," Ross replied confidently, and then turned his attention to the team's collator.

"Paul, I want you to concentrate on Aegis, find out exactly who they are, what they do and how far their influence in the field of oceanographic research reaches around the world."

Ferris nodded.

"Whatever you need to help with that inquiry, just ask. It's vital we know who and what we may be dealing with. It might turn out that Aegis is in the clear, no skeletons in their corporate cupboards, but that's fine too. It's just as important to eliminate potential suspects as it is to bring new ones on board in a case like this. Like I said, dig deep, and let me know immediately if you find the slightest hint of anything that doesn't look or sound right about them. The way they approached Sally Metcalfe was a bit odd to me and I wonder if they knew she was in a relationship with the son of a C.I.A officer before they made her that offer of sponsorship."

"I'll leave no stone unturned sir and no seashell either," Ferris replied.

"Oh no," Ross groaned. "Don't you start with the funnies too. Don't you think I've got enough to do just coping with my sergeant's little witticisms?"

Ferris smiled at the boss, and just laughed as he said, "Sorry sir, something of the sergeant's style must have rubbed off on me while I've been riding with you the last few days."

"Well, rub it off yourself, Ferris," Ross spoke light-heartedly. "I can't cope with all this frivolity and jocularity."

The rest of the team giggled like schoolboys and even Sam Gable joined in.

"Oh, and Tony, Nick, find out if Aaron went diving, you know, as in skin diving, aqualungs and so on. Sergeant Drake's had an idea."

"Good to know marriage hasn't blocked the old thought processes Sarge," D.C. Curtis quipped.

"Takes more than a wedding to put me off my stride, Tony," she replied, smiling at the young detective.

"Right," said Ross in a firm and commanding tone, "It's time to hit the streets. Sergeant Drake and I are going to talk to the father again, and probably the mother and brother too if they've arrived in town. Let's go find ourselves a murderer, people, and let's do it soon!"

CHAPTER 11

SECRET MISSIONS?

Jerome Decker III seemed to have aged ten years since Ross had first met him two days ago. Still immaculately dressed, his face looked drawn and haggard and his hair had a greasy sheen to it. The grief and stress that went with the loss of his youngest son was having an obvious effect on the man. Decker however, had been as charming as he could be on being introduced to Izzie Drake as she and Ross were admitted to Decker's suite at the hotel where he and his family were now firmly entrenched. Liverpool's Hilton may not have quite rivalled London's equivalent but was still one of the best hotels the city could offer. Decker explained that he and his wife had a suite of their own, while Peter and Kelly were sharing a second. Kelly adored her eldest brother and the pair had no qualms about sharing a suite so they could catch up with each other's news as well as share in their grief for their brother.

Ross's first surprise of the morning had been meeting Decker's wife for the first time. Elaine Decker was a beautiful woman, of that there was no doubt, but after doing a quick double-take, the inspector recognised her as being a well known former actress, known for her roles on both stage and screen. He realised that like millions of others, he'd never thought of her stage name as being just another tinsel town fabrication.

"I'm pleased to meet you, Mrs. Decker, though I wish the circumstances could have been happier. I'm so very sorry for the loss of your son and I assure you we're doing all we can to find the person who did this to Aaron."

"Thank you, Inspector. I'm sure you are, and I at least have faith in the great British police to handle the investigation thoroughly."

Those words led Ross to surmise that Elaine Decker and her husband had disagreed on how the investigation should proceed, with Elaine urging Jerome to stay out of it and leave it to the locals. *Good for her*, he thought.

"Thank you," Ross replied and he and Drake then found themselves being introduced to the two remaining Decker siblings. Peter looked so much like Aaron that the two could have been twins, despite the difference in ages. Facially, they were almost identical, much like the father and son resemblance Ross had noted on his first meeting with Decker senior.

Peter, however, differed markedly from his younger brother by sporting what Ross thought of as the trademark long hair of a rock guitarist and his clothes though looking unkempt and faded were clearly expensive and specially tailored to produce such an appearance. His handshake had been firm and his demeanour polite and respectful, and Ross found himself liking Peter Decker almost instantly.

Kelly, the Decker's eighteen year-old daughter was another kettle of fish entirely. The girl was obviously still distraught at the loss of her brother, her eyes red and puffy from crying. Dressed in a simple roll-neck sweater and jeans, she could hardly look Ross or Drake in the eye, and obviously wanted to be anywhere other than in the same room as the detectives, or Ross thought, her parents. Here was a young girl who clearly wanted to be alone, to grieve privately for her dead brother. Ross vowed to keep it as short as possible when it came to Kelly Decker, who lacked the composure her more mature brother had succeeded in maintaining through his own grief.

"So you're no nearer to finding my son's killer, Inspector Ross?" Decker said, as though he was expressing his dissatisfaction with what Ross had reported to him so far.

"Mr. Decker, no we are not," Ross spoke firmly, "though we might have moved a little faster had you been a little more forthcoming with us in the first place."

Ross had cleverly turned the heat in the other direction.

"I really don't know what you mean," Decker countered.

"Oh, come on, Mr. Decker. You're the C.I.A.'s Deputy Head of Station, London. Did you really think we wouldn't find out? If you did you've seriously underestimated the intelligence and efficiency of the British Police."

"See, Jerome, what did I tell you?" Elaine Decker interjected.

"Right, okay Honey," Decker tried to calm his wife. "You were right, and yes, Inspector, perhaps I should have told you right away instead of leaving you to find out by whatever means you have found out, but I didn't see it had any relevance to Aaron's death."

"No relevance?" Ross was astounded. "I think you should leave the detecting to me, Mr. Decker. I don't know how the C.I.A. actually works, but I'm sure as hell you're not trained as police detectives. For all you know, your son's death could well be connected to you and your position in the C.I.A. Speaking of which, was Aaron a diver?"

"A diver? Like deep sea diving? What's that got to do with me or Aaron's death?"

"I don't know if it has any connection yet, but please, answer the question."

"He was a very accomplished diver, Inspector Ross," Peter Decker answered. "Not deep sea stuff, but with an aqualung maybe in a few fathoms, he was fine. He loved being under the water, always said it was like being in another world."

"Thank you Peter," Ross smiled at the rock singer. He explained his question now.

"We have reason to believe that Aaron was researching a particular project that the company that is sponsoring his girlfriend, Sally through university is involved in. If he found something he shouldn't have found it's possible they took action to prevent him revealing that information."

"What project?" Decker senior asked.

"Aegis Oceanographic are apparently conducting a survey to discover the effects of the wreckage of ships in the English Channel on marine life and the environment."

"Aegis is sponsoring Sally Metcalfe?"

"Yes. I take it you didn't know, Mr. Decker. You've obviously heard of them?"

"You're correct that I didn't know, about the sponsorship and yes, I know of Aegis. They're a large organisation, with many worldwide interests in various areas of marine and oceanographic research. You think they may be involved in something shady?"

"At this stage I don't know anything," said Ross. "It's a theory we're looking into. Maybe you, with your contacts would know more about an American company than we do."

"Trust me, Inspector Ross, if there's anything going on at Aegis, I have no knowledge of it, and Aaron never said anything to me about any suspicions he may have had about them. But, by God, if there is anything illegal going on within Aegis Oceanographic, or the Aegis Institute, I'm damned sure I'll find out about it and I will let you know right away."

"I hoped you'd say that," said Ross, "but please, remember you're in England, Mr. Decker. You have no authority to take any kind of action over here, covert or otherwise, so don't even think of going off half-cocked and trying to deal with things by yourself. You and your people, if you discover anything, no matter how small, about Aegis, you ring it through to me, or I'll have no choice other than to arrest you for obstructing an investigation and I don't think your family would be too happy about that."

"You hear him, Jerome?" said Elaine Decker. "Do what the man says, you got that?"

"As long as I don't hear about it, you can investigate as much as you like," Ross grinned at the C.I.A. man. "Now, I think my sergeant has some questions she'd like to ask," Ross went on.

"Okay, okay, I've got it," Decker said, holding both hands up in surrender. "I promise, no rogue operations on UK soil, Inspector. But we will be investigating Aegis in our own way."

Decker looked at Izzie, unsure how to take this young woman, dressed in her smart skirt suit, her shoulder length hair perfectly in place and her eyes bright and intelligent. He waited as she looked around the room, taking in everything in sight, before beginning her questions. Izzie had been 'people watching' as Ross had spoken to the head of the family and now she looked directly at Kelly Decker, who she was certain had something to tell them. One of Drake's greatest attributes was her ability to read people's body language.

"Kelly, I think you have something to say."

"Me?"

"Yes, it's okay, please just tell us. If might help us in finding your brother's killer."

Kelly hesitated for no more than a second and then replied.

"Well, when Sally went away to the Antarctic last year, Aaron did go down South, to a place in Cornwall or Devon, I think it was. I don't know the name. I'm not that good on English geography yet, still finding my way around London, you know?"

"Sure, that's okay. It wasn't a big secret though, was it?"

"No, not a secret, but he said he was on a 'secret mission' as he called it, and he told me it might make him a lot of money, but I should keep quiet about his little trip. He didn't want me to say anything to Mom and Dad because Mom always worries when he goes diving and if she'd known he was diving on wrecks, well, her hair would have turned purple at the thought of it."

"Kelly!" her mother said.

"Sorry Mom, but that was what he said. "He also said Dad would tell him to keep his nose out of other people's business so it was best to say nothing to him either."

Decker senior scowled, a look not lost on Ross or Drake.

"Right," said Drake, "and did he tell you anything else about this 'secret mission' of his?"

"Not really, but he did send me some great photos that he'd taken with his underwater camera. He loved using it. Me and Peter had bought it for him two Christmases ago and he sent me copies of the digital photos he'd taken. I've still got them on my computer at home."

"Why didn't you tell us anything about this before?" Kelly's father asked, his voice filled with accusation.

"Dad, I…well, I never thought of it until now and how was I supposed to know they might be important or have anything to do with Aaron's death?"

Drake could see that Kelly was on the verge of tears and quickly stepped in to diffuse the developing situation.

"Mr. Decker, I think Kelly is quite right. She couldn't have known this had anything to do with Aaron's death and it may not have, but it is important we see those photos, Kelly. Did you print any of those photos?"

"Sure did. I've got half a dozen in my backpack in my room. I'll go get them if you like?"

"Fantastic," said Drake, and the smile on Kelly's face showed she enjoyed being appreciated, something that maybe didn't happen a lot in her life.

A couple of uncomfortable minutes passed as Ross and Drake waited for Kelly to return. Her father obviously felt she'd been keeping secrets from him and her mother looked perplexed and worried. Ross breathed a sigh of relief as the girl re-entered the suite, and quickly held out her hand, passing a small collection of seven by five inch colour prints into his hand.

"There you go, Inspector," she said. "There's a few more at home on the computer, but these were the best quality so they're the ones I printed out."

"Thank you, Kelly. These might be a big help," Ross said as he looked at the photographs one by one, passing each one to Drake after he'd perused them.

"These are very good quality prints," Drake observed.

"It's a really cool camera," Kelly enthused. "Ain't that right, Peter?"

"Yes, it is," her brother agreed. "We bought the best we could afford."

"What's this?" said Ross, peering at one photo in particular. "It looks like a warship of some kind, but look at the old gun turret. It's small, looks like it would only have held one gun, probably rotted away by now, but what kind of warship could be so small and only have a tiny little gun turret like that?"

"May I see, Inspector?" asked Decker, and Ross passed him the photograph.

"A corvette, if you ask me," the American said. "Small ships used during the war to provide convoy escorts or coastal protection duties. Some of them weren't much bigger than a trawler, but they did good work, Inspector Ross."

"Thanks, I take it you know something of the history of World War Two, Mr. Decker?"

"Something of a pet subject of mine, Inspector. What else we got there? I like to think that's how Aaron first found his love of history."

Ross passed the entire collection to Decker who mused over them for a few seconds.

"Wouldn't surprise me if that little corvette went down during the Dunkirk evacuation, or maybe later, perhaps it hit a mine or was sunk by a German E-Boat on a hit and run raid in the Channel. Some of these are interesting. If you have a maritime museum here in the city you may find someone who can give you more help than me."

"There's the maritime museum at the old Albert Dock, sir," said Drake.

"Yes, maybe we can find some help there," Ross agreed.

"Hmm," said Decker, thoughtfully. "This is really old, look."

He pointed to what appeared to be nothing more than a gathering of old wooden beams and a few pieces of twisted metal but his trained eye saw something more.

"It's an old wooden hulled ship, Inspector, and if I'm not mistaken those are the circular metal hoops that would have been parts of barrels the ship was carrying. Fascinating! Wait a minute. Look at this."

Something had excited the C.I.A. man and he held one of the photos up to the light near the expansive window of the suite. "My God, it really is what I thought."

"What is it, Mr. Decker" Ross wondered what he'd missed when he'd looked at the prints.

"Look closely at this one, Inspector. Tell me what you see."

Ross did as Decker asked. It was another photo of the corvette, taken from another angle, and was of the other side of the ship to the first photo. Ross looked closer, and then, as he focused his vision on the slightly blurred section at the bottom of the photo he saw what Decker was so excited about.

"Is that what I think it is?" Ross asked.

"What is it? What didn't we see?" Drake added.

"If you think you're seeing the business end, the bow and torpedo tubes of an old time submarine somehow embedded under the keel of that corvette, then you're right on the button, Inspector. By God, my son was one hell of an undersea photographer."

The sudden pride in Decker's voice was tinged with a hint of sadness as he remembered why they were gathered here in his hotel suite.

"But what does it mean? Is there some significance to that submarine being there?" Drake asked the obvious question.

"I don't know," Decker replied, "But my guess is that that is a German U-Boat, possibly sunk by the corvette. Maybe she was depth-charged or the little warship rammed her after the sub had torpedoed her or damaged her with fire from its deck gun. Hell, I don't know but your naval historians might be able to throw some light on the two ships being out there, locked together; embracing one another in death, as it were."

"That's all well and good," Ross was now playing Devil's advocate. "But can this have anything to do with Aaron's death? What possible connection can this have to his murder? Aegis is legitimately working with these old wrecks, after all. The whole purpose of their remit is apparently to study just how these wrecks have affected the environment around them."

"Wait sir," Drake butted in. "Kelly, you said Aaron told you that what he found could make him a lot of money, right?"

"Yes, that's what he said," Kelly agreed.

"So maybe it's not the corvette and submarine we should be looking at. What about the old wooden hulled ship?"

Decker and Ross both looked again at the photo of what appeared to be an old wooden ship, but couldn't make out any defining images from the photograph.

"At this point, anything's possible," Ross replied. So far, the only thing he knew for certain was that they knew virtually nothing. Andy Ross felt a frisson of excitement at what they'd just discovered, but the frustration he felt at a total lack of real progress pervaded his thoughts like a disease. He was sensible enough to acknowledge when he needed help or when he was out of his depth, he thought, ironically.

It would take an expert to try to identify what they were looking at, in terms of the wooden hulk. Another of the photos again showed the corvette, this one taken from what would have been the bow, and Ross could clearly see damage of some sort to the warship.

"Maybe the corvette was hit by a torpedo but had enough power or steerage way or whatever they call it in nautical terms left to ram the U-Boat," he theorised.

"But, what does any of this have to do with the murder of a young man?" Izzie Drake spoke up. "Okay, so these ships are war graves, but nothing about them would give anyone a motive for murder, surely. I'll bet Aegis have all the necessary permissions to dive on the wrecks in order to carry out their research."

"Maybe it's not a matter of who, but what?" said Decker.

"Pardon?" said Ross.

"The corvette wouldn't be involved, but it's possible the U-Boat may have been carrying something valuable. I know for a fact that the Germans often attempted to smuggle secret and expensive cargoes to countries sympathetic to their cause towards the end of the war. I think you need to identify that submarine, Inspector."

"I think you're right, Mr. Decker," Ross agreed.

"Can I make a point here, sir?"

"Go ahead, Sergeant," said Ross in response to Drake's question.

"The maritime museum at Albert Dock mostly relates to Liverpool's own seafaring history, and that was mostly based on the big liners that sailed from here, like Lusitania and Titanic. If we want to find out about warships then I think we need to direct our inquiry to the Royal Navy."

"A good point," Ross agreed. "We'll get on to that as soon as we return to headquarters. Meanwhile, give Ferris a ring, and ask him to find me the number for the Royal Naval Museum, which will probably be in Portsmouth unless I'm very much mistaken."

"Will do sir," and Drake moved to the far side of the room to make the call to Paul Ferris.

"What's this?" said Peter Decker, who'd picked up the photos from the table where his father had laid them. He was indicating one of the other photos that seemed to show a large seal swimming across the camera lens."

"That's a seal, Peter," said Kelly, derisorily.

"Not the seal, lunkhead," Peter laughed. "Look in the background."

Kelly did, and then passed the photo to Ross, pointing at the object Peter had noticed.

"Well, I'll be a monkey's uncle," said Ross.

"Okay, I'm hooked," said Decker senior. "What have you got?"

"I wish we had a magnifying glass here," Ross said gravely, "but I'm pretty sure that what your son Aaron accidentally photographed in the background, if you look very closely, is the dead body of a frogman. Aaron wasn't the only one interested in the wreck of the corvette and the U-Boat, obviously."

Jerome Decker took the photo from Ross, held it close to his eyes and squinted in deep concentration as he focused on the image. With an effort he could see what Peter and Ross had noticed. There, probably trapped by part of the wreck debris, the body floated, seemingly twisting slowly and gracefully with the movements of the current, in a macabre dance of death.

"Goddammit, Aaron," he finally exclaimed. "What the hell did you get yourself into?"

CHAPTER 12

FAMILY CONNECTIONS

Paul Ferris had been busy. While Ross and Drake were enjoying the luxury of the Decker's hotel suite, the detective constable had been slaving away over a hot keyboard, as he laughingly thought it, immersed in his research into the enormous, though previously unheard of, worldwide conglomerate that was Aegis Oceanographic. Ferris had found himself fascinated by much of the information he'd unearthed. Known as The Aegis Institute, or Aegis Oceanographic, or Aegis Maritime, depending on the discipline being undertaken, the company seemed to be almost octopus-like in having arms or branches in numerous countries around the world.

The Aegis Institute for example, took in the company's corporate head-quarters near Boston, Massachusetts, another major office in New York and the actual research institute, based close to the waterfront in the city of Portland, Maine, with various smaller facilities on both the Eastern and Western Seaboards of the USA. Ferris digressed from his main research for a few minutes, fascinated by the history of Portland, with its regenerated Old Port District, similar in some ways to Liverpool's newly regenerated docklands area, and possessing the oldest lighthouse in continuous use in the USA. The city even has a number of pubs more akin to the English equivalent than the traditional American 'bars' and was the home of the famed poet, Longfellow.

Bringing himself back to the matter in hand, Ferris dug further and found that Aegis had various facilities in Europe, based in England, Spain and Italy, and further but smaller locations in Asia and the Far East, including a new state of the art research unit in Japan. The English facility was of obvious interest, and Ferris spent ten minutes looking into the publicly reported activities of Aegis (UK) Limited, based not far from Falmouth in Cornwall, well off the beaten-track for such a dynamic company, Ferris thought. Apart from the research they were aware of into the effects of the rotting Channel wrecks on the environment, it seemed the UK division was doing little else at present, at least nothing that had been made known to the local press.

Ferris now had a moment of inspiration as his initiative kicked in. He remembered that his wife had a cousin who was a police officer down in Cornwall. Kareen, although raised in Liverpool from the age of four, had been born in England's southernmost county, her father having been skipper of a trawler sailing out of the village of St. Keverne, not far from Falmouth. The family had moved north when Sam Tremayne was offered the chance to skipper a new, larger deep sea trawler operating from the then vibrant port of Fleetwood on the Lancashire coast. Kareen's father had sailed and fished some of the most inhospitable waters in the northern hemisphere, but the eventual decline of the fishing industry saw him finally giving up the sea, and the family moved once again, settling in Liverpool where Sam found work on the famous Mersey Ferries. The thing that gave Paul Ferris his inspiration was the memory of the fact that Sam Tremayne had a younger brother who was a police officer in the Cornish Constabulary. As far as Ferris could recall, Reginald (Reg) Tremayne had been a constable in Redruth, located not too far from Falmouth. Although Kareen hadn't stayed in close contact with her uncle over the years, Ferris thought that the family connection might come in useful if Reg was still on the force, and still based in Redruth.

A quick phone call to the Redruth police brought Ferris a slice of information he thought almost too good to be true. A Sergeant Grant, to whom he was put through to at Redruth police station, informed Ferris that Reg, now Sergeant Tremayne was still on the force, but was no longer at Redruth. Ferris's initial disappointment turned to unexpected excitement when Grant told him that Reg Tremayne had transferred to Falmouth three years ago.

Reg was surprised and delighted to hear from Paul Ferris. Ferris had to take a minute or two to get used to hearing the rather slow drawling Cornish accent in order to accurately follow Reg's words. Kareen of course, had no trace of a Cornish accent, having lived in Liverpool almost all her life, and her father had lost most of his accent over the years, but Ferris soon came to terms with Reg's speech, and Reg likewise joked about trying to keep up with Paul's Scouse accent.

Reg was full of questions about Sam and his niece, Paul's wife and apologised for not keeping in closer touch through the years, though the disjointed family had continued to exchange cards at Christmas and birthdays. Ferris soon had to curb 'Uncle' Reg's enthusiasm for family news as he quickly explained the professional nature of his call.

"Bloody hell, Paul," Reg exclaimed after Ferris has outlined the nature of the case he was working on. "You be the third person to be making inquiries about that lot from Aegis in recent times."

"Really?" said a surprised Paul Ferris. "Who were the first and second?"

"Well now. First of all I strongly suspect it was yon young feller whose murder you be investigatin'."

"And when was this, Reg?"

"Well, it were last summer, like. I were on duty one day when this good lookin' young chap walks into the station when I was on the front desk and starts askin' me if I knows anything about the folks who work at the Aegis place just out of town."

Ferris smiled to himself. When Reg had mentioned 'recent times', he'd assumed he meant within a few weeks or a couple of months, not a year ago, but then he thought to himself, life certainly moves at a much slower pace down in Cornwall. But, at least he could be on to something.

"Were you able to tell him anything, Reg?"

"Well now Paul, it were a bit weird. I told him as how they were a pretty secretive bunch, and that they didn't take too kindly to strangers hangin' around their place, or getting' too close to their ship. He just laughed and said as how they wouldn't know he was there and that he was after findin' out if they were doin' anything illegal out at sea, where they were supposed to be investigatin' old wrecks, as he told me. I told him if he thought anything untoward was happenin' he should tell the police and coast guard, but he just said the police couldn't do anythin' about what they was up to and that he'd sort it out himself. To be honest I thought he were a young lad who were just full of hot air, like, and tried to tell him to stay away from private property. From what you're tellin' me, seems he didn't take too kindly to my warning."

"I think you're right, Reg, but listen, I'm probably asking you the same questions he did. Why don't the people at Aegis want anyone near their property, and what's this about them having a ship of their own down there?"

"Your guess is as good as mine, Paul. Their place is protected by a ten foot high fence, electrified, and floodlights at night light the place up like daytime. I don't know what they do in there, but it is private property and they are entitled to their privacy I suppose. As for the ship, it's apparently a research vessel, called *Poseidon*. A real modern vessel it is too. Only about three hundred feet, but carries lots of cranes, gantries and looks like it carries more than one submersible or ROVs on or below decks."

Ferris deferred to Reg Tremayne's nautical knowledge. He was after all from a family that had lived its life on or near the sea for many years, but he did have a question.

"Submersibles I'm familiar with, Reg, but explain ROV please."

"Them's remotely operated underwater vehicles, Paul. You know, like those things you might have seen in the movie, *Titanic*. They can go down real deep and send live pictures up to the mother ship on the surface."

"Right, I understand that, Reg. Thing is, none of that sounds out of order for a maritime research company does it?"

"I've got to agree with you, Paul. No, it doesn't."

"Then why did you use the word 'weird' earlier?"

"Ah, yes, well, that brings me to nosey parker number two, so to speak," said Tremayne.

"Do tell, please Reg," said Ferris, likening getting information from Kareen's uncle to pulling teeth from an unwilling patient.

"He were a German feller, this other chap. Turned up about a month after the last time I'd seen the young chap. Told me he were some sort of Naval Historian, looking into German naval activity in the English Channel and specially around the Channel Islands during World War Two. I presume you know the Germans occupied the Channel Islands during the war, young Paul?"

"Yes, I knew that," Ferris replied, trying to force the conversation forward. "So what did this German want? Did he give you his name?"

"Aye, that he did, Paul. Hold on a minute, whilst I check back in me notebook." Ferris heard a slight 'clunk' as Tremayne placed the phone down on his desk. A minute passed and Reg came back on the line.

"You still there, Paul?"

"Yes, Reg. Go ahead."

"He gave his name as Klaus Haller, from Hamburg he said, and before you ask why I never got the young man's name, that were because he just came making general enquiries at the front desk, but this Haller chap came and we had a long talk in a more formal way, as him turning up so soon after the young man sort of got my interest roused, if you know what I mean."

"Yes, I understand, Reg. I think I'd have done the same. So what was the upshot of your meeting with Haller?"

"Not much really. I told him I knew nothing about Aegis or what they were doing in the Channel. All I knew was that they had permission to be out there exploring the wrecks for some sort of environmental research project. For some reason he seemed to think we, meaning the police, had some sort of control over their activities. I told him things don't work like that in England. He did mention though that he'd been invited over by a young university student who thought he'd find something interesting in the work Aegis were doing. Again, I presumed it were the young chap who you're looking into. He also asked if I knew what area of the Channel

538

Aegis were operating in, and I had to tell him again I knew nothin' at all about what or where they were working. I told him he'd have to maybe hire a boat and follow their research vessel out to sea if he were so interested in them. He said he'd do that and that were the last I saw of him."

"Thanks, Reg, that's all very helpful," Ferris said, not sure if it was or not. He felt there was little else Reg Tremayne could tell him at that point, but it was interesting that young Decker had perhaps invited Haller to England to look into the activities of the Aegis group. Ferris was unaware at this point of the gruesome discovery that Ross and Drake had uncovered as a result of their interview with Decker's family. He said his good-byes to Reg Tremayne with a promise to ask Sam to call his brother in the near future and with Reg's message of love to Kareen and the Ferris's son, Aaron the last words from the slow-speaking Cornish police sergeant, the call ended.

Ferris returned to his computer, sure now that something about the Aegis organisation wasn't quite as it might appear to be on the surface. He needed to dig deeper if he was to discover exactly what they might be up to. And who the hell was Klaus Haller? Maybe the internet could help him.

CHAPTER 13

KIEL, GERMANY, 1945

The party was in full swing. Even though the Officers Mess stood some 200 metres from the guardhouse, the naval ratings on guard duty could hear the raucous sounds as they shivered in the cool night-time air. Most knew the war was going badly and the fact that their officers could still find cause for celebration and enjoyment escaped them.

"Hey, Max, come here. A drink for you, my friend."

Korvettankapitän Max Ritter forced his way through the small throng of bodies and found a beer being thrust into his hand by *Kapitän zur See*, Heinz Schmidt.

"To the future, Max," Schmidt shouted as Ritter took a swig from the beer glass.

"Sure, the future," Ritter replied, knowing only too well what the future of Germany would be over the coming weeks.

"The admiral would have been here himself to see you off in the morning, but, well, you know how busy he is," said Schmidt.

"Of course," said Ritter, knowing full well that the admiral never had any intention of coming to Kiel to see *U3000*, recently redesignated *U966* slip her moorings in the morning. He'd most likely be curled up with his latest mistress, so much more preferable than standing on a cold wet dockside as Ritter and his crew left Germany for what the U-Boat commander knew in his heart would probably be the last time.

"Come, Max, enjoy yourself. See, there are plenty of young ladies eager to make your acquaintance." The captain, a former U-Boat skipper himself, now aide to Admiral Werner Stein, called across the room, over the sound of the piano and the group of officers gathered around it, singing and swaying, and two young blonde women rose from a couch and walked through the throng on the small dance floor to reach them.

"Ladies, see, here is the hero, home from the sea," said Schmidt as the two women sidled up to Ritter, both immediately seeing and recognising the Knight's Cross with Oak Leaves worn around the young U-Boat commander's neck.

It had been a while since Ritter had been with a woman, and the availability of one, or perhaps both of the young blondes was sorely tempting. Ritter knew they were part of that strange group of young women who had allowed themselves to become 'whores for Hitler,' many of them actually sent by their proud and willing mothers to become nothing more than 'comfort women,' prostituting themselves to provide sexual comfort for the officers of the Third Reich.

Ritter gazed around the room. On one couch nearby a young brunette lay on her back, her skirt hoisted up around her waist, legs spread, as a young *Lieutnant* pleasured himself between her thighs.

Looking at the two smiling girls standing one on each of his arms, Ritter looked at the girl on his right, and asked her name.

"Claudia, Herr Kapitän," she replied.

Dressed in a low-cut, diaphanous white blouse, and a black pencil skirt that accentuated the girl's hips and rear as she walked on what to Ritter seemed painfully high heels, Claudia still retained something of an air of innocence about her, despite wearing a little too much make-up that added a red lustre to her lips and a dark sensuousness to her blue eyes. He guessed her age at no more than eighteen or nineteen. Looking at her obvious charms, barely hidden by the thin material of her blouse, he felt himself becoming aroused.

"Come with me," Ritter ordered, taking her by the hand. "I'll see you later, sir?" he said to Schmidt.

"Sure, have fun Max," Schmidt replied, as Ritter led the young blonde towards the stairs and the private rooms upstairs. "Don't be late."

"I'll be back on board by midnight," Ritter called over his shoulder as Claudia led the way upstairs, her young hips swaying as he followed her, her legs looking long and inviting from behind.

As Max and Claudia disappeared from his sight, Schmidt turned to the second girl. "How old are you, girl?"

"Seventeen, sir," she replied in a small voice.

"How long have you been here?"

"Almost three months."

"Good, come with me," he ordered and the girl followed obediently as Schmidt led her up the same stairs Ritter had trod a minute ago.

* * *

Three hours later, Ritter stood on the conning tower of *U3000*, a prototype of one of Germany's latest 'breed' of U-Boats, his second-in-command *Leutnant zur See* Heinrich Engel by his side. The two men were aware of the importance of their mission and as the truck carrying their cargo pulled up on the dock alongside the boat, Ritter simply tapped Engel on the shoulder and the young first officer saluted and dropped through the hatch into the submarine's control room loading, emerging again a minute later from the forward deck hatch. Ritter looked on as Engel supervised a number of wooden boxes as they were first deposited on the dock, before being manhandled through the deck hatch by half a dozen members of *U3000's* crew.

In the submarine's control room, a pair of boiler-suited dock workers were completing a task that had mystified the two officers, and Ritter felt uncomfortable and unsure of the reasons for their actions which had been sanctioned by a written order signed by no other than Grand Admiral Doenitz himself. Their work done in less than ten minutes the two men, who in reality were not civilian dock workers but members of Germany's military intelligence service, the *Abwehr*, headed by Admiral Wilhelm Canaris, departed the submarine without a word to anyone, and disappeared into the night.

Once their cargo was safely secured and the hatch battened down, Engel reported back to Ritter.

"All is secure, Kapitän. The boat is secured and ready for sea, but this subterfuge, those two men, I wonder…?"

"Excellent Heini, now we wait for Schmidt to finish screwing his whore. Once we receive our sealed orders we can get underway. Perhaps they will answer your question, mine too. It may be a long time before we see our homes and families again, my friend."

"We must do what we can for the Fatherland, my Kapitän," Engel replied, but Ritter simply nodded as he said,

"The Fatherland is all but defeated, Heini. What we do now, we do because we are officers of the Kriegsmarine and it is our duty to follow the orders of our senior officers, whether we think them right or wrong."

Engel looked askance at Ritter, the first time he'd heard his Captain speak in such a way. Engel knew Ritter well. He'd first found fame during the 'happy time' when the German U-Boat 'Wolf Packs' roamed the North Atlantic at will, sinking allied merchant shipping virtually unopposed after the outbreak of war. His first command came almost by accident during a surface battle with an armed merchantman, the *S.S. Cressida*, whose captain refused to surrender. The merchant ship opened fire on the U-Boat, a lucky shot hitting the conning tower and killing the sub's commander, Ritter's friend, Gunther Adel. As first officer, Ritter assumed command and withdrew from the surface fight, laying off far enough to send two torpedoes into the enemy vessel, sinking her with all hands. Three further merchant vessels plus a convoy escort were sunk under Ritter's command during the voyage and on return to base the young first officer was awarded his first Knight's Cross, promoted to *Oberleutnant zur See* and given command of his own U-Boat. He received the Oak Leaves to his Knight's Cross when saving the lives of two crewmen from the damaged rear torpedo room of his boat after a collision with a convoy escort destroyer in the North Atlantic, refusing to seal off the compartment and leaving them to drown, after which he'd single-mindedly stalked the destroyer despite the damage to his boat, eventually sinking his opponent with two well placed torpedoes.

For Engel to hear his skipper talk of Germany losing the war was a shock to the young first officer, who for the first time began to doubt much of the propaganda that tried to convince the German people of eventual victory over the allies. If Ritter thought the war was lost, Engel believed him.

Just after midnight, as the middle watch replaced those on the last, (second) dog watch, a black Mercedes car pulled up on the dock beside the still silent U-Boat. The driver climbed out of the car, opening the rear door to allow *Kapitän zur See* Schmidt to exit the car. The driver saluted smartly, his salute being barely acknowledged by Schmidt who stood looking up at the submarine's conning tower. Seeing Ritter looking down at him, he marched smartly up the gangplank that led to the narrow deck of the U-Boat, where he was briefly held at bay by the two seamen on armed guard at the base of the conning tower, before being admitted to the interior of the boat. By the time he'd been escorted to the control room, Ritter was already there, waiting for him, Ritter escorted him to the so-called 'Captain's cabin,' in fact little more than a small cubicle with a dark red curtain draped across the entrance to provide a modicum of privacy to the boat's commander.

Ritter poured them both a measure of Schnapps from a bottle beside his bunk as Schmidt seated himself on a small stool beside Ritter's chart table.

"To your health and the success of your mission, Max," Schmidt said, raising his glass to the U-Boat skipper.

"I'd drink to that a little easier if I knew exactly what our mission is," Ritter replied, at which point Schmidt reached into the black leather briefcase he'd carried on board and removed a large, sealed envelope from within, which he passed across to Ritter, who sat on his bunk awaiting some explanation of the forthcoming mission.

"You are to sail before first light, Max," Ritter began, "and you may open your sealed orders as soon as you have cleared the harbour and have reached the open sea. There can be no risks of anyone leaking the nature of this voyage, and once opened, you may divulge the true nature of your voyage to your first officer, and your engineering officer only. What you tell the rest of the crew is up to you, Max, but do not underestimate the importance of this mission. Is that understood?"

"Perfectly," Ritter replied, "but first, can you tell me why my boat's maker's plate has been changed? This is *U3000*, and yet now the plate identifies us *U966*. What is going on, Kapitän? Can you personally tell me nothing of what lies ahead for me and my crew?"

"I'm sorry, Max. My orders are as specific as yours. I was to deliver the sealed orders to you with your instructions, and no more. I can tell you however, that the change in your boat's designation was authorised at the highest level. From this moment, you are in command of *U966*. *U3000* no longer exists. The admiral was quite explicit in his orders."

"I'm sure he was," said Ritter sarcastically, unsure precisely which admiral. Stein or Doenitz, Schmidt referred to. "And what of the real *U966*?"

"No longer in service, lost in '43. Due to the nature of your cargo and the other…erm, special features of your boat, you are now a ghost ship, Max. Everything that could identify you as *U3000* has been systematically obliterated during the recent maintenance work on your boat."

Ritter knew he'd learn nothing more on the subject from Schmidt but wanted the answer to one more important question.

"Are you aware that while I was away from the boat earlier today, a dockyard crew under the command of an S.S. colonel, of all people, came on board and stripped out almost all my torpedoes? The rear torpedo compartment is bare of armaments and I've been left with the four torpedoes in the forward tubes and the rest have been similarly removed. We've been left almost defenceless."

"All will be revealed when you read your orders, Max, and now, I must go. You have a voyage to prepare for."

Schmidt stood, drained his glass and gave Ritter a perfect Nazi salute.

"Heil Hitler," he said, and then, "Good luck, Max. I hope we meet again when this is all over."

Ritter casually returned the salute. He'd always been a sailor, not a Nazi, and he had little regard for Hitler and what he saw as the fawning band of sycophants that surrounded him, but he'd sensibly kept such thoughts to himself through the hard years of war. In Nazi Germany, you never knew who was listening, ready to report supposed 'treasonous' activities to the Gestapo. More than one U-Boat commander of Max's acquaintance had been summoned to Kriegsmarine headquarters in the past, never to be seen again. A waste of good men, Max knew, but such was the way of life in the Fatherland.

Just before first light, the newly designated *U966* slipped her moorings, and under the power of her virtually silent, gently throbbing diesel motors, she slowly eased her way out of the submarine base and into the open sea, destination unknown.

CHAPTER 14

MEGAN ROSE

Sam Gable sat opposite Megan Rose in the same room Ross and Ferris had occupied when they'd interviewed Sally Metcalfe. A petite auburn-haired young woman of twenty-three, Megan had made tea for them both and expressed surprise that the police needed to speak with her about the death of Aaron Decker.

"There's nothing to be nervous about, Megan," said Gable. "We just need to speak to as many people who knew Aaron as possible so we can build up a better picture of what he was like and perhaps why someone might want to hurt him."

"I see, I think," Megan replied, "but I didn't know him very well, I'm afraid."

"Okay, so how often did you see him Megan?"

"Well, he'd often come round here to collect Sally if they were going out, and sometimes, Sally would cook a meal and they'd spend the evening here, but on those occasions I'd usually go out with friends, or even on my own to the cinema sometimes, not wanting to cramp their style, you know?"

"Yes, I understand. So, when he came to collect Sally, did you and he talk much?"

"Just small talk, you know? Like, how's things? Maybe I'd ask how his research was coming along, that kind of thing."

"You mean for his post-doc, right?"

"Yes, but he was never very forthcoming, so I steered clear of the subject. I'd talk about the weather, or his cricket or other sports. He liked to talk about that stuff. I think despite being a nice guy, Aaron was a bit full of himself at times, liked to blow his own trumpet a bit."

"You mean a bit of a big head?"

"Yes, no, not really. I think it was because he was American. They tend to be a bit more direct and outspoken, or at least that's how I've found the few who I've come into contact with at the university."

"I think I know what you mean, Megan. So you'd leave them to it if he came here, but did he ever spend the night with Sally, here I mean, not at his place?"

"No, he didn't. Well, he wasn't supposed to, but now and then, he'd stay really late, you know…? Part of the terms of our student rental is that no overnight visitors of the opposite sex are allowed and we're both well aware of it. This is a nice house, and we don't want to risk losing it."

"I can understand that. I'm not here to get you in trouble with the landlord if Aaron overstayed a bit later than he should have done now and then. Sally has already told us he stayed over now and then. Do you have a boyfriend, Megan?"

"Not at present, no. I went out with a lad from Huyton a while ago but it only lasted a couple of months. He said I was too wrapped up in my studies and didn't spend enough time with him. I think the truth of the matter was really that I wouldn't drop my knickers for him. He was one of those guys who thinks all students are an easy lay, if you know what I mean"

"Oh yes, I know exactly what you mean. Better off without him then, eh?"

"Definitely."

"So, did you ever meet any of Aaron's friends?"

"Only once or twice, when I went to the pub and him and Sally would ask me over for a drink. There were sometimes a few of his mates there, but I never got to know any of them."

"What about the two men he shared his house with?"

"Oh yes, Tim and er, Martin is it? I never met Martin but Tim was in the pub a couple of times when I saw them there. I always thought he leered at Sally a bit. She told me they went out a couple of times, ages ago before she met Aaron but Tim wasn't her type."

"Did she say why?"

"No, not really. I don't think it was anything specific, just that they didn't have much in common as far as I could make out. Anyway, they'd finished long before Aaron came on the scene. Sally is the one you need to talk to about that."

"Yes, of course and I'm sure we'll be doing that. So, you don't know of anyone who might have wanted to harm Aaron or Sally, or both of them, maybe?"

"No, of course not. It's just unbelievable, what's happened to Aaron.

Sally's so upset and she told me that someone had drugged her too with a powerful anaesthetic. Is that right?"

"I can't go into details of the case, Megan, but yes, Sally was attacked too."

"That's just awful. Are you close to catching whoever did it yet?"

"We're following a number of leads at present," Gable lied, not wanting to let Megan know the police were so far baffled by the killing.

"So, is that it? Do you want to know anything else from me?"

"Just about Sally. Did you know her before you both moved in here together?"

"Not really. We met at a party when we were both looking for digs and we hit it off and started going out together, then the idea came up to look for a place to rent, to share the expenses, and we got lucky finding this place."

"So you don't know much about her background?"

"Not really. I know she's fanatical about her Marine biology research and anything to so with the environment, not that she's what you'd call an activist or anything like that. Just passionate about her work is how I'd describe her."

"And you wouldn't know if she had any enemies, or just anyone who dislikes her enough to want to hurt her through Aaron?

"No way. Sally's always been popular with everyone. The only person I know who she's ever had 'words' with is Tim Knight."

"Really? In what way?"

"Well, like I said, they dated a couple of times, long before she got together with Aaron. But one day, when we were in the pub, I heard Tim saying something like *"I was never good enough for you, was I Sally?"* or words to that effect, and Sally told him to stop being a prat, and that he'd had too much to drink. I think Tim might have been feeling sorry for himself because he'd just broken up with Fiona Gregg, his girlfriend at that time, plus he'd had a few pints, you know?"

"Yes, that's probably all it was," Gable agreed while at the same time filing that little piece of information away in her mind and in her note-book. It was probably nothing, as Megan Rose said, but as Sam knew, you never took anything for granted or at face value in police work, especially in a murder investigation.

Sam left the house after thanking the young woman. On the whole, she hadn't learned anything of value, though she'd learned at least that Aaron Decker had definitely possessed a high opinion of himself, but, was that sufficient to provoke someone to commit murder? Stranger things had happened in the past, she reminded herself.

CHAPTER 15

A MEETING OF MINDS

Andy Ross and Izzie Drake returned to headquarters with their minds buzzing, having been shocked to see the dead frogman captured on Aaron Decker's underwater photograph. Ross was certain now that the wrecks of the Corvette and the submarine must in some way be connected to the death of young Decker. Drake agreed and also put forward her supposition that the Aegis Institute or whatever name they were using in the UK must have a part to play in the growing scenario.

As they walked in to the squad room, still unaware of Ferris's conversation with Reg Tremayne they found the rest of the team all in one place at the same time, something of a rare occurrence nowadays.

"Nothing to do, people?" Ross half-joked as he and Drake walked towards the large whiteboard that Paul Ferris, as team collator, always used to display any and all information or photographs pertaining to their current case.

Sam Gable was first to reply.

"Just back from talking to Megan Rose, sir, Sally Metcalfe's room mate, house sharer or whatever we want to call her. Not a lot to be gained there, I'm afraid, apart from the fact that Tim Knight and Sally had a small altercation soon after she and Decker got together."

"What kind of altercation?" Ross asked her.

"Oh, just a drunken moan I think, sir. Knight had drunk too much, had just split with his girlfriend at that time, and accused Sally of seeing him as not good enough for her. As he and Sally had dated all of twice, Megan thought it was just a case of Knight feeling sorry for himself and lashing out verbally at Sally for no good reason. I must say, I tend to agree with her assessment of the event."

"Yes, sounds about right for a testosterone filled young stud of Knight's age group," Izzie Drake said.

Ross smiled.

"Of course, Sergeant Drake would know all about that, eh, Sergeant?"

A small ripple of laughter rolled around the squad room.

"Oh, come on," said Izzie. "Anyone would think I was the only person who ever got married round here."

"You are," laughed Derek McLennan. "At least, the only one who's got married while being an active member of the team. Paul and the boss were both married before the team was formed, and the rest of us are single, so yeah, you are the only one."

"Alright, let's get serious," Ross ordered, as he brought the impromptu team meeting back on track. "I agree too, Sam. I don't think a two-date relationship constitutes a major cause of unrequited love leading to murder. How about you two?" he asked next, looking at Dodds and McLennan, who'd been assigned the task of conducting the initial interviews at the university.

Derek McLennan replied first.

"Again, not a lot to be gleaned there either, sir. One chap, a Professor Tilkowski, the 'w' is pronounced as a 'v' by the way, told us that Aaron Decker was one of the most single-minded students he'd ever encountered. Everything came second to his work and studies, even the cricket, the prof said."

"Yes," Nick Dodds chimed in. "Apparently a couple of the big professional County Cricket clubs had approached Decker about him turning professional with them, but he'd rejected their offers, saying he was happy being an amateur and that cricket was just a pastime, not a profession as far as he was concerned."

Ross pulled a face, as he imagined how the stuffed shirt brigades at some of the old established County Cricket clubs would have taken to being dismissed in such a cavalier fashion by young Aaron Decker.

McLennan took over again.

"We spoke to a few students who knew Decker. As it was explained to us more than once, as a post doctoral student, it wasn't as if Aaron was involved in loads of organised lectures or tutorials like the younger students just setting out on their degree courses. We felt a bit thick, to be truthful, sir, not knowing quite how university education and the various degrees, post-doc studies as they were referred to and other various study courses were organised. In the end no one could tell us anything of any significance, apart from talking about his sporting prowess. Seems he was a pretty good tennis player too."

Ross was beginning to think the two young detectives were fast turning into a well-versed double act, a thought reinforced as Nick Dodds spoke up once again.

"There was one other thing, sir. A young chap by the name of Robert Allen told us that Decker had recently taken up playing snooker as well. He must have been a pretty mean pool player back in the States, because he'd become a first class player in no time."

"A real life pool shark, eh?" Ross commented.

"Yeah, apparently Allen and some other guys from the university ran a kind of gaming society at the 147 Club over on Fleet Street and Decker was known to have won quite a bit of cash from some of the players."

Ross knew of the 147 Snooker and Pool Club, to give it its full title. Well placed to attract customers in the city centre of Liverpool, the club had really reached its heyday back in the eighties when snooker had enjoyed massive popularity thanks to television coverage of the major tournaments, but word around town was that the place was struggling and the management probably welcomed the potentially raucous but well-heeled young men from the university who doubtless spent a good deal over the bar, in addition to losing money to people like Aaron Decker.

"So there may have been one or two potential bad losers in the pack who may have had it in for him," Drake observed.

"Yeah, but not enough to kill him, surely," said Dodds.

"That might depend how much he won, and if anyone might not have had the money to pay up on the spot when they lost, and owed him money. Nick, see if you can visit the place. Have a word with the management and staff and see if they know what kind of stakes they were playing for. This may not be much, but if it had gone from a few simple friendly frames of snooker to some form of big money gambling, it could cast a new light on things."

"Right boss," Dodds acknowledged.

"Okay everyone," Ross now said, calling for the team's attention. As he spoke he attached the underwater photograph from Decker's camera to the whiteboard.

"Paul, can you stop what you're doing for a minute?" he called across the room to Ferris who had continued to search the internet for more information about Aegis while Ross had received everyone else's updates.

"Sure boss," said Ferris as he turned round in his swivel computer chair. "Still looking for the dirt on Aegis, if there is any."

"Oh, I think you'll find some, somewhere," said Ross as everyone's attention was drawn to the small photograph he'd just displayed.

Ferris walked right up to the board, took one look and said,

"Is that a body?"

"First prize for observation goes to Detective Constable Paul Ferris," Drake said, smiling.

"Too right it is," said Ross as the others gathered closer to get a good look.

"It's a bloody frogman," said Tony Curtis who'd been quiet until now.

"A dead frogman," McLennan concurred.

"And that's a bit of a submarine, if I'm not mistaken, crushed under the ship," Dodds added.

"A ship, a dead frogman and a submarine. What's it all mean, sir?" Sam Gable asked.

"Good question, D.C. Gable," Ross replied. "Ferris, take the photo, get it blown up and let's see if we can find anything else. This was taken by Aaron Decker during a trip he made last year to check out something Aegis was involved in. That's why I think you'll find something in the course of your probing into their affairs, Paul."

"It could also be a pointer as to what got him killed," Drake added.

"Er, sir," said Ferris.

"Yes, Paul, what's up?"

Ferris went on to relate the conversation he'd had with Reg Tremayne after finding the Cornish connection to Aegis in the UK.

As soon as he'd finished speaking, Drake said,

"Why do I suddenly think that dead frogman is none other than this Haller chap?"

"And why do I think you're absolutely right?" said Ross, who now made a quick decision.

"Paul, get that photo blown up right away. I'm going to go and talk to D.C.I. Agostini. It's clear we need to bring the Cornwall police in on this now, and maybe the Coast Guard too. The biggest problem we have is that we don't actually know where the wrecks are. The English Channel is a bloody big body of water. The next thing on the agenda is to contact the Royal Navy museum. They might be able to identify the corvette in the photo or at least the type of ship. If we can find out where this ship or this type of ship operated we might be able to get a rough idea where to look."

"We could always ask Aegis Oceanographic, sir," Curtis joked, receiving a stern look of rebuke from Ross.

"Not very funny, Tony, not funny at all."

"Sorry sir."

"Right. For that, you can get a copy of the enlarged photo when Paul's done it, and then make it your priority task to get in touch with the Royal Navy. I want to know everything they can tell us about that shipwreck, and while you're at it, ask them about that bloody submarine too."

"Right sir. I'll get on to it right away, well, soon as Paul enlarges the photo." They turned to find Paul Ferris was already walking away with the photo in his hand. They knew he wouldn't be long.

"Okay, Sergeant Drake and me are going to bring D.C.I. Agostini up to date. He'll need to be the one to make an approach to the police down south, and if needs be, to get the Coast Guard involved too. It's beginning to look as if poor Aaron Decker found something he shouldn't have found, got this Haller chap involved and it somehow cost them both their lives. We need to find out what that something was and how Aegis is involved. Everyone tread carefully on this one, until we have a better idea of what we're dealing with. Direct your inquiries towards finding out if any strangers were seen or heard from by either Sally or Aaron in the weeks leading up to his death."

"One question, sir," said McLennan.

"Yes, Derek?"

"Well, if Aaron Decker took this photo around a year ago, and if, as Paul says, this German chap turned up soon after Decker was seen making his inquiries, then doesn't it make more sense to think the frogman must have been down there when Decker made his initial dives and that would mean it can't be Haller?"

Ross scratched his head for a minute, and then realised McLennan could be right.

"Well done Derek. That makes sense, unless of course, the photos we have were taken later, after Haller's death. It's possible Aaron took some earlier photos, sent them to Haller and when the German came over here and disappeared, Decker went back, found the body, photographed it and tried to blackmail someone at Aegis with his knowledge. We need to find out if the Deckers have or can locate any other memory cards from Aaron's camera that may contain earlier photos."

"I hadn't thought of that, sir but you're right. It could have happened that way, too."

"Well, we obviously have a lot of digging to do before we find our answer," Ross said as he and Drake moved to leave the room, ready to give D.C.I Agostini the latest news on the extremely tangled web they were gradually revealing that seemed to surround the death of Aaron Decker.

CHAPTER 16

U966, THE BALTIC SEA, 1945

Two days out from Kiel, and already the interior of what was now officially *U966* was taking on the atmosphere of a submarine at war. The air was heavy with the smell of diesel fumes, mingled with the scent of the sweat of those who crewed the boat. Most of the young men who served in *U966* had stopped shaving as soon as they'd left their home base just two days ago, and soon the lack of proper sanitation, a deprivation standard to U-Boat crews would increase the heady atmosphere within the boat, which would only be relieved when Ritter ordered the submarine to surface to recharge its batteries, and the hatches could be opened.

As soon as the boat had cleared Kiel and headed north towards the coast of Denmark, Ritter had called Engel to his tiny berth where he solemnly opened the sealed orders handed to him by Schmidt. Ritter read through the orders, then silently handed the two sheets of paper and an accompanying map to his first officer.

Engel took the orders, read them slowly, his eyes widening as he did so.

"This is madness, Max," Engel said.

"Those are our orders, Heini," Ritter replied. "We are officers of the Kriegsmarine and we are honour bound to obey them."

"We are virtually unarmed and we are supposed to make this crazy voyage?"

"The torpedoes were removed to lessen the weight of the boat, obviously, and to compensate for the weight of our cargo. There is no going back, my friend. To do so would be to invite summary execution for us all.

You've read the orders and seen the signature at the bottom. They come directly from the Fuehrer himself."

"I can see that Max. But why us? Why *U966*? Come to that, why the change from *U3000*?"

"I can't answer that, Heini. Maybe my reputation for seeing my commands through tough voyages brought me to Hitler's attention. Maybe we just drew the short straw. There aren't many of us left. The days of the wolf packs are long gone; you know that as well as I do."

Ritter took a bottle of schnapps from under his bunk, together with two tin mugs, into which he poured a liberal measure for each of them.

"Come Heini, let us drink to what may be our last voyage together. We have a long way to go and if we are lucky, then who knows? We may see Berlin again after all."

"See Berlin again? I've never been there at all. Until I joined the Kriegsmarine I'd never left Bremen in my life."

"I never knew that. Well, if we do make it, and one day return to Germany I will personally take you to the finest restaurant in the city and then we will find a top class brothel and enjoy ourselves as never before, eh, Heini?"

Engel looked at his captain, and smiled in resignation. Like Ritter he knew their chances of pulling off this mission were slim, but they would do as Ritter said. They would obey their orders as any naval officer would.

Ritter held his mug up and Engel reached across, tapped the rim of his own against Ritter's and the two men drank a toast, not to the mission, or to the Fuehrer, not even to *U966*, but instead, they drank to life, long or short, and to each other.

* * *

"Attention, this is your Kapitän speaking."

The sound of Ritter's voice, calm and commanding sounded throughout *U966* as the tannoy system carried his voice to every man on board.

In the control room, as elsewhere on *U966* the crew fell silent. Ritter had earlier informed the crew that they were sailing under top secret sealed orders and that news of their mission would be communicated to them when he deemed it necessary. *Oberfänrich zue See*, (sub-lieutenant), Wilhelm (Willi) Becker, at nineteen years old, the sub's youngest officer, currently in command of the boat while Ritter and Engel were in conference stood beside the periscope, a cigarette dangling from his lips, hands in pockets, trying not to betray his nerves as Ritter spoke. Around the boat, the rest of the crew listened attentively, some with excitement, others with trepidation, as the nature of their mission became clear.

"We are now sailing to the north of Denmark, and before long we will head into the north sea, after which we will adopt a new course that will take us south, along the east coast of Scotland and then England until we turn to the west and make a run through the English Channel, breaking out into the Atlantic after which we face a long and arduous voyage across the ocean, until we reach our final destination, which for the moment must remain secret. Some of you will have seen that our boat's maker's plate has been changed to identify us as *U966*. Henceforth we are no longer *U3000*. Do not ask why. It is part of the mission that we adopt the new designation. The cargo some of you may have seen being loaded into our boat is of vital importance to the Third Reich, and the orders we sail under have been signed by none other than the Fuehrer himself. Some of you will have noticed that the majority of our torpedoes have been removed prior to leaving Kiel. This was done to lighten the boat, enabling us to run silent and deep for longer periods, and to compensate for the weight of the boxes loaded on board at Kiel. We will surface only when necessary to recharge our batteries, so the air might become a little rank in here at times."

This brought a few quiet ripples of laughter from a few of the men.

"I make no apologies for the possible hardships we face on this voyage. Remember, we are not on a search and destroy mission. We are under orders not to engage the enemy unless it is absolutely necessary, so we must use stealth as our watchword at all times. The most dangerous part of our outward voyage will be the dash through the English Channel which is heavily patrolled by the Royal Navy, as we all know. Silence will be strictly maintained as we navigate through those waters. For now, I can add little more. We sail on a mission of the greatest importance, and I know I can count on every man aboard to do his duty to The Fatherland. That is all."

Ritter flicked the 'off' button on the microphone, omitting the usual *Heil Hitler* at the end of his address to the crew, a mark of his dislike for the man he considered unfit to lead his country. Only then did he notice his hand was shaking. This damned voyage was getting to him already.

"That was some of the finest and most resounding bullshit I've ever heard in my life," Engel said quietly as Ritter placed the microphone back on the hook beside his bunk. "You almost had me cheering you and believing that codswallop about the importance of the mission, and doing it for The Fatherland."

"What did you want me say, Heini? Should I have told them the British, if they detect us, will hunt us down remorselessly and destroy us without giving us a second thought?"

"Why not?" said Heini. "After all, this is a U-Boat and the British would try to sink any U-Boat they came across anyway."

"True, but I need the crew to be on my side, to believe we can do this. It's a long, long voyage, Heini and we need the men with us, not grumbling and becoming discontented and rebellious."

Engel smiled.

"Okay, I'm convinced. Shall we get back to work my brave and silver-tongued Kapitän?"

"A good idea, Heini, a very good idea. Let's go and relieve poor Willi at the con. He's probably having kittens by now, poor kid."

"They get younger all the time, the ones they send us now," said Heini, ruefully, forgetting he was barely twenty-two himself, though after surviving five years in the service, he could be considered an old man by many.

"They're getting younger because we are running out of men to recruit," Ritter replied. "Come, my friend, we have a course change to calculate," and the two men left the relative privacy of Ritter's cabin, relieved Becker, much to his relief, in the control room and were soon bent over the chart table, plotting the next stage of their voyage.

"Take her down to fifty metres," Ritter ordered.

"Fifty metres, aye sir," the voice of *Bootsmannsmaat* (Coxwain) Boris Nagel, the helmsman, replied as the nose of the submarine tipped downwards and the boat began a shallow descent to the required depth, almost two hundred feet below the surface of the sea. It would be some time before they reached the dangerous waters of the North Sea and eventually the English Channel.

In *U966's* engine room, surrounded by the quiet hum of the boat's twin AEG electric motors, the submarine's resident doom and gloom merchant, Joseph Ziegler, bare chested and with three day's growth on his chin, turned to fellow seaman Karl Meister, eighteen and still struggling to grow any semblance of facial hair and said, as he sat sipping from a tin mug of ersatz coffee,

"No good'll come of it, this voyage, young Meister, I can feel it in my water."

"Really, Joseph?" the young and impressionable teenager replied. "Why do you say such things? Hasn't the Herr Kapitän always seen us safely home after every trip?"

"How many trips have you completed?" was Ziegler's reply.

"Six now, Joseph."

"Ha, I've done twelve in this sardine can, and twenty six before that in other boats. Don't you think I should know when things are different?"

"Different?"

"For the love of God, Meister. Look around you. We've been stripped of our main armaments, for a start. We normally carry fourteen fucking torpedoes, and they leave us with four up the spout in the for'ard tubes, enough for maybe one, two attempts to sink an enemy, if we're lucky. They load us up with a deck full of wooden crates carrying God knows what and then, our dear Fuehrer, old 'Adolf, head in the clouds' orders us to sail halfway round the fucking world to deliver them to God knows where. These boats weren't made for voyages of that length, and d'you know why we've got to stay submerged for so long?"

"Why, Joseph?" young Meister asked the seasoned hand.

"Diesel fuel, young Meister, that's why. These boats have limited fuel capacity. Unless we are intended to meet up with a refuelling tender somewhere in mid-fucking Atlantic, we barely carry enough diesel fuel to see us halfway there under normal conditions. Do you have any sodding idea how foul it's going to get in here if we have to run underwater almost all the way?"

"But we'll be surfacing to recharge the batteries won't we, Joseph?"

"That's what I mean," said Ziegler. "We'll surface to recharge the batteries and while we're up top we have to run on the diesels and the fuel will be getting lower and lower all the time."

"But, the kapitän would not take us into danger deliberately, would he?"

"No, Meister, but I tell you, this whole mission stinks, and I don't just mean the fucking air in this tin can."

"Stop trying to scare the lad, Ziegler, and get on with your job."

The sharp voice of the U-Boat's engineering officer, the blonde-haired, blue-eyed Aryan stereotype, Heinz Muller cut in to the conversation. Although he would have made a perfect advertisement for Hitler's Aryan superiority theme, Muller was a fierce anti-Nazi, though he managed to keep those thoughts to himself. He was first and foremost an engineer, in love with the pristine examples of German engineering that had been placed in his devoted care, and secondly, he considered himself a professional officer of the Kriegsmarine, a naval officer above thoughts of politics and race. He served the navy, and through the navy, he served his captain and his ship, which meant that for the time being, Heinz was madly in love with, and married to the engines that propelled the *U966*.

Ziegler grudgingly complied with Muller's order, sluicing away the dregs of his ersatz coffee, and turning back to his task of maintaining the efficient running of *U966s* engines. Muller wiped the sweat from his face with the oily rag that never seemed to leave his hand, the result leaving his face looking even dirtier than he'd appeared a few seconds earlier.

* * *

As *U966* silently crept around the northern coast of Denmark, the Royal Navel Dockyard at Portland in Dorset was as usual, a hive of activity. In one small corner of the docks, two 'Cathedral' Class corvettes stood, berthed side by side, being readied for sea. *H.M.S. Norwich* and *H.M.S. Ripon* were sister ships, small, poorly armed escort vessels normally assigned to convoy escort duties despite their apparent unsuitability for the task. Smaller than many of the ships they were ordered to protect, they carried a single 4 inch turret forward of the bridge, together with a number of ack-ack (anti-aircraft) guns positioned along the port and starboard sides of the ship, two depth charge launchers on each side, with twin torpedo launchers at the stern. For the crews of these two little ships, their current assignment on channel patrol was like being sent on a well needed holiday after their last stint of Atlantic convoy duty. Constantly cold and wet, unable to sleep in the rolling, pitching waves, and subject to repeated alerts and hours at battle stations, the Atlantic convoy routes were unforgiving on those whose duty it was to protect the merchant vessels that carried the goods and materials essential to Britain's war effort.

For the moment, both ships were engaged in regular patrols in the English Channel, on the lookout for raids by German E-Boats, that had recently been attacking lone trawlers and small merchant vessels that plied their trade close to the coast. The Royal Navy simply didn't have enough Motor Torpedo Boats (M.T.B.s) in home waters to counter the threat, hence the current assignment.

On board the *Norwich* her captain, Lieutenant Commander Giles Clarkson, stood on the bridge, watching the activity taking place both on board and on the dockside. The *Norwich* might not be a battleship or cruiser, not even a destroyer, but she was his ship, his first command and he was proud of her and her crew, who had served with distinction on their last voyage which had seen five of their number fail to return to port. Clarkson had spent an afternoon writing letters of condolence to the relatives of his fallen crewmen and now, with darkness falling, he needed to wind down, to relax, and as was his usual routine, he did so by keeping a close watch on everything that happened around the dockyard, always a fascinating scene for the twenty eight year old officer. A sound from his left signalled the arrival of a duffel coated figure who stepped over the side coaming onto the bridge to join him.

"Permission to join you sir?" asked Lieutenant Peter Hicks, his first officer.

"Of course Number One," he replied. "Everything alright below?"

"Totally ship-shape, sir. The stores will soon be fully loaded, armaments already done. The coaler will be coming alongside as soon as they've finished with *Ripon* and she's moved away to grant them access.

"Excellent. Well done, and well done to the men too. How's morale, Peter?"

"Still good, sir. Despite the losses on the last trip, they know we did a good job. It was a shame we just missed nailing that damn sub, though"

"True, but you never know, we may just get a chance to find some action on our next patrol."

"We still have four men to return tomorrow, sir. They were allowed compassionate leave, you recall, family losses in the bombings in London and Liverpool."

"Yes, of course, poor buggers. They go through bloody hell for weeks at a time at sea, and then come home to find their homes, families, kids all gone. God, Peter, I hate this damned war."

"As we all do, sir. But don't worry, the men will be ready for sea by tomorrow night, as scheduled."

"Good. Bloody awkward having to cast off after dusk but those damned E-Boats like to dash across the channel and hit our fishing vessels as they're returning to port, the cowardly bastards."

"Yes indeed, sir. So let's hope we can nail one or two of them this time, eh?"

"Definitely, Number One. It would be great for morale too if we could sink one of those bastards."

The sound of someone in clumping heavy sea boots sounded on the short bridge ladder and was quickly followed by the appearance of the smiling face of Chief Petty Officer Albert (Nobby) Clark, the ship's bosun. Clark's toothy grin seemed fixed in place, and even through the fiercest North Atlantic gale, the experienced and stalwart senior N.C.O. on board the *Norwich* always had a kind word or found the right thing to say to often fearful young ratings, many of whom had never served aboard a ship in their lives. As kindly as he was, however, Clark was a fierce taskmaster and didn't suffer fools gladly. Twenty years in the Navy had honed his skills as a manager of men to a fine art and Clarkson had often wondered how such a man had ended up on the *Norwich* when he could have served with distinction on a battleship or cruiser or one of the new breed of submarine hunting destroyers that helped turn the tide of the war at sea against Germany's underwater marauders. In a conversation with the Captain (D), in command of the destroyer squadron assigned to Portland, he'd eventually discovered that despite his previously excellent war record, Clark had been sent to the Corvette squadron as a kind of punishment for a breach of King's Regulations. Whilst serving on *H.M.S. Forester*, a cruiser of the Mediterranean fleet, Clark had countermanded the orders of a young Lieutenant who had ordered two men to release an anti aircraft gun mounting that had locked in place during an engagement with a small Italian cruiser. Clark knew there was no hope of them succeeding in the task and he'd seen the approach of two Italian *Macchi C200* fighter aircraft off the starboard beam, heading straight for the *Forester*. The two ratings would have been horribly exposed to the inevitable canon fire from the fighters and Clark had belayed the Lieutenant's order and commanded them to take cover instead. Seconds later a burst of shellfire from the leading fighter plane raked the ship's starboard side, totally destroying the anti-aircraft gun and its mounting, where the two men would have been working if they'd followed the inexperienced officer's order.

Rather than commend Clark for his foresight in anticipating the attack on the anti-aircraft guns, saving the lives of the two ratings, the Lieutenant instead placed Clark on report for inciting the men to disobey an order.

The captain of the cruiser, knowing in his heart that Clark was the hero of the hour, had little choice but to follow regulations, especially as Clark admitted to the charge and did the best he could by reprimanding the C.P.O. and arranging his transfer to another vessel. Hence, the *Forester's* loss was *Norwich's* gain. As for the Lieutenant who had been so pernickety in his observance of the letter of the law, he was lost soon afterwards when the *Forester* was torpedoed off the coast of Greece and went down in less than ten minutes with only twenty survivors from a crew of nine hundred men. The captain was one of those who survived, miraculously blown off his bridge and into the sea by the force of one of the explosions that tore his ship apart. In a touch of supreme irony, the captain, stunned and floating helplessly, close to his sinking ship and almost certain to be pulled under by the undertow when the ship went down, was pulled to safety by two young seamen in a collapsible life raft, the same two ratings saved by Clark's action a few weeks earlier.

Now, Clark saluted and stood before the captain of the *Norwich*, his usual smile fixed in place as though he hadn't a care in the world.

"Hello Bosun," said Clarkson. "To what do we owe this honour? It's a rare thing indeed to see our beloved bosun up here while we're preparing for sea."

"Evenin' sir," Clark replied. "Just thought as how you'd like to know the men have completed the repairs to that cracked boiler we was worried about. The dockyard people said as it would take at least three days of work, a deal of welding and what have you to get the job done. But our lads completed the job in just over twenty four hours. The ship will be ready to sail as ordered tomorrow, sir, that's definite. Like I said, just thought you'd want to know."

Clarkson knew the smile on Nobby Clark's face was not only genuine but was one of pride. In a few short weeks, the bosun had succeeded in doing his own spot of welding, having welded together a bunch of disparate personalities that included twenty ratings straight from training establishments, into a truly efficient fighting crew that possessed a fierce pride in their ship. The *Norwich* might be small and outgunned by almost every ship in the German navy, but she was their ship, and the pride Clark had instilled in them gave them an added edge when it came to going into action. Clarkson knew this only too well and was grateful he had the experience of the bosun to rely on when the *Norwich* was called into action once again.

Clarkson returned the bosun's smile.

"Thank you bosun. I had every faith in you and the men. When you told me you could do it I had no hesitation in telling Captain Hennessy we'd sail on time tomorrow."

Clark's smile grew a little broader.

"Thanks sir. They're good boys, most of 'em. A few's a bit raw, but they'll do. The couple of moaning minnies we inherited with the ship are learning they can't take liberties any more, not as long as I live and breathe, at any rate."

"I'm sure they are," Clarkson replied. "Why don't you go and get some sleep now, Chief? There's no need for you to burn the midnight oil tonight. We'll have plenty to do tomorrow and I do know you've worked without a break for over twelve hours."

"Well, if you say it's alright sir, I think I might do as you suggest. Couple of hours sleep sounds pretty good to me."

"Then go, rest a little. And Bosun?"

"Sir?"

"Tell the men well done from me, won't you?"

"I'll do that for certain, sir. Thanks."

With that, Clark disappeared as quickly as he'd arrived and Clarkson turned to Hicks and said, "Thank God for people like Clark, Number One. I think he could single handedly force this bloody ship to sea with the strength of his will if he had to."

"You might be right, sir," Hicks replied. "I think though, if I might make a suggestion, you should turn in too, as you've told Clark to. You need to rest too. I've got the watch for the next four hours. Nothing's going to happen to us while we're here and I can supervise the loading of the coal when the old *Farimond* arrives."

Clarkson yawned, clapped his first officer on the shoulder and said.

"You're right of course, Number One. I'll be off then. Goodnight."

"Goodnight sir," Hicks replied as Clarkson departed the bridge, leaving the first officer alone with his thoughts and the sounds of the ship at anchor as she and her crew settled down for the night.

CHAPTER 17

A PASSAGE TO WREXHAM?

Andy Ross and Izzie Drake sat opposite D.C.I. Oscar Agostini in his office. They'd spent an hour going through the entire case so far with the boss, and Agostini looked thoughtful as he contemplated all they'd learned so far.

"This is turning into a far more complex case than we first envisaged," Agostini mused. "The thing we need to do is go back to the beginning, Andy. First of all, where did the killer obtain the Ketamine? There can't be that many places where it can be easily obtained without a pharmaceutical licence. Next, how did the killer get into the house and young Decker's bedroom without the two other housemates hearing anything? Okay, it appears the front door was locked but the back door wasn't so there's a possibility, a strong one, the killer entered there and crept silently up the stairs. We just don't know yet. Third, we really need to find the motive for the crime. So far you have some tenuous links to this American Company, Aegis, who suddenly came along and offered some kind of sponsorship to Decker's girlfriend, with the offer of a job at the end of her university studies. We know young Decker felt there was something 'off' about them, hence his trip to dive on the wrecks in The Channel, but listen, how did he know exactly where to dive? There's a possibility someone on the inside was helping him.

You then have the frogman's body. Who is it? Could it be this German man, Klaus Haller? We need to find him. If he's alive and well, it makes identifying the body at the wreck site even harder. Then we have to take into consideration the fact that Decker's father is a senior officer in the bloody C.I.A. of all things. Is there some connection between the father's occupation and the murder of his son, or is it purely coincidental? And we need to try the Royal Navy for help in identifying the ship you saw in the photos, and maybe the submarine too. So tell me, Andy, where are you going next with all this?"

Ross leaned back in his chair, and thought long and hard for a minute before replying.

"Well sir, Ferris is still looking into the Aegis Institute and its various operations around the world. It's obvious we need to look very carefully at them if we're to push the case forward, but I can't just go blundering down to Cornwall and encroaching on another force's turf."

"Leave that to me," Agostini interrupted. "I'll speak to my counterpart at the Devon and Cornwall Constabulary, and elicit their help. You may have to make a trip down there and it might need a few days. I know you've just got married, Sergeant," he said to Drake, "so how will your husband feel if you go swanning off with D.I. Ross to the wilds of Cornwall?"

"Peter understands what my job entails, sir. It won't be a problem," she replied.

"Good, now, make it a priority to find out if this Haller chap is still alive, and if he is, where he is and what he's got to do with all this. It seems we have a real mystery on our hands, and I agree that the Aegis Institute is definitely connected to it in some way. You mentioned that young Decker said he felt whatever he'd discovered could be worth something. We need to find out what he meant by that. Did he mean financially or academically? You have a difficult path to follow I think, Andy. Try taking one step at a time."

"Yes, sir," Ross replied. "If there's nothing else for now, we'll get back to it, then."

"Yes, off you go, and I'll let you know as soon as I've spoken with the force down in Cornwall."

"Right, sir, thanks," said Ross and he and Drake made their way out of the D.C.I's office and back to the squad room.

As they walked in, Paul Ferris saw them and immediately beckoned the pair across to where he was sitting at his computer terminal.

"Please tell me you have something for me, Paul," Ross said, a hint of desperation in his voice.

"Perhaps, sir," Ferris responded. "It appears the Aegis Institute was set up fifty years ago by a wealthy philanthropist called Silas Wren, who all those years ago felt that the human race was slowly polluting and destroying the ecological balance of the world's oceans. Wren died twenty years ago and the institute suddenly blossomed into a true international conglomerate, controlled by a board of directors in Boston, U.S.A. Despite that they seem to work mostly out of massive office facilities in New York.

They spread their influence rapidly around the world, their facilities becoming bigger and better year on year. They own a fleet of ships, mostly research vessels and a massive number of submersibles, able to probe the deepest parts of the world's oceans. Now, if they were purely concerned with academic research and projects to protect the ecology of the oceans, there'd be nothing fishy, excuse the term, to find, but I found that Aegis has taken to doing a lot of what can only be called underwater archaeology, locating, investigating and in some cases downright plundering many of the sites they've worked on. There've been drowned cities, ancient and modern shipwrecks, some of which they've raised, amassing a small fortune in salvage fees in some cases, like a supertanker they raised with state of the art recovery technology. It seems as if the current Aegis Institute is more interested in making money that in being a kind of multinational Greenpeace type organisation."

"Very good, Paul. So you think they may be hiding a treasure hunting operation behind the veneer of oceanographic conservation, is that it?"

"That's exactly what I think, sir. The biggest problem we're going to have is proving it, and then proving that they're acting illegally."

"I have a feeling that's just what Aaron Decker did find out, Paul, and it cost that young man his life, because someone in that organisation is prepared to kill to protect whatever secrets they're hiding." Ross concluded.

"What about Klaus Haller?" Izzie Drake asked. "Did you have a chance to look him up, maybe find out if he's still alive?"

"I didn't have to," Ferris replied, much to their surprise. "Klaus Haller is alive and well and living in Wrexham."

"He lives in Wales?" Ross asked, astounded.

"Yes, sir. Derek McLennan did a simple search of his name on his computer, and located him in about ten minutes."

"I thought he told your wife's uncle he was from Hamburg," Izzie Drake said.

"He is from Hamburg, originally, but he's lived over here for the last five years. He's a genuine naval historian alright, in fact he's written three books on the subject of naval warfare. He probably told Reg he was from Hamburg from a sense of security if he was looking into the activities of Aegis. Anyway, Derek spoke to him and then took off in his car with Sam Gable. Wrexham isn't far so he phoned the guy and arranged to go and see him. They'll probably be there already."

"Well, that's initiative for you," said Ross, pleased that McLennan had taken it upon himself to go right away to interview a potentially important witness.

"Hold on though, let's rewind a minute," Izzie Drake said. "If Haller is in Wrexham, then who the hell is the frogman?"

"Precisely one of the points the D.C.I. brought up," Ross replied. "We have yet another layer to add to our growing mystery, it seems."

At that point in the conversation Curtis and Dodds strolled in to the squad room.

"Well, look who's back," said Izzie Drake. "It's the pool hall wizards."

"*Snooker and* pool hall, actually, Sarge," Curtis replied.

"Yes, but that doesn't fit with the song," Drake joked, referring to the old record, *Pinball Wizard* by The Who.

"Okay, okay, come on then, you two, what have you found out, if anything?"

"Well sir," Curtis began, "The manager at the 147 remembers Aaron Decker very well. He referred to him as 'The Yank' and said he took a lot of money off the other guys who he played with regularly. He didn't really know them by name, but he did say that more than one or two of them often got more than a little mad at the amount of money Decker won from them. Seems there were some heated arguments sometimes, when players lost to Decker and didn't have enough cash on them to pay up. Once, he heard someone refer to him as a hustler, but Decker just laughed."

"That's right," said Nick Dodds. "He also said that Decker played pool there as well, with similar results, though that was mostly against the local lads. They ended up refusing to play against him, he was that good."

"So young Aaron wasn't quite the paragon of virtue everyone holds him up to be," said Ross.

"Exactly, sir," said Dodds. "Seems he might have racked up a fair few enemies at the 147 club."

"Yes, but would any of them dislike him enough to murder him?" Ross mused.

* * *

Although located in North Wales, Wrexham is only 35 to 40 miles from Liverpool, depending on the route taken, so Derek McLennan and Sam Gable had arrived at the home of Klaus Haller about an hour after leaving the headquarters car park.

Haller lived in a small village on the outskirts of town, in a well kept period cottage, one of a small terrace of three that looked to have been built sometime during the nineteenth century. With its small windows, a front door at which anyone over five feet tall had to bend down to navigate entry into the home and its overhanging roof, it could have come straight out of a Dickens novel.

McLennan and Gable were seated opposite the German, on a chintz covered two seater sofa, the largest item of furniture in the small, cosy living room, which Gable thought might be best described as 'the parlour'. Haller was seated in the room's sole matching armchair, the only other items of note in the room being a small table in one corner holding a twenty four inch screen television, with a combined Video and DVD player seated on the shelf that ran along the underside of the table.

A compact portable CD player was precariously positioned on the window sill and a glass fronted cabinet against one wall held a number of model ships, a link to the resident's preoccupation in life. A small three-shelf oak bookcase finished off the room's furnishings. The carpet was thick and plush and on the bare stone interior walls, painted a subtle shade of cream, a couple of good quality prints of world war two warships took pride of place. Derek McLennan thought he recognised one of the ships as *Bismark*, having seen the film about the sinking of the great battleship some years ago.

Haller hadn't seemed surprised to have heard from McLennan, and having made his visitors a cup of the finest coffee McLennan had ever tasted, Haller sat back and waited for the two officers to begin their questions. Sam Gable would initially leave it to McLennan, who had done the work in locating Haller in the first place. She contented herself with studying the man they'd come to see as Derek began his questioning. Haller was of medium height, around five feet six or seven, and looked to be in his late fifties, maybe early sixties. His hair was almost pure white, and his clothes, though of good quality, betrayed the lack of female influence in Haller's life, Sam thought. The thing that caught her attention more than anything were the German's almost penetrating blue eyes, which despite the man's age, sparkled with life and vitality. Klaus Haller must have been an incredibly handsome man in his younger days, she concluded. Despite his height, Haller gave off the air of a much smaller man, appearing diminutive in stature, something Sam found odd, but put it down to the man's age and overall bearing and the architecture of their surroundings which made everything in the cottage appear miniaturised.

"Oh yes," Haller said in response to Derek McLennan's questioning, "young Aaron Decker came to me with his suspicions about Aegis Oceanographic's motives surrounding their Channel Project."

"But, why you, Herr Haller?"

"Ah, you see, Constable, Aaron and I had met a year previous to his seeking me out last year. I am regarded as something of an authority on the history of the war at sea during World War Two," and he reached one arm out from his chair towards the bookcase which stood close enough for him to pull a book from the top shelf, which he passed across to the detective. McLennan read the title, *A History of Naval Warfare in the Hitler Years*, and waited for Haller to explain.

In excellent English, Haller went on, "He was writing a paper about the events leading up to the sinking of the *Deutschland class* heavy cruiser, what you British called a 'pocket battleship' *Admiral Graf Spee*, under the command of Hans Langsdorff, sunk by the British off Montevideo in the Battle of the River Plate in December 1939."

Haller pointed to one of the prints on the wall.

"That's her in her glory days, during a review at Spithead in 1937, when she paid a visit to England."

The detectives followed Haller's pointing finger. McLennan could see the difference in size between the *Graf Spee* and the *Bismark*. Despite being smaller, *Graf Spee* seemed to simply bristle with gun turrets, large and small, giving her the appearance of a veritable floating arsenal. Now McLennan recalled seeing another old black and white movie, *The Battle of the River Plate*, which had told the story of her sinking by three British cruisers, the *Exeter*, the *Ajax* and the *Achilles*. McLennan mentioned this to Haller who smiled.

"Yes, a very stirring film, D.C. McLennan, and surprisingly accurate in the details considering when it was made, showing Langsdorff to be a real humanitarian in his treatment of prisoners. It was sad he felt he had to take his own life after scuttling his ship."

Klaus Haller sighed a sad sigh at the thought, and then continued.

"So, anyway, I had been of some use to Aaron in his research so when he had some doubts about the work the company that his girlfriend had contracted to work for, I suppose it was natural for him to contact me again."

"And you were living here in Wrexham at that time, Herr Haller?"

"Yes. I rent this charming cottage of course, it is not mine to own. I move around the world a lot in my work Detective Constable. Before this, I lived in the United States for four years, researching various aspects of the beginnings of the fledgling United States Navy, before that, in Norway, looking into the voyages made by the earliest Viking navigators, and so on. While here, I have been engaged in discovering much about the ships lost around the coast of Britain in the last two hundred years. For a relatively small island, Great Britain has some very treacherous coastal waters that have led to many shipwrecks over the years, I assure you."

"I see," said McLennan. "So you thought there may be something in what he told you?"

"I was not sure, to tell you the truth, but as I had great respect for the young man's dedication to his subject and his diligence in wishing to protect his lady friend, I thought it could do no harm to at least make some inquiries to see if he might be correct in his thoughts and assumptions."

"Please tell us what you discovered," said Sam Gable, now joining in the conversation.

"Well, it was all a little strange. I first of all contacted the man called William Evans, an American who was listed as the Research Director at the Aegis facility near Falmouth. I wrote to him and introduced myself as an author and historian and explained I wished to investigate certain aspects of the small engagements that occurred in the English Channel during World War Two. I told him I had been informed by a colleague that his company was currently working on an environmental project that included locating the wrecks of various ships on the sea bed and asked if he would be prepared to share the locations of such wrecks with me. He told me his company's work was confidential and that he was unable to furnish me with the information I required. This seemed odd to me. I have worked with many businesses over the years, involved in such work and could not understand his position. Surely, I thought, there is nothing of a confidential nature about the environmental effects of shipwrecks. I wondered if perhaps Aaron could be right so, my suspicions aroused, I travelled to Cornwall and sought out the local police at first to ask if they had any information on the activities of the Aegis people in their town. A sergeant told me that Aegis were very secretive and protective of their facility and did not encourage visitors. Undeterred, I paid a visit to Aegis but was turned away at the gatehouse to their private dock and told they did not allow unauthorised access to the site. Next, I asked if they at least had any information leaflets that I could take that gave any information on the company. Again I was rebuffed."

"You certainly tried hard, Herr Haller," said Gable.

"Ah, but I was not yet finished," Haller said, excitedly. "I returned to my hotel, where I placed a transatlantic call to the Aegis Institute in the USA. That was when I became convinced something was indeed not quite right about the situation."

"In what way, Herr Haller?" McLennan asked.

"After I introduced myself as an international author and well-known historian, I was put through to the publicity department where a lady called Hannah Ryker was very helpful and arranged to send me a dossier on the work of Aegis around the world, including the many historical sites they have helped to unearth beneath the oceans of the world. This seemed at odds with the words of Mr. William Evans, and I said so to Ms. Ryker. She was unaware of any secrecy surrounding any Aegis projects and said she would put me through to one of their research directors.

Mr. Francis Kelly spoke next to me. He told me that there was no real secrecy about their work in the English Channel, but the fact that the wrecks they had found were designated war graves meant they wished to ensure privacy as they had been subjected to protests from some people who thought they were desecrating the sites. Now, the thing is, constable, to be designated a war grave, a sunken ship must first be identified and all such wrecks are catalogued and their positions are common knowledge to anyone who knows where to look them up. So, I asked which ship or ships Aegis were currently working on, and Mr. Kelly became evasive. He said he was not privy to that information and as far as he knew the Aegis operation in the English Channel was currently centred on up to three unnamed wrecks they had located. That made no sense but I did not challenge his words. It was obvious he was not going to tell me any more, so I thanked him and hung up."

"Wow," said Sam Gable, "you are quite a tiger when you get going, eh, Herr Haller?"

"One does not become an expert in any field in life without being tenacious, young lady," Haller smiled as he spoke.

"So, you then reported back to Aaron Decker, I presume?" said McLennan.

"Oh no," Haller sounded offended that the D.C. assumed he'd given up. "I hired a boat."

"You hired a boat?" McLennan was incredulous. "What for?"

"To follow their research vessel of course. How else would I find out where they were working?"

"You're amazing," Sam Gable spoke to Haller with a hint of admiration in her voice.

"It was only a small boat of course, but I am an experienced sailor. I served in the German navy in the nineteen sixties, and was not put off by going to sea in a small craft. It was during my military service that I developed my love of naval history you see. Anyway, I found a vantage point from which I could see into the Aegis facility and when their vessel *Poseidon* was obviously preparing to leave port two days after my phone calls, I quickly drove down to the harbour, boarded my boat and took to sea, taking up a position from which I could see their vessel as it left port and headed out to sea. I simply followed them from a distance, my boat being small enough not to be seen by any lookouts they might have posted on deck. I assumed they would have radar, sonar and so on but didn't believe they would be looking for anyone tracking them, and it appeared I was right."

"Are you telling us you know where they were working, Herr Haller?" Gable asked.

"But of course," Haller said, "and upon my return to Falmouth, I immediately called Aaron and told him what I'd discovered. He had already been to Falmouth once, you see, but had been unable to find anything. He thanked me and said he would take it from there, and would come down to Falmouth again and arrange to dive on the wreck and see what they were doing. I am not a diver, and had no intention of joining him in his venture, but asked him to tell me if he found anything of historical significance, which he agreed to do."

"I see," said McLennan, "and did Aaron ever contact you again?"

"Yes, he did, a few weeks later, to tell me he'd been down to the wreck and that it was a badly decomposed merchant vessel of no significance and that he was sorry to have wasted my time, and that there was nothing to be concerned about. I never heard from him again and soon decided that whatever Aegis was up to was no longer any of my business."

"That's what he told you?"

"That's what he told me. I'm not an idiot, Constable. I thought he might have been holding out on me and when I saw the news the other day about his death, I realised that Aaron had lied to me. He did lie to me, didn't he?" Haller said with a note of sadness in his voice.

"Yes he did," Herr Haller," said Gable. "But tell me, do you still have the co-ordinates of the location of the wreck he dived on?"

"But of course." Haller stood and walked to the bookcase where he picked up a briefcase that lay on its side on the bottom shelf. Opening the case, he took out a small black book, flicked through the pages and finding the page he was looking for, simply tore it out and passed it to her.

"A good historian never loses anything that might be of help, Constable. Please take it. It is of no use to me any longer but if there is anything interesting from a historical point of view down there, I would appreciate hearing about it in due course."

"I'm sure my boss will be only too pleased to inform you of any historical information we discover," a smiling Sam Gable said.

"Thank you," said Haller. "It is sad that Aaron felt he had to be evasive with me. Perhaps he just did not want to share in whatever it was he had discovered, but still, a shame."

"Yes, I'm sorry too, had he done so perhaps things may have turned out differently. And thank you too, Herr Haller, you've been a great help," McLennan spoke, rising from the sofa and shaking the historian's hand.

The two detectives were soon on the road back to Liverpool, both aware that they may just be holding the key to unlocking the case and solving the murder of Aaron Decker on a small sheet of paper in Derek McLennan's jacket pocket.

CHAPTER 18

A SLEEPLESS NIGHT

"You're sure you don't mind me disappearing like this for a couple of days?" Izzie asked her husband of just over a week. The couple were sat together on the sofa in the lounge of their home, Izzie leaning back into Peter's chest with her knees curled up beneath her as the original *Star Wars* movie played quietly to itself on the TV.

"Mind? Of course I mind, but in the nicest possible way," Peter replied. "I knew what your job entailed before we married, so it's okay, really. It's just a shame that this comes so soon after the wedding."

"It'll only be for a couple of days, my darling, three at the most, I think, and I will of course make it up to you in the best possible way when I get back," Izzie said, flashing him an impish, highly suggestive smile."

"Oh yes?" he replied. "So how about a little bit of that making up right now, just to keep me going, as it where?"

"But what about *Star Wars*, Paul? It's one of your favourites."

"I've only seen it about fifty times so far," he jokingly replied. "I don't think the ending is about to change because we're up in the bedroom do you?"

"Well, what are we waiting for?" said Izzie as she slid off the sofa, stood up and took his hand, leading him out of the room and up the stairs to the bedroom, where their passion soon banished thoughts of Izzie's imminent departure for Cornwall in the company of D.I. Ross.

* * *

Andy and Maria Ross had also enjoyed the pleasures of an early night and now lay together in bed, Maria resting with her head on Andy's shoulder.

"It's really getting to you, isn't it darling, this case?" she said softly, almost reading his thoughts.

"Yes, it is," he confessed. "We seem to have very little in the way of concrete evidence so far, just lots of conjecture and suppositions, Maria, and you can't build a case of murder against a suspect based on those, not that we have a real suspect either."

"But I thought you said you were sure someone at this Aegis company must be involved?"

"Involved, maybe, but even if Aegis are behind it, we still don't know who actually carried out the murders. I can't get away from the thought that one or both of Aaron Decker's housemates must be implicated somehow. I think we need to dig deeper into their past lives to see if there's anything that would leave them open to persuasion to commit such an act."

"So, do you think this visit to Falmouth will help?"

"I hope so. Oscar has fixed it for us to meet with a D.I. Pascoe who knows the waters of the Channel very well apparently, being something of a weekend sailor himself, so Oscar was informed by his counterpart down there. The chap I spoke to at the Ministry of Defence was helpful too and some chap from the Admiralty is going to meet up with us too. Seems the Royal Navy has a special department dealing with wrecks and war graves that also happen to be former Royal Naval ships. That photo I told you about really does seem to have stirred up a hornet's nest of activity."

"What about the father, Andy? Do you still think this has anything to do with him being in the C.I.A?"

"I don't think so. That was just a dreadful and unfortunate coincidence I think."

"Well, if I'm going to be deprived of my husband for a few days, the least you can do is give me something to help me drop off to sleep," Maria said softly as she reached up, kissed her husband and then allowed her hand to wander down his chest, finally finding its target as Andy Ross groaned softly. He turned, kissed her hard on the lips in return, and then pushed his wife onto her back, Maria moaning softly in turn as his own hand found her wet and ready for him.

Later, as Maria slept peacefully beside him, Andy Ross lay awake until the small hours of the morning. He couldn't get the case out of his mind. The whole thing reeked of some form of corporate cover up by the Aegis Institute, but just what, he wondered for the hundredth time could they possibly be hiding? He'd been assured that the police inspector he was meeting knew the seas down there as well as anyone he could hope to encounter, and the local Coastguard station had also been informed of his visit and would send someone to meet him when he'd made contact with D.C.I. Trevelyan.

As the figures on the digital bedside clock read four o'clock in the morning, Maria stirred and turned to face him.

"You're awake aren't you, Andy?"

"Mmm," he replied. "Can't sleep. Sorry if I woke you."

"You didn't. It's this bloody case, isn't it?"

"U-huh. I have a feeling we're missing something. I'm just not sure what the hell it could be."

"I thought of something just before I fell asleep."

"What is it?"

"The two men who shared the house with your victim. You say they are technically the best suspects, but if I recall, you said they had a few drinks downstairs, probably fell asleep watching TV, and heard nothing, right?"

"That's right, so, what of it?"

"Just suppose, Andy, that someone spiked their drinks too, like the dead man and his girlfriend, just enough to make them drowsy enough to not realise someone had crept into the house. They could be totally innocent."

Ross could see the logic in Maria's words. As always, his wife's intuition had given his thought processes a nudge in a different direction. Her analytical medical mind had often come up with incisive thoughts and theories that had assisted him in solving tricky cases in the past.

"I'll hold that thought," he replied. "You may have a point my darling, though it's too late now to test any cans or bottles they may have drunk from and any knock out potion will have been purged from their systems by now."

"Ooh, I love it when you talk medical terminology at me," Maria giggled. "It gets me all turned on."

"Oh yes," Ross said, in a serious tone. "Then what, dear Doctor Ross, do you intend to do about it?"

As the first shafts of early morning sunshine forced their way through the tiny crack in the bedroom curtains, Maria rolled onto her back, and pulled her husband on top of her as she opened herself to him.

"How's this for starters?" she said in a husky, very sexy voice.

"Who am I to argue with the doctor?" Ross laughed as they made love once again before rising earlier than usual, as dawn broke over the city and all thoughts of tiredness were temporarily banished from his mind. An early breakfast was followed by Ross taking his time to pack a suitcase for his trip to Cornwall, helped by Maria who made sure he had enough pairs of matching socks, to last at least three days, plus one extra pair, just in case, as she put it.

"You always forget to pack enough socks, even when we go on holiday," she chastised him. "And what about underwear?"

"I've packed four pairs, *Mummy*," he playfully goaded her.

Maria laughed and equally playfully slapped her husband's bottom and he feigned pain and put his hands over his eyes, pretending to cry.

"You cruel, husband-beating woman," he pretended to sob.

"So, go call a policeman and have me arrested."

"Help, police," Ross shouted as Maria took him in her arms, held him close and kissed him into silence. Five minutes later he was in his car, Maria waving to him from the front door-step as he headed into town to headquarters. He'd a telephone conference arranged with a specialist at the Admiralty in order to pick the man's brains on potential ships that fit the description of the assumed corvette on the sea bed of the Channel. If he could identify the wreck, and get an idea where it went down, he might just know where the search for the dead frogman should be directed. He was as yet unaware of the information McLennan and Gable had discovered the previous day, the pair having arrived back in Liverpool after Ross had left for home.

With luck he and Izzie Drake would be able to set off on their journey south by lunchtime. D.C.I. Trevelyan would be calling him as well with details of the accommodation arranged for them in Falmouth. Bearing in mind the length of the journey, some three hundred and fifty miles, Ross thought it best if he and Drake settled in to their hotel on their arrival in Falmouth and began their investigation first thing the next morning.

CHAPTER 19

THE ENGLISH CHANNEL, 1945, AND THE MARY DEAL

"Everything alright, Number One?" Lieutenant Commander Giles Clarkson asked his first officer, Peter Hicks, as he stepped over the coaming on the bridge of *H.M.S. Norwich*. Clarkson had managed a couple of hours sleep as the *Norwich* completed her latest sweep around the Eastern approaches to the Channel with Hicks in charge on the bridge as officer of the watch.

"All quiet, sir," Hicks confirmed. "Radar reports no contacts and we've maintained constant Asdic scans as ordered. Not that I can envisage any U-Boats trying to make it through the Channel when they can take the easy route around Scotland and into the Atlantic that way. Lieutenant Bailey has plotted the course for a zig-zag run from east to west as ordered as soon as you give the order."

"Hello Bailey," said Clarkson as he looked across the bridge to the young navigator. Bailey was a member of the Royal Naval Volunteer Reserve, the so-called 'Wavy Navy' christened as such owing to the wave shaped stripes worn on the officer's sleeves. Before the war, Bailey had been training as a doctor and it was a continuing mystery to Clarkson how the young man had forsaken his medical career to join the war as a volunteer naval officer. Bailey had told no-one aboard *Norwich*, his first ship, of the early dawn when he'd left the training hospital after a long night on the wards only to find his home had been completely obliterated when an unexploded bomb, buried underground and left over from the days of the Blitz, had exploded almost immediately outside the front door, not only destroying the house, but taking the lives of his mother, father and two sisters. With nothing left to live for, so he felt, Bailey lost no time in giving up his medical studies and arranging to join the RNVR.

"Hello sir," Bailey replied to his captain, his face as always serious-looking and totally focused on the job in hand.

"You've settled in well, Bailey," Clarkson said, encouragingly. "You'll be a fine officer if you keep up your current performance."

"Thank you, sir," Bailey replied, but still no hint of a smile crossed the young officer's face.

Clarkson turned to his first officer once more.

"What's the latest weather report Number One?"

"We have a report of fog rolling in from the west, sir. We'll probably hit it somewhere in the region of Exeter or Plymouth if we maintain our current course and speed."

"Okay. Well, at least the fog should hamper the Jerries as much as it does us. Maintain course and speed and continue the zig-zag manoeuvre. If there are any E-Boats out here, we don't want to present ourselves as a sitting duck for them."

"Aye aye, sir," said Hicks, acknowledging Clarkson's orders.

"And Number one?"

"Sir?"

"Keep me posted on those weather reports. If that fog starts to roll in faster, I want to know about it."

"Of course sir."

"How many of our own ships do we have on the plot at present?"

Hicks drew Clarkson to one side, where he pointed to the chart table positioned under cover at the rear of the bridge. He quickly pointed to half a dozen red pins in various locations of the map.

"These three are trawlers, heading for home and already relatively safe. This one is our friend, the *Ripon*, giving close escort to a small tanker which was damaged in an attack on the convoy she was in, originally headed for Liverpool. She was ordered to break off and head for the safety of Port-land. One of the convoy escorts shadowed her as far as the Scilly Isles and *Ripon* took over from there."

"And the other two?" Clarkson asked, indicating the remaining pins on the chart.

"This one is one of our submarines, the *Altair*, sir," Hicks pointed to the closest pin. "She's running on the surface, making for Portland too. She was damaged in a surprise attack by a *Condor* long-range patrol aircraft. Her ballast tanks are damaged and she can't submerge, apparently. The last pin is the *Paragon*. We were warned we might encounter her before we left port, sir."

"Yes, of course. The cruiser heading to reinforce the Mediterranean fleet. She's fast, Number One. I should think she'll disappear off our plot by morning."

"I agree sir. So, nothing untowards as far as we can make out. Lookouts are posted as well though and we'll remain at action stations as per your order"

"Good, I'm going below then. I'll relieve you in two hours."

"Thank you sir," Hicks replied as Leading Seaman Charlie Knox appeared, smiling and handing Hicks and Bailey two steaming hot mugs of extra-thick cocoa in tin mugs, both precariously carried in one hand as he used his other hand to balance himself against the rolling motion of the ship in the undulating waves.

"Oh, sorry sir," he said to Clarkson. "I didn't know as you was up here."

"That's okay, Knox," Clarkson replied, smiling whilst inwardly groaning at Knox's awful grammar. "I shouldn't be here. Just popped up to see the first officer."

"Oh, right, sir. You'll not be wantin' a cup then?"

"No thank you, Knox. I'm going below now."

"I can bring you one to your cabin if you like, sir," the smiling young rating offered. Charlie Knox, twenty three, from the Spitalfields area of London's East End, was a perpetual optimist and his smiling face never failed to make others feel a little better when he was around. Clarkson was grateful to have the hard-working, cheerful young rating aboard his ship.

"Alright, that would be very nice, thank you, Knox."

If anything, Knox's smile grew even broader at the captain's reply.

"Right you are sir. Give me ten minutes to get back to the galley and mix you a brew."

"No hurry Knox, and, thank you."

"It's my pleasure, sir, honest it is," said Bailey, and Clarkson knew the young man actually meant it. As he sat on his bunk awaiting the arrival of Charlie Knox and his mug of almost sludge-like cocoa, Clarkson contemplated his command. The *Norwich*, though small, had proved to be an efficient ship, with its crew a mixture of disparate individuals from varying parts of Britain, and from equally varied social backgrounds, from elite public schools to middle-class grammars and back street secondary-moderns all working together in harmony to produce a vessel Clarkson was rightly proud of. Knox soon arrived with the cocoa that Clarkson had accepted more from politeness and not wishing to hurt the man's feelings than from want, but he accepted it gratefully. Before Knox departed for the galley once more, Clarkson said,

"Can I ask you a question, Knox?"

Knox stopped in his tracks, had he done something wrong?

"Of course, sir," he replied.

"Why the hell are you always so damned cheerful? We're in the middle of this bloody god-awful war, people are being killed around us, and at home, and here on the ship we're mostly cold, wet and miserable twenty four hours a day and yet you always have a smile on your face, and a good word for everyone."

"Well, sir, that's thanks to me dear old Mum, that is. When I were a nipper, there were six of us kids at home, me, three bruvvers and two sisters. Dad were a bus driver, and we was never well off but we always 'ad food to eat and shoes on our feet. Mum always said as there was always folks in this world far worse of then us an' we should always be 'appy that we 'ad our 'ealth and strength and was loved and cared for at 'ome. I never forgot that, sir, even when me two eldest bruvvers was killed, one at Dunkirk, and the other on the old *H.M.S Hood*. Our 'ouse was bombed in the blitz, but no one got 'urt, so we 'ave a lot to be thankful for. I've made some great mates on this ship too. She ain't no battleship, that's a fact, sir, but, well, she's a good ship, and she's my 'ome until either the war's over or the Admirals send me on to another ship."

Knox fell silent, his story over. Clarkson felt quite humbled by this young man from one of the poorest areas of London, who'd lost two brothers, seen his home all but destroyed and yet maintained the most positive outlook he'd ever encountered.

"Thanks for telling me, Knox. You're a credit to the ship, just thought you should know that."

Knox's face lit up again, his smile so infectious that Clarkson beamed back at him.

"Thank you, sir," Charlie Knox said, pulling himself up to his full height and saluting his captain, ignoring the fact he wasn't wearing his headgear. "And I'm proud to serve under you, too sir. I shan't ever let you down."

Clarkson returned the salute and then Knox was gone, and he was alone again, with the sounds of the ship at night his sole companions as he sipped at the turgid brew, then put it down on his small bedside cabinet and, keeping his sea boots on in case of emergencies, Clarkson stretched out on his bunk, closing his eyes, but not for one minute did he fall asleep. The *Norwich* sailed on; the rhythmic sound of her engines the captain's constant companion in his small and at times very lonely cabin.

* * *

U966 continued her clandestine crawl through the English Channel, her sleek black shape hidden well below the surface, though her crew were no less anxious for that fact after Ritter told them where they were. He'd successfully brought his boat through the Straits of Dover, the shallowest part of the Channel at just under 150 feet, and past the channel ports and major cities of Dover, Portsmouth, Southampton and Weymouth, with the nearby Portland Naval Base and their attendant defensive minefields, laid to take care of just such incursions as Ritter was doing his best to avoid.

His was a passive passage through the Channel, though the British wouldn't see it that way of course.

Ritter could feel the tension emanating from his crew, an almost palpable sensation. He still wondered privately why he'd been instructed to adopt this course, though he felt it was probably an attempt to take a day or two off the total journey time of his voyage.

Heini Engel stood quietly watching his captain as he quietly passed on his orders to the members of the control room crew with calm self-assurance. Engel admired Ritter more than he cared to admit. If ever there was a U-Boat captain he wished he could emulate it was the man who now gave the order to bring the *U966* up to periscope depth. Apart from his skills as a commander, Ritter possessed one vital quality missing from many officers in Hitler's much vaunted Third Reich, that of a sense of humanity. Not only did he care for those who served under him, but Ritter took no great delight in the deaths of those who died as a result of the actions of his boat. He had a job to do, a dirty job as a rule, that involved the sinking of enemy ships, both merchantmen and warships, and he carried out his task with a grim professionalism, but Engel knew, from his many conversations he'd had with his captain, that Ritter always felt a private sense of grief for those who died as a result of his successes. To Ritter they were sailors, as he was, and no matter their nationality, all sailors shared a bond that those who lived and worked on the land could never truly understand.

Heini knew this was a potentially dangerous moment, but equally, he understood Ritter's decision. They had almost successfully negotiated the dangerous passage through the narrow body of water separating England and France and would soon be passing the Scilly Isles and heading out in to the Atlantic, where they would need to remain submerged for the majority of their crossing. Engel knew what was in his captain's mind. If it was safe to do so, Ritter would surface and recharge the submarine's batteries, allowing him to stay below the Atlantic waves away from the prying radars and echo location devices employed by the British and American convoy escorts and patrolling warships they might encounter as they made their run towards their eventual destination.

The scope raised, Ritter swivelled his cap round, placing the peak to the rear of his head as he lowered the twin handles used to rotate the periscope, leaning both forearms laconically over the shining steel handles and peering into the scope's viewer.

"Fog," Ritter exclaimed almost immediately. "Thick fog, Heini. What the British call a 'pea souper' I think. I can't see a bloody thing up there, and you know what that means, my friends?" He spoke as though addressing the entire control room crew.

"What, sir?" Engel asked, feeling that Ritter's comment called for a reply from someone.

"It means the gods are smiling upon us, Heini," Ritter smiled. "If we can't see anything, then neither can the British. If we silence the boat, we can surface and recharge the batteries and be submerged again before anyone knows we were here."

"But the British will have their direction finding equipment, that damned Asdic working for them. We know they can locate us even in fog."

"Maybe so, Heini, but Asdic only works when we're submerged and in this fog, they'll find it difficult to pinpoint our exact position if they do detect us with their *verdammt* radar and we should have plenty of time to dive and be out of their range before they know what's happening. Plus, they won't expect us to be in this area and with luck may mistake us for one of their own submarines just long enough to breed a little confusion in any warship's captain, again giving us time to slip away safely."

"You may be right, Herr Kapitän," Engel replied, hoping his captain was right in his estimation of the British ability to locate and track them if they did identify them as a hostile craft. German technology lagged somewhat behind the British in its echo-location devices. The U-Boats depended on a less than totally convincing passive sonar system that required the boat to turn through a full one hundred and eighty degrees in order to scan the entire horizon, not perfect in a precarious and potentially deadly situation. Ritter ordered his hydrophone operators to be on full alert as he ordered *U966* to the surface.

Throughout the sub, despite any lurking danger above the waves, Ritter's crew looked forward to the chance to breathe some fresh air, certain that Ritter would go 'up top' to the conning tower once the sub surfaced. If all was well, they hoped to have a few minutes at least to open the hatches and let the interior of *U966* 'breathe' as well, a natural fumigation that would clear the submarine of some, if not all of the smell of unwashed bodies and poor sanitation.

The sea was as calm as the proverbial millpond as *U966* broke through the gently rolling waves nose first, with Ritter being the first to the top of the ladder leading to the conning tower hatch. As the submarine settled itself in the all-enveloping fog, he was followed by Engel and the two men gratefully breathed in the cool night air. Two lookouts joined them, armed with powerful binoculars, rendered useless by the enveloping fog.

The smell of the ocean acted as a panacea to both men, and Ritter quietly called down through the hatch for the forward deck hatch to be opened and the men allowed up top in small groups to take their first breaths of fresh air since leaving Kiel. Meanwhile, the U-Boat's chief engineer, Heinz Muller began the process of recharging the batteries that would need to be operating at their best if *U966* was to successfully complete her Atlantic crossing.

Meanwhile, out of earshot of Muller, Joseph Ziegler moaned about having to wait his turn to go up top and young Karl Meister worked beside him, as always hanging on the every word of the older and he thought, wiser man.

* * *

Five hours earlier, approximately two miles west of *U966's* current position, the trawler *Mary Deal* had run into a spot of bother on her return voyage to her home port of Mevagissey, a small fishing village some five miles south of St. Austell. Her skipper, Andrew Douglas, fifty five, had fished these waters all his life and had decided to try one last trawl while daylight allowed. Unfortunately for Douglas, the *Mary Deal's* radio had begun playing up on the outward leg of their current trip, and failed to hear the fog warning that had been broadcast to all shipping in the area. Consequently, the incoming bank of thick, grey fog appeared ghost-like from astern of the trawler, seemingly hell-bent on catching up with the small vessel and wrapping her in its impenetrable cocoon.

"Fog coming in fast, skipper," came a shout from Johnny Baldwin, the skipper's nephew and senior crewman, having sailed with his uncle for nearly ten years.

"Damn, where the hell did that come from?" Douglas neither expected nor received a reply to his rhetorical question.

"What do you want to do?" Johnny asked his uncle.

"We'd better haul the nets in and make a run for home," Douglas replied. As an experienced seaman, the skipper had no intention of being caught at sea in thick fog.

Together with sixteen year old Peter Evans and Davy Billings, Johnny Baldwin began the task of hauling in the *Mary Deal's* nets. Andrew Douglas cursed silently. An extra haul would have gone some way towards making this trip worthwhile. Recent catches had been poor, and earnings reduced as a result. Still, no need to take unnecessary risks, he knew. There was always tomorrow.

Suddenly a shout from Johnny brought the whole job to a halt.

"Bloody hell, skipper, there's a mine in the net."

"What?"

"A bloody great mine, Uncle Andrew," Johnny repeated with fear in his voice.

"Ain't no minefields in these parts, though," Douglas replied, keeping as calm as he possibly could. No sense in making the lads panic, which would only increase the chances of disaster.

"What should we do?" asked a terrified Peter Evans.

Douglas thought for less than two seconds before making the only decision he could.

"We'll have to cut the nets loose. The damn thing must have come adrift from its mooring in one of our own bloody minefields. Damn the

Royal bloody Navy. Can't even set a bloody minefield properly without endangering their own bloody fishermen."

"That's hardly fair, Uncle," said Johnny.

"Maybe not, but it's going to cost us dear, lad, having to cast adrift the net and whatever it holds. Now, set to it lads. Get that damned thing cut free and we'll have to report it when we get back home. Damn that bloody radio."

It was an unfortunate fact that occasionally, a mine would indeed break free from its moorings and float to the surface, presenting a dangerous hazard to shipping both friendly and enemy. Usually, a call to the appropriate authorities would result in the Royal Navy despatching a mine sweeper to the area to clear the offending floating ordnance and ensure the safety of our own vessels. Without his radio it would be at least a couple of hours before the *Mary Deal* could make port and allow Douglas to make a report on the floating mine.

"God knows how long it'll take the Navy to get a mine sweeper out here," he grumbled. "We'd best find new grounds to fish tomorrow."

"Let's hope nobody else runs into that bloody thing before the Navy can get a mine sweeper to clear it," said Johnny Baldwin as the *Mary Deal's* net together with its precious catch finally floated away from the trawler, the mine firmly enmeshed in it. The crew of the trawler breathed a collective sigh of relief as the mine disappeared from their view, where it was soon enveloped in the almost impenetrable shroud of fog that rolled inexorably into the English Chanel from the Atlantic.

Unknown to Johnny Baldwin, the young trawlerman's sadly prophetic words would soon herald a series of tragic and unforeseen events.

CHAPTER 20

THE HOPE AND ANCHOR

Ross intended to keep the morning briefing as short as possible. In under an hour he expected the scheduled call from a Captain Anthony Prendergast, whom the Royal Navy had informed Agostini was the man in the know as far as the history of the war in the English Channel was concerned. Agostini had made sure the Navy had all the details, including a copy of the photo that showed the dead frogman, in order to ensure their fullest co-operation. It had worked. The Naval historical branch at the Ministry of Defence had pledged their help in any way they could, not only to identify a possible 'lost' shipwreck, but to help the police in their search for a murderer.

"Okay everyone," Ross began as the room fell silent. "You all know Sergeant Drake and I will be gone for a couple of days, but I need you all to keep searching for clues at this end. Ferris, keep digging into Aegis and their various offshoots. I want you to speak with Jerome Decker. See if you can get him to use his C.I.A. position to do some further probing into their affairs. If he hesitates, remind him it's his son's murder we're investigating."

"Got that, sir, no problem," Paul Ferris replied.

"Next, on the basis that they're our only two viable suspects in terms of having the opportunity to commit the murder, I want both the housemates looked into closely, and when I say closely I mean *very* closely."

"Tony, I want you to take Tim Knight, and Derek, take Martin Lewis. Find out everything there is to know about these men, and I mean *everything*. Could one or both of them have been coerced or blackmailed into participating in the killing? Find out. If either or both of them had any reason, no matter how small, to have a grudge against young Aaron Decker, find it. Leave no stone unturned. I don't care if you have to tread on a few toes along the way. If there's anything in either man's past that gives you cause for concern, I want to know about it. Got it?"

Curtis and McLennan both nodded their understanding as Ross turned finally to Nick Dodds and Sam Gable.

"Nick, Sam, go and see Haller. Try to get him to open up about the historical side of things. Let's remember there was a submarine involved in this affair according to that photograph. I strongly suspect it may have been a German U-Boat. Take a blow up of the photograph. If we can find out what kind of sub it was we might be able to come up with a possible date for when this all took place. That's a long shot I know, but if he can say with any degree of certainty it's a model that entered the war after, say 1944, we can knock out the first four years of the war for starters."

"There's not a lot of the submarine showing sir. There might not be enough for him to identify it with any certainty. Maybe your Royal Navy chap will know when he sees it."

"And maybe he won't, Nick. We're getting nowhere fast at present so let's use every asset we can until we've exhausted all possibilities, Okay?"

"Okay sir, whatever you say."

"Good, and all of you, remember to keep Paul updated with whatever you discover. He's still our collator so Paul, if you log anything onto the board that you think I should know, you call me right away on my mobile, and if you can't get me, try Sergeant Drake."

"Will do, sir."

"Right everyone, off you go. I'll be checking in regularly with D.C Ferris and calling daily updates in to D.C.I. Agostini while we're away, so let's try and make some progress. If you need anything, go and talk to the D.C.I. He won't bite and he's promised to be available for any help or advice you need in my absence."

With that, Ross brought the briefing to a close and while Drake went to get them fresh coffee and waited in his office, he paid Oscar Agostini a very quick visit, brought him up to date on who was doing what while he was away, and then returned to join Izzie, and the pair could only wait for the call for the man from the Royal Navy. The Navy, being very security conscious had insisted on their man calling Ross, rather than the other way round. That way, they were certain they'd be going through the police switchboard and talking to a bona fide police officer.

Ross was pleased when Captain Prendergast phoned him two minutes ahead of the scheduled time. At least the man was prompt. Ross soon came to like the man he was speaking with on the telephone, and quickly lost his preconceptions of a stiff upper-lipped, stuffed shirt type of naval officer. Prendergast was affable, easy to talk to and sounded keen to help

Ross however he could. After listening to everything Ross had to say the line was silent for no more than five seconds.

"Well, I have to say, Inspector Ross, you and your people have done pretty well so far. I've taken a long hard look at the photo you sent us, and I've had our own people blow it up even larger. You were quite right in your assumption that the ship you saw is a corvette, though at present I can't give you a positive identification. You have to understand that during the war we used various types of corvettes, some purpose built, some bought or leased from the U.S.A. and a few were even converted merchant ships, though the one in the photograph does look like a true warship, I have to admit, possibly built later in the war. The raked bow tends to give it away."

"So do you think you will be able to identify her for us?" Ross asked, hoping for a positive reply.

"We stand a good chance, Inspector. It may be necessary to send divers down, but that shouldn't be a problem. Your Mr. Haller seems to have given you an accurate position for the wreck, and if it is a Royal Naval vessel previously uncharted, it is highly likely to be a war grave situation so we would want to check it out and clarify it."

"Captain Prendergast, you've just made my day. Thank you, sir," Ross said, feeling like punching the air with delight. If the Royal Navy became involved there was no way Aegis or anyone else could prevent them diving on the wreck and they just might have a chance of identifying the poor devil whose body was floating down there, somehow caught up in the wreckage.

"I really hope we can help you, Inspector Ross, and please call me Anthony, no need to be too formal, don't you agree?"

"Of course, thanks, Anthony, and do please call me Andy."

"Excellent," said Prendergast. "I understand you're heading down to Falmouth today, so how about I meet you there tomorrow at your hotel?"

"You're coming down yourself?" Ross sounded surprised, and Prendergast registered that surprise.

"But of course, Andy. I love to have an opportunity to get out of the office and I'd like to take a personal interest in this one. The chances of finding an unknown World War Two wreck after all these years are few and far between. I think it calls for a personal involvement."

"I must say I'm delighted to have your help, Anthony."

"Don't mention it. You might be interested to know the local Coast Guard commander down there is ex-R.N. too. He served with me in fact on the old *H.M.S. Lupus* back in the early eighties. We were much younger back then of course, but we've kept in touch over the years."

"You're kidding me?"

"Not at all, Andy. His name's George Baldacre, and I promise you he'll be all for diving in himself to help you out. Actually he was the diving officer on the old *Lupus*."

"Oh, so the *Lupus* was…"

"A submarine, Andy, quite right. She was a deep diving attack boat, but she was decommissioned soon after I left sea duty. I was the weapons officer at that time, otherwise known to all and sundry as "Weps.""

"Well, I'll be glad to have you both along," said Ross, impressed even more by Prendergast who he'd thought at first was probably a career desk officer rather then a former warship officer, much less one who'd served on a nuclear submarine, and now it appeared they were getting two for the price of one, so to speak. For the first time in this God-awful case, Andy Ross began to feel a hint of confidence creeping into his investigation. In fact, as he and Izzie were motoring along the M5 four hours later, having left the M6 behind where it linked up with the M5 near West Bromwich, another thought came to Ross as Izzie drove, the car eating up the miles as they headed towards the south coast.

"I've had an idea, Izzie," he suddenly said, as a light bulb seemed to illuminate in his brain.

"I thought I could hear the old brain cogs grinding in there," Izzie joked. "Come on, sir. What have you come up with?"

"Marriage hasn't done anything for your sense of humour, Sergeant," Ross quipped.

"Did you expect it to?" Drake giggled.

"Of course not."

"Well that's alright then," Drake grinned. "Now, what's this new idea of yours, boss?"

"Well, I'm glad you've remembered who's in charge. But seriously, Izzie, if Ferris comes up with anything that casts any doubt on Aegis and their activities over here, we might be able to make use of Miss Sally Metcalfe to draw them out."

"That's different," said Drake. "In what way, sir?"

"I'm pretty sure she's in the clear, so it's safe to assume she'll want to help us find Aaron's killer. So, we know she already has a job offer from Aegis after she finishes at the university, so what do you think might happen if she suddenly decides she wants to turn their offer down?"

"I think someone at Aegis might be a little pissed at her if she did that after they've invested in her already with the sponsorship."

"More than a little pissed, Izzie, if you ask me. So what might they do, do you think?"

"If it was me, I'd want to talk to her, try to get her to change her mind, sir."

"Right, my thoughts exactly. I'm hoping the head man at the Falmouth base will be ordered to invite her down there to talk things through, and if he does, we can prime Miss Metcalfe with a few prime questions and also get her to keep her eyes and ears open for anything in their set up that doesn't sit right with her. She's a marine biologist after all. She should know if something is out of place. I know it's along shot, but…"

"But it might bring dividends, I agree, sir. But won't we be putting her at risk?"

"Not if she is properly prepared with a few genuine concerns and I'm sure she can think of a few things that would qualify in that respect." "But what if she doesn't want to help, sir?"

"We'll cross that bridge when we come to it. For now, I could use a coffee. There's a Service Area in a mile. Let's pull over, have a drink and a rest and I'll take over the driving for a while when we get back on the road."

* * *

The strangely named Hope and Anchor Hotel stood in its own grounds, set back from the road, about five miles outside Falmouth. With Ross now taking a turn at the wheel, Izzie Drake had displayed her map reading skills in directing them to their destination without a single wrong turn along the way, a feat Ross wasn't sure he'd have accomplished. Map reading had never been his speciality, something to do with trying to translate the tiny squiggles and signs on a map into the real world, so he thought.

The receptionist had them booked in within a couple of minutes of their arrival, and before they were shown to their rooms, a large, rather corpulent and extremely jolly looking man with swept back grey hair came bustling into the reception area from what was clearly an office to the rear of the reception desk.

"Hello, hello," the man spoke as though welcoming two old friends. "You must be Detective Inspector Ross and Detective Sergeant Drake, am I right?"

"Yes, we are, and you are?" Ross replied.

"Thomas Severn, owner of the Hope and Anchor, at your service."

Severn held out his hand and Ross reflexively shook hands with the newcomer, who proceeded to follow the same routine with Izzie Drake.

"I wanted to be here to meet you, Inspector," Severn went on. "We tend to be used for visitors or guests of the local constabulary so wanted to be sure you were comfortable with your rooms."

"That's very welcoming of you, I'm sure," said Ross, feeling a little overwhelmed by the man's effusive nature. Not so, Izzie Drake, who immediately asked the proprietor of the hotel the question she knew Ross would also like the answer to.

"It's a rather unusual name, the Hope and Anchor, Mr. Severn. How did that come about?"

"Oh, no secret there, Sergeant," Severn replied. "This used to be an old coaching inn, and until I purchased it, it went by the name of The Coach and Four. It was looking a bit tired when I took over so we gave the place a makeover, and added the new wing out back. A new name seemed appropriate. Hope is my wife's first name and I added the anchor part as I used to be in the Navy, until I was invalided out." He tapped his right leg, which made a hollow sound as his hand connected with it. "Lost the leg in a shipboard accident. No way I could carry on in the Navy after that. I got a massive pay-off from the M.O.D. though, enough to secure the down-payment on this place. It's virtually doubled in value in the ten years I've owned it so it seems I made a bloody wise investment."

Severn gave no further explanation and Drake didn't press the point. She didn't feel it right to question their host on something so personal. For Ross, it perhaps explained why the local police were happy to book their visitors and guests into the Hope and Anchor. Severn seemed a totally reliable and friendly sort of character with what appeared to be an impeccable background.

Severn called for one of his staff, a young man called Lewis, who helped load their cases onto a small trolley and the owner led the way to their rooms, which were on the ground floor to the rear of the hotel, away from any road noise, and, as Severn put it, "Sound proofed from any noise from the lounge bar and dining room, so you won't be disturbed."

He left them to unpack and get settled with instructions to call upon him or his staff if they needed anything at all. Ross informed him they'd be having visitors the following morning and asked if Severn could make a room available to them for the purposes of a small meeting. Severn assured them there was no problem and he'd have a room ready for them when ever they needed it. He was impressed when Ross told him the visitors would be a Royal Naval Captain and the local Coast Guard commander. He apparently knew George Baldacre well and spoke highly of the Coast Guard man, telling Ross he knew the local waters better then anyone he knew.

Time was passing quickly, so Ross and Drake both took the opportunity to shower and change and then met in the lounge bar for a drink before dinner. Their rooms were at the rear of the hotel in the newer part of the building, and were decorated in a modern style, both had en-suite facilities and tea and coffee making facilities and were clean and warm, so passed muster with both detectives. Ross was pleased to find that the dining room was situated in the original coaching inn part of the establishment and was possessed of great charm and olde-worlde character. Pictures of sailing ships adorned the walls, and the tables were a dark oak in colour, to match the window frames and doors. Word of who the pair were must have got around, he thought, as none of the waiting staff took them for a courting couple and none of the other guests gave them disapproving stares, thinking of him as an older man carrying on an affair with a good looking younger woman.

"I don't know whether to be disappointed or not," he said to Izzie after making the point about the other guests especially.

"Well, what's to stop you corrupting a junior officer?" she joked. "We could always act a bit flirtatious, give 'em something to talk about, sir."

"Are you kidding?" he looked aghast. "The old biddy with the blue rinse over in the far corner would probably get up and come across and stab me with a knitting needle if I so much as wink at you. Have you seen the looks she's been giving me? If those aren't daggers in her eyes, I don't deserve to be a D.I."

"Oh, well, what do we do now?" Izzie asked, at the same time dropping her voice, smiling coquettishly and leaning forward across the table conspiratorially. To the elderly lady in the far corner of the room, seated with her ageing and decrepit looking husband, it would appear as if Drake was whispering to Ross, perhaps inviting him to enjoy a spot of after dinner enjoyment in her room. Andy Ross knew exactly what she was doing.

"Are you trying to incite that little old lady to commit grievous bodily harm against a police officer, Sergeant Drake? Because, if you are, be aware that the old biddy over there is now on the verge of throwing those aforementioned daggers at me. I warn you, if she comes and throws a bowl of soup over me, you can be the one to make the arrest. Should make for an interesting arrest report, for sure."

Drake grinned at him, the inviting smile was back again as she spoke in hushed tones. "Well, sir, I'm only asking you what we do next, after all. It's not as if I'm publicly inviting you to some illicit tryst, or shouting at you to rip my knickers off in front of the locals is it?"

"Izzie Drake, if you don't put a sock in it, I swear I'll have you demoted as soon as we return to Liverpool."

Izzie couldn't help herself. Her voice rose to its normal volume.

"Oh no, please, don't. I'll do what you say, sir. Please don't do that. What would my poor old Mum say? She'd think it was my fault."

Ross groaned in anguish. Izzie's twisted sense of humour had got the old lady in the corner well and truly fired up but instead of coming across the room to physically or verbally berate him, he heard her say loudly to her poor, and obviously long-suffering husband, "Walter, come along. We're finished here. We're going back to our room."

"But, my coffee…"

"Forget the coffee, Walter. We're leaving."

The poor man forced himself to rise and follow his overbearing wife as she stomped from the room, casting a disapproving glance in Ross's direction as she flounced out of the dining room doors, Walter trailing obediently at least five paces behind her.

As the two detectives collapsed in a fit of stupid giggles and laughter, a grinning Thomas Severn stepped towards them from behind one of the columns that rose from floor to ceiling of the dining room, clapping slowly but happily.

"Oh, I say, that's the most fun I've had in ages, priceless. A superb performance, Sergeant. You had old Mrs. Twining almost wetting herself, poor dear. I think she had you squirming a little too, Inspector Ross," Severn laughed.

"My sergeant has, shall we say, a certain sense of humour, Mr. Severn?" said Ross, grinning.

"I can see that, much like many of the lads from Liverpool I met during my time in the Navy."

"I presume at some point you'll tell the old lady we were only kidding?" Drake asked.

"Oh no," Severn exclaimed. "You'll be the highlight of her week, and the talk of Cheltenham when she returns home. I can see her telling her friends at the W.I. or whatever she belongs to about the brazen hussy and the exploitative policeman she met on her holiday. She'll probably embellish the whole thing until she virtually has the pair of you making love across the dining table in full view of the guests."

Now Ross was laughing, and Izzie joined in too.

"Now, what would you like to eat?" Severn asked.

Ross selected a simple Sirloin steak with chips and peas, while Izzie went for the grilled Sea Bass with new potatoes and seasonal vegetables. Both agreed the food was superb and Ross asked Thomas Severn to give their compliments to the chef.

"My wife will be delighted, thank you," Severn replied.

"Your wife's the chef?"

"She certainly is," Severn grinned. "Hope was trained as a chef in the Navy. We served together, you see, Inspector."

"Well, you certainly have a real diamond there, Mr. Severn. The food really was excellent."

After dinner, Ross and Drake retired to their rooms, where each phoned home to their respective partners. Ross related the story of the old lady at dinner to Maria, who, knowing Izzie only too well, found it highly amusing. Later, they met once more in the lounge bar where they enjoyed a nightcap before turning in for the night. Ross hoped for great things from tomorrow's meeting. Surely, the combined efforts of the Merseyside Police, the Royal Navy and the Coast Guard would help to move this case towards a conclusion. He slept surprisingly well, another compliment for the hotel he thought. On the rare occasions he'd stayed away from home in the past, sleep had proved elusive, usually because of uncomfortable hotel beds, but not so at the Hope and Anchor. The mattress simply moulded to his body and he slept like a baby, waking at six a.m. as usual. After showering and dressing, he made his way to the dining room where Izzie Drake was already seated, sipping coffee.

Knowing they had a potentially long and demanding day ahead of them, both availed themselves of the Hope and Anchor's full English breakfast, Bacon, eggs, sausage, mushrooms and beans, with fried bread. Again, the food was excellent, and this time, they were able to meet Hope Severn and compliment her in person.

"Thank you," she said when Ross told her how much he and Drake had enjoyed her cooking. "My husband told me something of why you're here. I was sad to hear of that poor young boy's murder."

"You knew him?" Ross sounded surprised.

"Oh no, not the young man, but I did meet the man who was helping him."

"You mean Herr Haller, the German historian?"

"No, no, the other man."

Ross was suddenly on full alert.

"What other man, Mrs. Severn? We weren't aware of anyone else working with Aaron Decker down here."

"Oh, I see. He was a youngish man, about twenty four to thirty, I'd say. He came here looking for the young man. I said we'd never heard of him, which was true, and the man said he knew his friend was staying in a hotel somewhere in Falmouth, but he didn't know which one."

"Can you describe him for us, Mrs. Severn? Apart from his age of course." said Drake.

"Brown hair, cut in an old fashioned short back and sides, a fisherman's sweater, blue with a red design of some sort I think, and jeans, and oh, yes, he had a local accent . It was over a year ago, Inspector, Sergeant. That's the best I can do."

"You've been a great help," Ross replied. "Do you know where he went after leaving here?"

"Sorry, no idea," said Hope.

Ross thanked her for her time and her information and as he and Drake finished their third cup of coffee, he looked into his sergeant's eyes, and voiced the thoughts he felt they both shared.

"If I'm not much mistaken, Izzie, we have a possible third diver here. If that man wasn't Haller, of course, and I'm sure Mrs. Severn knows the difference between a middle aged German, a local man and a twenty-something American. Do you know what I'm thinking?"

"That the man who came here looking for Aaron was working with him in his research into what ever Aegis was up to, and if I'm not mistaken, you also think that man is in all probability the poor sod in a wet-suit who's floating around at the bottom of the English Channel."

"Bingo," said Ross. "You've got it in one, Sergeant Drake."

CHAPTER 21

A MEETING OF MINDS

Captain Anthony Prendergast, R.N. (Retired) arrived a good ten minutes before their pre-arranged meeting time. Ross was luckily positioned in the reception area anyway so couldn't fail to witness his arrival, though Ross mentally kicked himself for expecting the man to be dressed in uniform, only realising as Prendergast walked through the doors of the Hope and anchor that as a retired officer, he'd be dressed in civvies. Prendergast still managed to stand out however, dressed in his black blazer with the submariner's blazer badge and shining brass buttons, crisp white shirt and tie that also bore the logo of the submarine service, and sharply pressed grey flannel trousers. His black shoes were polished to a resplendent finish, every inch an ex-military man.

He equally had no difficulty in recognising Ross and walked straight across the floor of the hotel lobby and greeted the detective, who shook hands and quickly led the captain along the corridor to the room Hope Severn had prepared for their use, where he was introduced to Izzie Drake.

"Very pleased indeed to meet you, Sergeant Drake."

"Pleased to meet you too, Captain Prendergast," she replied, and Ross could have sworn he detected a slight blush crept up Izzie's cheeks as Prendergast held gently on to her hand a second or two longer than necessary,

"Please call me Anthony," he said in a soft, yet gravelly voice that had probably charmed more then a few young ladies into his bed during his younger years. It amused Ross to think the old seadog appeared to have retained every ounce of his charm.

A knock on the door was followed by the smiling face of Hope Severn who announced that the final member of their quartet, the Coast Guard officer, George Baldacre, had arrived. Ross immediately left the room, returning barely a minute later with the latest arrival.

Baldacre was somewhat younger than Prendergast, Ross correctly recalling that Prendergast had told him they'd served together. Obviously, Ross realised, Baldacre had entered the service some years after the older man. As head of the local Coast Guard unit, Baldacre obviously was still fit enough for sea duty and indeed, he was often to be found at sea on any of the local Coast Guard vessels, usually observing the crews at work. Ross had found out that the Coast Guard unit covered a large section of coastline along the Cornish coast, and was not simply restricted to Falmouth. That made sense as anything else would have meant the UK Coast Guard Service would have needed a navy of its own.

Prendergast greeted the former diving control officer of *H.M.S Lupus* with enthusiasm, the two men engaging in a bear hug of mammoth proportions. Baldacre was easily six foot tall, and built like the proverbial battleship. He was dressed in the uniform of H.M. Coast Guard Service. His hair was all but gone; just a few wisps of grey seemed to be fighting a losing battle to remain in place across the top of his balding pate when he removed his peaked cap.

"George, you old renegade," said Prendergast as he pumped the younger man's hand. "How the devil are you?"

"I'm well, thank you, sir," Baldacre replied, confirming Ross's thought that Prendergast had been the other man's senior officer.

"Forget that old sir malarkey, those days are long gone. It's Anthony as you well know."

"Right, Anthony it is then," said Baldacre.

"Forgive us please, Inspector," Prendergast apologised to Ross. "It's been a few years since we met up. Too many years in fact."

"That's quite alright," Ross smiled at the pair, wondering at the same time how someone the size of Baldacre had managed in the confines of a nuclear submarine. Perhaps, he thought, the man had been smaller in those days, though his height would surely have been the same. His question would have to remain unanswered however, as they had pressing matters to attend to.

After all four had helped themselves to coffee from the large pot supplied by Hope Severn, they arranged themselves around the large table in the centre of the room, on which Anthony Prendergast spread a large map of the English Channel that he'd removed from his briefcase, carefully unfolding it to its full size.

Using his pen as a pointer he gave the others a quick resumé of what lay before them on the table.

"As you can see, this map indicates all of the known wreck sites pertaining to ships of the Royal Navy and others in the Channel. These blue dots are our ships, nothing more recent than the Second World War, and not many either. The black dots indicate the known remains of ships of the German Kriegsmarine from World War Two, we have no records from World War One of any such wrecks. The green dots indicate the few known wrecks of civilian ships, mostly the odd trawler and one or two cargo vessels that were lost in deeper waters."

"That's quite impressive," Ross interjected. "I never realised there'd be such an accurate and comprehensive record of the wrecks on the sea bed."

"Normally you'd be correct, of course," Prendergast replied, "but the English Channel is one of the busiest waterways in the world and it's important from a safety angle that any wreck that might at some time present any hazard to shipping, no matter how remote, is known about and charted."

"Of course, yes, I understand," Ross nodded.

"Now, that's what makes this case of yours interesting, Andy, because the co-ordinates given to you by Klaus Haller do not correspond to any of these known wreck sites. Either the man has deliberately misled you, or, his coordinates are incorrect, or…" Prendergast hesitated.

"Or what?" Ross asked, eager for the final part of the reply.

"I think what he's saying," Baldacre joined in the conversation, "is that the only other conclusion that we might come to here, and it's not one the Navy would really be too happy with, is that Herr Haller, or, more precisely, these people from the Aegis institute, appear to have stumbled on an unknown wreck site. That means in effect, that somewhere along the line the Navy has managed to lose a ship somewhere, right, Anthony?"

"Right," Prendergast confirmed.

"I'm not sure I'm following this exactly," said Ross. "When you say they've lost a ship…"

"Let me explain," Prendergast stopped him in mid-sentence. "When a Royal Navy vessel is in trouble, Andy, standard procedure is for the Captain to transmit its position, enabling search and rescue units to locate it and carry out their tasks. The same holds true now as it did during the war. As long as we know where the ship went down, we can co-ordinate the search for survivors, wreckage and so on. However, if the ship, for what-ever reason, transmits incorrect co-ordinates, or, worst of all, doesn't send out a distress call, we have no way of knowing where that ship is in reality. If the wrong position is transmitted the rescue craft could be searching miles away from where the ship went down."

"And if no distress call goes out?" Drake now asked the question.

"Well, Sergeant. In that case we would in effect have 'lost' a ship as George so succinctly put it. If we don't know it's been sunk, how the heck do we know we've got a missing ship until such times as it fails to report in or doesn't return from a patrol for example?"

"But surely," Drake said, "the Royal Navy knows when one of its ships is missing, presumed sunk, Captain? They must have records of such things."

"Anthony, please," Prendergast corrected her. "It's not always as simple as that, Sergeant."

"Izzie," she interrupted.

"Okay, Izzie, let me explain a little. You see, when World War Two was in progress, we obviously had ships at sea in virtually every ocean of the world. Now, say for the sake of argument the ship Aegis has discovered was part of a convoy escort, sailing from, let's say Halifax, Nova Scotia, to Liverpool, your home town…"

"But that's nowhere near the Channel," Drake persisted.

"No, but what if the convoy had been attacked by U-Boats, or perhaps a roving *Condor*, that was a German long range maritime patrol aircraft, by the way, and one or two merchant ships had been damaged but not sunk. If the ship, or ships were not too badly damaged and the commander of the convoy escort screen, normally the senior captain of the destroyers that often sailed as cover, together with perhaps two or three corvettes decided they stood a chance of making port, but not necessarily the original port of destination, he had the authority to detach those ships from the convoy, and send them to a closer port of safety and would usually send one of his escort vessels to accompany the stragglers to port. Depending on where the attack too place, it might have seemed sensible for him to direct the escorting vessel to see them safely to a port on the south coast, perhaps Plymouth, or Portsmouth, where they could have picked up Naval protection as they neared home waters."

"I'm getting the picture," Drake said. "I think you're saying that if a ship was lost after being detached from the convoy and didn't have a chance to send a distress signal, you, that is the Royal Navy, I mean wouldn't have a clue were it went down."

"Precisely. Now you're beginning to understand the problem. It's clear from the photograph young Decker took that the ship is in all probability a Royal Naval vessel, and we've already guessed it looks likely to be a corvette. So far, so good. However, since I was asked to look into the matter, and as I already explained, there are no records of any naval vessel going down at that position in the channel. So, we now need to look at any ships that may have mysteriously disappeared in the Channel or its approaches in the later years of the war. We know it had to be around that time by the design of the ship's bow. Earlier corvettes were built to a pretty dated design and had what you might call a 'sit up and beg' bow, fairly straight rather than the raked bow on later, more modern designs."

"And have your initial inquiries come up with anything, Anthony?" Ross asked, expecting the Captain to perhaps come up with a long list, knowing how many ships were lost during the war.

"As a matter of fact, they have, Andy" Prendergast smiled. "I have a list here…" Ross groaned, "of three possibilities." Ross perked up imme-diately.

"Only three?" he asked. "Are you sure?"

Prendergast smiled sympathetically, knowing Ross to be a little in the dark on this subject.

"The Royal Navy isn't now, and never has been in the business of totally losing track of long lists of our warships, Andy."

"I'm sorry, Anthony. No offence intended."

"None taken. It's a tricky thing to get your head round, I know."

"So, just three ships possible then," Ross repeated.

"That's all, Andy, and one is a definite favourite for your wreck"

"I'm all ears," Ross said as Prendergast pulled another sheet of paper from a compartment in his briefcase.

"Okay, first of all the three names. We have *H.M.S. Denbigh*, *H.M.S Violet* and *H.M.S. Norwich*, all reported missing without trace during 1945. Of the three, my money is on the *Norwich*.

Ross held a hand up to stop Prendergast.

"Hold on a minute, Anthony. I think we'd better have a coffee refill before you tell us this part."

Five agonising minutes passed, Ross wanted to hear Prendergast's theory as much as Izzie Drake, but he knew they'd all feel better for a little refreshment to go with it.

Finally they all sat round the table once more, and as Anthony Pren-dergast passed copies of a grainy black and white photograph of a small and insignificant looking warship to each of them, he began to relate, in as much detail as he could the tragic story surrounding the mysterious loss of *H.M.S. Norwich*.

CHAPTER 22

THE ENGLISH CHANNEL, 1945

Four hours after her encounter with the drifting mine, the *Mary Deal* was almost home. As the trawler crept through the fog, Andrew Douglas eventually breathed a minor sigh of relief as the ubiquitous sound of the foghorn positioned at the end of the small quay in the harbour of the tiny fishing village of his home at Mevagissey managed to claw its way through the all enveloping grey cloud finally reached his ears. He knew they were within reach of safety at last, and he called to his nephew, Johnny Baldwin to join him in the little trawler's wheelhouse.

"Listen lad, as soon as we tie up I want you to hop off and run as fast as you can to P.C. Pryde's house and tell him about that there mine."

"Right you are, Uncle Andrew," Johnny replied.

Douglas thrust a piece of paper into Johnny's hand.

"This 'ere piece o' paper's got the position of the mine written down on it, at least, where it were when we met up with it. Daresay it might have drifted a bit since then, but at least it'll give the Navy boys an idea where to look for the damned thing."

Young Baldwin nodded and fell silent as he watched his uncle guide the little trawler closer to safety, the sound of the foghorn growing louder as the *Mary Deal* crept along at little more than three knots. Then, like an angel beckoning them to Heaven the glow of the harbour light, complete with a spectrum-filled halo produced by the fog that shrouded the boat's approach broke through the dense cloying cloud. Andrew Douglas reduced power to the engine, which growled its acceptance of his touch on the throttle and the *Mary Deal* almost came to a stop but maintained enough steerage way under the command of her experienced skipper to slowly edge her way into the tiny harbour, where Douglas soon had her starboard side bumping up to the harbour wall, the thick tyres hanging along her side preventing damage to her hull.

Douglas instantly threw the engine into reverse, bringing the craft to an almost instant halt as Johnny Baldwin leapt upward onto the steps that led up from her berth to the top of the harbour wall. The young man quickly disappeared into the fog on his errand to report the mine to the authorities. Douglas switched off the engine and called for his remaining crew members to help him secure the boat and seal the hold. The few boxes containing the day's meagre catch could wait in the cold of the hold until morning as they were too late to offload and sell the catch thanks to the fog. Douglas cursed inwardly, fully expecting some of the catch, despite being packed in ice, to be useless by morning.

* * *

As Andrew Douglas threw the switch that turned off the *Mary Deal's* engine, the trawler shuddered for a moment from the last throb of the diesel motor, and then all was silent aboard the boat, apart from the lapping of the rippling harbour waves against the hull and the gentle creaking of the deck planking as she settled at her moorings.

Peter Evans and Davy Billings offered to stay with Douglas to await the return of Johnny Baldwin, but Douglas thanked the two younger men and told them to go home to their families.

"Your Mum will be worried about you, Peter," he said to Evans. "We're late enough coming back as it is. Go and put her mind to rest lad."

Left alone with his thoughts as he waited for his nephew to report back to him, Andrew Douglas sat in the *Mary Deal's* wheelhouse and took a small hip flask from his heavy seaman's duffle coat pocket. The flask contained the last of the trawlerman's supply of rum, a gift from a grateful destroyer captain when Douglas had presented him with a box of freshly caught fish when the two had met at sea some months earlier.

Sipping the amber liquid that sent an instant warmth down his throat and into his stomach, Douglas allowed himself to be lulled for a few seconds by the gentle movement of the *Mary Deal* as she swayed in time to the movement of the barely perceptible swell within the little harbour.

"I'm getting too old for this lark," he spoke aloud, his only audience being his boat, the ocean and the stars that he knew illuminated the night sky somewhere beyond the bank of fog that now seemed to be slowly clearing, with minor improvement to the overall visibility from his perch in the wheelhouse. "Perhaps Stella was right. Maybe it's time to pack it in, Andrew, me laddo, leave the sea to the young 'uns."

"Talking to yourself now, are you, Andrew?"

The deep voice of the local police constable, Sebastian Pryde, known to all as Seb, broke into his reverie. The muffling effect of the fog had prevented Douglas from hearing the approach of the policeman.

"Seb Pryde, you be careful, creepin' up on a man like that. You could have given me a heart attack. And where's that nephew o' mine?"

"Right here, Uncle Andrew," Johnny replied as he appeared almost wraith-like from behind the constable, an apparition materialising from the fog bank.

"I came to see you personally, Andrew," Pryde said, "and let you know I've telephoned the Royal Navy base at Portland. They said to say thank you for reportin' the mine and they'll be sendin' a mine sweeper along as soon as possible to clear it and make the shippin' lane safe again."

"Hmph," Douglas grumbled. "I doubt they apologised for allowin' the damn thing to drift away in the first place, puttin' my boat in jeopardy like that, did they?"

"Course not," said Pryde. "But at least they'll see to it, though I must say you were damn lucky you saw it rather than hittin' it. You and the *Mary Deal* and crew might never have been seen again if you had."

"That's what I was thinkin' afore you crept up on me," Douglas admitted. "Perhaps it's time to hang up me sea boots. How do you fancy skipperin' the *Mary Deal*, young Johnny?"

"Are you serious, Uncle?" an astounded Johnny Baldwin asked, his face a mask of total surprise.

"Aye lad, I am. You're aunty has been a' naggin' at me to give up the sea and I'm thinkin' tonight's just about done it for me. We'll talk with your father tomorrow and see about fixin' a decent wage for you, and the *Mary Deal* will have a new skipper the next time she puts to sea."

"I don't know what to say," said Johnny, and the policeman clapped him on the shoulder and congratulated him on his good fortune. Before leaving the two seamen, Pryde gave them a cautionary warning.

"Just be sure you and your crew don't go spreading it about that you almost hit one of our own mines, you hear me, Andrew?"

"I hear you, Seb. We'll call on the others on the way home and warn them off from sayin' anything, though they'll have told their families, I'm sure."

"Just make sure it goes no further," Pryde warned him. "It wouldn't be good for morale among the population if they thought our own ships were at risk from our own mines. That's why the Admiralty provide us with charts so our people don't end up in our minefields."

As Douglas and Baldwin followed P.C. Pryde as he led the way back towards the village, each man felt satisfied that he'd done his duty satisfactorily, the *Mary Deal* was left at her moorings, her deck silent and her engine making an occasional clicking sound as the metal machinery parts cooled in the night. She and her crew had played their part in what would become one of wartime's cameos of circumstance, a part none of the other participants would ever be aware of.

* * *

"Damn this fog," Engel cursed as he and Ritter stood together on the conning tower of *U966*, peering into the murk that surrounded them. Five hours had passed since the *Mary Deal* had passed this self-same position as she headed back towards Megavissey. Ritter and Engel of course, had never heard of the little trawler, nor would they in the time they had remaining to them.

Ritter placed a hand on his first officer's shoulder.

"What we can't see, neither can the enemy, Heini. We're as safe as we can be at present. Won't be long before we submerge and break out into the Atlantic."

"I'll feel a lot safer when we do," Engel moaned at his skipper who merely shook his head and said, "Don't be an old woman, Heini. Do you want to live forever?"

"Not forever, mein Kapitän, but at least until we see the coast of South America would be good for now."

"Then come, Heini, she should be ready now. Let's take a last deep breath of fresh air and go below. We'll submerge and make a dash for it. Perhaps you're right. Best not to push our luck too far, eh?"

"Yes, and by the way, did Kraus tell you some of the crates we were loaded with had come loose this afternoon? We had to tie them down again?"

Jurgen Kraus was in effect the bosun of the U-Boat, the senior non-commissioned officer on board. He was responsible for all aspects of ship-board discipline and other more mundane tasks at present, like overseeing the safety of the mysterious cargo.

"No, he didn't. Knowing Kraus he'll have seen to it without feeling any need of disturbing me with such matters of routine."

"It's just that, apart from cursing those blasted SS types who loaded them on board and wouldn't let the crew near them, Krauss told me he could hardly believe the weight of six of the crates. It took four men to manhandle them into the correct position so they could be lashed to the bulkheads properly this time. What the hell is in those things? The ones in the rear torpedo compartment and up for'ard are nowhere near as heavy, according to Kraus."

"Speculation is futile, my friend," Ritter replied as he and Engel dropped down the ladder into the control room. Looking back over his shoulder he said, "We sail on orders from the Fuehrer. What choice do we have?" Engel didn't reply.

"Secure the hatch," Ritter ordered and as soon as his order had been complied with he gave the order to dive. *U966* levelled out at ten metres below the surface and before Max Ritter could say another word a shout from Gerhard Shenke, from his position on the hydrophones brought everyone in the control room to attention.

"Kapitän, engines, I'm detecting engines in the water."

"Shit," Ritter exclaimed. "Location, course and speed, Shenke."

"Two kilometres to the west, sir, course two two zero, speed approximately twelve knots."

"What do you think, Shenke?"

Shenke was an experienced operator who could often identify the type of enemy quickly from the sound of her engines.

"I don't know, sir. If it was a destroyer it would be moving faster. Could be a merchantman, maybe a straggler from a convoy."

"I don't know either," said Ritter, removing his cap and scratching his head. "Even twelve knots is pretty good for most of the old rust buckets they send out in the convoys nowadays. I wish we'd remained on the surface for a few more minutes, and maybe got a look at it."

"But we probably wouldn't have been able to see it anyway with that bloody fog up there," Engel countered.

"True, Heini, very true."

Shenke spoke again, urgency in his voice.

"Whatever she is, she's got Asdic, sir. She's scanning. Maybe she heard us."

"Damn," said Ritter.

"What now?" Engel asked.

* * *

Having completed the outward leg of her patrol area, *H.M.S. Norwich* had turned for home twenty minutes earlier and was on a heading that Clarkson couldn't know would take her directly towards *U966*. As luck would have it, the fog had begun to lift in patches and *Norwich* had been blessed with a clear window for the last five miles of her passage. Even so, there was no way her lookouts could have seen the *U966* on the surface as she recharged her batteries. The submarine was still shrouded by fog. Unfortunately for *U966* however, when the crew had re-secured the mystery crates after they'd worked loose, a careless rating had left a wrench propped on a steam pipe that ran along the top of the passageway where the heaviest crates were stored. As the U-Boat slipped below the waves following Ritter's order to submerge, the wrench had slid from its place atop the pipe and clattered to the deck, the sound loud enough to be heard by the ever alert crewmen of the corvette.

"It's a U-Boat, sir, I'm sure of it," said petty officer Sykes as Clarkson stood beside him, the pinging echo of the Asdic resounding in the enclosed space, Sykes continually turning the control wheel as he followed the track of the target.

Clarkson ordered the *Norwich* to full speed ahead and in seconds, their routine patrol had turned into a deadly game of cat and mouse.

Peter Hicks had joined Giles Clarkson on the bridge, together with the young navigator Lieutenant Bailey, who stood beside the voice pipe ready to convey the skipper's orders to the engine room. Leading Seaman Charlie Knox, still smiling, was at the helm, and two young ratings, Adam Phelps and Albert Taylor stood, one on each wing of the bridge, binoculars in hand, surveying the surrounding waters, which were suddenly becoming more visible as a break in the fog seemed to be a heaven-sent gift to the hunters of the submerged submarine.

Below the waves, Max Ritter cursed his ill-fortune. Another ten minutes and he'd have been clear of the area, and secondly, if he'd remained up top, he'd have possibly escaped detection altogether, sheltered in the haven provided by the fog.

"Bring her up to periscope depth," he ordered with a hint of angst in his voice.

"But sir…"Engel began to protest.

"Now, Heini," he reiterated.

"Jawohl, Herr Kapitän," Engel replied, repeating the order to the helmsman.

"Up scope," Ritter snapped and quickly scanned the surrounding sea, surprised to see the fog dissipating by the second as the view became clearer. His eyes quickly picked out the approaching warship, its bow wave indicating she was probably at full speed, on a course that would put them right where *U966* was in less then a minute.

"It's a corvette, probably a convoy escort," he said as he calculated his best course of action, at the same time remembering his orders not to engage the enemy unless absolutely necessary.

"Damn Hitler's bloody 'special cargo'," he cursed.

"Your orders, Kapitän?" Heini spoke with respect, professionalism overtaking the bond of friendship that existed between the two men.

Ritter knew he had only seconds to make a decision; stay and fight, use his limited supply of torpedoes to attempt to sink the small warship, or save them for bigger prey that they may encounter on the voyage, or attempt to evade the corvette, which, by nature of its purpose as he well knew, would be armed with enough anti-submarine weapons, depth-charges and torpe-does of its own, to damage his boat, perhaps fatally.

As the sound of the *Norwich's* propellers filled the ears of the crew within the sleek but sealed interior of *U966*, growing louder by the second, Max Ritter, faithful to his orders, made his decision.

"Crash dive," he ordered. "Take her down, now. Helm hard right."

Almost immediately, the bow of *U966* noticeably dipped as the submarine made its attempt to reach the sea bed, out of range of any depth charges the warship might be about to release. Simultaneously, the sub began to turn to starboard, Ritter's ploy being to confuse the surface ship as to his true intent. He wanted the corvette's captain to believe he was trying to escape by turning to starboard and making an emergency course change. If he could make his adversary wary of the possibility he may be preparing to launch torpedoes against his ship, he might pause to think and in those precious seconds, *U966* would slip under the corvette and be on the sea bed in less than two minutes.

Aboard the *Norwich* the sense of excitement was palpable as the constant pinging of the Asdic penetrated almost every compartment of the corvette. On the bridge, Clarkson held on to the bridge railing with one hand, while holding his binoculars in the other. Turning to his yeoman of signals, Seaman Hurst, he said in a calm voice, betraying not a hint of emotion, "Send the following signal immediately, adding our position at the end."

He passed a slip of paper to Hurst with the ship's position clearly written upon it.

TO CAPTAIN (D) COMMANDING DESTROYER SQUADRON PORTLAND stop FROM CAPTAIN, H.M.S. NORWICH stop AM ENGAGING UBOAT stop CURRENT POSITION...

It was at that moment when all the laws of probability, happenstance and sheer bad luck overrode the best intentions of both Lieutenant Commander Giles Clarkson and Korvettankapitän Max Ritter and the vagaries of the sea took control of the battle between the *Norwich* and *U966*.

The madness took everyone by surprise. The excited shout of "Instantaneous echo" from the Asdic operator was followed immediately by Clarkson's order to fire a salvo of depth charges. The death-dealing, amatol-filled barrels of explosives arced away from the *Norwich's* port side as she raced over the position of the German submarine.

Aboard *U966* Ritter actually heard the sound of the depth-charges as they hit the surface of the sea. He hoped his ploy had gained him enough seconds for his boat to gain the depth he needed.

It worked. As the charges exploded, the concussion from the exploding amatol caused momentary panic on *U966* as the sub lurched almost onto its port side, the lights went out, various pipes burst and small leaks caused jets of freezing water into various compartments, steam into others, but after a few seconds the lights came back on, repair crews dashed to repair the leaks and the submarine stabilised and continued its controlled dive to the bottom, reaching safety a few seconds later. Ritter ordered full stop to the engine room and allied his order with the command for total silence aboard the boat. The corvette's captain would, he hoped, either think the *U966* had escaped to the South, or alternatively, might believe the sub to be fatally damaged and sunk, crippled to the bottom of the sea.

Just as Clarkson was about to order a turn to starboard, and as the ship's wireless operator was about to send the Captain's message to Portland the mine that had drifted some ten miles since its encounter with the *Mary Deal* entered the equation.

The *Norwich's* starboard lookout just had time to shout "Mine" before the ship's port side came into contact with the deadly prongs of the mine and an almighty explosion rocked the corvette. The explosion literally ripped the guts from the warship, the engine room and the magazine being holed and flooded in seconds, everyone in those areas killed almost instantly.

The corvette, almost cut in half by the exploding mine and her own armaments, began to sink immediately. The explosions had by then left the bridge a tangled mess of metal and human tragedy. Clarkson lay dazed beside the binnacle housing the ships compass. Peter Hicks was dead, his shocked, staring eyes peering upwards and unseeing. The helmsman, yeoman, and all but one other man on the bridge had also perished. A hand came to rest on Clarkson's arm.

"Come on, sir, please. Let me help you."

"Is that you, Knox?" Clarkson asked breathlessly, the wind having been knocked from him by his fall against the binnacle.

"Aye sir, it is. Let's get you out of 'ere, eh? Don't seem too 'ealthy to me up 'ere any more," said the ever smiling Leading Seaman.

"You're a bloody sight for sore eyes, Knox, that's what you are. What about the others?"

"Dead sir, sorry to 'ave to report. Mr 'icks is over there and poor Mr. Bailey copped it too, and 'urst and the others."

Clarkson tried to focus his sight on the devastation on the bridge. Sure enough, the body of the young, depressed navigator lay slumped in one corner, his head cleanly taken off by a shard of flying metal. The rest of the bridge crew lay dead around him and he felt the urgency in Charlie Knox's words.

"Sir, we need to get out of 'ere. She'll go under any minute."

Another voice seemed to appear from nowhere.

"He's right sir. Come on, let me help you get him to his feet, Knox," said Chief Petty Officer Nobby Clark.

"Chief," Clarkson gasped the word, "I might have known you'd turn up too."

Clark smiled at his captain, but looked with grief as he turned to Charlie Knox. The two men saw the blood as Clarkson coughed. Knox gently opened the captain's blood-soaked duffel coat and the two men saw the wound. A large piece of shrapnel had penetrated Clarkson's left lung and stuck out grotesquely from his torn and shattered body. Clark and

Knox knew enough to realise that attempting to remove it would only hasten their captain's death.

Clarkson seemed to know what was in their minds, and through his pain, and through gritted teeth he gave his last order to the two men.

"Leave me," he gasped. "Try and save yourselves."

Knox looked at Clark and pulled him to one side.

"I ain't leavin' 'im, Chiefy. 'E's a good man, and I can't leave 'im to die alone."

"You're a good man too, Charlie Knox," said the C.P.O. "We'll stay together, eh lad?"

Still smiling, Charlie Knox just nodded and turned back to his skipper. He eased himself onto the deck of the shattered bridge, gently placed an arm round Giles Clarkson and placed the captain's head on his own shoulder. Chief Petty Officer Nobby Clark took up a position on the other side and took the captain's hand in his own. Only then did Knox see that the Chief's left hand was missing, the end of his arm wrapped in an assortment of rags and pieces of other unknown materials. Blood dripped slowly through the makeshift dressing.

"Caught a bit of a packet yourself, eh Chiefy?" he said, not needing an answer, though Clark smiled back at him and replied,

"Anyone ever tell you you've got a great talent for stating the bleedin' obvious, Charlie boy?"

"Oh yeah, me Mum says that all the time, she does."

At that moment, for the first time since he'd known him, Nobby Clark saw the smile disappear from the face of Charlie Knox, only for a second, as he realised he wouldn't be seeing his mother again, and then it was back.

"We'll be alright though. We'll go together, eh Chiefy?"

Clark nodded, astounded at the cool bravery and stoicism of young Charlie Knox.

Clarkson looked up at the two men, and tried to smile at them.

"You're both bloody fools, you know that don't you? Stupid, idiotic, insubordinate bloody fools, and the two bravest men I've ever known. Thank you, thank you both"

"Don't mention it, Skipper," said Knox, smiling benignly at Clarkson, as the captain gripped Clark's hand in one final gesture of thanks, and his head lolled to one side on Knox's shoulder.

The two men looked at one another, no words necessary as they gently lowered Clarkson's lifeless body to the deck.

"What now then, Chiefy?" asked Knox.

"Can't do much, can we, Charlie?" Clark replied, supporting his wounded arm with the other as he looked at the devastation around him.

An ominous rumbling sound emanated from the bowels of the *Norwich* as the ship began to slide beneath the waves. Almost broken in two, but with her keel remaining intact enough to hold the bow and stern sections together.

"Does it 'urt much?" said Knox, indicating Clark's hand.

"Not for much longer, Charlie," Clark replied with a wry smile. The *Norwich* lurched suddenly as her forward compartments flooded beyond the point of no return and as she slipped below the waves,

Nobby Clark held tightly onto the arm of young Charlie Knox and said, "Been nice knowing you, Charlie Knox"

"Same here, Chiefy," Charlie replied, and the young man put an arm round the Chief Petty Officer, and smiled.

* * *

"What was that?" Engel said as the sound of the explosion filtered down through the waves to reach the *U966*.

"Sounded like our hunter blew herself up."

"But what, how?"

"I don't know, Heini. Maybe another U-Boat found her, perhaps she hit a mine, or her boilers exploded. I don't know."

"But there are no minefields in this area, surely?"

"Agreed, but maybe it was a drifting mine, broken loose from one of the Britishers' own minefields."

"So, what do we do?"

"We wait, Heini. We need to be sure there are no other warships in the area."

"But there may be men in the water," Engel said, his humanity for fellow sailors in trouble taking over."

"I'm sorry," said Ritter. "Our mission comes first. We must remain unseen and unknown."

Engel nodded his understanding.

Unfortunately for the men of *U966*, they couldn't know that the *Norwich* was now sinking fast, and heading straight for the position on the sea bed where the submarine lay in hiding.

As the crew of *U966* held their breath, wondering what Ritter would do next, none of them, Ritter included, could have known that the *Norwich*, her descent slowed by the waters of the Channel, was now headed inexorably for the stern section of the submarine. The sinking corvette now appeared to twist in a macabre death spiral as the current played with her dying shell.

For a few seconds, her spiralling motion made it appear as though she would narrowly miss the U-Boat but then, in a disastrous and cruel twist of fate the current tugged her back towards the submarine. Still, there was a chance of a narrow miss and the *Norwich's* stern settled on the sea bed, less than ten yards from where *U966* sat helplessly, unknowing. The stern quickly dug itself into the soft sea bed at an angle of about 45 degrees, leaving the bow section pointing up towards the surface, like an accusing finger. What remained of the ship's funnel now collapsed towards the stern and the sound as it was torn from its mounting by its weight and the action of the current transferred itself to the interior of *U966*, and a tremor of fear spread throughout the still and silent submarine.

"What the hell's happening out there?" Engel asked as he looked at Ritter, more in hope than expectation of a logical reply.

Ritter however, had a very good idea of what was taking place just yards from his boat.

"Sounds to me as if the warship just hit bottom quite close to us, Heini. That sound we heard was probably her funnel being torn from its mooring points."

"Bloody hell, Max, that was fucking close then. It must be our lucky day."

"I think you're right, Heini. It's time we weren't here, my friend. Let's get the hell out of here while we can."

"What if there are any other ships up there?" Engel asked.

"That's a chance we have to take," Ritter said, and a shudder ran through his body, a premonition, a warning, quite what it was he couldn't say. Pulling himself together, he grabbed the microphone that hung from the control room ceiling.

"This is the captain speaking. I know you're all wondering what's been happening. All I can tell you is that we encountered a British corvette which was making an attack run on us when it suddenly exploded after releasing a single spread of depth charges which failed to do any real damage. I do not know why. The loud noise we heard was the ship as it struck the sea bed not far from us. We appear to have had a narrow escape. We will now prepare to get under way and continue our mission. That is all."

Unfortunately for Ritter and his crew, the *Norwich* now began to move again as the bow section began to settle in a downward motion that saw the first twenty feet of the corvette's keel come to rest with a grinding sound across the stern section of *U966*. In a few horrendous seconds, the U-Boat found itself trapped, pinned to the sea floor by the weight of the *Norwich*. Somehow, the submarine's pressure hull withstood the impact. Instead of imploding and killing all on board, instead the deck buckled where the *Norwich* impacted upon it, and various leaks sprang around the rear compartments, but *U966* stood firm.

Sadly, Ritter, Engel and all those on board would soon realise that the initial reprieve would turn into something far worse than instant death. Pinned to the sea bed, the submarine was now incapable of movement, despite Ritter ordering full ahead, and then full astern, all in vain. Max knew that *U966* had become his tomb, and that of his crew. He knew the air in the boat would gradually grow fouler and fouler as they breathed in what remained of their good air and that slowly and inexorably, he and his crew would die a slow and agonising death by suffocation.

He made his grin announcement to the crew, keeping nothing from them. He felt it fair they should know the truth, enabling them to make their peace with whatever God some of them may follow.

"Shit, shit, shit," Joseph Ziegler had said to his young protégé Karl Meister as the news sank in to everyone's minds.

"Joseph? What is it?"

"Oh, nothing, young Meister. It's just that I always wanted to die in a Berlin brothel from a heart attack, lying on top of a buxom whore, not in this stinking rat trap of a sardine can."

Heinz Muller, the submarine's engineering officer took a tour around the engine room, stroking and polishing his beloved engines. Finally satisfied that all was as it should be, Muller sat down on the little stool that the crew had always called his perch, closed his eyes, and fell asleep. He would not wake up again.

Young Willi Becker succumbed early to the effects of oxygen deprivation. Ritter was glad, for the simple reason he had seen the white faced fear and panic in the young man's eyes. It was good, thought Ritter that Willi hadn't suffered for long.

As the hours passed, some of the men spent what time they had left praying, others slumped on their bunks looking at photographs of wives, sweethearts, children until the pictures blurred before their eyes, eventually slipping from their lifeless fingers.

Heini Engel stayed close to his captain, his hero, right to the very end. Both men felt the onset of that final unconsciousness around the same time, and somehow, found enough strength to reach out to each other and shake hands. Max Ritter leaned back against a bulkhead, sighed once, and everything turned black. Heini Engel lasted only seconds longer, his last thoughts being of Ritter's promise to take him to Berlin after the war, sad it would never happen. Then he too was gone.

Soon, all was quiet aboard *U966*. The only occasional sounds were those of the metal of her hull as it groaned against the pressure exerted by the warship nestled on her stern. No distress signal had been sent from the submarine, nor from the corvette, that had blown up before her radio had sent the report of the engagement with the u-boat. Together with their crews and Hitler's mystery cargo, *H.M.S Norwich* and *U966* finally settled deeper into the mud of the sea bed, lost and forgotten, missing, position unknown to the Admiralty or the Kriegsmarine.

CHAPTER 23

HANDS ACROSS THE SEA

Detective Constable Paul Ferris was happily typing search instructions into his computer when D.C.I. Agostini walked in to the squad room. The Chief Inspector placed a hand on Ferris's shoulder and the D.C almost jumped out of his skin.

"Wow, sorry about that, Ferris," the boss said with a smile. "You were miles away there, lost in your work I'm pleased to see."

Relaxing slightly, Ferris stood up as he replied.

"I was, sir. It can really pull you in once you get started searching the internet for information. I'm finding some very interesting stuff about Aegis, but nothing specifically illegal so far."

"I see, but it sounds as though you suspect there could be something there if you dig deeper, am I correct?"

"You are indeed, sir. I just get the feeling that they're too good to be true."

As Agostini was about to ask Ferris why he felt that way the phone on Ferris's desk rang.

"Excuse me a moment, sir," he said as Agostini nodded.

Ferris listened for a few second and then replied to the desk sergeant who'd called his extension, "Can you get someone to bring him up please Sarge? I'm with D.C.I. Agostini at present."

Replacing the phone on its cradle, he turned to the Chief Inspector.

"You might want to stay for a few minutes sir. Could be something interesting."

"Really?"

"Yes sir, Sergeant Cross on the front desk is sending Jerome Decker the third up. It seems Aaron Decker's father has something to tell us. As D.I. Ross and Sergeant Drake are away, you may want to hear what he says first hand."

"Interesting, and yes, Ferris, I'd love to hear what he has to say."

Two minutes later, Decker was shown into the squad room by a young woman in plain clothes, and Ferris greeted the C.I.A. man and introduced him to Agostini.

"Good to meet you, Detective Chief Inspector," said Decker as the two men shook hands."

"I believe you have some information for us Mr. Decker," Agostini wasted no time in saying.

"Yes, I do. Detective Inspector Ross asked me to use, shall we say, my connections to look a little more into Aegis from the U.S end and see if I could find anything that might be helpful to you. In short I asked one of our analysts to do some serious infiltration of the company without them being aware of it."

"You hacked them," Ferris said immediately.

"You said that, Mr. Ferris, not me," Decker smiled at the D.C.

"So, what did your analyst find, Mr. Decker?" Agostini asked.

"Okay, well there's something odd about the way the company is set up in some ways. No disrespect, Mr. Ferris, I know you're very good at what you do, but our people knew what to look for, whereas you're shooting pretty much in the dark."

"I don't mind if it helps the case," Ferris replied.

"So, the thing we've discovered is that the personnel Aegis employ varies greatly depending on where they're employed. We found that wherever they are involved in instances of underwater archaeology around any historic location, the head of the local operation is in fact a specialist in marine salvage. I can assure you that is not normal. That is the case with every one of Aegis's operations around Europe and in the Far East, Chief Inspector. So the immediate question that springs to mind is why they need a salvage expert in charge of what are supposed to be either historical or environmental investigations?"

"Because," Agostini surmised, "Aegis, or someone high up on their payroll, is plundering historical sites and lining their own pockets."

"That's exactly what my people think, Chief Inspector," Decker replied.

Both Ferris and Agostini could tell that Decker was now acting not as the bereaved father of young Aaron, but as a senior operative of the Central Intelligence Agency. There was a hint of steel in his voice, a determination to help them find out just what was going on within the Aegis operation on a worldwide basis.

"But how can they be getting away with this under the noses of the top people at Aegis?" Ferris asked, quite logically.

"Let's just say it depends how high up in the company this goes, Detective Ferris," Decker replied.

"A good point," Agostini agreed, and then introduced a note of caution to the conversation.

"Mr. Decker, we really appreciate you calling on your…professional resources to help us, but are you sure this isn't going to cause problems with your superiors, using C.I.A. resources to carry out these checks and passing information to us?"

"Chief Inspector. My son has been murdered and sure as hell, I want his killers brought to justice. The C.I.A's remit is to protect U.S. interests abroad. If an American company such as Aegis is carrying out clandestine operations to desecrate and or steal national treasures or valuable items belonging to friendly nations then it's totally within our purview to investigate. Further, if they are carrying out such actions against nations not overly friendly to Washington, it could lead to an international incident if discovered."

"Right," said Agostini. "So, is there any way to find out if any of the executives at Aegis might be dirty?"

"Bank accounts," said Ferris before Decker could reply. "If we could ascertain whether any of the people at the top have suddenly become richer than they should be, according to their status and salary, we might be on to something."

"Listen," said Decker. "Things are a little different in the States. Yes, it's possible someone might have a grossly inflated bank balance, but that would be too easy for the authorities to track. We have strict rules at home governing the amounts of money that can be paid into or withdrawn from domestic accounts. As it happens, I have a few friends at the F.B.I. who might help us look into the finances of the Aegis executives, but it's highly likely, if there are very large sums involved that the money they're making will be squirreled away in an offshore bank account, maybe in the Caymans or even in Switzerland. That would be almost impossible to trace."

"Lifestyle," Agostini said.

"Eh?" asked Decker.

"Lifestyle," the D.C.I. repeated. "If we have one or more bad guys at Aegis in the States, it's likely they are living an inflated lifestyle compared with the time before they started all this. Maybe a house they shouldn't really be able to afford, new cars for the kids, who knows?"

"Yes, I see what you mean," Decker agreed. "Looks like I need to speak with my friends at the Federal building."

"We appreciate this, Mr. Decker, and you may wish to start with a man named Francis Kelly, who spoke to Klaus Haller when he phoned Aegis in the States last year. Haller told us the man seemed evasive in his replies to his questions." said Agostini. "Meanwhile, I'll make sure D.I. Ross knows what's going on at our end when I speak with him later."

"Do you have any idea if he's made any progress on the coast yet?" Decker asked.

"He's meeting with representatives from the Royal Navy and the Coast Guard as we speak. I'm hoping for a report from him later this afternoon."

"He seems a good man, your D.I. Ross," Decker said before taking his leave of the Chief Inspector and D.C. Ferris.

"One of the best, Mr Decker, one of the best," Agostini agreed.

After Decker had departed, Agostini stood beside Ferris's desk for a minute, and then had an idea.

"Ferris, I want you to try and find out as much as you can about the man who heads up the Aegis facility in Falmouth, his name according to Haller is William Evans. It's all very well thinking as we now do that there's a worldwide web of corruption emanating from somewhere within Aegis, but it's here in England that we're going to find young Aaron Decker's killer or killers. If we can find something we can use to put pressure on the local head of the operation, you're the man to find it."

"Thank you for the confidence sir. I'll do what I can."

"Good man. It looks as if the Aegis thing is a large multi-pronged operation, like a many-headed Medusa. If we can find a way to cut off the head of the local snake-in-charge, we might actually discover how to take them all down."

"Wow, that would be bloody impressive, sir."

"Wouldn't it just, Ferris?" Agostini smiled and rubbed his hands together in anticipation. "Maybe we can teach the highly vaunted C.I.A. a thing or two eh?"

"Maybe we can, sir. I'll get right to it."

"Good man. And Ferris?"

"Sir?"

"This is between you and me at present, and D.I. Ross when I speak to him, got it? Let him be the one to tell the rest of the team what we're doing."

"Sure, sir. Mum's the word."

"The fewer people who know we're investigating Aegis, the less chance there is that they'll find out we're on to them, understood?"

"Of course sir. I understand."

"D.I. Ross will tell the others what we're up to, I'm sure, but I mean it, Ferris, keep your search as low-key as possible but leave no stone unturned, right?"

"Right sir," Ferris agreed as Agostini left him to peer at his computer screen as he began to type in a set of new search parameters.

CHAPTER 24

HOLMES AND WATSON?

Andy Ross had to admit to being impressed with the level of cooperation he was receiving from the Royal Navy and the Coast Guard. His next step was to arrange liaison with the Devon and Cornwall Police. Thanks to D.C.I. Agostini, the local force had been made aware that he and Drake were 'on their patch' and were expecting his call. He'd delayed contacting them until he'd spoken with the Navy and Coast Guard representatives. Now he was sure of their support he felt he could move to involve the locals. Agostini had furnished him with the name of the local Detective Inspector who'd been tasked with working with him and he placed a call to the local station and was put through to D.I. Brian Jones.

"Jones here. I've been expecting your call, D.I. Ross."

"It's Andy," Ross replied. "Thanks for agreeing to be my chaperone while I'm here."

"My pleasure, Andy. I'm Brian. From what your boss told my boss, and he told me, it sounds as if you have something quite interesting on your hands."

"That's one way to put it," said Ross. "Don't mind me saying this, but I was expecting to be working with a D.I. Pascoe."

"Sudden change of plan, Andy. Tommy Pascoe fell downstairs at home and broke his leg yesterday. He's in hospital, well and truly plastered at present, so you're stuck with me, I'm afraid."

"I'm sure you're every bit as good at your job Brian. I'm glad to have the chance to work with you."

"Same here," Jones replied. "Let's catch some bad guys eh?"

* * *

Two hours later, Ross and Drake walked into the small office occupied by D.I. Brian Jones at Falmouth Police Station. The pair were greeted cordially by Jones who introduced them to his own assistant, Sergeant Carole St. Clair. Drake was delighted to have the opportunity to work with another woman, and St. Clair seemed equally pleased when she also realised there'd be another woman on the team.

"So, how exactly can we help?" Jones asked, after the foursome had settled themselves in chairs around his desk, supplied with steaming mugs of coffee by a young constable who closed the door quietly on his way out.

"I'm not entirely sure, and that's being honest," Ross replied. "I think we need your local knowledge more than anything. It wouldn't do for me and Sergeant Drake to go blundering around on your patch without having the foggiest notion where we are or where we're going."

"True," said Jones, "though it sounds like you need a pair of babysitters more than anything else."

"I doubt that, sir," Drake piped up. "We could be up against some very nasty characters here and your knowledge of the area and the people will be invaluable to us."

"Very true," Ross agreed, "and after I've filled you in fully with all we know, you might see that there could be a little danger along the way."

"Now you're talking," Jones clapped his hands together. "Isn't he Carole?" he asked his sergeant, rhetorically, as it was clear the D.I needed no reply.

"Of course sir," she replied anyway, then, "Sorry about my gaffer sir," she said to Ross. "He loves a bit of excitement now and then and some-times lets his enthusiasm run away with him."

Jones laughed and Ross was pleased to see the D.I. and his sergeant appeared to enjoy a similar easy going relationship to him and Izzie.

"Been together long?" he asked.

"Afraid so," Jones smiled as he spoke. "I've had this one round my neck for three years now. Can't seem to get rid of her."

"Ha, more like you wouldn't know what to do without me," St Clair replied, grinning at her boss.

"Well, looks like we're in for a good time down here, Izzie," Ross said and Izzie Drake nodded in agreement.

Jones suddenly turned serious and said to St. Clair.

"Better tell our new friends here what we've found out so far, Carole."

"Right you are sir," she replied.

Carole St Clair was thirty, but looked younger, her short blonde hair and slim figure belying her quick mind and her black belt in judo, as many criminals had discovered to their cost over the years.

She lifted a pale brown folder from Jones's desk, opened it and began to read from a fact sheet she'd already prepared for the newcomers.

"Aegis International, as they're known round here are extremely secretive about their operations. The people who work there are, for the most part, brought in by the company either from their U.S operation of from other facilities around the world. Nothing wrong with that of course, but it had been thought they'd have given the local economy a boost by providing a number of jobs when they got the go-ahead to build their own docking facility close to the existing harbour. As far as we can tell, they only employ a small number of locals, mostly in low-grade jobs such as security guards, cooks for their staff dining room and a few cleaners. All of them are sworn to secrecy and will not reveal anything of what takes place at the facility, though from the jobs they do, I'd seriously doubt they'd know anything, anyway. The really odd thing is that the people Aegis has brought in never appear to socialise in the town. Aegis must have built an accommodation block or something on-site because none of their imported staff are ever seen in town, at the pubs or shops for example so it's assumed they live and work within the confines of the facility."

"That's more than a little strange," said Ross.

"That's what we thought too, Andy," Jones agreed. "There's something fishy about that place, and I'd love to know what it is they're trying to hide."

"Fishy? In Falmouth?" St Clair said, and laughter erupted between the pair again.

"You two are really corny, do you know that?" Ross said, joining in the momentary hilarity.

"Corn? Not in Falmouth, Andy," Jones quipped again, and this time, even Izzie Drake groaned.

"Okay, thanks," Ross said, trying to get back on track. "Joking aside, we really can't do much until we can get out to the wreck and see exactly what it was that young Aaron Decker was so fired up about."

"I understand the Navy and Coast Guard are willing to help you out on this one," said Jones.

"Yes, and we're going out on one of their ships tomorrow to the position Herr Haller gave us to see what all the fuss is about. I'd like you and Sergeant St Clair to join us."

"We can hardly refuse an offer like that, can we, Carole? A nice sea cruise and the wind in your hair. A fine day out if the weather holds, eh?"

"I'm not a very good sailor, sir, actually," Carole St Clair replied with a worried look on her face.

"Oh, I forgot. You get sea sick watching your rubber duck bobbing about in the bath don't you?"

"Ha, ha, very funny," she responded.

"You'll be fine, Carole," Izzie Drake leaped to her defence. "I'll get you some of those special anti-sea sickness pills on our way back to our hotel."

"Thanks," St Clair replied.

"Yeah, don't worry Carole. My daughter has some of those wrist bands that are supposed to counter motion sickness too. I'll bring 'em along in the morning," Jones said, more serious now.

"Hope they work," said St Clair.

"I'm sure they will," said Drake, feeling a little sorry for her Cornish counterpart.

* * *

Following a good night's sleep, preceded by another splendid meal provided by the redoubtable Hope Severn, Ross and Drake set off at a brisk walk, intending to time their arrival for 9 a.m. the time agreed for them to meet up with Captain Prendergast, Coast Guard George Baldacre and the two Falmouth detectives. Thankfully for the pair, most of the walk was downhill as the distance turned out to be a little further than they anticipated.

As they arrived at Falmouth's picturesque harbour, Ross and Drake could hardly believe their eyes as they easily recognised their ride for the morning. When Anthony Prendergast had told them the Royal Navy would be providing a ship to ferry them out to the wreck location, Andy Ross had expected a small launch or maybe something the size of a tug boat at most. Instead, tied up to the harbour wall, the two detectives saw a sleek, grey warship, which Prendergast would soon explain was in fact *H.M.S. Wyvern*, one of the Royal Navy's latest submarine hunting frigates.

"Impressive, isn't she?"

Prendergast's voice had taken the pair by surprise as he arrived from their rear, having walked across from the dockmaster's office.

"I should say so," Ross exclaimed. "I was expecting something a little…erm…smaller."

Prendergast laughed.

"I'm sorry if you're disappointed, Andy," he said, grinning.

"Oh, no, I didn't mean…"

"I know, I know, just pulling your leg," said the retired naval officer.

Within minutes, they were joined by George Baldacre, D.I Brian Jones and Sergeant Carole St Clair, the latter looking distinctly nervous as she looked up at the ship that appeared to tower above them.

"Well, ladies and gentlemen, shall we go aboard?"

Prendergast led them up the gangway, where they were met by a pair of Royal Marines who'd been expecting their arrival, and who, having examined their credentials, escorted them to the bridge where a tall, superbly groomed officer, with razor sharp creases in his uniform turned at the sound of their arrival.

"Welcome aboard the *Wyvern*, ladies and gentlemen," said Captain Charles Howell, commanding officer of the frigate.

Prendergast shook hands with the captain and introduced his companions, and then communicated Ross's surprise at the frigate being assigned to this particular mission. Howell smiled and then replied.

"Never let it be said that the Royal Navy ever gives up on its own, Detective Inspector. If one of our corvettes from World War Two is lying on the seabed, lost since the forties, it's time we found her and gave her crew the respect they deserve. The *Wyvern* is by design a submarine hunter, but that also makes her perfect for this job. We have the latest state-of-the-art technology on board that will help us in an underwater search. I won't bore you with the technical names or descriptions of everything we can put to use in the search but believe me, if there is a wreck down there, we will find it, that I can promise you."

"We're grateful, Captain," said Ross, "though a little surprised that the Navy has sent such a magnificent ship to assist us."

Charles Howell smiled as he replied, "Inspector, we go where their Lordships of the Admiralty send us, and you're in our backyard really, us being based at Portsmouth. Of course, it also helps that we're the best equipped vessel in the area to look for and find one of our own ships, even if it has been missing for over half a century. Now, let me introduce you to Lieutenant Ridley."

The tall figure who until now had remained standing ramrod-straight behind Howell now stepped forward, his outstretched hand reaching for Ross, who took it and winced at the sheer power he felt in a quick handshake with the lieutenant.

"Pleased to meet you, Inspector Ross," said the man. "I'm Gareth Ridley, Royal Marines."

Howell spoke again.

"Lieutenant Ridley and a team of twelve Royal Marines will be accompanying us on our little trip, Inspector Ross, just to ensure we have added security in case your killers come calling when they find we're diving on the wreck site."

"I'm delighted you're with us," Ross said to Ridley, who bowed graciously in the direction of Sergeants Izzie Drake and Carole St Clair.

"You two ladies must be Drake and St Clair," he said politely, a typical officer and gentleman, Ross surmised, but not one he'd care to take on in a fist fight, if his handshake was anything to go by.

Both sergeants smiled back at Ridley and D.I. Brian Jones politely coughed in the background and stepped forward.

"D.I. Brian Jones, Lieutenant," he said, introducing himself and offering his hand.

"Of course, my apologies," said Ridley as he almost mashed Jones's fingers to a friendly pulp.

"I don't know about the rest of you, but I find all this formality rather grim with so many of you police officers around," Howell interjected.

"I'm Charles, and Gareth won't mind you using his name so I suggest we dispense with all this Detective Inspector this, and Detective Inspector that, and the same for the two sergeants as well if that's agreeable."

"It would certainly save some time and breath," Ross smiled. "I'm Andy, Sergeant Drake is Izzie, and our friends from Falmouth are Brian and Carole."

"Righty-o," said Charles Howell, "glad we've sorted that out. We must of course maintain our ranks in front of the men, I hope you understand but for now, if you will show our friends to the wardroom, Lieutenant, I have work to do. I want to be under way in less than an hour."

Ross thanked Captain Howell and allowed himself and the others to be led from the bridge by the strapping marine officer, who escorted them to the wardroom or 'officers mess' of the ship, where tea and coffee was supplied along with a selection of biscuits, all very civilised and exactly as Ross imagined it would have been in those rare off-duty moments for the officers of the corvette they were seeking in those long ago, dark days of World War Two, before they and their ship met with their as yet unknown fate.

Carole St Clair thought the sea-sickness pills she'd taken before boarding the *Wyvern* must have worked. She felt okay, so far, though she soon realised the gentle motion of the ship at anchor would be totally different to the way the ship would behave once they left harbour and were exposed to the waves that would be waiting for them in the Channel. Her right hand subconsciously reached across and touched her left wrist, checking the 'sea band; was in place. Satisfied, she repeated the procedure with the other hand, making sure the so-called 'magic,' magnetic motion sickness bracelets were in the correct places on her wrists.

Izzie Drake saw her and reached a hand out and touched St Clair on the arm.

"You'll be fine, Carole. I heard the Captain say it's like a millpond out there today."

"Yes, but he probably feels at home in a force ten gale. What he calls a millpond might be pretty rough seas for someone like me."

"I say, er…Carole," Ridley interrupted. "I couldn't help overhearing your conversation. Am I correct in assuming you suffer from a touch of the old *mal de mere?*"

"I'm afraid so," St Clair replied a little shamefacedly.

"Not to worry," Ridley smiled and shouted for the wardroom steward who magically appeared as if from nowhere at his side.

618

"The sergeant here gets queasy at sea. Fix her up with a 'special' would you, there's a good chap?"

"Of course, sir. Won't take long, miss, er, sorry, Sergeant," the steward replied.

In reply to St Clair's puzzled look, Ridley explained, "Believe it or not, even seasoned sailors can often feel a bit under the weather at sea. There isn't a wardroom steward in the Navy who doesn't have a guaranteed antidote for the old wobbly tummy."

"I see," said Carole St Clair. "Thank you."

"Don't thank me, thank Leading Seaman Bowles. Ah, here he comes," said Ridley as the steward appeared, carrying a mug of something that resembled a mixture of ground charcoal and diesel fuel.

"Get that down you, Sergeant," he grinned and in response to her worried look, he went on, "and don't worry, it tastes better than it looks, honest."

It did, much to St Clair's relief.

"Mmm, not bad," she said. "Do I detect a touch of honey in there?"

"Indeed you do," Bowles smiled at her, "but don't ask what else is in it. That's top secret that is."

"He wouldn't reveal his secret recipe under torture, Carole," Ridley said, so straight-faced she actually believed him.

Very soon, there was a distinct feeling of anticipation in the air as they heard the sounds of running feet, the shouting of orders and felt a distinct increase in vibration from the deck, the engines increasing in the engines' revolutions as the *Wyvern* cast off and began to manoeuvre her way out of the harbour towards the open sea.

"Perhaps we should join the skipper on the bridge now," Ridley suggested. "He asked me to escort you back up there once we'd cleared our moorings."

"Right, thanks," Ross replied and he and the others followed the marine officer as he led them back to the bridge. In contrast to their earlier visit, the bridge of *H.M.S Wyvern* was now a hive of activity.

Ross and Jones in particular found themselves fascinated by the machinery, if it could be so described, that they'd failed to notice on their earlier visit. Unlike the controls of wartime warships they'd probably both seen in old action movies, the Wyvern's bridge was clean and uncluttered, with computer screens and controls arranged in banks at strategic points around the bridge. Even the steering could be controlled by computer although there was a wheel, which Ross somehow found comforting, though it was gleaming steel and smaller than the multi-pronged wooden ones he'd seen in those old films.

"Welcome back," said Howell as he acknowledged their return. "This is my first officer, Mike Sutherland," he said as he introduced them to his second-in-command. "Mike will be in overall command of the dive when we reach the wreck site. We'll be sending down two ship's divers, plus two of the marines who are also qualified to work in the submersibles we carry. Let me explain, 'ship's divers' are specifically trained to carry out any and all activities relating to underwater work. They are specialists and one will accompany each marine as they take a first look at the wreck you've located. Once we know what we're dealing with down there we can formulate a plan of action. I'm assuming you'll want to know as much as possible about the corvette and the submarine that you say is buried beneath her, and of course, there was some mention of a body?"

"Yes, a frogman, or at least a man n a wetsuit as far as we could make out," said Ross, who pulled a copy of the underwater photograph taken by Aaron Decker from his inside jacket pocket and handed it to Sutherland.

"Hmm, yes, I see. Under normal circumstances, a body would be carried away for miles by the current but it seems this poor chap was trapped, possibly by a cable or something similar,"

"Or maybe his killer anchored him to the wreck," Drake suggested, "maybe hoping he'd just decompose and disappear."

"He didn't know a lot then, did he?" said Ridley. "The wetsuit would afford a degree of protection against decomposition and the body would slowly break down within the suit but certainly wouldn't disappear. After all the bloody suit's made of neoprene and rubber," he went on.

"You seem well versed in such things, Gareth," Brian Jones said.

"I've dealt with a few recoveries of bodies from the sea," Ridley replied. "One gets used to the effects of the ocean on the human body after a few of those, I can tell you."

"Yes, Unfortunately, I suppose you do," said the Falmouth Detective.

Clearing the breakwater, *H.M.S Wyvern* headed out into the English Channel and Carole St Clair stood staring straight ahead through the bridge viewscreen, as the gently rolling waves lifted the sharp prow of the ship and then just as gently lowered it into its equally placid troughs. Amazingly, she felt fine, but deferred from moving from her position or looking around for fear the movement might bring on a bout of sea-sickness.

A voice spoke from beside her.

"How are you holding up, Carole?"

It was Gareth Ridley.

"Oh, fine so far, thank you. Your steward seems to know what he's doing with that concoction of his."

"I'm pleased to hear it. By the way, he's not 'my' steward. I don't usually serve aboard the *Wyvern*. I only met him when I came aboard last night."

"But than how did you know he could…?

"I told you in the wardroom. Every wardroom steward worth his salt has a recipe for something similar. It wouldn't do for the ordinary seamen to see one of their officers looking green around the gills with sea-sickness, so they all seem to come up with a sure-fire cure to keep their officers on their feet and fully operational."

"Well, I'm grateful to him, anyway," St Clair replied. "What was his name again?"

"Bowles, Leading Seaman Bowles."

"Well, I hope I get the chance to thank him before we leave the ship."

"I'm sure you'll get the opportunity," Ridley said, smiling at the attractive sergeant.

Izzie Drake couldn't help but notice the attention the handsome marine lieutenant was paying to the attractive Cornish detective and smiled to herself, suspecting a budding romance being born before her eyes.

For now though, they were heading further away from Falmouth with each passing minute and she moved to stand beside Andy Ross as they watched with interest as the bridge crew managed the running of the ship.

Ross felt comforted by the sight of the gun mounted on the deck ahead of the bridge. Though equipped with only one barrel as opposed to those massive three barrelled turrets he remembered from the battleships in the movies, this was a modern, computer controlled weapon that packed a deadly punch. No one would stand in their way as they explored the wreck, of that he was sure. Whatever fate had befallen the poor soul who remained floating above the wreck, nothing similar would happen today.

* * *

Ninety minutes later, the deck of the *Wyvern* was a veritable hive of activity as her crew prepared the equipment necessary for the forthcoming exploration of the sea bed. An air of quiet expectancy pervaded the ship, no more so than on the bridge, where Ross and the other police officers stood watching the myriad activities taking place around them, whilst feeling a little helpless not to be directly involved in this stage of the operation.

Together, they watched as the submersible being used for the dive was made ready for sea. Bright yellow, with twin Perspex bubbles that formed the viewing windows for the two man crew, the strange-looking craft possessed a series of mechanical 'arms' with various configurations at the end that could be used for underwater retrieval purposes, and what appeared to be powerful headlights mounted, front and rear, that would illuminate the depths around the craft.

Two men appeared on the bridge, and reported first to Captain Howell. They were the two man crew of the submersible, Lieutenant Dave Cox, and Chief Petty Officer Bob Lomax, affectionately known to the rest of the *Wyvern's* crew as *The X-Men* due to the matching letters at the end of their surnames.

"All ready, chaps?" Howell asked the pair.

"We are, sir," Cox replied for them both. "Any last instructions?"

"Better ask Detective Inspector Ross, Lieutenant. He might have something to add to your earlier briefing."

"Sir?" Cox asked, looking at Ross.

"I've nothing to add, Lieutenant Cox," Ross said. "Please remember that as far as we, that is the police are concerned, it's important to try and identify that body. So again, please do the best you can to recover it intact, if you can."

Cox snapped a quick salute at Ross.

"You can count on us sir, don't you worry."

"Better be on your way then," Howell said as the pair quickly left the bridge and made their way to their craft.

Five minutes later, the deck crew had lowered the submersible to the sea's surface and amid a large stream of bubbles, it slowly disappeared beneath the waves.

"It's a weird looking vehicle," Izzie Drake commented as she watched it dive under the waves.

"Looks can be deceptive, Sergeant," Howell replied. "It's American designed but built over here under licence. It can go where divers can't, can lift a payload ten times its own weight, and yet, in the right hands, its arms can pick up a seashell from the ocean bed without crushing it. If anyone can find anything to help you in your investigation, it's Cox and Lomax, and the *Watson*."

"Watson?" Brian Jones asked.

"Ah yes," Howell replied. "As I told you earlier, we have two submersibles on board and rather than refer to them by their identification numbers, which seemed a tad impersonal, the dive crews christened them *Holmes* and *Watson*. Seemed appropriate really, as they are used mostly for underwater investigative purposes."

"Good choice of names, Captain," the Cornish D.I. answered, approvingly.

"How long till they reach the wreck, Captain?" Carole St Clair asked, all her earlier seasickness having disappeared completely.

"Not long," said Lieutenant Commander Mike Sutherland, the *Wyvern's* first officer who was tracking the submersible's dive on a computer screen off to one side of the bridge. "I reckon she'll reach the bottom in another minute or so."

Sure enough, the cameras onboard the submersible were soon enabling them to see the sea bed. Cox and Lomax had stated that for safety's sake they would aim to arrive at the bottom some thirty yards or so west of the wreckage, then take a slow look around to ascertain there were no visible impediments to a close inspection of the wreck.

Ross, Drake and the two Falmouth police officers all gathered around the viewing monitor, watched in total fascination for the next twenty minutes as Cox and Lomax carried out their initial survey of the wreck. Next they swung the *Watson* round to approach the gently swaying body of the frogman.

Cox's voice came over the radio, loud and clear.

"It's a body alright, confirmed. Tell the inspector it definitely looks like murder. We're going in closer but we can see from here the body is attached to the wreck with a length of chain, and it's evident the poor bastard's air hose was cut."

Ross merely nodded. He could think of nothing to say for a moment, his thoughts focused on the horrible death the victim had endured. He'd drowned, his air piece cut though and his leg chained to the wreck, left to struggle as his air ran out and his lungs filled with seawater.

It was Izzie Drake who spoke first.

"Are you able to release the body and bring it up, Lieutenant Cox?"

"Yes, we are," Cox replied from the submersible. "It's evident from here however that there won't be much left. What hasn't decomposed has been picked off by the fishes as far as we can see."

"Inside a wet-suit?" St Clair added.

"Yes, sergeant," Cox answered. "The wet suit might look intact in the photos you showed us but there are numerous tears and rips in it which would have let our finny friends in."

"Damn," said Ross at last. "I suppose that buggers up our chances of identifying the poor guy."

"Not necessarily," came the voice of C.P.O. Lomax, speaking for the first time since the submersible had arrived over the wreck. "It's possible, if he used his own equipment, that you can trace him through the serial numbers on his air tanks."

"We can?" Ross asked.

"Yes, Inspector," said Lomax, "believe me, it can be done."

"Thanks, Lomax," said Ross.

They all watched fascinated as Cox and Lomax gently manoeuvred *Watson*, and using the mechanical arms, carefully cut the floating body free and lowered it into a metal cradle at the side of the submersible, which was then covered with a metal lid to ensure the contents couldn't float away.

"Moving on to inspect the rest of the wreckage now," said Cox as *Watson* slowly moved up and over what would have been the forward deck of the corvette.

The next hour saw *Watson* cover every inch of the wreck, and then move on to the remains of the submarine trapped under what remained of the corvette's keel. In close up, through the submersible's cameras, those watching were left in no doubt that they were seeing the shattered remains of a second world war German U-boat.

Cox and Lomax kept up a steady stream of comments and observations, and Ross noticed a young rating standing close to the captain, making copious notes of the submersible crew's words. Marine Lieutenant, Gareth Ridley noticed Ross and Drake looking quizzically at one another and stepped across to explain.

"That seaman is what's known as a 'Ship's Writer' and is obviously qualified in shorthand. He's taking down every word they're saying and will transcribe it when they come to the surface so we'll have a full record of everything that's happened down there. Normally, we'd just have the recordings taken during a dive but the captain thought, as this is a police case, you'd want the equivalent of a written statement of everything that transpires down there."

"That's really helpful," said Ross. "I'll remember to thank Captain Howell later."

Ross could see that Howell was busily engaged in a lively conversation with Captain Prendergast. The retired captain had become extremely animated from the moment the submersible had begun transmitting pictures of the wreck to the *Wyvern*. As the man responsible for looking into the case of the sunken corvette on behalf of the Navy's historical branch, Prendergast was now in his element. More than once, Ross heard him mention the name *Norwich* and he felt reasonably sure that the ship down on the sea bed was indeed the one Prendergast had hypothesised it to be.

An hour after it had first sunk beneath the waves, the submersible *Watson* returned to the surface, and was soon retrieved from the sea, and secured on deck. The hatches opened and Cox and Lomax exited the craft, stretching their cramped limbs as their feet came to rest on the *Wyvern's* deck once more.

The two men looked up towards the bridge, Cox giving a thumbs-up signal to those watching their disembarkation from *Watson*. The deck crew was already at work extricating the frogman's remains from *Watson's* cradle. It would soon be undergoing an examination by the ship's senior medical officer.

Captain Howell turned to the watching band of police officers and coast guard officer, and said, "We'll give them a half-hour to change and get some refreshment and then we'll hold the debriefing. From what we've heard already, it should be very interesting."

Ross agreed, and at Howell's invitation, the party of visitors, accompanied by Lieutenant Ridley, left the bridge, went below to the wardroom and were served fresh coffee and hot croissants as they waited somewhat impatiently for the arrival of Cox and Lomax, when they would learn in full the results of their preliminary inspection of the wrecks on the sea bed.

CHAPTER 25

PLOTS AND PLANS

William Evans was not a happy man. As head of Aegis's UK facility, life had been good to him so far. His wife loved England, they had a beautiful house overlooking the sea, and his kids had not only settled well into the local school, but they actually preferred British TV to that at home. Okay, so the coffee was crap, but what the hell, you couldn't have everything. Ten minutes earlier however, news reached him of a disquieting nature following a knock on his office door.

The door had opened to admit Ryan Newton, Deputy Director of the facility.

"Hello Ryan, what can I do for you?" he'd asked as Newton walked into the office.

"You wanted to know what the Royal Navy were doing here, William?"

"You've found out?"

"Yes, it was easy enough. I just asked the dock superintendant, in a very casual manner as I took a walk along the quayside."

"Okay, okay, and what did the man tell you?"

"Apparently, one of the crew told him they were here to search for a World War Two warship that was reported missing but never found. Seems they have an idea it might have sunk somewhere in our vicinity."

"I see," Evans had answered. "Did this man tell the superintendant anything else?"

"Only that for some reason, a delegation of police officers and the coastguard were sailing with them."

"I see, well, thanks Ryan. I don't suppose they will be interfering with us if they're on a glorified salvage mission,"

"Just what I thought too," Newton had replied. "Will there be anything else?"

"No, thanks for coming in to let me know, Ryan. As you say, nothing to concern us."

As soon as Ryan Newton closed the door on his way out, Evans's face darkened and his bunched up fist thumped into his desk top, the resulting vibration making pens and pencils dance off the edge of the desk and fall clattering to the floor.

"Damn, damn, damn," Evans cursed to himself.

In point of fact, there was much for Evans to worry about, despite his outward calm in front of his deputy. As soon as he was sure he had total privacy, the director picked up his phone, pressed the number 9 to give himself an outside line and dialled a number that was answered on the third ring.

"Finch," was the one word reply as the recipient of the call picked up at the other end.

"It's me," said Evans, knowing the other man would immediately recognise his voice."

"What's wrong," the man named Finch asked, instantly sensing the tension in Evans's voice. "You do realise what time it is here, don't you? Do we have a problem?"

"Yes I do and yes, we may have," Evans replied. "The bloody Royal Navy has turned up with a bloody great frigate, or salvage tug, I don't know what they call it. Some damned police officers from Liverpool and a couple of locals are with them. They sailed from Falmouth this morning. Our contact says they're searching for a missing ship from the war years."

"And you think it's our ship, right?"

"Oh, come on Finch, what do you think? It's too much of a coincidence them turning up like this, especially with coppers from Liverpool. It can't be any other ship, can it? They must have pieced some of it together. I said it was a fucking mistake getting rid of that kid who was nosing around."

"So what do you think we should have done? He'd already got Knowles involved and that German historian who was nosing around last year could have been in league with the kid too for all we know. Maybe we should have done him as well."

"Don't say that, Finch. You know as well as I do that Haller was too high profile, a respected expert in his field. Another disappearance would definitely have drawn attention to us. As it is they could well be on to us now."

"And maybe they're not. Stop panicking until you know more. Okay, the kid might have said something to someone and they know there's a ship down there, but they can't know for sure that Aegis has anything to do with it, or with the death of Decker."

"But what about Knowles? Those stupid goons we paid to get rid of him left him chained to the bloody wreck, for God's sake. They'll probably find his body and then they really will have something to be suspicious about."

"After over a year? I doubt there's anything left down there by now. The fishes will have feasted on Mr. Knowles long ago, I'm sure."

"Listen, Finch, whatever you say, as far as I'm concerned the whole operation's at risk now. We've almost finished our work on the wreck site as it is, but we need at least two more dives to complete the salvage operation. If only Aaron Decker had backed off and taken the money we offered him, everything would have been okay."

"But he didn't, did he, Billy Boy? Now, we have to make the best of the current circumstances."

Evans hated it when Finch called him that name. His over - familiarity grated on Evans. Just who the hell did Finch think he was talking to? William Evans was no two-bit lackey, for Christ's sake.

"So what do you suggest we do?" he asked, doing his best to control his temper.

"We wait, Billy Boy, that's what we do. We wait until the Navy comes back to port and you use your contacts, or bribe some new ones, to find out just what they've found and more to the point what they intend to do next. Just remember, the police have no idea what they're looking for down there, and with a bit of luck, they never will. Call me again when you have something real to report, and for Christ's sake, remember the time, Billy Boy."

The line went dead before William Evans could say another word. He banged the phone down on its cradle, more incensed by Finch's use of the name 'Billy Boy' than anything else the man had said. He knew only too well that what Finch had said made sense, but he couldn't help but feel that things were slowly slipping out of control here on the south coast of England and wished he could be back in Greece, where things had run much more smoothly on his last 'exploration'.

Back in the States, the man known as Finch now made a phone call, this time to Francis Kelly.

"Mr. Kelly," he said as soon as the other man replied. "William Evans sounds as if he's on the verge of panic in England."

"That's not like Evans," said Kelly.

"He thinks the police are on to something. They've got the Royal Navy searching for the *Norwich* as we speak."

"Ah," said Kelly, "perhaps I was remiss in saying too much to that German, Haller, last year. I should never have told him we were searching for three wrecks that could be undesignated war graves. At the time, I thought it would deflect him from our operations if he believed we were carrying out legitimate and authorised work and that he would take it no further. Looks like I was wrong. Damn these people. Why can't the historians and the police keep their noses out of other people's business? Are we anywhere near completion in the English channel, Finch?"

"Yes, sir, we are. Evans estimated another two dives and we'd have everything we can possibly expect to lift from the submarine, but as you know, we have had to leave a respectable time between our dives on the wreck, just in case anyone gets suspicious, and now that the Royal Navy is on site we look like missing out on those last two dives. Looks like we're left holding a busted flush, Mr. Kelly."

"Sadly, Mr. Finch, I do believe you're right. It may be time to cut our losses as far as the U.K. is concerned, if you follow my meaning."

Finch simply nodded his head as he understood exactly what Kelly was referring to.

"No loose ends I take it, sir?"

"You've got it, Mr. Finch, no loose ends. Time for you to visit your old homeland I believe.

* * *

With the dive crew changed into fresh clothes and rejuvenated by mugs of hot coffee, Cox and Lomax now sat opposite the gathered assembly of police officers, plus Prendergast and Baldacre, in the *Wyvern's* wardroom.

With Captain Howell, and Lieutenant Commander Mike Sutherland seated either side of the submersible crew, and Gareth Ridley and two of his marines guarding the door, Lieutenant Cox was the first to speak after Charles Howell asked him to begin.

"Based on what we were told before we began the dive, first thing to report is that the ship down there is definitely a World War Two designed corvette, and we're pretty sure it is the ship suggested by Captain Prendergast, *H.M.S. Norwich*. Despite the ravages of time and ocean currents, it's quite incredible that so much of the ship is still in once piece, though that may have something to do with the fact she's not entirely buried into the sea bed.

C.P.O Lomax and I are in agreement that, unbelievable as it may sound, the *Norwich* appears to have sunk and then landed on top of the submarine, which must have been lying silently on the bottom as part of her captain's evasion tactics. Sadly, he failed."

Cox now motioned to Lomax, who rose and turned on the screen of the monitor that stood at the end of the table. Instantly, those round the table found themselves watching a re-run of the *Watson's* progress as she made her dive on the wreck, with Cox now commentating.

"We can see quite clearly the damage to her starboard side," Cox went on.

"Would you say she was sunk by a torpedo?" George Baldacre, the Coast Guard asked.

"I'd say no," C.P.O. Lomax joined in the conversation. "A torpedo would have penetrated the hull and the explosive damage would have displayed a different pattern, with a smaller initial entry 'wound 'if you like, and more internal damage as the warhead exploded and the blast wave moved through the interior of the compartment where it struck. If you look at the bloody great hole in her side, and the way the plates have been blown inwards, I'd make an educated guess that she struck a mine."

"But surely the Germans weren't able to lay mines in the English Channel during the war?" Ross commented.

"No, Andy, they didn't," Charles Howell replied, "but we did."

"You mean she blundered into one of our own minefields?"

"No, Andy, that I very much doubt, but there were plenty of occasions where mines broke adrift from their moorings after being laid and were known as 'floaters', simply bobbing around in the open sea waiting to catch any ship unwary enough to run into them."

"Oh God," said Izzie Drake. "That brings a whole new meaning to the phrase 'friendly fire."

"I guess it does," Mike Sutherland said. "A whole ship's crew, by all accounts, lost to one of our own mines."

"A bad show, Mike," Howell agreed. "So, carry on gentlemen," he gestured to Cox and Lomax, who had waited patiently as the others talked, Lomax having used a remote control to pause the view on the monitor. He now set it going again and Cox took up the commentary once more.

Watson is of course too big for us to effect an entry into the wreck but we did send the ROV, that's a Remotely Operated Underwater Vehicle for our new friends," he explained, "in to have a quick look. You've probably seen similar things before if you've ever watched *Titanic*."

Ross and the others nodded in the affirmative as the small, bright yellow ROV appeared as it left the deck of the submersible and filled the viewer for a few seconds until it slowly entered the cavernous hole in the side of the *Norwich*.

"C.P.O. Lomax is piloting *Moriarty* in this sequence."

"You gave the ROV a name too?" Carole St. Clair asked with a hint of surprise.

"Of course," said Cox. "Makes it more fun, and gives the vehicle a touch of personality."

Carole St. Clair privately thought these Royal Navy types were definitely a classic case of boys and their toys, but kept her opinion to herself.

"So, here we go," said Lomax as the *Moriarty* moved into the dark interior of the *Norwich*, its path highlighted by a series of very powerful head-lights mounted on the ROV.

The others watched in awe as the little yellow vehicle made its way very slowly into the dark abyss of the *Norwich's* long dead compartments. It was evident to all that Chief Petty Officer Lomax was highly skilled in the operation of the ROV as it alternately glided and hovered as it probed deeper into the ship. It felt eerie to them as *Moriarty* showed empty corridors, twisted bulkheads and hundreds of tiny fishes, illuminated and twinkling like living stars by the ROV's powerful lights. A large crab scuttled across the sloping sand covered deck, startled by this alien invader into its current home. Ross and the others were relieved that no skeletal remains suddenly leaped out at them, disturbed by the movement of the ROV, but Lomax quickly put their minds at rest.

"Don't worry people, you won't see any bodies or human remains in there. They will have long ago disappeared. We didn't probe too far this time. We can go back again, but it was important to get an idea of the damage caused to the interior of the ship. We're moving into what would, I think, have been the wardroom now."

Having been so graciously entertained here in the *Wyvern's* wardroom, Ross and Drake especially felt the poignancy of seeing the smaller and long ago deserted wardroom of the *Norwich*. They could imagine the men who served on board this ship taking a few minutes in the midst of war to grab a quick bite to eat or a mug of tea, to rest between shifts or perhaps sit and write a letter to a loved one. Sitting beside Izzie Drake, Sergeant Carole St. Clair felt particularly affected by the sight, as she wondered if the *Norwich's* wardroom steward had had his own equally efficacious cure for sea-sickness, similar to that provided by Leading Seaman Bowles here on the *Wyvern* and a lump formed in her throat as she wondered what the final moments must have been like for him and his crewmates as the ship blew up and the seawater burst into her corridors and lower decks. Carole found herself hoping he hadn't suffered. A few remnants of dinner plates, a couple of spoons and what may have been a tin mug gleamed momentarily in *Moriarty's* lights and then were gone.

After another few minutes, and a brief examination of what remained of the bridge, Lomax had extricated the ROV from the interior of the wreck, satisfied there was nothing more he could do in the time he'd been allotted for this part of the mission.

Moriarty was slowly returned to its docking station on the submersible and then they watched, fascinated, as *Watson* glided imperiously over to the port side of the *Norwich* and closed in on the grim sight of whatever remained of the frogman's body, now fully illuminated by the powerful headlights of the *Watson*.

Lt. Cox took up the commentary again as the eerie sight came into closer focus.

"The poor bastard, excuse me ladies, is tethered to a surviving section of the port side dock rail. I'm not a pathologist or a specialist in forensics of course, but if you ask me, whoever did this chained him to the railing first then cut through his air hose with a diver's knife or similar instrument and he was left to thrash about, unable to get free as he drowned."

"The hallmark of a real sadist at work, I'd say," D.I. Jones spoke before anyone else could comment.

"I'd agree with that, Brian," Ross concurred.

The scene played on, on the monitor screen.

"Look closely," said Cox, "and I think you'll see that the diving suit is quite badly torn in places. The fact that water has entered the suit probably made you think it was a fully intact body when you saw those photographs you spoke of, but once we get our divers down there, I'm sure we'll find there's not much left of the poor bugger who was in that suit. But, the air tanks are still there and we should be able to trace them at least once we get the remains to the surface. Our second dive team is scheduled to go down in an hour now that we know the lay of the land, so to speak,"

"They're not using a submersible?" asked Izzie Drake.

"Yes, they are," Cox replied. "They're using *Holmes*, which differs from *Watson* in that it can be used for jobs like this. There's a hatch that allows one crew member to exit the craft to work outside while the other crewman keeps the vessel on station and can be called upon to use the mechanical arms as directed by the man outside."

Cox fell silent then, as the others watched the monitor closely, taking in the sad scene as the picture showed the dead frogman, or rather what was left of him, in much closer detail than they'd seen so far. As Cox had intimated, they could now see the holes and gashes in the wetsuit, where the denizens of the deep had made inroads into the suit and doubtless feasted on the flesh and bones of the dead man, presuming of course, Ross thought, that it was a man. He didn't think this was the best time to suggest it could just as easily have been a woman.

"Okay, now we move on again," said Cox as the picture on the screen seemed to tip on its side for a few seconds, which indicated *Watson's* progress over the side of the ship and subsequent nose down position as they moved to inspect what lay beneath the keel of the *Norwich*.

"This is where things get really interesting," Lomax took over the tour. "I know you officers are interested in the body of course, but look here."

As he spoke the lights of the *Watson* illuminated the unmistakeable, sleek black shape of the U-Boat.

"It's hard for you to make it all out clearly if you're not familiar with such things, but take it from me, this was one hell of a disaster. From the positions of the two vessels and the fact that the keel of the corvette is so well buried into the deck of the sub it looks as if the ship sank quickly and in doing so, by a stroke of awful bad luck, landed directly on top of the U-

Boat, trapping it on the sea bed. A lot of the stern end of the sub is buried well into the sea bed, but you can see the bow section clearly. Her bow planes are still in place, remarkably, in full horizontal position which tells us her captain had taken her down to the bottom and was holding position in the hope the corvette, which we assume was hunting him, passed over without sensing his presence."

They all watched enthralled as the sharp prow of the U-Boat came into clear view in the lights. They could make out the dark, threatening openings to the torpedo tubes and Andy Ross wondered how many times those tubes must have launched their cargoes of death in the months or years before the submarine met its own death here on the bottom of the English Channel. Lomax had fallen silent as he allowed the pictures on screen to speak for themselves. Everyone seemed to be watching in respectful silence as though all were aware that they were looking at the last resting place of maybe two hundred or more men in total.

Ross stood almost rigid as the lights of the submersible next picked out the U-Boat's deck gun, rusting and useless, but still looking lethal, pointing towards the surface of the sea as though waiting for the ghostly hands of her crew to spring to action stations to defend the sub from any and all comers. Ross shivered at the eerie thought. As though sensing his thoughts, in that strange way the two seemed to read each other's thoughts, Izzie Drake reached up to her full height and whispered in his ear.

"Still looks ready to fire, doesn't it, sir?"

"Hmm," Ross grunted, not able to say much as the emotion of the moment washed over him like a spectral hand.

The conning tower came next, its array of antennas and the periscope housing clearly still discernible though the small deck section had long since collapsed into the sub's interior. It was as the *Watson* slowly glided over the top of the conning tower and began to descend down the starboard side that Lomax spoke again.

"Now, this is where things get *really* interesting," he said, dragging out the word 'really' so it sounded like 'reeeeally'.

The others watched as the lights picked out a large hole in the side of the conning tower. One didn't need to be an expert to realise it had not been caused by the corvette landing on and crushing the sub into the sea bed.

"What the hell?" said Brian Jones.

"By jove," exclaimed Prendergast.

"Bloody hell," said Ross.

"Wow," Carole St. Clair frowned at the sight.

"Never seen anything like it," George Baldacre the coast guard added.

"Now, that's what I'd call unusual, not that I know much about it," Izzie Drake spoke quietly, putting things into some small degree of perspective.

In the few seconds they'd taken to make the array of comments, Ross had noticed that the hole in the side of the conning tower had quite obviously been made from the outside, as if a giant drill had somehow bored its way through the shell of the submarine and into the darkness that lay beyond.

"Looks like a giant lamprey's been feeding on it," Captain Howell now commented, having remained silent as they'd watched the images captured by his submersible crew.

"What's that?" Drake asked.

"A lamprey? It's a very archaic fish, Sergeant, I mean Izzie. It's an ugly little bugger with a big, round mouth at the end of its head. It latches on to its prey, for example a bigger fish, and literally bores its way into the other fish's body and eats it alive from the inside out."

"Blood hell," Drake exclaimed. "Sounds a real monster."

"In a way it is, said Howell, "but a very successful monster. The lamprey has been around for thousands of years and is still going strong, so it must be doing something right."

"Anyway, let's get back on course," said Prendergast. "What do you think you were looking at Lieutenant Cox?"

"Someone's been using some powerful underwater cutting equipment on her," said Cox. "They obviously knew what they were doing because it would have much harder for them to get through the double hull if they'd tried going through the sides of the sub, and the pressure hull, if still intact would have resisted even modern cutting equipment."

"So, it looks as if this is about the submarine and not the corvette," said Ross, thoughtfully.

"It must have been carrying something important," said Drake.

"Important and worth killing for," Brian Jones added.

"We need to find out what was on that submarine," Ross said.

"But to do that, we somehow have to identify the U-Boat," Prendergast added, "and that won't be easy, unless we can find something inside her to assist in the identification. Once upon a time, U-Boats carried their number on the conning tower, but the practice stopped during the war years." He seemed lost in thought for a few seconds and then something clicked in his memory. "Hang on though, there might be an easier way."

"We're listening, Captain." Ross said, expectantly.

"If my memory serves me right, and perhaps your friend Herr Haller can confirm this, the U-Boat builders were very proud of their craft and would usually inscribe the number of the boat they were working on into various parts of the boat, most commonly the periscope housing and the interiors of the torpedo tubes."

"Divers can check that out, sir, at least on the periscope housing," Lomax volunteered.

"That's right sir," Cox agreed. "I can brief Baines and Christie before

633

they go down and tell them to check out the periscope housing. I doubt they'll be able to gain access to the torpedo rooms though."

"It's worth a try," said Captain Howell. "Brief them as soon as we've finished here, please Lieutenant."

"Aye, sir," Cox replied.

"And, Lieutenant?"

"Sir?"

"Tell them there's been a change in plan. Double the dive team. I want four men down there this time, two on the corvette and two on the U-Boat. Let's get this job done as fast as we can."

"Aye, sir," said Cox again.

"Gareth," Howell said to the marine lieutenant, still positioned at the doorway, "your men are all dive trained and qualified, right?"

"Yes, sir, they are."

"Okay, I want two of your marines to form the second dive team. Your men can take the sub while our lads take the corvette."

"Got it sir. I'll go and brief my lads."

"Good man," said Howell and the young marine saluted and went to ready his men.

"Any particular reason you're sending marines down to the sub, Charles?" Ross asked the captain.

"You're an astute man, Andy," the captain smiled at him. "I very much doubt we're in any danger out here. No one in their right mind is going to attack a Royal Navy frigate in broad daylight, but that's not to say there might not be something nasty waiting for us down there."

It was the retired submarine commander, Captain Prendergast who reacted first to Howell's words.

"You're thinking whoever plundered the U-Boat wreck might have booby-trapped her, aren't you, Charles?"

"It's a possibility," Howell confirmed. "If you'd been responsible for stealing God knows what from that wreckage, and if it was valuable enough to kill for, wouldn't you want to make sure nobody else found out what you'd been up to?"

"But wouldn't it have been easier to just blow up the remains of the submarine and the warship?" D.I. Jones asked.

"Not as easy as that," C.P.O. Lomax provided his answer. "Put together, the corvette and the sub constitute a sizable chunk of scrap metal, stuck on the bottom of the sea bed. It would take a bloody great explosive charge to blow the lot to smithereens, and the explosion would probably have been big enough that any shipping in the vicinity could have heard or felt the pressure waves from it and reported it to the authorities. This way, if the skipper's right, they lay sneaky little traps to catch the unwary and no one's the wiser."

"Thank you for that erudite explanation, Lomax," the captain grinned.

"You're welcome sir," said Lomax. "Couldn't think of a better word than sneaky, begging your pardon, sir."

"Probably right on the mark, actually," Howell replied.

"I'm sure Ridley's boys know what they're doing sir," Cox asserted.

As scheduled by the *Wyvern's* captain, one hour later, the much larger submersible, the affectionately named *Holmes*, took to the water. She held the *Wyvern's* second dive team, Lieutenant Dave Baines and Petty Officer Lee Christie. A fifth man, Chief Petty Officer Chris Dowling was at the controls, a last minute addition to the team that would enable both pairs of divers to work as couples, both for safety and because, as Howell pointed out, two divers could produce twice the results in half the time possible for one. *Holmes* could carry up to six people and so now held Dowling, Christie and Baines and the two marine divers, both petty officers, Al Sharp and Billy Kendall. Those two would both dive on the U-Boat, keeping a sharp eye out for each other amidst the possible danger of booby traps, as they'd been briefed. Dowling would remain on board the Holmes, keeping the submersible on station as the divers carried out their exploration, monitoring their air supplies, dive times, crucial to ensuring the divers well being, as well as being in a position to assist in case of unforeseen accidents. Gareth Ridley spent a good five minutes explaining to their guests the dangers associated with diving on such wrecks, particularly once the divers entered the dark and potentially wreckage-strewn compartments of both the corvette and the U-Boat.

As Ross and his comrades again held a watching brief on the bridge of the *Wyvern*, he and Drake both shared the feeling that they were about to find some, if not all of the answers to the mystery surrounding Aaron Decker's seemingly senseless murder."

CHAPTER 26

"IT'S JUST NOT CRICKET, YOU KNOW"

Detective Chief Inspector Oscar Agostini placed the phone down on its cradle at the end of a most illuminating phone call. Andrew Montfort, one of the chief supporters of the university sports department, but especially the cricket club, had taken him by surprise with his call.

Agostini sat thinking for a minute and then picked up the phone again. When Paul Ferris answered his extension, Agostini asked him to find Sam Gable and Derek McLennan and send them to his office. Ten minutes later the two detectives found themselves in Agostini's office, wondering if they were about to receive some kind of reprimand for some unknown infraction they'd committed.

Seeing their body language and sensing their tension, the D.C.I. smiled and invited them to sit.

"Don't panic. You're not here for a bollocking. Far from it. You and the team have been working like Trojans in D.I. Ross and Sergeant Drake's absence, so just relax, okay?"

Both detective constables visibly relaxed their postures, and Sam Gable replied, "Thank you, sir. What can we do for you?"

Agostini looked at his desk, checking through the notes he'd made on an A4 pad as he'd listened to what Andrew Montfort had to say.

"Right, here goes. A few minutes ago I received a phone call from Andrew Montfort. Either of you heard of him?"

"I have, sir," Sam Gable said. "Isn't he some wealthy entrepreneur who supports various charities and good causes in the city?"

"That's right, he does," Agostini confirmed. "Well, apparently, he also gives his family name to an annual cricket match that takes place between Liverpool and Manchester Universities, the aptly named Montfort Trophy, no less. It seems Montfort is a great cricket fan and was there to watch this year's match, which Aaron Decker starred in apparently. He speaks very well, very posh, and rather olde worlde, if you know what I mean, all "I say, sir," and "Bad show" sort of thing. Seems he watched this year's trophy match, presented the trophy to the winners, Liverpool of course, and the man of the match prize to Decker and then jetted off the next day to Barbados where he has a private estate. He only returned to this country a few days ago and was shocked to hear of Aaron Decker's murder."

"And I take it he had something important to tell us, sir?" D.C. McLennan asked as Agostini paused for a second to draw breath.

"He did, McLennan, or rather, let's call it something of interest to us that may be of help in the investigation. According to Mr. Montfort, he was rather surprised when he first heard that Aaron Decker was sharing a house with Tim Knight."

Agostini paused again, for effect this time and it worked, as the looks on Gable and McLennan's faces confirmed.

"But we were led to believe they were good friends, sir, and the other lad in the house, Martin Lewis," said Gable.

"Yes, sir, all our inquiries so far have shown no evidence of any bad blood between them, apart from that one instance of Knight trying to pull Decker's girlfriend, but that was before Aaron and Sally got together so we couldn't see it being very significant and even Sally Metcalfe said it was all something and nothing," McLennan added.

"Hmm, well, all was not as clear cut as it appears according to Mr. Montfort." Agostini replied. "It would appear that Aaron Decker's closest friend on the team was the captain, Simon Dewar, and not, as he'd have you believe, Tim Knight. Montfort told me that when Decker was first spotted and included in the team there was some initial feeling against him among some of the players, this new arrival from America of all places, suddenly coming on the scene and showing our lads how the game should be played, but that soon passed as they realised what an asset young Decker was to the team. One man, however, apparently continued to hold something of a grudge against the new man."

"Tim Knight?"

"Correct," said Agostini in response to Gable's almost rhetorical question.

"Yes, and Montfort was quite adamant about it, told me that until Decker came along, Knight was the golden boy of the team, the one the girls wanted to be seen with and so on. That all changed when Decker joined the cricket team."

"So it's possible that Tim Knight did have a motive, however tenuous, for wishing Decker could be out of the way," said Gable, "though it's still a bit of a stretch to think he might have murdered Aaron Decker over being picked for a cricket team, surely, sir?"

"D.C. Gable, when you've been around as long as I have in this job, almost nothing will surprise you. I've seen murders committed for much less substantial reasons than being selected for the cricket team, I can assure you."

"Yes, of course sir, I just thought it unlikely."

"And under normal circumstances you'd probably be correct in your assumption, but remember this, both of you, murderers are not normal members of our society. Something sets them apart, something that allows them to step over the fine dividing line between what is and is not deemed acceptable behaviour by society. If everyone was like them, we'd be living under the laws of the jungle, kill or be killed, survival of the fittest and all that crap, if you understand my meaning."

"Yes, I see what you mean sir," Gable replied,

"That's an interesting way of putting it, sir," said Derek McLennan. "What you're really saying is you believe murderers may possess something like an aberrant gene, a fault in their genetic makeup that makes them somehow more prone to exhibiting the kill behaviour trait"

"Well done, McLennan, that's exactly what I'm saying, but of course, that's my own theory and there are others who would disagree with it I'm sure! Anyway, I want you two to go and see Mr. Montfort and get a signed statement from him. Once we have his words on paper, I think it'll be time for an official chat under caution with Mr. Tim Knight."

"You really think he's involved, sir?"

"As D.I. Ross said, Knight and Lewis are the obvious suspects, and sometimes, the obvious suspects are the best suspects, even though it might appear to be too simple a solution. But we'll wait until you've spoken with Montfort, so I suggest the two of you get a move on. Here's his address," Agostini said, handing a piece of paper across his desk, which McLennan took from him and took a quick look at the address.

"Nice," McLennan commented.

"Where are we going, Derek?" Sam Gable asked.

"Formby," McLennan responded. "Cheveley House, which I suppose will be some grand mansion overlooking the sea."

"I don't care if it's a hovel overlooking the Ribble in Clitheroe. Now go on, you two, we've a killer to catch."

McLennan and Gable were soon on their way, heading north towards Formby, after giving Paul Ferris a brief update on the news from the D.C.I. Paul Ferris took a break from his own computer search in order to key their information into his case file and then returned to his trawling of the internet for any inside information he might unearth relating to the Aegis organisation. So far, his efforts had proved frustratingly negative, but as always, optimism and his confidence that he would eventually find something, somewhere, kept him going as his fingers danced across the keyboard, his eyes intently scanning the screen on his desk.

* * *

"Do sit down, please," Andrew Montfort politely invited the two detectives after escorting them into a large sitting room in his Formby home. Not quite as large or as palatial as Derek McLennan expected, but it did overlook the sea, and did look rather grand from the outside, especially as visitors drove along a short but winding drive that was bordered on both sides by well established firs that formed an avenue, and then opened up to reveal full daylight as though exiting a tunnel, with the house sitting just beyond the gravel parking area, with a fountain situated in the centre, water gently cascading from the statue of a young woman holding a pail on her shoulder, from whence the water flowed.

The interior was even more imposing to Derek and indeed to Sam Gable, with what had to be genuine original oil paintings on the walls of the entrance hall, guarded it seemed by two gleaming suits of armour, each standing, holding vicious looking lances, either side of the large staircase that rose in a semi circle from the entrance hall towards the first floor. A mansion? Maybe not, but a beautiful country house for sure. Derek McLennan, brought up in a basic two-up, two-down semi-detached house in Crosby, was impressed!

Despite his obvious wealth and affiliation with the upper echelons of society, Andrew Montfort came across as easy to talk to and was warm and welcoming in his manner towards the two young detectives.

"I know your time is valuable so I took the liberty of ordering tea when I saw you pulling up outside. It will be here any time."

Right on cue, a young woman, dressed in traditional maid's uniform, black dress, white apron and a little white maid's cap, knocked and entered, carrying a silver tray, (McLennan guessed it had to be real silver), and walked across the room, placing the tray on the large coffee table that stood in between the sofa where McLennan and Gable sat and the large winged armchair in which Andrew Montfort had comfortably seated himself.

"Would you like me to pour, sir?" she asked, smiling at her employer as she spoke.

"No, thank you, Terri," Montfort replied, smiling back at the girl. "I'll see to it. I'll call if I need anything else."

"Okay, sir," said Terri, as she turned away and walked from the room, her heels clicking on the wooden border around the thick rug that took up the centre part of the room, finally closing the large, heavy looking door behind her

"Nice girl, Mr. Montfort," McLennan commented.

"Terri? Yes indeed, Mr. McLennan. I'm not one for all the old-fashioned master and servant stuff. Don't be fooled by the classic maid's uniform. Terri loves it, as if she's starring in an episode of *Upstairs, Downstairs*. She achieved a first class degree in English Literature last year and when she heard of my extensive collection of medieval English manuscripts she asked if I'd mind her visiting my library to carry out some post-doctoral research. I ended up hiring her to help me on a part-time basis over coffee and a discussion of Shakespeare's *The Merchant of Venice*. I did laugh when she asked if she could wear a 'proper' maid's uniform, but thought it did no harm to humour her request. If you weren't here, she'd be calling me Andrew and telling me about her latest boyfriend. But, you didn't come here to talk about my domestic arrangements. I presume you know what I told Detective Chief Inspector Agostini on the telephone?"

"Yes, sir," Sam Gable answered his question. "The D.C.I. would appreciate it if you'd go over what you told him once again with us and give us an official statement, for the record."

"Of course, Miss Gable," Montfort replied. "As I told Mr. Agostini on the phone when he asked if I'd see you right away, I'll do anything to help find poor Aaron's killer. I'm only sorry I was out of the country when it happened and only heard of his death on my return, or I'd have been in touch sooner."

"You mustn't feel bad about it," Gable said, reassuringly. Money or not, it was clear to her that Montfort had been shaken by the news of Decker's death and the old man was eager to help if he could. "There was nothing you could have done to prevent it, and you weren't to know what was about to happen when you left for Barbados."

"Quite," was Montfort's short response, which he followed up by shaking his head as he said in a quiet voice, "It just isn't cricket you know."

"Sir?" Gable was lost for a second.

"Sorry, Miss Gable, not cricket, you know? Bad form and all that, taking a young man's life when he had so much to live for."

"Yes, of course," she replied. "And you told D.C.I. Agostini you were surprised that Aaron Decker ended up sharing a dwelling with Tim Knight?"

"Very surprised, young lady, very surprised indeed."

Somehow, the fact that Montfort kept referring to them not by their ranks, but as Mr or Miss and in this case, young lady, seemed perfectly normal to Sam Gable, who wasn't in the least bit put out by what Agostini had described as his 'olde worlde' affectations and mannerisms.

"So, Tim Knight and Aaron Decker weren't the best of friends, as far as you knew?"

"Oh, don't get me wrong, they may have ended up as good friends, but back when young Decker first came on the scene, it wouldn't have taken a detective to work out that a certain amount of jealousy existed on young Tim's side of course. I only saw them on a few occasions back then, when I'd go along to watch the cricket team either in the nets at practice, or in Aaron's first few matches, when the jealousy seemed more apparent."

"So, are you saying the jealousy died away in time, sir?" Derek McLennan asked.

"On the surface, yes," Montfort said, "and of course, it's quite possible they did become closer as Aaron proved himself to be a quite magnificent cricketer, but it still came as a surprise when I learned they were sharing a house."

Thirty minutes later, armed with a signed statement taken down in her notebook by Sam Gable, the two detectives took their leave of Cheveley House, being waved off by the incongruous sight of Andrew Montfort and his erstwhile maid, Terri, standing side by side on the entrance steps of the house smiling together as the police car disappeared from view.

"I'll bet you any money the old boy's bonking that young maid of his," Derek McLennan said as he drove back in the direction of the city.

"Well if he is, that's their business, Derek, isn't it?" Sam replied. "She's not exactly under-age is she?"

"I know, but, I mean, he's old enough to be her father, maybe even her grandfather and, well, you know…"

"I do believe you're jealous of old Andrew Montfort, Derek," Sam grinned at him. "You can't believe an old chap like him might be getting in the pants of a young, gorgeous girl like Terri, where I have no doubt you'd very much like to find yourself, given half a chance."

"Sam!" Derek exclaimed.

"Oh, come on, McLennan," she laughed. "You're only human after all, and I must admit, she did have a great pair of legs, and the rest wasn't bad either."

Derek McLennan blushed bright red, his face an absolute picture as far as Sam Gable was concerned. No one on the team knew much about Derek's life out side of work, but Sam was now fairly certain that his out of work activities clearly didn't involve any young women at that time. *Was Derek a closet virgin?* she chuckled to herself.

"What?" Derek asked, hearing her quietly laughing to herself.

"Oh nothing, Derek," she replied. "Just wondering if Montfort keeps a harem of young women in reserve, waiting for him to summon them to his bedchamber, like some old lord of the manor. Then again, if Terri was the one who instigated the master and maid thing by asking if she could wear the uniform it could easily be her who's the one with the fetish for sex games and Montfort simply can't believe his luck."

"You've got a dirty mind, so you have, Samantha Gable,"

"Sometimes, yes Derek, I most definitely have," Gable smiled again and the two fell into a silence that lasted until they pulled in to the car park at Headquarters, and headed up to the fourth floor to report to D.C.I. Agostini, before hopefully heading out again to bring Tim Knight in for questioning.

CHAPTER 27

PRAYERS FOR THE DEAD

The second dive on the *Norwich* and the as yet unidentified *U3000/U966* had seemed to go on for ever to those waiting patiently on the bridge of *H.M.S. Wyvern*. Ross, Drake and the others had listened intently to the words being transmitted to the surface by the two dive teams, and Ross was at last beginning to understand just what the lure of the old German U-Boat had been for the crooked executives of the Aegis Institute, and why Aaron Decker had said that he thought he might be on to something that might make him a lot of money.

Team One had dived on the *Norwich* and despite no outwardly visible identification marks on the ship, Prendergast assured everyone it could only be the *Norwich*, based on its location and the type of corvette design she adhered to. Pictures coming up from the wreck reminded the watchers of those remarkable underwater shots of the *Titanic* as the divers with their hand held cameras moved silently through the eerie and long ago deserted corridors and companionways of *H.M.S. Norwich*. Meanwhile, everyone watched as the exploration of the wreck revealed one or two poignant reminders of the men who had served on board the corvette. As Baines and Christie swam slowly and carefully into the lower reaches of the corvette, their lights illuminated a familiar shape, trapped under a piece of collapsed and rusting metal, at one time part of a bulkhead. They all recognised it as a pipe, a personal item that belonged at one time to one of the men who bravely went to war on the *Norwich*. Most surprising and of even greater significance perhaps, was the discovery in the ship's engine room of the remains of an officer's cap, still hanging from one of the rusting handles of the ship's engine room telegraph, where possibly the chief engineer might have placed it while he wiped his sweat lined brow, perhaps seconds before *Norwich* struck the mine that destroyed her. Baines brought the telegraph into sharper focus and the watchers on board the *Wyvern* could see that the telegraph was set at 'full ahead' telling the Naval officers present that the *Norwich*, in all probability, had been at flank speed, searching for the submerged U-Boat at the moment she'd struck the mine.

Baines and Christie eventually arrived in the ship's forward section and there, about thirty feet from the bows, they came across the large, gaping hole in the ship's side, where she'd hit the mine, and seeing the twisted mass of metal, Captain Howell ordered them to take no chances by trying to explore further. He instructed the divers to exit the interior of the wreck, taking photos of any serial numbers they might be able to discern on any machinery that could help confirm the ship's identity and then to try to confirm that it had been a mine that had been the probable cause of the ship's demise. Charles Howell had seen enough and after a brief conversation with Anthony Prendergast, it was agreed that identification of the wreck as *H.M.S. Norwich* should be formally entered, provisionally into the *Wyvern's* log at that time.

Captain Anthony Prendergast, R.N. (Retired), knew his own work in connection with the *Norwich* would begin in earnest once he returned to shore, when the task of notifying any living relatives of the crew would begin with an extensive search to trace them, and procedures would be set in motion to have the wreck officially designated as a war grave.

No one felt like talking much at that point. Even Ross, Drake, Jones and St. Clair could sense the overwhelming sense of sadness that seemed to pervade all those present on the *Wyvern's* bridge.

Ross had by now come to understand that to the men of the Royal Navy, a ship was almost a living, breathing entity, an extension of the personalities of the men who crewed her, and in a case like this, the men who died with her. No sooner had those thoughts passed through his mind than he heard the sound of someone praying. Previously unnoticed by all except the Captain and First Officer, the ship's Chaplain had arrived on the bridge and was now praying for the souls lost at the time of the *Norwich's* sinking.

Everyone's attention now turned to the second bridge monitor, where the two marine divers, Sharp and Kendall were making very slow progress in their dive into the interior of the German U-Boat.

* * *

At the same time as Ross and his people were watching the underwater scenes from the wreck site, and as McLennan and Gable were reporting to D.C.I. Agostini on their interview with Andrew Montfort, the man known as Finch sat at a desk in his apartment in the Bay Ridge area of Brooklyn, New York. Finch had been busy planning his next move after his conversation with Francis Kelly. Finch knew exactly what needed to be done and after due consideration he'd made a decision. Finch never rushed into things, which was one of the reasons he'd survived and prospered for so long in his line of work. Few people knew his real name, and those that did had no idea that he was anything other than a successful broker who'd made a small fortune playing the stock exchange for many years. In fact, Finch hadn't set foot on Wall Street for many years, any financial investments he made, and they were numerous, were handled on his behalf by a large brokerage house in the city.

Jerome Decker III would have been surprised and extremely disappointed to know that Finch was a former C.I.A. operative who had turned 'rogue' many years ago, and now ran his very own private 'security' service, selling his and his operatives' skills to the highest bidder, becoming a very rich man in the process.

Finch picked up the phone and dialled an international number, which was answered on the third ring. It was a simple ploy used by Finch and his people. Answer too soon or too late and it would indicate a problem, which could be anything from an operative having been compromised, or just an inopportune moment to take a call. Either way, it meant Finch would call back in thirty minutes and try again.

"Robin here," came the voice over the phone.

"Robin, it's Finch, you ready to go to work?"

"I am indeed," Robin replied, his accent immediately identifying him as English.

"Good. Listen up my friend. Here's what I need you to do."

Robin listened carefully for five minutes as Finch outlined the task that lay ahead of him, taking notes that he would burn as soon the call was over and he'd had chance to memorise them.

"You got all that?" Finch asked after briefing Robin on the job.

"Sure have, Finch. When do you want me to expedite the package?"

"It's of the utmost urgency, Robin. I'd like it very much of you could ensure delivery today. There'll be a large monthly bonus heading your way if you can deliver on time."

"Consider it a done deal," said Robin, a former soldier-turned mercenary who'd found a new and more lucrative career since joining Finch's enterprise. "Any paperwork involved?" he asked, a subtle way of asking for photographs or maps to assist in his assignment.

"Check your email in five minutes," Finch replied.

"That all?"

"That's it. Let me know when the job's done. Usual payment arrangements."

"Okay, Finch."

"Goodbye Robin," said Finch as he hung up and Robin found himself holding a phone connected to dead space.

Exactly five minutes later, Robin's computer gave a single beep, telling him an email had arrived. As promised by Finch the two attachments showed him his targets and exact directions to their location. Robin printed them out, cursing the fact he'd have to travel no more than twenty miles to carry out his mission. He enjoyed long distance travel, warm destinations, pretty women by a swimming pool, but no, Finch was sending him to bloody Liverpool!

Robin quickly packed an overnight bag, not intending to stay the night in Liverpool, but you never knew when plans might need to be changed at a moment's notice and anyway, he needed something to carry the tools of his trade in. His last thoughts as he looked round his flat one last time before locking up was how he hated Finch's stupid idea of giving his operatives the names of birds. *Robin, for God's sake*, he thought. *What am I, Batman's little buddy or something?*

Five minutes later he was on the road, heading along the East Lancs Road to 'Scouseland' as he disparagingly referred to the city of Liverpool. At the same time, Finch was boarding a Delta Airlines transatlantic flight from New York's JFK International Airport to London Heathrow. Finch was heading home to the UK, where he could maintain hands-on control of any clean-up operations that might become necessary if things went pear-shaped with the current situation.

* * *

The interior of *U966* had been kindly treated by time. There was little interior degradation of the main control room or engine room, which was sealed off from the rest of the sub by its watertight doors and the two divers, having entered through the hole that had been cut in the side of the conning tower, were feeling a little spooked by the appearance of the silent eeriness of the U-Boat, which had withstood the ravages of time so well. Those watching from the bridge of the *Wyvern* watched, enthralled, as Sharp and Kendall slowly moved through the deserted interior. As they reached the engine room, the two men joined forces to slowly open the watertight door, and even though the sea immediately began to flood into the compartment, they could clearly see what awaited them.

"Oh shit," Petty Officer Sharp suddenly exclaimed and dropped his powerful hand-held halogen lamp.

"What is it, Sharp?" Gareth Ridley asked his man over the comm. system.

Without a word, Sharp swam down to the deck and retrieved his lamp and then pointed it towards whatever it was that had startled him.

"Oh, dear God," Ross now exclaimed as he too saw the last remains of a body, still dressed in the rags of his uniform, that lay, resting beside one of the submarine's large diesel engines. The atmosphere inside the watertight compartment of the engine room had helped to preserve the body that appeared to be sitting on a stool, peaked cap jauntily propped on the head, sloping to the left side. Before they could do anything, the seawater rushed past them, sweeping the corpse to the floor of the engine room. *U966's* engineering officer Heinz Muller had remained at his post for nearly sixty years, still guarding his precious engines.

"Go no further," Howell ordered. "If there are other sealed compartments they might also contain human remains. We have to respect the dead, no matter what side they were on. Stick to the areas the interlopers have already opened up and let's see if we can find what they were looking for."

"Aye sir, understood. They seem to have concentrated on the for'ard section, so we'll head that way," Sharp acknowledged.

"That was awful," said Carole St. Clair as she exhaled, realising she had been holding her breath as they'd taken in the sight of the skeleton in the engine room.

"If there are more compartments that have remained sealed watertight since the sinking, there could be more remains in there," said Charles Howell. Unlike the *Norwich*, it looks like the sub remained free from the sea's encroachment until our unknown 'friends' came along.

"Oh God, that's so awful to think about," St. Clair said.

"There's one thing that's been bugging me about all this," Izzie Drake now spoke, trying to get back to the real reason for them being here.

"Go on, Izzie, what is it?" Ross asked, knowing that she'd obviously been thinking hard all the time they'd been watching the underwater drama unfold on the bridge monitors.

"Well sir, we're here because someone killed Aaron Decker and in the course of our investigation we found out he was interested initially in researching the company that had offered his girlfriend a job and in the course of so doing he became suspicious about what they were doing in the English Channel. He travelled down here to check them out and then, I'm assuming he followed them out to sea in a boat of some kind and discovered this very spot and came back to investigate by himself later. At some point he involved the historian Haller, who would have been his logical choice, given his expertise in maritime history, and we know that Haller then came down here also, did his best to find out what Aegis were doing, even hiring a boat himself and presumably doing what Decker did in following them out here. Am I right in all that so far?"

"I'd say you are, Izzie. Go ahead, I know you have a point to make here, and I've a feeling I know what it is, but let's wait and see if we agree."

"Okay," Drake continued. "Until we know more about the poor sod who was chained to the wreck down there, we can only speculate as to who he or she may be and what their involvement is, but we're still left with one big burning question as far as I can see."

"Which is?" Ross prompted.

"Well, sir, it's quite simple really. Decker heard about it through his connection to Sally Metcalfe, Haller heard about it from Aaron Decker, but, and this is the sixty thousand dollar question, how the hell did Aegis know about it, and even more important, what led them to believe there was anything valuable to be found on either of the two wrecks?"

"Bravo, Izzie. The same thoughts have been going through my mind too. It seems to me that someone in the Aegis set up had to have had some prior knowledge of the possibility of some kind of valuable cargo existing down there, in all likelihood on the U-Boat. So who told them? Who knows enough about the war at sea and in particular the German U-Boat war to have given them the information that sent them searching in the area in the first place?"

A light went on in Drake's mind at Ross's question and she instantly replied, "Haller? You really think he could be involved in this?"

"Why not? He's an acknowledged expert in the field and like anyone else, he could probably be bought for a large enough sum."

"But he seems too straight, sir, too legit to become involved in something like this."

"I know, Izzie, but if not Haller, then who else do we have? At present, nobody, so it's time we got someone to drive back up to Wrexham and put a little more pressure on Herr Klaus Haller."

"You want me to call Headquarters and get someone out there now, sir?"

"Yes, please Izzie, and send Dodds and Ferris. It'll do Paul good to get away from his computer for a couple of hours, and he's damn good at asking probing questions. Tell them to be respectful but let Haller know we have suspicions. They're to try and get him to open up if he is involved, but if he truly isn't he may know someone who could be helping the murdering bastards at Aegis."

Izzie turned and walked across the bridge, walking out onto one of the bridge wings, where she could talk to the team back home in relative privacy. After speaking to Paul Ferris, she returned to watch the progress of the divers with the others.

* * *

Sharp and Kendall swam slowly through the flooded forward compartments of *U966*. Whoever had found the submarine and broken through into its interior quite clearly hadn't given a damn about preserving any human remains that might have been present. Any such remains would by now have floated clear of the U-Boat's hull and been lost to the

648

sea forever. Prendergast had vowed to himself that at some point in the future, he would contact the German Navy and arrange a joint recovery operation to access the sealed rear compartments of the submarine in the hope of recovering any preserved remains. For the time being though, he watched with the others as the two divers explored further into the eerie wreck.

Kendall was the first to break the silence that had accompanied their progress since the ill-fated foray into the engine room.

"I think we've found what they were looking for," he reported.

"What do you see, Kendall?" Captain Howell asked.

"Hang on a minute, sir," the diver replied.

Ross and the others watched as Sharp swam in front of the camera, which Kendall held steady as the other man reached down and indicated a large packing case, still attached to one of the forward torpedo room storage racks by thick canvas webbing straps that had stood the test of time remarkably well.

"There are two more of these boxes down here," said Kendall, "but by the looks of things there must have been others. There are more of these webbing straps here that look as if they've been recently cut. I'd say whoever has been working in here has only half-finished the job."

"But Decker was here a year ago, sir," Drake commented. "Why has it taken them so long to remove whatever they were after?"

"That's an easy question to answer, Sergeant Drake," Howell said. "Yes indeed," agreed George Baldacre, the coast guard, who hadn't spoken much at all since they'd begun to watch the dive operation. "I think what the captain was going to say, and excuse me for butting in Charles, is that you can't just turn up in the English Channel with a bloody great salvage tug and begin exploring the sea bed without anyone knowing about it. This is, remember, one of the busiest sea lanes in the world and they'd have been noticed and questions asked. I would guess they spent a long time in small boats or even in a submersible of their own, simply checking out the wreck site, and then eventually sending divers down much as we have, but only for short periods at a time so as not to arouse suspicion. The weather would have played an important role too. They set up their cover story to fool us and the other maritime authorities but I still don't understand how the hell they managed to force their way into the submarine's conning tower. What the hell did they use?"

Ross was impressed with Baldacre's theory which seemed to fit all the facts and he now came up with a theory of his own.

"You said they might have used a submersible, George. Charles, tell me, could a civilian organisation like Aegis have anything like the *Holmes* or *Watson*, you know, a submersible with all the mechanical grabs and arms and so on, at their disposal?"

"Of course," the captain replied. "Such things are not restricted to the

Royal Navy, Andy. Most ocean exploration companies have them nowadays."

"And is there such a thing as an underwater drill?" Ross ventured.

"Bloody hell, he's right sir" Ridley exclaimed. "That's how they did it. They must have used something like 'the worm.'

"Er, what's the worm?" Izzie asked.

"It's a special tool we have at our disposal," Howell replied. "It is, in effect a large drill bit, an augur that can slowly cut through the hull of a ship. We only use it for salvage purposes but if they have something similar, they could easily have used it as a break-in tool to gain access to the U-Boat's interior."

"Bloody hell, sir, look here," the startled voice of Petty Officer Kendall pulled all eyes back to the monitor.

"Jesus Christ," Sharp added as the beam from his lamp shone on one corner of the packing case which had become rotten and fallen away, probably since the sea had been allowed to encroach into the compartment thanks to the thieves as everyone now thought of them.

"Is that what we think it is, Kendall?" Captain Howell asked his diver.

"I believe so, sir. I think this is part of a horde of bloody Nazi gold. The bastards who did this are nothing but a bunch of murdering grave robbers."

"Gold!" D.I. Brian Jones exclaimed as his eyes took in the sight.

"And it's been down there all those years," his sergeant, Carole St. Clair added. "But like Izzie said earlier, how did the Aegis people know it was here?"

"Someone had to know it was on the submarine," Jones said. "Andy is probably right that this Haller chap must know something."

"But that doesn't add up either," Ross suddenly said.

"Why not, Andy?" Jones asked.

"Because he wouldn't have given us the exact location of the wreck site if he was part of the conspiracy. That would have been stupid beyond belief. No, there has to be someone, somewhere who knew about the cargo this sub was carrying and who got the Aegis people involved, probably for a share of the loot. Before we even begin to find out who it is, we need to identify the U-Boat, Captain Howell," Ross said to Charles Howell, in a seriously official tone of voice.

"Indeed we do," the captain replied and then he spoke to the divers.

"Sharp, Kendall, did either of you look for the maker's plate in the control room? It should have been bolted somewhere on the superstructure. They always did that, I think."

"That's right," said Prendergast, "like a birth certificate. It would have the boat's number, date of launch, where it was made and other specific information."

"We didn't see it, sir," Sharp replied, "But I don't think we need to look for it."

"And why's that, Sharp?" said Howell.

Sharp pointed towards the crate again and Kendall focused the camera to a close up view. The watchers could now see a series of stencilled numbers and letters on the packing case and what appeared to be some lettering below.

"Looks like one of the crew got bored and indulged in a spot of graffiti," said Sharp. "Anyone up there speak German?"

"I do," said Gareth Ridley. He moved to the front of the watchers and looked at the screen as the words came into focus.

One of the crew had indeed been busy during a few idle moments on the last voyage of *U966*. Underneath the official lettering, someone had etched *U966, Adolph postboten* into the side of the crate and filled the lettering in with what had probably been oil or diesel fuel oil, turning it black and still readable after almost 60 years.

"*U966* is obvious," said Ridley and the words translate as *Adolph's postman.*"

"Well done you two, and thank you, Lieutenant," Howell said, without revealing that he too spoke perfect German. Better to let young Ridley feel he'd contributed substantially to the mission.

"*U966*," said Ross. "Well, at least now we know the sub's number we might be able to discover more about her. Izzie, get back on the phone to Ferris. Tell him what we've found and make sure he knows Haller is no longer a viable suspect. Treat him as a valuable witness and find out if he knows anything of the history of *U966*. He's the expert historian after all."

"Right you are, sir," Drake replied as she stepped out on the port wing of the bridge again to call Paul Ferris.

Captain Howell meanwhile, had been in a huddle with his first officer, Mike Sutherland. Turning to Ross, he spoke in a hushed tone.

"Andy, I know this all began with your request for help in a murder investigation but now we know what we're dealing with, I'm sure you can see that as far as the Royal Navy is concerned, this matter goes much further than that. I will of course be reporting everything we've found to the Ministry of Defence and I'm sure they will launch a full scale inquiry into both wrecks down there, particularly as we seem to have unearthed an amount of Nazi treasure which it's clear to see was being transferred out of Germany to some secret location, possibly South America, knowing the Nazis had connections over there during the war. We'll continue to assist you of course but I think it's safe to say we'll be joined by a much larger salvage team and possibly a specialist salvage vessel sooner rather than later. Will you be expecting to stay and see what else we discover?"

Ross thought for a few seconds before replying.

"I don't think so, Charles. Once we get your doctor's report on the remains of the frogman and the remains sent to the local medical examiner, I think our usefulness here will be at an end. I'm sure D.I. Jones and Sergeant St. Clair will be happy to be our eyes and ears on the case down here while we go back to Liverpool to continue the investigation."

"We'll be more than happy to work the case from our end," Brian Jones replied. "We're only a phone call away at any time and you only have to let us know if we need to be doing anything to help push the investigation along and we'll be on it right away, won't we, Carole?"

"Without a doubt, sir," Carole St. Clair agreed.

"Thanks," said Ross as they all turned to watch the final minutes of the dive. Lieutenant Commander Douglas Sykes, the *Wyvern's* senior medical officer was still busy at work on the remains of the frogman and Ross was keen to find out what he'd discovered.

Leaving the others to watch the submersible begin its ascent from the deep, Ross and the other police officers now made their way to the *Wyvern's* sick bay, escorted by a young naval rating. Once there, Ross politely knocked on the bulkhead at the door to the sick bay and was ushered in by one of Sykes's sick berth attendants. The grim task of opening the wetsuit to examine the remains had already been undertaken by Sykes and two of his sick-berth attendants, and the rest of the procedure was now watched closely by Ross, Drake and the two Cornish police officers.

As expected, the denizens of the deep had made many a meal of the dead man, or woman, and Sykes and his men had been able to recover nothing more than a few well-picked bones from the interior of the wetsuit. Any hopes Ross might have had of identifying the body from its remains were dashed almost as soon as the examination had begun, but then, just as he was beginning to think they'd run into another brick wall in the investigation, Doctor Sykes suddenly perked up as his hands emerged from the wetsuit holding something silver in colour, attached to a thin chain of a similar metal.

"Aha," said Sykes, almost triumphantly, "what do we have here, I wonder?"

"What is it Doc?" Ross asked quickly, taking two steps towards the examination table in the centre of the *Wyvern's* sick bay treatment room.

"A silver St. Christopher medallion, Inspector, still with its chain attached." Sykes turned it over and smiled as he passed it to Ross.

"Take a look Inspector. It's engraved on the back."

Ross looked closely at the medallion, which was no more than an inch and a half in diameter, but big enough for him to clearly make out the engraving on the back.

"T.J.K. LOVE FROM J.D. 6.6.2000," he read aloud for all to hear. "If this doesn't help us to identify the body, nothing will."

"Oh Christ," Brian Jones exclaimed as Ross passed the St. Christopher around for the others to examine.

"Brian?" Ross questioned the Falmouth detective's reaction, without failing to notice Jones's face had turned pale as a sheet.

Replying to his own sergeant rather than directly replying to Ross, Jones spoke quietly as his shoulders appeared to sag.

"You know who this is, don't you. Carole?"

"Surely it can't be," St. Clair replied. "Everything pointed to him doing a runner, sir. We had evidence…"

"Faked evidence, obviously," Jones said, his voice cracking with emotion.

Ross had listened to the exchange between the Falmouth detectives and now tried again to reach past Jones's obvious shock.

"Brian, I'm sorry, but please talk to me. It sounds to me as if you both have a bloody good idea who our victim is. Take a deep breath, and tell me, for God's sake."

"Carole, would you…?" Jones said, turning away from the sight of the remains on the examination table and reaching out to the nearby bulkhead to support himself.

Carole St. Clair cleared her throat, nodded at her boss and turned to Ross.

"Sir, you'll recall we told you that only a few locals were ever employed by Aegis at their Falmouth facility, and even then, only in pretty menial jobs, nothing that would have given them access to anything important that Aegis might be working on?"

"I remember, Carole, please go on."

"Well sir, one of those locals was Thomas Joseph Knowles, known as T.J. to his friends. T.J. was employed as a security guard by Aegis. His job was restricted to patrolling the grounds of the facility at night, ensuring nobody broke into the place. None of the security guards have access to the main buildings there apparently. This was just routine exterior patrol work. T.J. was out of work for a while, so grabbed the chance to earn a few pounds when this job was advertised.

He'd been going out with a local girl, Julie Dakin for about two years when Julie announced she was pregnant. Next thing anyone knew, T.J. disappeared one day about a year ago. Julie received a text message from him saying he wasn't ready to be a father and he'd gone away to think things over, to decide what to do next. A week later, she received a postcard from London, saying he was staying in a B & B in Whitechapel, that he was well and didn't know if or when he'd be coming home. She kept trying to reach him by phone and text message, and received another text a fortnight after the postcard. He said he was sorry, but he couldn't be a dad. He said he loved her, told her to take care of herself and that was the last thing anyone heard from him."

St Clair paused for breath. Somehow, Ross had a feeling he knew how this story might end, but he waited and allowed her to carry on.

"When nothing was heard from T.J. after another two weeks passed, Julie, who was already beside herself with grief, asked her uncle to look into his apparent disappearance. Julie Dakin is D.I. Jones's niece, Inspector Ross."

"I guessed as much," said Ross. "Brian, I'm sorry, this has been a real shock for you, but we need to know what happened next."

Jones acknowledged Ross with a nod and gestured for St. Clair to continue.

"Everyone knew this to be out of character for T.J. He absolutely adored Julie. They were childhood friends, and their friendship turned to something more as they grew older. No way would he have run off and left her in the lurch, or so we all thought. Julie gave birth to a little girl a few months ago, called her Kerry."

Having finally composed himself, Brian Jones pushed himself away from the bulkhead and walked closer, looking down with sadness at Thomas Knowles's remains.

"We did all we could to find him, Andy. I even went up to London and trawled the B & B's in Whitechapel. Those bastards were clever, I'll give 'em that. I actually found a place where a young man matching T.J's description had apparently stayed for a week, before moving on, according to the landlady, who also said she hardly saw him, so her confirmation of his identity was a little suspect, but I couldn't argue about the fact that the handwriting on the postcard looked a perfect match for his. The bastards must have taken him and made him write it before killing him. They were too clever for me, I have to admit."

"But what would he have had to do with all this?" Izzie Drake asked.

"T.J. was an expert diver, Izzie. He was also round about the same age as Aaron Decker and it's possible that Aaron met him while he was down here, maybe in one of the pubs in town, found out he was employed by Aegis and somehow convinced T.J. to help him look into what they were up to. T.J had a great sense of adventure, and also knew right from wrong, so I could easily imagine him being talked into helping Aaron in his quest, particularly if Aaron offered him some kind of financial reward. Like I said, he'd been out of work for a time, so he'd have jumped at the chance to earn a few quid."

Ross had been thinking as Jones spoke and now voiced his agreement with the Falmouth detective's hypothesis.

"You know, Brian, I think that's probably exactly what happened. I can't see anyone other than Aaron, or at a push, Klaus Haller asking him to dive on the wreck site. In fact, it could have been Haller rather than Decker who recruited him. Decker could dive himself, Haller is too old, and might have wanted confirmation of what Decker had told him. But if he did get T.J. to help him, why didn't he mention it when my people spoke to him before?"

"Seems every mystery in your case leads to yet another one," Jones observed and Ross couldn't really argue with his point.

"Is there anything else you can tell us about the remains of…er, T.J., Doctor Sykes?" Ross asked, trying to return to a less personal perspective.

"Not really," said the *Wyvern's* medical officer. "There just isn't enough here to carry out a post mortem on, I'm afraid. Obviously, we'll forward the remains of Mr. Knowles to the medical examiner's office in Falmouth as soon as we dock, but I doubt you'll get much more from him, Inspector Ross."

Ross thanked the doctor and quietly signalled for Drake and St. Clair to follow him out of the medical centre. Seeing them and realising Ross's intent, Doctor Sykes also beckoned to the two sick berth attendants who likewise followed him through the door, leaving Detective Inspector Brian Jones alone with what remained of the man who was the father of his niece's baby girl.

CHAPTER 28

A HISTORY LESSON

Nick Dodds and Paul Ferris sat opposite Klaus Haller in his comfortable cottage in the Welsh town of Wrexham. Haller had welcomed them into his home and made them wait to talk to him while he'd made fresh coffee for the three of them.

He'd then listened intently as they'd conveyed the information they'd received from Izzie Drake.

"*U966*?" he mused. "I know the history of most of the better known U-Boats of the war, detectives, but you must forgive me if this one doesn't immediately spring to mind."

"But can you help us to trace its history, Herr Haller?" Dodds asked him.

"But of course. I did not mean that because I have no personal recollection of it that I cannot find out what you want. Please wait while I conduct a quick search."

Haller rose from his armchair and walked across the room, re-seating himself at his small desk that held his small personal computer, switching it on and then waiting as it whirred and finally beeped to signal it had fully booted up. The historian opened his personal files and within a minute, had located the one he was looking for.

"Ah, here we are, gentlemen," Haller said quietly, continuing to read as he spoke. "Now, this is a little odd."

"In what way, sir?" Ferris asked.

"Well, *U966* was one of the type VIIC boats, launched in 1943 and scuttled later that same year after being badly damaged by an aerial depth charge attack in the Bay of Biscay. Yet the shape of the vessel in the photos Aaron took resemble more the much later type IXD U-Boats, which were all built slightly later in the war. They were more than five hundred tons heavier and almost ten metres longer than their predecessors, but records indicate they had their torpedo tubes removed and were converted for transport purposes, essentially making them nothing more than freight carriers, but this boat looks to be a fully functional craft and there is something else about it that I cannot quite put my finger on at this moment. It may come to me in time. One thing I can tell you for certain though is that this U-Boat, whatever its maker's plate or any other identification marks may say, is most certainly not the original *U966*. For some reason, she was redesignated as *U966*, as a subterfuge, so there must be something secret about the U-Boat itself, or about someone or something on board when she sailed. You say she was being used to carry cargo of some kind?"

"That's correct, Herr Haller," Ferris confirmed. "Detective Inspector Ross has authorised us to give you certain information which he hopes you will keep in confidence."

"I wish nothing more than to help in this matter, so yes, you can be assured of my discretion in this matter, and you have really piqued my interest with the mention of this boat. Please wait while I see what else I can discover."

Dodds and Ferris looked on as Haller opened up page after page of information on his computer. Ferris, the murder investigation team's collator and resident computer expert was impressed by Haller's dexterity and speed in operating his machine. The historian soon had something to tell them, though his face betrayed a look of puzzlement, which Ferris noticed right away as Haller looked at them.

"What is it, Herr Haller? You look as if something is wrong."

"Now wrong, exactly, Constable Ferris, but, shall we say, a little odd?"

"Please explain, sir."

"Well, it would appear that *U966*, that is to say, the ersatz, you would say, false *U966* was placed in reserve at the beginning of 1945. In essence, she was being kept in port, in Kiel, and held in a constant state of readiness for what were deemed 'special operations.' That term could have meant almost anything in those days, but what interests me is that she'd been operating at sea for some time and her captain was a highly decorated officer who had previously commanded a most successful U-Boat during the Battle of the Atlantic. His previous boat had been badly damaged and needed extensive repairs after his part in a Wolf Pack operation against allied convoys, and he was then transferred, along with a sizable number of his crew to the *U3000*. But we know that *U966* was sunk two years earlier so someone went to great trouble to create a false record for this 'new' *U966*, long before she sailed from Kiel, possibly before her captain was even aware of it."

"That sounds suspiciously like a clever cover story," said Nick Dodds.

"Ja, very much so, Constable, especially as the records then go on to state the boat was lost with all hands, in May of 1945, having sailed from Kiel in March but gives no approximate position or even what heading she was last reported to be following. That is not like the usual German efficiency. It sounds as if *U966*, it is easier for you if we stick to that number I think, was dispatched on a secret mission around a month before Hitler's suicide. If, as you say, she was carrying gold bullion it is likely to be either a cargo of part of the immense of amounts of gold the Nazis stole from occupied countries, or part of Germany's own gold reserves. Hitler remained convinced almost to the end that he could revive Germany's war effort and rumour has it that he was ferrying looted art treasures and gold bullion to sympathetic nations in South America for some time in the final months of the war. Let me see next, what we can discover about her captain. Ah, here we are, *Korvettankapitän* Max Ritter, holder of the Knight's Cross with Oak Leaves, a much respected U-Boat commander, gentlemen. Now, his name I do recognise, though how he ended up on this *U966*, ferrying gold across the sea, I do not know. Someone in high authority must have been involved to have had such a man's records changed to include this false 'cover story' as you call it. I can think of only one man who would be responsible for this."

"And who would that be?" Ferris asked.

"Admiral Wilhelm Canaris, Constable, head of the *Abwehr*, the Nazi's military intelligence service, probably in collusion with Admiral Doenitz, who headed the U-Boat arm of the Kriegsmarine. They obviously went to great lengths to disguise this boat, its crew and its mission."

"Even I've watched enough on the history channel to know that the decorations you quote mean Ritter was highly decorated, Herr Haller," said Ferris. "But if he was so well thought of, is it not possible he was selected for the mission precisely because of his bravery and loyalty to the Reich, that he was well aware of his mission all along? A good officer would go along with such a subterfuge if it was for the benefit of the war effort, surely."

"Yes, of course," Haller replied thoughtfully, "and there may be something in that after all when you consider who he worked under."

"Such as?" Dodds asked.

"Well it says here that his immediate superior was *Kapitän zur See*, Heinz Schmidt, who was himself the close aide to Admiral Werner Stein. Stein was well known to be close to Hitler and Schmidt was an ardent Nazi, so I can easily believe them selecting Ritter for such a task, but it is strange…" his voice tailed off thoughtfully.

"What's bothering you, Herr Haller?" Ferris asked, seeing the historian appearing to debate something in his own mind.

"Her course, Constable Ferris, her course is all wrong, but wait, no, perhaps not so crazy after all."

"Do you mind explaining, sir?" Ferris pressed Haller to elaborate on his thoughts.

"How is your German geography, gentlemen? Oh never mind, just look here." Haller beckoned the two detectives to come and look at a map he'd just opened up on his desk. Using a pencil as a pointer, he began to explain. "Here's Kiel," he indicated and then using the pencil, he traced what would have been a U-Boat's usual route around the coast of Denmark, across the North Sea and into the Atlantic via the northern route, past the northern British Isles and on towards Greenland. He then traced a totally different route, one which placed *U966* in the English Channel before breaking out into the Western Atlantic.

"I would wager that Schmidt planned a route that sent *U966* on a circuitous route, away from the usual U-Boat areas of activity, thinking there was less chance of accidental interception of the submarine by patrolling warships."

"He got that bit badly wrong then, didn't he?" Dodds commented.

"You appear to be correct," Haller agreed. "I think also, that if the ultimate destination of *U966* was South America or perhaps one of the island chains, The Bahamas for example, it would in fact save time and fuel by taking this route, especially if Ritter was under orders to remain submerged as long as possible."

Dodds and Ferris looked at the plot that Haller had drawn on the map and it did appear to both men that the overall length of the voyage would have been shorter using the route he'd mapped out.

Ferris now asked the same question that had been niggling at Izzie Drake down in Falmouth.

"Herr Haller, even accepting the truth of all you've told us, how did the people at Aegis learn of the position of the submarine, or even learn of its existence?"

"I have been thinking of that question as we have been talking," Haller said, "and it seems to me there are only two people who might know the answer to that."

"You know who they are, Herr Haller?" Dodds asked, feeling stupid as he did so, *Obviously Haller knows or he wouldn't have said there were two people would he?* Nick Dodds thought.

"While we have been talking I have checked on the histories of both Schmidt and Stein, gentlemen. Stein died in 1965, but was survived by a son, Ralph, who was born in 1946 which would make him fifty-seven years old now. Schmidt was thirty when the war ended and is, as far as I know, still alive, obviously in his eighties now, and my records show he was last known to be living in a retirement home near Rothenburg in Bavaria. It is possible that Schmidt knew the course that *U966* was to follow and may now be trying to locate the gold or, perhaps, Stein left the same details for his son to find and he is now working in league with the people at Aegis to take the gold and share it with them in return for them doing the work of recovering it."

"Do your records show where Ralph Stein lives, Herr Haller?"

At that point, Haller paused as if for dramatic effect before replying.

"My records show only information relating to persons who have served in the Kriegsmarine, or since its inception the modern-day German Navy which replaced the Kriegsmarine after it was disbanded after the war, gentlemen, but luck is with us. Ralph Stein served for eight years in the navy and his last known address places him in Rostock, close to the Baltic Sea."

"Which by itself means little of course," said Ferris, unless…" he hesitated. "Can you do a search please, Herr Haller and see if Aegis has any business interests in that area of Germany, please?"

"Of course, let me see now…ah, here it is. Constable Ferris, you are indeed a clever man. When Communism fell and Rostock became part of the new reunified Germany, they invited many foreign companies to the town to assist with rebuilding and modernisation and the Aegis Corporation is listed as one of those companies and indeed they still maintain an office in the city and a small facility on the coast near the city's Baltic port at Warnemünde a few miles away. I explain, of course. Rostock is a few miles inland from the coast and its port facility is actually on the Baltic at the head of the river Warnow, on which Rostock stands."

"Herr Haller, you have been a great help," Ferris said. "Please, can you print this information for us? We may need to talk again and in the meantime, as we asked earlier…"

"I will say nothing of your visit, Constable, I promise. I only hope I am helpful in finding out who killed that poor young man. It is for me a great pity that the life of any person is considered less than the value of a few gold bars. In the meantime I will continue to investigate the anomaly of the change in the U-Boat's number and if I find anything I will of course telephone you or your superiors in Liverpool."

Ferris and Dodds thanked Klaus Haller, and were soon motoring back to Liverpool, eager to speak to Andy Ross as soon as they could. Hopefully his mobile phone would be in range by the time they got there.

CHAPTER 29

AGOSTINI'S 'LIGHTBULB'

Detective Chief Inspector Oscar Agostini had until recently shared the same rank as Andy Ross. When his predecessor as head of the murder investigation team, Harry Porteous, announced his retirement, his job and a promotion was offered to Ross, who turned it down, preferring to remain 'in the field' on active investigations. Ross was delighted when his old friend and one-time partner, Detective Inspector Oscar Agostini was promoted and handed the job.

The two men had worked together many years earlier and had remained firm friends ever since, and Ross had no problem in working for Agostini, the pair retaining a respectful but friendly working relationship during office hours whilst being able to remain as before in their own time.

As Agostini waited for Ross and Drake to return from Falmouth, and as the rest of the team continued to gather other pieces of the jigsaw this case had become, he sat at his desk, pondering. Though not out on the streets any longer, Agostini was still a detective and a damn good one at that and this case had so far proved something of a nightmare.

The D.C.I. now decided to use one of his old techniques, one that had proved valuable in the past. He began to mentally sift the facts and the fictions of the case so far. By the fictions, he meant the idle suppositions and wild theories that often enter into difficult inquiries.

As he saw it, the case began not with the murder of Aaron Decker, but long before that when someone gave information to another person at the Aegis Institute about the possibility of there being a cache of Nazi gold on a shipwreck in the English Channel. He now believed, with the informa-

661

tion gleaned from Klaus Haller, that that person had to be either Ralph Stein or Heinz Schmidt.

There had to be a crooked executive or group of executives within the Aegis organisation. The company was respected around the world and it was inconceivable that the entire set-up was involved in illegal activity. No, Agostini concluded, there had to be a rogue element present and he and his team, possibly with help from Interpol and perhaps the resources of Jerome Decker's C.I.A. affiliates had to find whoever was leading that group. His personal favourite at present was Francis Kelly. He was sure that at the time of Aaron Decker becoming involved in the case, the perpetrators quite possibly knew nothing about his father and his position in the C.I.A. their first big mistake, Agostini concluded.

At some point in the case, Aegis Oceanogaphics made a job offer out of the blue to Sally Metcalfe, Aaron's girlfriend. Sally's father owns a haulage company that had done some work for Aegis in the past and apparently Sally was offered the job based on this connection.

Aaron had decided to check out her prospective future employers and something aroused his suspicions about Aegis's activities. He consults a respected historian, Klaus Haller who in trying to help Aaron gets cold-shouldered by Aegis, but cleverly follows their ship out to the wreck site from a distance and notes the location. He passes this to Aaron who goes to Cornwall, dives on the wreck, and later manages to hire this local lad, T.J. to help him. T.J. Agostini supposes, gets found out and eliminated by the Aegis people, so when he doesn't hear from him, Aaron returns to Cornwall, dives on the wreck himself and takes the photos we now have.

Agostini paused in his reflections. Why had so much time passed between Aaron finding the body chained to the wreck and his murder? Only one answer. Agostini recalls Aaron having told someone, was it the girlfriend, that he'd found something that could make him a lot of money? Perhaps he didn't mean the gold on the submarine, as he probably wasn't really aware of the cargo on the submarine, but he could have been blackmailing someone at Aegis, by threatening to reveal the presence of the body and where the wreck site was. That was surely a motive for murder. At this time, Agostini couldn't know that Aegis had tried and failed to buy Aaron Decker's silence.

Aaron was killed while his two housemates, Tim Knight and Martin Lewis were in the house, asleep by their own testimony. Sally was also drugged but not sufficiently to harm her permanently. Why?

By the Occam's razor principal, Knight and Lewis were the only possible killers but there was no evidence to link them to the murder, and no apparent motive for either of them to want to harm Aaron.

"Bloody hell," Oscar Agostini shouted out to the walls of his office. He'd had a personal 'light bulb' moment thanks to his old tried and tested method of singularly brainstorming the case in his head.

He suddenly felt he knew what they'd been missing. The key to cracking the case lay not below the English Channel or on the university cricket pitch, or in a care home in Bavaria, or on the Baltic coast though he was sure that was probably where it all began but somewhere and with someone they hadn't even considered up to this point. Sitting quietly at the periphery of the case was someone they hadn't even spoken to so far. Again, Agostini asked himself that one final question just to make sure of his thoughts. Why hadn't Sally Metcalfe been murdered along with Aaron Decker? It would surely have been easy enough to kill her at the same time, and would leave less chance of her being a witness to anything. The answer was still the same one he'd just arrived at. Was Sally Metcalfe a killer? Did she collude with Knight and Lewis to murder her boyfriend? No, of course she didn't, but the man who was probably responsible for carrying the pilfered gold from Cornwall to its final destination, somewhere in Europe to one of Aegis's facilities on the continent, and who must have known what was planned for Decker could only be her bloody father!

Oscar Agostini picked up the phone. He had some calls to make.

CHAPTER 30

ROBIN

Robin parked the stolen Land Rover a little way down the road from the house shared by Tim Knight and Martin Lewis. Thankfully, most of the residents were still at work, college or whatever, he didn't really care. The email he'd received from Finch had been wonderfully comprehensive and Robin was fully conversant with their day to day routine.

Knight was at cricket practice, so could wait a little. Lewis was at home, but his file indicated he'd be leaving home any time now to spend an hour at the gym three streets away, which he visited twice a week. Luckily for Robin, this was one of those days.

Sure enough, five minutes later a man matching the photograph Robin held in his left hand emerged from the house with a back pack over his shoulder, headphones in place as he listened to some kind of music and began a slow jog along the pavement in the opposite direction from where Robin was parked. Perfect!

Lewis reached the end of the street and pressed the button on the pedestrian crossing, and waited for the lights to turn green in his favour, red for the traffic. Robin calmly pulled out of his parking space, and with military precision, judged his moment perfectly, flooring the accelerator pedal just as the lights switched and Lewis started to cross the road. At the very last second, Lewis heard, maybe sensed the sound and approach of the onrushing vehicle as it came towards him and too late, tried to avoid it. The Land Rover literally propelled Martin Lewis like a rag doll into the air, his body bouncing up off the bonnet of the vehicle before sailing over the roof to land in the road, broken, bloody, and very, very dead. It all happened so quickly, Robin was clean away before a young woman, pushing a toddler in a pushchair, realised what had happened before her eyes and began to scream. A full twenty seconds passed before another car turned into the quiet street, the woman frantically flagging it down and the driver running to the nearest phone box to dial 999 to summon the emergency services.

Robin drove carefully, keeping to the speed limit, and returned the Land Rover to the multi-storey car park he'd taken it from, deliberately leaving it on a level higher than he'd stolen it from. Confuse the enemy; that was his strategy. He walked to where he'd left his own car and casually drove out of the car park towards his next 'appointment' with death.

As the virtually new, 2003 model Lexus carrying Robin sedately proceeded towards his next target, another car, this one carrying Ferris and Dodds happened to pass him travelling in the opposite direction. The two detectives, having reported to D.C.I. Agostini were on their way to pick up Knight and Lewis for further questioning, hoping to find the two men at home at that late hour in the afternoon. The Lexus was Robin's own car, hadn't been reported as stolen, was adhering to the speed limit, so there was nothing overtly suspicious about it, just another car on the road, eliciting barely a glance from either man as they passed side by side for a brief second with the killer of Martin Lewis. Robin was using his own vehicle so he could carry out part two of his mission and then simply drive away, home in time for supper.

A few minutes later, Ferris pulled up as they took in the scene ahead. Two police patrol cars, an ambulance and a scene of general pandemonium greeted them as they attempted to approach the house on Manor Court.

Despite the terrible injuries caused by the impact of the Land Rover on the body of Martin Lewis, his face, though bloodied, was instantly recognisable to Ferris and Dodds.

"Shit, shit, shit," Ferris shouted. Holding up his warrant card, he barked at the nearest constable, "What the fuck happened here?"

"Looks like a hit-and-run," said the young officer. "The young woman over there with the kid in the pushchair seems to be the only witness, but she said it all happened so fast, it hardly registered with her mind at first. By the time she realised what had happened and started screaming her lungs out, the car that hit him was long gone."

Ferris shared Ross's belief that coincidences were often just too convenient in explaining away sudden events like this. It had to have been deliberate.

"Nick, for fuck's sake get to the house. Check and see if Knight's there. I think this was a cold-blooded murder. Someone wants to make sure we don't talk to this pair of scallys."

Nick Dodds set off at a run towards the house as Ferris got on the radio to headquarters, quickly being patched through to D.C.I. Agostini.

The horrified chief inspector cursed and immediately asked if Knight was safe in the house.

"Dodds is checking, sir. Hang on, he's coming back."

Still running, Dodds breathlessly shouted to Ferris from ten yards away, "Not there Paul."

"I heard that," Agostini said. "Where the hell is he?"

"I don't know, sir. Any suggestions?"

"Let me think, Ferris. It sounds as if the bastards know we're getting close, and are trying to eliminate anyone who can connect them to the case. Looks like we were right to eventually latch on to Knight and Martin."

"But why would they kill their friend, sir?"

"Probably for the oldest motive in the world, Ferris, money. When this is over, I'll bet we find those two were paid a handsome sum to eliminate poor Aaron Decker."

"Bastards," Ferris said loudly, and then, "Sorry, sir."

"Don't apologise, Ferris. Those are my thoughts too. Look, you and Dodds knock on a few doors, and get those uniformed lads on the scene to help you. See if any neighbours are at home and if any of them know anything about Knight's routine. We might get lucky if one of them knows where he might be."

"Okay, sir. I'll get back to you ASAP if we find anything out."

"Good lad, Ferris. Now go, don't waste time. Tim Knight is in danger. I'm certain of it."

As the ambulance carrying Martin Lewis's body pulled away slowly with no need for sirens or flashing lights, Ferris and Dodds, in company with the four uniformed constables from the patrol cars, began knocking on doors.

Nick Dodds appeared to have struck lucky when one elderly man who lived opposite Knight and Lewis and who had come out to see what the commotion in the street was all about informed the detective that he often talked to Knight about cricket, being a fan himself, and he knew Knight often went to net practice after completing his studies. He knew this to be one of those days as he'd seen Tim Knight leaving his home that morning carrying his cricket bag, containing his bat and pads.

"Thanks, Mr. Collins. You wouldn't happen to know where Tim goes for net practice would you?" Dodds asked hopefully, though his luck ran out at that point.

"Sorry, young man," said Collins. "I've no idea, but you could try the university. That's who he plays for isn't it?"

"Yes, of course," Dodds replied. He knew full well that the university was a large and sprawling microcosm of a community, with more than one playing field in more than one location. If Tim Knight was in imminent danger, he realised they needed to move fast in locating him.

"Damn," said Ferris when Dodds reported Mr. Collins's information to him. "They wouldn't hold net practice on the main playing surface would they? I know sod all about cricket, Nick. I'm a soccer fan, like you."

"So who might know?" Dodds mused aloud and then brightened up as he said, "Sally Metcalfe."

"His girlfriend?"

"Sure. She must have gone along now and then to watch him practice and then maybe gone on to the pub for a drink or back to the house for a sweaty shag?"

"Nick, you've got a dirty mind mate," Ferris grinned.

"Yeah, I know," Dodds laughed, "but she's a bit fit that girl of his, you must admit, with that long blonde hair, great legs and a nice pair up top. I wouldn't mind a quickie with her, that's for sure."

"Nick, we don't have time for this, and I'm a married man, remember? We need her number, now, you bloody pervert."

"Hey, just fantasising, you know? I don't know her number, do you?"

"No, but wait," said Ferris quickly putting in a call to Sam Gable at headquarters.

"Sam's got it," he said triumphantly, "and she just phoned Sally while I held on. The nets are at the Mile End playing field, let's go."

Leaving the uniformed officers to continue their house to house inquiries for witnesses to the death of Martin Lewis, the two detectives dived into their car and sped off with a squeal of tyres in hopes of reaching Tim Knight before the as yet unidentified assailant. Meanwhile, Control were sending the nearest uniform branch patrol car to the Mile End Sports Ground as back up. If possible they would detain Knight until the detectives arrived.

Tim Knight, knowing nothing of the events of the last hour or so had showered and changed at the end of practice, and was walking out of the practice ground with Simon Dewar. At the car park, Dewar offered Knight a lift in his car, but fatefully, Tim Knight said he would walk to the nearby pub, The Journeyman, have a drink or two and then get a taxi home. Tim waved at Dewar as he pulled out of the car park and began to walk towards the pub. He had only gone a few yards when a voice from behind made him stop.

"Mr. Knight?" said a tall uniformed policeman.

"Yes?" Knight replied. "Can I help you?"

"Actually you can, sir," said the officer who came closer to Tim and smiled.

"Is this to do with Aaron?" Knight asked.

"Oh, yes, you could say that," the policeman replied, quickly checking there was no one else around and then removing his right hand from the pocket into which he'd slipped it when he first saw Knight.

Before Tim Knight could react, the man raised his hand and quickly stabbed a tiny, dart shaped needle into the young man's neck.

"What the hell? What do you think you're…"

Tim Knight never got to finish his sentence as the fast acting poison hit his nervous system. His body appeared to go into an instant seizure, breathing arrested and cardiac arrest followed in seconds, and the young man was dead before his body hit the ground.

Robin walked away without hesitating, job done. As he climbed into his car, parked around the corner from the street where Knight lay dead, a police patrol car sped past on its way to the sports ground. The two constables, seeing what appeared to be another of their own, waved and Robin waved back. That was the moment when they first saw the body of Tim Knight lying on the ground and the senior man in the car made a leap of faith in his decision making and told his partner to swing the car round and go after the officer they'd seen a few moments ago. Constable Les Dunn had quickly realised a uniformed officer wouldn't be driving an unmarked car and was convinced the man was bogus, and probably the killer of the man on the ground.

"Radio it in, now," he shouted at Constable Danny Jewel as he switched on the siren and lights and set off in pursuit of the blue Lexus driven by Robin.

Less than twenty seconds later, Ferris and Dodds arrived on the scene and almost simultaneously heard Jewel's message to control and saw the body of Tim Knight on the ground.

Making a fast decision, Ferris dropped Dodds off at the scene to call headquarters and await the arrival of the forensic and medical teams. He then sped off to join in the pursuit of the Lexus.

Robin couldn't believe his bad luck. He'd almost been clean away when those stupid plods had arrived in the patrol car, and put two and two together. Now, he threw the car round turn after turn as the police Peugeot screamed along within a hundred yards of his rear. It had been six years since his last foray into Merseyside in general and Liverpool in particular and that had been solely for the purpose of visiting Goodison Park on a rare meet-up with his younger brother, Malcolm, to watch an Everton versus Manchester United football match. Mal, married with two kids and a pretty wife, and neat semi-detached suburban house was nothing like his brother, lived in a smart suburb of Chester and the pair found it easier to maintain a passing relationship rather than a close one, exchanging cards on birthdays or at Christmas, only meeting once or twice a year when Mal would bore him to death with happy family news and the latest on their mother's failing state of health. Robin always wondered how the old girl had lasted so long, her lungs buggered up from a lifetime of smoking twenty a day and her joints riddled with arthritis.

His unfamiliarity with his surroundings now meant that Robin was lost in a maze of unknown streets and roads that could lead anywhere. The damned patrol car seemed to be getting closer. Another slice of ill fortune for Robin had placed Les Dunn behind the wheel of the chasing car. Dunn was qualified as a high-speed chase driver and his skills behind the wheel were honed to a fine art. Whatever Robin could do, Dunn could react to instantly.

Back at headquarters, Oscar Agostini wasn't sitting idle either. Galvanised by the opportunity to apprehend the killer and perhaps grasp an opportunity to crack the case wide open, the D.C.I. soon had an all points bulletin out on the airwaves, and consequently, every patrol car and beat officer in the city was quickly appraised of the ongoing chase and was on the lookout for the blue Lexus, its registration plate number having been provided by P.C. Jewel in the chasing car.

Robin, determined not to be taken lightly, reached under his fake policeman's jacket and withdrew his trusty Glock from its shoulder holster. He only took a couple of seconds to extract it and place it on the passenger seat but that momentary lapse in concentration would cost him dear.

Seemingly appearing from nowhere a second police patrol car suddenly pulled out from a side road to join in the pursuit of the Lexus. Seeing the new chaser in his rear view mirror, Robin instantly pushed his foot down hard on the accelerator, and as he did so, an elderly lady in an old black Fiat Panda pulled out of a side road directly in front of Robin, who tried, too late, to swerve around her. The Lexus swiped the rear quarter of the Panda, hit a parked Ford Focus and bounced into the air, turning an almost graceful cartwheel as it flew over the Ford, almost in slow motion in the eyes of those watching and struck a lamp post head-on with a sickening sound of crunching, tearing metal as the pre-stressed concrete structure buried its steel reinforced body into the speeding car's engine compartment. As the car's air-bags deployed, Robin was aware of a sharp pain in both legs as the car's momentum continued its forward motion and his legs were crushed as the lamppost broke into the passenger compartment of the Lexus, and then, everything went black.

Ferris appeared on the scene within minutes, and ran swiftly from the car to take stock of the situation. The old woman in the Panda appeared to be fine and Ferris gave her into the care of one of the constables to await the arrival of the medics.

"Is he alive?" Ferris asked P.C. Dunn immediately as he stepped closer to the crashed car.

"I think so," Dunn replied. "It's my guess the airbag saved him from fatal head damage, but he's out cold, that's for sure."

"That was some nifty driving by the way," Ferris complimented him, and Dunn basked for a moment in the congratulations.

"Thanks. I'm assuming we arrived after he'd killed that poor guy in the street back at the sports ground?"

"That's right," Ferris confirmed. "And another one at Manor Court before that."

"Bloody hell," said Dunn. "A real busy chap eh?"

"Looks that way," Ferris said. "Look, we need to seal the road off until the medics arrive. Can I leave you and your lads to see to it? I need to follow this one up."

"Sure," Dunn replied and he led Jewel and the two officers from the second patrol car to take care of making the area secure, just as the ambulance arrived, blues and twos announcing their arrival well in advance.

"How is he?" Ferris asked the paramedic who had just finished examining the man in the Lexus.

"Both legs broken and probably a severe concussion, maybe other internal injuries. We'll know when we get him back to the Royal," referring to the Royal Liverpool University Hospital, which Ferris found rather ironic considering the circumstances.

"What about getting him out of the car?"

"The fire brigade will be here in a minute. We'll need their help to get him out without damaging his legs further."

A quick examination of the old lady in the Fiat confirmed she was shaken up but not badly hurt, leaving Ferris to concentrate on his number one priority.

Right on cue, the fire brigade arrived on the scene, the crew quickly assessing the situation and Ferris stood well back and watched as the firefighters used cutting equipment to extricate the man from the concertinaed front end of the Lexus.

As soon as they'd managed to extract him from the shattered front compartment of the car, the paramedics took over, immediately hooking Robin up to a drip and immobilising both legs and his neck.

Ferris radioed to Control, asking them to instruct Nick Dodds to meet him at the Royal and then followed the ambulance as it sped through the busy city streets to the hospital, where Robin was rushed through the Accident and Emergency Department and into surgery, where the doctors began their work.

Ferris was soon in touch with D.C.I. Agostini, who instructed him and Dodds to remain at the hospital until he arranged for uniformed firearms trained officers to be sent to mount a round the clock armed guard on the killer. Agostini would also ensure a detective presence to be in close proximity to the killer at all times, and would send someone to relieve Ferris and Dodds as soon as possible. He wanted a full and detailed report on the events of the afternoon.

Ross and Drake were arriving back at headquarters just as D.C.I. Agostini was being informed by Sam Gable of the results of the search to identify the owner of the blue Lexus.

CHAPTER 31

HAIL, HAIL, THE GANG'S ALL HERE

Ross and Drake walked in to the squad room within minutes of Ferris and Dodds having returned from the hospital. Oscar Agostini welcomed them home, at the same time berating them for coming into headquarters instead of going home after their long journey from Cornwall.

"We both needed to check in here first, sir," said Ross, "just to make sure the place was still in one piece," he grinned.

"We can manage to blunder along quite well in your absence, Andy," Agostini countered and then proceeded to give the pair a brief update of their progress while Ross and Drake had been on the South Coast.

Ross was delighted with the news that they had the killer of Knight and Martin under wraps in the hospital, even more so when Derek McLennan, looking up from his desk, added a piece of new information.

"I've got a name for the driver of the Lexus, sir. Well, at least I'm assuming it's him. A check with D.V.L.C. indicates the registered keeper of the Lexus as a Graham Young, with an address in Manchester. Wonder why he was stupid enough to use his own car?"

Everyone knew that the Driver and Vehicle Licensing Centre in Swansea was the fount of all knowledge when it came to information relating to cars on Britain's roads, but that the 'registered keeper' of a vehicle was not always the actual owner, though in most cases it was. They hoped this would be the case with the Lexus.

"Probably expected a quick in and out job and less chance of being pulled than in a stolen car. Do we have anything on this Graham Young?" Ross asked.

"Haven't had time to check him out yet," McLennan apologised. "I'm getting on it now, sir."

"Good lad Derek." Ross said, giving Derek an encouraging pat on the shoulder.

"It's good to have you both back," Sam Gable added as she handed mugs of coffee to each of them.

"Thanks, Sam. We needed this," Izzie Drake said in thanks.

"Where's D.C. Curtis?" Ross asked, noticing the missing face from his team.

"At the hospital, keeping an eye on the Lexus driver," Agostini provided the answer. "He volunteered to take the first shift. I was willing to bring in some help from Division but the team wanted to keep it within the squad as we've come so far."

"I'm taking over from Tony later, sir," said McLennan.

"And I'll be relieving Derek in the morning," Sam Gable added.

"Nick and I will cover the rest of the day tomorrow," Ferris said, as Ross felt a sense of real pride in his team.

"Right, you two," Agostini now said, putting on his most forceful tone of voice, "I'm ordering you both to go home to your spouses, have a hot bath or shower, enjoy your evening, and come in bright and fresh in the morning. We all want to hear your news from Falmouth, but it's getting late in the day and we're not going to get much more done today. Andy, just give me ten minutes in my office first before you go."

"Right, sir. You're the boss," said Ross, who sent Izzie Drake off home while he accompanied the boss into his inner sanctum. Agostini spent five minutes appraising Ross of his theory regarding Sally Metcalfe's father. Ross, who'd seen Agostini perform this particular 'trick' before with his single minded brainstorming sessions agreed it made sense.

"Why the hell didn't I make that connection myself?" he asked.

"Not your fault, Andy," Agostini replied. "You, like the rest of us, had to take in so many facts and theories at once, the glaringly obvious got lost in the middle of everything that was happening around us."

"Hmm, kind of like not seeing the wood for the trees," Ross agreed. "Like bloody Knight and Martin. We should have pressured them more to begin with, but we had no evidence at all to link them with the murder of Aaron Decker."

"Again, not your fault, Andy. We're up against some very clever people here, mark my words. They've been very good at covering their tracks so far but they've suddenly slipped up today."

"Yes, they have. I wonder why?" Ross mused, thinking aloud.

"I have a theory they thought we were closer than we really were, Andy. You and Drake going down to Falmouth and the Royal Navy sending the frigate to help in the investigation must have really put the frighteners on them. They obviously want to silence anyone who can connect Aegis to the killings and the wreck site."

"I agree, Oscar," said Ross, using his friend's first name as they were used to doing in private. "But that means anyone who knew about the wreck who wasn't involved in their operation could be in danger too."

"Don't worry, I thought the same thing. A couple of detectives from the North Wales Constabulary picked Klaus Haller up a couple of hours ago and he's in protective custody. They're going to transfer him into our care tomorrow. We'll put him under guard in a safe house until we catch these bastards."

"Let's hope we catch them soon, then," Ross said. "They're a bunch of cold, heartless bastards, for sure. Young Decker, the lad T.J, in Cornwall, Knight and Martin, though I can't feel too sorry for them, and God knows how many more, all dead in order to satisfy someone's lust for bloody gold."

"I know, Andy, I know. I've been in touch with D.I. Jones and his boss in Falmouth while you and Sergeant Drake were on the road, and they're aware of what's happened here today. Jones's boss, D.C.I. Small, has agreed to institute round the clock surveillance on the Aegis facility in Falmouth. As soon as we get one slightest scrap of evidence that links them to the wreck or even one of the murders, his people will swarm over the place like a pack of angry wasps."

"We're getting closer, and catching this fellow this afternoon could just be the break we need to open up the whole can of worms."

"I hope so, Andy, now do me a bloody favour and go home to Maria. You look bloody knackered!"

"Okay, I get the point," Ross laughed. "See you in the morning."

"Sleep well, Andy," Oscar Agostini said as Andy Ross walked from the office.

"You too, boss," Ross said as he quietly closed the door behind him, looking forward to an evening at home with his wife. He knew tomorrow would likely prove to be a very busy day.

* * *

Sam Gable was the only member of the team missing from the following morning's briefing. She was at the hospital, keeping watch on the man they now knew to be Graham Young. Curtis and McLennan, despite having both spent most of their night in a similar role, had both arrived for the briefing, anxious to hear what Ross and Drake had discovered in Falmouth and to be involved in the continuing investigation. Both men had decided that sleep could come later,

Ross looked his usual self again, the tiredness of the previous day wiped out by a romantic evening spent with Maria, who'd ensured her

674

husband received a fitting welcome home, a great meal, one of his favourite DVDs to relax with, followed by a couple of hours of conjugal bliss before they'd fallen asleep in each others' arms.

Izzie Drake had enjoyed a similar return to her new husband. Peter had swept her off her feet as soon as she'd walked through the door and in a reverse of Ross's evening timetable, had immediately whisked her off to bed, from where they emerged much later, before showering, ordering a meal from their favourite Chinese takeaway, and then skipping the movie part of the evening as they fell into bed once more. Eventually, they ended up much the same as Andy Ross and Maria, fast asleep, holding each other in a loving embrace.

Both inspector and sergeant felt ready to push the case towards a conclusion, but unusually for him, Ross announced he was initially handing the briefing over to D.C.I. Agostini. His reason for doing so soon became clear as the chief inspector quickly outlined his theory relating to the potential involvement of Sally Metcalfe's father.

As he came to the conclusion of his idea, Agostini summed things up.

"Like a lot of police officers, we may have blundered a little in the beginning, not by anyone being at fault, but because the simple solution actually looked the most unlikely one, and didn't appear to fit any of the known facts. As the case grew more and more complicated we lost sight of the little things, the obvious things, as our very clever adversaries probably expected us to.

I decided to strip the case bare of all its complications, start from scratch, and see if a dog is just a dog is just a dog after all."

"Eh?" Curtis said quietly, only to receive a dig in the ribs from Derek McLennan. Agostini had heard him though.

"D.C. Curtis, all I mean is that just because you start out thinking a dog stole your sausages, but then someone tells you they saw a boy running behind a dog with a string of sausages in his mouth, and then a man appeared on the street offering cheap sausages for sale, it doesn't mean the man and boy were responsible for the dog stealing the sausages. The boy could have been trying to catch the dog to get the sausages back, and the man was probably a legitimate door to door butcher, got it?"

"Er, not really sir, sorry."

"Oh well, never mind," said the chief. "D.C. Ferris, I want you to use your extensive skills on the computer to check out Metcalfe Logistics. I ran a quick search on my own computer before coming to the meeting. Sally's father is Jeffrey Metcalfe, aged fifty five, and the company has depots here and in Spain as she told us in her statement. But, it would appear they own a subsidiary company, Advance Transportation, which operates an international freight service, which could be very useful for anyone wanting to ferry illicit goods from country to country. Use every tool at your disposal, Ferris and see what you can find."

"Right sir," said Ferris.

"Now, I'm sure D.I. Ross has a lot to tell us about his trip to Falmouth, so please, let's hear it, Andy."

"Thank you, sir," said Ross and between them, he and Izzie Drake spent the next twenty minutes giving the team the full run down on the events of the last few days on the south coast, the identification of the wreck of the *Norwich*, the revelation of the gold bullion on board the old U-Boat, and the final, tragic identification of the frogman who they'd all seen in the photos taken originally by Aaron Decker."

"So, D.I. Jones is continuing the investigation from Falmouth too, sir? Dodds asked.

"Yes, he and Sergeant St. Clair will be in daily contact with us, so be ready to speak to them if you happen to answer the phone when they call, introduce yourselves and work with them. We're all on the same case, remember that."

"Okay, sir, no problem," said Dodds.

"Do we know how this T.J. character came to be involved with the case, sir?" Derek McLennan asked.

"We don't know for sure," Ross replied, "but we think it's a safe assumption that Aaron Decker found out he worked at the Aegis facility and made contact with him and somehow convinced him to help dig up the dirt on his employers."

"So, what now, boss?" Curtis asked.

"Now, Tony, we first hope we can get something from Graham Young. Sergeant Drake and I are going over to the Royal in a while to see if he's ready and able to talk yet. With a case like this, I want him out of the hospital and safely under lock and key as soon as possible. If his employers know we have him and are afraid he'll talk, they might try to have him eliminated before he can spill the beans and blow their operation out of the water."

"Nice analogy, sir," Drake smiled.

"What? Oh, yeah, out of the water. Completely unintentional I assure you," he grinned back at her.

"Meanwhile, Klaus Haller is being brought to Liverpool today. He'll go straight to the designated safe house where we can keep him protected at all times. Thanks to D.C.I. Agostini, Interpol are looking into the activities of Ralph Stein and Heinz Schmidt. If either of them is involved, as I suspect will be the case, we'll soon know about it. Derek, you seem to get on well with Herr Haller. Once he's in the safe house, go and see him. Try and find out if there's any way he can help us trace any other living relatives of the men who sailed on *U966*, or *U3000*, or whatever the Germans called her. Bloody confusing, changing the number the way they did."

"But they must have had a reason sir," Drake said, after having been silent for some minutes. "What if the U-Boat itself formed part of the secret?"

"Go on, Izzie, what are you thinking?"

"Well sir, changing the number of the submarine only makes sense if the Germans didn't want it identified it were sunk or captured by the allies. What if it held some secrets that they wanted to cover up at any cost?"

"Such as?"

"I've no idea, sir. It was just an idea."

In fact, Ross thought it a very good idea that could help their case if they could discover exactly what the extent of the Nazis subterfuge really added up to.

"Derek," he looked at McLennan.

"I know sir, ask Haller."

"Good lad, Derek," Ross said, at the same time thinking what an excellent and intuitive detective Derek McLennan had become in the four years he'd worked under Ross. From a young, idealistic, and naïve young man, McLennan had grown to be a first class investigator with a quick brain and a burning desire to see justice prevail in every case he worked.

* * *

Despite his wife being a doctor, Andy Ross hated hospitals. Something about the smell, the almost institutional colour scheme so typical of such places, the stagnant over-heated air-conditioned air, an all-pervading smell of overcooked cabbage and the constant hubbub of sounds that assaulted his ears on every corridor, made him want to turn and run back out into the fresh air as soon as humanly possible.

After pausing to say hello to Sam Gable and then sending her to the cafeteria to grab a coffee and a bite to eat, Ross and Drake nodded their hellos to the uniformed guards on duty outside the door to the room where Graham Young lay, both legs elevated and securely wrapped in plaster casts. His head was also bandaged, Gable having informed them the doctor had recently informed her that Young was also suffering from intra-cranial bleeding and might need additional surgery to relieve the pressure on his brain.

While travelling to the Royal in their car, Ross and Drake learned more about Young, when Agostini himself contacted them to let them know that Young's fingerprints had led to a positive identification. They now knew that Young was a former sergeant in the Parachute Regiment, who had been dishonourably discharged following an assault on a superior officer. Young had served twelve months in the military prison at Colchester after first striking and then breaking the arm of a Lieutenant who had reprimanded him for smelling of drink while on duty. Since his discharge, Young had apparently been working as a mercenary for some years, but had recently fallen off the grid and his whereabouts and employment details for the last three years were a blank to the authorities.

"Well, well," Ross said, looking down at the figure lying in the bed before him, "looks like you have quite a chequered past, you murdering bastard."

"Do you think he can hear us, sir?" Drake quietly whispered in Ross's ear.

"I doubt it, Izzie, not yet anyway. When he comes round, I want one of our people with him with a recorder so anything he says won't be missed. If we're lucky, he'll be a bit disorientated when he starts to wake up and you never know what he might inadvertently blurt out without him realising he's said it."

"You're a sneaky bastard sometimes, Detective Inspector, you know that don't you?" she smiled.

"But of course, Sergeant Drake," he smiled back at her. "When we get back to headquarters, draw up a rota, Izzie, so we've got someone with Young every minute, day and night, until he wakes up."

"Right sir. Why don't we go see if the doctors can tell us when that's likely to be?"

"You go, Izzie. I want to stay here and get a good long look at this piece of dung. There's a lot he can tell us if we can break him down, but given his background, that's not likely to be an easy task."

"Okay, won't be long," Drake said and she was gone in a second, leaving Ross alone with the killer of Tim Knight and Martin Lewis, themselves a pair of cold-blooded killers for money as far as Ross was concerned.

As Ross waited for Izzie's return, Young stirred, and much to Ross's surprise, his eyes suddenly snapped open. Seeing Ross towering over his bed, Young seemed to sense just who and what Ross was. In a rasping, dry voice he croaked, "Fuck off, copper," and then closed his eyes again.

Ross quickly went to the door, and ordered one of the constables on guard duty to go and summon a doctor. The nurses station was mere yards away and the P.C. reported that the patient was conscious. A doctor appeared as if by magic within a minute and joined Ross in the room at Young's bedside.

"Good morning, Inspector. I'm Doctor Starling," the doctor introduced himself.

"He woke up, swore at me, then closed his eyes again, Doc," Ross informed the doctor, who proceeded to examine the patient. When he lifted Young's eyelid, Young sprang to life again, protesting at Starling's intrusion.

"Ah, good to see some response from you, Mister Young," Starling said, completely unfazed by Young's reaction. "Try to lie still. You're in the

Royal University Hospital. You have two broken legs and scans show you have an intra-cranial bleed."

"Meaning?" Young croaked.

"Meaning you have a potentially serious injury. We may have to operate to prevent pressure building in your head and in turn putting pressure on your brain."

"Can I talk to him, Doctor Starling?" Ross interrupted.

"In a minute, please, Inspector," Starling rebuffed him, as Izzie walked back into the room, surprised to see the doctor with Ross.

"Oh, I just got back from talking to Doctor Clemence," she said, "he got the call from the nurse to say Young was awake and…" and in less than a second, Ross leaped at Starling, knocking him down and pinning him to the floor.

"Cuffs, Izzie, *now,*" he shouted and Drake responded instantly, handcuffing the man on the floor as Ross kept him pinned down. Once the prisoner was secure, Ross pulled him to his feet. Starling scowled at Ross and Drake, but could do nothing to prevent Ross from delving into the pockets of his white coat, his right hand emerging with a syringe loaded with a clear liquid.

"Well now, what have we here?" Ross said as he held the hypodermic up for Young to see. "It would appear someone didn't want to take a risk on you talking to us, Mister Young."

"Bastards," was the monosyllabic reply from the man in the bed.

"I take it my return was a timely one," Drake observed.

"Definitely," Ross confirmed as the door opened to admit Doctor Clemence.

"Oh, hope I'm not intruding," Clemence said, as though seeing a man dressed a doctor being held in handcuffs by two police officers in a patient's room was a normal, everyday occurrence in his life.

"Not all, Doctor," Ross replied. "Just a minute and we'll get this impostor out of your way."

Ross called the armed constables into the room and handed Starling over to them.

"Get this piece of scum down to headquarters," he ordered. "I'll let them know you're on your way in. Sergeant Drake and I will stay with the patient, along with D.C. Gable when she gets back, until you return."

"Yes sir," the two men echoed each other as Ross took out his mobile phone and called D.C.I. Agostini, who would personally begin interrogating Starling as soon as he was delivered to headquarters.

"Perhaps you'd like to check him over, Doctor?" Ross said to Clemence, who nodded at the detective and then carried out his examination of the patient.

Young remained silent throughout, and Clemence finally stood back from the bed, and turned to Ross.

"He's going to make a full recovery, Inspector, though it will be a while before he's walking again."

"Good," said Ross.

"Yes, well, whatever he's done, he's still my patient and it's my job to patch him up the best I can."

"I know, Doc, but it just seems a waste of taxpayers money to pay for all that treatment for a piece of murdering shite like him."

"Not for me to debate," said Clemence.

"Sure, I won't make it difficult for you," said Ross. "I just want to talk to him."

"Well, I have no objection to that. If you need me, I'll be outside for a few minutes at the nurse's station."

"Thanks, Doc," said Ross and Clemence made his way out of the room, leaving Ross and Drake with Graham Young.

"Well now, that was a turn up for the books wasn't it? Your friends certainly didn't waste any time in trying to silence you, did they?" Ross said to Young who glared back at him.

"Don't tell me you're going to keep silent to protect them after that?" Drake asked. "You ought to be bloody grateful to Detective Inspector Ross here for saving your worthless life."

"Worthless to you maybe, darlin' but not to me," Young replied in his hoarse, croaking voice.

"Well if you don't want your pals coming back to try again, I suggest you tell us what we need to know," Ross said as he stood staring hard at the man in the bed.

Young stared back, still perhaps feeling the effects of the anaesthetic, his eyes seeming to lose focus for a few seconds. In fact, he was quickly mentally weighing up his options. As soon as the bogus doctor had introduced himself to Ross as 'Doctor Starling' Young had instantly realised that the man was another of Finch's operatives and could only be in his room for one purpose. He'd been unable to react quickly or shout a warning to the policeman, but thankfully the real doctor coming in to the room together with Izzie Drake's words had alerted Ross, who'd reacted with surprising speed in taking the man down. Young could only guess at the contents of the syringe Ross had taken from Starling's pocket, but guessed it would probably prove to be the same cyanide compound he'd used on Tim Knight. Fast acting and bloody awful way to die, but over in seconds. Finch obviously didn't trust him to keep his mouth shut, or maybe that was the American's way of dealing with any of his operatives he felt had failed him. Either way, Graham Young knew he had to make a decision, and as self-preservation was always his priority, the appeal of living to fight another day over-rode any thoughts of 'honour among thieves' or any of that old-fashioned malarkey.

Young appeared to Ross to slump back against his pillows and exhaled a deep and almost reluctant breath as he looked up at the Detective who'd just saved his life, and pointed to the water jug on the cabinet beside his bed. Ross nodded to Izzie Drake who filled a small plastic drinking cup with a straw from the jug and held it out to Young. He managed to take and hold the cup while he took a few sips of the already slightly warm water, enough to lubricate his dry throat.

He passed the cup back to Drake without a word, and Izzie placed it back on the cabinet as Ross began to lose patience.

"Well, come on, Young, what's it to be? We know you murdered Tim Knight and Martin Lewis, so you're caught bang to rights on those killings. If you don't want us to start digging further, maybe get Interpol to look into a few unsolved murders across the continent, I suggest you talk to us." Ross turned to Drake, winking at her as he spoke.

"You never know, Izzie, this bastard might have killed more people over the years, maybe in Germany, Greece, Albania, Turkey, oh yes, Turkey or Albania would be good ones. I don't think Mr. Young here would receive a very warm welcome in either a Turkish or Albanian prison would he? Of course, if he confesses all, we might be able to keep him here and make sure he serves a nice, long, warm and comfortable sentence in a good old, civilised British prison, but just think of the things we've heard about what happens to good looking chaps like Mr. Young at the hands of the guards, never mind the inmates in Turkish jails especially. Brings tears to your eyes just thinking about it."

"God yes, it does sir. Must say I've never understood what makes men want to do that to other men, but hey, whatever floats your boat, and all that."

Young had heard enough. Ross may have been bluffing about Interpol, but then again, maybe not, and he certainly didn't want them to know about the jobs he'd carried out over the years, including a couple in Turkey. No way was Graham Young going to allow himself to become a faggot for some fat, dirty, unwashed Turkish bastard of a prison guard. He actually subconsciously cinched the cheeks of his backside together as he sighed again and looked up at Ross, who knew instinctively he'd got his man.

"Well, Young? Anything to say?" he asked once again.

Graham Young almost choked on the words as he finally spoke, hatred for his adversary still clear in his eyes, but the words he spoke were just what Andy Ross wanted to hear.

"Alright," he said. "What do you want to know?"

CHAPTER 32

FINCH UNMASKED

The excitement among the team at headquarters was palpable as everyone began to believe they were finally closing in on the solution to the case. No sooner had Ross and Drake arrived in the squad room, after arranging for Graham Young to be transferred to another hospital room, under a false name, with armed guards present inside the room rather than outside the door, than the squad received an unexpected visitor.

Jerome Decker III appeared to have aged ten years since the case began with the murder of his son. He at first expressed total surprise at the revelation that his son had been murdered by his two housemates, two men Decker had met and thought to be Aaron's friends. Ross had made him sit down and compose himself as memories began to flood the C.I.A. man's mind.

After a couple of minutes, Decker stood and walked across to where Ross was in a huddle with Agostini and Drake.

"I actually came to bring you some information," Decker said, as he walked up behind them, making them jump in unison.

"Oh, sorry," he apologised.

"No, please, go on Mr. Decker," Agostini said. "I'm presuming those inquiries you were going to get your people to make have borne fruit?"

"In a way, yes," Decker replied. "It seems that the Aegis Institute is to all intents and purposes innocent of any collective or corporate wrongdoing, Chief Inspector, but, my operatives in various locations, have, shall we say, unearthed something interesting?"

"Go on, please," said Ross.

"Okay, with the reports I was receiving, a pattern gradually emerged. You guys already know that for some reason, Aegis has been employing salvage experts to head up some of their facilities and where we identified such people we concentrated our inquiries. We found the men employed to run those facilities all appear to live a little too well, you know what I mean, cars or houses a bit too extravagant for their status in the company and so on. Taken individually it wouldn't add up to a hill of beans and they wouldn't ever have expected a major investigation into their little scam, well a big scam in fact. Everywhere that Aegis has carried out supposed environmental studies or oceanographic research into coastal erosion by wave action or whatever, some kind of historical site has been found nearby, or an ancient wreck or the ruins of an underwater city, and so on. Pretty innocent so far, yes?"

Everyone in the room was listening now and they collectively nodded, like puppets being manipulated by invisible strings, Paul Ferris thought to himself. Decker continued.

"Okay, but, in these cases, it seems that Aegis only arrived on the scene after they made representations to the governments or at least the local regional governments responsible for these locations."

"They weren't invited, then?" Ross asked.

"Not in one single case," Decker confirmed, "and in all those cases the man who made first contact was none other than Francis Kelly, whose official title by the way is Executive Vice President in charge of Overseas Development. My friends at the F.B.I have informed me that Kelly lives in a house comparable with that of Aegis's CEO, but that he also owns a large beach front property in Malibu, a condo in Florida and holiday villas in four European countries, all countries that have an Aegis facility present on their shores."

"But okay," said Ross, "I can accept that Kelly is running a crooked operation, ripping off governments around the world, stealing national treasures or items of historical significance, but my question is, how the hell are they locating these sites in the first place?"

Instead of a reply, Decker picked up a large manila envelope he'd earlier placed on a nearby desk and extricated a large ten by eight inch photograph that he first passed to Ross, who in turn passed it on to Agostini and the others.

"Are you serious?" Ross asked.

"Deadly," said Decker.

"But that's a…a"

"Submarine, Sergeant Drake, exactly," said Decker as Izzie hesitated with the shock of the revelation.

"You're telling us that Aegis has the use of a submarine?" She gasped.

"No, Sergeant, not *a* submarine, *four* of the damned things."

"Where the hell did they get them from?" Ross asked incredulously.

683

"In 1991, the Soviet Navy effectively ceased to exist with the fall of Communism," said Decker. "You've maybe heard stories of the old Soviet Fleet lying rusting away in various dockyards around the old Soviet Union. Well, that's true but some enterprising Russian entrepreneurs, usually high up in the new democratic but equally corrupt government have made millions of dollars over the years by secretly selling off various parts of the fleet, at least parts that were still operational. The sub in that photo is a Kilo class boat, non-nuclear diesel electric powered. We think they have two of those, plus a couple of Juliett class guided missile subs."

"That's almost unbelievable," a shocked Oscar Agostini managed to gasp.

"Unbelievable but true," said Decker.

"And is that what I think it is behind the conning tower?" Ross asked, looking closely at the photo.

"They call it the 'sail' nowadays, Inspector, not the conning tower," Decker pointed out.

"Oh, right, I stand corrected, but the question remains, is that a bloody great submersible on the deck behind the…sail?"

"It is," Decker confirmed, "and that's how they are finding these sites. They have modern submarine technology with the ability to scan the terrain of the sea bed, and carrying their own submersibles means they can carry our covert examinations of the target areas to see if they're worth 'grave robbing' for want of a better term."

"So they find themselves a possible target, check it out, and if it's a possible source of wealth, they move in with some sort of legitimate offer to the relevant authorities and then proceed to strip the assets from the poor sods who think Aegis is doing them a service."

"That's exactly the way my people read it, Inspector," Decker confirmed.

"But how is this Kelly guy keeping all this secret from his bosses?" Drake asked.

"Easy," said Decker. "As far as the executives of Aegis know, Kelly's people are carrying out legitimate research or whatever, and Kelly and his cronies carry on doing what they do under a cloak of legitimacy."

"But what about the submarines? Why don't they tell the countries they are working for about them?" asked Derek McLennan.

"Politics, Detective," said Decker. "No way do the Aegis board want anyone to know they are sailing around the oceans in a small fleet of former Soviet attack submarines, for obvious reasons."

"Sure, I see," said McLennan.

"It seems clear to me," said Decker. "Kelly and his highly specialised team of crooked operatives have gained control of one or more of the submarines, and using some form of intelligence gathering system that I'd love to infiltrate, they are managing to target specific areas that might yield

684

massive personal profits if they can first of all negotiate a legitimate contract with the relevant government, and then they send one of their subs in to confirm the possibility for profit. If there is nothing in it for them, they allow a normal Aegis research team or exploration vessel to carry out the contract and everything is perfectly legit, a perfect cover in fact for the shady operations that develop when they identify potential, illegal profit making enterprises. It also serves a purpose by keeping the main board of the Aegis out of the loop because all they see are normal, oceanographic studies or environmental investigations being carried out by their people and equipment."

"But, how do they cover up the crooked operations?" Ross asked the C.I.A. man.

"That should be no problem for Kelly either," Decker replied. "Look at the Falmouth job, as I'll call it. Aegis Oceanographic in the States are aware only of the legitimate side of the operation taking place in the English Channel, as Herr Heller discovered when he contacted them. So, they have instant plausible deniability which is genuine because Kelly's people are running the salvage and plundering of the wreck site as what we'd call a 'Black Op' with only a small number of people aware of the true nature of what they're up to. I'll bet if we could access their records, we'd find a team of scientists and underwater specialists are in fact gathering data on the environmental issues surrounding not just this site, but others in the English Channel, with only Kelly's gangsters actually working this particular site."

"That's absolutely diabolically brilliant," Oscar Agostini grudgingly admitted.

"Yes it is," said Decker, "and Kelly obviously has enough personal finance behind him to run these special operations without disturbing the company's finances and raising suspicion."

Ross had remained virtually silent throughout Decker's report, realising also just how far reaching the intelligence gathering skills of the C.I.A, could reach into the lives and the operations of people and organisations around the world. Having heard what Decker had to say, he felt it an opportune moment to fill in the assembled group of detectives and Decker on what he and Drake had learned in their time at the bedside of Graham Young.

"All you've said makes sense, Mr. Decker and tends to fit what we've learned from Kelly's hired killer, Graham Young. As soon as he realised that Kelly had sent a man to eliminate him after he'd fallen into our hands, he became a little less reluctant to cover up for his employer who must be one hell of a ruthless man,"

"He did what?" Decker asked and Ross, realising that Decker wasn't aware of recent events at the hospital, quickly brought him up to date with what had occurred in Young's room.

"Holy cow," Decker retorted. "Ruthless indeed. Please go on, Inspector Ross. Sorry for the interruption."

"Well," Ross began again, "according to Young, the boss as he put it, employs a team of specialist 'damage limitation experts' as they call themselves to make sure the illegal operations remain secure from outside interference. The man who heads up this team, mostly former mercenaries and Special Forces personnel, is known only as Mr. Finch. All the members of the team are known by code names, in Young's case, his is 'Robin'. That's what gave the bogus doctor away to Young at the hospital although he couldn't cry out to warn us at the time. When he introduced himself to me as Doctor Starling, another bird's name, Young knew right away he was as good as dead. If the real doctor hadn't come in to the room at that moment, with our own 'bird,' Sergeant Drake of course, it's likely Starling would have asked us to leave while he carried out some bogus examination of the patient and would have injected Young with the assumed poisonous contents of the syringe we took from him."

"Sorry to interrupt again," said Decker, "but where is this Starling guy right now?"

"In custody," said Ross, "cooling his heels under guard in an interview room waiting for me and Sergeant Drake to question him." "That's great," Decker enthused. "So, you have two of the bastards under lock and key."

"Yes," Ross agreed, "but from what Young told us, each of these men is a highly trained killer, ready to kill at a minutes notice without conscience. None of them are privy to the running of the organisation and all work for the man known as Finch who in Young's case at least, contacted him initially by email. After a few messages between them, a meeting was set up and Young was hired as a 'security consultant' and given the name 'Robin'. I doubt any of them has access to Kelly. Young says he's never heard of him, and I tend to believe him. Having someone try to kill you in your hospital bed tends to focus the mind and destroy any old allegiances in my experience."

"So, how we can use them in trying to crack the case, sir?" asked Derek McLennan.

"Well, Sergeant Drake and I have concocted a plan," Ross replied and nodded to Drake, who continued.

"We hope to use Young as bait," she said. "Young doesn't want to spend the rest of his life looking over his shoulder, so he's agreed to help us. In return, we'll recommend he be tried over here and not handed over for extradition if anyone else comes seeking him for previous crimes. He knows we can't make promises but he's trusting us to do our best. We'll let word slip out that Young is talking and is being held in a safe house, which he will be, but not at the address we'll leak.

Young thinks it likely that Finch might just try to finish him off himself once word leaks that Starling failed. He says Finch is an arrogant so and so and it would be just the way he'd work things to make sure Young is out of the way for good. If he can't trust Starling then he'll try to finish the job himself."

"But why eliminate Young if he can't tie them to Kelly?" McLennan asked.

"Because Young ties in to Finch, and Finch is obviously connected to Kelly and if we establish that link we might just be able to bring the whole house of cards down. Finch must be worried and therefore Kelly is too."

"So really the man we want is Finch?"

"That's right, Derek," Ross replied this time. "Even Young thinks Finch knows enough to identify Kelly as the brains behind the operation. He's bragged to 'Robin' that he knows enough to cause trouble for the paymasters if they try to dupe or double cross him."

"But I thought Finch was in America," McLennan probed further.

"Young doesn't think so," said Ross. "Kelly is, but not Finch. Young believes Finch is the head of security for the UK, maybe Europe too, but even though Finch talks with a U.S accent and tries to make Young believe he's in the States when he speaks on the phone, Young says sometimes there are none of the distinctive sounds present on the line like you get from an international call when he speaks to Finch. He's convinced Finch spends time in both countries and if this is where the action is this is where he'll be."

"This Finch guy sounds a slippery customer," Jerome Decker interjected.

"Yes he does, Mr. Decker, and listen to this. Young told us he believes Finch is ex-C.I.A."

"What?" Decker exploded. "I need to find out who that rat is. I'll personally drown his ass in your River Mersey if I can get my hands on his sorry throat. Did Young or Robin, whatever his name is give you a description?"

"Yes he did," Izzie Drake replied to his question, taking out her notebook from her shoulder bag. "Young says he only met Finch once, when the other man interviewed him for the job."

The others coughed and almost laughed at the description of hiring a hitman at an interview.

"I know, I know," said Drake, knowing what they were chuckling at, "but that's what Young called it. Anyway, he says Finch was around forty to forty-five years old, just short of six feet tall he thought, though the man was seated most of the time. Young has travelled extensively and he was certain Finch's accent put him as being from New York, though he'd tried to refine it a little. He had brown hair, thinning on top with a hint of grey at the sides, brown eyes, and had an Italian look about him."

Ross couldn't help but notice a look of intense concentration on Decker's face, one eye was almost closed, and his head was slightly tilted to one side, as though he was accessing some long buried memory bank in his brain. Meanwhile, Izzie Drake continued.

"Young said the one feature that made Finch stand out was something he only noticed when he shook hands with Finch as they were parting company. He said he couldn't help noticing that Finch had no little finger on his right hand and something made him look at the other hand and Finch was missing the little finger on that hand too."

Jerome Decker virtually exploded as recognition swept through him.

"Lambert," he shouted so loud everyone in the room was totally shocked by his outburst. "Fucking Randolph Lambert," his voice grew even louder.

Ross placed a hand on Decker's right shoulder in an attempt to calm him down.

"Mr. Decker, please, calm down. I take it you know who this man is?"

"I do, Inspector Ross," said Decker, lowering his voice to a reasonable decibel level. "Randolph Lambert was a first class operative until he was captured on a covert mission into Iraq during the first Gulf War. Saddam's Secret Police had him for nearly three months, tried everything to get him to betray his two fellow agents who were with him in Tikrit. They cut one of his fingers off and he didn't talk. They cut off his other little finger and he still didn't talk. When they cut off the things you didn't see, two toes from each foot, and then began beating his bleeding feet, Lambert cracked. Who could blame him? Thing is, before the Secret Police could act on his information, the building they were in was assaulted by an extraction team ordered in by his co-agents in the town. They took one look at what those bastards had done to Lambert and shot them where they stood. Lambert was treated and repatriated to the States but due to his injuries he wasn't considered suitable for field work any longer. He was given a desk job but it soon became evident his mind had gone. He blamed the Agency for what had happened to him, said we should have got him out sooner, which we would have done if we'd known where they were holding him. He was subjected to a psyche evaluation which deemed him unfit for service so he was pensioned off, invalided out of the service. He made a lot of noise at the time, saying he'd been betrayed by those he'd fought to protect and was eventually placed in a psychiatric hospital. He was resourceful though and escaped and has been living off the grid until now. He's obviously using his former skills to run his own squad of highly paid mercenaries in a pseudo-security operation on sale to the highest bidder."

"You sound as if you knew him well, Mr. Decker," said Ross, speculating that there was a punch line to all this.

"I did, Inspector Ross," Decker confirmed. "I was the person he blamed the most for his capture. You see, I was his handler, his superior officer. I sent Randy to Iraq in the first place. His mind somehow twisted into holding me responsible for his capture, incarceration and torture. The fact that I organised the team that eventually broke him out of there and took him home got lost somewhere along the trail. Now he's responsible for the death of my son."

Decker's head slumped into his shoulders as his words dried up.

The room fell silent. For a while, nobody could think of a word to say. Ross, Drake, Agostini and the rest of the team quickly realised that finding those responsible for Aaron's murder had now taken on an even greater significance for Jerome Decker III.

"You can't think Lambert knew right from the start that Aaron would become involved, surely?" Drake asked the American.

"No, Sergeant Drake, I don't. But once he knew someone was poking around in his UK operation and then discovered it was Aaron, he would have had a perverse sense of revenge in ordering his murder. Gentlemen, ladies, rest assured, I will do everything in my power, personally and professionally to bring him down, and all those connected with him. Aaron's killers may be dead, but the ones who ordered his death and maybe others are still free. I hope this doesn't close the case for you, Inspector Ross?"

"Far from it," Ross replied. "There's still the matter of the death of T.J. Knowles in Cornwall and the involvement of Sally Metcalfe's father in transporting stolen artefacts and bullion to be taken into consideration, plus his possible connection to Aaron's death."

Decker appeared stunned.

"You really think Metcalfe could have been involved in Aaron's death? He was his daughter's boyfriend for Christ sakes."

"Someone helped to set up the whole scenario here in Liverpool. Someone told them where Aaron and Sally would be that night. Who better than her own father?" Ross added.

"Jesus H. Christ," Decker exclaimed. "This gets worse by the minute."

"Yes it does, Mr. Decker, and now I need to ask you to let us get on with our jobs and try to close the net on these bastards. Any help you and your people can give, as long as it remains focussed outside the United Kingdom, will of course be appreciated."

Decker nodded his agreement.

"Anything, Inspector, anything at all."

"Thank you," said Ross as his face seemed to set into a hard and determined look as he spoke to his team.

"For now, everyone, we have a sting to set up, a trap to bait."

CHAPTER 33

A SINGING CANARY AND A HISTORY LESSON FOR TONY CURTIS

In order to put their plan to lure the man known as Finch into their trap into operation, Ross and Drake spent an hour in the company of Graham Young, the killer now so concerned with his own self-preservation that he was to use Ross's awful pun, 'singing like a canary' in his efforts to deflect blame onto those responsible for the plot that had led to the deaths of Aaron Decker, T.J. Knowles, and the two housemates, Tim Knight and Martin Lewis.

Everything he knew, he told the detectives, until eventually they managed to build up the best picture they possibly could of the man known as Finch, a.k.a. Randolph (Randy) Lambert.

Ross's next move was to contact D.I. Brian Jones in Falmouth. He needed to give the Cornish detective the news of Young's capture.

"Brian," Ross said as Jones answered his extension at the police station in Falmouth, "glad to catch you in the office."

"Hello, Andy. Something tells me, by the sound of your voice, that you have news to impart."

"Very astute my friend, and yes, I do. We have the killer of T.J. Knowles in custody, though not before he'd managed to kill the two men who carried out the murder of Aaron Decker."

"Bloody hell," Jones said loudly down the phone. "Sounds like you've been busy up there."

"We have, Brian, but I'm only sad we were one step behind them most

690

of the way and just too late to save Knight and Lewis, Aaron Decker's housemates."

"Why the hell did they kill their own friend?" Jones asked an obvious question.

"Money, mostly, Brian. According to Young, Knight had the bigger incentive, because believe it or not he was jealous of Aaron's prowess at cricket and he also coveted Sally Metcalfe, Aaron's girlfriend. Lewis was the follower, the weaker of the two, but he'd run up some nasty gambling debts and saw this as a way out of hock, and a new start."

"Bloody hell," Jones's Cornish accent seemed to grow stronger as he became more animated. "I can scarce believe it. Andy, did this Young character tell you what happened to T.J?"

"He did, Brian. Seems young Aaron met him in a pub in Falmouth as we thought, got talking to him and found he worked for Aegis. T.J. must have shot his mouth off a little about being fed up with the poor wages Aegis was paying to their U.K staff and Aaron targeted him as a potential helper. When he told T.J what he thought Aegis was up to, T.J was happy to join forces in the hopes that there'd be something in it for him. Aaron must have told him there was the potential to make some money. I think Aaron's real plan was to find out what Aegis was up to and simply blackmail them. Gold bullion was outside the realms of what Aaron could possibly carry or sell on so blackmail makes sense. All he had to do was come up with enough proof of exactly what they were up to. I think he was killed because he'd made contact with Aegis and tried to put his blackmail plan into operation. He used Haller to establish the credentials of the wrecks once he knew Aegis was diving on the site. God knows how many dives he and T.J. made over the months but they eventually figured it out. Of course, we all know how it all turned out, Brian."

After a moment's silence, Jones asked Ross the inevitable question.

"So, what happens now, Andy?"

Ross outlined his plan, as agreed with Agostini, which met with immediate approval from Brian Jones.

"Anything we can do to help, let me know," the Falmouth detective offered.

"I'm sure we'll need you and your people at some point, Brian. Probably be an idea to let your guvnor know the score, and be ready for a call. We're obviously going to have to hit the Aegis facility down there before long, but first we need to get our hands on this Finch character and hopefully cause some panic in the minds of the top man in the organisation."

"And you think it's this Kelly character, right?"

"Maybe, but there's a possibility he may be the front man for someone higher up in the Aegis hierarchy."

"Bloody hell, Andy. Just how far does this thing reach?"

"Hopefully, we're not far from finding out, my friend. By the way, how are our Navy friends getting on down there?"

"I thought you'd never ask," Jones replied. "The *Wyvern* was joined on station as they call it by a Royal Fleet Auxiliary salvage tug, the *Whitehaven Castle*. Don't be fooled by the word 'tug' Andy. I had a mental picture of something like you see pushing ocean liners around in the movies, but God, this thing anchored off Falmouth the day before yesterday and it's bloody massive, even bigger then the *Wyvern*. She's not a very pretty ship, nothing like a sleek warship like the *Wyvern* but Cap'n Howell says the *Whitehaven Castle* has instantly speeded things up and they anticipate completing their investigation of the wreck of the *Norwich* in a few days time, after which she will be designated as an official war grave. The Navy is holding a memorial service at sea for the crews of the sub and the *Norwich* too and I'd really like you and Izzie to come down and see that short ceremony of dedication, if you're able to, Andy."

"Of course we'll be there, Brian. I'll get it cleared with D.C.I. Agostini today and you can then book us in to the Hope and Anchor again if you don't mind."

"No problem, Andy."

"Any news on the U-Boat, Brian?"

"They're working on the submarine today. I'll call you as soon as I know anything with an update."

"I'd appreciate that, thanks Brian."

"So what's next for you guys up there?" Jones inquired.

"My D.C.I. is talking with his boss, Detective Chief Superintendent Hollingsworth about involving our friends across the pond. We are going to need the Americans' help if we're to bring Kelly to justice. We can't touch him as long as he's in the States, but the F.B.I. can. And then of course, we've got Aaron's father, the C.I.A. man and his contacts working the Continental Europe angle. Hollingsworth will also liaise with the other European police forces in countries affected by Aegis's crooked operations. Hopefully we can bring the whole lot down in one fell swoop in a single well co-ordinated operation."

"Blimey," said Jones. "You make the whole thing sound like a bloody military operation, Andy."

"It seems like it, doesn't it? Anyway, this whole thing harks back to World War Two with the sinking of the *Norwich* and the *U966*, or *U3000*, or whichever you want to call it, Brian, so it's rather appropriate we should use military style planning to bring these murdering bastards down, don't you think?"

"There's no arguing with that," Jones agreed. "So this Chief Super of yours, do you think he can swing it with the Yanks and all the Euro-forces."

"He's a she, actually," Ross corrected his Cornish counterpart. "D.C.S. Sarah Hollingsworth is one damned tough cookie, Brian. Good looking, brains, and a clinical and analytical mind. She's been in the job three years now and I can tell you, if anyone can pull it all together in a short space of time, she can."

"Wow, she sounds like a real firebreather," Jones quipped.

"Well, I've heard she can be a bit of a dragon in meetings," Ross joked and the two men shared a brief few seconds of laughter.

* * *

Klaus Haller was in his element. Safely ensconced in a safe house organised by Merseyside Police, located a few miles east of the city in St. Helens, with two armed police officers inside and two more outside for his protection, plus the company of Detective Constable Tony Curtis, who'd been sent to check on his progress, Haller was a busy man. Curtis had taken the place of Derek McLennan in visiting the historian when Ross informed them that McLennan was needed for a special assignment, related to the current case. Very mysterious, Curtis thought, but Ross said no more.

The German historian was proving a real asset to the investigation. Even as Ross and his team were thinking along the same lines, Haller had decided that someone with a connection to the strange circumstances surrounding the false *U966's* last mission had to be connected to the current case. Of course, there was old Hans Schmidt and Ralph Stein, but Haller's own inquiries showed that Schmidt, now old and infirm, was suffering from Alzheimer's disease and could be easily eliminated as a suspect. Stein was a possibility but though he lived close to an Aegis facility, his life since leaving the Kriegsmarine had been an exemplary one and his chances of being involved, at least to Haller, seemed tenuous to say the least.

Being the historian that he was, an established academic and expert in his field, Haller had devised a new theory, one he now sat explaining to D.C. Curtis.

"We must remember," Haller began, "that the boat we are now referring to as *U966* was in fact *U3000*, sailing under a false designation. We know there were no survivors from the sinking of the U-Boat, but we Germans, and the Nazis in particular have always been known for keeping scrupulous records, D.C. Curtis. So, the crew records for *U3000* must have been altered to show the men of *U3000* to be serving on the false *U966*. There is no way the boat would have sailed without a full crew and cargo manifest being compiled, which leads me to believe we may have missed another person, two perhaps, who may have been aware of the nature of this *U966's* mission."

Tony Curtis was a bright and quick-thinking young detective and without further prompting, he quickly latched on to Haller's train of thought.

"Clerks, administrative staff, that's what you're getting at, isn't it, Herr Haller?"

"*Sehr gut*, forgive me, I mean to say, very good. Yes, that is what I am getting at. Now, my research while I have been in this nice house you have accommodated me in has thrown up two names. The first was the senior dockyard superintendent's secretary at the Kiel Submarine base, Brigitte Kraus, who was responsible for maintaining all such manifests as I previously mentioned. The second is Helene Schneider."

Haller paused and waited for Curtis to accept the bait in his hesitancy.

"And she is, or rather, was?"

"Helene Schneider, Detective Curtis, was at the time of the redesignated *U966's* voyage, the personal secretary to Admiral Stein. She was only twenty at the time, and is now seventy-eight years old, but in full health, as I have discovered."

"You think this Helene Schneider is the one, don't you, Herr Haller?" Curtis astutely observed.

"Oh yes, I do, I most certainly do, Mr. Curtis," said Haller as the excitement in his voice grew by the second, "though not directly. Fraulein Schneider married in 1950, and records show she gave birth to three children in the next ten years. Helene married a former naval officer, Jürgen Reinhardt, who was unconnected to the U-Boat arm of the service. Now for the interesting part, D.C. Curtis. She had two daughters, Lotte and Inge, and a son, Anton. Life in post-war Germany was hard, though the Reinhardt family were fortunate to live in that part of Germany you called West Germany, and not in the so-called German Democratic Republic, East Germany to you, and controlled by the Soviet Union. The best way to make a good life in those times was through a good education and Helene and Jürgen encouraged their children to make a good future for themselves.

To cut this short, Anton went to university in Heidelberg and is now a respected research chemist working for a large pharmaceutical company, involved in developing new drugs to combat various cancers. Lotte never married and is a journalist for a feminist magazine based in Munich, where she lives with her lesbian lover, Hilda Neumann. This leaves us with Helene's youngest daughter, Inge. Whether by coincidence or design I cannot say, but Inge Reinhardt, while studying history, much like Aaron Decker met and fell in love with a much older man, named Robert Ackermann."

Haller paused for breath and took a sip from the glass of water on the table in front of him. Curtis did the same. He found it strangely enthralling listening to the passionate way the German historian related this story to him. History had never been a favourite subject of his at school, but somehow, Klaus Haller had the knack of making the events and the people he talked about come to life in the listener's mind. After audibly clearing his throat, Haller continued with his story.

"Now, where was I? Ah, yes, Robert Ackermann. You will not have heard of this man, D.C. Curtis…"

"Oh for God's sake, Herr Haller, call me Tony, please. No more of the D.C. Curtis or 'detective' and all that crap. It'll save a lot of time."

"Very well, and thank you," Haller smiled at Curtis, feeling he had made a friend of sorts in this young and very attentive detective.

"So, as to Robert Ackermann. During the war, Tony, Ackermann was on the staff of Grand Admiral Karl Dönitz, head of the U-Boat arm, close confidant to Adolf Hitler and later President of Germany for a short time following Hitler's death. Inge was not concerned with Ackermann's war service, quite clearly and she and Robert later had a son, born in 1960, who they named Erich. Now, in 2003, Erich Ackermann is of course a grown man of forty-three years of age, and this is where I believe you should make a phone call to Detective Inspector Ross, Tony."

Haller sighed, fell silent and leaned back in his chair, a knowing smile on his face.

Curtis in turn smiled back, and waited.

"Okay, Herr Haller, let's hear it," he said after a few moments' silence. "I can feel a punchline coming on."

"Haha," Haller giggled quietly. "I am aware of this phrase, punchline, and yes maybe you will take it as such when I tell you that Erich Ackermann is a financial genius, who has made a small fortune, as I believe it is called, by playing the world's stock markets, and by speculating on some very risky financial ventures over the years, but he is also the European Head of Finance for the Aegis Institute, a position he acquired as a result of being listed as a major shareholder in the company. Not only do I suspect Ackermann of having inherited his father's papers, including details of the voyage of *U966*, but I think you will find he has been the driving force behind the Aegis plan to steal the gold from the wreck of the submarine."

Tony Curtis fell silent; his mouth moved a couple of times though no sound came forth as he assimilated Haller's information.

"Herr Haller, you're a genius. How the heck did you find all this information? We're supposed to be the police, not you, and yet you've uncovered all this in no time at all."

"I thank you for the compliment, Tony, but it took no genius to fathom this conundrum out. You must remember that I am German, my friend, and so when it comes to researching anything to do with the Kriegsmarine and the modern German Navy, first of all I am a world-renowned expert on the subject, and have access to many databases your people would not know exist, many written in German of course and by the same token I can also access information about their families and descendants in a similar way, though that takes a little more expertise and the opening of a few, how do you say, back doors?"

"You mean you've hacked into their systems?" an incredulous Curtis ventured, surprised that a man like Klaus Haller would not only have the skills to be a computer hacker, but was prepared to use them.

Haller chuckled. "Sometimes, in order to get at the truth it is necessary to take a crooked path, do you not think, my young friend."

"Well, yes, I suppose so," Curtis agreed, not sure if by doing so he was condoning an illegal act, *but what the hell*, he thought, *if it helps catch a killer…*

Allowing his mind to end its personal internal ethical debate, Detective Constable Tony Curtis pulled his mobile phone from his pocket and dialled D.I. Ross's number.

CHAPTER 34

THE TRAITOR

Andy Ross was pleased with the way his plan was coming together. He'd been delighted beyond belief with Klaus Haller's information, and thanks to Oscar Agostini's intervention with Detective Chief Superintendent Sarah Hollingsworth, not only had the New York office of the F.B.I been brought into the case, actively investigating the internal finances of the Aegis Institute and also having placed a watch on the activities of Francis Kelly but D.C.S. Hollingsworth had acted immediately on the information supplied by Haller, and now the German police in the form of the *Bundeskriminalamt*, Germany's Federal Police Force was involved and were now investigating Erick Ackermann and the activities of Aegis in Germany. The Germans were also liaising with their counterparts in Greece, Italy and Turkey, all countries where the arms of the Aegis octopus of criminal activity was thought to have spread its tentacles.

In order to bring the case to a logical conclusion in the UK, however, it remained for Ross and his team, together with Brian Jones of the Devon and Cornwall Constabulary, to link the deaths of Aaron Decker, T.J. Knowles, Tim Knight and Martin Lewis to Francis Kelly in New York and secondly, to bring Sally Metcalfe's father to justice for his part in the operation in transporting the stolen bullion around Europe and possibly setting Aaron Decker up to be murdered. Ross and Drake had concluded that Metcalfe must have had modifications carried out to Advance Transportation's vehicles in order to conceal the whereabouts of the gold when they crossed various borders on the continent, a theory Agostini wholeheartedly agreed with.

Now that the various European police forces were actively investigating the activities of Aegis Oceanographics, Ross could concentrate on the next phase of his plan, that of luring the man known as Finch, a.k.a Randolph Lambert into the open and then using him to implicate Kelly.

When Oscar Agostini asked Ross how he planned to execute such a plan he replied,

"Easy, Oscar, one of our detectives is corrupt, a leak and is ready to reveal the details of our investigation to Kelly."

Agostini smiled, knowing Ross had a plan up his sleeve.

"Okay, Andy, and just who is this bad cop?"

"Derek McLennan, sir. Of course, he doesn't know it yet, but I'm sure he'll want to volunteer once I explain the plan to him."

"Is your D.I. serious?" Agostini asked Izzie Drake, who was standing behind Ross, her bottom resting on the edge of his desk as the three of them discussed Ross's plan in his small office.

"Deadly serious, sir," she replied. "Derek'll be made up to have the chance to play James Bond."

"You've considered the potential danger to McLennan I presume?" Agostini said.

"We'll have men watching him all the time, sir. Derek McLennan is a top class detective. He can do this. We have a good cover story for him. He sat his sergeant's exams recently. We don't know the actual results yet but we can put the word out that he's failed and he's really bitter at not getting the opportunity to move up in rank."

"You really think you can pull it off, Andy?"

"Yes, I do, sir. Finch is bound to be panicking, knowing we have both Starling and Robin in custody. If Derek can convince him they are both spilling their guts to us, he's going to want to silence them. The fact we haven't got them in a regular prison, or prison hospital in Robin's case, adds to the fact that he will see we're trying to keep them well out of reach of him or any hired killers he might be able to use behind bars. So he'll be desperate to eliminate the pair of them before they can do irreparable damage to his organisation. Derek will contact Finch on Robin's mobile phone, which he'll have supposedly 'borrowed' from the evidence locker, and offer to sell him the locations of both men, but only on a cash basis and at a one to one meeting."

Agostini thought it through for a minute before making his decision.

"Okay, Andy. If McLennan is willing to try, let's do it."

Relieved, Ross could only thank the D.C.I. and he and Drake left to brief Derek McLennan on Ross's proposal. The detective constable was immediately enthusiastic about the idea, and was grateful to Ross for the faith the D.I. was willing to place in him and his abilities. Derek had indeed come a long way since those early days as a young, rather gauche and naïve D.C. Now, he realised, Andy Ross trusted him totally and he intended to repay that trust by carrying off the undercover sting to the best of his ability.

It was agreed that before they went ahead, the Press Liaison Officer, George Thompson would be brought on board. Thompson would 'plant' a story in the Liverpool Echo's evening edition through his contact there, Terry Wallace, a reporter Ross knew could be trusted, having dealt with him during the Brendan Kane and Marie Doyle case four years previously in 1999. The story would report that two men, believed to be connected to the death of local student and sporting hero Aaron Decker, had been apprehended in two separate incidents in the city, and were now under guard in separate locations where they were providing the investigating officers with a plethora of useful information which the police hoped would lead to an early arrest of those behind the murder of the popular young sportsman.

* * *

Paul Ferris, meanwhile, had been far from idle. His investigation into the activities of Jeffrey Metcalfe and his two businesses, Metcalfe Logistics and Advance Transportation was proving interesting. Although Metcalfe Logistics appeared to be perfectly up front and legal in every respect, Ferris had discovered that the subsidiary business, Advance Logistics, had originally been set up and incorporated on the island of Jersey in the Channel Islands, well known for its status as a virtual tax haven for many companies.

It had become evident to Ferris that any business carried out on behalf of the Aegis group over the last three years had been directed through Advance Transportation and not Metcalfe Logistics. Even more interesting to the team's computer whizz-kid was the fact that although Metcalfe Logistics was listed as a Public Liability Company with shares readily available through any legitimate broker, Advance Transportation was a simple private company, sole proprietor, Jeffrey Metcalfe. In other words, the activities of Advance were under the sole control of its owner.

Having found that much, Ferris had moved on to trying to trace the movements of Advance Transportation's small fleet of lorries. To do so, he needed to call on a certain outside resource, a computer geek, a friend, and one of the finest hackers he knew that wasn't actually in jail.

Frankie Trout's saving grace was that he never actually obtained any financial reward as a result of his 'prying' into other people's business. Ferris had met him when he'd caught him trying to hack into the Merseyside Police Personnel Records. Frankie, horrified at being discovered 'with his hands in Aunty's panties,' as he himself described it, thought he'd been apprehended by a 'super hacker' and only later found that Ferris had stumbled on him quite by accident.

Frankie had been able to assure Ferris he only did it to prove to himself he could, which was true of most of his more outlandish 'adventures' in the world of cyberspace. As a result, Ferris was able to use Frankie's expertise in cases where an 'invisible' presence was required, and here and now was one of those occasions.

Five feet five in height, with hair that resembled a young John Lennon during his Maharishi days, and pale green eyes sunken into his head through an apparent lack of a good night's sleep in the last ten years, Frankie answered the phone on the first ring, automatically recalling and recognising Ferris's mobile phone number as it showed on his screen.

"Paul Ferris, my friend," he replied, knowing full well this was no social call. "Tell me what you need."

"You don't mess about, Frankie, do you? Let's get straight to the point huh?"

"Why beat about the bush? We both know you only call me when you want me to do something illegal for you, *Detective Ferris*." He emphasised Ferris's name and rank as he smiled into the phone.

"Watch your mouth, there Frankie. If not for me, you'd be doing ten years in Walton jail, mate, so be grateful I let you do me these little favours now and then."

"Yeah, yeah, right. I'm real grateful, Mr. Ferris, sir. You do realise if any of my geeky mates find out about me helping you I'll probably get chucked out of the Liverpool Geeks and Weirdos Society."

Not sure at first if Frankie was serious, Ferris merely laughed, then realised his tame hacker was simply being facetious.

Frankie laughed along for a few seconds and then asked Ferris what he needed. The detective explained, assuming of course that Metcalfe, like most modern businessmen kept his company records on computer. He warned Frankie that the man might keep anything illegal or secret on a separate, personal computer.

"No problem, Mr. Ferris," Frankie said when Ferris fell silent. "Just tell me where the mark lives. I'll be able to trace any IP addresses located at his home or work. Just leave it to me. Shouldn't take long."

"Really?" Ferris queried.

"Simple task really," Frankie replied. "Ah well, maybe one day you'll bring me a real challenge."

"What, like hacking into the accounts of the Bank of England?" Ferris laughed.

"Oh no, been there, done that. I mean something really difficult."

Ferris stopped laughing.

"Frankie, you haven't? Wait, don't answer that. Just get on with what I want, okay?"

"Sure, Mr. Ferris," Frankie replied. "I'll get back to you soon."

The phone went dead as Frankie hung up and Ferris sat looking at the silent device he held in his hand, wondering, *The Bank of England?* No, surely not. Then again…

CHAPTER 35

NO HEADSTONE ON A SAILOR'S GRAVE

With plans in place for the operation to lure Randolph Lambert, a.k.a. Finch to Liverpool, Ross and Drake once again made the long journey to Falmouth, where the evening found them in familiar surroundings, enjoying a meal at the Hope and Anchor, prepared expertly by Hope Severn. Her husband Thomas had welcomed the two detectives back to his establishment and insisted they call him Tommy. Now they were returning guests, they were regulars as far as he was concerned and thus classed as friends.

This time, there was no old Mrs. Twining or her equivalent in the dining room as they enjoyed their meal. They were however, joined for dinner by Brian Jones and his sergeant Carole St. Clair. The two Cornish detectives were there to bring Ross and Drake up to date on the salvage operations in the Channel.

There had proved nothing unusual or remarkable about the wreck of the *Norwich* apparently, but the team from the Fleet Auxiliary vessel *Whitehaven Castle* had made a remarkable discovery. The wreck of the *U966*, finally revealed in the brilliant high powered underwater lights of the *Whitehaven Castle's* submersibles and dive teams, had given up a secret nobody had expected.

Brian Jones explained as the four enjoyed the redoubtable Hope Severn's superb cooking.

"Charles Howell on the *Wyvern* and his chief engineer tried their best to explain it to us. We saw what looked like an extra torpedo tube on each side of the U-Boat but the tube looked wrong and seemed to run all the way along the lower part of the submarine's hull with corresponding tube exits at the stern. Once the divers identified the exterior anomaly they explored further within the sub's interior until they found what they were looking for.

It seems *U966* was an experimental craft, Andy. She not only carried the gold that Hitler wanted to reach his ex-pat Nazis in South America but she was fitted with what the Navy guys are calling a Hydrodynamic propulsion system."

"I see," said Ross, "and what is a Hydrodynamic propulsion system?"

"Explained in simple terms, Andy, it's a system that sucks in seawater from the front, passes it through something like a ramjet inside the sub and then expels it at great pressure from the rear to propel it at great speed, virtually silently. Imagine if that bloody technology had been put to use by the Nazis. They would have had a 'stealth submarine' as early as 1945, and the ability to strike at our naval and civilian vessels and attack our ports and coastal towns from a fleet of undetectable submarines."

"In other words, that one U-Boat might have changed the course of the war," said Izzie Drake.

"Well, yes and no," Jones responded.

"How come?" Ross asked.

Jones coughed as a piece of food caught in his throat. As he sipped from a glass of water, Carole St. Clair continued.

"It was probably too late in the war for it to have had any real effect on the outcome of the conflict according to Captains Howell, and Prendergast. Anthony Prendergast knows the history of the war at sea better than anyone else in the UK according to Charles Howell. Anthony says that Germany was already on the verge of collapse by the time *U966* or *3000* left Kiel. God it's bloody confusing, these two different numbers, don't you think?"

"Let's stick with *U966*," Ross decided, as that's the number she sailed under, okay?"

"Suits me," Jones agreed, and Carole St. Clair added, "It'll save space in my notebook too."

"Good enough," said Jones. "So anyway, Anthony Prendergast says that Hitler was so out of touch with reality by then he probably did think he could still win the war and in all seriousness, he ordered the experimental U-Boat to set sail for a secret destination, carrying enough stolen gold to finance the building of a fleet of his new super U-Boats. Prendergast thinks the sub was probably headed for a rendezvous with Nazi sympathisers in Argentina. I am left wondering why they didn't use the new propulsion system on that last voyage."

"Why Argentina?" Izzie asked, as she added, "Maybe it wasn't working properly."

"That would make sense," Jones tried to give a rational explanation.

"I've been reading up on the history of the Second World War since we got involved in this case, and after the divers found evidence of this Hydrodynamic thingy system, I went a bit further and looked up as much as I could on the Nazis and their search for new technology."

"And what did you find, Brian? Anything interesting?" Ross asked his Cornish counterpart, impressed with the fact he'd delved into the mists of time to try to pour light on the present."

"I was amazed," Jones replied. "The Nazis were obsessed with developing so-called Super Weapons. They used their best scientific brains, plus God knows how many captive scientists and engineers in Hitler's almost manic quest to come up with what we'd call 'weapons of mass destruction' today. Most of us have heard of the V1 and V2 rockets of course but it seems they were working on much more, including the equivalent of today's inter-continental ballistic missiles which could have drastically changed the course of the war. Historians have actually found the ruins of several test sites and underground research facilities where these projects were worked on. They used slave labour to excavate these sites and again to do the manual labour of maintaining them, simply killing the poor bastards when they couldn't work any more."

"That's inhuman," said Izzie.

"True," said Carole St. Clair, who'd obviously been aiding her D.I. in his research, "but they did far worse, Izzie. At one site, the historians found the remains of hundreds of bodies, hastily buried in pits dug only a few feet into the ground. Forensic anthropologists who examined the bones found many of them contained traces of radiation."

"Radiation?"

"Exactly," Jones re-entered the conversation. "They concluded, together with the historians and archaeologists, that the Nazis probably tested the contents of the experimental warheads on those poor sods, who the anthropologists identified as being mostly of Slavic or Jewish origins, so probably they were Russian P.O.W.s and concentration camp inmates, shipped to the site to be used as human guinea pigs."

"Fucking hell, Brian," was all Ross could manage to say.

"My thoughts exactly, Andy," said Jones. "Anyway, the Nazis had lots of similar facilities all over occupied Europe, working on new aircraft designs, ships, submarines, poison gas filled torpedoes, all sorts of diabolical stuff. Thankfully they never got to develop most of them. Seems the RAF, thanks to some bloody great intelligence work by the resistance in some countries and by their own aerial reconnaissance, identified a lot of these sites and bombed the bastard things out of existence."

"Thank God they did," Izzie Drake replied as Jones fell silent.

"So you think they developed this new propulsion system at one of these sites and then tried to smuggle the technology out of Germany when it looked like they might be losing the war in Europe?"

Jones now returned to Izzie's earlier question regarding Argentina being a possible destination for the disguised submarine.

"There's evidence, according to Prendergast, that a large group of Nazi military personnel and scientists were gradually ferried across the Atlantic towards the end of the war, first of all to escape the constant bombardment of Germany's cities by the RAF and the U.S. Army Air Force, and secondly to continue their work on various Nazi super-weapons, designed to give Hitler a final decisive victory in the war. In case you're wondering the U.S. Air Force as we know it today didn't become a separate force until late in 1947, according to the great sage, Prendergast." Jones smiled and the others smiled with him.

"So, come on, Brian, what does Prendergast think the Germans intended to do if the U-Boat had made it to Argentina?"

"He thinks the Nazis had set up a secret base, run by senior naval officers and crack scientists, where the production of these super-subs could be carried out. It was probably Grand Admiral Doenitz's plan to continue the war after the fall of Berlin, but even he couldn't have anticipated Hitler's suicide and the rapid decline and fall of the Third Reich after his death as the Allies overran the Fatherland and its occupied territories. It was interesting to note the actual spelling of his name was Dönitz. Doenitz is the Anglicised spelling apparently. The old bastard lived until 1980 and died peacefully at the age of 89. Anyway, the point is, bringing things bang up to date, that the technology employed by these new U-Boats was so advanced that even today, it could be worth a fortune, not specifically for submarines, which have changed dramatically since the advent of nuclear propulsion but simply as a highly efficient system of propulsion for surface vessels, reducing the dependence on oil for any nation possessing it."

"Sounds to me as if the technology for this hydrodynamic propulsion system could actually be worth more in the long run than the gold the *U966* was carrying," said Ross.

"Exactly," Jones agreed, "and that, Andy, definitely gives anyone who wants to possess the technology a bloody big motive for murder to obtain it, develop it commercially and to prevent others getting their hands on it."

"Brian, my friend, I think between us all, and with thanks to you and Anthony Prendergast, we may have arrived at the true reason behind everything that's happened."

"There is another option we haven't considered too, sir," said Drake, who'd been following the conversation closely.

"Go on, Izzie, what have we missed?"

"Well sir, I was just thinking; we're all presuming that the whole idea of this exercise was for Aegis to steal and develop the new technology themselves, right?"

"Yes, that's how it seems."

"But with the world's dependence on oil, what if Aegis was being paid by a separate interested party to get hold of the Nazi technology and sell it on to them?"

"And who are you thinking of, Izzie?"

"The people who would stand to lose most if such technology came into being of course, sir."

"Of course," Ross realised what Drake was thinking. "You mean the Arabs."

"Exactly sir. It might be unlikely, but it does bear thinking about. Some of the Arab nations would stand to lose billions of dollars if this new propulsion system came into being."

"But surely," Jones interjected, "it would make more sense for Aegis to just go ahead and develop the system themselves, and make a fortune from building ships and so on that used these engines and selling them to shipping companies all over the world."

"If this Kelly chap is as greedy as we think, I'd say that would depend on how many billions the Arabs would pay to possess and bury that technology," Drake replied.

"A good point, Izzie," Ross said, "and certainly an option we shouldn't discount out of hand until we know more. Thanks for your input. Good to see your brain hasn't been totally befuddled by the joys of marital bliss."

Laughter ensued as everyone took a few seconds to escape from the gravity of the discussion, but then Ross motioned for them to return to the matter in hand.

He went on to explain in detail the information provided by Klaus Haller. It now appeared that the path to the solution to this complicated and convoluted case both began and ended with Erich Ackermann. Now they knew that, and once Ross explained the basis of his plan to bring Finch out into the open as a means of getting to Kelly, he felt it was only a matter of time before they brought those responsible for so many deaths to justice.

Dinner over, the four detectives retired to the bar where they sat and enjoyed a single drink together, a nightcap to bring the evening to a close. Jones and St. Clair bade the Liverpool duo goodnight when their shared taxi arrived, the two living quite near to each other, or, as St. Clair put it, "Tight bugger won't stump up for a second taxi for me when he can get away with only paying for one."

"Now come on Carole, you know very well I've got a wife, a mortgage and three credit cards to support."

The group enjoyed a quiet laugh on the steps of the Hope and Anchor, and as the taxi's rear lights disappeared from view, Ross and Drake made their way to their rooms, both phoning their respective spouses before going to bed, ready for a good night's sleep and a busy day in the morning.

* * *

"You were right, Brian," Ross observed as the helicopter that had picked them up from Falmouth neared the Royal Fleet Auxiliary Vessel, *Whitehaven Castle*. "She's certainly an ugly duckling, that's for sure."

"Ugly maybe, but from what we've seen she's a hell of a ship," Brian Jones said with clear admiration in his voice. The Westland Lynx Mk8 banked slightly to port, giving the passengers a better view of the R.F.A. ship as they turned to make their landing approach.

The dull grey ship had an ungainly appearance, its upper decks seemingly a mass of derricks, cranes and gantries, the few crewmen visible from the Lynx resembling ants scurrying around as they made their way towards the ship's helicopter landing pad, clearly identifiable by the large white 'H' painted on a section of the upper rear deck. A little way to the south of the salvage tug, the sleek lines of *H.M.S. Wyvern* could be seen by the Lynx's passengers, the raked bow and narrow beam of the warship contrasting sharply with the ungainly behemoth of a ship that waited to greet them. Quite clearly, the *Whitehaven Castle* was the type of ship that, had it been a child, only a mother could love. The closer the Lynx got to the ship, the smaller that 'H' and its surrounding circle of clear deck appeared to Ross and his companions.

Closer and closer, the deck appeared to be rising from the ocean to meet their rapid, (in Ross's mind), descent. Ross, never a great flyer, was about to start saying a prayer when the pilot pulled back on the collective, and the helicopter flared out and made its final approach to the deck, seeming to Ross to literally thump on to the *Whitehaven Castle*, despite the obvious suspension springs in the undercarriage easing the shock of final touchdown. Realising he'd been holding his breath, Ross let out a massive sigh. Izzie Drake, who'd noticed her boss's nervousness on the final approach, touched his arm and gave him a reassuring smile.

"Nice soft landing that," she said facetiously.

"Yes, hardly knew we'd touched down," Carole St. Clair added, obviously much happier flying than sailing.

"You alright, Andy?" Jones asked. "Your knuckles have turned a bit white."

Seeing them all grinning sheepishly at him, Ross knew they were having a laugh at his expense.

"Alright you horrible lot," he said, regaining his composure. "Let's get out of here. There's a reception committee waiting for us by the look of it."

Despite his best efforts, Andy Ross still managed to stagger a little as his legs touched the deck, and it took him a couple of seconds to regain full equilibrium. As he did, Captain Charles Howell of the *Wyvern*, Anthony Prendergast of the Royal Navy's Archives Section, and another man strode towards them.

Charles Howell made the introductions, as the new man, a reasonable replica of Captain Birdseye with his long white beard, rotund figure and an unlit pipe dangling from his mouth smiled at the newcomers. The man was a veritable giant, too. Ross estimated his height at around six feet four or five.

"Ladies and gentlemen, say hello to the master of the *Whitehaven Castle*, Captain James Ramsey. James, this is Detective Inspector Andy Ross from Liverpool, D.I Brian Jones from Falmouth and Sergeants Izzie Drake and Carole St. Clair."

"Welcome aboard to you all," Ramsey spoke as he reached out to shake hands with each of his visitors. Ross thought the captain had a handshake that could crush granite, firm and assured, and the man exuded confidence. He'd already been informed by Jones that the Royal Fleet Auxiliary was manned by civilians, not Royal Naval personnel and he could instantly see the difference as he took in the appearance of Ramsey's uniform. Similar in some respects to the military uniform it was however different enough to the naked eye to make the distinction between civilian and military.

"Please follow me," Ramsey said as he turned and beckoned the newcomers to follow him as he led them from the exposed helipad to the warmth that awaited them as they passed through a large steel door and entered one of the ship's many large 'warehouse' facilities where repairs and other vital work could be carried out. For now though, this particular area had been set up as the control room or 'hub' for the continuing exploration of the wreck site. Numerous monitors stood against one bulkhead, each one manned by a seaman who appeared to be analysing everything that had been previously recorded by the dive teams, frame by frame, missing nothing as they searched for anything that would add to the historical records of what had taken place between these two old adversaries during the cold dark days of World War Two.

Captain Ramsey excused himself for a minute, allowing them to take in their surroundings. Ross and the others were amazed at the array of information presented on the various screens. They were able to see the record of everything that the crew of the *Whitehaven Castle* had achieved since arriving on the scene of the dual wreck site. Some of the screens were replaying the same footage over and again as analysts busily examined the pictures in detail, recording their findings and opinions onto voice recorders as they picked up on every tiny detail from earlier dives, and other screens showed static images, those which the experts wanted to examine in closer detail, or that presented them with evidence to help in the examination of the wreckage of both the corvette and the U-Boat.

Ross sensed a presence behind him and turned to see Captain Ramsey approaching with three newcomers in close attendance. Ramsey wasted no time in introducing Ross and his companions to the smiling trio who accompanied him.

"Ladies, gentlemen, please say hello to these gentlemen who will be carrying out our simple act of remembrance for the crews of the *Norwich* and the *U966*, or, as we have been informed of its correct designation, the *U3000*."

Ramsey then introduced Father Roland Green representing the Roman Catholic Faith, Giles Parker from the Church of England and finally, Pastor Konrad Völler from the German Evangelical Church, representing the German Navy.

Father Green spoke for the others after a round of handshakes was completed.

"Detective Inspector Ross, and all of you who have helped in this finding of the two vessels that lie below us on the seabed, on behalf of myself and my colleagues in Christ, I thank you for your dogged determination and your efforts to ensure that the men who were lost on that fateful night in 1945 will no longer be merely part of a forgotten page in history."

Ross went to speak but Green held a hand up, stopping him as his words began.

"No, please, do not be modest, as I'm sure you were about to be. We are here to ensure those men are commemorated today, not as men of war, as they surely were at the time, but as human beings, as husbands, fathers, sons, brothers. You and your people, police officers and naval personnel have all contributed to this moment, and we thank you."

Andy Ross felt a lump in his throat, touched by the simple gratitude expressed by the priest and echoed by his two fellow ministers.

"Thank you," he said, struggling to find words appropriate to the moment. "We were just doing our jobs, all of us, but I'm sure I speak for everyone involved in locating these two ships, and that includes my team back in Liverpool, even young Aaron Decker and TJ Knowles, whose deaths, in retrospect, led to us being here today. Anyway, thank you."

As Ross fell silent, feeling slightly awkward and a little embarrassed, the sound of a helicopter could clearly be heard as it landed on the deck outside the hangar-like room they occupied.

Charles Howell spoke up at that point.

"Aha, sounds like our other guests are arriving. Do excuse me for a few minutes," and he turned on his heel and marched out through the nearest bulkhead door.

"It's beginning to look like we're having a real gathering here today, Andy," Brian Jones commented. "I wonder who's arriving now."

The answer arrived soon afterwards as Captain Howell led another officer, resplendent in the full dress uniform of the German Navy into the operations centre, as they'd by now been given its title.

"Let me introduce you to Kapitän Franz Steiger," Howell said as the German officer snapped to attention and saluted the small group. "He's the official representative of the German Navy. He has a small contingent of naval ratings on deck who will join with men from the *Wyvern* in firing a salute to the dead after the short service of remembrance.

Steiger greeted Ross warmly and the next hour passed quickly for everyone as final arrangements were made for the service to commemorate those who'd died all those years ago.

When the time came, Ross was particularly moved by the words of Pastor Völler, which included:

"These men, who never met face-to-face, but who were forever joined in death, served and died for their countries. In the case of the crew of the *U3000*, sailing under false identity as *U966* they were all young men who served an evil regime, but these were not evil men. The Germany they lived in was not like the Germany of today. It was not possible to be a conscientious objector to the war in my country during those dark days, as many priests, much like me, discovered to their cost. It was a case of serve or die, perhaps quickly at the end of a rope or slowly in a concentration camp, so they served, whether they believed in the cause or not. Yes, it is true that some followed the ravings of the madman who rose to power in our nation at that time, but the vast majority did not. They were ordinary men, sailors of the Kriegsmarine, and their foremost pride was in their *Kapitän* and their boat. They did their jobs, as did the brave men of *H.M.S. Norwich*, without thought for themselves, only for their fellow crewmen and their ship. How these men died that night long ago is less important than the fact that they died in the service of their countries, in the cold, dark, moonlit waters of the sea, far from home and family, one minute vibrant, alive, maybe sharing a joke with their fellows, and then pitched into the darkness of death, either in the water, in an explosion, or in the case of the men in the submarine, from a slow, lingering death as their air ran out. We remember them not as foes, but as human beings, as brave men and we salute them all and commend their souls to God."

The other two ministers spoke similar words, and Izzie Drake wiped a tear from her face as Kapitän Steiger now stepped forward, side by side with Captain Howell, each man carrying a large wreath, Howell's in a mix of red and white flowers, the colours of the Royal Navy's white ensign, and Steiger's in the red and yellow of the German Navy ensign with black ribbons to complete the colours of their flag.

Steiger spoke briefly.

"It is my wish to recite for you a poem," he said. "It was written by your English poet, Brian Porter, and is called *No Headstone on a Sailor's Grave*. It was, I understand written to commemorate the men of your Merchant Navy, many of whom lost their lives during the Second World War, but I believe the sentiments of the poem are appropriate to the events of today."

Taking a piece of paper from his pocket, Steiger cleared his throat, and began by reading the title, followed by the words of the poem.

"NO HEADSTONE ON A SAILOR'S GRAVE

Third day now, and still no sign of any rescue boat,
Please God, how much longer on this ocean must we float.
Poor Lofty's fell asleep again, I'm afraid he's getting weaker.
Truth be told, I think that our chances are getting bleaker.

She went down so very quickly, it happened all so fast.
Torpedo in the hold I think, judging by the blast.
So cold, wet and hungry, no fresh water to drink.
Must keep baling though, don't want this thing to sink.

Lofty seems delirious, he thinks he's home in bed,
Strange how things like this put all these daft things in your head.
Maybe my mind will start to go, if we're not found quite soon.
Maybe tonight I'll be looking up, and howling at the moon!

I wish someone would find us, I'd kill for a cup of tea.
But all I can see for miles around is nothing but open sea.
Perhaps they'll never find us, don't even know we're here.
Wasn't much time for a mayday call, will anyone shed a tear?

I'm sleepy now, I must admit, can't go on for very long,
I think I'll soon be listening to the sound of Neptune's song.
If anyone should find these words, say a prayer for Lofty and me.
And please, throw a few rose petals on our grave beneath the sea."

* No Headstone on a Sailor's Grave is from Lest We Forget, An Anthology of
Remembrance, by Brian L Porter, published by Next Chapter.

Steiger bowed his head as he came to the end of the poem, and then walked slowly to the deck rail of the *Whitehaven Castle*, where he stood silently and saluted over the rolling waves of the Channel, as he cast the page containing the poem into the breeze. The assembled group watched as the light breeze caught the flimsy sheet of A4 paper, and for a few seconds the poem and its poignant words seemed to fly of its own volition, swirling up and down, back and forth as though on wings of faith, until the breeze relented for a few seconds and the page floated gently to land, printed side up, on the undulating swell of the ocean, where it remained for at least a minute until, saturated by the waters of the English Channel, *No Headstone for a Sailor's grave*, silently and with an uncanny sense of reverence, slowly disappeared beneath the waves, gently floating down in a silent pirouette towards the shattered remains of the two former warships, where, perhaps, the ghosts of those who'd sailed in them waited to receive it. Charles Howell next walked forward to join him at the ship's rail and together the two men threw their respective wreaths onto the waters below in their final, joint act of remembrance, each man saluting in farewell and respect to those who'd met their deaths in a watery grave, almost sixty years earlier.

Not a word had been spoken by anyone on deck as Steiger had read the poem, or as the wreaths were thrown down to the sea and everyone present had been moved not just by the poet's words, but by the German officer's emotional delivery of them.

Now, as though by prearranged signal, the single deck gun of the *Wyvern* burst into life, a single round fired in salute to those who'd perished on the two vessels on the seabed. Next, a loud command of 'fire' from none other than Marine Lieutenant Gareth Ridley who had appeared as if by magic as far as Ross's party could see, was followed by a fusillade of rifle fire from the joint contingent of Royal Naval and German Naval ratings in a second and reverberating salute.

Ross and Drake, and the others couldn't fail to be moved by the ceremony, which was then brought to a close by the Reverend Giles Parker, who led those present in the Lord's prayer, after which, another surprise for the visitors as a small company of youngsters were led onto the deck by the choirmaster of Exeter Cathedral and as they began their rendition of *'For those in peril on the sea'* with the officers and men on deck joining in lustily, Ross saw tears streaking the face of Izzie Drake. Never had he seen his sergeant so moved and emotional. At the same time, he noticed Brian Jones and Carole St. Clair also appeared highly emotional, remembering of course the family connection for Brian Jones to T.J. Knowles.

Lunch was served soon afterwards, with Captain James Ramsey proving to be a genial host, and the food served by the *Whitehaven Castle's* chef, quite superb. Ramsey explained that their chef was a former Cunard employee, who had served aboard the *Q.E.2* for some years. When asked by Carole St. Clair how he came to be serving on a Royal Fleet Auxiliary salvage tug, Ramsey simply tapped the side of his nose with one finger and with a knowing wink, replied "Don't ask."

The Naval personnel, plus the visiting clerics were all keen for Ross to tell them the story of how they all came to be meeting on this day and the D.I. did his best to inform them without giving away too many salient details of the case, which as he explained, was still an ongoing criminal investigation. He explained that he would love to say more, but knew they'd understand his reticence, which they all of course reluctantly accepted.

Their hosts however were not so reluctant in divulging their knowledge of the underwater examinations of the two wrecks.

First of all, Charles Howell went into more detail about the submarine's revolutionary technology, the hydrodynamic propulsion system. As a former submariner himself, Anthony Prendergast was especially interested in knowing as much as they could tell him about the discovery. The system, as far as Howell was able to describe it worked like a sort of snake, propelling the submarine along using the same principles as jet engine propulsion, but using water instead of air as the medium by which to create the necessary energy.

Ramsey explained that they had finally broken through to the still watertight areas of the U-Boat and by using state of the art compressed air technology had succeeded in preventing them becoming totally flooded. In so doing, they had found the decomposed remains of another twenty five of the *U3000/U966's* crew. Most of them had been identified from their identity tags. A couple, obviously in breech of regulations hadn't been wearing theirs and would remain unidentified.

He went on to say that they were welcome to view the films taken by the divers who had located the remains if they wished to, though Ross and his people couldn't decide if they wanted to take that step, as Ross himself felt it to be perhaps an intrusion too far into what was in effect the grave of those who'd died in her.

Charles Howell agreed with Ross to a point but he explained that by identifying those men, the German Navy had been able to locate a number of surviving family members, descendants of the dead men and it was hoped to invite them, as well as any other legitimate family members of the known crew, plus the living relatives of the crew of the *Norwich*, to attend a joint service of remembrance in the near future, probably in Exeter Cathedral. Everyone thought that to be a good idea and by the time came for Ross and his party to board their helicopter for the journey back to Falmouth, friendships had been formed and promises made to keep in touch, which everyone intended to keep. Ross was especially touched when Anthony Prendergast, on behalf of the Ministry of Defence, passed on an invitation for Ross's entire team from Liverpool to attend that service when it took place, as a way of thanking them all for finally helping the dead to be properly acknowledged and their last resting place confirmed. Ross felt proud of his team, and said he'd do his best but it would depend on their case load at the time of the service. Brian Jones and Carole St. Clair were also invited, and they gratefully accepted right away.

The return flight in the Lynx was smoother than the outgoing leg of their day's journey, but Andy Ross was glad to finally find his feet on *terra firma* later that day and after he and Drake said their farewells to Jones and St. Clair and picking up their bags from the Hope and Anchor, they began the long and arduous journey back along the motorway system towards Liverpool where the next day, Ross hoped, just might prove decisive in bringing the case to its finale.

CHAPTER 36

A SET-UP

Randolph (Finch) Lambert lay on the bed in his hotel room, situated in a quiet street in Bloomsbury, London. The television was playing quietly in one corner of the room, the sound turned down so low that its effect was little more than white noise on Lambert's senses. The flickering picture depicted some inane comedy movie he'd never seen before and certainly had no wish to see again in the future.

Lambert was planning, working out how to first of all find out where Robin and Starling were being held, and secondly how he would then find a way past the inevitable police defences around each man. Lambert was certain the police would have put armed guards in place. He was confident enough to assume Starling's silence but Robin was another matter. He wasn't stupid and must have realised that Finch had sent Starling to eliminate him. He was, as far as Lambert knew, still unconscious in hospital. The police had only released the information that the man responsible for two murders in the city was being treated for multiple injuries and may have suffered brain damage. Brain damaged or not, he needed to make sure that Robin never recovered sufficiently to tell the police what he knew about Finch's organisation. As one of his most trusted operatives, Robin knew more than most, perhaps too much, Lambert thought in retrospect.

Having flown to Heathrow as Ralph Kerr, one of his many aliases, he was confident that he had arrived unnoticed into the United Kingdom. Sadly for Lambert, that was his first mistake. Unbeknown to him, Graham Young, (Robin), was recovering well from his injuries and was proving to be a veritable goldmine of information in his attempts to avoid being potentially handed over to one of the foreign powers with a less than civilised policy towards imprisoned killers. He knew of more than one member of his profession for example who had been sentenced to lengthy spells in Turkish prisons, only to suffer appalling and inhuman cruelty at the hands of sadistic warders, including gang rape, severed fingers and toes, starvation and brutal whippings and beatings. By contrast, a prison sentence in Britain would be the equivalent to a stay in a holiday camp.

His thoughts were interrupted by the ring tone of his mobile phone. Lambert reached out, picking the phone up from its place on his bedside cabinet. Looking at the screen, a puzzled look appeared on his face as he recognised the caller's number. With one eyebrow rising, Spock-like he saw Robin's number displayed. *How the hell could he be calling me?* he thought, knowing only too well that the man was in police custody, supposedly unconscious and unable to communicate.

More curious than suspicious, Lambert pressed the green answer button on the phone, held it to his ear and listened without saying a word.

"Hello?" an unknown voice with a distinct though not overly heavy Liverpool accent spoke to him. Lambert remained silent, waiting.

"Hello? Mr. Finch?"

Lambert continued to wait, saying nothing, trying to draw the unknown caller out.

"I know you can hear me," the voice said. "If you're wondering who I am and why I have Robin's phone, let's just say for now, that I'm someone who can help you."

"And just how can you help me? Just what do you have that I want, and who the fuck are you, some copper trying to get me to talk?"

"As it happens, Mr. Finch, I am a police officer, but one who may be prepared to provide you with information that could prove to be beneficial to both of us."

Lambert fell silent for a few seconds, his mind quickly evaluating the information from the unknown caller. This could be a godsend or it could be a trap. He needed to know more. A bent copper on the investigating team could prove to be manna from heaven if this guy knew how he could get to Robin and Starling, and could help him in his quest to eliminate them.

"Do you think I'm some sort of moron?" he asked the mystery caller. "You call me on Robin's phone, but you could be anyone, a passer-by who picked it up at the scene of the accident, a thieving hospital orderly, almost anybody in fact. Why should I believe you're a copper or that you want to help me?"

At the other end of the line, Derek McLennan smiled to himself. Detective Chief Inspector Oscar Agostini, listening to every word through an ear-piece connected to Derek's phone nodded to McLennan to move onto the next part of the attempt to 'hook' Finch.

"Okay, I know you're suspicious," said McLennan. "I would be too, so just listen, okay? I'm not going to give you my name yet, that could prove to be bad for my health in the long term, but I am part of the team investigating the murders of Tim Knight and Martin Lewis. I've sort of 'borrowed' his phone from the evidence locker. They know a lot about what's going on, Mr. Finch. They also know it was probably you who sent Starling to kill Robin, and that means you have unfinished business to take care of."

"Even if that's true, and I'm admitting nothing," Finch replied,

"why should I trust you?"

"Because I'm your only hope of getting to both men without being gunned down by armed police officers before you can reach them; that's why. Okay, you want to know why I'm prepared to help you, right?"

"It would help," said Lambert.

"I've been a police officer for nearly ten years, Mr. Finch. I was ambitious, and a good copper too. Thing is, I've taken my sergeant's exams three times, and just because I'm no bloody good at taking exams, I've failed every time. My chances of ever making sergeant or going any higher are just about zero. I don't intend to be a lowly detective constable for the rest of my life, ending up in some out of the way station out in the sticks because I never had what it took to climb the promotion ladder. I've seen enough old stagers like that already in my time, just plodding along towards early retirement, sitting behind a desk doing the Daily Mail crossword until another piece of paper comes along to be filed. I want money, Mr. Finch and I'd rather have it while I'm young enough to enjoy it."

Randolph Lambert said nothing for a few seconds, wondering if he could take a chance on this unknown man being straight with him. There was still the possibility he was a plant, a Trojan Horse, and a part of a ploy to entrap him. Finally, he made a decision.

"Okay, I still don't know if I can trust you, but let's say you're telling the truth. Tell me something that the police know that isn't general knowledge. Convince me you're close enough to the investigation that I can trust you to be able to get me what I want."

"Okay," said McLennan. "We've found out that Robin and Starling work for you in a 'mercenary for hire' security organisation, hiring yourselves out to the highest bidder, At present you're working for the Aegis Institute, and you need to eliminate anyone, including your own people, who might be able to tie you into your boss in the States, thus compromising both him and you. The only evidence we have is circumstantial at present but if Robin and Starling agree to talk, then we can probably get enough evidence to come after you and your boss, Mr. Finch. It would appear your only hope of preventing them from talking, which I'm sure Robin will be happy to do when he learns you tried to have him killed, is to make sure neither man is ever in a position to implicate you directly."

"I think you and I should meet," Lambert said after a brief pause for thought. "If I think I can trust you, maybe we can come to a deal. If not, then I promise you that your future will be a very short one. Do I make myself clear?"

"Clear as crystal," Derek replied, his voice confident and unwavering.

"Give me a name I can call you," Lambert said.

"I tell you what, you can call me Raven," said McLennan. "That should sit nicely with your obsession with our feathered friends."

"Right, Raven it is." Lambert checked his watch, estimating how quickly he could get to Liverpool. If this copper was actively working on the investigation there was no way he could leave the city to meet him halfway.

"When do you go off duty, today, Mister Raven?"

"Six p.m." McLennan replied, "assuming nothing crops up needing overtime."

Lambert had visited the city of Liverpool twice in the past and his knowledge of the place was limited so he decided on a nice, public place where both he and his would-be informant could meet without being over-heard, and where he would be able to spot any surveillance team in an instant. After all, that was part of his business. They couldn't fool him.

"Is there still a McDonald's on the concourse at Lime Street Station?" he asked.

"There is," said Derek.

"Seven thirty this evening; be there. I'll be wearing jeans and a black leather jacket and a New York Yankees baseball cap. I want this done quickly, so whatever you think you can do for me, it has to be done tonight. I don't want to be in your damn city when the sun rises tomorrow, got that? And you'd better not be trying to trap me, copper," he said, his voice suddenly full of latent menace.

"Trust me, Mr. Finch. Ordinarily I would never even dream of doing something like this, but Starling and Robin are just a pair of murdering bastards who probably deserve nothing better than a bullet in the head. What I have planned to get you to them can be done tonight, tomorrow, any time at all, so there's no problem there, and, like you say, the sooner the better really. What you do to them won't make me lose a minute's sleep, but there's a condition to me helping you."

"Oh yeah, and what's that?"

"Nobody else gets hurt, okay? I don't want any fellow officers ending up as collateral damage. If you can't agree to that, then the deal's off."

"Okay," Lambert agreed readily, obviously lying, as McLennan knew. "We'll do it your way. Now, how will I know you, Mister Raven?"

"You won't," said Derek. "But I'll know you from the description you just gave me. Sit anywhere you like and I'll come to you."

"Okay," said Lambert, "but you haven't told me how much you want for this information."

"Oh, don't worry; it'll be something you can afford. We'll discuss it when we meet," McLennan said, growing more in confidence with every second.

"Okay, Raven, don't be late," Lambert said and before Derek could say another word, the line went dead.

Derek McLennan hadn't noticed until the phone went dead in his hand, that he was shaking from the raw emotion of talking to the cold-blooded killer on the other end of that call. Agostini however, congratulated the young D.C. having been impressed by his handling of the conversation.

"Thanks a lot sir," Derek said in response to the D.C.I's flattery. "I hope I sounded more confident than I felt."

"You were great, McLennan, really. I wasn't sure you could pull it off but you did. I think you've actually got him hooked."

Ross had been listening from the next room, knowing his presence might serve to make Derek more nervous than needs be, and now came smiling into the room, accompanied by Izzie Drake, adding his congratulations to those of their boss.

"You were damn good there, Derek. Well done."

"Thanks, sir," McLennan replied.

"Of course, tonight will be the tricky part," Ross went on. "You're going to have to be totally convincing, Derek. This is no amateur we're dealing with. One slip and you could be in real danger, you do know that don't you?"

"Yes, I do sir. I wouldn't have volunteered if I didn't think I could pull it off."

"Good lad," Ross smiled again and patted McLennan on the shoulder. "Don't forget, we'll have you under surveillance all the time you're with him. Don't worry; he won't be able to make our people. Sam Gable will be there as a Mum with a baby in a pram, not a real one of course, and Izzie and Tony will be a courting couple, canoodling in McDonalds. I'll be a ticket inspector, already agreed with the station authorities, who think we're looking for a drug dealer. And just to be on the safe side, we'll have a police marksman up in the roof, with a rifle trained on Finch the second he's in view on the concourse and another couple of armed officers will be positioned in a diesel locomotive that will be conveniently stood at the buffers closest to the concourse."

"Tell me again why we can't just pick this bastard up the minute he sets foot in Liverpool?" Izzie suddenly asked; her concern for Derek uppermost in her tone of voice.

"Because, Sergeant Drake," Agostini provided the reply, "as much as we may know just who and what this man is, we have no hard evidence that proves he's committed an offence on British soil. He's clever, and covers his tracks very well indeed. We have to have something concrete to pin on him. We need him to attempt to kill one or both of his men and then, by God, we'll have the bastard."

"What about attempting to bribe an officer? Didn't he just do that with Derek?"

"No, he didn't. McLennan called him, remember, and offered to sell us out to him. His phone will no doubt have a record of the call he received so all he'd need to do is prove we called him and then claim entrapment. We have to do it this way. I know you're concerned for McLennan, but he's a big boy, and he can handle the situation."

"I'll be fine, Sarge," McLennan reassured her. "All I have to do is convince him I can lead him to Graham Young and we'll have him."

"I hope you're right, Derek," Drake said, not entirely convinced.

* * *

The evening traffic had eased off by the time Derek McLennan made his way into Lime Street Station. He couldn't help but be impressed every time he entered the place. The architecture of the railway station, with its arches and façade that was once the North Western Hotel, reminiscent of a French Chateaux was without doubt one of the most impressive mainline stations in Britain but for now, Derek pulled his mind away from such thoughts and made his way towards the arranged meeting place.

Finch wasn't there yet, so he bought a coffee and seated himself at a table that afforded him a good view through the large plate glass window, enabling him to see anyone coming or going from the restaurant. He knew that Ross was already in place, having seen him at the ticket barrier as he walked along the concourse. Somewhere above him, he knew a police marksman was hidden, rifle in hand, ready to act if Derek needed immediate help. He'd noticed a diesel locomotive standing just where Ross had said it would be, and knew two more armed officers, dressed in railway uniform would be scanning the concourse continuously.

Sipping his coffee, Derek checked his watch. He was too early, Lambert, or Finch wasn't due for ten minutes unless he too put in an early appearance. The double glass doors swung inwards as a couple entered, laughing and talking, eyes only for one another. A swift double-take told McLennan his close back-up had arrived. Izzie Drake was virtually unrecognisable from her day to day on-duty appearance. Her hair had changed from its usual shoulder-length brunette to long, blond tresses, with a sexy fringe, (Derek thought). For a second he couldn't take his eyes from Izzie's legs. In her short, black mini skirt and two inch heels, she looked incredible, Derek decided. The silky white blouse accentuated her breasts and Derek McLennan almost fell off his seat as he finally realised it *was* Sergeant Izzie Drake he was ogling. Pulling himself back to reality he now realised the man she was with was his friend and colleague, D.C. Tony Curtis. With long but neatly styled hair, which Derek had to assume was a wig, expensive shoes and a sharp three piece suit in a pale blue pinstripe, Curtis reminded Derek of a well-heeled pimp or drug dealer. Maybe that was his cover, Derek smiled to himself.

"See something funny, or maybe something you like, Mr. Raven?"

McLennan looked up to see the man he was due to meet standing at his shoulder, dressed as Finch had said he'd be, down to the New York Yankees cap. He'd been so engrossed in watching Izzie Drake's totally transformed look that he'd taken his eye off the door for a few vital seconds, allowing Finch to take him by surprise, a mistake he rapidly decided he mustn't repeat if he was to succeed in his undercover role.

Looking up at the new arrival, Derek could only say, "Finch?"

"That's Mister Finch to you, Raven. Not much of a copper are you? You were so busy ogling the Tom over there; I could have walked right up to you and blown your fucking head off."

Derek decided to play dumb, to play along with Finch's initial impression of him.

"You think she's a prossie?"

"Are you thick? Of course she is. Skirt that short, almost showing everything she's got? Nice shapely ass and great legs though, I'll grant you, but I'll bet you she opens 'em more times in one night than you get laid in a year. Her pimp's probably brought her here to deliver her to a client for the evening. Less chance of being picked up by your lot if he hands her over in a place like this."

"Right, yeah, I see what you mean," said Derek. "So, anyway, why don't you sit down? Can I get you a coffee or tea or something?"

"This isn't a social call," Finch replied. "Let's talk," and the man sat down opposite McLennan, who couldn't help noticing his eyes. Finch's eyes were dark pools, almost lifeless in their appearance as though he saw the world through a soulless veneer with not a hint of emotion visible in his countenance. As Finch/Lambert took his seat, Sam Gable entered the cafeteria, pushing the door open with her bottom as she reversed into the place with her 'baby' in the pram that she towed in with her. Unlike Izzie Drake, Sam was 'dressed down' in a quilted jacket that had seen better days, well worn jeans and a harassed look on her face as she looked around for a place to sit and park the pram without causing an obstruction. She didn't give the two men at the table a second glance, just hurried past, another stressed out, care-worn young mother, eager for a cup of tea and a sit down.

Finch wanted to get his business concluded as fast as he could.

"Assuming you've got information that I want to buy, just how much do you expect me to pay you for it, Raven?"

"Short and to the point, I like that," McLennan replied, now recovered from his earlier lapse and getting back into the role of bent copper. "I want twenty thousand for each location."

"Twenty thousand pounds? You can't be serious, Raven. You must think I'm stupid."

"Far from it," McLennan replied. "If either of those men talks, it could completely compromise you and give my bosses a good reason to pick you up and charge you with conspiracy to commit murder. I'd say forty grand for the two of them is a bargain if it helps to keep you out of jail. Oh yes, and another thing; I'm not sure how your bosses would react if you did get arrested, Mr. Finch. Maybe you'd be the next one with a contract taken out on your life. I'll bet you know enough to bring your bosses down, Think about it."

Derek McLennan was growing into his role by the second, any earlier hesitancy completely gone. He felt he almost had Finch hooked. Now, the only question was whether Finch would accept his terms or try to negotiate. Finch had to be desperate; he had no other way of locating the two men, or of finding a way to actually get close to them. Derek represented that chance and both men knew it. A few seconds passed in an awkward silence before Finch suddenly reached a hand across the table and said "Done, you thieving bastard."

Derek reached across and the two shook hands on the deal.

"You won't regret it, Mr. Finch," he said as he sat back in his uncomfortable plastic chair again.

"I'd better not," Finch grinned at him as he went on, "I'd have paid twice that amount if you'd pushed me, so I guess I got a good deal. It's easy to see this is the first time you've done anything like this."

"Yeah, well, I just want enough to maybe resign from the force, start a little business of my own maybe, somewhere new, you know; a fresh start."

"Right, well, I don't give a shit what you do with the money. Just tell me what I need to know."

"Not so fast," said McLennan. "I want fifty percent up front, the rest when you're satisfied the job's done."

Finch smiled as he reached into his inside pocket, so intent on his dealings with McLennan that he failed to notice the 'hooker' sitting at the far side of the cafeteria as she fiddled with something in her handbag. In fact Izzie Drake was pressing the shutter button on the camera cleverly hidden in the clasp of her handbag, a handy gadget Ross had borrowed at short notice from a friend in the drug squad. They now had, if nothing else, Randolph Lambert passing money to Derek, as payment for information that would lead to attempted murder.

"There's ten grand in there," Finch said to Derek. "Take it or leave it as a down-payment. You don't think I'd carry all that cash around for a first meeting do you? You get the rest after the first hit. I'll know you can be trusted then and I sure don't intend to hang around after the second one to have a nice chat with you to hand over the rest. You won't see me again after that, you have to appear clean, so we have to make it look good. I don't want your friends realising you've sold them out and closing the door on my escape."

"So what do you suggest?"

"You get me in to Robin's room. I take care of business. We meet at a place of your choice, in the car park, wherever you want. I hand over the cash and head off to take care of Starling."

"Wait a minute. I've already thought of an easy, painless way in."

"Go on, I'm listening."

"I can come and go as part of the team, so I propose I go in with a nice flask of coffee, suitably drugged and as soon as they fall asleep, I get out of there, and drive to the next location, ready to meet you there. I then call you in, give you the directions to Starling's location and you do what you have to do. You get what you want and no one gets hurt."

"Apart from Robin of course," Finch grinned. "I like it. You're sure you can pull the drugged coffee thing off?"

"Of course, I can later say I left my flask unattended for a few minutes at the nurses' station and you must have crept up and dropped something in it while the nurse was taking me to see the duty doctor. Don't worry, I'll make sure she and I are away long enough for it to have happened in theory."

Finch was obviously so keen to see the end of Robin that he accepted the plan without too much thought, as Ross had imagined he would.

"What time do we go in?" Finch asked.

"Three in the morning, that'll be the best time right in the middle of the night shift. There's only one nurse on duty at that time, and I can deal with her and the guys on guard, no problem. All you'll have to do is walk in and do the job and walk out again. Nobody will even see you. Here, take this."

McLennan passed a cheap basic pay-as-you-go mobile phone to Finch. I have one like it. Yours has my number programmed into it. This is how we stay in touch. Once the job's over, you can dispose of it."

"You've worked it all out, haven't you?"

"Yes, Mr. Finch, I have. I'm not as stupid as you may have thought."

"Okay, Mr. Raven, so you want me, where, just before 3 a.m?"

"Be in the main car park of the Royal Hospital. I'll tell you where to find Robin when I meet up with you."

"Okay. But listen to me, Raven. This had better work or you will live to regret it."

"Trust me, it'll work," said Derek.

Without another word, Finch rose and walked out of the cafeteria. None of the undercover officers approached Derek or made any contact with him, just in case Finch was lurking somewhere nearby, watching Derek in case of a double-cross.

Derek waited two minutes before he also got up from his seat and walked out to the car park. He drove all the way home before picking up the phone and calling Andy Ross who was delighted things had gone so well. Everything was set up, now all they had to do was wait for dead of night to fall on the hospital.

CHAPTER 37

GERMAN EFFICIENCY

Following the telephone update from McLennan, and with Derek safely at home with instructions to get something to eat and then put his feet up for a couple of hours, Ross and Drake joined D.C.I. Agostini and the rest of the team in the squad room where they held a quick debriefing session on Derek's meeting with Randolph (Finch) Lambert.

"He did a good job, that's for sure," Ross said.

"I'm pleased to hear it," Oscar Agostini replied. "It could have all gone badly if Lambert had caught on to our little plot."

"Derek was rather amazing, sir," Sam Gable observed with real admiration in her voice for her colleague.

"He was," Curtis agreed, "but I thought his eyes were going to pop out when saw you in that mini-skirt, Sarge," he said to Drake.

"I'm just glad Peter couldn't see me dressed like that," Drake said. "His eyes would have popped out of his head at the sight of me in that skirt," she grinned.

"Hey, Sarge, you never know, he might fancy you looking like that, want to go in for some dressing up games at bedtime; you know what I mean?"

"You're a cheeky bastard, D.C. Curtis," Izzie said, mock seriously.

"I'd have given you fifty for an hour," Curtis joked and flinched as Drake slapped him across his right shoulder.

"Cheapskate!" she shouted at him and laughed. "You couldn't afford me, Tony."

The whole room exploded in laughter, Agostini included as the brief exchange allowed them all a release of the tension that had built up during McLennan's meeting with Lambert.

"Anyway, those legs of yours did the trick, Izzie. Lambert made you as a prossie right away and never gave you a second thought," said Ross.

"Oh, thank you sir," Drake said, "Easily forgotten eh, legs or no legs?"

"You know what I mean, Izzie," Ross grinned.

"You're forgiven, sir," she replied.

"Ahem," Agostini interrupted. "Sorry everyone, but we need to make sure we're all focussed on tonight. Have you made the necessary arrangements with the hospital, Andy?"

"I have sir, as you said, and the hospital authorities have been very cooperative. Our people will replace their staff before McLennan gives Lambert the room number. There are only four patients on that private wing at present and they're being moved to another floor temporarily until our operation concludes. Everything should go smoothly tonight."

"Excellent," Agostini said as the door to the squad room opened and much to everyone's surprise, Detective Chief Superintendant Sarah Hollingsworth walked in to the room, accompanied by her aide, Inspector Mark Bennings.

"Ma'am," Agostini acknowledged his immediate superior officer as she walked to the front of the gathered officers, Bennings by her side.

Ross and Drake exchanged surprised glances. It was rare for the Chief Super to make an unannounced appearance at an impromptu briefing like this, so rare in fact that Ross couldn't recall it having happened at all in his living memory. Whatever had caused Hollingsworth to appear like this had to be important.

"My apologies for barging in like this," she began, "but I've just received news that I think you'll want to hear. As D.C.I Agostini has no doubt informed you, I've been in touch with various friendly police forces across Europe in relation to your current case and have just received a phone call from Germany."

A ripple of murmurs circulated among the detectives present, quickly silenced as Hollingsworth held a hand up.

"I'm not great with German pronunciation so let's just say that Joseph Lenz is of an equivalent rank to myself. Herr Lenz is with the *Bundespolizei* who it appears, were alerted to our case by Stephan Jung, my contact at the *Bundeskriminalamt*.

I've just come from a very illuminating telephone conversation with Herr Lenz. I think you'll all be as surprised as I was to learn that Erich Ackermann is currently in a cell in the police station in Rostock. He was arrested at his home three hours ago."

Andy Ross stared at Hollingsworth. Another ripple of murmurs ran round the room, that quickly fell silent as the Chief Superintendent cleared her throat and carried on.

"It appears the German police have had their eyes on Herr Acker-mann for some time, suspecting him of financial irregularities in his busi-ness dealings. In short, Joseph Lenz heads up a crack team that investigates serious fraud cases, not small run-of-the-mill everyday fraud, we're talking about cases where the amounts involved run into millions of *Deutschmarks,* or, since last year, 2002, the Euro of course and involve large scale move-ments of money across international borders. Like many such investiga-tions, it can be a long and often frustrating maze for investigators to negotiate as we know only too well from the efforts of our own Serious Fraud Squad. However, as so often happen, it can be one small thing, maybe totally unrelated directly to the actual investigation in progress that leads to a positive resolution to the case.

Just such an instance has taken place in Germany today, thanks to you and your people, D.I. Ross."

"Really Ma'am?" Ross exclaimed in some surprise.

"Really," Hollingsworth replied. "Erich Ackermann has always sailed a little close to the wind in his business dealings apparently. Perhaps that's why he's been so successful, never being afraid to gamble, take a chance on speculative ventures, high risks for high profits, according to Lenz. A few years ago his various dealings saw his financial investment business take a massive hit, losses mounted, investors were becoming angry and deserting him in droves. Then apparently overnight all was well again. One of Ackermann's investors became suspicious when Ackermann began buying up large tracts of land and then making a fortune from subsequent devel-opments. Where had all the new money come from? This investor knew it couldn't be from Ackermann's dealings on the financial markets as he spoke to a number of acquaintances, also clients of Erich Ackermann, all of whom reported their investments going down, not up.

The police listened to the investor, and instinct told their investigators that Ackermann was either involved with organised crime, money laun-dering was an obvious guess, or had become involved in other, illegal activ-ities that were bringing in sudden large sums of money.

They quickly discovered that Erich Ackermann was also bankrolling a radical neo-Nazi political group calling itself *neue Morgendämmerung,* that's 'New Dawn' in English. That was enough to place him firmly in the sights of not only the Fraud Squad but the anti-terrorist police as well, which put him on the *Bundeskriminalamt's* radar too."

"Bloody hell, Ma'am," Ross couldn't help interrupting. "Sounds like this guy is a far bigger fish than we thought."

"Precisely, Detective Inspector Ross, which is why I'm so pleased that D.C.I. Agostini had the sense to alert me when this case of yours suddenly appeared to have far greater ramifications than the murder of young Aaron Decker first led us to believe. Anyway, the one thing the police needed was a thread to hang on Ackermann, something that would enable them to bring him in and sweat him, try to get him to crack a little and maybe open a floodgate. You've given them that thread. They knew about his connection to Aegis and once we told them what to look for, they were able to pinpoint every deal he'd set up with every bent official in various governments, Turkey, Greece, Italy etc.

Anyway, they picked him up from his own office, in front of his staff, and as soon as they got him into an interview room they went at him hard from the start.

"Ve haf vays of making you talk," Tony Curtis mimicked in a terrible German accent, with a Liverpudlian twang.

"Yes, thank you Constable Curtis," Hollingsworth said and Curtis turned red. She went on:

"Yes, well, it does seem like our German friends are allowed a little more latitude than we are when it comes to interviewing suspects and within a short time, they had him talking. Although they're sure he had nothing to do with the murders over here, apart from financing the whole operation, Lenz told him they'd got him lined up as an accessory to at least four murders in England and that they were quite prepared to ship him over here to stand trial. Lenz told him that English prisons are a hotbed of homosexual rape, with new prisoners subject to daily sodomy attacks by multiple hardened criminals and that he'd get at least ten years for his part in the conspiracy to murder, plenty of time for him to get used to it. Lenz told me he'd never seen the blood drain from a man's face so fast in his life. Ackermann is talking even as we speak. Ackermann, with his ingrained Nazi beliefs, is actually appalled by and terrified of homosexuality and Lenz knew it. So, it seems our man rose quickly in the Aegis hierarchy thanks to him bankrolling the purchase of the four submarines they use for their underwater survey work. He also negotiated crooked deals with certain officials once they'd located valuable historical sites. He siphoned off vast sums of plundered wealth into accounts Aegis knew nothing about in order to finance his search for the *U3000.*"

Hollingsworth fell silent, as she allowed her last words to penetrate the minds of Ross and his team.

"This was all about the U-Boat, right from the start?" Ross said, incredulously.

"Indeed," the D.C.S. confirmed. "He knew exactly what the submarine was carrying, the gold and artworks of course, but more importantly he knew about the new technology she incorporated. He knew that if he could get his hands on it, and the final plans and drawings for the working prototype were supposed to be sealed in the U-Boat's safe, he knew the potential for profit was virtually limitless. Imagine a process that could literally revolutionise the worldwide shipping industry, removing the need for oil as a fuel source, with the only raw material necessary to operate even a massive supertanker being nothing more complicated then water. Ackermann thought it would make him the richest man in the world."

"So in the end it was still about money," Drake said with distaste. "All those people dead, and for what? A money making scheme that he didn't even know would work."

"Oh, but the thing is, he knew it does work," Sergeant. "Apparently he has the documents that show the Nazis tested the new system for over three months in the *U3000* before she was sent on her last fateful voyage. It was a mostly proven system and only the fact that Germany was by then almost defeated prevented Hitler having a fleet of those submarines and maybe even surface ships built that could have swung the war in his favour. Ackermann believed that any flaws in the original system could be ironed out and an improved design produced by Aegis's engineers. Anyway, that's by the bye, now. He's talking to Lenz who has promised to drop the conspiracy to murder charges if he tells all and names every crooked Aegis employee he's corrupted in his evil scheme."

"That's wonderful, Ma'am, so what do we do?"

"We go on as before," Inspector Ross. "We still have to nail those responsible for the crimes committed here in Liverpool and the UK in general. You have a sting operation in place for tonight, I understand from D.C.I. Agostini?"

"Yes, Ma'am," said Ross. "And if we can bring this man Lambert in and get him to talk, we may be able to pass on enough to the F.B.I to give them the information they need to prosecute the head of the American arm of the corrupt Aegis octopus."

"Ah yes, Mr. Kelly. Ackermann has mentioned him to Lenz, but hasn't given him any details that can be used to link him to the murders. It seems Mr. Kelly decided to take the murderous path towards their goal without consulting Ackermann, who wasn't interested in how Kelly got results, as long as he got them. Basically, he's a coward and a narcissist who really had developed a kind of Fuehrer complex. He actually thought he was going to be so damned rich he'd have a stranglehold on world commerce through what he saw as 'his' revolutionary propulsion process. So going back to Kelly, I know the father of the Decker boy has been helpful and I've spoken to the Supervisory Special Agent in Charge of the F.B.I. team who are investigating Kelly and they are willing to pick him up as soon as we can give them confirmation that this Finch chap will testify that Kelly gave the orders for the murders of Aaron Decker and T.J Knowles. I understand you used the threat of a Turkish prison on one of the men you already have in custody, D.I. Ross?"

"Erm, yes, I did, Ma'am. I know it's not..."

"Oh, don't apologise, Ross. I quite like the idea. Now I understand this Finch chappie wouldn't be very happy at the thought of returning to Iraq, for example?"

Ross smiled and then laughed out loud at the connotations of the D.C.S's words.

"No Ma'am, I don't suppose he would."

"Well then, we'll leave it at that shall we?"

"Yes, of course, Ma'am, thank you."

Hollingsworth had said what she'd come to say and nodded to her aide, who prepared to leave with her. Before she left the room she had one last thing to say.

"D.I. Ross, please wish your young detective constable, I believe his name is McLennan, the best of luck tonight. He's a very brave young man going up against an extremely dangerous killer. For his sake I hope all goes well for you all. I don't care what time you conclude this operation tonight, Oscar," she said to Agostini. "You call me and let me know the outcome, you hear me?"

"I hear you Ma'am," Agostini replied and with that, she was gone.

CHAPTER 38

CLOSING THE NET

"I knew I could count on you, Frankie," Paul Ferris exclaimed as his 'tame' computer geek and hacker Frankie Trout exultantly relayed the findings of his short but extremely productive foray into the innards of the computers owned by both Advance Transportation and Jeffrey Metcalfe.

"Yes, well, I did say it wouldn't take long didn't I?" said Frankie. "When have I ever let you down, eh, Mr. Ferris?"

"Never, Frankie, and that's why I come to you when I need a favour. Now, this is important. What you've just told me, there's no chance you've made any mistakes or misinterpreted any of the data you just relayed to me?"

"I'm sending you a copy of everything by email right now, Mr. Ferris, encrypted as usual of course. Only you and I have the key to access it, so please, for my sake keep it that way okay?"

"No one will know you're helping me, Frankie, you have my word. This is just what we needed. You've done well, my friend."

"Yeah, looks like your target has been naughty in their dealings. Like I told you, Advance Transportation's confidential files show their lorries arriving at various European coastal locations on or around the same dates as Aegis Oceanographic registered ships arrived in the same ports. The next day, in each case, the lorries departed carrying freight for onward forwarding to an Aegis facility near the port of Brindisi in Southern Italy. Brindisi is a major centre for trade with the Middle East and Greece. By the time those lorries leave Brindisi their cargo has apparently been offloaded and new cargoes loaded, for transport back to the UK, so they're clean by the time they return. I've done some tracking via satellite records and soon after Metcalfe's lorries made their drop off at the Aegis facility an Aegis supply vessel left port, bound for Egypt, which is where the trail goes cold. I suspect that whatever is taken to Egypt is offloaded and later flown to the States or wherever your crooked guy at Aegis wants it in one of their fleet of private aircraft."

"You've done well, Frankie," Ferris said, satisfied he had enough for the team to move against Jeffrey Metcalfe.

"Oh, one last thing," Frankie went on. "The weights, Mr. Ferris. You do know that these big intercontinental trucks are sort of 'weighed in' and 'weighed out' at the beginning and end of each journey, right?"

"Yes, I knew that, Frankie."

"Well, the freight that those lorries was carrying on the trips to Brindisi was always far heavier than whatever they carried back to the UK. I don't know if that's significant, but thought I'd mention it."

"It could be Frankie. Thanks again. You've been really helpful."

"Yeah, well, I hope you catch the bad guys, Mr. Ferris."

"Me too, Frankie, me too."

Frankie hung up and Ferris saw the 'email received' icon flashing on is computer screen. He soon had Frankie's information printed and after checking it through and making notes that he could use to explain things clearly to D.I. Ross, he set off in search of his boss.

He found Ross, together with Drake and Agostini in the Headquarters Central Control Room, where they were making arrangements for extra officers to be drafted in to the area around the hospital during the time they expected the take-down of Randolph Lambert to occur. They were to be kept out of sight in surrounding streets, ready to add assistance if needed. No chances were being taken. Even traffic patrol cars were being diverted from their normal patrol areas to be on hand if needed in the vicinity of the Royal Liverpool University Hospital.

Ross saw Paul Ferris as soon as the D.C. walked into the control room and beckoned him across to join him.

"Your smile tells me you have some good news for me," Ross said, his eyes drawn to the folder Ferris held in his left hand.

"I do sir. It's mostly circumstantial, but I think we've got enough to bring Jeffrey Metcalfe in for questioning. These records are enough to link his fleet of lorries to the movements of Aegis ships arriving at a central point, in this case Brindisi, which is where I believe Kelly has set up his central clearing house for their plundered treasures. He moves them from there to Egypt, and then flies them out to either the States or wherever he wants them, maybe to illicit buyers, who knows?"

Ferris passed the folder to Ross who took a good look at the contents, passing it to Agostini in turn.

"Yes, it may be circumstantial but it's pretty damning," said Ross. "It's definitely enough to have him picked up and brought in. He's not a career criminal, so I doubt he'll hold up for long. If we hit him with some hard questioning he'll cave in, in no time."

"I agree," Agostini concurred. "Let's get a warrant issued for his arrest, send a couple of burly uniformed officers up to Lancaster to carry out the arrest and put the fear of God into him. Have him brought here, let him sweat for a while in an interview room and then threaten to charge him as an accessory to the murder of his daughter's boyfriend and I bet he'll crack and spill everything he knows."

"You're a hard man D.C.I Agostini," Ross smiled at his friend and his guvnor, who smiled back.

"We're two of a kind, Andy. Let's finish this and put this nest of bloody vipers behind bars for a bloody long time."

"Damn right, sir," Ross agreed, taking the folder back from the boss and passing it to Izzie Drake who quickly familiarized herself with the contents.

"Seems to me he's one cold and callous bastard," she commented as she placed the folder on a nearby desk. "Not to mention greedy and without any scruples whatsoever. What is his daughter going to think of her father, when she learns what he's done? Then there's his wife of course. Why do people do these things? There he was, nicely set up with a couple of companies making a decent living, certainly enough to keep his family in a small degree of luxury and then he gets involved in something like this."

"Money, Izzie," said Ross. "The root of all evil as they say. We can't say how much is involved yet, but it must run into millions of dollars at least."

Paul Ferris then added his own surprise, one which he knew might add weight to their case against Metcalfe.

"Oh, by the way, there's just one other point that I should mention. My source also did some digging and although Metcalfe is listed as sole owner of Advance Transportation, fifty percent of the company's equity is held by…any guesses anyone?"

"Aegis Oceanographic?" Drake proffered.

"Right," said Ferris. "I think that's enough, don't you sir?"

"Well done, Ferris," said Ross. "Yes, I think that proves Metcalfe is well in bed with Aegis, certainly enough to tie him in to their illegal cross-border activities."

Agostini, his mind working at almost computer-like speed had been listening carefully to all that was being said around him and now, bearing in mind the time, and that in a few hours Derek McLennan would be putting the final stage of their plan to snare Finch into operation, he made a decision to try to expedite things.

"Right, I want Metcalfe in this building ASAP, and there's only one way to get that done quickly. We don't have time to send someone up there to bring him back before we have to turn all out attention to matters at the hospital."

"You have an idea, sir?" Drake asked.

"Indeed I do, Sergeant Drake," the D.C.I. replied as he walked across to the nearest telephone, picked it up and asked the switchboard operator to connect him with Lancaster Police Headquarters on Thurnham Street in the university city. The others watched intently. Unlike his predecessor, D.C.I. Harry Porteous, Agostini certainly wasn't averse to getting directly involved in a hands-on manner with an investigation and was pouring all his efforts into an all-out effort to support his men and women in the field, rather leading from behind a desk.

Agostini was soon connected to Chief Inspector Mitch Wells, who at one time in the past had been his 'guvnor' when he was a uniformed sergeant. The two had remained in fairly close touch over the years and Agostini was confident Wells would accede to his urgent request.

"No problem, Oscar," was the immediate response from Wells. "I'll send Inspector Barry Houseman and Sergeant Pat Norman to pick him up and have him taken straight to you. Houseman is my best man, big and burly as you asked for, and can be very intimidating, so should put the fear of God into this Metcalfe character."

"Thanks, Mitch," Agostini replied. "And Norman?"

"Ah yes, Patricia Norman is a hell of a good copper. A black belt in three different martial art forms, and takes no crap from anyone. They'll have him wetting himself, believe me. He should be glad to get to Liverpool and ready to talk by the time he gets there if he's half the coward you think he is."

"Sounds good. I'd better go and let you get them on the road."

The two men said their goodbyes, and Agostini, smiling, turned to Ross and the others.

"Sorted," he said, firmly and with conviction, confident his old boss would have already dispatched Houseman and Norman to the address he'd provided to Wells, who'd whistled through his teeth as Agostini read it to him, well aware of the upmarket location of the Metcalfe home.

* * *

The arrest of Jeffrey Metcalfe couldn't have gone better as far as the police were concerned. His wife, Dorothy, had answered the loud knocking on the front door of their large, mansion sized residence on the outskirts of Lancaster, Houseman purposely using his fist on the door rather then using the polite approach of pressing the doorbell or using the ornate brass doorknocker in the shape of a stag's head.

"Police, Ma'am," Houseman announced in a loud voice, as though the uniform didn't tell the story. "We'd like to speak to your husband please. Is he at home?"

Dorothy Metcalfe could only nod in surprise at the sudden arrival of the police on her doorstep and quickly showed them into a large and beautifully furnished sitting room where her husband sat in a large, winged armchair, reading a newspaper. As luck would have it, Sally Metcalfe was seated on a nearby sofa, her legs curled beneath her, stroking a small tan-coloured dachshund that lazily opened a sleepy eye at the two interlopers to its domain and then promptly curled up and went back to its doggie dream world. Having been briefed by Wells, Houseman wondered if some of the antique statuary and paintings that adorned the room might be part of the man's ill-gotten gains from his crimes.

Looking up, Metcalfe's face registered first surprise and then a hint of apprehension as he took in the hard stares of the two police officers as they strode purposely into his inner sanctum, straight towards him, stopping just a few feet in front of his chair.

"Officers?" he said, trying to appear composed while his mind tried to work out why the police were in his home. "Is there something I can help you with?"

"Jeffrey Metcalfe," Houseman spoke without preamble. "My name is Inspector Barry Houseman, and this is Sergeant Norman, Lancaster Police. I'm arresting you on charges relating to the murder of Aaron Decker and of participation in the theft and international trafficking of stolen and contraband antiques, historical artifacts, and currency."

After completing the statutory warning relating to his right to silence and the possible use of his word being used against him in court, Houseman fell silent as he watched the colour drain from Metcalfe's face, his mouth opening and closing in shock, speechless at the Inspector's words. Behind the two officers, Dorothy Metcalfe stood stock still, frozen in place like one of the Roman style statues that stood either side of the interior of the sitting room door. On the sofa, Sally Metcalfe however, leapt up in shock, the poor dachshund sent scrabbling to the floor where it quickly ran and hid under the large oak sideboard that stood against one wall of the room.

"Daddy," she almost screamed. "What the hell are they talking about? What do they mean, by *charges relating to the murder of Aaron*? Please tell me they're making a mistake."

"Sally…I…" before he could say more, Sergeant Norman took hold of his elbow as he moved to lever himself from his chair and as he reached a standing position she swiftly pulled his arms behind his back and snapped a pair of handcuffs in place, closing tightly around his wrists, bringing an audible gasp from the man and equal gasps of shock from his wife and daughter."

"Are those really necessary?" his wife asked pleadingly, referring to the handcuffs.

"I'm afraid so," said Houseman. "Your husband faces serious charges, Mrs. Metcalfe. We're transporting him immediately to Merseyside Police Headquarters in Liverpool, where he'll be questioned by the detectives conducting the investigation."

"But Aaron was my boyfriend" said Sally. "My father couldn't possibly have had anything to do with his murder. I mean, even I was drugged at the time, and he wouldn't have…"

Sally stopped in mid sentence as doubt suddenly crept in. She'd wondered why, when Aaron was murdered, she'd only been knocked out for a few hours. Was it really possible her own father was involved in this nightmare?"

"I'm sorry Miss, we don't have time for this. They're waiting to speak to your father in Liverpool."

Houseman and Norman had then quickly and efficiently ushered the handcuffed figure of Jeffrey Metcalfe from his home, still in a state of apparent shock, leaving his wife and daughter in tears, clinging to each other on the steps of their grandiose home, which to both women suddenly seemed a cold and empty place as the reality of the situation took hold of the pair. Houseman and Norman maintained a planned, ominous silence during the journey to Liverpool increasing Metcalfe's agitation and trepidation as they steadfastly refused to respond to his attempts to illicit any information from them regarding his future. By the time Houseman delivered his prisoner into the custody of Merseyside Police, Metcalfe appeared on the verge of a panic attack. After ensuring he was fit enough to be questioned he was placed in interview room two, where he was left under the guard of a uniformed constable, to await the arrival of Ross and Drake who would be conducting his interview.

Ross and Drake had in the meantime greeted and thanked Houseman and Norman, who reported their own satisfaction with their own role in the affair, being pleased to have helped and as Houseman put it, "Glad to have helped bring a little bit of the soft criminal underbelly to the surface. I hope you now proceed to sink the bastard without trace."

The pair stayed long enough to also meet Oscar Agostini, who asked them to pass on his personal thanks to Chief Inspector Wells, after which, following a hot coffee in the cafeteria, the two uniformed officers took their leave of Liverpool, returning to Lancaster within an hour of their arrival in the big city.

Ross next sent the remaining members of the team home to get a couple of hours rest. They would all return later that night to take part in the operation supporting Derek McLennan. Last to leave was Paul Ferris, who was collected by his wife Kareen and young son, another Aaron. Ross, Drake and Agostini made a fuss of young Aaron, who had undergone painful sessions of kidney dialysis when younger, eventually receiving a kidney transplant at the tender age of six years. Now a well developed ten year-old, Aaron was something of a favourite among the members of the Murder Investigation Team, an unofficial mascot almost. Having only arrived quite recently Oscar Agostini didn't know the lad as well as the others but that didn't prevent him from ushering Aaron into his office, from where he emerged a few minutes later with a Merseyside Police wall shield, which Ross knew had been displayed on Agostini's office wall up until that time.

Ferris thanked the D.C.I. for his kindness and Agostini just winked at him as he patted Aaron on the shoulder, telling him he was almost a grown up now, and to look after his Mum while his Dad was busy at work. Young Aaron's chest swelled with pride at that, and Ferris and Kareen were both grateful to Agostini for giving Aaron that bit of self-importance and inner confidence.

With the Ferris family gone, the squad room took on an air of desertion, like a ship left without a crew, drifting at sea. Agostini followed Ross and Drake as they walked solemnly towards interview room two. He then entered the door to the viewing room where he would observe Metcalfe's interview through the room's large one way mirror, listening in through the built-in intercom system.

Jeffrey Metcalfe almost jumped out of his skin when the door opened to admit Ross and Drake. After introducing himself and Sergeant Drake, and starting the tapes that would record the suspect's interview, Ross wasted no time in getting straight to the point.

"You're in some really deep shit, Mr. Metcalfe," he began. "I doubt poor Sally is going to forgive you when she hears how you conspired to kill her boyfriend, or how her job offer from the Aegis Institute came about through your own criminal connections with Francis Kelly and his bunch of thieves and cutthroats."

With those opening words, Ross had successfully peeled away the last veneer of Metcalfe's slim hopes of avoiding serious charges. To Metcalfe, that brief opening statement from Ross, and the use of Kelly's name had him believing the police knew everything there was to know about his activities. As had happened at the time of his arrest his mouth opened and closed but no words came out.

"Got nothing to say, Metcalfe?" Ross asked. "Well, let me fill in a couple of the blanks for you. It all probably began innocently enough with a genuine tender by your company to carry out a regular freight contract for Aegis's European Division. Then, somewhere along the way, you met Kelly, probably on one of his visits to the UK, and Kelly quickly saw you could be bought and manipulated into carrying out some of his less than legitimate business, am I right?"

Metcalfe nodded, and in a hushed voice, spoke at last. "It was a company golfing weekend, where we met. I told him about Sally. He said he could help her career, and things started from there."

"I thought so," Ross replied. "Now listen to me, you corrupt, greedy piece of shite; I hate killers and I hate people who hide behind killers almost as much. Unless you want to spend the rest of your natural life behind bars, I suggest you tell us everything about your involvement with Aegis from the time you met Francis Kelly. I want to know about the shipments, the false compartments built into the trucks of your subsidiary company and how the hell you let yourself be talked into setting up poor Aaron Decker and allowed your own daughter to be given a dangerous drug that might have killed her at the same time."

"You're not a man," Izzie Drake added as Ross drew breath. "You're the lowest form of animal life, Metcalfe. But the more you tell us, the easier the judge might be when we tell him you've cooperated fully with our investigation, got it?"

Metcalfe nodded, and after taking a deep breath, he talked. The tapes carried on turning, and Drake made copious notes as he revealed the full story of his involvement with Kelly and his plot to steal from and defraud not only those who'd employed his company, the innocent and legitimate wing of The Aegis Institute who had naïvely awarded him contracts on Kelly's recommendations, but governments who trusted Aegis to work for them, and how Kelly and his trusted security force would ruthlessly eliminate anyone perceived as being a threat to their activities, including Aaron Decker.

Andy Ross had dealt with men like Metcalfe in the past, ordinary men who allowed greed and avarice to completely overtake their sense of social responsibility. The temptation to turn a fast profit from what initially must have seemed a simple get rich quick scheme had ensnared many men before Metcalfe and would do so again in future. For now though, Ross and Drake were content that within an hour, Jeffrey Metcalfe, mostly inspired by fear of his now unknown future had provided them with enough to convict him of multiple offences and sufficient information the F.B.I. and C.I.A. would be able to use against Francis Kelly. The net was tightening, and now all they needed was success with their plan to bring Finch, a.k.a. Randolph Lambert into custody.

CHAPTER 39

A HOSPITAL OPERATION

There was no doubt in the minds of Ross and Drake that the net was now firmly closing on those concerned with what had turned out to be a case with so many international ramifications.

"To think this started with the death of a young university cricket star, sir, and look where it's led us," Drake commented, as she and Ross sat in his office, doing their best to relax a little after finally handing Jeffrey Metcalfe over to the custody sergeant to be officially processed into the system. He'd be held overnight in the holding cells and brought up before the magistrates in the morning, when he'd be officially arraigned and transferred to prison to await his trial.

"True enough Izzie," Ross replied, his voice calm and quiet as he sipped from a mug of barely warm coffee. "But you know, it may have started for us with the death of Aaron Decker, but really it began on a cold night in Kiel, Germany back in 1945 when that submarine slipped its moorings and set to sea on Hitler's orders. Everything we've been involved with in this case all stems from that damned secret voyage."

"You're right, of course, sir," she agreed, "but we didn't know about any of that when we started out did we?"

"No, we didn't. And can those involved in this bloody catalogue of crime say it was worth it? With the number of years in prison they're going to serve, I doubt it, and don't forget how many people have lost their lives through the greed of people like Ackermann, Kelly and Metcalfe."

"Do you think we'll get enough on Kelly for the Americans to act against him?" Izzie asked.

"We will," Ross said firmly. "Derek McLennan will snare us this bloody Finch character tonight and we'll make him talk one way or another. He's the man who can link everything that's happened back to Kelly. I had a quick call from Jerome Decker earlier. Apparently Supervisory Special Agent David Lee and a special F.B.I Task Force is ready to move against Kelly. The F.B.I. has informed the Aegis senior executives of their suspicions regarding Kelly, and the board of directors is horrified and supportive of the Bureau's initiative. If we can send them a recording that implicates Kelly in murder, they will pick him up right away. Under U.S. laws, it appears Kelly is guilty of a number of serious financial offences already, so murder on top of that should wrap their case against him up nicely."

"Are you sure Derek will be okay?" Izzie said, switching back to the night's sting operation set up to entrap Finch/Lambert.

"I know what you're thinking," Ross said straight away. "Randolph Lambert is a dangerous man for sure, but Derek will be out of the way before the arrest goes down, and Lambert won't have a chance to get at him."

"I hope you're right, sir," Izzie said, worried for their colleague.

"He's a first class copper, Izzie. He knows what's at stake tonight and is professional enough to handle whatever happens."

"I know sir. He's come a long way since he first joined the team. Sometimes I forget he's all grown up now and isn't that wet behind the ears young D.C. any more. I'm sure he'll be fine."

"Listen, why don't you go home for a couple of hours? Peter must have forgotten what you look like. As long as we're all back here by midnight, there's no reason for you to hang around here."

Izzie stretched both arms upwards, suddenly realising how tense and weary she was.

"Well, I wouldn't mind having a quick shower and a change of clothes. As you say, Peter will be pleased to have me home for a little while. Hey, you never know, we might even be able to…"

"Enough, no more, too much information," Ross laughed, thinking of the newly-weds falling into bed together for a 'quickie' before Izzie reported back for work.

Izzie laughed too.

"I was going to say, we might be able to grab a quick meal together for the first time this week," the smile on her face growing broader as she spoke.

"Oh, right, yes of course you were," Ross replied, looking suitably chastised. "Just my dirty mind at work again."

"Yeah, don't I know it?" Izzie giggled.

"Go on, get off home," Ross smiled again. "I'll see you later."

"Okay, sir, you should go home too. Give Maria a treat."

"Izzie…" Ross warned playfully, throwing a crumpled-up piece of paper at his sergeant.

"Just saying," Izzie joked as she disappeared out of Ross's office, leaving him alone with his thoughts in the ensuing silence.

Ross spent a few minutes tidying a few pieces of paper of no great importance that littered his desk and then picked up the phone.

"Order us a Chinese, Darling," he said when his wife, Maria answered his call. "I'm coming home for couple of hours. Have to come back later; got a big op on tonight."

"It'll be here by the time you get home, Andy," Maria replied, glad her husband would be home soon, for however brief a time. She'd been married to a detective long enough to accept the unusual hours he had to work from time to time. "Drive carefully."

Ross turned the lights off as he left his office, and the silence in that small enclave within the headquarters building was instant as the overhead buzzing of the fluorescent tubes ceased instantly. He allowed himself a few moments of reflection in the squad room before leaving for home. A case that had begun with the death of a young man who appeared to have a great future ahead of him, an American, no less, who excelled at the very British game of cricket and whose record for bowling maiden overs had made him the darling of the university cricketing fraternity had turned into a case involving international conspiracy, multiple murder and a large helping of greed and avarice. Ross glanced at the large whiteboard at the far side of the room, now in semi-darkness and briefly contemplated each face placed there by Paul Ferris as the case had developed.

So many people, here in Liverpool and elsewhere had contributed to him being close to resolving the case. The Royal Navy, a German historian, the Devon and Cornwall Constabulary, even the C.I.A. and the F.B.I. for God's sake, not forgetting the most recent contribution from the police in Lancaster. Cross border cooperation? If ever a case had proved that crime prevention organisations around the world could work together to successfully crack such a wide-sweeping international conspiracy, this was it, he concluded. He knew Oscar Agostini would still be in his office on the upper floor of the building and pondered on calling in to see him before going home, but the thoughts of spending a couple of hard-earned hours with Maria overrode that option and he quickly made his way out of the building and was soon driving home.

Marie Ross was as good as her word. The Chinese takeaway had been delivered a few minutes before her husband's arrival at their neat detached home in Prescot. After enjoying a selection of dishes Marie had selected to tempt his palate, Ross made his way up stairs to take a shower and indulge in a change of clothes before heading back to work.

Andy Ross stepped from the en-suite bathroom with a towel around his waist, another in his hand, his hair still wet from the shower, to find Marie sitting on the bed, her legs crossed provocatively, her skirt having ridden up far enough to display a tempting glimpse of thigh.

"Feel better?" she asked as he used the hand towel to briskly rub his hair almost dry.

"Much better," he replied.

Marie patted the bed and beckoned him to come and sit beside her.

He'd given her a run down of the case as they'd eaten and she sensed he had a few reservations about the final stage of his plan.

"You're worried about Derek McLennan, aren't you?"

"Not so much worried as just a bit on-edge. Derek can take care of himself but the man we're after tonight has very little to lose at this stage and could be unpredictable. I just don't want Derek to get over confident and blow the whole plan as a result."

"Do you trust Derek?"

"Of course I do."

"So stop worrying and give him the credit he deserves, Andy. He's been with you a while now, so you should know whether he can do the job."

"Of course he can. It's just me being over-protective I suppose."

Marie smiled at her husband as she took his hand and placed it gently on her right knee.

"Well, well, Detective Inspector Andy Ross, the great mother hen. I can think of something to take your mind off your worries for a while. You did say you weren't going back to the office for a couple of hours, didn't you?"

"Yes, I did," said Ross as he caught the glint in Marie's eye as she slowly began to manipulate his hand further up her leg until he began to move independently and his hand found its way under the hem of her skirt. Clothes quickly discarded, the pair found themselves naked on the bed in no time and the next thirty minutes were spent in enjoying a brief interlude of intimacy that took Ross's mind far away from thoughts of death and conspiracy for a short time.

As they lay together in the warm afterglow of their lovemaking a large smile appeared on Andy Ross's face. Seeing his grin, Marie kissed him and then asked, "Are you going to tell me what's amusing you so much, just after you've made mad passionate love to your wife?"

"Oh, nothing really," Ross replied. "It's just that I suggested something similar to what we've just done to Izzie before sending her home and now...well, here we are, you know?"

"Andy!" Marie exclaimed. "You mean you actually told your sergeant to go home and get laid?"

"Well, sort of, I suppose."

"Yes, well, I know all about your 'sort of,' suggestions, poor girl. Anyway, I hope she took your advice," and the two of them laughed out loud together as Ross kissed her back and hopped off the bed, walking across to the wardrobe to select a suitable change of clothes for the late night operation at the hospital.

* * *

The office was buzzing with activity when Ross walked in shortly before midnight Almost everyone had beaten him to it, anticipating the operation that would take place in a few hours. Nick Dodds had arrived just before Ross. The detective constable had begged to be allowed to be part of the team that finally brought Finch in. Ross had agreed to him leaving Klaus Haller under the protection of his armed police guard at the safe house in St. Helens, after sending an extra uniformed officer to support them. As much as Dodds enjoyed Haller's company, he felt frustrated at being a glorified 'baby sitter' as he put it. Ross felt Haller would be safe enough as they knew precisely where Finch would be during the coming hours. Even Izzie Drake was there before him, grinning like a Cheshire cat at him as she sat on the corner of Paul Ferris's desk as the team's collator sat busily typing information into the computer.

"Something happen to hold you up, sir?" she grinned at him.

"I had a very enjoyable couple of hours at home, thank you, Sergeant Drake, Chinese takeaway in fact." Ross grinned back at her. "I take it you also took advantage of the short break to spend some quality time with Peter?"

"Oh yes, sir. As you suggested, we did enjoy spending some time together. Chinsese takeaway, eh? So that's what they're calling it nowadays is it?" Izzie replied, a red blush and a grin on her face as she spoke.

Ross merely winked at her and beckoned her to join him in his office, where Derek McLennan was already waiting for him, in company with D.C.I. Agostini. McLennan had handed the envelope containing the down payment from Finch, which would remain in Agostini's care for the time being.

"You alright, Derek?" Ross asked as Drake closed the door behind them as they entered the office.

"Fine thanks, sir," McLennan responded. The young detective constable had gone to a lot of trouble to look the part for this evening's operation. He wore a black leather jacket, faded blue jeans and heavy Dr. Martens boots. His hair was slicked back with gel and if anyone looked like a 'bent' copper, somehow Derek gave off just the right aura.

"You look…different," said Drake who, like Ross was used to seeing Derek in either his work suit or at worst, a casual jacket and trousers and open-necked shirt as opposed to the plain white t-shirt he currently wore under his jacket.

"Thought this look made me look a bit tougher," Derek replied with a sheepish grin.

"Oh, for God's sake Derek. You already met the man earlier. He knows just what you look like, and you haven't exactly grown much stubble in the last few hours," Drake added, a reference to his not having shaved.

"Oh, well, never mind," he said quietly.

"Leave him alone, Izzie," Ross said. "As long as Derek feels comfortable with his appearance, that'll do for me."

"Right sir. Sorry Derek," Izzie apologised.

"No problem, Sarge," Derek responded.

Back in the squad room a few minutes later with the whole team present, Ross quickly phoned Agostini who had asked to be present at the team briefing. Five minutes later, the D.C.I added his presence to that of the others in the room and Ross began his briefing as silence descended on the squad room.

"Okay everyone, you all know why we're here. I hope you all managed a meal, some rest and maybe a shower in the couple of hours you got to go home, and thank you all for volunteering to be part of tonight's operation."

A small ripple of polite laughter ran round the room. Nobody would have dared not to 'volunteer' of course and everyone did after all want to be there when Finch was brought to heel.

"You all know the essence of tonight's set up. We aim to take down the man known as Finch, real name Randolph Lambert. Lambert is the man, the only man as far as we know who can give us the intelligence we need to lay murder charges against this Francis Kelly character in the States. He's sort of like Kelly's first lieutenant, his enforcer, whatever you want to call it. As you know, Derek has laid the bait for Kelly, playing the role of a bent copper prepared to sell out the location of the two members of Lambert's so-called security force, in other words his hired killers that we currently hold in custody. It's obvious that Kelly wants no living witnesses that can tie him to this whole sorry business and it's our guess that Lambert, if given time, would probably see through our plan, but we're lucky that he's under pressure from Kelly, and it appears he believes that either Robin or Starling are willing to talk to us about their part in his schemes. Derek has already hinted that Robin, a.k.a Graham Young is the easiest target and has arranged to meet Lambert at the hospital and give him Young's location, at the same time as he disables the guards with drugged coffee. Of course, Graham Young has already been moved to a safe location, and our friend Lambert is due to receive something of a shock when he tries to do away with the patient in room 414.

You all know the roles assigned to each of you. Sam, you're the duty nurse, Nick and Tony, you're the two uniformed officers outside the room, drugged of course, and Paul Ferris and Sergeant Drake will be taking the part of the two uniformed officers inside the room. Make sure you all have your vests on. I don't think for one minute that Lambert will draw attention to himself by using a gun in the hospital when he feels sure he can achieve his aims with poison and a syringe, which seems to be one of the trademarks of his people's method of eliminating their enemies. It's quick, quiet and efficient. Seems Lambert picked up plenty of sneaky tricks during his time in the C.I.A. We're being supported by a dozen uniforms who will all be firearms trained and strategically placed at major exit points of the hospital and in the car park, just in case something goes wrong and Lambert evades us in the hospital. Derek will meet him as arranged, and in return for the information Lambert needs, he will hopefully keep to his side of the bargain and pay Derek his blood money before entering the building."

"Isn't it assuming a lot to think he's just going to hand over a wad of cash to Derek before checking that Robin is really where Derek says he is, sir?" Tony Curtis asked.

"That's a good question, Tony," Ross replied, "and ordinarily I'd agree with you, but as I said earlier, Lambert is under pressure, and will want to be in and out as quickly as possible. If he had any sense, yes, he'd check it out first, and he may still do that, just to keep Derek dangling. If he does, Derek, just protest for a minute that he's changing the arrangement you made with him, but then kind of grudgingly accept what he says and agree to wait in the car park or wherever Lambert suggests, okay?"

"Okay, sir. Don't worry; I'll be prepared for any eventuality."

"Good man, Derek."

At this point, D.C.I. Agostini reached across and placed a silencing hand on Ross's shoulder. The D.I. immediately gave way to the boss, who obviously had something to say.

"Sorry to butt in, D.I. Ross, but I just want to say something at this point. First of all, thank you for going ahead with this one, D.C. McLennan. I know you'll be well supported but still, you're the front man and thus the most exposed of us all. Your bravery won't go unnoticed, young man."

Derek McLennan actually blushed at the praise from the Chief Inspector.

"As for the rest of you, I know you'll all do your jobs as well as I know you can, but please let me stress that Randolph Lambert is a dangerous man. I learned earlier from Jerome Decker that before being recruited into the C.I.A. he was a member of one of the U.S. Army's crack fighting units, so he has plenty of experience in the art of killing, so I'm saying, be careful out there tonight."

There followed a general round of nods, and voices in agreement with Agostini's instructions.

"Mr. Decker also gave me more information on the prime target, Francis Kelly. Prior to joining Aegis, Kelly worked as a deputy director at USUMRA, the United States Underwater Marine Research Agency. He's a genuinely qualified marine biologist and salvage expert, but get this, before taking his degrees and as a younger man, Kelly was a member of the U.S. Navy Seals."

"I've heard of them, sir. They're a bunch of tough cookies, a bit like the SAS as far as I know," said Drake.

"Correct Sergeant, though a better comparison would be with the Royal Navy's Special Boat Service, the SBS, who are a direct equivalent of the Seals."

"So that probably explains why Kelly went for a man like Lambert to head up his private security force, and also why most of the men Lambert then recruited would also appear to be predominantly former Special Forces people and highly paid mercenaries," Ross concluded.

"Exactly," said Agostini, "so again, I stress that the watchword for tonight is 'extreme care', ladies and gents."

Ross had no desire to over-complicate things, so with everyone knowing what was expected of them in a few hours, he brought the briefing to a close. The team rose as one from their seats and most made their way to the coffee machine for a quick caffeine boost.

Ross and Drake spoke with Agostini and with Derek McLennan for a few minutes, finalising the plans and then McLennan became the first of the team to leave the building. Just in case Lambert had set up any kind of surveillance on him, they wanted McLennan well away from headquarters before any of the team made their own departures. He'd visit a couple of late night clubs looking for all the world like a regular punter, certainly not an on-duty police officer, before making his way to the hospital at the allotted time.

* * *

The early morning hours were usually the most peaceful in and around the Royal Liverpool University Hospital. As the clock ticked past two forty-five a.m. Derek McLennan made his way out of the hospital's main entrance, looking as though he was coming from inside the building. In fact, he'd entered by a rear exit some ten minutes earlier, met up with Ross and Drake and was now standing in the car park, looking up into a clear night sky. Myriad stars twinkled in that clear sky, McLennan was even able to recognise The Plough, one of the few constellations he knew by sight. Not a cloud showed, nothing at all to obscure the brightness of the moon which hung above him like a shimmering orb of light, a shining beacon in Space, watching over the Earth and its denizens as they slept, or, in some cases, worked.

Derek's daydream, or should it be night dream (?) was interrupted by the arrival of a car in the car park. Dazzled at first by its headlights, as soon as the driver killed the lights Derek saw it to be an almost new Ford Focus, exactly the car Lambert had told him to expect.

Derek walked confidently towards the parked car, even though the driver made no attempt to exit the vehicle. He knew Lambert, he must remember to call him Finch, would be sizing him up. Any sly glances behind him or hesitancy in his manner might be enough to blow his cover.

A quiet 'swish' was the only sound that heralded the opening of the driver's side window as Derek drew level with the Focus.

"'Well, well right on time, Mr. Raven. The punctuality of the British Bobby eh?"

Lambert flicked a cigarette out of the open window, its embers breaking up into tiny red flares as it hit the ground.

"Mr. Finch, good to see you," Derek responded.

"I hope our patient is well. I'm looking forward to seeing him very soon," Finch said without preamble.

"Everything's set up," said Derek. "Ten minutes from now, every member of the night staff in the side ward on the tenth floor will be fast asleep. All you have to do is walk in and walk out again. I'm presuming it won't take long?"

"You presume correctly, Raven."

"So, what about my money?" Derek asked quite brazenly.

"Not so fast there," the man in the car said as the door slowly opened and Derek stood back as Finch got out, closed the door and held a brown envelope in his hand. He was dressed in a convincing doctor's coat, had a stethoscope round his neck, and a name badge that read, of course, Finch.

"Here's your money, but it stays with me until the job's done."

"But, that's not how we agreed things," Derek protested, having been warned by Ross that this was likely to happen.

"Let's just call it a slight change of plan. You can wait here until I've eliminated my friend Robin, then when I come down here again you get half the contents of this envelope. Then you'll lead me to wherever they're holding Starling and then, and only then, will you receive the rest of your thirty pieces of silver."

Derek looked crestfallen, as he was supposed to. Ross had warned him to expect just such a move by Lambert. It was likely the man would try to evade paying McLennan a penny, the only danger being he'd try to eliminate the detective at the same time. McLennan was confident that Lambert would not be coming back down from the upper floor of the hospital, so his fears were minimal

"But that's not fair. You'll know I'm on the up and up as soon as you get up there," he gestured up at the hospital building.

"You'd better hope that's true, won't you? You get paid when I say so and not before."

Derek McLennan shrugged his shoulders in a show of resignation.

"I don't seem to have much choice, do I?"

"No, you don't, Mr. Raven. Now, where do I go to find Robin?"

Derek quickly gave the killer the directions to the side ward on the tenth floor where he could find Robin. He stressed that the staff and police guards would remain drugged for at least two hours, giving them plenty of time to move on to their next target, the fake Doctor Starling.

"You'd better be here when I get back," Finch ordered as he turned to walk towards the hospital entrance.

"I've nowhere else to go," Derek replied. "I'm putting my entire career on the line here, Mr. Finch. I'm relying on you as much as you're relying on me."

Lambert simply grunted and walked away. Randolph Lambert exited the lift on the tenth floor. All had gone well so far. No one had challenged him and he felt confident as soon as he saw the 'night nurse' slumped over her desk a few yards from the lift. He stepped confidently passed her, and rounded the corner that led onto the corridor holding Robin's room, so he believed. There, he saw two uniformed police officers, one asleep on a plastic hospital chair, the other spread-eagled on the corridor floor where he'd apparently slid from his chair as 'Raven's' drug had taken effect.

Without wanting to waste time, the killer stepped past the two policemen and quietly opened the door to the room they'd been guarding.

Randolph Lambert repressed a quiet chuckle as he found exactly what 'Raven' had told him to expect. Two more uniformed constables were slumped in their seats, one a female, their heads resting on their chests. The man was actually snoring! Just to be sure all was as it should be Lambert swung a kick at the right leg of the female officer, who made a convincing groaning sound and fell off the chair onto the floor.

In the bed, the patient lay sleeping, apparently, though Lambert couldn't be sure due to the swathe of bandages that covered his head. He was hooked to various machines, all of which he assumed to be recording various life signs or recording his bodily functions.

Lambert reached into the right hand pocket of his white coat and with-drew a pre-loaded hypodermic containing a lethal dose of ketamine as used to dispatch young Aaron Decker. Seeing the patient was hooked up to a saline drip, Lambert simply used the syringe to inject the lethal chemical into the drip, and then stood back to wait for the man in the bed to react. A few convulsions should be all that showed as Robin's system went into terminal shock with death following in seconds.

Instead, what happened next seemed to play out in slow motion in Randolph Lambert's mind as, like a zombie rising from the grave, the figure in the bed, far from going into convulsions, slowly sat up, it's right hand reaching up to the head, from where is slowly began to unwrap the swathe of bandages that covered the face.

As it did so, and as Lambert stood rooted to the spot in almost morbid fascination, the left hand, which had been under the bedcovers until that moment, suddenly appeared, holding a rather lethal looking handgun, which he instantly recognised as a Glock 26, used by many of Britain's police forces.

"Surprise, Randy boy," said the man in the bed as the final bandages fell away to reveal the smiling face of a stranger.

"Yeah, surprise, surprise" said a female voice from behind him and he turned his head enough to find himself facing two more Glocks, held by Izzie Drake and 'snoring' Paul Ferris.

"Very clever," said Lambert, knowing he'd been outmanoeuvred and well and truly conned. "I suppose this means Mr. Raven isn't as bent as he led me to believe," he added as Andy Ross stepped from the bed, demonstrating as he did so that the catheter that led from the drip wasn't actually fitted to his wrist but was merely taped in place. The lethal dose of ketamine was simply flowing into a plastic bag that was attached to the end of the feed line under the blankets, sufficient evidence to convict him of attempted murder.

"Oh no," Ross said. "Your Mr. Raven is one of mine, and straight as a die, Mr. Lambert, or should I say Finch?"

"My, my, you do know a lot, don't you, copper?"

"It's Detective Inspector Ross to you, Lambert, and yes, we know a lot more than you might imagine, seeing as Graham Young didn't take too kindly to you trying to kill him and has been talking to us as though his life depended on it."

Lambert's face fell as he realised the extent of the con that the police had pulled on him and inwardly cursed his own stupidity at not being more meticulous in checking out the credentials of the so-called 'bent' police officer who'd led him into this carefully laid police trap.

Before he knew it, Lambert's hands were roughly pulled behind his back by Paul Ferris, as Izzie Drake opened the door to summon the remaining 'sleeping' policemen into the room. As Dodds and Curtis made their entrance, Izzie Drake suddenly swung her leg and kicked Lambert firmly across his right shin.

"Ow, you bitch. Did you see that? She kicked me. That's assault, police fucking brutality," he complained to the others.

"Did she? I never saw a thing, did any of you see the sergeant assault this man?" said Ross, as he nodded at Izzie as she took her revenge for the kick Lambert had landed on her leg on entering the room.

Dodds and Curtis both shook their heads, and Lambert growled, "Bastards, fucking police bastards."

"Now, now, that's not very nice, is it, Mr. Lambert, especially as we've got a nice heated cell and maybe even a cup of weak tea waiting for you after you've been processed into our custody suite? I think it will be a long, long time before you see the light of day again, unless it's through a barred window," Ross added. "Though we might think of something that might mitigate the length of time you spend behind bars, Lambert."

"What are you talking about?"

"Later," said Ross. "Take the bastard away lads."

Dodds, Curtis and Ferris jointly hustled Lambert from the room, where they were joined by Sam Gable, still dressed in her nurse's uniform, in the outer corridor.

"You too, eh?" Lambert said quietly as he realised the 'nurse' was yet another police officer.

"Yeah, me too. Life's a bitch, isn't it, Finch?" Sam said, grinning at the handcuffed killer. The small team of detectives were feeling pleased with themselves as they led Lambert away, leaving Izzie Drake to help Andy Ross to divest himself of the rest of his 'patient' disguise. Soon after, they followed the others after Ross first made a call to the hospital administrator, informing him the operation had gone smoothly and thanking him and his staff for their cooperation.

As Ross and Drake arrived in the car park, they caught up with the others just as Lambert was being forcibly loaded into the back seat of a police patrol car. Any hopes he'd harboured of attempting to break away from his police escort had disappeared when he arrived with them at the hospital exit to find a ring of armed uniformed officers waiting to ensure he was safely taken into custody.

As the car carrying their prisoner drove away at speed, escorted by two more cars and two police motorcyclists as outriders, Ross gathered his team around him.

"Well done everyone. I can't believe how smoothly that went. Anybody seen Derek? He should have been out here waiting for us."

They all looked around, each of them realising that they hadn't seen Derek since exiting the hospital. A feeling of dread gripped them all as they realised Lambert could have done something to Derek McLennan before entering the hospital. Ross called the sergeant in charge of the extra uniformed officers across but he confirmed that neither he nor any of his men had seen Ross's undercover detective since they'd taken up their positions.

"Sir, you don't think Lambert's done something to Derek do you?" a worried Sam Gable asked, her face betraying her feelings as she tried to envisage what could have happened.

"I don't know, Sam," Ross replied as a sliver of trepidation ran down his spine. Had they congratulated each other too soon?

"Search the car park," he ordered. "Look behind and under every vehicle, every bush and tree in the grounds. If Lambert did do something to McLennan, he didn't have time to go far to dispose of him, so he must be close by."

As the uniformed officers and the rest of the murder team, one dressed as a nurse, the others as uniformed officers themselves began to spread out to search the car park with Ross resembling an escapee from Doctor

Frankenstein's laboratory in his hospital garb, with tubes and other paraphernalia dangling from his arms and green hospital gown, Ross was
brought up in his tracks by a voice that came from somewhere behind him.

"What's up, sir, someone lost something?"

Derek McLennan was striding towards him from the direction of the
hospital entrance.

"Derek, where the bloody hell have you been? We thought Lambert
had topped you or something?" Ross virtually bellowed at him.

McLennan immediately adopted a sheepish grin as he admitted.

"Oh God, sorry sir, I was bloody desperate for the toilet."

Ross could only gape at him in disbelief, but Izzie Drake walked right
up to the Detective Constable and without a second's hesitation, slapped
him across the back of the head.

"You bloody dickhead," she bawled in his face. "Here we are thinking
you're lying dead or injured somewhere and you're off having a bloody
crap."

"Sorry Sarge, but I just had to go."

"Some bloody James Bond you are," Drake said with disdain as Derek
stood looking crestfallen, until Izzie stepped closer and put her arms
around him.

"Never mind, Derek," she said. "You're still the hero of the hour. We
got the bastard, all according to plan."

"That's great," said McLennan. "Congratulations sir," he said,
directing his words at Ross.

"Yes, well, it's congratulations to all of us," Ross replied. "Let's head
back to headquarters. I want to see Lambert booked and behind bars
before we go home. I want to interview him as early as possible in the
morning, so it'll be a short night's sleep for us tonight, Izzie."

"No problem, sir," Drake answered.

"You go home, Derek, You've earned a good night's sleep, and Derek?"

"Sir?"

"Next time, put a bloody plug in it okay?"

"Okay sir," McLennan replied. "Sorry to cause all that trouble."

"Forget it, Derek. Really, it's forgotten. We were worried, that's all."

Within minutes the car park of the Royal Liverpool University
Hospital stood deserted, the police presence gone as quickly as it had
appeared, the moon and stars in silent vigil as always. Ross was looking
forward to the morning, when hopefully, following his questioning of
Randolph Lambert the final pieces of this convoluted and complicated
case might just fall into place.

CHAPTER 40

THE MORNING AFTER THE NIGHT BEFORE

Andy Ross, Izzie Drake and the rest of the team were back in the office at seven thirty a.m. Most of them had managed no more than an hour or two of sleep after being sent home at three-thirty or thereabouts. Some, like Tony Curtis and Nick Dodds had simply returned to their homes, showered, changed and slumped in a chair for an hour or so, almost afraid to climb into bed in case sleep claimed them and refused to release them in time to return to headquarters. Both men placed their alarm clocks close to them as they slept fitfully in their uncomfortable positions. Sam Gable went home as ordered, showered, fell into bed totally naked, and woke an hour later, feeling cold as she'd been so tired she'd failed to pull the duvet over herself. Another hot shower revitalised her and she was soon dressed and ready to go back to work. Paul Ferris, as Ross and Drake had done the previous evening, enjoyed the pleasure of spending almost two hours in bed with Kareen, who woke instantly when she sensed his weight on the bed. If Kareen hadn't set their alarm clock for six thirty, post coital slumber would definitely have made Ferris late, but thankfully he just made it into the squad room before Ross's arrival.

Detective Chief Inspector Oscar Agostini was there, smiling with satisfaction at the results of the operation to apprehend Randolph Lambert. He also had an announcement to make, one he quickly shared in private with Ross before speaking directly to the team.

Ross raised a hand, and the team fell silent as they waited for the early morning briefing to begin. Ross couldn't help but notice a few yawns and stretches taking place but he knew it was simply fatigue and not boredom that was taking its toll on his people.

"Good morning everyone," Agostini addressed the small gathering.

Muttered but polite replies came from a few of the detectives.

"First of all, my congratulations to all of you on a successful completion of Operation Cuckoo last night," referring to the name he'd given the plan to apprehend Lambert at the last minute, "or should I say earlier this morning? Anyway, D.I. Ross has kindly allowed me to talk to you all this morning as I have some information to share with you with relation to the case."

That seemed to bring everyone to attention and their eyes and ears appeared to perk up as they waited to hear what the D.C.I had to say.

"As soon as Randolph Lambert was brought into custody, I informed Detective Chief Superintendant Hollingsworth. She in turn made contact with those agencies who share an interest in Lambert's activities. As a result of those calls, certain...erm...arrangements have been made that we will implement if D.I. Ross and Sergeant Drake are able to extract the information we want from Lambert."

Agostini certainly had the team's full attention now, though Ross's face was giving nothing away despite most of his team looking questioningly at him.

"I'm not going to go into all the details of what's been decided upon. That, as I'm sure you'll understand, doesn't really concern us, being a decision made at command level."

With those words, a few more whispers and mutterings could be heard as some of the team suspected they might not like what was coming. Agostini continued.

"As you all know, this case has morphed into something much bigger than we at first thought, and carries certain international ramifications that have had to be considered. The chief super has been in contact through the night with all those concerned and this is what has been decided.

If we can get a confession from Lambert that provides us with details of times and dates of crimes of violence, including murder, that directly implicates Francis Kelly, the U.S. authorities will immediately issue a warrant for Kelly's arrest. The F.B.I's serious crimes unit have already unearthed information relating to illegal financial activities perpetrated by Kelly, but the fear is that a team of clever and very expensive lawyers could find a way to secure bail for him if he was arrested on those charges, with the chance that might find a way to flee the country. A charge, or charges of multiple murder however could persuade a judge to deny bail and allow time for further inquiries to be made that will in all likelihood result in further charges being laid against him. Erich Ackermann in Germany is also incriminating Kelly in various illegal activities relating to Aegis Oceanographic's European operations, with the theft of antiquities and the pillaging of historical sites being at the top of the list. Kelly's biggest mistake in all this would seem to be allying himself with people who are not what we'd call career criminals. Most of them, like Ackermann for example are simply those who sought to exploit their knowledge and power to enrich their bank accounts. In other words, a bunch of greedy bastards."

That remark brought a round of laughter from the detectives, immediately followed by a question that came from Izzie Drake.

"Sir, I get the feeling this is leading up to something we might not like. Are you telling us that Lambert is going to be let off because he's being offered a deal of some sort by the Americans?"

Agostini smiled a knowing smile before replying to Drake's question.

"Very astute of you Sergeant Drake," he said, "and you're correct to an extent, though rest assured, Lambert is not getting away with anything."

"Then what, sir, if you don't mind me pressing you for an answer?"

"I don't mind at all, Sergeant. You and D.I. Ross will interview Lambert when we leave this room. Thanks to the efforts of Aaron Decker's father, the C.I.A. has been active in the last week and through their efforts, a number of countries including Greece, Turkey, Italy, Azerbaijan, Turkmenistan, and of all places, Japan, have all issued arrest warrants for Randolph Lambert and every member of his security force. You and D.I. Ross will at some point in the interview inform Lambert of the precarious nature of his situation. Although some of those nations probably have fairly modern and humane correctional institutions, I doubt Lambert will relish the possibility that he may end up incarcerated in a jail cell in Azerbaijan, for example , much less Turkmenistan or even Japan where he'd have a severe language problem for sure. If, on the other hand he is willing to tell us what we need to know, he will be tried in this country, and following sentencing, the United Sates will make an application for his extradition, which will of course be agreed to by the Home Office. Once on U.S. territory, Lambert will be charged with numerous offences but again, in return for his cooperation in the case against Francis Kelly he will be spared the death sentence for murder, and will receive a reduced sentence. At some point down the line, in consideration of his previous work for his country as a C.I.A. operative, he will be moved to a lower category prison from where he will eventually be released with a new identity, under close supervision by both the C.I.A. and the F.B.I."

It was Paul Ferris who was the first to fully comprehend the hidden agenda behind Agostini's words.

"What you're telling us, sir, is that the C.I.A. are going to put him back to work for them, isn't it?"

"I told you they'd soon catch on, sir," Ross smiled at his boss.

Agostini nodded, sagely, as he turned to face Paul Ferris.

"You, Detective Constable Ferris, are a very intelligent and perceptive officer, too good to remain a constable for much longer. Yes, you're quite correct in your assumption, but, let me reassure you all that if Lambert agrees to this deal, any operations he carries out in future for the C.I.A. will be extremely high risk 'black ops' with a very strong likelihood that he may not return in one piece, not that he'll be told that of course."

This time, the murmurs that sprang up around the room were of a more approving nature.

"So, any questions, ladies and gentlemen, or shall we allow D.I Ross and Sergeant Drake to go and talk to Mr. Lambert?"

"Just one question, sir, if I may?" asked Tony Curtis.

"Yes, D.C. Curtis, what is it?"

"I was just wondering when D.C. McLennan will be receiving his licence to kill, sir."

The explosion of laughter that instantly filled the room in response to Curtis's remark instantly relieved any lingering tension that Agostinis's announcement might have caused.

Even Oscar Agostini couldn't help himself and joined in the amusement. As he stopped laughing, he managed to keep a straight face as he replied to Curtis's facetious remark.

"Good point, constable. I think we'll leave that one to 'M's' discretion."

The D.C.I was pleased to receive another round of laughter in return.

"Right, everyone, that's enough," Ross said, taking charge of the situation, "sorry, sir, but we'd best get on."

"Yes, of course, D.I. Ross," Agostini grinned at the fact that Ross had taken control after his slight lapse into levity. "Everyone better get back to work, plenty of reports to be written up after yesterday, I believe."

Oscar Agostini shook hands with Andy Ross before departing the room with another remark of thanks for a job well done.

"Okay then, Izzie, let's go talk to our prisoner," Ross said firmly as the pair made their way to interview room one."

* * *

Randolph Lambert looked calm and assured, seated at the metal table that stood in the middle of the interview room, a uniformed officer on guard at the door, as Ross and Drake made their entrance and seated themselves opposite him.

The two detectives had interviewed hundreds of prisoners in their time together and would follow their usual procedure this morning. Ross would lead and Drake would intervene as and when she felt it advantageous to do so. It wasn't a 'good cop, bad cop' routine but it had always worked well for them, with Drake's seemingly random interventions often proving a decisive tactic.

"Mr. Lambert, good morning," Ross said politely, as he took his seat. "I'm D.I. Ross and this is Sergeant Drake."

"Yeah, we met last night. You were dressed as The Mummy," Lambert replied.

"Indeed we did. I hope you're not going to be difficult this morning. We've already got enough on you to put you away for a long, long time."

"So, what's the point of all this, then?" Lambert replied, feeling confident that he, not the police was in control of the situation. All that changed when Drake opened the folder she'd carried into the room with her, looked at the first page she came to and suddenly said.

"Randolph Lambert, U.S. citizen, also known as Finch, leader of Francis Kelly's private security force and wanted for various crimes including murder in Greece, Turkey, Italy, Azerbaijan, Turkmenistan, and Japan. Also caught red-handed attempting to murder a police inspector, namely D.I. Ross here, at approximately three oh-five this morning."

Lambert's face lost its composure for a few seconds before he replied.

"So, do you think I'm worried about it? I can bring in some real high powered lawyers to get me out of this."

"That's where you're wrong, Lambert," Ross said. "If you're thinking you can call on Kelly's lawyers, we should let you know that Francis Kelly is already in custody in the States," he lied, knowing the F.B.I. were waiting on the results of his interview with Lambert. "The F.B.I have been watching him for some time and I don't think he'll be wanting to even acknowledge your existence if it means he can cut a deal to save his own skin."

Lambert hesitated.

"Look," he said, "I don't understand where you're going with this. Fair enough, you got me on the attempted murder, but that's all. You can't prove anything else against me. I'm an American citizen and I want to speak to someone from my embassy."

"Funny you should say that," Ross smiled at him. "Someone from your embassy is very keen to speak to you, too. You might have heard of him. He's the deputy station chief for the C.I.A. in London at present, a certain Jerome Decker."

"Decker?"

"Yes, the man whose son you had killed, Lambert, the man you used to work for and the man who is going to 'nail your ass to the wall,' to use his own words. It seems the United States is willing to waive it's right to apply for your extradition if any of the aforementioned countries apply to have you passed into their jurisdiction for trial and either imprisonment or execution. They do have the death penalty in Azerbaijan, don't they, Sergeant Drake?"

"Oh, yes they do, sir, and in Turkmenistan, I understand. They use the old fashioned way of hanging there I believe; slow strangulation hanging from a long rope, no nice neat scaffold like we used to have here. I looked it up this morning. It can take up to half an hour for a prisoner to die that way, dancing and dangling at the end of the rope, pissing themselves and losing bowel control whilst choking their guts out as they die horribly and slowly."

Lambert visibly paled.

"Hmm, Turkmenistan sounds favourite to me then. What about Azerbaijan?"

"Looked that up too, sir. Could be firing squad, could be hanging, it's up to the judge. Oh, yes, they like to do it in public too over there. Makes for good entertainment for the masses, helps to deter crime too."

Ross and Drake had hardly glanced at Lambert as they'd exchanged those few words, but Ross now looked him in the eye and could see the first hint of uncertainty in the man's demeanour.

"You guys wouldn't deport me to one of those places," he said.

"Why not?" Ross asked. "After all, you were quick to point out you're a U.S. citizen and Jerome Decker says they don't care what we do with you, so why don't we save the British taxpayer a fortune in keeping you locked up and fed in a nice soft British jail when we can accept the request of one of the other nations who want you and let them mete out some swift justice? Give me a good reason, Lambert, just one good reason why I should do anything that will save your miserable, murdering hide."

Ross knew they were winning. He and Drake had planted a seed in Lambert's mind and what came next would, as far as Lambert was concerned, be all his own idea. He glanced sideways at Izzie Drake, who gave him a sly smile in return. She knew, too.

"I can tell you stuff," Lambert suddenly blurted out. "Stuff that will help the Feds take Kelly down for far more than they probably know about. I can tell you enough to tear his organisation to pieces."

"Really? That's interesting, Mr. Lambert," Ross replied. "And what would you expect in return for this information?"

"A guarantee that I wouldn't be extradited to any of those places you mentioned. And immunity from prosecution over here and in the States."

Ross laughed out loud and Izzie joined in at Lambert's outrageous demand.

"You've got balls, Lambert, I'll give you that," said Ross. "You haven't a snowflake in hell's chance of getting off scot-free. We do, however, have an alternative proposal for you. I'd seriously suggest you give it some thought before replying."

"I'm listening," Lambert said, sitting back in the hard plastic chair and trying, unsuccessfully, to appear calm and unruffled.

Andy Ross spent the next few minutes outlining the C.I.A's proposal, stressing to Lambert that it had been ratified by the Home Office, and was thus officially sanctioned by the British government.

"If it was up to me, Lambert, I'd let you go to trial and be sentenced to life without parole," Ross snarled at the killer. "Sadly, I'm just a pawn of those in higher authority so I've been forced to make you an offer that I consider generous in the extreme."

Lambert looked pensive as he considered Ross's offer. Deep down, he knew it was the best, in fact the only offer he was likely to receive, and one that would enable him at some time, to taste freedom again, albeit under the control of his former paymasters at the C.I.A.

Finally, knowing he was out of options, Lambert nodded, almost imperceptibly, and Izzie Drake reached again into the folder she'd brought into the room with her and removed a two page document that she simply pushed across the desk towards Lambert, together with a ballpoint pen. Lambert cast no more then a cursory glance at the pages and then picked up the pen and signed in the appropriate place, pushing both document and pen back to her.

Inwardly, Ross sighed in satisfaction. It maybe wasn't the perfect result as far as he was concerned, but it would suffice and would certainly take a whole lot of criminals out of circulation once the various international law enforcement agencies made their moves. Most importantly, Lambert's testimony would now help to convict Francis Kelly of multiple murder, conspiracy to commit murder and more.

"We'll send someone to take your statement," Ross said as he and Izzie rose from their seats, leaving Lambert sitting under the watchful eye of P.C. Henderson.

Ross and Drake wasted no time in delivering Lambert's signed agreement to D.C.I Agostini.

"Well done Andy," said Agostini, who immediately phoned D.C.S Hollingsworth with the news. A minute later, after hanging up the phone, he turned to Ross and confirmed that Hollingsworth had already set in motion the international effort to bring down the whole of Francis Kelly's organisation. The board of directors at the Aegis Institute had given the American authorities *carte blanche* to enter any of their facilities in cooperation with the relevant local law enforcement agencies.

"What's happening with Lambert now?" Agostini asked.

"Paul Ferris and Sam Gable are with him. Ferris is the perfect man to take Lambert's statement, with his background in computers and knowledge of the business world, he'll make better sense of what Lambert's telling us, and Sam Gable will keep him on edge, make sure he doesn't try to keep us in the dark about any aspect of the case. She's good at that."

"Excellent," Agostini said. "As soon as Ferris gives us that statement, I want it copied and we can then send a copy to each of the police forces involved around the world."

"Sounds weird, that, sir."

"What? Around the world?"

"Yes. Who'd have thought it?"

"I agree, Andy, but it just goes to prove that the criminal fraternity has tendrils everywhere nowadays. It seems no section of the community is exempt from being infected by the desire to circumvent the law."

* * *

Lambert's statement took two hours to relate, after which, Paul Ferris and Sam Gable saw him being safely locked in a cell before heading back to the squad room. From there, as Agostini had requested, copies of that statement were sent to all the relevant forces involved in the investigation. Agostini and D.C.S. Hollingsworth both received a copy and at a meeting with Sarah Hollingsworth later that day, Oscar Agostini expressed his amazement at just how much information Randolph Lambert had given them.

"It looks as if Lambert always thought he might have to turn on his boss," he said to the Chief Superintendant. "He must have used his position of trust within Kelly's inner circle to gather and retain enough information to give himself a little insurance if ever he needed it."

"Well, he certainly needed it today," Hollingsworth agreed. "I spoke with the F.B.I. soon after you sent me a copy of the statement and they were ready to move against Kelly. I was assured they'd be taking action to arrest him within an hour of my call. I'm expecting to hear that he's in custody very soon. Ross was clever, telling Lambert that Kelly was already in custody. That gave him a sizable push to get his story in first, in case Kelly tried to put too much blame on his shoulders."

As Agostini nodded, Hollingsworth's phone rang and she looked at the instrument as though she could read its message just by doing so.

"This could be the call I've been expecting," she said as she lifted the receiver to her ear. After listening for a few seconds, she mouthed "F.B.I." at Agostini, and then exchanged pleasantries, listened, and then Agostini sensed something wasn't right.

"He what?" Hollingsworth shouted into the phone. "But how? I thought your people had him under constant surveillance?"

Agostini felt a sinking feeling in his stomach, knowing very well what Hollingsworth was hearing on the phone. The Chief Superintendant continued talking for a minute or two before hanging up angrily.

"Kelly gave them the slip," she almost shouted at Oscar Agostini. "The bastard must have been tipped off."

"A leak?"

"Either in the F.B.I, or maybe someone on the Aegis board of directors perhaps. That was Special Agent-in-Charge Hal Morrow. He's bloody mad as hell, couldn't apologise enough. Seems Kelly left the building no more than twenty minutes before his agents arrived. Somehow, he made it to La

758

Guardia airport where he boarded a private plane and was last seen heading in the direction of the Canadian border."

"Fucking hell, Ma'am, after all our work."

"I know, but Morrow says he hasn't given up yet. Kelly forgot in his panic to escape that his plane has a transponder and U.S. air traffic controllers are monitoring his flight. As long as he stays on his current heading, Morrow thinks he's heading for Alaska, where Aegis owns a massive deep water port facility and where their submarines are based when not at sea."

"Shall I tell Ross and his team?"

"Yes, do that, but make sure he knows the F.B.I. people are still tracking him."

Ross and Drake virtually mirrored Hollingsworth's and Agostini's reaction to the news, but refused to be downhearted. Andy Ross was certain that Kelly wouldn't get away, and his belief was vindicated soon afterwards when word came down from D.C.S. Hollingsworth that Kelly's short-lived bid for freedom had ended in his capture and arrest.

Agostini and Ross were soon seated in Hollingsworth's office, eagerly waiting for her to tell them more. She looked far more relaxed than she'd been during Agostini's earlier visit as she invited both men to help themselves to coffee from her rather plush and expensive percolator, both men availing themselves of this unheard of generosity.

"Well, gentlemen, it appears our Mr. Kelly was fast, but not fast, or clever enough. This is what I've just been told, much of which fits with what we talked about earlier, Oscar. The Americans were able to track his aircraft and with the cooperation of the Canadian Air Traffic Controllers, were soon able to plot his potential point of landing. His overflying of Canada was clever but it was soon evident he was heading for Alaska. As I explained, Aegis has its own private deep-water port facility there, not far from the settlement of Port Lions on Kodiac Island. They really can be predictably original in naming places, our American friends. The place was named after The Lions Club who helped pay for the building of the settlement apparently."

"Never heard of it, Ma'am," Ross observed.

"Neither had I until a few minutes ago," the D.C.S. replied. "But it appears Kodiac is a large island off the coast of Alaska, mostly visited by tourists who go there to see Brown Bears. The island is a bit bigger than Cyprus," she said as she turned her computer screen towards them, displaying a map of Kodiac she'd just found on the internet. "So anyway, Hal Morrow of the F.B.I's special task force told me that since obtaining permission from the CEO of Aegis, they'd already sent a team of agents to the inspirationally named, *Aegis Seaport* facility, as they have to every facility run by one of Kelly's salvage experts. It's been quite simple for them to target the Aegis installations run by Kelly's people; just look for the salvage people he'd infiltrated into the organisation. Oh, before I forget, they soon found the leak. One of Aegis's board of directors was conspicuous by his absence at a meeting last night and he was also picked up by the F.B.I. at Miami airport trying to board a connecting flight to the Bahamas with a case full of money, after being traced to a flight to Florida. He was sitting in the departure lounge, bold as brass, thinking he was on his way to a life of luxury in the sun, paid for by Kelly's dirty money. He'd tipped Kelly off about the F.B.I, being ready to move against him and then done a runner, the idiot. If he'd stayed put he may have been able to remain under our radar and got away in a few months, assuming Kelly didn't drop him in it once we got him. So, where was I? Oh, yes, Kelly was really stupid running as he did, with no thought about his flight being tracked. The pilot was an innocent in all this, just a regular company employee, used to flying executives anywhere they needed to go, often at short notice, so he wouldn't have thought to try and cover up their destination.

So, Kelly's plane landed at Aegis's small private airfield on Kodiac Island, from where he was picked up in car driven, unknown to him of course, by an F.B.I. agent who drove him straight to the base. From there, he walked to the Aegis base control centre, made sure the submarine that had been renamed *Aegis Explorer* was ready for sea, and gave orders that the base be placed on alert for a potential terrorist attack, with further orders to shoot to kill if any unauthorised people attempted to assault the base, crafty bastard. Of course, all the 'security' personnel at the base had already been detained and replaced by F.B.I agents. Kelly knew none of the local security operatives personally so the 'Feds' as the Americans call them weren't worried about him not recognising the security staff. He did know the head of security however who played his part in the deception with an F.B.I. gun at his back as he spoke to Kelly."

As she paused for breath, Agostini took the opportunity to speak.

"Sounds to me as though the F.B.I. ran a bloody good operation, all things considered, Ma'am."

"Yes," Ross agreed, "especially as they had to move fast once they knew he'd slipped through their fingers in New York."

"Very true, gents," Hollingsworth agreed, "though they were already on site of course, which none of Kelly's people, even the crooked director knew about. Anyway, here's the best bit, according to Morrow. Kelly walked through the Aegis facility as if he owned the place, and took the elevator that led to the lower levels where the submarine pens had been built. They could accommodate any two of their four modified subs there at any given time. In fact, the original modifications to the former military submarines had been carried out in Alaska, far from prying eyes, we now know.

Kelly was as confident as he could possibly be that he'd evaded capture according to the agents who observed his behaviour and body language as he marched along the underground dockside to the *Aegis Explorer*. He saw the gangplank waiting for him, leading straight to the door at the base of the 'sail' which I still think of as the conning tower, sounds better to me. Who thinks of a submarine having a bloody sail after all? So, he walked on board the submarine into the control room where he was met by the skipper of the sub, one of his trusted inner circle of cohorts, who was also being 'worked' by an F.B.I agent close behind him.

"Ready for sea?" Kelly asked.

"Aye, sir," the captain, a man named Ryan replied. "Do you have a destination for me yet?"

"Here you are," Kelly replied, handing Ryan a piece of paper. Ryan scrutinised it and then gave the agents spread around the control room a pre-arranged signal and they instantly encircled Kelly, identified themselves as Federal agents and took him into custody. His face was an absolute picture, according to Morrow, who described it as 'a perfect take-down.'

"You bastard, Ryan," was all Kelly could say as the captain of the sub handed the piece of paper to the senior agent in the control tower. It appears Kelly was running to The Seychelles, where he probably has a nice little hideaway prepared, a bolt-hole ready for a time when he might have to disappear. They'll soon have it located now they have the sailing co-ordinates. It's possibly where all Kelly's private records are secreted away, as Ryan confirmed, after Kelly had been led away, that he'd taken his boss there on a couple of occasions in the past, always to different locations. There are over a hundred islands that go to make up The Seychelles, so it was important for them to get Kelly's own directions to his captain, to make sure the knew exactly where in the world he was headed."

"Brilliant," Agostini enthused. "You have to hand it to them. The F.B.I. has gone up a ton in my estimation."

"Mine too," said Ross. "Nothing like in the movies eh?" he smiled.

"They are a very efficient and dedicated force for law enforcement, gentlemen. I'm glad we had them with us on this one or Kelly might never have been brought to justice."

Detective Chief Superintendent Sarah Hollingsworth then took Andy Ross by surprise. Rising from her chair, she walked around her desk until she stood in front of the seated D.I. who promptly stood up to face her. Hollingsworth reached out her right hand and Ross automatically did the same as she proceeded to shake his hand vigorously.

"Well done, Detective Inspector," she said effusively. "You and your team have done a wonderful job on this case. How on earth you pulled all the threads together I have no idea, but I do know that D.C.I. Agostini has been singing your praises in my ear for days now."

"Really, Ma'am, I mean, thank you, Ma'am, you too, sir," Ross gabbled as he turned to Agostini who simply grinned at him.

"I know the two of you came up through the ranks together,"

Hollingsworth went on, "so I suggest the pair of you get together outside work hours of course, and enjoy a celebratory drink together. It might be nice to include the rest of your team, of course, D.I. Ross."

With that, Sarah Hollingsworth reached behind her to where her black leather bag stood on her desk. Reaching into it, she removed her purse and extracted a roll of ten pound notes, a hundred pounds in total, which she pressed into Ross's hand.

"A small token of appreciation for a job well done," she said. "I haven't lost my memories of the feelings that come from solving a big case you know. I stood where you are once, D.I. Ross. I wasn't always a Chief Super. Now go, you too, Mr. Agostini, and give my thanks to all your team on a job well done."

"Thanks a lot, Ma'am," said Agostini as he led an almost speechless Andy Ross from the room.

* * *

The lounge bar of the Fullers Arms reverberated to the sounds of raucous laughter and old but good jokes as Ross's team enjoyed a couple of hours of celebration after he'd returned to the squad room with the news of Kelly's eventual arrest. As is the case with close knit teams in many occupations, they had worked hard and now they felt they could play hard. The beers were flowing, at least in most cases, though Izzie Drake and Sam Gable were enjoying themselves with the fruits of Bacchus, red for Izzie, white for Sam.

"No one beats us, that's for sure," Tony Curtis slurred as his fourth pint began to take effect on his equilibrium.

"We're the best," Nick Dodds agreed.

"You two are drunk," Izzie Drake said to the two constables, accusingly.

"Not quite, Sarge, but we will be in a minute or two," Dodds said and another round of laughter filled the room.

"Hey, Derek," Curtis called out to Derek McLennan, who was threading his way back to the table from the direction of the gents.

"What's up, Tony?" McLennan called to him.

"Where you been, lad?"

"You know where I've been," Derek hiccupped.

"Oh yes, I forgot. Derek McLennan, Undercover Toilet Agent."

Derek blushed as everyone around the table, even Ross and Agostini joined in the laughter. Sam Gable sidled up to him and put a protective arm around his shoulder.

"You lot leave our Derek alone. He's my hero, he is, licensed to thrill is our Derek."

"Yeah, as long as there's a gents in the vicinity, just in case," Tony Curtis quipped, cueing more laughter.

Oscar Agostini stood up, banged his empty beer glass on the table and called for attention.

"Listen to me," he ordered. "You've all done a great job, but don't be late for work in the morning. You've still got lots and lots of reports to make out before we can officially close this case, so don't get too drunk, will you?"

As he was grinning like a Cheshire cat as he said it, his statement was greeted by boos and catcalls from the team.

As the general hubbub and air of celebration continued around them, Drake pulled Ross to one side.

"What's up, Izzie?" Ross asked.

"Just wondered if you'd phoned D.I. Jones in Falmouth, sir. He'd be pleased to know we got them all in the end."

"I phoned him before we left headquarters, Izzie, while you and Sam were adjusting your make up in the ladies loo."

"How was he? And Carole of course?"

"They're fine, Izzie. Brian was over the moon with the news. Sergeant St. Clair was out on a job when I called, but she'll be made up with the news too, no doubt. Now that we're on the cusp of cleaning out this nest of vipers, I asked D.I. Jones if he'd like to lead the team that hits the local Aegis facility down there. He'll have already spoken to his boss by now and they won't be wasting any time in moving in on the place. He can't wait to snap the cuffs on that Evans character who runs the Aegis operation, and his cronies."

"Surely not all the Aegis employees at the site are crooked, sir."

"No, they're not, but the first thing the local force down there will do is go in fast and hard, lock the place down and arrest Evans. Then they'll interview every employee and it shouldn't be difficult to weed out the good from the bad. Here's the best bit. I also phoned the Ministry of Defence, and it seems *H.M.S. Wyvern* is still on station as they call it, in the Channel and they're sending her to effect the arrest and impounding of Aegis's research and salvage vessel. Captain Howell will liaise with the Devon and Cornwall Constabulary to coordinate everything. Brian Jones is hoping they can hit the facility from land and sea at the same time in a joint assault, as he put it."

"Sounds as if he's looking forward to it, sir."

"He definitely is, Izzie. He reckons he owes Evans and his crew a bloody nose, figuratively speaking of course."

"Having met D.I. Jones and Sergeant St. Clair, I wouldn't be at all surprised if the bloody noses are more real than figurative when he and his people force their way into that place," Izzie smiled as she spoke.

"You know, Izzie, you could be right," Ross grinned back at her. "Now, let's go grab one last drink and then we'd better head for home. Marie will want to hear all about tonight from me and I'm sure Peter will want the same from you."

"Oh, I think that can wait, sir. Peter will have something else on his mind when I get home, I'm sure."

Ross groaned in mock indignation.

"Oh no, I really don't need to know that. I keep forgetting you newly wed types are all at it like rabbits for the first year or two."

"I'm hoping it will last a darn sight longer than that," Izzie laughed as she pushed off through the crowded bar, shouting "Same again sir?" as she went, a big grin on her face.

Ross laughed and nodded, unable to make himself heard above the general din in the Fullers Arms. His team were enjoying themselves, letting their hair down, and deserved to. Ross saw Izzie heading back in his direction, threading her way through the crush of bodies and thought, *Maybe Marie could be persuaded to wait for the full story until later…*

CHAPTER 41

EXETER CATHEDRAL, SIX WEEKS LATER

"A wonderful, moving service, I thought," said Captain Richard Prendergast, Royal Navy, (Retired), the Navy's archivist as he and the others gathered on the steps of Exeter Cathedral after the memorial service, jointly organised by the Royal Navy and the German Navy. A large congregation, including descendants of the crew members of *H.M.S. Norwich* and *U3000*, later known as *U966*, had attended the service of remembrance that took place on a warmer than usual late Autumn day.

"It was indeed," Oscar Agostini agreed, having travelled down from Liverpool with Ross and his team specifically to meet the rest of the people who'd been involved in one of the most difficult and complex cases he could personally remember during his long and varied career.

A number of the latter-day relatives, both British and German had sought out the group they knew to be responsible for finding their ancestors' last resting place, and there'd been much hand shaking, back slapping and a few tears as well as emotions ran high that day.

"I'd like to say a big thank you to Captain Howell and his crew and you too, George," Ross nodded in the direction of Coast Guard George Baldacre. You were all superb and worked so hard to assist us." The rest of Ross's team were there, all meeting the Royal Naval personnel, the Coast Guard, D.I. Brian Jones and Sergeant Carole St. Clair for the first time.

"Shall we walk a little, gentlemen, ladies?" Charles Howell asked, indicating the path that led through the grounds of the great cathedral, famous for possessing the longest unbroken Gothic ceiling in the world and so the little group did just that, breaking away from the immediate vicinity of the towering church structure to a slightly more peaceful, private part of the grounds.

A minute later, Howell stopped, and almost as one, the group seated themselves on the grass beside the path. Howell had signalled to one of his crew members as they'd walked away from the cathedral steps and the rating had proceeded to thoughtfully place a thick tartan design throw on the grass for Izzie, Sam and Carole to sit on and avoid getting grass stains on the outfits they'd worn for the occasion.

"I thought it might be nice, as it's probably the last time we'll all be together, if we could sit here and let Detective Inspector Ross enthral us with the final details of the case as I'm sure some of us haven't as yet heard the full story."

"Good idea, Charles," Prendergast agreed, "if you don't mind of course, Andy?"

"Not at all," Ross replied and in the space of the next fifteen minutes he tried to give the others as much detail as he could of those final days and more importantly, the final hours of the operation to bring Francis Kelly and his cohorts to justice.

"I have to say, we wouldn't have achieved anything at all in the end if it hadn't been for the help and perceptions of our special guest here today." Ross indicated the diminutive figure of Klaus Haller, who'd been invited along as a gesture of thanks. He had, after all, been instrumental in identifying much of the Hydra-like formation at the head of the Aegis operation to murder, steal and defraud on an international scale hitherto unknown to Ross and his team.

Haller rose to his feet and bowed, saying only, "I thank you, Inspector Ross, for allowing me to help you and your excellent officers. It was an honour."

Haller blushed as the others gave him a brief round of polite applause. Captain Howell wasn't finished however. "We found so much more, as you now know, when we completed our examination of the remains of *U3000*. In one of the as yet undisturbed packing cases, instead of gold, we found a number of art treasures, sadly damaged by water seepage over the years, that may have been worth a small fortune back in 1945, and which were probably intended to help pay for the development of the new, revolutionary hydrodynamic drive."

"I thought that was the purpose of the gold," Brian Jones commented.

"So did we at first, Detective Inspector, but when we raised the safe from Max Ritter's cabin, which remained watertight through the years, we found a copy of his sealed orders. Apparently the gold was intended to be one of four similar shipments being made to a secret location in Argentina where the Nazis hoped to regroup and raise a new political party and a new army, with the stated intention of continuing Hitler's policies and eventually giving birth to a 'Fourth Reich' as stated in the orders."

"Four shipments?" Oscar Agostini asked. "So what happened to the other three?"

"A very good question, Detective Chief Inspector," Howell replied. He and Agostini had got on from the moment they'd met before the service. "We can only guess at present. Maybe all or some of those shipments reached their destination, maybe they ended up on the bottom of the sea. We were kind of hoping that a very clever and well respected naval historian might be willing to work with a joint committee from the Royal Naval Archives Branch and their German counterparts in trying to trace just what did happen to those shipments."

He looked directly at Klaus Haller who, realising that Howell was referring to him, clasped his hands together in excitement and exclaimed,

"I would be honoured, highly honoured, thank you."

"No, it is we who thank you, Herr Haller."

"So the hydrodynamic engine never saw operational service?" Ross asked the captain.

"No Andy, not during the war at any rate. The experimental engine fitted to *U3000* had undergone sea trials with limited success and Ritter might have been able to evade the entire British and American navies if it had been operational when he made his Channel dash, but he'd been forbidden from using it. The risks were too great of it malfunctioning at great depth and causing the loss of the U-Boat. It's rather ironic when you think how things turned out for Max Ritter and his crew.

So, anyway, what happens next to the bad guys you've now got safely in custody?"

"Oh, the law will take its course," Ross said. "Kelly will be tried in his own country of course and I believe when the United States hand out life sentences, they tend to mean life, so I don't think he'll be seeing the light of day again, and that's if he manages to escape a death sentence."

"And the men you arrested in Liverpool?"

"Ah well, Graham Young, a.k.a. Robin is singing like a canary, forgive the pun, and the one known as Starling, real name Billy Figgis, is being all big and brave, and a real hard case and won't talk, but we don't need his testimony, what with all we've learned from Young and of course, the big cheese, Randolph Lambert, known to his minions as Finch. Lambert is doing all he can to push as much blame onto Kelly as he can in an effort to lessen his sentence and avoid being extradited to some nasty country that might not be too humane in their treatment of prisoners."

This precipitated a round of laughter from the others.

"And what about Jeffrey Metcalfe?" Captain Howell asked. "D.I. Jones really surprised me when he told me of his involvement."

"Well, he won't be seeing freedom for some time either," Ross said, his face suddenly adopting a look of disgust at the mention of the man's name. "He's probably one of the most black-hearted, cold and calculating bastards I've ever encountered. When we questioned him, he cracked completely and told us everything. It seems he was more involved in Aaron Decker's murder than we thought. When Sally Metcalfe was offered the job with Aegis, Aaron was intrigued and he did everything we already knew about, but there was something else. While he was down in Falmouth, he happened to see a number of Advance Transportation's lorries coming and going from the Aegis facility. At that time, Aaron of course suspected that Aegis were up to no good, and innocently, he became concerned that his girlfriend's father might have been unwittingly dragged into their plot, by them using his trucks for nefarious purposes. Not believing Sally's father could be part of the criminal activities, Aaron went to him with his suspicions. He might as well have signed his own death warrant, because there was no way Jeffrey Metcalfe was going to risk losing the vast sums of money he was making through his involvement with Francis Kelly. Metcalfe reported straight to Kelly, and Lambert was tasked with ensuring that Aaron Decker was 'taken care of' as Metcalfe coldly put it."

"What a bastard," said Prendergast, then, "do excuse my language, ladies."

Izzie and the other women smiled. They were used to much worse in their day to day work with the police. Izzie completed that part of the story while Ross took a breather.

"We all thought Aaron was targeted because he'd found out what they were up to and tried to blackmail those responsible, but in fact, when he'd said he thought he could make some money out of his discovery, it was because, in his own way, he probably thought he could make a few pounds from the story of the discovery of the two previously unknown World War Two shipwrecks. Aegis went as far as trying to buy him off, paying him to go away, but that only made him more suspicious apparently. Of course, once he found out what was really going on, his sole motive was to protect his girlfriend, Sally, from what he thought were unscrupulous people who might have conned her father. He paid a high price for his naïve attempt at chivalry."

Everyone fell silent for a few seconds. Thoughts of a young man imbued with old-fashioned standards of 'doing the right thing' filling most of their minds.

"Where is Aaron's father by the way, Inspector?" George Baldacre asked. "I thought he and his family would be here today."

"He very much wanted to be here," Ross replied, "but Jerome Decker was recently appointed as head of a new C.I.A. international task force, set up to trace every last vestige of the crimes perpetrated by Kelly and his people. He and his family left London two weeks ago and I really don't know where they are now. Knowing Mr. Decker, he'll never rest until every last minion of Kelly's, down to the most insignificant customs official or museum employee around the world is brought to justice. The U.S. embassy was represented here today though, and I'm wondering where he is, as a matter of fact. Last I saw, he was chatting to one of the Members of Parliament who showed up today."

Right on cue a loud voice could be heard calling, "Andy, Andy Ross," and they all turned to see a tall, immaculately dressed man striding along the path towards them. Ross stood up to greet the newcomer.

"Ethan, it's good to see you," he said as he shook hands with his old friend. "Everyone, please say hello to Ethan Tiffen. Ethan works for the U.S. Immigration Service and was here to represent the Decker family and the embassy today. Ethan and I have known each other since he helped me out on a case a few years ago."

"Sorry I couldn't get away sooner, Andy," Tiffen apologised "Those M.P.s of your sure can talk. Anyway, good to meet you all. Jerome Decker sends his good wishes and apologies but our government decided he was needed somewhere else and fast. As he said, they've already buried Aaron and held his funeral service and memorial service so this was really more for the families of those boys who were lost at sea all those years ago. He hopes you all understand."

"Of course we do, Ethan. If you ever talk to him in the future, tell him we all wish him well, his family too, and thank him for the help he gave us in our investigation, okay?"

"You got it, Andy, no problem."

"So you don't know where Mr. Decker is?" Agostini asked the question.

"I don't, I'm afraid, and even if I did I'm afraid that information would be regarded as highly confidential."

"I won't say another word," Agostini said, as Ethan Tiffen reached into the inside pocket of his jacket, pulled something from it and passed it to Andy Ross.

Ross looked at the postcard Tiffen had given him and saw a picture of the Great Pyramid of Giza. Turning it over, Ross saw nothing had been written on the card, leaving nothing but a blank space. His brow furrowed for a second until he saw Tiffen wink at him. Ross nodded back, so imperceptibly no one else would have noticed. Jerome Decker was in Egypt, he was certain, taking up the chase for the missing antiquities and treasure that he knew had been passed through Cairo on their way to various dealers and collectors. Ross almost felt sorry for those who were about to be hunted down by Decker and his fellow C.I.A. operatives. He'd heard a few stories about the ways in which the C.I.A. worked within foreign borders, and the methods they sometimes employed and he had no doubt that more than a few lives would never be the same again once Jerome and his team tracked them down.

"So, that just about wraps everything up, I suppose," Charles Howell said. "I can only say that it's been something of a privilege working with you all. Seeing the way in which you gradually pieced the case together has been, well, educational to say the least."

"Whoa there, Charles," Ross said forcefully. "Let's get this straight. Without the initial help of Captain Prendergast, followed by the wonderful cooperation from the Navy, and you and your crew and those on the *White-haven Castle*, all that technology, the submersibles and so on we'd never have solved a thing. All of us are grateful to you and everyone else who helped us."

"We are quite the mutual admiration society today, are we not?" Klaus Haller smiled as he spoke.

"And you all deserve to be, Herr Haller," Oscar Agostini told the little German historian. "I've been a policeman for more years than I care to remember and I can honestly say I've never seen such wonderful inter-agency and international cooperation and determination to succeed as I have in this case. My boss, Detective Chief Superintendant Sarah Hollingsworth has authorised me to invite you all to lunch before we go our separate ways, courtesy of the Merseyside Police."

A round of spontaneous applause broke out among the little group seated there on the grass in the shadow of Exeter's beautiful Gothic cathedral.

"Wow," said Brian Jones. "I wish our Chief Super would be so generous once in a while."

"Ha, not much chance of that," Sergeant St. Clair added.

Three hours later, after a superb meal in one of Exeter's finest restaurants, the group finally began to break up, with the Royal Naval Captain, Charles Howell the first to depart, needing to return to his ship before evening, followed soon after by Captain Prendergast, who had a long journey to London ahead of him. Promises were made to keep in touch in future, such were the bonds that had been formed during the case, perhaps none as strong as those between Ross and Drake and their Cornish counterparts, Jones and St. Clair.

Relieved the case was over, and pleased to have put the perpetrators of so many crimes behind bars, it was nonetheless with a sense of some regret that Andy Ross and Izzie Drake finally drove away from Exeter later that day, followed by McLennan, Dodds, and Curtis in one car, and Oscar Agostini in another, driven by Sam Gable.

For now, their time on the south coast was over. As Izzie put it,

"Let's try not to have to take too many sea cruises in future, eh sir?"

"Feet on dry land, Izzie, that's a promise."

He couldn't have been more wrong.

EPILOGUE

LIVERPOOL A MONTH LATER.

"I can't see her, sir, can you?" Izzie Drake asked as she and Ross walked along the waterfront. Behind them, the world famous Royal Liver Building, The Cunard Building and the Port of Liverpool Building, collectively known as the Three Graces dominated the skyline, as they have done for over a century. Their brickwork glistened in the autumn sunshine, the three buildings providing a majestic vista for those arriving by sea at the port of Liverpool.

"Not yet, Izzie, but she asked us to meet her here. Maybe she's been delayed."

The two detectives walked slowly, the path lined by young trees planted to add a touch of natural beauty to the overall effect of Liverpool's already impressive waterfront. The phone call Ross had received earlier had taken him by surprise but he felt a sense of obligation to answer the plea from Sally Metcalfe to meet her right where they now sought her.

"Look sir, is that her, over there?" Izzie pointed to where a young woman, dressed all in black, sat on the wall close to the water's edge a hundred yards away, seemingly staring out over the water.

The detectives quickened their pace and sure enough, as they drew closer, they both recognised the hunched figure as being that of Sally Metcalfe.

"Sally?" said Ross quietly, not wanting to startle the young woman, who slowly turned to face them. Ross could see she'd been crying, and was even now fighting hard to control her emotions. "Is everything alright?"

"Inspector Ross. Sergeant Drake, thank you for coming," Sally replied, ignoring Ross's direct question.

"You look upset, Sally," Drake said quietly. "What can we do for you?"

Sally hopped down from the wall, and began to walk along, towards the pier head. Ross and Drake looked at one another and followed, quickly catching her up and walking with her, one to her left the other on her right. After they'd walked for about ten seconds in a silence that seemed like a lifetime to the detectives, Sally at last began to speak.

"I'm leaving Liverpool for good, Inspector, the university, everything. None of it means anything any more. I wanted you to know that."

"I see," Ross replied. "You're going home to Lancaster, I presume?"

"No, I can't go back there either. The shame of knowing what my Dad did is just too great. My Mum's a broken woman, Inspector. All those years she loved him, lived with him, even worked with him and never knew what a black-hearted villain he really was, it's proved too much for her. She's moved out of the house, has filed for divorce and is staying with her sister in Leyland until she figures out what she intends to do"

"I see," Ross said, a little confused, "so you …?"

"I'm staying with a friend in New Brighton until I begin my new job."

"A new job? But your post-grad studies, the offer from Aegis?" Izzie asked.

"I could never work for the Aegis Institute after what my father did, Sergeant Drake. Oh, I know the actual Institute is genuine and legal, but it's still Aegis isn't it? My father had poor Aaron killed when all he tried to do was protect me, didn't he, Inspector Ross?"

Ross nodded, unable to deny the truth of Sally's words.

"I'm afraid so, Sally," was his short reply.

"So, what job are you talking about, Sally?" Drake asked.

"I've managed to secure a post with the British Antarctic Survey," Sally replied. "I'll be sailing on the *Ocean Venturer* in six weeks. I'm qualified to fill a number of scientific study posts and they're glad to have me. The pay isn't fantastic but the experience will be terrific for me and help with my future."

"Well, we can only wish you well, Sally, and I really mean that," said Ross.

Sally Metcalfe halted in her stride, looking out over the water for a few seconds. Ross could sense she wanted to say more and knew that silence was often the best way to get a witness to talk, just give them time to pull their thoughts together. Sure enough, Sally turned to face him and asked the question that must have been burning into her brain since she first found out the truth behind Aaron Decker's murder.

"Why did they use Tim and Martin, Inspector Ross? What on earth could have turned Aaron's friends, well, I thought they were his friends, into killers?"

Ross looked at Sally with a sadness in his eyes that he couldn't hide. He really felt for this girl who had unwittingly been a pawn in the deadly game that had been played out across continents, but that had come home to roost directly in her own back yard, figuratively speaking.

"Money, Sally, one of the oldest motivators in the book, allied in Tim's case with a large slice of jealousy."

"Tim was jealous of me?"

"Well, of you being with Aaron, yes."

"I thought that was all over, that he knew it was never going to happen between us."

"The thing is, Sally, his mind never actually accepted that you didn't 'fancy' him. He thought that if you hadn't met Aaron he'd have still had a chance with you. Then of course, there was the cricket."

"You're not seriously telling me that boring old cricket formed part of his motive for murder?"

"I'm afraid it did," Ross said, shaking his head as he spoke. "When Aaron came along, Tim lost what he thought was his place as the pin-up boy of the university cricket team. All of a sudden, along came this American who could play cricket better than a native, and as Aaron racked up more and more playing records, so Tim's inner resentment grew. Aaron quickly established a record for bowling the most maiden overs in a season, followed by the best batting returns anyone could remember for a long time, and when you combined those statistics with Tim's latent and irrational thoughts about his relationship with you, it added up to a motive for murder, which a man called Randolph Lambert, who worked for Francis Kelly, the man behind the illegal activities being conducted under the Aegis name was quick to exploit."

"But how did he know all this about Tim? And what about Martin? Why did he get involved?"

"Let me explain, Sally," Izzie Drake said, giving Ross a break. "When your father passed all the information relating to Aaron to Francis Kelly, it was passed on to Lambert, head of Kelly's internal security force. Usually Lambert would have sent one of his hired killers to do the job, but he saw a way to get the job done without involving his people, using Tim and Martin, who was up to his neck in debt to some not very understanding people and this was his chance to clear that debt and get a fresh start. Lambert's people are clever and resourceful. He simply sent a couple of his men along to find out the easiest way to eliminate Aaron."

Sally physically flinched at Izzie's words.

"Sorry, Sally but there's no way to sugar coat what took place. They must have spent time on campus, learning all they could about Aaron, probably even befriended him, bought him a few drinks, same with his two housemates, which is how they probably learned of Tim Knight's feelings for you and his resentment of Aaron. They probably came here intending

773

to do the job themselves but when they identified the possibility of using a couple of outside dupes to do their dirty work it was too good an opportunity to pass up. We later found out that your father was the source of the ketamine used in the murder, through a pharmaceutical company he'd done work for."

By now, Sally Metcalfe was in tears, understandably, and Ross gave Izzie a look that said he thought they'd told the young woman enough.

Izzie dutifully fell silent and instead took a pace towards Sally, wrapping a comforting arm around her shoulder until the girl managed to stop crying and with a heave of her shoulders, composed herself once again.

"Thank you for telling me everything," she said eventually, at the same time withdrawing an envelope from her handbag, which she passed to Ross.

"I really asked you to meet me today because I wanted you to have these, Inspector Ross," she said as Ross slowly opened the unsealed flap of the envelope and removed the contents.

The first of the two photographs Ross extracted showed Aaron Decker in his wet suit, his head bare, seated on a quayside he recognised from his visit to Falmouth. Aaron was smiling and giving a thumbs-up sign to the camera. The second photo showed an equally happy and smiling T.J. Knowles, dressed in t-shirt and brightly coloured floral patterned knee-length shorts, looking for all the world like an eager surfer, ready to ride the waves. Ross smiled at the sight of the two young men, and wondered why Sally wanted Sally wanted him to have them.

"You never met or knew Aaron, Inspector," she explained. "You worked so hard to solve his murder, and I just wanted you to see him when he was alive, happy and with his whole life ahead of him, so you won't just think of him as a dead body in future when you recall any thoughts you may have of him. The same goes for the other man. I never knew him either, but it's obvious they became good friends and it's better to remember him like this than as a floating body, shackled to a sunken ship, don't you think?"

Ross understood and felt privileged that Sally Metcalfe had chosen to share these memories of Aaron Decker and T.J. Knowles with him, but still had a question for her.

"I really appreciate these, Sally, thank you, and I know exactly what you're telling me by giving them to me, but where did they come from? They might have proved useful earlier in the investigation. And, don't you want to keep these yourself?"

"I only received them a few days ago," Sally replied. "One of Aaron's tutors found them tucked in between the pages of a book Aaron had been using for some research matter, and he'd not looked at it for some time. He picked it up and they fell out and he thought I might like to have them. The ones I've given you are copies, I still have the originals."

"Well, thank you again, Sally," Ross said. "They certainly will help me in remembering Aaron and T.J. in the proper manner. I never forget the victims in any investigation I carry out, but these photos will serve to remind me of the humanity of those who I seek justice for."

Ross couldn't think of anything else to say, and just placed the photos back in the envelope and transferred it to the inside pocket of his jacket. Izzie Drake gave Sally a hug, and added her thanks to those of her boss.

"I doubt we'll meet again, Inspector," Sally said as she prepared to take her leave of the detectives. "I've no desire to stay in England any longer than I have to and I've certainly no wish to return in a hurry once I've left all this pain and heartbreak behind."

Ross understood the young woman's feelings, but knew he had to say something to remind her there were still certain realities she'd have to face in the future.

"I know how you must feel, Sally, but there's still the matter of your father's trial. You may be needed as a witness."

"Oh, I hadn't thought of that," Sally said with a hurt look on her face.

"Well, there's a chance you won't have to give evidence," he replied, giving her a straw to clutch at. "Your father has admitted everything in his statements to us and if he pleads guilty to all charges when his trial opens, the judge might sentence him without need for you to give evidence."

"Oh, I do hope so," Sally said, hope appearing in her expression as she spoke. "We haven't been informed of a trial date yet, but as far as I'm concerned he can rot on remand for ever until it's time. He used to be a decent man, Inspector. If there's a shred of decency left in him, he'll do the right thing and save me and my poor Mum from having to testify against him."

"I hope he will, too Sally. It certainly won't do his case any good for a jury to see and hear his own wife and daughter testifying against him on such serious charges."

With that, Sally Metcalfe took Andy Ross completely by surprise as she stepped in front of him, stood on tiptoe, threw her arms around his neck and planted a kiss on his cheek before pulling away, saying a quiet "Thank you," and standing in front of him again smiling up at him.

"Wow," said Ross. "What did I do to deserve that?"

"You just gave me hope," Sally replied. "If I do have to come back, perhaps the British Antarctic Survey People will be able to get me home, given enough notice. They have planes as well as ships, so we'll cross that bridge if and when we come to it."

"I had to tell you about the trial, Sally, you understand that don't you?"

"Yes, but I don't think my father will want either me or my mother testifying against him in court, so it's likely he'll plead guilty, I think. He wasn't always a bad man, so maybe he still has a spark of decency in him, somewhere."

"Let's hope so, eh, Sally?"

Izzie reached out and gave Sally a quick girlie hug and whispered, "good luck," in her ear, and then stood back.

Sally Metcalfe looked as if she was about to speak again, but instead she simply flashed a big smile at the two detectives, and took a step backwards.

"Well, better be off then," she suddenly said and turned on her heel before anyone could say another word and with that, Sally Metcalfe walked away from the two detectives, who watched as her diminutive figure grew ever smaller as she drew further away from them until she eventually disappeared into a small crowd of people walking in the same direction she was.

"Well, that was unusual," Ross said to Izzie Drake, who smiled at him.

"What, the photos or the kiss?" she grinned.

"Well, both, I suppose," Ross replied. "I feel sorry for that young woman. She's lost her boyfriend, her family's effectively been destroyed, her father's facing trial and facing life imprisonment and her career's destroyed before it had even begun, and yet she still has more humanity and depth of feeling in her than many people twice her age. I think I'll always remember Sally Metcalfe as The Mersey Maiden, in honour of the case and its cricketing connections."

"You're just an old softy at heart, sir, you know that don't you?"

"Hey, I'm just a well worn old copper, Izzie, one who's been round the block a few too many times, but can still be surprised now and then."

"Yeah, sure, I'll believe you," Drake smiled at her boss.

"She's going to need a lot of mental strength to get through the next couple of years, that's for sure,"

"I have a feeling she'll make it alright, sir."

Andy Ross nodded in response to Izzie's words. There seemed little he could add.

Ross and Drake took a slow walk back to headquarters, for the most part both being content with a companionable silence, each lost in their own private thoughts on the immensely complex and at times emotionally upsetting case they finally felt was drawing to a close. They still had information to glean from Lambert and Young, and maybe even Starling if and when he cracked, and the Americans would doubtless learn much from Francis Kelly, but until the trials, their involvement was almost over.

* * *

Later, alone in his office, Andy Ross sat at his desk looking at the two photographs Sally Metcalfe had presented him with. He opened the top drawer of his desk, and removed two drawing pins from a small container. Rising, he walked across to where a corkboard hung on the wall opposite his desk and carefully pinned the photos in place directly in the centre, amidst duty rosters, various flyers and notices pertaining to routine police business. Returning to his desk, he sat down, opened the bottom drawer of his desk and removed a bottle of Glenmorangie and a small whisky glass, placing them on the desk in front of him. He kept the whisky for special occasions, and it had been quite a while since the bottle last saw the light of day. After wiping the whisky tumbler out with a tissue, he poured himself a small measure, stood up and looked across his office at the photographs of Aaron Decker and T.J. Knowles.

Ross held the glass up in front of his face for a second, surveying the amber liquid within, then gestured with the glass towards the cork board on the opposite wall.

"I won't forget you lads, or your Mersey Maiden, Aaron, that's a promise," Ross said, and then gulped the fiery Scotch down in one in a final toast to the two young men.

He'd just returned the bottle to the drawer, leaving the glass on his desk to rinse later when Izzie Drake knocked and entered his office, balancing two coffees on a plastic tray.

"Thought you might want one," she said and Ross motioned for her to come in and sit down.

"Aha, caught you," she smiled, seeing the whisky glass and easily being able to smell the lingering fumes of Glenmorangie.

"Guilty pleasures, Izzie," he smiled in return. "Want one?"

"No thanks," she declined his offer. You know I'm not big on spirits. Got any red wine in that drawer?"

"Sorry," he apologised.

"Oh well, maybe another time. Suppose the coffee will have to do for now."

Ross was about to speak when the phone on his desk rang. Ross lifted the receiver, then recognised the voice at the other end of the line and gestured to Izzie, who pressed the button on the base unit of the phone that switched on the speakerphone facility. He obviously wanted her to hear this conversation.

"Mr. Decker," Ross said in surprise. "Good to hear from you. Where are you calling from?"

"I can't tell you that, Inspector, but please, call me Jerome. I think we've worked together long enough for you to use my given name. Did you get my message from Ethan by the way?"

"I did, thanks," Ross acknowledged, knowing that Decker was in Cairo though he wouldn't say so on an open telephone line. "And call me Andy, please."

"Okay Andy, that's great. How's that beautiful, sexy little sergeant of yours?"

"I'm fine, thank you Mr. Decker," Izzie said, knowing Decker was unaware they were on speakerphone.

"Ouch, you got me, Sergeant Drake," Decker half laughed.

"Don't worry," Izzie replied. "I might have been offended if you'd said *'How's that fat ugly little sergeant of yours?'* but beautiful and sexy I can live with, thanks."

"Okay," Decker laughed again.

"So, Jerome, what can I do for you today?" Ross asked, intrigued to be hearing from the C.I.A. man.

"Oh, it's kind of more what I can do for you, Andy. I have some information you might find useful in putting the case to bed."

"Really? Please go on, you have my full attention."

"Right, well, I suppose you'd call this more of a postscript to the case really. It's just that it has such a twist to it that I just knew you'd want to hear about it."

"Okay, you've baited the hook and now you've got me dangling, Sergeant Drake too, so please tell me what you've got."

"Ah, well, it wouldn't do to keep a beautiful, sexy lady waiting would it?"

Izzie Drake visibly blushed this time. Decker continued.

"So, here goes. As you know, I'm in charge of certain matters pertaining to our friend in New York," an obvious reference to Francis Kelly. "Among other things, it was a priority to locate and impound those submarines. Kelly tried to escape in the *Aegis Explorer* and thanks to the cooperation of the Aegis Institute's CEO, we soon located and had orders sent to the *Aegis Wanderer,* and *Aegis Seascape* to return to port where their crews were arrested and the vessels impounded."

Decker paused long enough for Ross to realise there was a 'but' coming. Ross again took the bait.

"That's only three subs accounted for, Jerome. You're going to tell me there was a problem with number four."

"You got it, Andy. The final submarine, one of the Kilo class vessels renamed the *Aegis Seaquest* received identical orders to the others but failed to respond at first. That's when the Aegis executives launched their own inquiry and found out that the *Aegis Seaquest* had undergone an extensive overhaul and engine modification when she last docked in Alaska."

"What kind of engine modification, Jerome?"

"Aha, you're quick, Andy, I'll give you that. It seems that Erich Ackermann possessed what he thought was a duplicate set of plans for the hydrodynamic propulsion system as installed on *U3000* or whatever goddamn number you want to give it. His mother either appropriated the plans or was given them to look after by the admirals at Kiel when the war looked lost. Somehow they survived and were eventually passed to Ackermann. Of course, they wanted to get their hands on the actual engine, which is partly why they tried to get their hands on *U3000*, but Kelly also ordered the engineers at the Kodiac Island facility to use the plans Ackermann gave him to retrofit the *Seaquest* with an updated version of the system, adding a few modern refinements."

"Kelly told you all this?"

"No, Andy. The engineers at the Kodiac base carried out the work in innocence, after Kelly told the Aegis board that his own research scientists and engineers had developed a potentially environmentally friendly means of ship and submarine propulsion. With no reason to disbelieve him, the board sanctioned the development costs and the project went ahead. The system was only installed on the *Aegis Seaquest* three months ago and was still undergoing extensive sea trials. The problem is, we believe the plans Ackermann's mother possessed were either incomplete or just a draft copy, one that was later modified before being fitted into Max Ritter's submarine. When he was told the submarine was missing, Kelly clammed up and wouldn't talk so the F.B.I. called the Germans who must have threatened Ackermann with God knows what if he didn't talk because he told them all he knew. He said he thought Kelly would use the plans in conjunction with the actual engines when they salvaged them, to create an improved version of the original. He never thought Kelly would try and build a system based on the draft plans alone.

Anyway, returning to the *Aegis Seaquest*, it transpired that after a day's silence from the sub following the recall order the Aegis Seaport facility received a short but frantic transmission from *Seaquest* which read, and I quote, *'Hydrodynamic system failure, unable to disengage. Nose down attitude, no control. Diesel override inoperative. Stuck on seabed, depth 200 fathoms.'* This was followed by her position. Two hundred fathoms is one thousand, two hundred feet, Andy."

"My God, this sounds reminiscent of the *U3000's* predicament," Ross said quietly. The look on Izzie Drake's face mirrored his own. "Don't mind me asking, Jerome, but just when did this take place?"

There was a silence at the other end of the line, just a few seconds before Decker replied, but enough for Ross to guess the answer wasn't going to be a positive one. Finally, Decker spoke again.

"A week ago."

"A week? And what's been done to find the submarine since then?"

"The Aegis board, by now fully aware of Kelly's crimes remember, contacted the F.B.I. and the U.S. Coastguard immediately. The biggest problem was that the submarine's last reported position placed her four hundred miles from land, west of Santiago in a relatively shallow section of the Pacific Ocean, off the coast of Chile. The Chilean government were made aware of the situation but possessed no ships capable of helping and the submarine was after all in international waters, so the U.S. Navy sent two destroyers and two of their best deep sea salvage vessels to the sub's last reported position."

"I have a feeling you wouldn't be telling me this unless there's some bad news involved, Jerome." Ross felt he had to comment.

"Yeah, you're right," Decker said, a hint of sadness in his voice. "I know you and the sergeant there will know what the salvage guys went through after your own recent experiences, you know, sending submersibles down and so on. To cut a long story short, by the time they reached the submarine it was too late. The *Seaquest* had literally nosedived into the seabed and become embedded in the mud and silt at the bottom of the ocean. Their air had run out Andy. Thirty men suffocated to death."

Decker fell silent.

"Tragic," Izzie Drake said as she and Ross assimilated the information.

"Even more deaths that, morally at least, can be laid at Kelly's door," Ross said eventually.

"Yes," Decker agreed. "It could have been more if she'd been fully crewed. The Russians originally used a crew of fifty-two on the Kilos, but of course, in civilian use, no weapons technicians and other specialists were needed."

"So that's it then?" Ross asked. "A bitter end to Kelly's plans."

"Well, yes, apart from another tragic little twist you'll be interested in," Decker replied. "You see, back in 1945, it seems the skipper of *U3000* or *U966*, whatever, slept with a young whore named Claudia Rheinhardt in a Kiel brothel just before sailing. She was young and inexperienced and part of a programme known as 'Whores for Hitler' where young women volunteered or in some cases were sent by their parents to work in up-market brothels, servicing German officers and high ranking civilian officials."

"That's sick," Drake shouted.

"True, Sergeant Drake, but they really believed they were helping the war effort, helping the Fuehrer by keeping his elite troops supplied with good sex."

"Yuk."

"So, anyway, soon after Ritter sailed Claudia Rheinhardt found herself pregnant. Even in the Nazi's organised brothels, birth control could be a hit-and-miss affair. Under normal circumstances the baby would have been born and sent into the Lebensborn programme, brought up in an orphanage, or adopted and raised by an approved couple to be part of Hitler's future master race. The war ended before that could happen and so the child was eventually born and raised by his mother who told the young growing boy many made-up stories of his war hero father. He was brought up bearing his mother's name and was in quite a lot of trouble as an adolescent; fights, petty crime and so on. He finally changed his name and joined the German Navy when he was eighteen, virtually disowned by Claudia, who died two years ago and left under a cloud years later after striking a senior officer. He was a submariner though, and was later recruited by Ackermann to command one of the submarines he'd paid for on behalf of the Aegis Institute. This was the man who was in command of the *Aegis Seaquest*. When he changed his name, he took the name of the man his mother told him was his father. Andy the captain of the *Aegis Seaquest* was Max Ritter."

"Bloody hell," said Ross.

"Oh my God," Drake exclaimed as she threw a hand over her mouth in shock.

"That's unbelievable," Ross added.

"I know, Andy, I know," said Decker. "He was nearly fifty eight years old and was Kelly's most trusted captain. He must have been told about his father's last mission by Ackermann and would probably have relished the opportunity to use the propulsion system his father first trialled at sea all those years ago."

"And he met an identical death to his father," Drake said softly.

"And in a similar way, he was working for an evil and unscrupulous leader," Ross added. "Thanks for telling us, Jerome. I suppose it's fitting that the case ends with a submarine disaster, after all that's taken place from the war through to today."

"Yes, I thought you'd think that way," Decker said. "Now, I'd better go back to work. I still have lots of people to see, places to go, you know what I mean?"

"I do, and I wish you luck, Jerome Decker the third," Ross said with great gravitas in his voice.

"And the same to you, Detective Inspector Ross, Sergeant Drake," Decker said and then, before they knew it, the line went dead. Decker was gone.

"Typical Yank," said Ross. "Always in a hurry."

"Nice of him to call though, eh sir?"

"Yes, it was Izzie. I suppose that really is the end of the case for us now, until the trials."

"I wonder…"

"What?" Ross asked.

"If the child born to Claudia Rheinhardt really was Max Ritter's? I mean, she was a whore after all. She must have slept with hundreds of men while working in that brothel. How could she be sure Ritter was the father?"

"We'll never know, Izzie, will we? Max Ritter was a hero at the time though, with his Knight's Cross and Oak Leaves. Maybe she thought it romantic to assume the father of her child was a famous U-Boat commander rather than one of the many run-of-the-mill officers she had to sleep with during her time in the brothel."

"I can understand that," Drake said softly. "She was little more than a kid herself when young Max was born. She probably wanted him to have a father figure to be proud of, rather than telling him he was the result of her copulating with dozens of unknown men in a seedy Nazi brothel. I wonder if he ever found out the truth about his birth?"

"That's just one more unanswerable question, Izzie, something nobody can answer. With her being dead and the younger Max too, it really does feel like the real end of the case, thank God."

"I can't say I'll miss it," Drake sighed, "even if we did meet some interesting people along the way. It's weird to think that it really started and ended with a man named Max Ritter. If you don't mind, I'll call Carole St. Clair later and give her and Brian the news about the submarine and the younger Max Ritter. I'd like to think we might work with her and D.I. Jones again one day."

"Same here, and yes, by all means give her a call, say hello to her and Brian from me," said Ross, as he rose from his chair. "Come on Izzie, let's go tell the others about Decker's news. Better not forget the D.C.I. too."

"He's okay to work for, Mr. Agostini, isn't he, sir?"

"He's a good bloke, yes. We worked together in our younger days, you know that of course?"

"Yes, heard all about it. You two got up to some real tricks back in the day, so I hear."

"Right, well, enough of that," Ross laughed. "Let's go talk to the team, and you know what, Izzie?"

"What, sir?"

"I'm going to give everyone the rest of the day off, including me and you."

"But what about D.C.I. Agostini, sir?"

"Oh alright, he can have the rest of the day off too."

Drake's laughter was so loud, so infectious that Ross couldn't stop himself from joining in. It was good to laugh again.

Little did they know however, that at that moment, on the continent that the original Max Ritter had been heading for many years earlier, the seeds of their next case had already been sown…

ABOUT THE AUTHOR

Brian L Porter is a multiple award-winning, best-selling author and poet. He's best known for his successful Mersey Mystery series and his true life, bestselling Family of Rescue Dogs Series. He also writes children's books as Harry Porter and romantic poetry as Juan Pablo Jalisco, (Of Aztecs and Conquistadors).

He is a grandfather, a former member of the Royal Air Force, is married to Juliet and together they live in the North of England, sharing their home with their canine family of nine rescued dogs.

* * *

To learn more about Brian L. Porter and discover more Next Chapter authors, visit our website at www.nextchapter.pub.

Mersey Murder Mysteries Collection - Books 1-3
ISBN: 978-4-82417-479-6
Paperback Edition

Published by
Next Chapter
2-5-6 SANNO
SANNO BRIDGE
143-0023 Ota-Ku, Tokyo
+818035793528

4th April 2023

MERSEY MURDER MYSTERIES COLLECTION

Books 1-3

BRIAN L. PORTER